The Short Fiction of
CHARLES W. CHESNUTT

The Short Fiction of
CHARLES
W.
CHESNUTT

Edited and With an Introduction by

Sylvia Lyons Render

HOWARD UNIVERSITY PRESS

Washington, D.C.

1974

Printed in the United States of America.

Library of Congress Cataloging in Publication Data

Chesnutt, Charles Waddell, 1858-1932.
    The short fiction of Charles W. Chesnutt.

I. Title.
PZ3.C4253Sh [PS1292.C6]   813'.4
ISBN 0-88258-012-4   73-88973

To my parents and all others who dreamed dreams that inspired their children to have visions.

Acknowledgments

I WISH TO EXPRESS my deepest appreciation to relatives of Charles W. Chesnutt who provided me with information not of record, gave me access to Chesnutt materials not otherwise available, and granted me permission to publish the Chesnutt manuscripts in this volume. Among them Helen Chesnutt, Arna Bontemps (both deceased) Dean H. Keller and Carr Liggett.

I am also very grateful to the Fisk University Library Special Collections staff, headed by Mrs. Ann Schockley, for providing me with copies of many of the selections which appear in this collection and to The Western Reserve Historical Society for the copy of "Jim's Romance," also included in the work. I am likewise deeply indebted to librarians at George Peabody College for Teachers, North Carolina Central University, Duke University, and Fayetteville State University for their help in locating Chesnutt manuscripts and publications.

Special thanks are due to Dr. C. W. Foster, Prof. Warren I. Titus and to the editors of *CLA Journal* to excerpt my article, "Tarheelia in Chesnutt," which appeared in the September, 1965, issue of the *Journal*. I also appreciate those grants which helped make it possible for me to assemble and comment upon Chesnutt's short fiction. I am indebted to the American Philosophical Society, the North Carolina Central University Faculty Research Committee. The Cooperative Program in the Humanities conducted jointly by Duke University and The University of North Carolina at Chapel Hill, and The Ford Foundation.

This manuscript would never have reached its present form without the industry of my typist, Mrs. Gladys Harrison, and the critical reading of Mrs. Elizabeth Jezierski, Mrs. Julia Harris, Miss Audrey Dupuy, and Miss Paula Giddings.

Contents

The Short Stories

Prefatory Note

All of the anecdotes, tales, and short stories in this volume are appearing for the first time in book form. Excluding the sixteen tales and short stories published in *The Conjure Woman* and *The Wife of His Youth and Other Stories of the Color Line,* this volume contains all but four of Chesnutt's pieces of short fiction for which there is any evidence of publication.

The seven Uncle Julius tales which were not originally included in *The Conjure Woman,* Chesnutt's most popular work, are in this collection. Five have been previously published in periodicals, and two have never before appeared in print. The former are "A Victim of Heredity" and "The Dumb Witness," and the latter, "A Deep Sleeper," "Tobe's Tribulations," and "The Marked Tree."

The Introduction does include discussion of all of Chesnutt's short fiction including the tales and short stories published in the two volumes. They are:

The Conjure Woman. Boston: Houghton Mifflin Company, 1899.
   The Goophered Grapevine
   Po' Sandy
   Mars Jeems's Nightmare
   The Conjurer's Revenge
   Sis' Becky's Pickaninny
   The Gray Wolf's Ha'nt
   Hot-Foot Hannibal

The Wife of His Youth and Other Stories of the Color Line. Boston: Houghton Mifflin Company, 1899.
   The Wife of His Youth
   Her Virginia Mammy
   The Sheriff's Children
   A Matter of Principle
   Cicely's Dream
   The Passing of Grandison
   Uncle Wellington's Wives
   The Bouquet
   The Web of Circumstance

Introduction

CHARLES WADDELL CHESNUTT merits recognition as a significant writer because of his extraordinary ability to blend his African and European heritages into distinctly American forms. Nowhere is this more evident than in his short fiction. Many of his eighty-odd anecdotes, tales, and short stories are not only outstanding examples of those forms as they evolved during the late nineteenth century but also reflect the author's ability to refract the American experience through the double vision of one whose racial antecedents placed him on the color line rather than on either side of it.

As a "voluntary" Negro—"one who, though so fair in complexion as to be indistinguishable from a Caucasian, chooses not to 'pass' "—Chesnutt could easily have denied his ethnic identity and become lost in the anonymity of whiteness, as many of his relatives and thousands of other mixed-bloods have done. Instead, he chose to remain identified as an Afro-American and sought to remove rather than to avoid various forms of discrimination.

Color—or caste, as he more correctly called it—served both as motivation and subject matter in most of his writings. The major pieces of short fiction in this volume have unmistakably autobiographical overtones and reflect the impact of racial discrimination and injustice upon Chesnutt.

Those stories that treat the South are set almost exclusively in the Cape Fear (North Carolina) River area where Chesnutt's ancestors originated and where he lived from age eight to twenty-five. Chesnutt eventually moved North after resolving that he would not expose his children to the "social and intellectual proscription" he had suffered, and the remainder of his fiction records Chesnutt's impressions of life there.

Chesnutt's leaving the South was reminiscent of a move made in 1856 by a group of "free colored people" in North Carolina. Among them were Andrew Jackson Chesnutt, Ann Maria Sampson, and her mother, Chloe Sampson. "Jack" fell in love with Ann Maria during the course of that trying wagon-train trip organized by blacks willing to risk the unknown rather than adjust to the increasingly oppressive "Southern way of life."

3

"Jack" Chesnutt was bound for Indiana to live with an uncle who had
crossed the color line; the Sampsons were headed for Cleveland, where they
were to retain their Afro-American identity. Reciprocated love drew Chesnutt
back to Cleveland in 1857; there he and Ann Maria were married and settled
with Chloe in her neat little cottage in a German neighborhood. There also
Charles Waddell was born June 20, 1858.

The Chesnutts soon moved to Oberlin, where three other children were
born (Lewis, Andrew, and a girl who died in infancy) before the family returned to Cleveland and "Jack" joined the Union Army as a teamster. At the
end of the war, he accepted the offer of his father, apparently a man of means,
to set him up in the grocery business in Fayetteville, North Carolina. This
prospect influenced "Jack," upon his return to Cleveland, to overrule his wife's
strenuous objections to taking up residence again in the South.

Life in the South

Young Charles apparently retained few impressions of his first eight years in
Ohio. On the other hand, his private journals afford penetrating insights into
his sixteen years in North Carolina. Until he was thirteen, when his mother
died, the boy's life was better than that of most blacks in Cumberland County.
He attended the Howard School, named in honor of General O. O. Howard
of the Freedman's Bureau and built largely through the efforts of public-spirited
black citizens, including Andrew J. Chesnutt.

After school Charles helped his father in the family store located near the
Market House, still a major historical Fayetteville landmark. and absorbed the
miscellany of fact and fantasy which he heard there. In the evenings and before
school he helped his mother with the household chores and with the younger
children.

When Mrs. Chesnutt became incapacitated, her mother came down from
Cleveland to help out; she remained after her daughter's death until she persuaded Mary Ochiltree, a young niece who lived in an adjacent rural area,
to replace her as housekeeper. In exchange for her services Mary had the opportunity to go to Howard School.

Before very long, however, Charles's life changed drastically. First, his
father married Miss Ochiltree, whom the children addressed customarily as
"Cousin Mary." Then the elder Chesnutt lost his store because of his overly
generous credit policies. To compensate in part for the subsequent loss in income, he moved his family to a farm down on the Wilmington Road and informed Charles that he would have to stop school to help support the still-
growing family, which finally included twelve living children. However, the
principal of the school, Robert Harris, who was also a family friend and Charles's confidant after Mrs. Chesnutt's death, prevailed upon the father to let
Charles take a pupil-teacher job at Howard School and turn his modest salary

over to him. Thus Chesnutt's formal education ended before he had a chance to finish high school.

A lifelong passion for books and love of reading served well in his self-education thereafter, particularly during adolescence, when he was both eager and impressionable. His fondness for the printed page, apparently shared with and encouraged only by his mother, was a standing family joke before he started school. The white owner of a bookstore near the Chesnutt grocery gave the boy the run of his premises. Later, Charles had access to a local private library, composed largely of European and English classics and reputedly the finest in the area.

To help provide for the family, Charles also peddled wares over the countryside. In addition he assisted and taught, first in Fayetteville and later in Charlotte, during the regular school terms, and wherever he could find a colored school available in adjacent areas during the short summer terms. At the same time he followed a planned course of reading and study that encompassed algebra, natural philosophy, theory of education, Latin, American history, and literature. Charles Dickens, Harriet Beecher Stowe, Byron, Thackeray, Cowper, Burns, Sir Walter Scott, Shakespeare, and the Bible were among Chesnutt's early favorites. He added Homer, Virgil, Horace, Herodotus, Seneca, Ovid, Catiline, Cicero, Macaulay, Alexandre Dumas, Albion W. Tourgée, Benjamin Franklin, Horace Greeley, Francis Jeffrey, Washington Irving, Samuel Pepys, Le Sage, Molière, Joseph Addison, and Richard Steele to the list before he migrated North in 1883. When Charles received the first salary check over which he had complete control, $37.50 for his first month of teaching near Spartanburg, South Carolina, in August, 1875, he guiltily splurged $1.50 on a copy of Dickens's *Barnaby Rudge.*[1]

Chesnutt returned to Fayetteville permanently in the fall of 1877 to become first assistant to Robert Harris, who had just been named principal of the new state normal school for the preparation of colored teachers, located on the second floor of Howard School. At the same time he expanded his activities considerably to include teaching "reading, writing, spelling, composition, and related subjects," advising the literary society, practicing piano and organ, continuing his self-education, and courting Miss Susan U. Perry, who had begun teaching at Howard School while Chesnutt was in Charlotte. Marriage to Susan the following summer and the birth of their first child, Ethel, in April, 1879, moved Chesnutt to accelerate rather than abate his largely solitary efforts at self-improvement. His routine that summer called for one hour's attention daily to Latin, German, French, literary composition, and the garden; on the other hand, he set no time limit for his practice of shorthand, miscellaneous reading, "and tending to the baby."[2] By 1881, having served two years as full principal of the normal school after the demise of Robert Harris, Chesnutt had added Greek to the languages he was trying to master. His private journals show that he also devoted some time to "history, biography, shorthand . . . composition . . . music [and] domestic economy."³ Besides striving to share his increasing knowledge with his pupils, Chesnutt sought also to inspire them. As adviser to the Normal Literary Society, he often addressed the group on such subjects as "The Advantages of a Well-Conducted Literary Society," "Etiquette: Good Manners," and "Self-Made Men."⁴ Some of the latter, including Frederick Douglass, were black men of distinction, who were Chesnutt's favorite subjects. Later testimonials from former students indicate that the teacher himself provided for them the same kind of motivating image.⁵

Chesnutt's diligence, community activity, and excellent decorum won for him the most remunerative position (seventy-five dollars per month) open to an Afro-American in Fayetteville when he was only twenty-two. At the same time, however, spending so many hours in solitary pursuits had deepened a natural introversion. Moreover, his growing appreciation of Western literature and music further alienated him from people of color; he seemed to have no friends who shared his enthusiasms. During this period he served as organist, choirmaster, and Sunday-school superintendent of the historic Evans Chapel African Methodist Episcopal Zion Church; entertained important visitors in his home; and gave private piano, organ, voice, and Latin lessons. Nevertheless, on March 7, 1882, he still found himself in his study "without the companionship of one congenial mind" with whom to "enjoy the society of the greatest wits and scholars of England . . . the greatest men of earth."⁶

Local mores continued to bar him from associating as an equal with whites whose tastes were similar to his own—and for him no compromise was acceptable. Though he appreciated the self-reliance which he gained from his "solitary studies," he complained in a private journal entry of October 16, 1878:

> I love music. I live in a town where there is some musical culture; I have studied and practised till I can understand and appreciate good music, but I never hear what little there is to be heard. I have studied German, and have no one to converse with but a few Jewish merchants who can talk of nothing but business. As to procuring instruction in Latin, French, German or music, that is entirely out of the question. First class teachers would not teach a "nigger," and I would have no other sort.⁷

Many more forceful notations fairly burn in their delineation of the resentment, frustration, and humiliation which "niggers"—himself included—experienced as Redemption succeeded Reconstruction in the South.⁸ Sometimes the slights, slurs, and scorn were intentionally more pronounced because, through no fault of his own, Chesnutt had been taken on face value and assumed to be white. He recalled in 1880 that he had "possessed such opportunities for observation and conversation with the better class of white men in the South as to understand their modes of thinking."⁹ Such an ability had a direct bearing on blacks' quality and quantity of life. Paradoxically, after Emancipation, in too many places in the United States a black man had to be increasingly on his guard to maintain his self-respect and at the same time to live long enough to die a natural death.

The lukewarm attitude of the Andrew Johnson administration toward blacks, the failure of the Supreme Court to enforce vigorously the Fourteenth and Fifteenth Amendments, the repeal of the Civil Rights Act of 1875, the Hayes-Tilden Compromise of 1877, and the eagerness of Northern capitalists to establish profitable relationships with Southern landowners and industrialists doomed the efforts of Afro-Americans and their few white supporters to gain equal rights for any blacks, regardless of their pre-Civil War status. Emboldened by the permissiveness of the national government and goaded by fear of the potential power of a fully equal black citizenry, the majority of white Southerners used fiat and force to relegate blacks to the lowest possible status.

All the Southern states ignored President Johnson's recommendation that literate or property-owning Negroes be permitted to vote. Moreover, Dixie legislatures passed laws sharply restricting the activities of blacks. They could own or rent property—sometimes on a limited basis only—sue and be sued, make contracts, and marry. On the other hand, however, besides being denied the franchise, Afro-Americans could not intermarry, serve on juries, testify in court against a white person, carry a gun, be unemployed, or freely quit a job.[10] Freemen and freedmen alike were also psychologically harassed and physically abused—at times even murdered—"by the Ku Klux Klan, Knights of the White Camellia, Knights of the White Rose, Pale Faces, Red Jacks, Knights of the Black Cross, White Brotherhood, and Constitutional Guards."[11]

According to Frenise A. Logan, North Carolina blacks were so unfairly treated that "James H. Harris, a prominent Negro politician," called a meeting of " 'representative colored men' in Raleigh in January of 1880" to air grievances which had prompted a mounting emigration of blacks from the state. The complaints concerned exorbitant rents for land and inflated prices for supplies in rural areas, "the nefarious Landlord and Tenant Act" which enabled "unscrupulous landlords" to defraud black tenants, the election of justices of the peace by the state legislature rather than by the local constituency, the denial of jury duty to black men, the denial of the right of blacks to select their own committeemen and through them the teachers for Negro schools, and the denial of equal justice under the law in many counties of the state.[12]

In 1879 Chesnutt had praised North Carolina for its progress in race relations and had expressed optimism about a reconciliation of the races throughout the South. However his own as well as the group experience forced him to recognize the increasingly hopeless plight of Southern blacks. His father, for example, had served both as a county commissioner and a justice of the peace in the late 1860's, but when Chesnutt accepted the nomination for town commissioner at a Republican convention at the Fayetteville Market House in 1880, white advisers "put so many 'fleas in [his] ear' " that he withdrew. Aware of a further deterioration of race relations by the following year, Chesnutt concluded that the pronouncement of a poor-white store clerk in Fayetteville was the prevailing sentiment on the "Negro Question." While conceding to an ex-slave that Chesnutt was "a perfect gentleman in every respect, a hard student, a shorthand writer," and an individual who thought himself as good as a white man, the clerk doggedly insisted, "Well, he's a nigger; and with me a nigger is a nigger, and nothing in the world can make him anything else but a nigger."[13] The attitude of higher-class whites was little better, though expressed more diplomatically. A letter of recommendation which Chesnutt took with him to Raleigh to apply for the principalship of the normal school stated, "His morality is high-toned, and although colored, he is a gentleman."

Such assaults on his pride made him wish to go North at once. Nevertheless, Chesnutt left the South only after much deliberation and planning. On April 23, 1879, he had vowed effusively:

> I will go to the North, where although the prejudice sticks, like a foul blot on the fair scutcheon of American liberty, yet a man may enjoy these privileges [of associating with people of similar taste and interests] if he has the money to pay for them. I will live down the prejudice; I will crush it out. If I can exalt my race, if I can gain the applause of the good, the approbation of God, the thoughts of the ignorant and prejudiced will not concern me.[14]

He tendered his resignation to the Board of Managers of the State Colored Normal School, effective at the close of the session in June. It was hard for his wife, expecting their third child in September, and other relatives and friends to understand his compulsion to sacrifice a secure future for the hazards of a new occupation in strange surroundings.

However, believing that racial discrimination was less pervasive in the North, he determined to take the economic risk and suffer the loneliness of the temporary separation from his family in order to provide his children a better climate for growing up than he had had.

Chesnutt also thought the North would afford him a better environment to realize a dream he had been nurturing since childhood: to become a writer. A local weekly Negro newspaper in 1872 had serialized a little didactic piece in which he condemned the reading of dime novels. Private journal entries between 1874 and 1882 include repeated references to a driving urge to become an author interspersed with amateurish efforts to compose and his reactions to popular writers of the period. He recorded in 1874 what he called his "first real attempt at literature" and labeled it "Lost in a Swamp." By 1875 he wanted to write like Dickens. In 1877, inspired by Thackeray, he had changed his purpose for keeping a journal from improving himself "in the art of composition" to recording "my impressions of men and things, and such incidents or conversations which take place within my knowledge, with a view to future use in literary work."[15]

Tourgée's novel *A Fool's Errand* (1880) and Harriet Beecher Stowe's *Uncle Tom's Cabin* (1852) awoke Chesnutt to the possibility of helping his own people at the same time that he sought to satisfy his persistent urge to write fiction. The would-be author reasoned that if Judge Tourgée, a relative newcomer to the South, could write such an appealing novel about regional social conditions, he, Chesnutt, could compose a better book than either Tourgée or Mrs. Stowe had produced—if he possessed the same ability. He was more familiar than either of them with the thought processes of both black and white Southerners and had a comparable knowledge of history.

Out of such deliberations Chesnutt evolved his "high and holy purpose" for writing, enunciated on May 8, 1880:

> The object of my writings would not be so much the elevation of the colored people as the elevation of the whites—for I consider the unjust spirit of caste which is so insidious as to pervade a whole nation, and so powerful as to subject a whole race and all connected with it to scorn and social ostracism—I consider this a barrier to the moral progress of the American people; and I would be one of the first to head a determined, organized crusade against it. Not a fierce indiscriminate onset, not an appeal to force, for this is something that force can but slightly affect, but a moral revolution which must be brought about in a different manner. . . .
>
> This work is of a two-fold character. The Negro's part is to prepare himself for recognition and equality, and it is the province of literature to open the way for him to get it—to accustom the public mind to the idea; to lead people on, imperceptibly, unconsciously, step by step, to the desired state of feeling. If I can do anything to further this work, and can see any likelihood of obtaining success in it, I would gladly devote my life to it.[16]

Life in the North

More than twenty years would have to pass before Chesnutt could afford to devote all his time to writing. In the meantime he spent about five months in New York City as a reporter for Dow, Jones and Company and a columnist for the *New York Mail and Express*. In November, 1883, however, after a "fit of lonesomeness" he moved on to Cleveland, Ohio, where he had relatives and friends. His family joined him the following April. Chesnutt was employed in the Cleveland office of the Nickel Plate Railroad Company, first as a clerk and later as a stenographer for the firm's legal counsel, Judge Samuel Williamson, in whose office he studied law. During this period Judge Williamson offered to finance Chesnutt's moving abroad, but Chesnutt preferred to remain in the United States. In 1887 he passed the Ohio bar with the highest grade in his group.

In the meantime, Chesnutt employed the techniques of Dickens, Swift, Twain, Cable, Defoe, and other popular writers in shaping his observations into narratives which he thought would appeal particularly to newspapers and lesser magazines ranging from *Puck* to *Youth's Companion*. Apparently, the demands of writing and of operating the legal stenographic service which he established in 1890, making him the most prosperous Negro in Cleveland for a time, caused him to discontinue the revelatory journals which he had kept since he was a teen-ager. However, voluminous correspondence between Chesnutt and various publishers attest to his persistent struggle for recognition as a writer. He received his first rejection slip in 1882, before he left Fayetteville. Many more came before the McClure Syndicate paid him ten dollars for "Uncle Peter's House," which appeared in the *Cleveland News and Herald* in December, 1885. He made Afro-American literary history with "The Goophered Grapevine" in the *Atlantic Monthly* of August, 1887, although his ethnic identity was not then known to the editors.

Chesnutt, however, was not attempting to pass. He knew that black writers were not always expected to meet the high literary standards demanded of white writers; he knew also that works by blacks sometimes received less consideration because of race. Therefore, to insure that his work was considered solely on its merit, Chesnutt did not initially announce that he was an Afro-American. On the other hand, long before he described himself as "an American of acknowledged African descent" in a letter of September 8, 1891, to Houghton, Mifflin Company seeking publication of a collection of stories, Chesnutt's racial identity was generally known in literary circles. The publishers delayed official disclosure until 1899 because of a proper regard for Chesnutt's right to personal privacy and also because of their concern about less favorable public reception of his works.

At the outset Chesnutt attracted the attention of well-known authors such as Tourgée and Cable, the latter of whom sought him out in 1888. Cable gave Chesnutt literary advice for a number of years, and Chesnutt supplied him with information on the "Negro Question" for use in the Open Letter Club, a forum which Cable organized to promote debate by outstanding blacks and whites on the nation's most crucial issue. Walter Hines Page, a native North Carolinian, was more helpful. As an *Atlantic Monthly* editor, he facilitated publication of some stories which Chesnutt submitted to the most prestigious literary magazine of the day. Page not only gave him valuable editorial assistance but also implemented the publication of *The Conjure Woman*, which brought Chesnutt international attention in 1899, and of *The Colonel's Dream*, the last of his novels to appear in print, in 1905.

During these years Chesnutt had devoted many hours to writing nonfiction as well as fiction in his efforts to give black people "their day in court." Further, from the time he set up his own legal stenographic service he set aside funds to support his family should his writing attract enough attention to serve as his vocation rather than as an avocation.

During this period the Chesnutts were active in social groups such as the Cleveland Social Circle and the Tresart Club. The Social Circle, which probably served as the model for Chesnutt's fictional Blue Veins of Groveland,[17] was organized in 1869 by "a small number of friends" who believed that "the formation of a society for the promotion of social intercourse and improvement [for] the welfare of the young people of Cleveland [was] essential."[18] One of the Chesnutt daughters described it as "a very exclusive organization" whose members were "better educated people of color."[19] A literary and musical program was a feature of every meeting and the group circulated privately *The Social Circle Journal.* A few undistinguished poems and some better epigrams by Chesnutt are included in the miscellany of its offerings.

According to Mary Dickerson Donahey, one of the founders of the Tresart Club, it was organized in the first decade of this century to provide musicians, writers, and painters an easy means of sharing common interests. She revealed that Chesnutt's indisputable position as "the most famous writer in the state" overrode the reluctance of most of the all-white membership to invite him to join when his name was first mentioned.[20]

On the other hand, however, Chesnutt was nominated three times before being approved to affiliate with the Rowfant Club in 1910. This exclusively male group was—and still is—interested primarily in fine books and printing, and has since published special editions of Chesnutt's *The Conjure Woman* and "Baxter's Procrustes." Later, in response to an inquiry about the course of his life after he left Fayetteville, Chesnutt mentioned that the club roster included "half a dozen millionaires, a former United States Senator, a former Ambassador to France, and three gentlemen who have been decorated by the French Government. . . . It is needless to say that it is not wealth or blood or birth that makes me acceptable in such company."[21]

Chesnutt joined these organizations because he found in them congenial individuals who shared his enjoyment of literature and music. Nevertheless, he chided them for their snobbery: the Social Circle mildly in "The Wife of His Youth" and caustically in "A Matter of Principle," and the Rowfanters in "Baxter's Procrustes." Chesnutt also insisted upon complete freedom in choosing his friends, according to firsthand observations of the retired educator Russell H. Davis, a lifelong resident of Cleveland.[22] In an Associated Negro Press syndicated feature eulogizing Chesnutt shortly after his death in 1932, N. D. Brascher, who claimed a long-term friendship with the writer, declared that Chesnutt "believed in no inhibition of race."[23]

Chesnutt—the Writer

In September, 1900, emboldened by the initial public reception of *The Conjure Woman, The Wife of His Youth,* and *Frederick Douglass,* all published in 1899, Chesnutt closed down his business so that he could write and lecture full time.

The author was forty-one years old when he embarked on his new career—one in which no blacks and relatively few whites had succeeded up to that time in this country. Moreover, he was risking his own savings in this venture, fully aware that the thrust of his writing was diametrically opposed to the largely pejorative treatment of Negroes by popular white authors. Adherents of the plantation school, particularly Thomas Nelson Page, portrayed Negroes as being very limited in either aspiration or capacity, and incapable of self-government. In *The Leopard's Spots* and *The Clansman,* Thomas Dixon painted Afro-Americans as degenerate and dangerous, a threat to the country when educated and on any level a menace to the racial integrity of Anglo-Saxons. George Harris in *The Leopard's Spots* and Lydia Brown and Gus in *The Clansman* are typical.

Moreover, writers of nonimaginative literature also sought to show the alleged Afro-American inherent inferiority and thus justify a status of second-class citizenship. The denunciation of Negroes in Congress on December 20, 1898, by Representative John Sharp Williams of Mississippi, "who was perhaps a little more polished than the other demagogues," is typical:

> You could shipwreck 10,000 illiterate white Americans on a desert island, and in three weeks they would have a fairly good government conceived and administered upon fairly democratic lines. You could shipwreck 10,000 Negroes, every one of them a graduate of Harvard University, and in less than three years, they would have retrograded governmentally, half of the men would have been killed, and the other half would have two wives apiece.[24]

Chesnutt recalled this situation years later while relating the circumstances under which he first came to national attention as a writer in 1899:

> Thomas Dixon was writing the Negro down industriously and with marked popular success. Thomas Nelson Page was disguising the harshness of slavery under the mask of sentiment. The trend of public sentiment at the moment was distinctly away from the Negro. He had not developed any real political or business standing; socially he was outcast. His musical and stage successes were still for the most part unmade, and on the whole he was a small frog in a large pond, and there was a feeling of pessimism in regard to his future.[25]

Despite these handicaps Chesnutt published many pieces of short fiction, one biography, a number of speeches and essays, and three novels between 1885 and 1930. Available manuscripts attributed to him include one play, five poems, six novels, fifty-three essays and speeches, and eighteen short stories. Some are incomplete.

The author came nearest to perfecting his art in short fiction, achieving a felicitous blend in his handling of basic narrative elements developed to serve a predetermined artistic—and often didactic—end. The high level of his accomplishment is especially significant because he had no formal training in either creative writing or literary criticism. Further, during his formative years he had no meaningful contacts with authors or any other persons seriously interested in writing. According to a private journal entry, dated May, 1880, his only tools for writing consisted of

> a fair knowledge of the classics, a speaking acquaintance with the modern languages, an intimate friendship with literature . . . seven years experience in the school room, two years of married life, and a habit of studying character.[26]

Perhaps cognizance of his lack of preparation for writing fiction made Chesnutt more willing to imitate the models of contemporary writers. Experience also dictated that if he wanted to be published, he had to give the public stories following current trends through publishers who were willing to consider the work of a beginner. Therefore, since there was constant demand in the United States for humor peculiarly American and for pathos characteristic of the contemporary romanticism which had not yet capitulated even to the reticent realism of William Dean Howells, Chesnutt concentrated on very short narratives during the 1880's. Generally light in tone, they were on conventional subjects preferred by periodicals like *Family Fiction, Puck,* and *Tid Bits,* and by newspaper syndicates like that of S. S. McClure. The latter firm circulated the first story Chesnutt is known to have published as an adult, "Uncle Peter's House," which appeared in the *Cleveland News and Herald* in December, 1885.

This rambling narrative is unlike most of the others of this stage of Chesnutt's writing. It is more pathetic than humorous, and treats seriously, though superficially, most of the themes and issues which Chesnutt handles in greater detail in later stores: the cruelties of slavery, especially miscegenation and the forceful separation of close-knit families and sweethearts; the malicious thwarting of ambitious freedmen; unfair labor practices; dishonest selling practices; sharecropping; convict labor; and exorbitant legal fees. It is a capsule review of the dark days before and after the Civil War.

As Chesnutt developed his writing skill and his stories appeared with some regularity in columns of newspapers and magazines, he began to write longer fiction. The author seems to have published no anecdotes after 1891. Most of the stories he contributed to periodicals and published in collections after 1890 differ in form, tone, and focus from earlier works. The mood is more serious, the humor increasingly subtle and satirical, the irony more apparent, and the focus of the more developed action largely upon Afro-Americans. Further, instead of using contemporary settings repeatedly, Chesnutt lets most of his characters move around in the Cape Fear area of North Carolina during the trying times of slavery, Reconstruction, and Redemption.

At this time Chesnutt did not appreciate the literary value of the folklore of his region, nor did he make a conscious effort to familiarize himself with it. The author later acknowledged this lack of awareness and appreciation in "Superstitions and Folk Lore of the South" in the May, 1901, issue of *Modern*

Culture. As Cable did with the Creoles of Louisiana, so Chesnutt called attention to the ills of the present by pointing up the injustices of the past. However, he replaced Cable's romanticism with his particular brand of revelatory realism.

Realism in Chesnutt's fiction ranges from the implicit, with overtones of romanticism, to the explicit which borders on naturalism. His infrequent use of surrealism usually emphasizes the impact upon an individual's subconscious of some harsh aspect(s) of life. All of the varieties of literary temper can be found in the fourteen Uncle Julius "frame" stories, some of which represent Chesnutt's greatest literary achievement.

In the later short stories, as typified by those in *The Wife of His Youth and Other Stories of the Color Line,* and the novels, Chesnutt is consistent in his accurate portrayal of historical fact and contemporary life, especially from the perspective of the disadvantaged and dispossessed. His primary concerns are post-Civil War problems between and within ethnic groups. Chesnutt's treatment of slavery is a refreshing departure from the literature of the period, as in his "The Passing of Grandison" and "The Sheriff's Children." "The Averted Strike," "The March of Progress," "Uncle Wellington's Wives," "The Bouquet," "The Web of Circumstance," "Aunt Lucy's Search," and "The Partners" belong to the relatively large group of stories showing how the freedmen coped with manifold problems of self-determination after Emancipation. The author also described how the sometimes fatherless black family remained cohesive despite systematic assaults on it during slavery. The deep devotion of mothers is confirmed in "Aunt Lucy's Search" and "Aunt Mimy's Son," of fathers in "The Conjurer's Revenge" and "The Doll," of husbands and wives in "Po' Sandy" and "The Gray Wolf's Ha'nt," and of other relatives in "The Passing of Grandison" and "Lonesome Ben," among others. Black family relationships are dealt with in "The Sway-Backed House" and "A Limb of Satan." "Mr. Taylor's Funeral" is concerned with sectarian rivalry, while "The Doll" explores racial antagonisms rooted in the past.

Characters struggle with the problems of naiveté in "Walter Knox's Record" and "A Metropolitan Experience," of class and color in "The Wife of His Youth" and "A Matter of Principle," and with those of racial identity in "Her Virginia Mammy" and "Cicely's Dream." The love interest is overriding in "Jim's Romance," "A Fool's Paradise," "The Kiss," "White Weeds," "How He Met Her," "A Miscarriage of Justice," and "The Exception"; Chesnutt's legal and business backgrounds are equally apparent in "Stryker's Waterloo," "A Miscarriage of Justice," "The Exception," and "Walter Knox's Record." Human failings and foibles are treated lightly in "Wine and Water," "How Dasdy Came Through," "A Doubtful Success," "The Shadow of My Past," and "Tom's Warm Welcome."

"Concerning Father" (1930), Chesnutt's last published short story, touches in the same manner upon color and racial identity which is the most recurrent subject in his works. Father's conclusion that "any way you look at it, this is a queer world, and a great many peculiar things happen in it," echoing Uncle Julius's words in "The Conjurer's Revenge" (1889), is doubtless an opinion which life had painfully reinforced in Chesnutt through the years.

Though imitative in his choice of forms, Chesnutt was innovative enough to adapt them to his own purposes of entertainment and didacticism. As he had conjectured years before, the struggles of Afro-Americans, enslaved and free, to enjoy first-class citizenship since about 1850 provided all the drama necessary for gripping narratives. Further, Chesnutt was astute enough to limit his story materials to his own experiences and the firsthand accounts of other people. He was also aware that the lives of persons of mixed African and European, and sometimes Indian, ancestry, such as the North Carolina mulattos, were new and potentially rewarding literary subjects (in an essay on the subject Chesnutt refers to the latter as "the free colored people of North Carolina").[27] In short, Chesnutt was adapting to his own ends the realistic and "local color" movements then in vogue.

Local Color

Chesnutt's penchant for realistic writing influenced the Flaubertian accuracy of the descriptions of his main settings, the Cape Fear River and Cleveland, Ohio. His fidelity to a localized setting, to the appearance and peculiarities of the people of the area—including their folkways, dialects, and superstitions— justifies recognition of him as a local-color writer.

The vicinity of "Patesville" (actually Fayetteville), a town of "four or five thousand inhabitants, with all shades of complexion," on the banks of a navigable river, furnishes the background for most of Chesnutt's North Carolina stories.

A surprising number of people of color had lived in this region, as well as in all North Carolina, where the number of mixed-bloods during the 1870's (37,441 or 9.6 per cent) and 1890's (77,201 or 13.8 per cent) was exceeded only by those in Virginia and Georgia among the South Atlantic states, according to the *Thirteenth Census of the United States*, 1910.[28] Uncle Julius is a good example of a local-color Negro, being typical of lower-class Afro-Americans who lived in the Cape Fear area of North Carolina during the latter half of the nineteenth century. This venerable-looking colored man is described in "The Goophered Grapevine" by John, the narrator, as

> . . . a tall man, though slightly bowed by the weight of years, apparently quite vigorous. He was not entirely black, and this fact, together with the quality of his hair, which was about six inches long and very bushy, except on the top of his head, where he was quite bald, suggested a slight strain of other than Negro blood. There was a shrewdness in his eyes, too, which was not altogether African, and which . . . was indicative of a corresponding shrewdness in his character.[29]

Chesnutt suggests the pervasiveness and variety of this mixing in several of his characters. Besides Viney in "The Dumb Witness," with her triple ethnic heritage, and the mulatto Uncle Wellington in "Uncle Wellington's Wives," with his father's Caucasian features and his mother's color, Uncle Solomon Grundy in "The Sway-Backed House" shows his racially mixed background in his dark color, straight nose, kinky hair, thin lips, and blue eyes. Cicely in "Cicely's Dream" is a "bronze Venus"—a brown not deep enough to blot out the redness from another race in her cheeks. She and her grandparents decide that the wounded young man she finds in the woods is "one er dem bright mulatters, f'om Robeson County—some of 'em calls deyse'ves Croatan Injins," a group who by legend descended from Sir Walter Raleigh's lost colony and still reside mostly in the North Carolina sandhills country.

The natural features of the Cape Fear section also figure prominently in many of the stories. John finds the climate perfect and the soil ideal for the grape-culture he contemplates; a cousin already in residence is in the turpentine business, one of the chief industries of nineteenth-century North Carolina. The walnuts, chinquapins, and wild grapes which Cicely and her ward John gather, the dried peas they pick, the corn they pull, and the fodder they strip may all be found in abundance in the Tarheel State. The animals into which Aun' Peggy changes people, and the birds and insects which she uses as emissaries are native to this part of the country, as are the sandy surfaces, the pine stands, and the shallow streams bordered by bays and willows.

Chesnutt displays another facet of his artistry in the skillful manner in which he uses indigenous materials. In many cases he establishes a precedent in his choice or use of these materials, especially to reflect regional superstitions which John in "Tobe's Tribulations" describes as

> dim reflections of ancestral fetishism; . . . the supersitions, filtered through the Negro intellect, of the Scotch settlers who had founded their homes on Cape Fear at a time when a kelpie haunted every Highland glen, and witches, like bats, darkened the air as they flew by in their nocturnal wanderings.

For example, Tenie turns Sandy into a pine tree in "Po' Sandy" because pine was so plentiful that the appearance of a new tree would hardly be noticed. Later, after that tree is tapped for turpentine once (Sandy shows the resultant mutilation when he resumes his natural form), Tenie sends a hornet to protect him from further injury by stinging the would-be tapper.

Likewise, Aun' Peggy uses the hornet to sting the knees of the racehorse in "Sis' Becky's Pickaninny" to hasten the retrading of Sis' Becky and the horse to their original owners. In the same story the conjure woman changes little Mose into a mockingbird, so that he may fly swiftly to the other plantation and cheer his grieving mother with his lilting notes. The kind of black bear into which Aun' Peggy changes Tobe in "Tobe's Tribulations" once roamed the North Carolina hills. Its fondness for sweet potatoes and honey and its habit of hibernating are responsible for Tobe's first failure to reach the North.

The old woman also employs the homely sweet potato, a staple of the Southeast, in "Mars Jeems's Nightmare" to restore Mars Jeems to his natural state. The scuppernongs which she goophers at the request of Mars Dugal' were so plentiful that grape-culture was a profitable enterprise at the time. The new scuppernong wine which Primus as mule consumes in "The Conjurer's Revenge" was a favorite drink. The Spencer oak in "The Marked Tree" is of a variety which adds to the majestic beauty of the North Carolina landscape. Moreover, the clay in which these oaks often spread their roots constitutes in "Lonesome Ben" a main item of Ben's diet and causes his complexion to change from beautiful black to jaundice yellow.

The diction and dialectical pronunciation of many of Chesnutt's characters likewise identify them with the Virginia-Carolina-Georgia region, the Tarheel State, and the Fayetteville area; in Hans Kurath's *Word Geography of the Eastern United States* the latter is located in the southeastern region composed of the valleys of the Cape Fear and Pee Dee Rivers. Through Uncle Julius, Chesnutt introduced into literature the terms *Jim Crow* (meaning a crude comb resembling a currycomb) and *goopher*.[30] Many other words or expressions used in the tales are identified with North Carolina. The scuppernong, imported from France under another name, bears its present name because it first flourished along the Scuppernong River. Other terms associated with the state by long-term or widespread general usage include *slat bonnet, piggin, ax* (for *ask* or *asked*), *biggety, sometimey, crick* (for *creek*), *passell, branch, you all, lighterd* (for *lightwood*), *monst'us, patteroles* (for *patrollers*), and *cape jessamine* (for *cape jasmine*). Although they were no doubt used by both ethnic groups, *buckra, conjure, conjuration, coming through, hoe cake,* and *working his* (or *her*) *roots* probably occur more often in black speech; *rockaway, piggin,* and *piazza* are used more frequently by whites. White sandhillers of Uncle Julius's class substitute *fresh* for *freshet, riz* for *rose,* and *jist* or *jest* for *just.* A constant use of the plural verb with a singular subject ("Pete were"; "Pete air") distinguishes the speech patterns of the mountain whites in "The Prophet Peter."

Uncle Julius's language is rich in the diction, flow, and imagery which lend a special vitality to folk speech. Describing Mars Dugal' McAdoo, in "The Goophered Grapevine," Julius says,

> Now, ef you 'd 'a' knowed ole Mars Dugal' McAdoo, you 'd 'a' knowed dat it ha' ter be a might rainy day when he could n' fine sump'n fer his niggers ter do, en it ha' ter be a might little hole he could n' crawl thoo, en ha' ter be a monst'us cloudy night when a dollar git by him in de dahkness. . . .[31]

He also recalls that his mammy told him "Mars Jeems's Nightmare" when he "wa'n't mo' d'n knee-high ter a hopper-grass."[32] Again, his phrasing of Tenie's proposal to Sandy that he permit her to change him into some other form, "Ef you'll des say de word, I kin turn you ter w'atever you wanter be, en you kin stay right whar you wanter, ez long ez you mineter"[33] has a rhyming rhythm which is characteristic of Negro folk speech.

The distinctive flavor of this ethnic diction is also conveyed in Brother Gabriel Gainey's explanation in "The Fall of Adam," this time in the stirring cadence of the black preacher:

Adam started to run—de Lawd right aftuh 'im; Adam jumped ovuh de tree of life—de Lawd right aftuh 'im; run roun' de worl'—de Lawd right aftuh 'im; swum ovuh de sea—de Lawd right aftuh 'im; jumped ovuh Jupiter—de Lawd gainin' on 'im; jumped ovuh de moon—de Lawd close behin'. When he got to de sun, he was so tired he couldn' jump high 'nuff, an' de bright light blind' 'im so he couldn' see whar' he was goin', an' he fell—fell right down into the rivuh Jordan an' befo' he could pull hisse'f out'n de mud at de bottom, de Lawd cotch 'im—an' sich anuthuh whippin' de Lawd give Adam de worl' have nevah hearn tell uv sence. An' dat 'splains, bro'rs an' sisters, de fall of Adam.

C. W. Foster, in his doctoral dissertation, "The Representation of Negro Dialect in Charles W. Chesnutt's *The Conjure Woman*," (University of Alabama, 1968), has determined that the phonology of *The Conjure Woman* is "significantly different" from that of Page's *In Ole Virginia*. He also notes that although Chesnutt followed the pattern of the literary dialect of Joel Chandler Harris and Thomas Nelson Page when it suited his purposes, as in the use of *marster* for *master* (pronounced to rhyme with *imposter*), he was bound by no pattern or established practice in trying to represent the speech of the characters treated. Depending less upon eye-spelling than most, Chesnutt devised combinations which let the word remain recognizable and thereby elicit a phonemic response from the reader, as with *aidge* for *edge* and *watermillyum* for *watermelon*. The author's representation of *point* as *pint*, of *took* as *tuck*, of *year* for *ear*, and his spelling of *shut, touch, brush, scarce, hearth, hoof, yonder, crop, neither,* and *because* so that the pronunciation will rhyme with *bet, stretch, mesh, lace, path, puff, gander, flap, brother,* and *daze* (some of the archaisms are traceable to British pronunciations) was the basis of Foster's conclusion that, according to *The Linguistic Atlas of the United States and Canada,* such a combination of pronunciations would characterize the speech of an individual in a lower socioeconomic class in the Fayetteville, North Carolina, area. Thus, as Foster observed, "Chesnutt's representation of dialect is so accurate, and his ear for dialect so acute, that it is actually possible to locate the provenience of Uncle Julius *from his dialect.*"[34]

Chesnutt is equally meticulous in his representation of the speech of other characters and likewise reflects differences of locale, race, social class and economic level in their speech patterns. He shows the slight variance in the speech of lower-class blacks and whites by respelling a greater proportion of the words spoken by blacks. Foster confirmed that there is little difference in the speech patterns of the two groups on this level. All of the educated people, North and South, use standard English colored slightly by the sex, temperament, and mood of the speaker. The narrator of *The Conjure Woman,* for example, uses diction easily understandable to an average reader, though occasionally high-flown; but Davis, a member of the sciolistic Bodleian Club in "Baxter's Procrustes," borders on obscurantism in one vague, heavily polysyllabic statement: "Well . . . it is not exactly Spencerian, although it squints at the Spencerian view, with a slight deflection toward Hegelianism."

Chesnutt describes Northern scenes and people less extensively. However, he clearly delineates Groveland to be recognized as Cleveland, as is evident in "Uncle Wellington's Wives," when Mr. Johnson is showing Uncle Wellington the sights of the city.

Cleveland, a principal center then, had attracted an especially large number of Afro-Americans from North Carolina since at least the 1850's. Many of them were very fair, their appearance having been greatly affected by their European, Indian, or other ancestry. In Cleveland, as in other black communities, they were called Blue Veins by their fellow Afro-Americans. However, the standards for acceptance in such groups varied in various localities, as Chesnutt indicates in his writings. Mr. Ryder in "The Wife of His Youth" and the Clayton father and daughter in "A Matter of Principle" are typical members of the Groveland Blue Vein Society organized at the close of the Civil War "to establish and maintain correct social standards among people of color." Character and culture are stated requisites for membership; light color and free birth, alleged requirements.

Mr. Ryder, the dean of the group, has features "of a refined type," almost straight hair; and irreproachable manners. Moreover, his dress is as neat as his morals are above suspicion. Although he has had little formal education, he has a responsible white-collar position and is well read. A practice of economy has enabled him to purchase a comfortable house in a good neighborhood, and his home furnishes ample evidence of his interest in poetry, painting, and music.

Mr. Clayton, on the other hand, has by business acumen become the richest colored man in Groveland. With his olive complexion and Latin-American features accentuated by a Van Dyke beard and pointed mustache, he strikingly complements his "nearly white" daughter, Alice. She, though pretty, accomplished, amiable, and tasteful in her dress, is as color-conscious as her father.

The Groveland Blue Veins speak standard English, as do most of Chesnutt's Northern white characters. Less fortunate blacks who have more recently migrated from the South, including 'Liza Jane in "The Wife of His Youth" and Uncle Wellington in "Uncle Wellington's Wives," still use a dialect hardly distinguishable from that of Uncle Julius. The most distinctive dialect of the Northern whites is that of the garrulous Mrs. Flannigan in "Uncle Wellington's Wives." In a thick Irish brogue which bespeaks her recent arrival in

the United States, she opines to her fellow-worker, Uncle Wellington, that
". . . it must be an awful lonesome life ye've been afther l'adin', as a single
man, wid no one to cook fer ye, or look afther ye."

Character

In pleading the black man's cause, Chesnutt depicts many types of characters,
black and white, used by American short-story writers during the last half of
the nineteenth century, as well as by Afro-American writers of short fiction
until the Harlem Renaissance of the 1920's. The stereotypes most frequently
portrayed were identified in the 1930's by Sterling Brown as the following:
the contented slave, the wretched freeman, the brute Negro, the tragic mulatto,
the comic Negro, and the exotic primitive.[35] Later, Nick Aaron Ford added
to the list the worshipful servant and the superstitious Negro—two characters
for whom Chesnutt provides no clear-cut example.[36] According to James W.
Byrd, between 1900 and 1950 the benevolent white father of mulattos, the kind
aristocrat, the Northern champion of the poor, the mean planter, the brutal
overseer, and the poor white villain appear regularly in the short fiction of
black writers.[37] Professional men such as lawyers, politicians, and ministers particularly, as well as actors, businessmen, and soldiers, are almost wholly identified by white writers as white in short stories of the late nineteenth century.
Children, preachers, politicians, banjo players, fiddlers, and voodooists have
the ethnic identity of their black creators.·

Chesnutt usually added another facet to some of the popular black stereotypes which he found more acceptable, thus investing them with new depth
and dimension. On the other hand, he kept his depiction of derogatory Negro
stereotypes at a minimum, for one of his chief purposes was to counteract the
increasingly pejorative treatment of the Afro-American character in contemporary literature. Chesnutt apparently felt that no enslaved black could be contented, for the contentment of his seemingly contented slave is only a pose in
"The Passing of Grandison." The supposedly stupid slave Grandison tells
Colonel Owens, who is "de bes' marster any nigger ever had in dis worl',"
that he is "better off . . . dan . . . lowdown free niggers" and that he
"would n' low none er dem cussed, low-down abolitioners ter come nigh" him
if he is permitted to go North as young Mars Dick's body servant.[38] But Grandison's subsequent actions prove that—like many others who in real life traveled on the Underground Railroad—he cherishes his freedom, he is willing to
risk it to free his family, and he is capable of completely outwitting the colonel,
his son, and their friends in the process.

Ben in "Lonesome Ben," though likewise discontented, never wins his
freedom. A runaway lurking on the outskirts of his master's plantation, hoping
to catch a glimpse of his family, he is mistaken for a wretched freeman.

Apparently Chesnutt considered a wretched freeman as much of an anomaly as a contented slave, for all his freemen have forceful personalities which usually bring them success rather than failure in their endeavors. In addition to Mr. Ryder, the Claytons, and other progressive blacks in the North, Aun' Peggy and Uncle Jube demonstrate their special powers in the South. A pivotal figure in a number of the Uncle Julius tales, Aun' Peggy is respected by all the blacks and whites around. She is also feared by most of them for occult powers which are surpassed only by those of Uncle Jube in "The Gray Wolf's Ha'nt." Aun' Peggy is set up in the "conjuh" business down by "de Wim'l'ton Road" in a settlement of free Negroes; in her cabin are "roots en go'ds en snake' skins en yuther cunjuh-fixin's, en a big black cat wid yaller eyes, settin' on de h'a'th," according to Uncle Julius. "She could wuk de mos' powerfulles' kin' er goopher,—could make people hab fits, er rheumatiz, er make 'em des dwinel away en die; en dey say she went out ridin' de niggers at night, fer she wuz a witch 'sides bein' a cunjuh 'oman."[39] A shrewd business woman and student of human nature, she requires remuneration according to the ability of the client to pay and the difficulty of the task to be performed. She complains about the small mess of peas which in "Sis' Becky's Pickaninny" poor old Aun' Nancy brings the first time she asks Aun' Peggy to reunite Sis' Becky and little Mose. The conjure woman accepts as her due the basket of chicken, the pound cake, and the bottle of scuppernong wine which helps evoke Mars Dugal's request that she stop the slaves from eating his scuppernongs. When in "A Victim of Heredity" the avaricious Mars Donal' McDonal' pays her with a lead dollar, she makes it appear to be a twenty-dollar gold piece and gets him to change it for her, thus making McDonal' nineteen dollars poorer for trying to cheat her. The only exception is young Mars Tom McDonal' in the same story. Because he has saved her from drowning she offers to help him become solvent financially and even advances him money for the necessary business transactions.

Aun' Peggy follows definite procedures to get the desired results. In "The Goophered Grapevine," for example, she performs her rites as ceremoniously as the high priestess of an ancient nature cult.

> She sa'ntered 'roun' 'mongst de vimes, en tuk a leaf fum dis one, en a grape-hull fum dat one, en a grape-seed fum anudder one; en den a little twig fum here, en a little pinch er dirt fum dere—en put it all in a big black cat's tail, en den fill' de bottle wid scuppernon' wine. W'en she got de goopher all ready en fix', she tuk 'n went out in de woods en buried it under de root uv a red oak tree, en den come back en tole one er de niggers she done goopher de grape-vimes, en a'er nigger w'at eat dem grapes 'ud be sho ter die inside 'n twel' mont's.[40]

Other "mixtrys" variously cause a white plantation owner to turn into a Negro and back again and make a slave invisible ("Mars Jeems's Nightmare"); reduce the appetite of a plantation work force ("A Victim of Heredity"); and change people into animals and birds ("Sis' Becky's Pickaninny" and "Tobe's Tribulations"). In "Hot-Foot Hannibal" she fashions a baby doll to put a spell on Hannibal; in "The Gray Wolf's Ha'nt" she prepares a life charm to ward off the effects of a spell cast by Uncle Jube. Whenever her goopher is ineffective, as in "The Gray Wolf's Ha'nt" or "Tobe's Tribulations," human fallibility rather than the inefficacy of her magic may be the cause.

Aun' Peggy acknowledges at the outset that Uncle Jube is more powerful than she; this he proves conclusively in "The Gray Wolf's Ha'nt." Already a veteran in "de [cunjah] business" in Patesville when Aun' Peggy was just beginning, Uncle Jube has a jaybird familiar so smart that "de niggers 'lowed he wuz de ole Debbil hisse'f."[41] With the bird's help and his keen insight into human nature, the old conjure man is able to avenge his son's death in a diabolical manner despite Aun' Peggy's best efforts to save her client.

No Negro brutes appear in Chesnutt's short fiction, and only one character in his published novels, the mulatto Jeff Wain in *The House Behind the Cedars,* qualifies for such a classification. Conditions justified this restriction. Chesnutt was well aware of the tendency of the majority to accuse—and sometimes to execute summarily by lynching—an unbelievably large number of black men for alleged sexual intimacies with white women. Moreover, as a child of nine he was nearby when a Negro man being taken up for arraignment for "the nameless crime" was fatally shot, as previously plotted, at the Fayetteville Market House. The press consistently gave undue attention to all crimes attributed to Afro-Americans. Further, the black male as brute was serving increasingly as a scapegoat in fiction at the turn of the century, especially in Thomas Dixon's works.

Likewise, only one of Chesnutt's major characters, Rena Walden in *The House Behind the Cedars,* has any of the passivity usually attributed to the tragic mulatto. The lives of the mulattos in his short fiction may be shattered, but not so seriously as to prevent their reacting aggressively. Viney, a volatile combination of black, white, and Indian, in "The Dumb Witness," is incensed when her paramour-master, Malcolm Murchison, informs her that he is about to marry a rich widow. When her remonstrances to him are of no avail, her revelation of the mesalliance to the prospective bride causes the latter to break the engagement. The master, thwarted and enraged, beats Viney mercilessly. She, apparently unable to speak, divulges only after his death years later the whereabouts of legal documents which would have made Murchison financially secure; they had been left in her care during the short interval he was away ascertaining whether Viney had destroyed his romance. If depth of feeling were the only criterion, Phillis in "The Marked Tree," Tenie in "Po' Sandy," and Chloe in "Hot-Foot Hannibal" could be placed among the tragic mulattos; their skin color, however, is nowhere even suggested.

Chesnutt's comic Afro-American characters are likewise relatively few in number and different from the stereotype. The majority of them serve other literary purposes as well. Because of his experience as a black and because of the total race experience in the United States, Chesnutt often used an edged humor to convey a serious message. As he indicated to George W. Cable, most of his writings up to that time had been humorous. "But," he qualified, "my position, my surroundings, are not such as to make me take a humorous view of life. They rather tend the other way . . . a humorous Jew is a rarity . . . the reason is to be sought in their past history."[42]

The stereotypic comic Afro-American, always ludicrous and sometimes unbelievable in his good-natured stupidity, was already being given assiduous attention by James Lane Allen, Virginia Boyle, Harry Stillwell Edwards, Irwin Russell, Francis Hopkinson Smith, and Ruth McEnery Stuart. Chesnutt, however, is careful not to demean his black characters while he pokes fun at them. The lightning reversal of attitude expressed in "A Limb of Satan" by old Ebenezer Johnson and Sis' Jane Walker toward one another and toward her little son, Sammy, who has wrought havoc on Johnson's possessions and person with his slingshot, evokes sympathetic laughter. Discovery that they are closely related changes the old man's insults and threats of dire bodily harm to concord, caresses, and candy. In "A Tight Boot" Chesnutt moralizes about the sin of vanity and shows the highly discomforting wages Bob pays for wearing to a late night party the boots of an overnight guest at his master's inn. The stuttering Bob is unable to remove one of the boots even after the owner repeatedly calls for them the next morning. His frantic farcical antics subsequently involve his irate master as well as other slave help in the kitchen. On the other hand, the deeper import of "Appreciation" is only implied. In it an old freedman, after smilingly accepting a playful kick from a young white man, requests and receives from the donor some "terbacker."

Although "A Roman Antique" and "The Origin of the Hatchet Story" also feature comic characters of color, a greater number of whites play light humorous roles in Chesnutt's short fiction. Lovesick Tom in "Tom's Warm Welcome," vinous old Peter Hardcase in "Wine and Water," the overly apprehensive Mrs. Baird in "The Doctor's Wife," and the nightmare-ridden narrator of "A Midnight Adventure" are among the more fully delineated characters in ludicrous situations.

The worshipful servant vied with the comic Negro for treatment in post-Civil War fiction and gained ascendancy in serious works of the plantation school led by Thomas Nelson Page, who was followed closely by Joel Chandler Harris. However, no worshipful servants fawn on their employers in Chesnutt's short works, though Uncle Julius, who recalls events of slavery which are in turn related by the narrator John in *The Conjure Woman* and at least seven other tales, is unmistakably modeled on Harris's Uncle Remus. But Uncle Julius McAdoo, probably Chesnutt's most popular character, completely overshadows his literary inspiration. Uncle Remus is simply the mouthpiece for the African animal stories which Harris heard the slaves tell; Uncle Julius spins tales combining myth, superstition, and the sometimes terrifying realities of life. Moreover, by these three tenuous threads he usually manipulates one or more persons to act in accordance with his wishes. The old freedman's motives thus organically connect the action of the frame and that of the inner stories, giving these tales a structural compactness lacking in those of Harris. As the narrator observes in "The Marked Tree," Julius "took the crude legends and vague superstitions of the neighborhood and embodied them in stories as complete, in their way, as the Sagas of Iceland or the primitive tales of ancient Greece." Further, in the words of John in "The Gray Wolf's Ha'nt," this "venerable-looking colored man" seemed to possess an exhaustless store of tales of the old slavery days,

> . . . some weirdly grotesque, some broadly humorous, some bearing the stamp of truth, faint, perhaps, but still discernible; others palpable inventions, whether his own or not we never knew, though his fancy doubtless embellished them. But even the wildest was not without an element of pathos,—the tragedy, it might be, of the story itself; the shadow, never absent, of slavery and of ignorance; the sadness, always, of life as seen by the fading light of an old man's memory.[43]

Significantly, neither Julius's experiences as a slave nor advancing age seems to have lessened his shrewdness. Like most normal human beings, he seems to be trying to get something for himself; the coveted items include food, drink, money for clothing, a job for a relative, and a building to serve as a church. These items fall into two significant categories: basic necessities of life and support for the most important institutions of the black culture of the time, the family and the church. Julius also shows concern for the few whites whom he really likes. He is altogether altruistic in letting his favorite, Miss Annie (a name which is surely a take-off on the derisive "Miss Ann"), keep and use his priceless rabbit foot to improve her health in "Sis' Becky's Pickaninny." His evident fondness for Mabel is enough for him to set the stage for patching the lovers' quarrel between her and Malcolm Murchison, although a little bribe from the latter may also be a motivating factor. It is therefore evident that though Uncle Julius is obviously self-serving and has no scruples about practicing chicanery when it suits his purpose, he is not altogether selfish or mercenary. His concern for those he cares about transcends gain, and his friendship cannot be bought.

An equally steadfast belief in superstitions has an unmistakable effect on Uncle Julius's personality. His complete faith in the efficacy of "de lef hin'-foot er a grabe-ya'd rabbit, killt by a cross-eyed nigger on a da'k night in de full er de moon' " is complete.[44] In this aspect of his character he illustrates the stereotype of the superstitious Negro. The ignorance resulting from lack of formal training (he indignantly rejects the heliocentric theory of the universe in "The Conjurer's Revenge" as violating what he sees with his own eyes!), the limited outlook of one who has traveled hardly twenty miles from his birthplace, his withering scorn of the poor-white, and the psychological conditioning of slavery likewise manifest themselves. Nevertheless, Uncle Julius is fascinating as a character whose depths have not been completely plumbed.

The narrator becomes increasingly aware of the subtleties which underlie the bland surfaces of the Negro's behavior, especially after the watermelon disappears in "A Deep Sleeper." Perhaps Chesnutt is suggesting that John's initial blindness parallels that of Southern and Northern whites who underestimated blacks—especially the slaves—in the antebellum period. Uncle Julius is not a participant in the action of the inner tales; yet he stands at the center of the action of the frame stories as a whole. Despite such prominence Chesnutt never reveals where the freedman's innocence ends and his guile begins. Consequently, the old man emerges as the most characteristic, complex, and completely drawn of all the figures in Chesnutt's short fiction.

Chesnutt's realistic rather than romantic concept of the Old South is reflected in the absence of the benevolent white father of mulattos, the kind aristocrat, and the Northern champion of the poor in his short fiction; the latter two are well represented in two of his novels, however. Conversely, the plantation- and slave-owners Dugal' McAdoo (Uncle Julius's "ole marster"), Marrabo McSwayne, Jeems McLean, Colonel Pendleton, Aleck Spencer, Malcolm Murchison, Colonel Owens, Donal' McDonal', and Sheriff Campbell in composite form emerge as the mean planter. They are self-indulgent rather than self-controlled, imperious, avaricious, cruel, unprincipled, and sometimes hypocritical. Regarding their slaves as chattel rather than as persons, they sell or trade them at will. McSwayne in "Po' Sandy" swaps Sandy's loving wife for another slave because he can get "big boot" on the deal; he consoles Sandy with a dollar! The once very wealthy Spencer, in "The Marked Tree," urged by his wife, sells Phillis's only son, Isham—Phillis "had be'n impident tuh huh one time"—to finance Marse Johnny's wedding; and because he cannot raise the thousand dollars cash the owner demands, Pendleton swaps Sis' Becky for a racehorse he *must* have. He declares hypocritically that he feels so bad about separating the young slave from her baby that he can't bear to tell her she has been sold—he even tries to give the baby away when the horse trader refuses to buy it. McDonal' is so eager to make slavery more profitable that he gets Aun' Peggy to prepare for him a goopher mixture that will reduce the slaves' appetites but not affect their capacity to work.

According to Uncle Julius, "Mars Jeems" McLean is vicious:

> His niggers wuz bleedzd ter slabe frum daylight ter da'k . . en dey didn' get no mo' ter eat dan dey oughter, en dat de coa'ses' kin'. Dey wa'n't 'lowed ter sing, ner dance, ner play de banjo w'en Mars Jeems wuz roun' de place, fer Mars Jeems say he would n' hab no sech gwines-on,—said he bought his han's ter wuk, en not ter play, en we'en night come dey mus' sleep en res', so dey'd be ready ter get up soon in de mawnin' en go ter dey wuk fresh en strong.[45]

McLean also forbids courting and separates slaves who want to get married. His unvarying response to complaints is forty lashes. "Mars Jeems didn' make no 'lowance fer nachul bawn laz'ness, ner sickness, ner trouble in de min', ner nuffin; he wuz des gwine ter git so much wuk outer eve' han', er know de reason w'y.' "[46] Later, when his love affair sours, he vents his frustrations on the hapless slaves.

Though in "Mars Jeems's Nightmare" the slaves suffer greatly under the direct supervision of their owner, Mars Jeems McLean, they fare even worse under "po'-w'ite" Nick Johnson, who is obviously a stereotype of the brutal overseer. His "big yaller [snaggle] teef," his constant snapping of a rawhide which he always carried, and his penchant for hard driving are not the only reasons the slaves call him "Ole Nick" behind his back.

> He wuz wusser 'n Mars Jeems ever da'ed ter be. Co'se de darkies did n' lack de way Mars Jeems used 'em, but he wuz de marster, en had a right ter do ez he please'; but dis yer Ole Nick wa'n't nuffin' but a po' buckrah, en all de niggers 'spised 'im ez much ez dey hated 'im, fer he did n' own nobody, en wa'n't no bettah 'n a nigger, fer in dem days any 'spectable pusson would rather be a nigger dan a po' w'ite man.[47]

Johnson finally leaves the plantation suspected of fraud after his extreme cruelty boomerangs.

In tracing the rise of Mars McDonal', Chesnutt reveals that some wealthy planters are not of patrician stock. Details of the unethical means they employed in becoming prosperous plantation owners justify their classification as poor-white villains early in their careers. The writer shows that some of the blue-bloods are unscrupulous too. Pressed for cash, Sheriff Campbell in "The Sheriff's Children" sells one of his young mulatto concubines and their child in a fit of anger. Malcolm Murchison in "The Dumb Witness" beats his housekeeper-paramour mercilessly because she spoils his plans to marry a rich white widow. In "The Goophered Grapevine" Mars Dugal' McAdoo makes a profitable business of selling Henry at a prime rate in the spring when he is robust and buying him back as a bargain in the fall when he ages prematurely and appears on the verge of dying. *Nouveau riche* Donal' McDonal' even tries to give Aun' Peggy a worthless lead dollar instead of a silver one for reducing the cost of feeding his slaves in "A Victim of Heredity."

Among the professionals frequently characterized in fiction, Chesnutt gives teachers preferred treatment, no doubt both because he observed firsthand the praiseworthy efforts of Northern whites "to transform three millions of slaves into intelligent freemen" and because he himself had served in the classroom for nine years. The Misses Henrietta Noble in "The March of Progress," Mary Myrover in "The Bouquet," and Martha Chandler in "Cicely's Dream" are sympathetically drawn and are saved from the blight of idealization by having personal as well as altruistic reasons for their self-sacrificial but fulfilling work.

In "Uncle Wellington's Wives" Chesnutt presents a lively version of one unlisted white stereotype, that of the Irish immigrants who were pouring into the Northern cities during the last decades of the nineteenth century. Mrs. Flan-

nigan, a volatile, uninhibited widow who has decided she is still too young
to remain unmarried, uses her advantages as cook in a wealthy household to
attract likely prospects for matrimony, including the "very good-looking" mulatto Uncle Wellington. Her buxom figure, agile tongue, and "a natural
freshness of complexion deepened to a fiery red by the heat of a kitchen range"
further vitalize one of the liveliest and most natural of Chesnutt's white female
characters.[48]

One of Chesnutt's noteworthy contributions was to introduce a black who
fits no sterotypic pattern. This is all the more striking when the story seems
to carry no weighty message. In the anecdote "An Eloquent Appeal," the door-
to-door salesman who comes into the narrator's office attempting a "hard sell"
is "a tall, tolerably well-dressed and somewhat distinguished-looking colored
man" who uses high-flown English. In the course of the largely one-sided conversation, he points out the wrongs inflicted upon the Negro from the introduction of slavery in this country to the present, suggests that some whites are
becoming aware that they owe him reparations for the indignities he has suffered (a surprisingly modern sentiment), and asks his listener, "As a member
of the dominant race, do you not feel it your duty to do what you can toward
lifting my race to a higher level—toward repaving, in some small degree, the debt
this country owes them?"

The narrator, obviously white, maintains an attitude of attentive objectivity
while tacitly acknowledging the truth of the Negro's argument. The only emotion he expresses is astonishment at finding himself the possessor of a stick
of "Magic Corn Cure" in exchange for a quarter he can ill afford to spend.
The incongruity of the seller's presentation and of his product invests the episode with American humor, but does not divest the Afro-American of any of
his dignity. This black character gains in stature when contrasted with the
white book salesman in "Gratitude," another anecdote describing an almost
identical situation. In that short piece, the "tall, cadaverous-looking individual,
clad in a faded brown ulster" and kicked downstairs, is "ever so much obliged"
for being let off alive while the Negro in "An Eloquent Appeal" bows out with a
sale and a flourish.

In the short stories with a more serious tone, the mulatto Tom in "The
Sheriff's Children" stands out. With his back literally to the wall of a jail
cell, he faces the equally hopeless alternatives of escaping and probably being
lynched by a mob or of remaining to be tried and being hanged by the authorities for a murder he has not committed. The sheriff, who has protected the
youth from the mob, suddenly finds himself threatened by his own pistol in
the hands of his desperate prisoner. When reproached, the young man reveals
their relationship and berates his father: "Did you give me your name, or even
your protection? Other white men gave their colored sons freedom and money,
and sent them to the free States. *You* sold *me* to the rice swamps."[49] Having
spoken bitterly about the limitations imposed on him by his color despite his

education, Tom is forestalled from taking the sheriff's life by a bullet in his shooting arm from the sheriff's daughter. Now facing almost certain death for a crime he has not committed, the youth recalls that all his life his color—and hence his condition—has been the primary cause of his misfortunes. Totally despairing, Tom lets his hurts and hates flow out with his lifeblood when he tears the bandages from his wound during "the silent watches of the night."

In his works Chesnutt acknowledged the deleterious effects of traumatic everyday living upon blacks. Nevertheless, though he depicts them as degraded and sometimes destroyed, they are never dehumanized. Rather, they display considerable emotional depth in coping with their problems. The slaves Tenie in "Po' Sandy," Ben in "Lonesome Ben," and Chloe in "Hot-Foot Hannibal" love so intensely that each loses his will to live after being separated by death or circumstance from husband, wife, or intended. Sis' Becky in "Sis' Becky's Pickaninny" is so devoted to her little son, Mose, "de cutes', blackes', shiny-eyedes' little nigger you eber laid eyes on," and he to her that only the conjuration of Aun' Peggy keeps mother and baby from dying of loneliness when Sis' Becky is sold away from her child after having lost her husband the same way. Again, in "The Doll" the unusual action is psychological rather than physical or thaumaturgical: the Groveland barber Tom Taylor controls his understandably driving urge for bloody revenge so that he may continue to protect his little daughter rather than die a convicted murderer.

Without violating the truth of the times Chesnutt shows how Afro-American characters, usually less favorably placed, still manage to get what they want by using their heads. Techniques used may be telling a story with a point, as Uncle Julius does; enlisting the aid of a conjurer as related in "Mars Jeems's Nightmare"; charting a course of strategic action such as Dasdy follows in "How Dasdy Came Through"; outwitting the other fellow in the manner of Jack in "A Matter of Principle"; combining Dasdy's and Jack's tactics on a grander scale with the fortitude Grandison exhibits in "The Passing of Grandison"; or simply keeping one's mouth shut, a tactic Viney in "The Dumb Witness" (later incorporated in modified form in *The Colonel's Dream*) and Tom Taylor in "The Doll" find preferable to creating a scene. All these methods assure victory for the weak who are wise enough to know they cannot compete successfully in open confrontation. Sometimes even a loss can lead to a moral triumph such as Mrs. Harper enjoys in "Her Virginia Mammy" and Mr. Ryder in "The Wife of His Youth."

Chesnutt's black characters are also very fond of their friends, regardless of race. Uncle Julius has a rabbit foot of a kind so "ska'ce" that no amount of money can buy it; in "Sis' Becky's Pickaninny" he does, however, lend it to Miss Annie, whom he evidently "sot sto' by," to help rouse her out of a deep depression. Freedman William Cain, an almost unbelievably noble character in "The Partners," demonstrates to what great lengths he will go to live up to his pact of friendship with the less skilled ex-slave Rufus Green.

In "The March of Progress" when Miss Henrietta Noble is about to be summarily replaced by a young black teacher at the Patesville colored school, Old Abe Johnson, father of fourteen, smites the consciences of the other school-board members by recalling Miss Noble's many kindnesses during the "fifteen yeahs dat she has libbed 'mongs' us an' made herse'f one of us, an' endyoed havin' her own people look down on her." Sophy Tucker's devotion to her white teacher, Miss Mary Myrover, in "The Bouquet," transcends death. Barred from the Myrover parlor and the church by Mrs. Myrover's rabid race prejudice and from the cemetery by custom, she is reduced to using Miss Myrover's pet dog as her proxy. Obedient to Sophy's command, the dog carefully takes the now-faded bouquet of yellow roses and drops it among the other floral pieces on his mistress's last resting place.

Zeal for the cause of his people notwithstanding, however, Chesnutt was too good a craftsman to make all his black characters flawless or nearly so. The motivations of those who transgress, particularly because of jealousy, revenge, fear, and covetousness, are common to all mankind. One of the meanest characters is Wiley in "Dave's Neckliss," "one er dese yer shiny-eyed, double-headed little niggers, sha'p ez a steel trap, en sly ez de fox w'at keep out'n it." Wiley is losing Dilsey, "a monst'us peart, good-lookin', gingybread-colored gal—one er dese yer high-steppin' gals w'at hol's dey head up, en won' stan' no foolishness fum no man," to exemplary Dave. Wiley "wuz one er dese yer 'ceitful niggers, en w'ile he wuz làffin' en jokin' wid de yuther han's bout Dave en Dilsey," he was also planting a ham under Dave's cabin floor and prompting the overseer to discover it there.

A similar strong implication is apparent in "The Web of Circumstance." It seems that the young mulatto Tom secretes Colonel Thornton's whip in the blacksmith shop of Ben Davis, his employer, in order to get Davis's "good-looking yellow wife" for himself. Neither Ben's protestations of innocence, his spotless record, nor his obvious ability to buy such a whip saves him from being sentenced to five years at hard labor. In a lighter vein, jealous hatred causes Miss Dasdy Williams, while in the writhing throes of "coming through," to reduce to fragments the silk and velvet finery with which 'Lizah Davis has temporarily lured away Dasdy's somewhat inconstant sweetheart, Adolphus Sampson.

Other miscreants are appealing despite their wrongdoing. In "The Conjurer's Revenge," for example, party-going Primus, homeward bound at two in the morning and traveling a back road to avoid "de Patteroles," cannot resist appropriating "a fine, fat shote":

> . . . somehow er 'nudder he could n' git away fum dat shote; w'en he tuk one step for'ards wid one foot, de yuther foot 'peared ter take two steps back'ards, en so he kep' nachly gittin' closeter en closeter ter de shote. . . . De shote des 'peared ter cha'm Primus, en fus' thing you know Primus foun' hisse'f way up de road wid de shote on his back.[50]

Jack, the poor but clever cousin of the affluent Blue Vein Cicero Clayton family in "A Matter of Principle," is morally responsible, but can hardly be blamed for taking advantage of the Clayton phobia against dark skin tones to rid himself of a more powerful rival for the hand of the popular "nearly white, accomplished and amiable" Miss Alice Clayton. His name, Jack, suggests strongly that he is cast in the role of the trickster, a popular figure in Negro folk literature.

Chestnutt's writing, however, reflects none of the color prejudice often attributed to very fair Negroes; on the contrary, he roundly condemned it, as he did any such discrimination in real life. In a posthumous tribute W. E. B. Du Bois noted:

> Chestnutt was of that group of white folk who because of a more or less remote Negro ancestor identified himself voluntarily with the darker group, studied them, expressed them, defended them, and yet never forgot the absurdity of this artificial position and always refused to admit its logic or its ethical sanction. He was not a Negro; he was a man. But this fact never drove him to the opposite extreme. He did not repudiate persons of Negro blood as social equals and close friends. If his white friends (and he had legion) could not tolerate colored friends, they need not come to Mr. Chestnutt's home. If colored friends demanded racial segregation and hatred, he had no patience with them. Merit and friendship in his broad and tolerant mind knew no lines of color or race, and all men, good, bad and indifferent, were simply men.[51]

The consensus of the Blue Veins in "The Wife of His Youth" that Mr. Ryder should acknowledge the homely but faithful wife of his youth instead of the highly eligible Mrs. Dixon, and Miss Alice Clayton's loss of the biggest catch of her life, Congressman H. M. Brown, to her archrival, Miss Lura Watkins, in "A Matter of Principle," both reflect Chestnutt's attitude and his actions with regard to color prejudice.

Moreover, Chestnutt saw beauty in all the rich variegation of color among his people, "from a white almost as clear as [that of a Caucasian] to the darkest livery of the sun," and was partial to no complexion in his characterization. Miss Clayton's obvious attractiveness is marred by her abhorrence of black men (the acceptability of dark brown with "good hair" underscores the illogic at the base of all prejudices). Ben Davis's wife in "The Web of Circumstance" is yellow, Cicely in "Cicely's Dream" bronze, Tom Taylor in "The Doll" brown, and both Dasdy Williams and 'Lizah Davis in "How Dasdy Came Through" "dusky." Significantly, black is beautiful in "Lonesome Ben." Ben, the central figure "wuz one er dese yer big black niggers—he wuz mo' d'n six foot high an' black ez coal"—a "fine-lookin' man" to his wife, Dasdy. After running away from a promised flogging by his master, Ben subsists on yellow clay and creek water while waiting for a chance to see his family. This diet causes the fugitive slave to lose his color and with it his appeal—and, symbolically, his identity. Dasdy takes him for a "low-down free nigger," his son breaks away and runs from him in fear, a friend calls him "de mos' mis'-able lookin' merlatter I eber seed," and his master disowns him indignantly, declaring, "Ben wuz black ez a coal an' straight ez a' arrer. Youer yaller ez dat claybank, an' crooked ez a bair'-hoop." On the whole, Chesnutt's white characters are fewer and have less depth, vitality, and originality than his black ones. This is due not only to the fact that Afro-Americans concerned him most but also to his deliberate delay in presenting what he considered his choicest materials about blacks until he had gained more writing skill. Chesnutt also treated more white characters in his earlier work because he was trying to gain a foothold as an author and he realized that such stories had a much better chance of being published than those featuring blacks. This, however, did not keep Chesnutt from portraying whites realistically.

The author's experiences as a member of the oppressed black minority is also reflected in his sympathetic treatment of disadvantaged whites, in his unromantic portrayal of more fortunate Euro-Americans, and in his empathy for the American Indian. Tom in "Tom's Warm Welcome," though of a lower class, wins, weds, and outlives pretty, well-to-do Jinnie Campbell; Hank Skinner relates in "The Shadow of My Past" that he is able to overcome the handicaps of orphanhood and poverty to marry the daughter of a stockholder of the bank which employs him as a teller; stupid seer Peter in "The Prophet Peter" is saved by friends; and crippled elevator operator Jim finally wins the statuesque blonde office worker Mamie, to whom he remains devoted despite constant disappointment.

Mrs. Laura Wharton, the protagonist in "A Grass Widow," is as conscienceless in eloping with the husband of her friend and hostess as Polly Poppleton is in transferring her attentions from her young suitor Frank to his rich father in "A Doubtful Success." Mamie in "Jim's Romance" is as heartlessly opportunistic as the former Miss Ida Ferrand, who dupes three husbands, including the narrator, in "A Fool's Paradise." Mars Donal' McDonal' in "A Victim of Heredity" no more hesitates to cheat his nephew Tom out of his inheritance than Mars Dugal' McAdoo in "The Goophered Grapevine" demurs about selling Henry each spring and buying him back in the fall. Again, "Kunnel Pen'leton" and the horse trader in "Sis' Becky's Pickaninny" both try to foist back on the original seller what each considers a bad bargain. "A Midnight Adventure" affords striking evidence of Chesnutt's advanced ideas. The main character, who is also the unnamed narrator, during an alcohol-induced nightmare finds to his dismay that his typical smug attitude of white superiority to the Indians brings their righteous wrath down upon him for rejecting one of their maidens.

The selections cited and others in this volume illustrate Chesnutt's conviction that, regardless of race, color, and condition, individuals respond alike to basic inner drives and outward motivating forces.

Though Chesnutt's accurate mirroring of human nature invests his stories with universality, some of them seem specially directed to whites while others have a particular message for blacks. By using the folk-motif of transformation in "Mars Jeems's Nightmare," for instance, Chesnutt literally turns the master into the slave so that he may himself experience the physical and psychological degradation of involuntary servitude.

When Mars Jeems, goophered, turns up on his own plantation with temporary amnesia, the mental outlook of a slave-owner, and the identity of a slave, his trouble compound. When the overseer interprets his truthful but misleading remarks about his identity as impudence,

> . . . Mars Johnson haul' off wid his rawhide en hit de noo nigger once. De noo man look' at Mars Johnson fer a minute ez ef he did n' know w'at ter make er dis yer kin' er l'arnin'. But w'en de oberseah rais' his w'ip ter hit him ag'in, de noo nigger des haul' off en made fer Mars Johnson, en ef some er de yuther niggers had n' stop' 'im, it 'peared ez ef he mought 'a' made it wa'm fer Ole Nick dere for a w'ile.[52]

In retaliation Johnson makes it hot for the "noo nigger." The slave-breaker constantly lashes, curses, cuffs, and starves the bewildered slave, who is not only inept but also "could n' 'pear ter git it th'oo his min' dat he wuz a slabe en had ter wuk en min' de w'ite folks."[53] Thus if a white reader has difficulty identifying with a black character, he may by this means feel more empathy for a white one.

The next step for all but bigots is to sympathize with any person in such a terrible predicament. Chesnutt apparently hoped that anyone who has the power to determine, direct, or influence the course of another's life will take his responsibilities more seriously after seeing how self-indulgence in "The Sheriff's Children" and "Sis' Becky's Pickaninny," faulty judgment in "Dave's Neckliss" and "The Web of Circumstance," and cruel and inhuman treatment in "Lonesome Ben" and "The Dumb Witness" lead to tragic outcomes. In "A Victim of Heredity" Uncle Julius emphasizes that whites are responsible for so-called characteristic Negro faults such as stealing, lying, laziness, impudence, and sexual looseness, which the power structure condemns and punishes severely.

"A Matter of Principle" and "The Wife of His Youth" emphasize through contrast the corrosive effects of color and class prejudice among blacks. "The Partners" is clearly a bid for a pooling of racial talent for joint enterprise; "Tobe's Tribulations" and "Uncle Wellington's Wives" show that blacks must have industry and some kind of salable skill if they wish to avoid following Tobe and Uncle Wellington down to the dead end of failure. "The March of Progress" strongly suggests that blacks should not mistreat persons who have served them well in the past when they are no longer needed.

Besides creating an unprecedented variety of characters with the complexities and contradictions which mark real-life individuals, Chesnutt sought through the actions of his characters to treat both perennial situations and contemporary issues. The author's sympathies are expressed to varying degrees in the course of the action, but each outcome inevitably accords with the realities of the times.

Point of View

Chesnutt also makes his characters come alive through his versatility and innovation in handling point of view. He utilized more variations of both the first- and third-person point of view than most of his contemporaries. Possibly influenced by Henry James, whom he admired, Chesnutt came to employ the third-person point of view in several ways: with an aloof stance, as in "Busy Day in a Lawyer's Office"; tentatively, through the consciousness of one or more characters, as with Cicely in "Cicely's Dream" and Tom Taylor in "The Doll"; and with intrusive omniscience in the manner of Thackeray, as in "Aunt Lucy's Search." However, he seemed to prefer diversified narrating in the first person, with its possibilities of greater authenticity, a closer though more limited view of the action, and heightened suspense.

The author thus makes it possible for a reader to relive experiences through the eyes of a peripheral or central character involved more or less in the action. In "Cartwright's Mistake" Walton, the first-person narrator, is literally an observer (as the story opens he is following the movements of a ship through binoculars) and reporter who relates the actions of the main characters, whom he knows, with minimal personal reaction. Like Walton, the narrator of "Aunt Mimy's Son" does not participate in the main action of the story. This is revealed through letters the young man sends to his proud mother from time to time. The narrator, though not identified by name, is the John of the Uncle Julius stories, who, upon coming South and buying the old McAdoo plantation, has hired the capable but illiterate Aunt Mimy to cook for him and Miss Annie. One day, in the absence of the niece who usually reads to Aunt Mimy her letters from her son Tom, the ex-slave asks her employer to read one. He recollects:

> Among other things it said, in substance, that the writer had found banking a somewhat uncertain business, that it had its ups and downs, that it had opened the way for him, however, to a place in a state institution, where he would be sure of steady employment for a year or two, and would know what his earnings would be, and that he expected to be so busy that he might not be able to write to her with his usual regularity.

The narrator makes no comment on these richly ambiguous revelations, which Aunt Mimy interprets as Tom's having "be'n 'lected to de legislatur or sump'n." However, the suspicion of the reader that upstanding citizen Tom is but a mirage of mother love is strengthened bit by bit thereafter and confirmed in the narrator's glimpse of a grieving, enlightened Aunt Mimy at the end of the story.

In this way Chesnutt not only imbues a set of usual circumstances with unusual drama but also provides himself an effective means of suggesting certain parts of the action. By utilizing such telescoping, which also requires greater reader participation, Chesnutt was enabled to produce the complete but shorter narratives coming more into vogue at the turn of the century.

On the other hand, the character who relates "Baxter's Procrustes" is involved in the action of that vignette, but he, along with Davis and Thompson on the "Procrustes" committee, is so busy conforming to the practices of the club that the brilliant individualistic Baxter dupes him as completely as he does the other two.

Besides employing point of view as a technique to reveal character and expand action, Chesnutt found it especially useful in promoting the involvement of the indifferent white majority in the problems of class and caste for which they had to furnish "the ultimate solutions." He had a need to express his "vision of himself in relation to his world—a vision eventually encompassing all dispossessed Americans—in attempting to change that world's vision of him. He had found that even "the best white people" were loath to discuss problems which beset Afro-Americans. Chesnutt also felt that whites avoided thinking about their injustices to blacks and thereby invited the danger inherent in the denial of evil which Hawthorne had pointed out earlier in the nineteenth century.

In order to stir his readers to action, the author realized that he needed the immediacy of the first-person point of view with the narrator having a primary involvement in the action. The Reverend Samuel Thompson relates a traumatic experience in "A Virginia Chicken." The one-time cook for Union troops in the Civil War recalls that when his Confederate captors decided "there's nuthin' ter do but to shoot 'im . . . my heart sank down into my boots, went out at the toes, and ran off in the woods." At the same time Chesnutt also knew that he had to maintain an attitude of objectivity; with hardly a cursory glance his prospective readers would dismiss his works as biased if they suspected his intent. Moreover, forthright forceful statements about conditions and issues could also alienate the people whose active cooperation was necessary for the changes Chesnutt sought.

His artistic combination of both the first- and third-person points of view within the double structure of the frame story, as illustrated repeatedly in the Uncle Julius tales, helped reduce the difficulty of accomplishing his didactic aims. The narrator, John, can realistically maintain a suitable air of detached objectivity since all the situations which Julius describes are outside his experience. A Yankee born and bred, he has no knowledge of the peculiar ways of the South and has had no direct contacts with slavery. Viewing himself as sophisticated, John gives short shrift both to his wife's sympathetic responses and Uncle Julius's grassroots manner of relating to others. Bred in a tradition of empiricism, he limits his world to one of demonstrable truth which completely discredits Uncle Julius's faith in the accounts of the marvelous. Thus, by relating the tales with the slight air of mockery and disbelief which the average reader brings to them, John provides latitude for acceptance of the stories by believers and unbelievers alike. Julius, in his telling, is properly self-effacing and apologetic in a manner calculated to remove the sting from the slightest criticism of the system which spawned and shaped him. The narrator notices this in "Dave's Neckliss":

> While he mentioned with a warm appreciation the acts of kindness which those in authority had shown to him and his people, he would speak of a cruel deed, not with the indignation of one accustomed to quick feeling and spontaneous expression, but with a furtive disapproval which suggested to us a doubt in his own mind as to whether he had a right to think or to feel.

The resultant filtering of the stories through the narrator makes them seem "shown" rather than told and allows more leeway for interpretation. Within the context of each narrator's editorial comments, every story lends itself to two interpretations according to the inclination of the reader. The true meaning, however, depends upon a realization that both John and Uncle Julius are fallible narrators and that what Chesnutt intended probably lies somewhere in between the extremes of their statements and interpretations. The author may have favored the position of Miss Annie, which by a blending of the two sometimes divergent views affords different insights. "Sis' Becky's Pickaninny," she declares, "bears the stamp of truth, if ever a story did." Unable to explain the roles of the hummingbird, the mockingbird, the sparrow, and the hornet in terms of natural history when challenged by her matter-of-fact husband, she shrugs these off as "mere ornamental details and not at all essential. The story is true to nature."[54] Though John never admits belief in superstition and the marvelous, influenced both by his wife and Julius he becomes increasingly humane; his more understanding attitude is especially apparent in "A Victim of Heredity."

Tone

Chesnutt's sensitivity to the traumatic nature of everyday living for Afro-Americans evoked the somber tone of most of his fiction. Chesnutt occasionally bowed to the contemporary demand for typical romantic endings, as in "The Wife of His Youth," "The Kiss," "A Metropolitan Experience," "White Weeds," and "Jim's Romance"—the latter at a publisher's request. But Chesnutt depicts varying degrees of sadness better than he does those of happiness. "Uncle Peter's House," "Aunt Mimy's Son," "The Bouquet," "A Grass Widow," "Cicely's Dream," and "Her Virginia Mammy" are among the stories which evoke sentimental tears and a resultant mild catharsis which readers of his generation thoroughly enjoyed. On the other hand, the tragic implications or outcomes of engrossing stories like "The Doll," "The Marked Tree," "Po'

Sandy," "Hot-Foot Hannibal," "The Sheriff's Children," "Dave's Neckliss," and "The Web of Circumstance" penetrate remote emotional recesses; they usually provoke reflection and sometimes, as Chesnutt hoped, remedial action.

Moreover, without violating the authenticity of the surroundings, Chesnutt always designed his settings so that each helps to establish and enhance the mood of the story of which it is an integral part. The sunny warmth in which "A Deep Sleeper" opens indicates a happy ending for the story; in contrast, decay, desolation, dissolution, and disaster (symbolized by the rattlesnake) mark the opening of "The Dumb Witness." Chesnutt's skill as a writer is also apparent in the gray clouds and steady downpour of rain occasionally punctuated by muted thunder which provided Julius the opportunity to trace the tragedy in "The Gray Wolf's Ha'nt."

Humor, Satire, and Irony

Chesnutt's wide use of humor, satire, and irony saturates his short fiction. No institution or individual was too sacrosanct for such treatment, for Chesnutt followed the neoclassical practice of using laughter to reduce man's prejudices and presumptions. The Afro-American *joie de vivre* pulsates in church-related activities in "The Fall of Adam," "The Conjurer's Revenge," "How Dasdy Came Through," and "Mr. Taylor's Funeral." In the first story Chesnutt tells how a plantation preacher gets his own church and flock after "de wah" and describes, with a trace of facetiousness, the Sunday service at Hallelujah Chapel, including the opening prayer "by a longwinded brother," who is encouraged by "groans and exclamations" of several "happy" sisters. "He might have gone on and on forever . . . had not Brother Gabriel . . . at last brought the prayer to a close by interjecting a sonorous 'Amen' when the eloquent and perspiring orator paused to breathe." Before Brother Gabriel can begin his vision-inspired sermon on "The Fall of Adam and the Origin of Races" he has to adjust his spectacles, pour out a glass of water, open the Bible at random, take out his handkerchief—"a large square of snowy linen"—blow his nose in a dignified manner, place the handkerchief under one side of the Bible, and announce his text. That portion of the moving rhythmic discourse which explains why some people are white and others are black is an ingeniously contrived tall tale which has all the hallmarks of a folk myth. It is also a classic example of the humorous folk sermon, Afro-American style.

Chesnutt's use of bland humor in portraying Hallelujah Chapel and its congregation extended to other groups in the country. The other selections, however, range in tone from the uncritically ludicrous to the critically serious and in type from anecdote to short story. Many of the techniques he employed to provoke laughter are in the nineteenth-century American tradition, such as situations rife with slapstick comedy, reminiscent of those of George W. Harris's Sut Lovingwood. In "A Tight Boot," while trying to help Bob get a guest's boot off his foot, buxom Aunt Lyddy loses her balance and sits "down in the big pot of hot water on the hearth." In the same vein the wife in "She Reminded Him" gives her husband a jolting uppercut; and Primus, changed into a mule by the conjure man in "The Conjurer's Revenge," first manhandles and later kicks the unsuspecting Dan, who is replacing Primus in the affections of his wife. Elements of the tall tale of the kind which brought fame to T. B. Thorpe appear in this tale also. Primus as mule on one occasion eats two whole rows of tobacco plants; on another, he gets dead drunk from consuming several gallons of wine "making" (fermenting) in a barrel; finally, one night he gets out of the pasture, goes to the quarters cabin which Sally and Dan are now sharing together, and terrifies Dan by trying to break in.

> Dan wuz layin' dere on his pallet, w'en he heard sump'n bangin' erway at de side er his cabin. He raise' up on one shoulder en look' roun', w'en w'at should he see but de noo mule's head stickin' in de winder, wid his lips drawed back over his toofs, grinnin' en snappin' at Dan des' lack he wanter eat 'im up.[55]

The literary quality of the tale is enhanced by the skillful manner in which Chesnutt characterizes Primus so that the animal into which he is transformed will have verisimilitude within the context of the action and at the same time manifest the personality traits of Primus.

By means of tall tales mythic, farcical, and fantastic Chesnutt criticizes excessive hero-worship in "The Origin of the Hatchet Story," and scores gradualism as a means of solving the race problem in "A Roman Antique." Satirical touches lighten his resigned acceptance of the inexplicable behavior of women in "An Original Sentiment," "Cartwright's Mistake," and "The Doctor's Wife," but do not veil his contempt for the Uncle Tomism displayed in "Appreciation."

Among "the great many peculiar things" which happen in this "queer world" about which the protagonist, Father, speaks in general terms in "Concerning Father" and which Chesnutt satirizes in other short fiction are the capriciousness of the public in "The Shadow of My Past," "How a Good Man Went Wrong," and "The Web of Circumstance"; the fraudulence of people in "Stryker's Waterloo"; the mendacity of women in "A Doubtful Success" and "A Fool's Paradise"; the covetousness of Professor Revels in "The Sway-Backed House"; and the gullibility of individuals and groups alike in "A Fool's Paradise" and "The Prophet Peter."

The writer bizarrely censures race prejudice in "White Weeds." Professor Carson literally worries himself to death because his wife will neither affirm nor deny the allegation in an anonymous letter he receives on the eve of their wedding that she is not "all white." When she asks how white one must be "to come within the protection of the code of Southern chivalry," he explains:

> There are no degrees. . . . To me, and those who think like me, men and women are either white or black. Those who are not all white are all black. Were I

married in fact to a woman even seemingly as white as you, yet not entirely
white, I should feel guilty of mortal sin. I should lie awake at night, dreading
lest my children should show traces of their descent from an inferior and degraded race. I should never know a moment's happiness.

The new Mrs. Carson's justification for refusing to commit herself is that she
must be loved for what she is.

By accident or design Chesnutt makes most effective use in his frame tales
of three types of incongruity for comic appeal identified in *Native American
Humor (1800-1900)* by Walter Blair. Chesnutt's juxtaposition of the educated,
practical, conventional Northerner John as narrator with the illiterate, crafty,
imaginative ex-slave Uncle Julius provides the incongruity between the gram-
matical, highly rhetorical language of John in the framework on the one hand
and, on the other, the racy ungrammatical dialect of Uncle Julius, the teller
of the internal stories. Consequently, there is a world of difference in the calm
balance of John's literary appraisal of Patesville in "The Goophered Grapevine"

> Indeed, when I first saw the town, there brooded over it a calm that seemed
> almost sabbatic in its restfulness, though I learned later on that underneath its
> somnolent exterior the deeper currents of life—love and hatred, joy and despair,
> ambition and avarice, faith and friendship—flowed not less steadily than in livelier
> latitudes[56]

and the stringing-out of short, simple statements characteristic of the unedu-
cated, as illustrated when Uncle Julius advises him on their first meeting:

> Well, suh, you is a stranger ter me, en I is a stranger ter you, en we is bofe
> strangers ter one anudder, but 'f I 'uz in yo' place, I would n' buy dis vimya'd.[57]

Likewise, in Uncle Julius's recounting to his employers of events which
occurred long before the Civil War, the sharp contrast between the tranquil
comfort of the immediate environs—often the piazza of the couple's newly constructed dwelling—and the unpleasant setting of the tale provides the
incongruity between the situation when the yarn is being told and the situation
described in the yarn itself. "A Deep Sleeper," exceptional for its humorous
episodes, provides such a contrast. John describes the setting in which Uncle
Julius tells the tale:

> It was four o'clock on Sunday afternoon, in the month of July. The air had been
> hot and sultry, but a light, cool breeze had sprung up, and occasional cirrus clouds
> overspread the sun, and for a while subdued his fierceness. We were all out
> on the piazza—as the coolest place we could find—my wife, my sister-in-law and
> I. The only sounds that broke the Sabbath stillness were the hum of an occasional
> vagrant bumblebee, or the fragmentary song of a mockingbird in a neighboring
> elm, who lazily trolled out a stave of melody, now and then, as a sample of
> what he could do in the cool of the morning, or after a light shower, when the
> conditions would be favorable to exertion.

Thus, even the most timorous of Uncle Julius's listeners is amused rather than afraid at that climactic point of the story when one evening down in the swamp " 'a great big black ha'nt 'bout ten feet high, en' wid a fence-rail in its han's jump out'n de bushes en' chase [a terrified slave] cl'ar up in de co'n fiel'."

The Uncle Julius tales abound in incongruity between realism in the framework and fantasy in the enclosed narrative because of the important role conjuring and goophering play in the action. Among the fantastic aspects which have humorous overtones are the peculiar behavior patterns of Skundus in "A Deep Sleeper" and of Hannibal in "Hot-Foot Hannibal." Skundus will fall asleep anywhere:

> He went ter sleep walk'n' 'long de road oncet, en' might nigh bus't his head open 'gin a tree he run inter. I did heah he oncet went ter sleep while he wuz in swimmin'. He wuz floatin' at de time, en' come mighty nigh gittin' drownded befo' he woke up.

Hannibal's trouble, on the other hand, is that he moves too fast. This is due to the influence of the little doll with pepper feet which Aun' Peggy has prepared and Jeff has buried under the doorsill.

> W'en dinner-time come, en Hannibal wuz help'n de cook kyar de dinner f'm de kitchen inter de big house, en wuz gittin' close ter de do' whar he had ter go in, his feet sta'ted ter bu'n en his head begun to swim, en he let de big dish er chicken en dumplin's fall right down in de dirt, in de middle er de ya'd.

The psychological reactions of the characters are supported to a surprising degree by the most modern behavioral theories. For example, Skundus, who is probably Chesnutt's satirical reaction to the widespread belief that all Negroes are lazy, is using here one of the most popular means of avoiding a problem, never-ending work, which he has no viable means of solving. Sis' Becky in "Sis' Becky's Pickaninny" and Henry in "The Goophered Grapevine" would certainly have died had they not come to believe that they had been willed to live by a power outside themselves. Dan in "The Gray Wolf's Ha'nt" is impervious to the conjure man's spells until he lets down his guard. Chesnutt makes Dan, who is "big en strong en hearty en peaceable en goodnachu'd most er de time, but dange'ous ter aggervate," a heroic figure. He is more invulnerable than the fabled Achilles, for the rattlesnake which the conjurer sends to sting him "say de nigger's heel wuz so ha'd he couldn' git his sting in." The implied comparison evokes the amusement which accompanies the juxtaposition of opposites.

Chesnutt appreciated the sterling qualities of the common people, black or white, as much as did Bret Harte, with whom he has been compared. Further, he not only portrays their shortcomings more realistically but also champions the cause of the more defenseless among them with greater vigor than his contemporary does. In these respects and in his constant use of satire and irony he is similar to Mark Twain. However, perhaps because early in his life he had to develop a philosophy which would enable him to live as an Afro-American and still keep his sanity and self-respect, he did not follow Twain into the bitter misanthrophy discernible in "The Mysterious Stranger." When America continued after 1900 to withhold from blacks the freedoms she dispensed with largesse to successive waves of European immigrants, Chesnutt instead retreated from time to time into a world of comic fantasy heralded in the early "A Roman Antique" and "The Origin of the Hatchet Story," and illustrated finally in his last short story, "Concerning Father."

In treating lighter subjects, not concerned primarily with race and rights, Chesnutt could give his artistry freer rein. The funeral in "Mr. Taylor's Funeral" is obviously farcical, with two ministers and two choirs conducting funeral services simultaneously in opposite rooms of the funeral site. The startling reappearance of Mr. Taylor at the close of the service underscores the comic element and provides Chesnutt the opportunity to moralize. Many more of the selections, especially the anecdotes, are lightly satirical, clearly and cleverly showing Chesnutt's awareness and condemnation of certain aspects of American society. Like A. B. Longstreet, "he saw ridicule as a weapon against vice." Attorney Sharp, Mrs. Rogg, Judge Flipp, Dr. Vaseline, Mr. De Bullion, Bloke, and Sneak—with names following the pattern of nomenclature used in the old English morality plays—and their activities in "Busy Day in a Lawyer's Office" suggest the unethical state of the legal profession; the ironically titled "A Soulless Corporation" and "A Cause Célèbre" reveal the questionable integrity of the lay public and the equally poor state of our system of justice. The epistolary form of the latter follows a tradition traceable to Samuel Richardson in English literature and given comic overtones in later times by Seba Smith's Jack Downing, James Russell Lowell's *Biglow Papers,* and William T. Thompson's Major Jones. The atrocious spelling follows that of Artemus Ward, the literary creation of Charles Farrar Browne (who was also a Clevelander), and of Josh Billings (Henry Wheeler Shaw).

Some humorously ironic sidelights also emerge in "Wine and Water," set in a time when temperance was a burning national issue and most religious sects, especially in the Southern Bible Belt, were bone dry in precept if not in practice. Peter Hardcase, a confirmed tippler, is trapped in the most sacred section of the church, the pulpit platform. He takes refuge in the baptismal tank and is literally saved by immersing himself in the water which nevertheless remains lower in Peter's estimation than the communion wine he has stolen and risked his life to keep. Hardcase, an independent thinker, is not suddenly converted by his narrow escape, and later relishes the bottle without a qualm.

In "Baxter's Procrustes," Chesnutt's raillery of the stuffy Bodleian Club's preoccupation with the form rather than the substance of the books which are the core of the group's activities results in his most polished satire. The exclusive Rowfant Club, of Cleveland, Ohio, inspired this story, which so suavely jolts the posture of pretension. As was often the case in Chesnutt's narratives, the title is witty; even the term *Procrustes,* the name of a legendary Greek, is in keeping with the nature of the club, the cultural level of its members, and the resolution of the situation in the story. Baxter, the main character, is slightly suggestive of Chesnutt in appearance, avocation, and attitude. He is evidently a nonconformist; by 1904 Chesnutt was being forced by circumstances to realize more than ever that living in the United States was, for a black person, too much like lying on Procrustes' bed. In his book published by the club Baxter expresses most ingeniously his disdain for the members' literary standards. Chesnutt must sometimes have been annoyed that as an influential body this club remained silent on racial issues.

"Baxter's Procrustes," universally considered as Chesnutt's best story, suggests the heights to which his creative imagination might have soared had it been free of the trammels of social purpose. Many writers rise to new heights of creativity when fired by causes; others, thrown off balance by their deep emotional involvement, tend to produce tracts rather than works of art. Chesnutt seems to have been aware of the latter danger, although this obviously did not affect his choice of subject matter. When asked, "What are Negroes to do when they are continually painted at their worst and judged by the public as they are painted?"—and this was the situation while he was writing—he responded that the writer was obligated "to protest and to paint a better type of Negro." This obligation, however, might make Negro writings "too subjective."

> The colored writer, generally speaking, has not yet passed the point of thinking of himself first as a Negro, burdened with the responsibility of defending and uplifting his race. Such a frame of mind, however praiseworthy from a moral standpoint, is bad for art.[58]

When Chesnutt turned from the pastimes of the privileged to the problems of his people, his satire became increasingly ironical, especially in the Uncle Julius stories. Uncle Julius must be considered as an ironic character. He is projected exclusively through John, a fallible narrator, whose accounts cannot be taken at face value and must be viewed within the context of each story. Since the stories themselves also come from a fallible narrator, Uncle Julius's words must be interpreted with even greater care. His great naiveté could be justified by the limitations of his early life as an illiterate slave field-hand and later as a freedman in a world little larger than the old McAdoo plantation. On the other hand, his experiences as a bondman may have taught him to be more devious than direct in achieving his ends.

Therefore, John's assessment of Uncle Julius as a creature nearer the brute than the human level in "Mars Jeems's Nightmare" may seem less appropriate at the end of the tale than at the beginning. Uncle Julius's identification of what had been the great oak tree on the old Spencer place as "a U-pass tree" has an increasingly ironic significance, of which the old man may be unaware. Although Uncle Julius does not know the symbolic significance of the term *U-pass (Upas)* and although the difference of opinion on the cause of the tree-connected tragedies cannot be resolved, the illiterate black Julius McAdoo and the educated white Aleck Spencer perceive alike the occult bond between the latter's family and the tree. Again, Uncle Julius's seemingly guileless invitation to the newcomers in "The Goophered Grapevine" to listen "ter a ole nigger run on a minute er two w'ile you er restin' " may be seen in a different light when the story concludes. Similar turns of events in the other tales lend more credence to the theory that a facile intelligence has in each case charted a course of action to reach predetermined ends.

Chesnutt shows in other ways how the prevailing doctrine of white superiority–black inferiority influenced individuals' concepts of themselves and of others, often creating ironic situations. Uncle Wellington, who fancies himself to be quite a man because of his mulatto handsomeness, unwittingly equates himself with animals when he tells Mr. Peterson, "I wuz rais' 'mongs' hosses." Sis' Becky in "Sis' Becky's Pickaninny" is traded for a horse and "de noo nigger" in "Mars Jeems's Nightmare" is the payment for a bet made during a friendly card game. In "Her Virginia Mammy" all of Miss Hohlfelder's worst fears about her ancestry turn out to be true; yet her fiancé, whose lineage she finally comes to believe is less distinguished than hers, knows the truth about her and accepts her in a way she would probably be unable to accept herself. Similarly, in "A Matter of Principle," Cicero Clayton, who earned the sobriquet "Brotherhood" by his oft-repeated statement that "what our country needs most in its treatment of the race problem . . . is a clearer conception of the brotherhood of man," nevertheless flagrantly violates the principle every day of his life.[59]

Old man Murchison in "The Dumb Witness" spends many years searching for proof of an inheritance which has been concealed in his favorite chair all the while. His failure to locate the papers is due to the truthful but enigmatic response Viney makes to his incessant questioning. Chesnutt reveals the unpleasant truths about Tom in "Aunt Mimy's Son" and the former Miss Ida Ferrand in "A Fool's Paradise" by means of the ironic ambiguity of the letters sent to Aunt Mimy and the diary entries of Paul Dunlap. Aunt Mimy's belief that Tom is to be a legislator and Dunlap's that he himself is the most fortunate of men, hardly deserving of the happiness of being married to Ida, are especially ironic. Again using dramatic irony, Chesnutt shows in "The Web of Circumstance" the blindness of Ben Davis to the infidelity of his wife. Ben does not realize that the "rattlesnake out in de gyahden"—a perfect symbol—which his wife Nancy says she has just seen is in reality his young mulatto helper, Tom, or that his own wife is the "gal" that Tom has on his mind. Referring editorially to Davis's trial for the theft of Colonel Thornton's whip, Chesnutt observes ironically that "the law in its wisdom did not permit the defendant to testify in his own behalf."[60]

Irony heightens the suspense of the situation in "The Doll," in which Tom Taylor, a Negro barber, is made aware that his customer, Colonel Forsyth, is his father's murderer. Years earlier the father had remonstrated about the treatment of Tom's sister in the Forsyth home and had been shot on the spot. Forsyth deliberately expounds, within earshot of the barber, his conviction that to keep the Negro in his place would solve the Negro problem. The Bourbon also reiterates, "I want a close shave," and Taylor, in his trembling desire for revenge, literally comes within a hair of cutting his customer's throat. A disclosure at the end of the story reveals another element of irony, thus doubling its emotional impact. Forsyth's estimate of Negroes,

> They are born to serve and to submit. If they had been worthy of equality they would never have endured slavery. They have no proper self-respect; they will neither resent an insult, nor defend a right, nor avenge a wrong,

like John's early belief, in "The Goophered Grapevine," that Julius's shrewdness is traceable to his white blood, is a satirical commentary upon the popular notion—not an agreement with it, as some readers might assume—and an ironic statement when viewed in context.

"The Passing of Grandison" is especially rich in dramatic irony. Young Dick Owens, eager to win the hand of his quixotic sweetheart, determines to free one of his father's slaves. He immediately plans a trip north to provide the opportunity for a bondman to escape. Colonel Owens, a white who thinks he understands blacks perfectly, believes that his slave Grandison is both too stupid and "too fond of good eating to risk losing regular meals." Therefore the father, equally concerned about retaining his human property, lets Grandison rather than the regular body servant of Dick accompany the latter. The slave, however, reveals another side of himself through his actions at the surprise ending of the story. Thus most of the conversations have ironic overtones and the action itself has several ironic twists. The father does not know that his son's real mission is to give the slave opportunity to seek asylum in Canada; the slave, ostensibly unaware of the son's motives, refuses to take advantage of the many chances for freedom literally thrust upon him. Finally, in desperation Dick has Grandison kidnaped and forcibly held in Canada until he himself can return to his Kentucky home. The reader, aware of the son's intentions, can immediately appreciate the irony in his statements to father and slave. However, the full extent of the irony in the dialogue of the latter two is not immediately apparent. The colonel's warning Grandison

> against these cussed abolitionists (heartless monsters) who try to entice servants from their comfortable homes and their indulgent masters, from the blue skies, the green fields, and the warm sunlight of their southern home, and send them

away off yonder to Canada, a dreary country where the woods are full of wildcats and wolves and bears, where the snow lies up to the eaves of the houses for six months of the year and the cold is so severe that it freezes your breath and curdles your blood; and where, when runaway niggers get sick and can't work, they are turned out to starve and die, unloved and uncared for. . . . But if you stick close to your young master and remember always that he is your best friend and understands your real needs, and has your true interests at heart, and if you will be careful to avoid strangers who try to talk to you, you'll stand a fair chance of getting back to your home and friends[61]

is, of course, a satirical thrust at the "kind" master of the Thomas Nelson Page type. Likewise the assenting, ingratiating responses of Grandison as a contented slave are so exaggerated as to suggest satire. Further, Grandison's actions after he makes his way back home voluntarily and is exhibited as a model slave reveal that all he said had a deeply ironic import.

Chesnutt transmutes human nature and history into literature mainly by his masterful handling of ridicule, satire, and irony. These literary conventions lend themselves well to the black experience because that experience in America is in many ways ridiculous, satiric, and ironic. One way black folks have protected themselves in this primarily hostile environment has been to employ the three literary conventions in their oral communication in a mode called *signifying*.

In this context *to signify* means to criticize in a special way, such as to heckle or deride subtly, to ridicule, to satirize, to "put (a person) down," to "pick"; to lie about an individual, to meddle in his business, or to cause him trouble by making insinuating remarks about him. Success in signifying depends more on the manner of delivery than on the message. When done properly, the procedure is apparent only to the initiated or to the very astute student of human nature. Signifying has been a favorite pastime of the masses of Afro-Americans since slavery.

The stories in this volume abound in illustrative statements and episodes, some of which have already been cited for other reasons. Viewed in this light, however, even the most ingenuous remark may have serious overtones. Before beginning the internal narrative in "A Deep Sleeper," Uncle Julius explains that some of Tom's ancestors were named "Skundus," "Tushus," "Cottus," and "Squinchus" by ole Marse Dugal' McAdoo, who

named all de babies w'at wuz bawn on de plantation. Dese young un's mammy wanted ter call 'em sump'n plain en' simple, like "Rastus" er "Caesar" er "George Wash'n'ton"; but ole Marse say no, he wants all de niggers on his place ter hab diffe'nt names, so he kin tell 'em apart. He'd done use' up all de common names, so he had ter take sump'n else. Dem names he gun Skundus en' his brudders is Hebrew names en' wuz tuk out'n de Bible.

Chesnutt is no doubt signifying, using Uncle Julius's naiveté as his medium. The writer is condemning the system which denies the mother, representing the family, the right to name her own child and thus, from the outset, also denies him his identity. The inability of the master to distinguish among his human chattel except by their different names also strongly implies that he sees them as things without distinguishing personality traits. The fact that all the common names are used up calls to mind the degrading practice of breeding slaves to sell which was widespread during the mid-1800's. Mention of the desire of the mothers to give them the "plain and simple" names listed permits Chesnutt to score what was a practice of many unlettered black folk and also to suggest the tragic irony of giving such names as Caesar and George Washington to individuals whom slavery would never permit to attain the eminence of the men whose names they bore.

That Chesnutt is signifying about the efforts to subvert the humanity of blacks is supported by the fact that the names given the brothers are actually the Latin terms *secundus, tertius, quartus,* and *quintus,* meaning *second, third, fourth,* and *fifth,* spelled in such a way as to approximate Uncle Julius's pronunciation of them. Having a number for a name helps reduce a human being to an object. Responsibility for identifying these names as Hebrew and Biblical cannot be assigned within the context of the tale. Chesnutt may also be satirizing the practice of slaveholders to cite the Bible as the authority or guide for their slave policies. Moreover, his playful humor, suggestive of Swift's manner when writing to Stella, seems to be challenging the reader to get the full import of all his words rather than to accept them at face value.

Themes

The most recurrent themes of Chesnutt's fiction are the humanity of the Afro-American, the mistreatment of minorities—especially blacks in this country—and the universal fallibility of human nature. Chesnutt's delineation of character and manipulation of situation result in outcomes which reflect these central ideas. Thus the reader is impelled to recognize the issues inherent in the different aspects of the themes. Chesnutt also treats these themes more directly in his essays and speeches, and at greater length in his three novels—mostly from the perspective of an Afro-American.

Chesnutt treats the faulty application of our democratic principles more often than he does any other aspect of American life. His use of miscegenation suggests that he considered it one of the most deleterious of our social ills. Miscegenation is a chief motivating force in "The Dumb Witness," "The Sheriff's Children," and *The House Behind the Cedars.* It is prominent though not central in *The Marrow of Tradition.* In "The Dumb Witness" Malcolm Murchison has no compunction about putting Viney aside. He threatens that if she continues to remonstrate, she will be punished by having to serve her former paramour's new wife in the same household where her authority had long been recognized. Intentionally or not, in the other three selections all the white fathers either permit their mixed-blood children to be born in a state of slavery or make no adequate provisions to save them from conditions little better than servitude.

In the economic sphere the black is accorded little more respect. "The Averted Strike" shows that race deters well-merited advancement in employment. Had Walker not saved the daughter of the plant owner and her friend from a fiery death, he would never have been accepted by less deserving white workers as their supervisor. Chesnutt was too much of a realist to let this deserved promotion take place routinely. Moreover, the climactic fire lends an additional dimension of truth and suspense to the story. That Walker is able to keep his new job attests to Chesnutt's optimistic attitude at the time.

The Colonel's Dream reflects the constantly worsening race relations in this country. When the protagonist, Colonel French, makes a proficient Afro-American the foreman of a group of bricklayers and rejects as invalid all objections to the promotion, some of the white workers walk off the job. This violation of a Southern custom sets into motion a chain of events so vicious that French leaves the South convinced that racial harmony cannot be achieved there immediately or in the foreseeable future.

Negroes suffer other injustices above as well as below the Mason-Dixon line. Installment buying is too costly in "A Limb of Satan" and law practices are questionable in "The Partners." The law is permissive in dealing with white offenders and legal services are too costly in "Uncle Peter's House." "The Web of Circumstance" reveals the worthlessness of such services and the vicious effects of the convict-labor system. All these abuses hit the Afro-American where he is most vulnerable—in the spheres of civil rights and economics. He has not had time to accumulate either substantial capital or sufficient understanding of legal procedures. And even when, like Ben Davis in "The Web of Circumstance," he is both prosperous and respected, he cannot get justice in a court system over which he has no influence as a voting citizen. This aspect of the story is obviously Chesnutt's fictional repudiation of Booker T. Washington's theory that the Negro should forego the franchise until he had an economic foothold.

Among Chesnutt's black folk meaningful relationships outweigh economic gain. Thus the slaves suffer greatly when personal associations are ignored in favor of arrangements which their owners prefer. Hannibal in "Hot-Foot Hannibal" is made a servant at the "big house" and told that he may marry Chloe in the spring despite her expressed preference for Jeff. In "A Deep Sleeper" Cindy's mistress overrides the master's reluctance to let her leave the plantation and her husband-to-be, Skundus, for temporary service with relatives of her owners. "Cindy didn' want ter go en' said so." But "ole Miss" decided that the impending marriage doan' cut no figger. Dey's too much er dis foolishness 'bout husban's en' wibes 'mongs' de niggers nowadays. One nigger man is de same as ernudder, en' dey'll be plenty un 'em down ter Wash'n'ton's plantation.

Cindy and Skundus as well as Sis' Becky and little Mose in "Sis' Becky's Pickaninny" are among the few slaves fortunate enough to be reunited. The reason for their reunion is not their master's compassion for their grief, but his financial gain. The majority, including Tenie and Sandy in "Po' Sandy," Chloe and Jeff in "Hot-Foot Hannibal," and Dave and Dilsey in "Dave's Neckliss," are separated forever despite their earnest efforts to remain together.

The antipathy of whites for people of color, extending from the cradle to the grave, blights individual lives and personal ties. Miss Hohlfelder in "Her Virginia Mammy" unknowingly sacrifices her mother to white supremacy, and Professor Carson in "White Weeds" prefers to sacrifice his life to this pernicious ideal. In "The Sheriff's Children" Tom's belief that even father and son cannot bridge the chasm between the races triggers his suicide. Color prejudice among Negroes causes Miss Alice Clayton in "A Matter of Principle" and Professor Revels in "The Sway-Backed House" to forfeit happiness they could have enjoyed. Rose is a victim of white class prejudice in "A Secret Ally." Immoral behavior or unethical practices as delineated in "The Exception," "A Soulless Corporation," "Stryker's Waterloo," "Jim's Romance," "The Kiss," "The Partners," and "Walter Knox's Record" bring sorrow and sometimes disaster to the guilty and innocent alike.

Chesnutt recognized that transgression is no respecter of race or class and gave ample evidence of this principle in the catholic manner in which he delineated his characters. At the same time, however, he recognized that blacks in the America of his time would not so often have acted nefariously had they had the same chances in life as others with whom they had to cope. Slaves, some freemen, and most freedmen had to devise unusual ways of protecting themselves and their interest. "Mars Jeems's Nightmare" is perhaps the author's most imaginative portrayal of such a procedure. In it Uncle Julius makes the point

dat w'ite folks w'at is so ha'd en stric', en doan make no 'lowance fer po' ign'ant niggers w'at ain' had no chanst ter l'arn, is li'ble ter hab bad dreams, ter say de leas', en dat dem w'at is kin' en good ter po' people is sho' ter prosper en git 'long in de worl.[62]

The slave expresses these sentiments more bluntly in "A Deep Sleeper" by telling Mabel, "Hit ain' my fault dat I ain't able ter read de Bible." John recognizes the old man's latent ability in "The Marked Tree" by noting, "Had Julius lived in a happier age for men of his complexion the world might have had a black Aesop or Grimm or Hoffman."

To hasten the coming of such an age was the main thrust of Chesnutt's writings. His themes, pointing up the injustices of the system, reflect the major issues of his day—and ours.

Style

Chesnutt's style is marked by directness, precision, forcefulness often characterized by understatement, and use of comic relief or irony. Except when striving for comic effects, he speaks solemnly about weighty matters and casually about trivial ones. His periods are sufficiently varied to avoid monotony and are marked by a restrained grace easily traceable to the Greek and Roman rhetoricians whom he read in the original as well as to his legal training and practice. His work is also distinguished by the use of the alliteration, antithesis, paradox, parallelism, puns, and repetition all approved by the classical masters and by the outstanding orators of his own time, including Abraham Lincoln. His mastery of dialect and admirable choice of diction have already been noted. Foster, who analyzed Uncle Julius's dialect, believes the former is attributable in part to Chesnutt's mastery of shorthand; the author's extensive vocabulary is certainly due to his wide reading.

Chesnutt also had the observant eye of the poet, which caught and recorded minute detail, as in the architecture of the church in which Peter Hardcase is trapped by fire in "Wine and Water."

Embellishment by figurative language traceable to both African and European influences lends added color and vitality to his work. In "Wine and Water," for example, the fire becomes a living entity:

> The fire then burst into a little flame, slowly consuming the pile of half-dried rubbish. This only whetted its appetite. It seized a bit of carpet on the floor, and, crawling under the nearest pew, reached up to the cushions on the seats, and greedily devoured them. Then, running along the carpet in the aisle on the right, it caught the ends of the pews, and wrapping itself around the pillars, reached long tongues of flame up toward the gallery, which extended along the sides of the church.

Here and elsewhere the imagery is often symbolic. In the same story "the sparkle of liquor in a glass charmed [Peter] like the eye of a serpent," and "the fire fastened its fangs into the pulpit floor." The heart of the "U-pass" tree in "The Marked Tree" is rotten, appropriately suggesting the moral deterioration of the Spencer family. In "The Dumb Witness" Murchison sits in "a massive armchair of carved oak," but Viney occupies "a splint-bottomed chair."

Many of the early fictional pieces reflect the haste with which they were written, being obviously contrived and formulaic. A train wreck, for example, is too often the means of disposing of a character or hastening resolution of the action of a story. Some of the works are more nearly sketches than stories; the characters are flat and stereotypic, and the action pedestrian. Like many other writers of the age, he depended too much on coincidence to suit the modern reader. Chesnutt's first stories, as a whole, have too little direct discourse and too much obvious didacticism. Occasionally, too, the pathos is overdone, as in "Aunt Lucy's Search."

Chesnutt's strengths as a writer, however, far outweigh his weaknesses. Except for fleeting lapses in emotional control, none of the faults mentioned are apparent in the author's later and longer narratives. The Douglass biography and the expository pieces are all well done, and are highlighted by eloquent and moving passages. The stories in this volume alone are sufficient to insure Chesnutt's place as a major writer of late-nineteenth-century American fiction, as a minor writer (in terms of the comparative quality of his works) in the whole range of American literature, as a social historian, and as the first black American to receive critical acclaim for his fiction.

He is claimed by both Ohio and North Carolina, having been the most important writer to have resided in either Cleveland or Fayetteville until his death in 1932. He was the first author to give extensive treatment to the heterogeneous inhabitants of the Cape Fear area. By introducing Buckeye and Tarheel Blue Veins and by exploring their problems, he earned the title of "pioneer of the color line." Chesnutt's depiction of blacks is unquestionably superior to that of his contemporaries. For accurate, objective, and perceptive thumbnail characterizations of blacks and whites on all the social levels he explored he also deserves to be called the Jean de la Bruyère of his period.

Chesnutt was able to utilize social history as fictional material without distortion; he was the first American writer to use local Negro folk life and folklore for social purpose. Writing realistically in traditional forms carefully modified to suit his preconceived ends, Chesnutt treated current issues forthrightly. In the course of his writing he depicted the greatest variety of black characters delineated in American fiction up to that time; concurrently he treated or anticipated every important theme and tone used by Negro writers through the Second World War. He is truly the father of twentieth-century Afro-American fiction.

Chesnutt was thoroughly imbued with every aspect of Afro-American culture and this way of life was the greatest single influence on his writing. It is therefore natural—perhaps inevitable—that the author would mirror the culture in his works. The expert manner in which he manifests his Negro-ness—expresses his "soul"—especially through the characters in the frame tales, is probably Chesnutt's most important contribution to American letters.

Public Reception

As has been the case with many other writers of distinction, Chesnutt was not properly appreciated by his generation. Although he realized that he was ahead of his time, this awareness could not have altogether relieved the pain of rejection for writing works that promoted American ideals, according to acceptable contemporary literary standards, in popular American forms, published by the most reputable firms. Ironically, the contemporary Paul Laurence Dunbar, a poetic prodigy and able fictionist, became almost universally known in Negro communities across the country while the name of Chesnutt still has no significance for most blacks. Both writers had enthusiastic white readers, but Chesnutt's popularity—which never had a chance to develop among his people—diminished while Dunbar's increased. That relatively few blacks had read any of Chesnutt's works initially or were made aware of them later may account for this paradoxical trend. The main reason is that Dunbar focused largely on an idealized past cherished by whites while Chesnutt exposed the hypocritical nature of race relations in the United States and suggested remedies within the framework of the Constitution.

For a few years, beginning in 1899, Chesnutt's work received widespread attention both from the leading critics of the day and from the general public. Initially the reactions were overwhelmingly favorable; however, as Chesnutt began to explore aspects of race relations usually avoided by established writers, he stirred up lively debates about his fiction. *The Conjure Woman* tales were warmly received as unique, enlightening, "of entrancing interest and of finished literary execution." A reader who had known Frederick Douglass wrote that Chesnutt's biography gave him "a fuller and closer estimate of the man than ever before." The "finished style" and "interpretive" nature of this volume led Vernon Loggins to declare that its general excellence was sufficient to win for Chesnutt "a place of importance in Negro literature."[63]

The author's "great delicacy and sympathy" in exploring some of the unacknowledged dilemmas of "the educated and well-to-do of the race" aroused strong feelings, often dictated by the personal or sectional bias of the reviewers. The Bridgeport, Connecticut, *Standard* found Chesnutt's disclosures of the underlying facts and inevitable conditions of the race situation in the color-line stories helpful to the reader's understanding, but Nancy Huston Banks in *The Bookman* (February, 1900) found only "The Wife of His Youth" wholly acceptable. While admitting that both "Uncle Wellington's Wives" and "The Sheriff's Children" were believable, she declared that Chesnutt showed "a lamentable lack of tact and reckless disregard of matters respected by more experienced writers in publishing the stories."[64] (She was doubtless referring to Chesnutt's frank discussion of race-mixing, with and without the benefit of clergy. The traditional treatment of this subject by both blacks and whites was less realistic than Chesnutt's; some aspects of it were carefully avoided.) A similar dichotomy of opinion was expressed about some of his novels. *The House Behind the Cedars* (1900) was a bold treatment of "passing" and miscegenation, and unusual in its sympathetic treatment of the major Negro characters.

Chesnutt's unusually forthright treatment of personal race relations from the Afro-American point of view prompted William Dean Howells, dean of American literary critics, to acknowledge in the May, 1900, *Atlantic Monthly:*

We had known the nethermost world of the grotesque and comical Negro and
the terrible and tragic Negro through the white observer on the outside . . . but
it had remained with Mr. Chesnutt to acquaint us with those regions where the
paler shades dwell.[65]

This appraisal is objective. However, after reading *The Marrow of Tradition*
(1901), Chesnutt's most fiery and controversial novel, Howells let Chesnutt's race
color his reaction in part by declaring in the December, 1901, issue of the *North
American Review* that

At his worst, he [Chesnutt] is no worse than the higher average of the ordinary
novelist, but he ought always to be very much better, for he began better, and
he is of that race which has, first of all, to get rid of the cakewalk. . . . [66]

The critic redeemed himself somewhat later in the review of the same novel.
Though Howells found the novel too bitter, he could find no fault with Chesnutt's aesthetics or ethics. In essence he forecast the inevitable dissolution of
the color bars which Chesnutt sought vainly to remove.[67]

The Colonel's Dream (1905) was anticlimactic. Though clearly conciliatory
in tone and lacking the confrontations between blacks and whites which had
especially aroused the public ire against the other novels, this book found few
readers. Critics received it more kindly; its truth was generally conceded and
a few rated it as Chesnutt's best work. However, most of the reading public,
who were predominantly white, obviously reflected the general attitude of a nation setting out to become a world power based upon a doctrine of white supremacy and manifest destiny. They therefore rejected Chesnutt's increasingly
explicit appeals for implementation of the principles of democracy on which
this country had ostensibly been founded.

Because Chesnutt did not receive the recognition his artistry merited, he
reopened his legal stenography firm in 1901. At that time too few black people,
regardless of their views or their financial ability, bought enough books to support any writer. Moreover, the majority of the white reading public were either
too censorious of or indifferent to Chesnutt's position on race relations to buy
enough of his works to make authorship even supportive. Inevitably discouraged
by the poor market, the publishers ceased more than routine promotion of Chesnutt's books. Invited to address a literary association in Boston, in 1902, Chesnutt wrote Monroe Trotter:

If I were making any considerable sums out of these race problem books, I would
cheerfully spend it in such ways (taking trips and making speeches gratis or for
partial expenses); but books in sympathy with the higher aspirations of the Negro
do not sell by the tens of thousands, and mine have cost me more to write, in
time spent, than I have got out of them.[68]

Chesnutt could recoup financial losses incurred while writing full time,
but apparently he would not have a second chance to achieve his "high and
holy purpose." As a writer whose works would not sell, he no longer had

at his disposal the only practicable means of reaching the people he wanted to influence. He was too realistic to expect any publisher to handle writings promoting unpopular causes and too honest to assume a stance contrary to his convictions.

Ironically, Chesnutt was more successful in breaking down racial barriers in the United States by his own life than through any movement actuated by his writings. He became one of Cleveland's first citizens. Modest and proud, shy and witty, unassuming and outspoken, and more at home with individuals than with crowds, Chesnutt was wise to bypass the political career for which his legal training and skill as a public speaker would have been assets. Instead, he used his knowledge of the law and a perennial interest in politics to secure and protect the rights of the black minority in the community and in the courts. Politically active as a private citizen, he came to urge his people to abandon blind party loyalties and to support responsive candidates regardless of their political affiliations. He was a participating member of many local and national groups, including the Cleveland Chamber of Commerce, the Cleveland Bar Association, the Cleveland Council on Sociology (as its first secretary and later as president), the Playhouse Settlement, now famous as Karamu House (also as the presiding officer), Booker T. Washington's Committee of Twelve, and the General Committee of the National Association for the Advancement of Colored People, hereafter referred to as NAACP, which he supported from its inception as the National Negro Committee in 1909 until his death.

Chesnutt enjoyed a warm friendship with Washington, dating from the time of his visit to Tuskegee during his tour of black Southern schools in 1901 and lasting until the educator's death in 1915. Chesnutt and Du Bois seemed to have mutual respect and admiration. Recognizing that both these great leaders had the same ultimate goals and that one great need of Afro-Americans was unity, Chesnutt championed neither man publicly during the years of the Washington-Du Bois debates. Instead, he supported to some extent and constructively criticized the philosophies of both. Chesnutt was also adamant in his refusal to participate in the personal vilification of either by partisans of the other.

Many letters in the voluminous correspondence between Chesnutt and Washington constitute a debate on the black man's use of the ballot. Chesnutt once wrote to Washington:

> I am squarely opposed to any restriction of the franchise in the South on any basis now proposed. It is wholly and solely an effort in my opinion to deprive the Negro of every vestige of power and every particle of representation. How completely this leaves him in the power of the whites and exposes him to their cruelty and contempt, is indicated in the disclosure of the peonage investigation now in progress in your State. I have no faith in the Southern people's sense of justice as far as the Negro's rights are concerned.[69]

Within two months Chesnutt addressed another long letter to Washington in which he announced that he had expressed in print his disagreement with his friend on voting, but at the same time recognized his "valuable services to the country."[70] Chesnutt also treated the educational biases of Washington and Du Bois, which he considered irrelevant in connection with the ballot:

> You Southern educators are all bound up with some cause or other, devotion to which sometimes unconsciously warps your opinions as to what is best for the general welfare of the race. You are conducting an industrial school, and naturally you place stress upon that sort of education, with perfect honesty and sincerity, but with the zeal of the advocate, before whose eyes his clients's case always looms up so as to dwarf the other side. Unfortunately, those who would discourage the higher education of the Negro, use your words for that purpose. Du Bois is in much the same situation. He is connected with Atlanta [University] and it is hard for him to discuss the abstract rights of the Negro without ringing in the higher education. Neither sort of education has anything directly to do with the civil and political rights of the Negro—these would be just as vital and fundamental as if there were not a single school of any kind in the Southern States. . . ."[71]

When, in 1910, asked by Du Bois to sign a protest, "Race Relations in the United States," which repudiated statements made by Washington during an interview published in the London *Morning Post,* Chesnutt responded with a reasoned refusal.[72] Through the years he had consistently avoided attacking Washington in the columns of *The* (Boston) *Guardian,* though invited to do so constantly by its courageous and impetuous editor, William Monroe Trotter, a Harvard college mate and partisan of Du Bois who served a short jail sentence for heckling Washington when he spoke in Boston in July, 1903.

On the other hand, however, Chesnutt spoke out unequivocally against any misrepresentation of facts about blacks, regardless of the race of the perpetrator. Largely through his efforts, the Macmillan Company withdrew from sale the libelous *The American Negro* (1901) by a Negro, William Hannibal Thomas. Chesnutt gathered evidence to show that the author was a fraud, presented it to the publishers, and scathed the scoundrel.[73]

Chesnutt also served continuously as a source of information on Afro-American life and culture. He condemned the Supreme Court for increasingly depriving blacks of their rights. He expressed his views concerning contemporary or perennial problems on pending legislation to local, state, and national lawmakers as well as to other influential people on all these levels. He lobbied locally against an anti-intermarriage bill (later defeated with the help of the Cleveland delegation) before the Ohio Legislature in 1913 and another in the United States House of Representatives in 1914. In 1915, Chesnutt prodded the governor of Ohio into action which forbade the showing of *The Birth of a Nation* to about one thousand Ohio teen-agers who were visiting Philadelphia. During the First World War he protested the treatment of Negro soldiers, and in the Senate Judiciary Committee hearings of 1928 opposed the Shipstead Anti-Injunction Bill because of the anti-Negro practices of labor unions.

Chesnutt spoke on many other occasions and also published articles on various aspects of Negro life and art in this country and abroad. He always emphasized the accomplishments of his fellow-blacks; he did not "think it the part of policy to be always dwelling upon the weakness of the Negro race." Moreover, he insisted on their inherent right to all the privileges of American citizenship and strongly criticized all obstructing forces.

Signal recognition came to Chesnutt in many ways. He was among the literary figures (the only Clevelander) invited to attend Mark Twain's seventieth birthday party at Delmonico's in New York City in 1905. He was twice chosen to serve as president of the Ohio State Stenographers' Association. Besides being a member of the bibliophile Rowfant Club from 1910 until his death, he was elected to membership in the National Arts Club in 1917. Wilberforce University conferred the LL.D. degree upon Chesnutt when he spoke there in 1913, and he was awarded the NAACP Spingarn Medal in 1928 as the black person who that year had rendered "the most distinguished service in some field of honorable endeavor."

It is now imperative that Chesnutt and all other accomplished black writers be given the same exposure and critical attention that other authors receive. The time has come in our civilization when all peoples must learn to accept and appreciate the superficial differences which should enliven and enrich rather than embroil our lives.

I hope that these stories will inspire every reader to share Chesnutt's vision and enthusiasm to work for "another golden age, when all men will dwell together in love and harmony, and when peace and righteousness shall prevail for a thousand years.

Notes to the Introduction

1. Charles W. Chesnutt, Journals, entry, August 13, 1875, and *passim,* Charles W. Chesnutt Collection (Fisk University Library, Nashville, Tennessee). Cited hereafter as CC.
2. Helen M. Chesnutt, *Charles Waddell Chesnutt: Pioneer of the Color Line* (Chapel Hill: The University of North Carolina Press, 1952), p. 19.
3. Charles W. Chesnutt (referred to hereafter as CWC), Journals, entry, June 25, 1881.
4. Manuscripts, CC.
5. See letter dated May 4, 1907, to Chesnutt from F. H. Hill, who had been a pastor for fifteen years. He was then serving as "private stenographer and typewriter for the Board of Bishops" of the A. M. E. Zion Church, and was aspiring "to become the next editor of our Sunday School Literature." See also statements by Mrs. Emma J. Council and Charles M. Williams, both longtime Fayetteville public school teachers in John W. Parker, "Chesnutt as a Southern Town Remembers Him," *The Crisis,* Vol. 56 (July, 1949), pp. 205–6.
6. CWC, Journals, entry, March 7, 1882, CC.
7. CWC, Journals, CC.
8. As explained by Monroe Lee Billington on p. 208 of *The American South: A Brief History* (New York: Charles Schribner's Sons, 1971), "Redemption" is one of several similar terms;

it designates but does not properly describe the period between 1869 and 1900 when native Southerners were regaining control of their formerly Confederate states. During the Civil War, whenever one of these states capitulated to Union forces, it had to accept a military governor. Such control was supposed to continue until at least 10 per cent of the people who had voted in the 1860 elections had complied with President Lincoln's 1863 proclamation on Reconstruction, which stipulated the conditions necessary for the re-establishment of civil governments loyal to the federal government. However, before this procedure was fully effected, the harsher Reconstruction Act of 1867 was implemented. For a more detailed account see John Hope Franklin, *From Slavery to Freedom,* third edition (New York: Alfred A. Knopf, Inc., 1969), pp. 301–6.

9. CWC, Journals, CC entry, March 16, 1880.
10. Billington, *op. cit.,* pp. 188-9.
11. Kenneth G. Goode, *From Africa to the United States and Then . . . A Concise Afro-American History* (Glenview, Illinois: Scott, Foresman Company, 1969), p. 84.
12. Frenise A. Logan, *The Negro in North Carolina, 1876–1894* (Chapel Hill: The University of North Carolina Press, 1964), p. 119.
13. CWC, Journals, entry, January 21, 1881, CC.
14. CWC, Journals, entry, April 23, 1879, CC.
15. CWC, Journals, 1874–82, *passim,* CC.
16. CWC, Journals, entry, May 8, 1880, CC.
17. The appellation "Blue Vein" reflects a practice in the Afro-American culture of so designating all blacks so fair in complexion that the blue of the venous blood at their wrists is clearly discernible.
18. "The Social Circle," *The Social Circle Journal,* XVIII (October, 1886), 2.
19. Helen M. Chesnutt, *op. cit.,* p. 61.
20. *Ibid.,* p. 187.
21. Letter dated October 16, 1961, from Chesnutt to E. J. Lilly, Correspondence, CC.
22. Statement by Davis during an interview with Sylvia Lyons Render, January, 1971.
23. N. D. Brascher, "Tells of Personal Experiencees with Late Charles W. Chesnutt," n. p., n.d., clipping, CC.
24. Quoted in Rayford W. Logan, *The Betrayal of the Negro: From Rutherford B. Hayes to Woodrow Wilson* (New York: Collier Books, 1965), p. 99. See also Hugh M. Gloster, *Negro Voices in American Fiction* (Chapel Hill: The University of North Carolina Press, 1948), pp. 7–11.
25. CWC, "Post-Bellum—Pre-Harlem," *Breaking Into Print,* Elmer Adler, ed. (New York: Simon and Schuster, 1937), p. 51.
26. Journals, entry, May, 1880, CC.
27. CWC, "The Free Colored People of North Carolina," *Southern Workman,* XXX (May, 1901), 136–41.
28. *Thirteenth Census of the United States, Taken in the Year 1910: Population,* I (Washington: Government Printing Office, 1913).
29. CWC, "The Goophered Grapevine," *The Conjure Woman* (Ann Arbor Paperback: The University of Michigan Press, 1969), pp. 9–10.
30. *Goopher,* also spelled *goofer,* is derived from the African term *gufa.* As a verb it is a synonym for *conjure;* both mean to put a spell on by means of incantation, by the placing of specially treated objects in the vicinity of individual(s) to be "fixed" or by giving the intended victim(s) specially treated food or drink. The object prepared is often called a *goopher.* The procedure followed by the conjurer is called *working (his* or *her) roots.*
31. CWC, "The Goophered Grapevine," p. 24.
32. CWC, "Mars Jeems's Nightmare," *The Conjure Woman,* p. 101.
33. CWC, "Po' Sandy," *The Conjure Woman,* p. 46.
34. Letter from Charles W. Foster to Sylvia Lyons Render, August 13, 1968.
35. Sterling Brown, *Negro Poetry and Drama and The Negro in American Fiction* (New York: Atheneum, 1969), p. 2
36. Nick Aaron Ford, "The Negro Author's Use of Propaganda in Imaginative Literature" (unpublished Ph.D. Dissertation, State University of Iowa, Iowa City, 1945), p. 14
37. James Wilburn Byrd, "The Portrayal of White Character by Negro Novelists 1900-1950"

(unpublished Ph.D. Dissertation, George Peabody College for Teachers, Nashville, 1955), p. 351.

38. CWC, "The Passing of Grandison," *The Wife of His Youth and Other Stories of the Color Line* (Ann Arbor Paperback: The University of Michigan Press, 1969), pp. 178, 180, 182.

39. CWC, "The Goophered Grapevine," p. 15.

40. *Ibid.,* p. 16.

41. CWC, "The Gray Wolf's Ha'nt," *The Conjure Woman,* p. 176.

42. Letter from Chesnutt to Cable, June 5, 1890, Correspondence, CC.

43. CWC, "The Gray Wolf's Ha'nt," pp. 167–8.

44. CWC, "Sis' Becky's Pickaninny," *The Conjure Woman,* p. 135.

45. CWC, "Mars Jeems's Nightmare," p. 71.

46. *Ibid.,* p. 72.

47. *Ibid.,* p. 75.

48. CWC, "Uncle Wellington's Wives," *The Wife of His Youth and Other Stories* . . ., p. 237.

49. CWC, "The Sheriff's Children," *The Wife of His Youth and Other Stories* . . ., p. 85.

50. CWC, "The Conjurer's Revenge," *The Conjure Woman,* p. 110.

51. W. E. Burghardt Du Bois, "Postscript: Chesnutt," *The Crisis,* XL (January, 1933), 20.

52. CWC, "Mars Jeems's Nightmare," p. 82.

53. *Ibid.,* p. 84.

54. CWC, "Sis' Becky's Pickaninny," p. 159.

55. CWC, "The Conjurer's Revenge," p. 119.

56. CWC, "The Goophered Grapevine," p. 4.

57. *Ibid,* p. 11.

58. CWC, "The Negro in Art," *The Crisis,* XXXIII (November, 1926), 28–9.

59. CWC, "A Matter of Principle" *The Wife of His Youth and Other Stories* . . ., p. 95,

60. CWC, "The Web of Circumstance," *The Wife of His Youth and Other Stories* . . ., p. 302.

61. CWC, "The Passing of Grandison," pp. 180–81.

62. CWC, "Mars Jeems's Nightmare," p. 100.

63. Vernon Loggins, *The Negro Author: His Development in America to 1900* (Port Washington, N.Y.: Kennikat Press, Inc.,), p. 270.

64. "Novel Notes," *The Bookman,* X (February, 1900), 597–8.

65. "Mr. Charles W. Chesnutt's Stories," *Atlantic Monthly,* LXXXV (May, 1900), 701.

66. "A Psychological Counter Current in Recent Fiction," *North American Review,* CLXXII (December, 1901) p. 882

67. *Ibid.,* p. 882.

68. Letter from Chesnutt to Trotter, December 17, 1902, Correspondence, CC.

69. Letter from Chesnutt to Washington, June 27, 1903, Correspondence, CC.

70. Letter from Chesnutt to Washington, August 11, 1903, Correspondence, CC.

71. CWC, "The Disfranchisement of the Negro," *The Negro Problem: A Series of Articles by Representative Negroes of To-Day* (New York: James Pott & Company, 1903), 74–124.

72. Letter from Chesnutt to Du Bois, November 21, 1910, quoted in Helen M. Chesnutt, *op. cit.,* pp. 240–44.

73. See Chesnutt's letter to Robert C. Ogden, May 27, 1904, in which he enclosed copies of communications on this matter, Correspondence, CC. See also CWC, "A Defamer of His Race," *The Critic,* XXXVIII (April, 1901), 350–51.

74. CWC, Journals, CC.

ANECDOTES

A TIGHT BOOT

Some years before the war Squire Mirabeau MacKinnon kept the Jefferson House at Macedonia, the county seat of one of the up-country counties of North Carolina. The hotel was a big two-story frame house, fronting on the Court House Square, with broad piazzas running along both stories, front and rear. A row of big elms along the sidewalk made a pleasant shade for loiterers on the front piazza, and sheltered from the summer heat the horses that were fastened to the dozen or more hitching-posts. Beyond the sidewalk a well and a watering-trough furnished additional facilities for the accommodation of the public. Back of the house, and separated from it by the clean-swept yard, stood the big red kitchen. The yard was perfectly innocent of grass or herbage of any kind—unless the elms and china trees might be included under that head—and by constant trampling was as hard and white as an ancient threshing-floor.

During the greater part of the year the Jefferson House did not do a very large business. The farmers on their way down to the larger towns on the navigable rivers or near the coast, with wagon-loads of cotton and tobacco, would stop at the Jefferson overnight, settling their bills when they came back with plenty of money and supplies of sugar, coffee, calico and other luxuries which were not produced on their plantations. A few town folks came up to Macedonia to spend a few weeks of the hot summer; and unquestionably it was a pleasant place.

Court week was the busy season at the Jefferson House. Court was in session for a week or ten days several times a year, and on these occasions the hotel was filled to overflowing, and in summer hammocks were swung on the piazzas and in winter pallets were made on the floor for those whom there were not beds to accommodate. The judges, the lawyers, and the county dignitaries who came in from their plantations to attend court all put up at the Jefferson House and kept Squire and Mrs. MacKinnon and their corps of servants very busy.

The duty of blacking the boots for the guests devolved upon a colored man by the name of "Bob". Under ordinary circumstances Bob enjoyed a sinecure, and was only consoled for his hard lot during the court week by the numerous dimes and quarters which he extorted from the good-natured gentlemen whose boots were the objects of his gentle ministrations.

One evening during the summer term Bob went around about ten o'clock to the rooms of such guests as had retired, and collected the boots for cleaning. He took them to the kitchen, and in order to lessen his work in the morning, blacked about half the lot. He wanted to attend a colored dance at a cabin a mile from the hotel, and while his orders were to stay at home, he thought he might slip away an hour or two without his absence being noticed.

While he was reveling in the anticipation of the fine time he would have, and keeping time with the blacking brush to the strains of an imaginary banjo, he took up a remarkably neat boot. It was a big boot, but made of fine leather, and quite new. It struck Bob that that boot was just about his size, and it looked so neat he thought he would try it on. It went on without difficulty, though it was a little tight about the hollow of the foot and the heel. Then it occurred to Bob that those boots would look nice on him at the ball. He drew on the other, and jumping over the back fence, made his way to the house where the ball was in progress.

The laws forbade any assemblage of the slaves, and when they had their balls, prayer meetings, etc., it was customary to station sentinels along the roads and paths which led to the meeting place to watch for the patrol—or "patterole," as the natives called it—a sort of mounted police, whose special duty it was to keep the slaves under surveillance at night. Bob avoided the patrol by going through the woods, passed the sentinels, and was soon swinging the girls around, and displaying the new boots, to the inspiring strains of "Camptown Races" and "Old Dan Tucker" as rendered by the combined exertions of a banjo, a fiddle, and a pair of bones.

The fun was at its height when someone dashed up to the door and yelled "Patterole!" Instantly the candles were blown out, a bucket of water was thrown on the fire, and the crowd rapidly dispersed through the various openings of the cabin—one frightened fellow going out through the big chimney. It was a false alarm, given by some ill-natured darky who had not been invited to the ball; but Bob did not know this, so he dodged into the bushes, and by cutting across the plantations, kept clear of the patrol and reached the hotel at about two o'clock in the morning.

He tried to pull the boots off, but either the peculiar conformation of his heel prevented it, or his feet were so swollen by his recent exertions that the boot would not come off. As Bob was very tired and sleepy, he spread a quilt on the kitchen floor and went to sleep, confident that in the morning the boot would come off without difficulty.

The cook, Aunt Lyddy, went in the kitchen in the morning to begin preparations for breakfast and there Bob was asleep on the floor. She called him, but got only a grunt in response. Finally a gourd of water thrown into his face brought about the desired result, and Bob got up, rolled up his pallet and put it away, grumbling at Aunt Lyddy's cruelty.

"Better g'long an' black dem boots," said Aunt Lyddy, who was a woman of few words.

"Wait till I git dis boot off, Aun' Lyddy," replied Bob; he had pulled off one boot, and as he began an account of the ball the night before, he took hold of the other with the confident expectation that it would slip off easily. His confidence was somewhat shaken when the boot showed no sign of yielding. He had no better success with a bootjack, and Bob began to get just a little anxious. Breakfast time was drawing near and the gentlemen would want their boots. One of them came to the top of the stairs and called:

"Boy!"

Squire MacKinnon, who was not yet dressed himself, heard the call and came to his bedroom door.

"Well, what is it, Colonel?" he asked.

"Tell that boy to bring my boots, if you please, Squire."

Squire MacKinnon went to the back door and called across the yard in his sharp way:

"Bob, you Bob!"

"S–s–s–s–ah!" replied Bob, who labored under a slight impediment in his speech, which came out strong when he was excited.

"Colonel Tyson wants his boots!"

"Y–a–a–s, s–s–s–ah!" replied Bob, tugging away desperately. The sweat had collected in great beads on his forehead and rolled in dirty streams down his cheeks.

"Fur de Lawd' sake, Aun' Lyddy, he'p me git dis boot off," he said imploringly.

"I can't take my han's out'n de dough," said Aunt Lyddy, who was filling a big pan with biscuits. But she called in another servant from the yard—Isham—and he added his efforts to those of Bob; but all in vain. The boot stuck—closer than a porous plaster—closer than poor relations—closer than Sinbad's Old Man of the Sea—as closely as though it were glued to his foot.

The Colonel was growing impatient. He came to the door again, and called:

"Boy, I want them boots right off!" The Colonel was more anxious about his boots than his grammar.

Squire MacKinnon, in shirt and trousers, came to the back door again.

"Bob, Bob, you Bob!"

"Ya–a–a–s, Marse!" came from the kitchen in anxious tones.

"Bring Colonel Tyson's boots right away!"

Bob was now in despair. He knew his master's disposition, and trembled for the probable consequences if he did not get that boot off very soon. His shirt was wet with perspiration, and his eyes stood out like a couple of dinner plates. Aunt Lyddy, who had finished the biscuits, Phyllis, Chloe, Isham, and another boy who had come in from the stable—all united in the fruitless attempt to get that boot off. Isham had hold of the boot in front and Aunt Lyddy had Bob by the waist; the others were ranged behind her and Isham respectively, all pulling hard, but with no success. The stubborn boot would not come off.

The Colonel came out on the upper floor of the piazza and thundered out:

"I want them boots, blacked or not blacked, and I want 'em quick!"

"Wha-a-at!" said the Squire, as he heard the Colonel's loud tones, and ran out, still half-dressed upon the lower floor piazza.

The other gentlemen had begun to come for their boots, and Squire Mac-Kinnon, fearful of offending his guests, walked quickly across the yard to the kitchen to see what was the matter. Bob and his friends were still pulling away in sheer desperation. The sweat had accumulated in little puddles on the floor, and the boot had begun to rip a little at the heel. Squire MacKinnon was puzzled for a moment, and then the full meaning of the situation dawned upon him.

"What the d—l does this mean?" demanded he.

"I j–j–j–is' put the boot on to black it better, Marse, and it won't come off no mo'," replied the trembling Bob.

The Squire pushed the others aside, caught the boot by the heel, and jerking the unfortunate Bob from the chair, dragged him around the kitchen. As he went around Bob caught at whatever came in his way; he overturned several chairs; he caught the leg of the table, and the dishes came down with a crash; and as the Squire, in his mad career, whirled him around again, he caught Aunt Lyddy by the ankle, causing that amiable woman and accomplished cook to lose her balance and sit down in the big pot of hot water on the hearth. It is needless to say that she lost no time in getting up again.

As the angry Squire made more circuits of the kitchen, Bob caught by the door frame and held on like grim death. The Squire gave one "long, last, last, long lingering" pull, and off came the boot!

The said boot continued to play an important part in the scene that followed for a few minutes, and Bob had ample time, while recovering from his bruises, to reflect on the sin of vanity, of the evil consequences of which his experience had certainly qualified him to think intelligently. He stayed at the Jefferson House until near the end of the war, when he drifted off in the wake of Sherman's army. Up to that time, however, he was not known to indulge again in the luxury of wearing other men's boots.

Gratitude

"**G**ood morning, sir."

I glanced from my desk at a tall, cadaverous-looking individual, clad in a faded brown ulster.

"I hope I don't disturb you?"

"You haven't yet," I observed.

"Thank you, very much. If it isn't troubling you, would you be kind enough to permit me to show you the advance sheets of our new work on 'Art in the Middle Ages'?"

"I don't want it."

"Thank you; but I don't ask you to buy it, but merely to look at it."

I am of a very obliging disposition. I turned over a few pages hastily, without giving him an opportunity to recite his usual lecture.

"Yes," I said, as I handed the book back to him, "it seems to be a pretty good book, but I'm not able to buy it."

"I'm very much obliged to you for the opportunity of showing it to you."

"Not at all," I replied, turning to my balance sheet.

"Couldn't I offer you some inducement in the way of easy terms?"

"I can't afford it on any terms at present."

"I am sorry," he said, as he started reluctantly toward the door, "but as it is, I owe you a debt of gratitude for permitting me to talk to you about it. The life of a book agent, sir, is hard; and it is like an oasis in a desert to meet a man who will permit an agent to describe his book. Good morning, sir."

I was half-way down a column of figures when he came back and remarked, over my shoulder, insinuatingly:

"Would fifty cents a month bring it within your means?"

"No," I said, with a touch of impatience; "I can't buy it at any price. I'm too busy to talk about it now, anyhow."

"Well, good morning, sir. I'm sorry to have disturbed you, but I'm more than obliged to you for the opportunity of showing you the work and letting you know what it is."

I started down the column of figures again, and had reached a total of two hundred and fifty-seven, when a voice remarked, apologetically, close to my ear:

"Excuse me, sir, but would you object to my inquiring when you think it is possible that you will be likely to have leisure to examine the work a little more thoroughly?"

I could bear no more. I arose from my desk and calmly but firmly took my visitor by the collar and led him out into the hall and to the head of the stairs. Then, with a skill derived from long practice, I kicked him downstairs.

I stood and watched his abrupt and somewhat undignified descent. The sound of breaking bones came up the hallway. A moment later the book agent picked himself up, slowly and painfully, and called back to me in a broken but grateful voice, as he limped away:

"Thank you, sir, I am ever so much obliged to you for letting me off alive."

Appreciation

Old Pilgrim Gainey moved to the North several years ago and the people of our Missouri town had about forgotten him, when he turned up again the other day. I met him on the corner by the Market-house.

"Hello, Uncle Pilgrim! You're back home again, are you? You've come on a visit, I suppose?"

"No, sah—no, sah—I ain't come on no visit, sah; I's come ter stay."

"How did you like the North, Uncle Pilgrim?"

"Well—er—jes' middlin', Mistah Dixon, jes' middlin'."

"Didn't you get along well up there?"

"Jes' middlin' well—middlin' well."

"Get good wages?"

"Yas, I s'pose I got good wages. I made twice as much ez I does heah."

"You could vote as you pleased, couldn't you?"

"O, Lawd, yas! Why, dey runs cullu'd men fuh de legislatur' on de Dimicratic ticket up dar!"

"Up there you had civil rights, didn't you? Your children went to school with the white children? You could stop at the hotels, ride in first-class cars, and sit in any part of the theatres and churches, couldn't you?"

"Well, 'bout de chil'en, I didn' had none. 'Bout de chu'ches, I nevah went ter no white chu'ches. But I b'leeves dat dem as has de money doan hab no trouble 'bout gittin' what dey wants."

"I don't see why you don't like the North, Uncle Pilgrim?"

"Well, I tell yer jes' how it is, Mistah Dixon. Yer kin git plenty wu'k, an' big pay, an' yer has all de privilege yer wants; but de rale fac' is, dat cullu'd people ain't 'preciated at de Norf. Dat's what's de mattah!"

Just then, young Tom Macmillan came up behind the old man, knocked his hat off, and saluted him with a playful kick.

"Look a' heah, Marse Tom, you stop dat now!" said Pilgrim with a delighted grin, which displayed all his wealth of ivory. "Is yer got any terbacker, Marse Tom?"

Tom tossed the old man a half-plug of chewing tobacco.

"Now, dat's what I calls 'preciation," said Uncle Pilgrim, filling his mouth with the savory weed. "I nevah had dat much terbacker give ter me all de time I wus at de Norf!"

An Eloquent Appeal

A tall, tolerably well-dressed and somewhat distinguished-looking colored man came into my office the other morning.

"Can you spare me a moment of your valuable time?" he inquired, in excellent English.

"Certainly," I replied. (My time was not very valuable, but I didn't feel called upon to say so.)

"Sir," he continued: "you see in me the representative of a despised and down-trodden race. For centuries the race with which you are identified held my people in a bondage more cruel than death, and lived lapped in luxury while their black bondmen toiled beneath the burning sun."

"That's largely true," I remarked, as he paused. He fixed me with his eye, and continued:

"When at last the exigencies of war made the abolition of slavery necessary for the preservation of the Union, your statesmen reluctantly granted us the tardy boon of liberty."

I was unable to deny this, and he went on:

"You gave us a theoretical liberty, and turned us loose, penniless and ignorant, among the people who had oppressed us. Is not this true?"

"Substantially true," I assented.

"The catalogue of our wrongs is a long and bloody one. But I notice now a growing sentiment among the white people of this country—a feeling that, in merely giving the Negro back the liberty they had forcibly taken from him, they have not done their whole duty toward him, but that they owe him reparation for the wrongs he has suffered."

I remarked, at this point of the interview, that I had an engagement which would require me to leave the office in a very short time.

"Just one moment," he continued: "As a member of the dominant race, do you not feel it your duty to do what you can toward lifting my race to a higher level—toward repaying, in some small degree, the debt this country owes them?"

I remarked that I was willing enough, but that I happened to be financially embarrassed just at that particular time.

"You misconstrue me," he replied, with dignity: "I do not seek charity for myself, or for others. I mean business. If, for instance, you could confer a favor on my race, with profit to yourself at the same time, would you do it?"

I answered in the affirmative.

"Then," he said, running his hand into his coat-pocket, you will certainly take a stick of my 'Magic Corn Cure,' warranted to remove hard or soft corns on one application; or if used occasionally, to entirely prevent their formation. Will one stick be enough?"

Before I could recover from my astonishment, he had collected a quarter from me, and left the office with a bow that would have done credit to any headwaiter in America.

A Cause Célèbre

The following correspondence illustrates the uncertainties of trial by jury, and also explains why the claim agent of the Brass Bound R. R. has received instructions to settle all claims, if possible, without litigation:

Coon Creek, Ohio,
December 8th, 1890

Mr. Clame Agunt.—Dere sur:

Yore rale rode killed a fine Cotswold buck sheap belonging to me last weak. Sheap was wuth fifteen dollars. Pleaze settle rite away and save trubble.

Yors trooly,
Josh Hayrick

New York, December 10th, 1890

Oliver Ollright, Esq., *Div. Sup't Brass Bound R.*
Dear Sir:

I enclose a letter of J. Hayrick, making claim for one sheep, valued at $15.00, killed on this railway week of November 30th–December 6th. Please have matter investigated, and report to me as soon as possible.

Yours, &c.,
U. B. Quick, *Claim Ag't*

Chipmunk J'c'n, Ohio, December 13th, 1890

U. B. Quick, Esq., *Claim Agent*
Dear Sir:

Have had section foreman look up claim of J. Hayrick for sheep killed. He reports that sheep was killed December 4th, by passenger train; that it was a lamb about six weeks old, and not larger than a good-sized cat; that he did not even think it necessary to bury carcass, but took it by the leg and tossed it over in the adjoining field; is of opinion that $2.00 would be a large price to pay for sheep.

> Yours truly,
> O. Ollright, *Div. Sup't*

New York, December 15th, 1890

J. Hayrick, Esq.

I have investigated your claim for sheep killed, and we are willing to allow you two dollars in full settlement of same, you to sign a proper release in full of all claims.

> Yours truly,
> U. B. Quick, *Claim Ag't*

Coon Creek, Ohio, December 17th, 1890

U. B. Quick.—Sur:

Yore insultin noat reseeved and returned unoapened.

> Josh Hayrick

New York, December 22nd, 1890

C. D. Sharp, Esq., *Attorney at Law*

Dear Sir:

I enclose summons in the case of *Hayrick vs. The Brass Bound R. R. Co.,* brought to recover for sheep killed. Please give the matter proper attention.

> Yours, &c.,
> B. F. Hytone, *Gen'l Counsel*

Columbus, Ohio, January 8th, 1891

B. F. Hytone, *Gen'l Counsel*

Dear Sir:

The case of *Hayrick vs. Company* was tried yesterday, to a jury. We introduced the testimony of three witnesses as to the value of sheep; but plaintiff produced ten witnesses, who swore positively that sheep was worth all the way from fifteen to twenty dollars. Verdict for plaintiff twenty dollars and costs, making a total of $42.17, which please remit to clerk of court. I have a clerk at present employed in making out my own bill for services, which I will forward some time this week, as soon as completed.

> Very truly yours,
> C. D. Sharp, *Att'y*

A Soulless Corporation

The claim agent of the Brass Bound R. R. Company sat in his office, his desk piled high with correspondence. He had disposed of sixteen claims for cows killed, thirteen sheep claims, and several personal injuries—about the usual daily average of accidents—when the office door opened, and a tall, angular woman entered.

"Be you the claim agent?" she demanded, with a voice which sounded like a cross between a buzz-saw and a steam whistle.

"I be," responded that official, briefly.

"I come up here to git pay for the trunk I lost in the Coon Creek collision."

There had been a bad smashup on the road a few weeks before and this was one of the claims growing out of it, which remained unadjusted.

"What is your name?" asked the agent.

"Mrs. Lovelock, of Geneva," she replied.

"Ah, yes," said the claim agent, "I remember now. How much do you think your trunk was worth, Mrs. Lovelock?"

"Well, I dunno exactly, but I sh'd think about two hundred dollars would be nigh the value of it, and I wouldn't want you should pay me any more'n it was worth."

"That is pretty steep," mused the claim agent, looking at his notebook. "Let's see how you make it. What was the trunk itself worth, for instance?"

"Well, it was a fine, large, new trunk, an' I had jest paid fifteen dollars for it before I started."

The claim agent made a note of the fifteen dollars. "Well, what was in the trunk?" he asked.

"Lemme see—there was my best Sunday dress—a black silk—the material in it cost twenty-five dollars, an' the makin' ten—that makes thirty-five. Then there was an alpaca dress, worth about fifteen dollars, an' a new bunnit I had jest paid fifteen dollars for."

70

The claim agent kept track of the items. "That makes seventy-eight dollars; now what else."

"Well," she said, "there was consid'able other clothin'."

"What was that worth?"

"I dunno exactly, but I guess about fifty dollars."

"Well, what else now?"

Her memory seemed to fail her at this point, but after a moment she continued: "There was about seventy-five dollars worth o' jewelry in the trunk."

"That makes something over two hundred dollars," said the claim agent.

"Well," she said magnanimously, "I don't want to be hard on the Comp'ny, so we'll call it jest an even two hundred."

"Trunk have any marks on it?" asked the claim agent, casually.

"It had a kyard with my name on it," she answered.

"Got the check?"

She produced it.

"Seems to me you are a little hard on us," said the claim agent. "Don't you think you could reduce the amount a little?"

"No, sir," she said, "an' if you don't pay, I'll sue."

"Sorry to go to law with you, ma'am, but we won't pay that claim."

She flounced out of her chair, and started for the door.

"Wait a minute," said the claim agent, soothingly. "I guess we can make some arrangement."

She sat down again, and the claim agent stepped out into the hall. When he came back a porter followed him, bringing under one arm a small, yellow trunk, tied about with a rope, and somewhat the worse for wear. It could have been bought anywhere for a dollar and a half. The claim agent looked at the card and compared the checks. "Is that your trunk?" he asked.

Her face was red as a beet, as she acknowledged, with very bad grace, that it was.

"The trunk hasn't been hurt at all," said the claim agent, "except by the wetting it got when the baggage car fell into the creek. If you've got the key there, we'll open it, and see what the damage was."

"I—I've—lost the key," she stammered.

"Oh, well, then we'll break it open," said the claim agent, cheerfully.

"Oh, no, don't do that," she remonstrated. "It—it—ain't my trunk—I borrered it from my sister, an' she wouldn't like that I should break the lock. I'd rather take less money."

"I guess you *would*," said the claim agent, with a chuckle. "I ain't been claim agent on this road for five years without meeting lots of people like you. We'll give you fifteen dollars for what damage the water may have done to your baggage—or, I'll open the trunk, and you can bring your lawsuit."

"I'll take the fifteen dollars," she replied, quickly, but snappishly. And when she had got the money and signed a receipt, she relieved her mind by saying, as she left the office:

"I wouldn't a thought a rich comp'ny like this would insult a lady that way. But all men ain't gentlemen, and corporations ain't got no soul nohow."

Busy Day in a Lawyer's Office

Attorney Sharp sat in his office waiting for the morning's business to begin. A somewhat pretty, frail-looking young woman entered.

"Ah! good morning, madam," said the lawyer, with a smile of recognition, placing a chair for the client. "How are you getting along with your last husband, Mrs.—, I forget your present name?"

"Mrs. Rogg. Oh, we've quarreled already, and I want a divorce."

"Let me see," said the attorney, reflectively, "this is the—"

"The fifth," replied the young woman. "You promised to make a reduction of ten per cent each time."

"Yes, I remember now. On what ground do you wish to base the action?"

"Gross neglect. He has refused me the money to buy a sealskin sacque."

"Hum-hum—Well, I guess it can be managed if we can get the case tried before Judge Flipp. Have you got any witnesses?"

"No."

"Well, I'll take the case for twenty-five dollars and witnesses found, or for fifteen dollars, and you furnish them."

The pretty young woman tripped out of the office, and tried to make a "mash" on a dude of the most pronounced type whom she met at the door.

"Good morning, Mr. De Bullion," said the attorney, with effusive politeness.

Mr. De Bullion stated his business. He wished to contest his father's will.

"Upon what ground do you want the will set aside?"

"That's just what I wished to consult you about."

"What did the old gentleman die of?"

"He choked to death in a fit of laughter."

"Very good, very good!" chuckled the lawyer; "and what was he laughing at?"

"The jokes in a humorous paper."

"Have you got the paper? What did it contain?" asked Mr. Sharp, leaning forward, eagerly.

73

"I have preserved the paper, folded just at the page he was reading. It contains an essay on the mule and a story about a mother-in-law."

"That is quite enough. We will contest the will on the ground of mental imbecility. My fees will be two hundred dollars down, and seventy-five per cent of the estate if I win the case."

Mr. De Bullion having dropped his eyeglass, and being somewhat near-sighted, almost ran into a portly gentleman who entered the office as he went out.

"Doctor, I am glad to see you. Be seated. To get to business, I wished to talk to you about that case of Bloke against the Brass Bound Railroad. You see, the thing stands just this way: If we can't show anything but a broken thumb and a sprained ankle we won't recover much; but if it can be shown that Bloke suffered serious internal injuries the case may prove a bonanza, sir. I am authorized by my client to expend twenty-five per cent of the amount recovered for contingent expenses. I hope you will make another examination."

"Why, certainly," said Dr. Vaseline, rubbing his oily hands together. "My first examination was somewhat hurried, but I will investigate the case more thoroughly."

As the doctor made his exit the lawyer put on his hat and said to his clerk, "James, I'm going over to the jail to coach Blood up on the insanity symptoms, and then I'll be at Police Court awhile to look after that little larceny case. Don't forget to look up some witnesses for Sneak's good character; and if you see any professional jurors about, set out the best cigars, understand?"

A Roman Antique

It was a warm day in summer and I seated myself for a moment on one of the benches in Washington Square. A few minutes later an old, white-haired Negro came hobbling along with the aid of a stick and seated himself at the other end of the bench, lifting his battered hat to me deferentially as he did so.

I was both surprised and flattered at such a manifestation of politeness in New York, and remarked to the old man in a friendly tone:

"A fine day, Uncle."

"Yas, suh it *is* a fine day, boss, sho' 'nuff. Dish yer weathah min's me er de kin' er weathah we useter hab in Rome."

"So you have lived in Rome, have you? I came from Rome myself."

"Lawd, boss, you doan' look ner talk lack no Roman. Anybody 'ud take you ter be'n bawn en raise' is dis country."

"Certainly I was," I replied. "I was born in Rome, New York."

The old man made no rejoinder, and struck by his apparent great age, I asked:

"How old are you, Uncle?"

"Lawd, chile," he answered with a silent chuckle, which exposed his toothless gums, "I doan' know—I done los' track un it. I wuz fifteen year ole w'en de wah broke out."

"That's impossible," I replied; "that wouldn't make you over forty, and you can't be less than seventy-five."

"I reckon I's 'bout nineteen hund'ed," said the old man, reflectively, after a short pause. "I useter be Mars Julius Caesar's fav'rite body-sarven', en I reckon you knows 'bout how long he's be'n dead. I wuz fifteen years ole w'en de las' wah wid Gaul broke out. I kin 'member de battle ob Alesia des ez well ez ef it wuz yistiday. De arrers wuz flyin' thoo de aiah thick ez flies 'roun' a merlasses jug, de jav'lins wuz w'izzin', en I wuz lookin' on fum de rare, w'en I seed a archer aim a arrer at Mars Julius. I grab' up a shiel', en rush inter de thick er de fight, en wuz des in time ter ketch 'im ez he fell f'um his hoss. I got a arrer thoo my side ez I wuz totin' 'im off, en wuz laid up fer two or th'ee mont's atterwuds. W'en I got well, Mars Julius gun me a quarter, en w'en he died, he lef' directions in his will fer me ter be gradu'lly 'mancipated, so I 'ud be free w'en I wuz a hund'ed years ole. Ah, but dem wuz good ole times!" he added, with a sigh of regret.

"I's done spent de quartah Mars Julius gun me," he remarked, giving me a sidelong look, "en I needs ernudder fer ter git some liniment fer my rheumatiz. Is yer got any small change 'bout yo' clo's, boss?"

A vision of imperial Rome rose up before me, with all its glory and magnificence and power. In a fit of abstraction I handed the old man a twenty-dollar gold piece, and when I started from my reverie, he had disappeared behind a clump of shrubbery in the direction of Sixth Avenue.

She Reminded Him

When Jones married Miss Joyntstock, Eastern culture, acting upon a naturally quiet and plastic temperament, had apparently eradicated all traces of that lady's early training—or lack of training—in the not very remote period when her father was a common, everyday Nevada miner. Jones is a clever young fellow, and knows it, and as a natural consequence is a trifle conceited, of which he is also conscious at times. He went to a party the other night, and, under the stimulus of good company and good champagne, talked a great deal—in fact, too much. The next morning, while dressing, he remarked to his wife:

"My dear, I wish you had more of that—that vivacity of intellect—that—that—spontaneity of expression, that—er—in short, more of that snap which makes some women's influence upon persons of the opposite sex so far-reaching and beneficent. For instance: When you hear me talking too much, it would be the simplest thing in the world for you to make an incidental remark, or drop a hint, that would keep me from making a fool of myself."

"Do you think so, dear?" she said quietly. "Then I'll try to do so. And in order not to lose any time," she continued softly, after a moment's pause, "I'll begin now."

When Jones recovered consciousness, his wife was bending solicitously over him, holding with one hand a damp towel to his head, and with the other a glass to his lips.

"Drink this, dear," she murmured, in her usual quiet way, "and you'll feel better. I'm awfully sorry for you, but you forgot that I was raised in a mining town."

An Original Sentiment

"**M**y dear," said Mrs. Thompson one evening last week, "I want you to help me get up a sentiment for Ella Miller's autograph album; won't you?"

"Certainly," said Thompson, laying down the paper. "How's this: 'May peace and happiness attend thy journey through life.' "

"Er—ah don't you think a nice quotation would be better? Something appropriate, you know."

"Why, yes," said Thompson, "have you looked in Shakespeare?"

"I think Shakespeare is a little antiquated. I'd rather have something more modern."

"How's Tennyson?"

"Tennyson's too sentimental, don't you think?"

"Longfellow?"

"Rather commonplace. I want something modern and at the same time effective and appropriate. Let's look through this pile of magazines," said Mrs. Thompson.

Thompson demurred a little, but dutifully began to overhaul the magazines. Half an hour elapsed but nothing suitable was found.

"Don't you think something original would be better?" said Thompson. "How's this, for instance?

" 'Dear Ella: You have a good head and a good heart. May you have good health, a good husband and a good time.' "

"Please say it again."

Thompson repeated it.

"I don't think it nice to tell people what they have already," said Mrs. Thompson.

"Umph!" said her husband, "my experience is that people like to be told of their good points."

"Besides," continued Mrs. Thompson, "it seems to me rather coarse to wish a girl a husband. I don't think it the height of a girl's ambition to get married."

"Oh, no," said Thompson sarcastically, "you were seventeen when you married, I believe. If you had waited as long as Ella Miller has, you would know how to appreciate a husband."

"And I'm not sure that I would wish a friend of mine any husband at all," she continued, reflectively.

"That's very complimentary to me," said Thompson, throwing down a magazine in a rage. "After wasting an hour and a half of my time waiting on you, I am to be insulted by your as good as wishing point blank that you had never married."

"I said nothing of the sort, Mr. Thompson, and I don't see how you could put such a construction on my language. If I made my living by writing," she added spitefully, "and couldn't compose a decent autograph, I wouldn't try to cover up my ignorance by blustering about it in that way."

"Don't you think this would do pretty well," she continued sweetly, while Thompson breathed hard. 'May peace and happiness attend thy journey through life..' "

"Excellent," replied Thompson, who was anxious to get out of it. "It includes everything you could wish."

"Don't you think it just about the right thing to say?" she asked meditatively.

"The most natural and proper thing in the world to say," he replied. "So much so that it is probably what Adam wrote in Eve's autograph album," and he couldn't refrain from adding, "It's what I told you to write at first."

"Why, Mr. Thompson, it is *not;* it's my own sentiment; and I wouldn't write anything in an album that wasn't quite original."

Whereupon she spent twenty minutes in practicing painfully on loose paper before she transferred Thompson's sentiment to the album.

THE TALES

The Origin of the Hatchet Story

When I first heard of George Washington and his Little Hatchet, I thought it was a very affecting incident, and I determined to emulate so worthy an example. The next time I heard the story, it had lost some of its freshness, but was still interesting. But afterward, as I had it dinned into my ears and the example of Washington held up to me early and late, and very frequently in a close and painful personal connection, I began to hate the very name of Washington. When I grew older and took up the study of American history, I perceived the nobility of his character and felt it a patriotic duty to place his name first on my list of heroes. But that fatal anecdote and its associations stood in the way; I could not do it.

Growing to manhood, a fondness for foreign travel and archaeological research took me one beautiful spring on an extended voyage up the Nile in the good steamer Wm. E. Gladstone. On our return trip the fuel gave out; and, being unable to obtain wood, the captain purchased a job-lot of mummies from a speculator near Bab-el-Mezook. In handling one of the mummies, a small roll dropped from the folds of the cotton cloth in which the mummy was enveloped. The engineer brought it to me; and, carefully moistening the dry roll and cautiously unrolling it, I found it to be a papyrus of the 19th Dynasty. It contained a legend of the childhood of Rameses III, and, from the simple character of the illustrations, was evidently designed for the instruction of youth. It ran as follows:

"When Rameses III returned from the conquest of Libya, he rested from warlike deeds for a year and twelve months, a great part of which he spent in the personal supervision of the education of his son, afterward Rameses IV, a child of fine parts, but too much under the influence of the priests to please his royal father, who wished him trained for a career of war and conquest.

"One day after the noontide meal, Rameses III, being in a pleasant mood, gave his son a small curved sword, or scimitar, of exquisite workmanship. Little Rammy, as he was called, went about the palace trying the temper of his new blade. First he neatly sliced off the ear of the Nubian eunuch who waited at the door of the royal presence chamber. Then, toddling to the apartments of his mama, he deftly sliced off the headdress of one of the ladies in waiting, taking quite a slice of the scalp along with it; and, proceeding to the palace kitchen, skillfully·amputated the little finger of one of the cooks, whose hand happened to be in a position convenient for the experiment.

"Passing thence out into the courtyard, he came up, unperceived, behind a servant who was kneeling before a wooden bench, polishing the royal crown with a soft brick. His head was bent forward, exposing the back of his neck in such a manner that Rammy could not resist the temptation, and playfully raising his puny right arm, he severed the head from the servant's body with one stroke—such was the keenness of his blade. What was his embarrassment, however, to discover, when the head rolled over at his feet, that he had slain his father's favorite Hebrew slave, Abednego.

"The situation was a painful one, and he did not have time to reflect upon it before he heard the footsteps of his royal father approaching. Yielding to the impulse of the moment, the royal infant hastily concealed himself in a large earthen water-jar which stood close by.

"When Rameses III saw the dead body of his favorite slave, his rage at first knew no bounds: 'Who slew my Hebrew slave?' he cried.

"In a moment all the members of the household had gathered in the court-yard. They, one and all, had disclaimed any responsibility for the slave's unfortunate death when the head of young Rammy appeared above the rim of the water-jar, from which he lightly sprang and prostrated himself at his father's feet.

" 'Sire,' he said, 'I cannot tell a lie. I did it with my little scimitar.'

"For a moment Rameses III was speechless with conflicting emotions. Then the trembling bystanders saw the great monarch's face soften, and heard him exclaim in feeling tones:

" 'Come to my arms, my son! I would rather you had killed a thousand Hebrew slaves than to have told a lie. I thank Isis that she has given me such a son.' "

The perusal of this interesting papyrus at once convinced me that the hated Hatchet Story was merely one of those myths which, floating down the stream of tradition, become attached in successive generations to popular heroes, and that, consequently, no obstacle stood in the way of my complete veneration of the name of Washington.

A Midnight Adventure

One afternoon last summer I went out to our local baseball park to witness the performance of one of the Wild West shows which
have become a feature of our national amusements. I was accompanied by the
young lady to whom I am engaged. We had good seats in the grand stand
and enjoyed the performance very much. The marksmanship was good, the
horsemanship excellent, the cowboys were rough enough to have come from
the most distant frontier and the Indians were typical representatives of the
modern Red man. There was one old squaw who figured in a camping scene,
and who impressed me as the ugliest human being I had ever gazed upon;
there were also several young women who were not bad-looking, in spite of
their rather stolid expression of countenance. I turned to Bella and remarked,
during the course of the performance:

"How thankful we ought to be that the accident of birth has made us
children of a civilized and progressive race! Just imagine the fate of one connected by birth or marriage with these untutored children of the forest and
compelled to pass his whole life among them!"

Bella responded with some remark to the effect that if one had been born
an Indian, one probably wouldn't find anything uncommon or disagreeable
about it, and that as for marrying one of them, there was no necessity or reason
for either of us to make such a sacrifice, when a startling feat of horsemanship
performed by a half-breed Apache excited her interest and put an end to my
moralizing.

I did not call at Bella's that evening, having been with her all the afternoon. As I was sauntering downtown after supper, who should I run across
but Bilkins, a young friend of mine, of sporting proclivities. Bilkins proposed
that we have a game of billiards. We played one game—two games—half a
dozen games—during the course of which I smoked several cigars and imbibed
a number of mixed drinks.

I started home about eleven o'clock. I was feeling a little tired from having
stood on my feet so much during the evening, and as I passed through a small
public park which lay in my homeward route, I sat down on an iron bench

to rest for a moment. The bench which I occupied was just across the walk from a life-sized bronze statue of an Indian, clad in the traditional garb of the forest, of a period antecedent to the introduction by the white man of whiskey and blankets.

I had been looking at this statue for several minutes when it seemed to me that the bronze plume which decorated the warrior's scalp-lock began to wave to and fro in the gentle wind. Of course the idea was preposterous and I had formed a satisfactory hypothesis to account for the delusion, when the statue upset my theory by stepping from its granite pedestal and advancing with a stately stride to the place where I sat.

"Ugh!" said the voice of the statue, with a metallic ring which sounded just a little out of the common.

"The same to you," I answered politely, not knowing exactly what it meant.

"I am Worm-in-the Bud, the last of the Ojibways."

"Pleased to meet you," I murmured. "My name is Jones."

The statue—or I may say, the Indian—glared at me a moment, and then extending his right arm with a commanding movement swept it slowly from right to left.

"This was once the hunting ground of my fathers," he said, and then paused as though he expected me to say something. But the circumstances were so unusual that I could not think of anything appropriate.

"Through the forest which adorned these shores once roamed the red deer and the moose, where now the streetcar horse toils wearily; the war whoop of the Ojibways resounded where now the shrill piping of the hand-organ announces the return of spring. Who has wrought these changes?" and he paused again.

I was about to remark that the great American people had wrought these changes, and that he would find a complete description of it in Bancroft's "History of the United States," when the Indian continued fiercely:

" 'Tis the paleface! The false-hearted paleface who has stolen our inheritance. But we shall be avenged. You are my prisoner. Come!" And he grasped his tomahawk so significantly that I did not stop to argue the point, but arose and followed him.

We went to the edge of the park and took a streetcar. There were several passengers aboard, and I might have raised an alarm and made my escape; but I hated to make a scene in public, and so sat quietly by the side of my bronze companion.

We had taken the car which went past the baseball park, and a ride of about fifteen minutes brought us to the entrance, at which we alighted. My companion put his hand to his mouth and emitted the cry of the screech owl. A guttural voice murmured something in the darkness, and the gate swung open before us.

In a moment the place was swarming with Indians—every copper-colored attaché of the show was evidently on hand. Somehow they seemed different in the moonlight from what they had appeared in the afternoon: their faces wore a fiercer expression, they walked with a longer stride and freer movement, and much of their cheap modern clothing had been replaced with deer and buffalo skins, and a profusion of feathers.

"Braves and squaws," said my captor to the crowd, which had surrounded us closely, "this is one of the accursed palefaces who have stolen our hunting grounds, dug up the bones of our fathers, and driven our tribe to the barren mountains of the far West. What shall we do with him?"

Several voices spoke confusedly together, but I could not distinguish what they said, and only knew that a discussion was going on. Finally a conclusion seemed to have been reached. An Indian broke away from the circle and brought a square block of building stone, which he placed in the center of the group, while another brought forward a sledgehammer, ordinarily used for driving tent poles.

I was wondering what this meant when I was firmly seized from behind, and a rawhide lariat wrapped around me half a dozen times and tied securely. I was then laid upon the ground, face downward, with my nose resting upon the cold stone. Twisting my head a little to one side, I saw a burly brave spit on his hands and grasp the sledgehammer. Still I said nothing, for I was curious to see how far the red devils would go with their tomfoolery. Worm-in-the Bud gave a signal and the sledgehammer was raised, when I heard a shrill voice exclaim, in pretty fair English:

"Hold! He shall not die! I will adopt him for my husband."

The sledgehammer sank to the ground, and an expression of disappointment gathered in the faces of the crowd. But it was their custom, and they did not think of opposing it. I was raised to a sitting posture, which gave me an opportunity to get a good look at the squaw to whom I owed my life. As I turned my head, I felt a sinking of the heart, a presentiment of evil, which was realized when I recognized in the speaker the old squaw whom I had observed in the afternoon. She looked ten times more hideous in the moonlight than she had seemed in the daytime. It was evident that she had been forced to adopt a husband for the reason that she could never have obtained one in the natural and ordinary way. The lariat had been partially removed when I remarked:

"Stop a moment. Is this the only way in which I can escape death?"

"It is the only way," replied Worm-in-the Bud.

"Cannot one of those younger women be substituted for this venerable relic?"

"By no means," he replied, frowning, "you must either marry Nokomis or die."

"Then let the execution proceed," I said calmly, but decisively, and laid my head upon the block. Once more the bronze chieftain gave the signal; once more the fatal sledgehammer was raised, and began its descent—when I awoke to find the cold club of a policeman resting quietly across my upturned nose, and to hear a blue-coated myrmidon of the law remark, in peremptory accents:

"Well, now, move on, will you. This park is no hotel."

I moved, and as I looked back, I could distinctly see a scowl of disappointment on the bronze face of the statue.

Concerning Father

Father is a peculiar man. To be peculiar is not unusual, but father's peculiarity is, perhaps I should say was, so very unusual that we all hope it will not break out again, because, while it was interesting and no harm came of it, it was rather wearing upon the family while it lasted, and it is easy to imagine a different and a tragic outcome. Suppose, for instance, father hadn't waked up at all?

The particular incident I refer to transpired more than ten years ago, just before and reaching over the end of the Great War.

It was an evening about ten days before the armistice was signed, while the Meuse-Argonne drive was at its height. We were all in the living room after supper—father, mother, my elder sister Imogene, who is a high school teacher; her fiancé, Percival Biggs; my younger sister, Helen, who was taking a business course in Commercial High School, and my young brother Billy. Father was seated in a cushioned armchair by the table, on which stood the electric reading lamp. He had been reading aloud, from the *Boston Evening Transcript,* which is delivered in our town in the late afternoon, the latest news of the progress of the fighting, and the predictions of experts as to the probable duration of hostilities. Percival, who was a stenographer in a law office, and was studying law in a night law course, and who was regarded by father as a very intelligent young man, had made several comments. Imogene, who had been doing war relief work on several committees, had contributed to the discussion. Mother had expressed what turned out to be the vain hope that the end of the war might soon bring prices down, when father again took the floor. Father loves to talk, in which respect he is not at all peculiar.

"For my part," he said, "the way Foch and Pershing have got them bottled up, the Huns can't advance much farther. Their supplies are so nearly exhausted that they couldn't do much fighting if they did, and their morale and their transportation system is so shot to pieces that they can't retreat rapidly, and if they could, we'd follow 'em to Berlin, and then where'd they be?"

He straightened himself up and leaned forward with both hands grasping the arms of the chair.

"In my opinion," he announced, "this war will come to an end on the . . ."

He stopped abruptly, and continued silent, while we waited for him to finish his sentence. Finally, after several moments, Percival spoke up.

"You were saying, sir?"

There was no response. We waited, breathlessly at first, then with a vague feeling of uneasiness, but still there was no answering sound. We saw that father's eyes were closed, and the natural assumption was that he had fallen asleep. But somehow this assumption was not convincing. His posture was not consistent with slumber. Had he fallen asleep he would have slumped back into the comfortable depths of the chair.

"For heaven's sake!" exclaimed mother, "it isn't at all like your pa to go to sleep that way, all of a sudden. Sam," she said, coming closer to him, "wake up, and go on upstairs if you're sleepy. We'll excuse you."

She reached over, took him by the shoulder, and tried to shake him.

"Well, I declare," she exclaimed, "he's as stiff as a board. I can't move him alone. Maybe Percival'll help me get him upstairs."

Percival came over and took him by one arm and mother by the other, but they were not able to budge him.

"Maybe he's dead," said Billy tremulously. "Teddy Wickham's grandpa had a stroke last week and dropped dead out in the garden while he was pulling carrots."

"No," said I—I had attended some Red Cross first aid classes, and had read more or less about death and its attendant incidents—"if he were dead, rigor mortis wouldn't set in for several hours, and, as mother says, he is stiff already."

"Hadn't we better call a doctor?" suggested Percival.

Mother had seated herself a short distance away, and was apparently deep in thought.

"No, children," she said, after a moment, "we won't call a doctor, and we needn't be alarmed. Your pa slept a whole day and two nights once before, when Imogene was a baby. I couldn't wake him up, and we sent for the doctor, and he said it was all right, at least for a day or two. And on the morning of the second day your pa woke up just as usual and went on about his business. And when I told him how scared I'd been, he told me never to bother about anything he did, that he had a peculiar streak in him that might crop out now and then, but it always came out right in the end, and that I wasn't to say anything about it, because he was a businessman and any reputation for being peculiar would hurt his business. So we'll just leave him where he is—I'll throw a blanket over him—and maybe he'll wake up in the morning, and if he doesn't within a day or two, we'll consider the matter further. So I guess we'd better calm ourselves and go to bed and get our night's rest. Don't say a word about this outside of the house, because I know that's what your pa would wish."

So we separated for the evening. Imogene, who was to be married as soon as Percival was admitted to the bar and began to practice, went out into the hall with him to bid him good night. Mother brought a double blanket and tucked it around father, turned out the lights, and we all went upstairs to bed.

Only mother and Billy slept well, and Imogene and I were the first ones up next morning. We woke mother and Billy, and then went somewhat fearfully downstairs to light the kitchen stove and get the breakfast started. We had given up our maid because of the war, and were doing our own housework, except the laundry work. On the way to the kitchen we peeped into the living room. Father was just as we had left him the night before. He had not moved a line, so far as we could perceive, and the blanket was still tucked around him as mother had arranged it.

We had the breakfast started when mother came down, and then, before sitting down at the table, we all went into the living room.

I took my courage in my hands and applied some of the theoretical knowledge I had acquired in my Red Cross course. I sent Billy upstairs to my bedroom for a hand mirror and held it before father's lips. There was a faint moisture upon the surface of the glass, very faint, but enough to prove that he was still breathing, however lightly. I felt his pulse. It was very feeble, almost imperceptible, but enough to show that his heart was still beating. His flesh wasn't exactly warm, but it wasn't cold. I had a clinical thermometer, which I managed to get into his mouth through the vacant space from which a loose tooth had been recently extracted, which he had meant to get replaced with a false one when he got around to it. His temperature was away below normal, but he still had a temperature.

When I had announced these reassuring conclusions, mother said:

"Well, now, children, your father's alive, and he'll come out of this trance, or whatever it is, when he gets good and ready, and we needn't worry about it, as long as he doesn't change from what he is now. In the meantime, keep your mouths shut. I know it'll be easy for you girls, but I'm not so sure about Willie. If anybody asks about your pa, tell 'em he went away on a business trip. So he did, a week ago, but you needn't tell 'em he came back today. Now, Willie, if you breathe a word about your pa's being home or about his condition, you'll have to deal with me, and with him later. But if you keep perfectly quiet, when your pa comes around I'll see that you get that new bicycle you've been pestering him about."

So we went in to breakfast. Percival called before we had scattered to our various daily pursuits, and we told him that father's condition remained the same, and that he was to say nothing about it, but to come around that evening as usual.

Percival came after supper. He had gone to the Public Library after leaving the office, and had been reading up on cataleptic trances, suspended consciousness and other abnormal physical conditions. He expected, he said, that his cousin, a distinguished nerve specialist who had been in France for a year in the army service, would return to his home in Boston on leave within a week, and whether father had recovered or not by that time, that he would write him a letter, stating a hypothetical case corresponding to father's and ask him for an opinion.

A week or more passed without any apparent change in father's condition. Of course so well known a man as he couldn't disappear without evoking some curiosity among his friends and business associates, but we managed to stave off any discovery or suspicion. We received callers in the library and kept the door between it and the living room locked. We arranged a screen to prevent anyone from looking in the living room windows from the outside and seeing father, and put the shades down at night. We indeed got so accustomed to the situation that we resumed our evening gatherings in the living room, and even got accustomed to father's silence, which we had never had an opportunity to do before, because father had rarely been silent when there was anything being said. I sometimes wondered, somewhat unfilially, I suspect, if nature were not taking this means of evening up things by giving him a long rest from speech. It might have seemed to an outsider a little uncanny, but we became accustomed to the situation, and mother, who was of course the person most concerned, did not seem to worry.

"We'll wait a while yet," she would say, "and give him a chance. He's no worse than he was, and he'll come around all right. He told me not to worry if he did anything out of the common, and I'm not worrying. It won't last much longer, because he's got to be at the office on the fifteenth to attend the annual meeting. The office called up today and asked where he was. I said he'd been called away on private business—as he certainly was—so that was no lie. They asked would I give them his address so that they could telephone or write him. I said no, he didn't want anybody to know where he was, but I said he'd be back in time for the meeting, and if they wanted to write they could address the letter to the house and I'd forward it."

Two weeks had passed without any apparent change in father's condition, and we were all becoming a little nervous and apprehensive. Even mother's Olympian calm was beginning to crack, and she had about decided to call the doctor, when our troubles came to an end without any intervention on our part.

On the thirteenth day of November, 1918, we were all gathered in the living room—mother, Percival, Imogene, Helen, Billy and I, the same company that were present when father became unconscious. Father, still rigid and immovable, was leaning forward in his chair as usual. For two days the town had been a constant din of loud and strident noises. Cannon had been shot

off, church bells rung, factory whistles sounded. On the night before, the signing of the armistice had been celebrated by a procession which had passed by
our house with a clamor sufficient to have awakened the dead, so to speak,
but none of these noises had disturbed father. Percival, who had developed quite
a flow of speech during father's silence and had taken the lead in our evening
discussions, was reading the details of the armistice from the *Transcript,* when
a slight noise sounded from father's direction, as though he were clearing his
throat. Suddenly he spoke, in a somewhat dry and husky voice:

". . . on the eleventh day of November, at eleven o'clock in the
morning!"

We were all too surprised to scream, and sat in a dead silence. Father
stretched himself a moment and then went on.

"Good gracious, Susie"—which was the familiar form of my mother's giv-
en name, "I feel mighty stiff in the joints. I guess I'll go to bed. I never was
so sleepy in my life."

He tried to rise, but mother and Percival caught him as he tottered.

"I guess it's a touch of rheumatism," he said. "You let Lizzie take your
place, ma, and help me upstairs, while you make me a good stiff toddy and
bring it up."

I am named Elizabeth, after the Virgin Queen, as was one of my grand-
mothers before me, but I have never been able to train father and mother to
use anything but the vulgar old diminutive in addressing me, which was sufficiently annoying before it was adapted as the pseudonym of a cheap tin motor
car, after which it became utterly unspeakable. The persistence of elderly people
in clinging to old and reprehensible habits of speech and social conduct is one
of the trials of the younger generation from which there seems no way of escape.

We got father to bed, and asked Percival to come to breakfast the next
morning at seven-thirty. It was a holiday and Imogene and the younger children
would not have to go to school, nor Percival to the office, so we would have
plenty of time to talk things over. Then we all went to bed, and slept, I imagine,
not much more than we did the first night we had left father sitting alone
in the parlor.

It had been agreed between us the night before to say nothing to father
about his strange experience until we met at the breakfast table. In the surprise
and confusion of the evening before we had not quite grasped the significance
of what father had said, or drawn any implications from it, at least I had
not; but in the still watches of the night it was borne in upon me that, connecting up the two ends of his broken sentence, and eliminating the period of lapsed
consciousness which had intervened, he had predicted two weeks in advance
the exact date and hour when the armistice was signed and the fighting ceased.
However, I did not try to solve the riddle but tried to go to sleep, which I
eventually succeeded in doing.

We were all seated at table when father came down. He greeted us cheerfully, and we responded in kind. He then, after his usual custom, picked up the morning paper.

"Well, by Godfrey!" he exclaimed, "that's a funny mistake for the *Bugle* to make. This paper is dated November fourteenth, when it should be October thirty-first. And what's all this," he went on, as he ran his eye along the head-lines. " 'Germans retiring beyond the Rhine. More details of terms of armistice. People of allied nations wild with joy at end of war!' What in the world does this mean? All these things couldn't have happened overnight!"

Then mother explained, with occasional assistance from others of us, that they were the events of a fortnight, during which he had been unconscious.

"We didn't call the doctor," said mother, "because you'll remember you told me, once before, not to worry if anything peculiar happened to you. And nobody outside of the family, except Percival, knows anything at all about it."

"We haven't been able," said Percival, "in the absence of expert opinion, to determine just what your condition was, or what was the cause of it; but we thought, in view of what you had said to Mrs. Beckett, that you might be able to enlighten us."

"Well," replied father slowly, as he ate his cereal—father could do almost anything and talk at the same time, he even talked in his normal sleep—"maybe what I'm going to tell you will explain it and maybe it won't; you can take it for what it's worth. It begins with a bit of family history about the middle of the eighteenth century. I've never told any of you about it, not even you, ma, for reasons which will be apparent as I go along.

"My ancestors, the Becketts, whose name we have inherited in the direct male line, were seafaring people. This town was the principal seaport for the Chinese and Indian trade. My great-great-grandfather, Jonadab Beckett, was not a vessel owner, but was captain of a ship that traded in the eastern waters, in silks and tea and ivory, exchanging for them American trade goods which suited the Eastern market. On his return from one of his voyages he brought home with him an Indian wife."

"Gee!" exclaimed Billy, "like Pocahontas."

"Be quiet, Willie," said mother, "and don't interrupt your pa."

"No, Billy," continued father, "Pocahontas was an American Indian, and my great-great-grandmother was an East Indian, a Hindoo, I guess you'd call her."

"Of what caste was she?" asked Imogene.

"I don't know," said father. "I don't even know what her Indian name was. They had been married on board another ship in Calcutta harbor, by the captain, according to maritime law, but when great-great-grandfather Jonadab brought her home, he was persuaded, in order to keep peace in the family, to have her baptized with a Christian name, and the minister of their church remarried them so as to cure any possible informality of the maritime rite. I gather that while they didn't exactly like the marriage, they wanted to make sure, for the sake of possible children as well as on moral grounds that it was an iron-bound copper-riveted marriage. So they took no chances. You'll find her name in the old Beckett family Bible, at your Uncle Joe's, in Plymouth; I think it was 'Grace Abounding'—I don't remember her Indian name, although I have heard it.

"I doubt if she ever knew the meaning of her Christian name, and her new religion, I imagine, was never more than skin deep. My grandfather, Abel Beckett, who told me these things when he was a very old man, said that at home, in the privacy of her own house, she would sometimes dress in a silk or satin gown which her husband had brought with her from India, put on a necklace of gold coins or green beads—"

"Rupees and jade!" murmured Imogene.

"With silver bracelets," father went on, "and sit motionless for hours staring into space or gazing at some little bronze or ivory image."

"She was homesick," interjected mother, "like I was when your father brought me here from Portsmouth."

"She was undoubtedly," suggested Percival, "a high-caste woman, a Brahmin, and of a fair complexion."

"Yes," said Imogene dreamily, "I can see her now reclining in a cushioned, silk-curtained palanquin, borne by two stalwart coolies, going to shop in the bazaars or to make a visit upon the women of the zenana of some friendly family. She had a complexion of creamy old ivory, with a rosebud mouth and teeth like pearls."

"But pa says he don't know," interposed Billy, "and she may have been a black, low-caste dancing girl, like the one in my geography, with bracelets on her ankles and a ring in her nose."

"Now you shut right up, Willie Beckett," said mother, severely, "and stop slandering your great-great-grandmother at once!"

"I never heard what she was," said father, "or how he came to know her. I don't know whether he bought her, or kidnapped her, or whether she came with him willingly. But he must have loved her, or he wouldn't have brought her home, and she must have been respectable or he wouldn't have married her.

"At any rate, New England didn't agree with her. I understand she never learned much of the English language. She stood the climate and the Yankee ways about three years, and then died, one cold, raw spring, of pnuemonia, leaving one child, my great-grandfather, and was given Christian burial. As I say, she couldn't have been very dark, because none of my ancestors or relations ever showed any color, except her son, my great-grandfather, who had a slightly yellowish cast and very black hair and eyes. But he married a red-headed Garford, and all his descendants, so far as I know, have been fair-complexioned with light hair. I've never said anything about my East Indian ancestry, because, while I have no prejudice against color myself, and consider one man as good as another, other things being equal, yet I know how most people feel about such matters, and it's just as well not raise the question.

"I never did take a great deal of stock in this heredity," he went on. "I believe God makes each man by himself. But if there is such a thing as a hereditary throwback, it may be that I inherited from my great-great-grand-mother some obscure faculty or tendency which has made me go off into a trance once or twice in my life."

At this point Billy butted into the conversation again. It was the only way he could get in.

"I wonder," he said, "if I inherited enough of her blood to learn to be a snake charmer, or a conjurer, and make a tree grow from a seed while you look at it?"

"Didn't I tell you to shut up, Willie?" said mother. "Don't let me have to tell you again. You've got entirely too much to say. You'll need all your time the next four or five years to learn your lessons in school."

"But," interposed Percival, "even that doesn't quite explain how you were able to predict to the hour the signing of the armistice, unless your ancestress's power to go into a trance was accompanied by the gift of prophecy."

"Well, now," said father, "it was hardly a prediction, was it? It was spoken after the event."

"But without any consciousness on your part," I suggested.

"Perhaps," resumed Percival, "while you were sitting quietly in the living room, your astral body was floating over the blood-stained battlefield of France, watching the ebb and flow of the conflict. Perhaps you were present at the war councils of the leaders and learned at first hand what Hindenburg and Ludendorff and Foch and Pershing were saying."

"Well," said father, "I don't know that I'd have understood it if I had, for I don't speak either German or French."

"You wouldn't have needed to," said Percival. "Your astral body could have read their thoughts, and then, when it returned to your physical body, conveyed them to your subconscious mind, which found expression unwittingly when you spoke."

"Well," said father as he rose from the table, "be that as it may, it was a close guess. I hope you saved the newspapers for me, Susie; I'll have to do a lot of back reading to catch up and keep from making a fool of myself. After all, any way you look at it, this is a queer world, and a great many peculiar things happen in it."

In which opinion of father's I heartily concur.

Tobe's Tribulations

About half a mile from our house on the North Carolina sandhills there lay, at the foot of a vine-clad slope, and separated from my scuppernong vineyard by a rail fence, a marsh of some extent. It was drained at a somewhat later date, but at the time to which I now refer spread for half a mile in length and a quarter of a mile in breadth. Having been planted in rice many years before, it therefore contained no large trees, but was grown up chiefly in reeds and coarse grasses, with here and there a young sycamore or cypress. Though this marsh was not visible from our house, nor from any road that we used, it was nevertheless one of the most prominent features of our environment. We might sometimes forget its existence in the daytime, but it never failed to thrust itself upon our attention after night had fallen.

It may be that other localities in our neighborhood were infested with frogs; but if so, their vocal efforts were quite overborne by the volume of sound that issued nightly from this particular marsh. As soon as the red disk of the sun had set behind the pines the performance would begin, first perhaps with occasional shrill pipings, followed by a confused chattering; then, as the number of participants increased, growing into a steady drumming, punctuated every moment by the hoarse bellowing note of some monstrous bullfrog. If the day had perchance been rainy, the volume of noise would be greater. For a while after we went to live in the neighborhood, this ceaseless, strident din made night hideous, and we would gladly have dispensed with it. But as time wore on we grew accustomed to our nocturnal concert; we began to differentiate its notes and to distinguish a sort of rude harmony in these voices of the night; and after we had become thoroughly accustomed to it, I doubt whether we could have slept comfortably without their lullaby.

But I had not been living long in the vicinity of this frog-pond before its possibilities as a source of food supply suggested themselves to my somewhat practical mind. I was unable to learn that any of my white neighbors indulged in the delicate article of diet which frogs' legs might be made to supply; and strangely enough, among the Negroes, who would have found in the tender flesh of the batrachian a toothsome and bountiful addition to the coarse food that formed the staple of their diet, its use for that purpose was entirely unknown.

One day I went frog-fishing and brought home a catch of half a dozen. Our colored cook did not know how to prepare them, and looked on the whole proceeding with ill-concealed disgust. So my wife, with the aid of a cookbook, dressed the hind legs quite successfully in the old-fashioned way, and they were served at supper. We enjoyed the meal very much, and I determined that thereafter we would have the same dish often.

Our supper had been somewhat later than usual, and it was dusk before we left the table and took our seats on the piazza. We had been there but a little while when old Julius, our colored coachman, came around the house and, approaching the steps, asked for some instructions with reference to the stable-work. As the matter required talking over, I asked him to sit down.

When we had finished our talk, the old man did not go away immediately, and we all sat for a few moments without speaking. The night was warm but not sultry; there was a sort of gentle melancholy in the air, and the chorus from the distant frog-pond seemed pitched this night in something of a minor key.

"Dem frogs is makin' dey yuzh'al racket ternight," observed the old man, breaking the silence.

"Yes," I replied, "they are very much in evidence. By the way, Annie, perhaps Julius would like some of those frogs' legs. I see Nancy hasn't cleared the table yet."

"No ma'm," responded Julius quickly, "I's much obleedzd, but I doan eat no frog-laigs; no, *suh*, no *ma'm*, I doan eat no frog-laigs, not ef I knows w'at I's eatin'!"

"Why not, Julius?" I asked. "They are excellent eating."

"You listen right close, suh," he answered, "en you'll heah a pertic'ler bull-frog down yander in dat ma'sh. Listen! Dere he goes now—callin', callin', callin'! sad en mo'nful, des lak somebody w'at's los' somewhar, en can't fin' de way back."

"I hear it distinctly," said my wife after a moment. "It sounds like the lament of a lost soul."

I had never heard the vocal expression of a lost soul, but I tried, without success, to imagine that I could distinguish one individual croak from another.

"Well, what is there about that frog, Julius," I inquired, "that makes it any different from the others?"

"Dat's po' Tobe," he responded solemnly, "callin' Aun' Peggy—po' ole Aun' Peggy w'at's dead en gone ter de good Marster, yeahs en yeahs ago."

"Tell us about Tobe, Julius," I asked. I could think of no more appropriate time for one of the old man's stories. His views of life were so entirely foreign to our own, that for a time after we got acquainted with him his conversations were a never-failing source of novelty and interest. He had seen life from what was to us a new point of view—from the bottom, as it were; and there clung to his mind, like barnacles to the submerged portion of a ship, all sorts of extravagant beliefs. The simplest phenomena of life were to him fraught with hidden meaning—some prophecy of good, some presage of evil. The source of these notions I never traced, though they doubtless could be easily accounted for. Some perhaps were dim reflections of ancestral fetishism; more were the superstitions, filtered through the Negro intellect, of the Scotch settlers who had founded their homes on Cape Fear at a time when a kelpie haunted every Highland glen, and witches, like bats, darkened the air as they flew by in their nocturnal wanderings. But from his own imagination, I take it—for I never heard quite the same stories from anyone else—he gave to the raw material of folklore and superstition a fancifulness of touch that truly made of it, to borrow a homely phrase, a silk purse out of a sow's ear. And if perhaps, at times, his stories might turn out to have a purpose apart from any esthetic or didactic end, he probably reasoned, with a philosophy for which there is high warrant, that the laborer was worthy of his hire.

" 'Bout fo'ty years ago," began Julius, "ole Mars Dugal McAdoo—*my* ole marster—useter own a man name' Tobe. Dis yer Tobe wuz a slow kind er nigger, en w'iles he'd alluz git his tas' done, he'd hafter wuk harder'n any yuther nigger on de place ter do it. One time he had a monst'us nice 'oman fer a wife, but she got bit by a rattlesnake one summer en died, en dat lef' Tobe kind er lonesome. En mo' d'n dat, Tobe's wife had be'n cook at de big house, en eve'y night she'd fetch sump'n down ter her cabin fer Tobe; en he foun' it mighty ha'd ter go back ter bacon en co'n-bread atter libbin' off'n de fat er de lan' all dese yeahs.

"Des 'bout a mont' er so atter Tobe's wife died, dez wuz a nigger run 'way fum ole Mars Marrabo McSwayne's—de nex' plantation—en in spite er all de w'ite folks could do, dis yer nigger got clean off ter a free state in de Norf, en bimeby he writ a sassy letter back to Mars Marrabo, en sont 'im a bill fer de wuk he done fer 'im fer twenty yeahs er mo', at a dollah en a half a day—w'at he say he wuz gittin' at de Norf. One er de gals w'at wukked roun' de big house heared de w'ite folks gwine on 'bout it, en she says Mars Marrabo cusst en swo' des tarrable, en ole missis 'mos' wep' fer ter think how ongrateful dat nigger wuz, not on'y ter run 'way, but to write back sich wick-'niss ter w'ite folks w'at had alluz treated 'im good, fed 'im, en clothed 'im, en nussed 'im w'en he wuz sick, en nebber let 'im suffer fer nuffin' all his life.

"But Tobe heared 'bout dis yer nigger, en he tuk a notion he'd lak ter run 'way en go ter de Norf en be free en git a dollah en a half a day, too. But de mo' he studied 'bout it, de ha'der it 'peared ter be. In de fus' place, de Norf wuz a monst'us long ways off, en de dawgs mought track 'im, er de patteroles mought ketch 'im, er he mought sta've ter def ca'se he couldn' git nuffin' ter eat on de way' en ef he wuz cotch' he wuz lakly ter be sol' so fur Souf dat he'd nebber hab no chance ter git free er eber see his ole frien's nuther.

"But Tobe kep' on studyin' 'bout runnin' 'way 'tel fin'lly he 'lowed he'd go en see ole Aun' Peggy, de cunjuh 'oman down by de Wim'l'ton Road, en ax her w'at wuz de bes' way fer him ter sta't. So he tuk a pa'r er pullets down ter Aun' Peggy one night en tol' her all 'bout his hank'in's en his longin's, en ax' her w'at he'd hafter do fer ter tun 'way en git free.

" 'W'at you wanter be free fer?' sez Aun' Peggy. 'Doan you git ernuff ter eat?'

" 'Yas, I gits ernuff ter eat, but I'll hab better vittles w'en I's free.'

" 'Doan you git ernuff sleep?'

" 'Yas, but I'll sleep mo' w'en I's free.'

" 'Does you wuk too ha'd?'

" 'No, I doan wuk too ha'd fer a slabe nigger, but ef I wuz free I wouldn' wuk a-tall 'less'n I felt lak it.'

"Aun' Peggy shuck her head. 'I dunno, nigger,' sez she, 'whuther you gwine ter fin' w'at you er huntin' fer er no. But w'at is it you wants me ter do fer you?'

" 'I wants you ter tell me de bes' en easies' way fer ter git ter de Norf en be free.'

" 'Well,' sez Aun' Peggy, 'I's feared dey ain' no easy way. De bes' way fer you ter do is ter fix yo' eye on de Norf Stah en sta't. You kin put some tar on yo' feet ter th'ow de houn's off'n de scent, en ef you come ter a crick you mought wade 'long fer a mile er so. I sh'd say you bettah sta't on Sad'day night, fer den mos' lakly you won' be miss' 'tel Monday mawnin', en you kin git a good sta't on yo' jou'ney. En den maybe in a mont' er so you'll retch de Norf en you'll be free, en whar you kin eat all you want, ef you kin git it, en sleep ez long ez you mineter, ef you kin 'ford it, en whar you won't hafter wuk ef you'd ruther go to jail.'

" 'But w'at is I gwine ter eat dyo'in' er dis yer mont' I's trabblin'?' ax' Tobe. 'It makes me sick ef I doan git my reg'lar meals.'

" 'Doan ax me,' sez Aun' Peggy. 'I ain' nebber seed de nigger yit w'at can't fin' sump'n ter eat.'

"Tobe scratch' his head. 'En whar is I gwine to sleep dyo'in er dat mont'? I'll hafter hab my reg'lar res'.'

" 'Doan ax me,' sez Aun' Peggy. 'You kin sleep in de woods in de daytime, en do yo' trabblin' at night.'

" 'But s'pose'n a snake bites me?'

" 'I kin gib you a cha'm fer ter kyo snake-bite.'

" 'But s'pose'n' de patteroles ketch me?'

" 'Look a heah, nigger,' sez Aun' Peggy, 'I's ti'ed er yo' s'pose'n', en I's was'e all de time on you I's gwine ter fer two chick'ns. I's feared you wants ter git free too easy. I s'pose you des wants ter lay down at night, do yo' trabblin' in yo' sleep, en wake free in de mawn'in'. You wants ter git a thousan' dollah nigger fer nuffin' en dat's mo' d'n anybody but de sma'test w'ite folks kin do. Go 'long back ter yo' wuk, man, en doan come back ter me 'less'n you kin fetch me sump'n mo'.'

"Now, Tobe knowed well ernuff dat ole Aun' Peggy'd des be'n talkin' ter heah herse'f talk, en so two er th'ee nights later he tuk a side er bacon en kyared it down ter her cabin.

" 'Uh huh,' sez Aun' Peggy, 'at is sump'n lak it. I s'pose you still 'lows you'd lak ter be free, so you kin eat w'at you mineter, en sleep all you wanter, en res' w'eneber you feels dat erway?'

" 'Yas'm, I wants ter be free, en I wants you ter fix things so I kin be sho' ter git ter de Norf widout much trouble; fer I sho'ly does hate en 'spise trouble.'

"Aun' Peggy studied fer a w'ile, en den she tuk down a go'd off'n de she'f, en sez she:

" 'I's got a goopher mixtry heah w'at'll tu'n you ter a b'ar.' You know dey use' ter be b'ars roun' heah in dem ole days.

"Den she tuk down ernudder go'd. 'En,' she went on, 'ef I puts some er dis yuther mixtry wid it, you'll tu'n back ag'in in des a week er mont' er two mont's, 'cordin' ter how much I puts in. Now, ef I tu'n you ter a b'ar fer, say a mont', en you is keerful en keeps 'way fum de hunters, you kin feed yo'se'f ez you goes 'long, en by de een' er de mont' you'll be ter de Norf; en w'en you tu'n back you'll tu'n back ter a free nigger, whar you kin do w'at you wanter, en go whar you mineter, en sleep ez long ez you please.'

"So Tobe say all right, en Aun' Peggy mix' de goopher, en put it on Tobe en turn't 'im ter a big black b'ar.

"Tobe sta'ted out to'ds de Norf, en went fifteen er twenty miles widout stoppin'. Des befo' day in de mawnin' he come ter a 'tater patch, en bein' ez he wuz feelin' sorter hongry, he stop' fer a hour er so 'tel he got all de 'taters he could hol'. Den he sta'ted out ag'in, en bimeby he run 'cross a bee-tree en eat all de honey he could. 'Long to'ds ebenin' he come ter a holler tree, en bein' ez he felt kinder sleepy lak, he 'lowed he'd crawl in en take a nap. So he crawled in en went ter sleep.

"Meanw'ile, Monday mawnin' w'en de niggers went out in de fiel' ter wuk, Tobe wuz missin'. All de niggers 'nied seein' 'im, en ole Mars Dugal sont up ter town en hi'ed some dawgs, en gun 'em de scent, en dey follered it ter ole Aun' Peggy's cabin. Aun' Peggy 'lowed yas, a nigger had be'n ter her cabin Sad'day night, en she had gun 'im a cha'm fer ter keep off de rheuma-tiz, en he had sta'ted off down to'ds de ribber, sayin' he wuz ti'ed wukkin' en wuz gwine fishin' fer a mont' er so. De w'ite folks hunted en hunted, but co'se dey didn' fin' Tobe.

" 'Bout a mont' atter Tobe had run 'way, en w'en Aun' Peggy had mos' fergot 'bout 'im, she wuz sett'n' in her cabin one night, wukkin' her roots, w'en somebody knock' at her do'.

" 'Who dere?' sez she.

" 'It's me, Tobe; open de do', Aun' Peggy.'

"Sho' 'nuff, w'en Aun' Peggy tuk down de do'-bar, who sh'd be stan'in' dere but Tobe.

" 'Whar is you come fum, nigger?' ax' Aun' Peggy, 'I 'lowed you mus' be ter de Norf by dis time, en free, en libben' off'n de fat er de lan'.'

" 'You must 'a' 'spected me ter trabbel monst'us fas' den,' sez Tobe, 'fer I des sta'ted fum heah yistiddy mawnin', en heah I is turn't back ter a nigger ag'in befo' I'd ha'dly got useter walkin' on all-fours. Dey's sump'n de matter wid dat goopher er yo'n, fer yo' cunj'in' ain' wuk right dis time. I crawled in a holler tree 'bout six o'clock en went ter sleep, en w'en I woke up in de mawnin' I wuz tu'nt back ag'in, en bein' ez I hadn' got no fu'ther'n Rockfish Crick, I des 'lowed I'd come back en git dat goopher w'at I paid fer fix' right.'

"Aun' Peggy scratch' her head en studied a minute, en den sez she:

" 'Uh huh! I sees des w'at de trouble is. I is tu'nt you ter a b'ar heah in de fall, en w'en you come ter a holler tree you crawls in en goes ter sleep fer de winter, des lak any yuther b'ar 'd do; en ef I hadn' mix' dat yuther goopher in fer ter tu'n you back in a mont', you'd a slep' all th'oo de winter. I had des plum' fergot 'bout dat, so I reckon I'll hafter try sumpin' diff'ent. I 'spec' I better tu'n you ter a fox. En bein' ez a fox is a good runner, you oughter git ter de Norf in less time dan a b'ar, so I'll fix dis yer goopher so you'll tu'n back ter a nigger en des th'ee weeks, en you'll be able ter enjoy yo' freedom a week sooner.'

"So Aun' Peggy tu'nt Tobe ter a fox, en he sta'ted down de road in great has'e, en made mo' d'n ten miles, w'en he 'mence' ter feel kinder hongry. So w'en he come ter a henhouse he tuk a hen en eat it, en lay down in de woods ter git his night's res'. In de mawnin', w'en he woke up, he 'lowed he mought's well hab ernudder chick'n fer breakfus', so he tuk a fat pullet en eat dat.

"Now, Tobe had be'n monst'us fon' er chick'n befo' he wuz tu'nt ter a fox, but he hadn' nebber had ez much ez he could eat befo'. En bein' ez dere wuz so many chick'ns in dis naberhood, en dey mought be ska'se whar he wuz gwine, he 'lowed he better stay 'roun' dere 'tel he got kinder fat, so he could stan' bein' hongry a day er so ef he sh'd fin' slim pickin's fu'ther 'long. So he dug hisse'f a nice hole under a tree in de woods, en des stayed dere en eat chick'n fer a couple er weeks er so. He wuz so comf'table, eatin' w'at he laked, en restin' w'en he wa'n't eatin', he des kinder los' track er de time, 'tel befo' he notice' it his th'ee weeks wuz mos' up.

"But bimeby de people w'at own dese yer chick'ns 'mence' ter miss 'em, en dey 'lowed dey wuz a fox som'ers 'roun'. So dey got out dey houn's en dey hawns en dey hosses, en sta'ted off fer a fox-hunt. En sho' nuff de houn's got de scent, en wuz on po' Tobe's track in a' hour er so.

"W'en Tobe heared 'em comin' he wuz mos' skeered ter def, en he 'mence' ter run ez ha'd ez he could, en bein' ez de houn's wuz on de Norf side, he run to'ds de Souf, en soon foun' hisse'f back in de woods right whar he wuz bawn en raise'. He jumped a crick en doubled en twisted, en done eve'ything he could fer ter th'ow de houn's off'n de scent but 't wa'n't no use, fer day des kep' gittin' closeter, en closeter, en closeter.

"Ez soon ez Tobe got back to'ds home en 'skivered whar he wuz, he sta'ted fer ole Aun' Peggy's cabin fer ter git her ter he'p 'im, en des ez he got ter her do', lo en behol'! he tu'nt back ter a nigger ag'in, fer de th'ee weeks wuz up des ter a minute. He knock' at dē do', en hollered:

" 'Lemme in, Aun' Peggy, lemme in! De dawgs is atter me!'

"Aun' Peggy open' de do'.

" 'Fer de Lawd sake! nigger, whar is you come fum dis time?' sez she. 'I 'lowed you wuz done got ter de Norf, en free long ago. W'at's de matter wid you now?'

"So Tobe up'n' tol' her 'bout how he had been stop' by dem chick'ns, en how ha'd it wuz ter git 'way fum 'em. En w'iles he wuz talkin' ter Aun' Peggy dey heared de dawgs comin' closeter, en closter, en closter.

" 'Tu'n me ter sump'n' e'se, Aun' Peggy,' sez Tobe, 'fer dat fox scent runs right up ter de do', en dey'll be 'bleedzd ter come in, en dey'll fin' me en kyar me back home, en lamb me, en mos' lakly sell me 'way. Tu'n me ter sump'n', quick, I doan keer w'at, fer I doan want dem dawgs ner dem w'ite folks ter ketch me.'

"Aun' Peggy look' 'roun' de cabin, en sez she, takin' down a go'd fum de chimbly:

" 'I ain' got no goopher made up terday, Tobe, but dis yer bull-frog mixtry. I'll tu'n you ter a bull-frog, en I'll put in ernuff er dis yuther mixtry fer ter take de goopher off in a day er so, en meanw'iles you kin hop down yander ter dat ma'sh en stay, en w'en de dawgs is all gone en you tu'ns back, you kin come ter me en I'll tu'n you ter a sparrer er sump'n' w'at kin fly swif', en den maybe you'll be able ter git 'way en be free widout all dis yer foolishness you's b'en goin' th'oo.'

"By dis time de dawgs wuz scratchin' at de do' en howlin', en Aun' Peggy en Tobe could heah de hawns er de hunters blowin' close behin'. All dis yer racket made Aun' Peggy sorter narvous, en w'en she went ter po' dis yuther mixtry in fer ter lif' de bull-frog goopher off'n Tobe in a day er so, her han' shuck so she spilt it ober de side er de yuther go'd en didn' notice dat it hadn' gone in. En Tobe wuz so busy lis'nin' en watchin' de do', dat he didn' notice nuther, en so w'en Aun' Peggy put de goopher on Tobe en tu'nt 'im inter a bull-frog, dey wa'n't none er dis yuther mixtry in it w'atsomeber.

"Tobe le'p' out'n a crack 'twix' de logs, en Aun' Peggy open' de do', en de dawgs run 'roun', en de w'ite folks come en inqui'ed, en w'en dey seed Aun' Peggy's roots en go'ds en snakeskins en yuther cunjun-fixin's, en a big black cat wid yaller eyes, settin' on de h'a'th, dey 'lowed dey wuz wastin' dey time, so dey des cusst a little en run 'long back home widout de fox dey had come atter.

"De nex' day Aun' Peggy stayed roun' home all day, makin' a mixtry fer ter tu'n Tobe ter a sparrer, en 'spectin' 'im eve'y minute fer ter come in. But he nebber come. En bein' ez he didn' 'pear no mo', Aun' Peggy 'lowed he'd got ti'ed er dis yer animal bizness en w'en he had tu'nt back fum de bull-frog had runned 'way on his own 'sponsibility, lak she 'vised 'im at fus'. So Aun' Peggy went on 'bout her own bizness en didn' paid no mo' 'tention ter Tobe.

"Ez fer po' Tobe, he had hop' off down ter dat ma'sh en had jump' in de water, en had waited fer hisse'f ter tu'n back. But w'en he didn' tu'n back de fus' day, he 'lowed Aun' Peggy had put in too much er de mixtry, en bein' ez de ma'sh wuz full er minners en snails en crawfish en yuther things w'at bull-frogs laks ter eat, he 'lowed he mought's well be comf'table en enjoy hisse'f 'tel his bull-frog time wuz up.

"But bimeby, w'en a mont' roll' by, en two mont's, en th'ee mont's, en a yeah, Tobe kinder 'lowed dey wuz sump'n' wrong 'bout dat goopher, en so he 'mence' ter go up on de dry lan' en look fer Aun' Peggy. En one day w'en she came 'long by de ma'sh, he got in front er her, en croak' en croak'; but Aun' Peggy wuz studyin' 'bout sump'n' e'se; en 'sides, she 'lowed Tobe wuz done gone 'way en got free long, long befo', so she didn' pay no 'tention ter de big bull-frog she met in de path, 'cep'n ter push him out'n de road wid her stick.

"So Tobe went back ter his ma'sh, en dere he's be'n eber sence. It's be'n fifty yeahs er mo', en Tobe mus' be 'bout ten yeahs older'n I is. But he ain' nebber got ti'ed er wantin' ter be tu'nt back ter hisse'f, er ter sump'n' w'at could run erway ter de Norf. Co'se ef he had waited lak de res' un us he'd a be'n free long ago; but he didn' know dat, en he doan know it yet. En eve'y night, w'en de frogs sta'ts up, dem w'at knows 'bout Tobe kin reco'nize his voice en heah 'im callin', callin', callin' ole Aun' Peggy fer ter come en tu'n 'im back, des ez ef Aun' Peggy hadn' be'n restin' in Aberham's bosom fer fo'ty yeahs er mo'. Oncet in a w'ile I notices dat Tobe doan say nuffin' fer a night er so, en so I 'lows he's gittin' ole en po'ly, en trouble' wid hoa'seness er rheumatiz er sump'n' er 'nuther, fum bein' in de water so long. I doan 'spec' he's gwine to be dere many mo' yeahs; but w'iles he is dere, it 'pears ter me he oughter be 'lowed ter lib out de res' er his days in peace.

"Dat's de reason w'y," the old man concluded, "I doan lak ter see nobody eat'n' frogs laigs out'n dat ma'sh. Ouch!" he added suddenly, putting his hand to the pit of his stomach, "Ouch!"

"What's the matter, Uncle Julius?" my wife inquired with solicitude.

"Oh, nuffin', ma'm, nuffin' wuf noticin'—des a little tech er mis'ry in my innards. I s'pose talkin' 'bout po' old Tobe, in dat col', wet ma'sh, wid nobody ter 'sociate wid but frogs en crawfish en water moccasins en sich, en wid nuffin' fittin' ter eat, is des sorter upsot me mo' er less. If you is anyways int'rusted in a ole nigger's feelin's, I ruther 'spec' a drap er dem bitters out'n dat little flat jimmyjohn er yo'n git me shet er dis mis'ry quicker'n anythin' e'se I knows."

Lonesome Ben

T here had been some talk among local capitalists about building a cotton mill on Beaver Creek, a few miles from my place on the sandhills in North Carolina, and I had been approached as likely to take an interest in such an enterprise. While I had the matter under advisement it was suggested, as an inducement to my co-operation, that I might have the brick for the mill made on my place—there being clay there suitable for the purpose—and thus reduce the amount of my actual cash investment. Most of my land was sandy, though I had observed several outcroppings of clay along the little creek or branch forming one of my boundaries.

One afternoon in summer, when the sun was low and the heat less oppressive than it had been earlier in the day, I ordered Julius, our old colored coachman, to harness the mare to the rockaway and drive me to look at the clay-banks. When we were ready, my wife, who wished to go with me for the sake of the drive, came out and took her seat by my side.

We reached our first point of destination by a road running across the plantation, between a field of dark-green maize on the one hand and a broad expanse of scuppernong vines on the other. The road led us past a cabin occupied by one of my farmhands. As the carriage went by at a walk, the woman of the house came to the door and curtsied. My wife made some inquiry about her health, and she replied that it was poor. I noticed that her complexion, which naturally was of a ruddy brown, was of a rather sickly hue. Indeed, I had observed a greater sallowness among both the colored people and the poor whites thereabouts than the hygienic conditions of the neighborhood seemed to justify.

After leaving this house our road lay through a cotton field for a short distance, and then we entered a strip of woods, through which ran the little stream beside which I had observed the clay. We stopped at the creek, the road by which we had come crossing it and continuing over the land of my neighbor, Colonel Pemberton. By the roadside, on my own land, a bank of clay rose in almost a sheer perpendicular for about ten feet, evidently extending back some distance into the low, pine-clad hill behind it, and having also frontage upon the creek. There were marks of bare feet on the ground along the base of the bank, and the face of it seemed freshly disturbed and scored with finger marks, as though children had been playing there.

"Do you think that clay would make good brick, Julius?" I asked the old man, who had been unusually quiet during the drive. He generally played with the whip, making little feints at the mare, or slapping her lightly with the reins, or admonishing her in a familiar way; but on this occasion the heat or some other cause had rendered him less demonstrative than usual.

"Yas, suh, I know it would," he answered.

"How do you know? Has it ever been used for that purpose?"

"No, suh; but I got my reasons fer sayin' so. Ole Mars Dugal' useter hab a brickya'd fu'ther up de branch—I dunno as yer noticed it, fer it's all growed ober wid weeds an' grass. Mars Dugal' said dis yer clay wouldn' make good brick, but I knowed better."

I judged from the appearance of the clay that it was probably deficient in iron. It was of a yellowish-white tint and had a sort of greasy look.

"Well," I said, "we'll drive up to the other place and get a sample of that clay, and then we'll come back this way."

"Hold on a minute, dear," said my wife, looking at her watch, "Mabel has been over to Colonel Pemberton's all the afternoon. She said she'd be back at five. If we wait here a little while she'll be along and we can take her with us."

"All right," I said, "we'll wait for her. Drive up a little farther, Julius, by that jessamine vine."

While we were waiting, a white woman wearing a homespun dress and slat-bonnet came down the road from the other side of the creek, and lifting her skirts slightly, waded with bare feet across the shallow stream. Reaching the clay-bank she stooped and gathered from it, with the aid of a convenient stick, a quantity of the clay which she pressed together in the form of a ball. She had not seen us at first, the bushes partially screening us; but when, having secured the clay, she turned her face in our direction and caught sight of us watching her, she hid the lump of clay in her pocket with a shamefaced look, and hurried away by the road she had come.

"What is she going to do with that, Uncle Julius?" asked my wife. We were Northern settlers, and still new to some of the customs of the locality, concerning which we often looked to Julius for information. He had lived on the place many years and knew the neighborhood thoroughly.

"She's gwineter eat it, Miss Annie," he replied, "w'en she gits outer sight."

"Ugh!" said my wife with a grimace, "you don't mean she's going to eat that great lump of clay?"

"Yas'm I does; dat's jes' w'at I means—gwineter eat eve'y bit un it, an' den come back bimeby fer mo'."

"I should think it would make them sick," she said.

"Dey gits use' ter it," said Julius. "Howsomeber, ef dey eats too much it does make 'em sick; an' I knows w'at I'm er-talkin' erbout. I doan min' w'at dem kinder folks does," he added, looking contemptuously after the retreating figure of the poor-white woman, "but w'eneber I sees black folks eat'n clay off'n dat partic'lar clay-bank, it alluz sets me ter studyin' 'bout po' lonesome Ben."

"What was the matter with Ben?" asked my wife. "You can tell us while we're waiting for Mabel."

Old Julius often beguiled our leisure with stories of plantation life, some of them folklore stories, which we found to be in general circulation among the colored people; some of them tales of real life as Julius had seen it in the old slave days; but the most striking were, we suspected, purely imaginary, or so colored by old Julius's fancy as to make us speculate at times upon how many original minds, which might have added to the world's wealth of literature and art, had been buried in the ocean of slavery.

"W'en ole Mars Marrabo McSwayne owned dat place ober de branch dere, w'at Kunnel Pembe'ton owns now," the old man began, "he useter hab a nigger man name' Ben. Ben wuz one er dese yer big black niggers—he was mo' d'n six foot high an' black ez coal. He wuz a fiel'-han' an' a good wukker, but he had one little failin'—he would take a drap er so oncet in a w'ile. Co'se eve'ybody laks a drap now an' den, but it 'peared ter 'fec' Ben mo' d'n it did yuther folks. He didn' hab much chance dat-a-way, but eve'y now an' den he'd git holt er sump'n' somewhar, an' sho's he did, he'd git out'n de narrer road. Mars Marrabo kep' on wa'nin' 'im 'bout it, an' fin'lly he tol' 'im ef he eber ketch 'im in dat shape ag'in he 'uz gwineter give 'im fo'ty. Ben knowed ole Mars Marrabo had a good 'memb'ance an' alluz done w'at he said, so he wuz monst'us keerful not ter gib 'im no 'casion fer ter use his 'memb'ance on him. An' so fer mos' a whole yeah Ben 'nied hisse'f an' nebber teched a drap er nuffin'.

"But it's ha'd wuk ter larn a ole dog new tricks, er ter make him fergit de ole uns, an' po' Ben's time come bimeby, jes' lak eve'ybody e'se's does. Mars Marrabo sent 'im ober ter dis yer plantation one day wid a bundle er cotton-sacks fer Mars Dugal', an' w'iles he wuz ober yere, de ole Debbil sent a 'oman w'at had cas' her eyes on 'im an' knowed his weakness, fer ter temp' po' Ben wid some licker. Mars Whiskey wuz right dere an' Mars Marrabo wuz a mile erway, an' so Ben minded Mars Whiskey an' fergot 'bout Mars Marrabo. W'en he got back home he couldn' skasely tell Mars Marrabo de message w'at Mars Dugal' had sent back ter 'im.

"Mars Marrabo listen' at 'im 'temp' ter tell it; and den he says, kinder col' and cuttin'-like—he didn' 'pear ter get mad ner nuffin':

" 'Youer drunk, Ben.'

"De way his marster spoke sorter sobered Ben, an' he 'nied it of co'se.

" 'Who? Me, Mars Marrabo? *I* ain' drunk; no, marster, *I* ain' drunk. I ain' teched a drap er nuffin' sence las' Chris'mas, suh.'

" 'Youer drunk, Ben, an' don't you dare ter 'spute my wo'd, er I'll kill you in yo' tracks! I'll talk ter you Sad'day night, suh, w'en you'll be sober, an' w'en you'll hab Sunday ter 'flect ober ou' conve'sation an' nuss yo' woun's.'

"W'en Mars Marrabo got th'oo talkin' Ben wuz mo' sober dan he wuz befo' he got drunk. It wuz Wednesday w'en Ben's marster tol' 'im dis, an' 'twix' den and Friday night Ben done a heap er studyin'. An' de mo' he studied de mo' he didn' lak de way Mars Marrabo talked. He hadn' much trouble wid Mars Marrabo befo', but he knowed his ways, an' he knowed dat de longer Mars Marrabo waited to do a thing de wusser he got 'stid er gittin' better lak mos' folks. An' Ben fin'lly made up his min' he wa'n't gwineter take dat cow-hidin'. He 'lowed dat ef he wuz little, like some er de dahkies on de plantation, he wouldn' min' it so much; but he wuz so big dey'd be mo' groun' fer Mars Marrabo ter cover, an' it would hurt dat much mo'. So Ben 'cided ter run erway.

"He had a wife an' two chil'en, an dey had a little cabin ter dese'ves down in de quahters. His wife Dasdy wuz a good-lookin', good-natu'd 'oman, an' 'peared ter set a heap er sto' by Ben. De little boy wuz name' Pete; he wuz 'bout eight er nine years ole, an' had already 'menced ter go out in de fiel' an' he'p his mammy pick cotton, fer Mars Marrabo wuz one er dese yer folks w'at wants ter make eve'y aidge cut. Dis yer little Pete wuz a mighty soople dancer, an' w'en his daddy would set out in de yahd an' pick de banjo fer 'im, Pete could teach de ole folks noo steps—dancin' jes' seemed to come nachul ter 'im. Dey wuz a little gal too; Ben didn't pay much 'tention ter de gal, but he wuz monst'us fond er Dasdy an' de boy. He wuz sorry ter leab 'em, an' he didn' tell 'em nuffin' 'bout it fer fear day'd make a fuss. But on Friday night Ben tuk all de bread an' meat dey wuz in de cabin an' made fer de woods.

"W'en Sad'day come an' Ben didn' 'pear, an' nobody didn' know nuffin' 'bout 'im, Mars Marrabo 'lowed of co'se dat Ben had runned erway. He got up a pahty an' tuk de dawgs out an' follered de scen' down ter de crick an' los' it. Fer Ben had tuk a go'd-full er tar 'long wid 'im, an' w'en he got ter de crick he had 'n'inted his feet wid tar, an' dat th'owed de houn's off'n de scent. Dey sarched de woods an' follered de roads an' kep' watchin' fer a week, but dey couldn' fin' no sign er Ben. An' den Mars Marrabo got mo' stric', an' wukked his niggers hahder'n eber, ez ef he wanted ter try ter make up fer his loss.

"W'en Ben stahted out he wanted ter go ter de No'th. He didn' know how fur it wuz, but he 'lowed he retch dar in fo' er five days. He knowed de No'th Stah, an' de fus' night he kep' gwine right straight to'ds it. But de nex' night it wuz rainin', an' fer two er th'ee nights it stayed cloudy, an' Ben couldn' see de No'th Stah. Howsomeber, he knowed he had got stahted right an' he kep' gwine right straight on de same way fer a week er mo' 'spectin' ter git ter de No'th eve'y day, w'en one mawnin' early, atter he had b'en walkin' all night, he come right smack out on de crick jes' whar he had stahted f'om.

"Co'se Ben wuz monst'us disapp'inted. He had been wond'rin' w'y he hadn' got ter de No'th befo', an' behol', heah he wuz back on de ole plantation. He couldn' un'erstan' it at fus', but he wuz so hongry he didn' hab time ter study 'bout nuffin' fer a little w'ile but jes' ter git sump'n' ter eat; fer he had done eat up de bread an' meat he tuk away wid 'im, an' had been libbin' on roas'n-ears an' sweet'n 'taters he'd slip out'n de woods an' fin' in co'n fiel's an' 'tater-patches. He look 'cross de crick, an' seed dis yer clay-bank, an' he waded ober an' got all he could eat, an' den tuk a lump wid 'im, an' hid in de woods ag'in 'til he could study de matter ober some.

"Fus' he 'lowed dat he better gib hisse'f up an' take his lammin'. But jes' den he 'membered de way Mars Marrabo looked at 'im an' w'at he said 'bout Sad'day night; an' den he 'lowed dat ef Mars Marrabo ketch 'im now, he'd wear 'im ter a frazzle an' chaw up de frazzle, so dey wouldn' be nuffin' lef' un 'im at all, an' dat Mars Marrabo would make a' 'xample an' a warnin' of 'im fer all de niggers in de naberhood. Fac' is Mars Marrabo prob'ly wouldn' a' done much ter 'im fer it 'ud be monst'us po' 'couragement fer runaway niggers ter come back, ef dey gwineter git killed w'en dey come. An' so Ben waited 'til night, an' den he went back an' got some mo' clay an' eat it an' hid hisse'f in de woods ag'in.

"Well, hit wuz quare 'bout Ben, but he stayed roun' heah fer a mont', hidin' in de woods in de daytime, an' slippin' out nights an' gittin' clay ter eat an' water f'om de crick yander ter drink. De water in dat crick wuz cl'ar in dem days, stidder bein' yaller lak it is now."

We had observed that the water, like that of most streams that take their rise in swamps, had an amber tint to which the sand and clay background of the bed of the stream imparted an even yellower hue.

"What did he do then, Julius?" asked my wife, who liked to hear the end of a story.

"Well, Miss, he made up his min' den dat he wuz gwineter staht fer de No'th ag'in. But w'iles he b'en layin' 'roun' in de woods he had 'mence' ter feel monst'us lonesome, an' it 'peared ter him dat he jes' couldn' go widout seein' Dasdy an' little Pete. Fus' he 'lowed he'd go up ter de cabin, but he though 'bout de dogs 'roun' de yahd, an' dat de yuther dahkies mought see 'im, and so he 'cided he'd better watch fer 'em 'til dey come 'long de road— it wuz dis yer same road—w'en he could come out'n de woods an' talk ter 'em. An' he eben 'lowed he mought 'suade 'em ter run erway wid 'im an' dey could all get ter de No'th, fer de nights wuz cl'ar now, an' he couldn' lose de No'th Stah.

"So he waited two er th'ee days, an' sho' nuff long come Dasdy one mornin', comin' over to Mars Dugal's fer ter fetch some things fer her missis. She wuz lookin' kinder down in de mouf, fer she thought a heap er Ben, an' wuz monst'us sorry ter lose 'im, w'iles at de same time she wuz glad he wuz free, fer she 'lowed he'd done got ter de No'th long befo'. An' she wuz studyin' 'bout Ben, w'at a fine-lookin' man he wuz, an' wond'rin' ef she'd eber see 'im any mo'.

"W'en Ben seed her comin' he waited 'til she got close by, an' den he stepped out'n de woods an' come face ter face wid her. She didn' 'pear to know who he wuz, an' seem kinder skeered.

" 'Hoddy, Dasdy, honey,' he said.

" 'Huh!' she said,' 'pears ter me youer mighty fermilyer on sho't acquantance.'

" 'Sho't acquantance! Why, doan yer know me, Dasdy?'

" 'No. I doan know yer f'om a skeerscrow. I nebber seed yer befo' in my life, an' nebber wants ter see yer ag'in. Whar did yer come f'om anyhow? Whose nigger is yer? Er is yer some low-down free nigger dat doan b'long ter nobody an' doan own nobody?'

" 'W'at fer you talk ter me like dat, honey? I's Ben, yo' Ben. Why doan you know yo' own man?'

"He put out his ahms fer ter draw her ter 'im, but she jes' gib one yell, an' stahted ter run. Ben wuz so 'stonish' he didn' know w'at ter do, an' he stood dere in de road 'til he heared somebody e'se comin', w'en he dahted in de woods ag'in.

"Po' Ben wuz so 'sturbed in his min' dat he couldn' hahdly eat any clay dat day. He couldn' make out w'at wuz de matter wid Dasdy but he 'lowed maybe she'd heared he wuz dead er sump'n', an' thought he wuz a ha'nt, an' dat wuz w'y she had run away. So he watch' by de side er de road, an' nex' mornin' who should come erlong but little Pete, wid a reed ober his shoulder, an' a go'd-full er bait, gwine fishin' in de crick.

"Ben called 'im: 'Pete, O Pete! *Little* Pete.'

"Little Pete cocked up his ears an' listened. 'Peared lak he'd heared dat voice befo'. He stahted fer de woods fer ter see who it wuz callin' 'im, but befo' he got dere Ben stepped out an' retched fer 'im.

" 'Come heah, honey, an' see yo' daddy, who ain' seen yer fer so long.'

"But little Pete tuk one look at 'im, an' den 'mence' ter holler an' squeal an' kick an' bite an' scratch. Ben wuz so 'stonish' dat he couldn' hol' de boy, who slipped out'n his han's an' run to'ds de house ez fas' ez his legs would tote 'im.

"Po' Ben kep' gittin' wus an' wus mixed up. He couldn' make out fer de life er 'im w'at could be de matter. Nobody didn' 'pear ter wanter own 'im. He felt so cas' down dat he didn' notice a nigger man comin' 'long de road 'til he got right close up on 'im, an' didn' heah dis man w'en he said 'Hoddy' ter 'im.

" 'W'at's de matter wid yer?' said de yuther man w'en Ben didn' 'spon'. 'W'at jedge er member er de legislater er hotel-keeper does you b'long ter dat you can't speak ter a man w'en he says hoddy ter yer?'

"Ben kinder come ter hisse'f an' seed it wuz Primus, who b'long ter his marster an' knowed 'im as well as anybody. But befo' he could git de words out'n his mouf Primus went on talkin'.

" 'Youer de mos' mis'able lookin' merlatter I eber seed. Dem rags look lak dey be'n run th'oo a sawmill. My marster doan 'low no strange niggers 'roun' dis yer plantation, an' yo' better take yo' yaller hide 'way f'um yer as fas' as yo' kin.'

"Ben almos' 'lowed he wuz gwine out'n his min', he wuz so 'stonished an' 'mazed at none er dese yer folks reco'-nizin' 'im. He went back in de woods ag'in an' stayed dere all day, wond'rin' w'at he wuz gwineter do. Oncet er twicet he seed folks comin' 'long de road, an' stahted out ter speak ter 'em, but changed his min' an' slip' back ag'in.

"Co'se ef Mars Marrabo had been huntin' Ben he would 'a' foun' 'im. But he had long sence los' all hope er seein' 'im ag'in, an' so nobody didn' 'sturb Ben in de woods. He stayed hid a day er two mo' an' den he got so lonesome an' homesick fer Dasdy an' little Pete an' de yuther dahkies—somebody ter talk ter—dat he jes' made up his min' ter go right up ter de house an' gib hisse'f up an' take his med'cine. Mars Marrabo couldn' do nuffin' mo' d'n kill 'im an' he mought's well be dead as hidin' in de woods wid nobody ter talk ter er look at ner nuffin'. He had jes' come out'n de woods an' stahted up dis ve'y road, w'en who sh'd come 'long in a hoss'n buggy but ole Mars Marrabo, drivin' ober ter dat yuther brickyahd youer gwineter see now. Ben run out'n de woods, an' fell down on his knees in de road right in front er Mars Marrabo. Mars Marrabo had to pull on de lines an' hol' de hoss up ter keep 'im f'um runnin' ober Ben.

" 'Git out'n de road, you fool nigger,' says Mars Marrabo, 'does yer wanter git run ober? Whose nigger is you anyhow?'

" 'I's yo' nigger, Mars Marrabo; doan yer know Ben, w'at runned erway?'

" 'Yas, I knows my Ben w'at runned erway. Does you know whar he is?'

" 'Why, I's yo' Ben, Mars Marrabo. Doan yer know me, marster?'

" 'No, I doan know yer, yer yaller rascal! W'at de debbil yer mean by tellin' me sich a lie? Ben wuz black ez a coal an' straight ez a' arrer. Youer yaller ez dat claybank, an' crooked ez a bair'-hoop. I reckon youer some 'stracted nigger, turn't out by some marster w'at doan wanter take keer er yer. You git off'n my plantation, an' doan show yo' clay-cull'ud hide aroun' yer no more, er I'll hab yer sent ter jail an' whip'.'

"Mars Marrabo drove erway an' lef' po' Ben mo' dead 'n alive. He crep' back in de bushes an' laid down an' wep' lak a baby. He didn' hab no wife, no chile, no frien's, no marster—he'd be'n willin' ernuff to git 'long widout a marster w'en he had one, but it 'peared lak a sin fer his own marster ter 'ny 'im an' cas' 'im off dat-a-way. It 'peared ter 'im he mought jes' ez well be dead ez livin', fer he wuz all alone in de worl', wid nowhar ter go, an' nobody didn' hab nuffin' ter say ter 'im but ter 'buse 'im an' drive 'im erway.

"Atter he got ober his grievin' spell he 'mence' ter wonder w'at Mars Marrabo meant by callin' 'im yaller, an' ez long ez nobody didn' seem ter keer whuther dey seed 'im er not, he went down by de crick in broad daylight, an' kneel down by de water an' looked at his face. Fus' he didn' reco'nize hisse'f an' glanshed back ter see ef dey wa'n't somebody lookin' ober his shoulder—but dey wa'n't. An' w'en he looked back in de water he seed de same thing—he wa'n't' black no mo', but had turnt ter a light yaller.

"Ben didn' knowed w'at ter make er it fer a minute er so. Fus' he 'lowed he must hab de yaller fever, er de yaller janders, er sump'n lak dat! But he had knowed rale dark folks ter hab janders befo', and it hadn' nebber 'fected 'em dat-a-way. But bimeby he go up off'n 'is han's an' knees an' wuz stan'in lookin' ober de crick at de clay-bank, an' wond'rin' ef de clay he'd b'en eat'n' hadn' turnt 'im yaller w'en he heared sump'n say jes' ez plain ez wo'ds.

" 'Turnt ter Clay! turnt ter clay! turnt ter clay!'

"He looked all roun', but he couldn' see nobody but a big bull-frog settin' on a log on de yuther side er de crick. An' w'en he turnt roun' an' sta'ted back in de woods, he heared de same thing behin' 'im.

" 'Turnt ter clay! turnt ter clay! turnt ter clay!'

"Dem wo'ds kep' ringin' in 'is yeahs 'til he fin'lly 'lowed dey wuz boun' ter be so, er e'se dey wouldn' a b'en tol' ter 'im, an' dat he had libbed on clay so long an' had eat so much, dat he mus 'a' jes' nach'ly turnt ter clay!"

" 'Imperious Caesar, dead and turned to clay,
Might stop a hole to keep the wind away,' " I murmured parenthentically.

"Yas, suh," said the old man, "turnt ter clay. But you's mistook in de name, suh; hit wuz Ben, you 'member, not Caesar. Ole Mars Marrabo did hab a nigger name' Caesar., but dat wuz anudder one."

"Don't interrupt him, John," said my wife impatiently. "What happened then, Julius?"

"Well, po' Ben didn' know w'at ter do. He had be'n lonesome ernuff befo', but now he didn' eben hab his own se'f ter 'so'ciate wid, fer he felt mo' lak a stranger 'n he did lak Ben. In a day er so mo' he 'mence' ter wonder whuther he wuz libbin' er not. He had hearn 'bout folks turnin' ter clay w'en dey wuz dead, an' he 'lowed maybe he wuz dead an' didn' knowed it, an' dat wuz de reason w'y eve'y body run erway f'm 'im an' wouldn' hab nuffin' ter do wid 'im. An' ennyhow, he 'lowed ef he wa'n't dead, he mought's well be. He wande'ed 'roun' a day er so mo', an' fin'lly de lonesomeness, an' de sleepin' out in de woods, 'mongs' de snakes an' sco'pions, an' not habbin' nuffin' fit ter eat, 'mence' ter tell on him, mo' an' mo', an' he kep' gittin' weakah an' weakah 'til one day, w'en he went down by de crick fer ter git a drink er water, he foun' his limbs gittin' so stiff hit 'uz all he could do ter crawl up on de bank an' lay down in de sun. He laid dere 'til he died, an' de sun beat down on 'im, an' beat down on 'im, an' beat down on 'im, fer th'ee er fo' days, 'til it baked 'im as ha'd as a brick. An' den a big win' come erlong an' blowed a tree down, an' it fell on 'im an' smashed 'im all ter pieces, an' groun' 'im ter powder. An' den a big rain come erlong, an' washed 'im in de crick, an' eber sence den de water in dat crick's b'en jes' as yer sees it now. An dat wuz de een' er po' lonesome Ben, an' dat's de reason w'y I knows dat clay'll make brick an' w'y I doan nebber lak ter see no black folks eat'n it."

My wife came of a family of reformers, who could never contemplate an evil without seeking an immediate remedy. When I decided that the bank of edible clay was not fit for brickmaking, she asked me if I would not have it carted away, suggesting at the same time that it could be used to fill a low place in another part of the plantation.

"It would be too expensive," I said.

"Oh, no," she replied, "I don't think so. I have been talking with Uncle Julius about it, and he says he has a nephew who is out of employment, and who will take the contract for ten dollars, if you will furnish the mule and cart, and board him while the job lasts."

As I had no desire to add another permanent member to my household, I told her it would be useless; that if the people did not get clay there they would find it elsewhere, and perhaps an inferior quality which might do greater harm, and that the best way to stop them from eating it was to teach them self-respect, when she had opportunity, and those habits of industry and thrift whereby they could get their living from the soil in a manner less direct but more commendable.

A Deep Sleeper

It was four o'clock on Sunday afternoon, in the month of July. The air had been hot and sultry, but a light, cool breeze had sprung up; and occasional cirrus clouds overspread the sun, and for a while subdued his fierceness. We were all out on the piazza—as the coolest place we could find—my wife, my sister-in-law and I. The only sounds that broke the Sabbath stillness were the hum of an occasional vagrant bumblebee, or the fragmentary song of a mockingbird in a neighboring elm, who lazily trolled a stave of melody, now and then, as a sample of what he could do in the cool of the morning, or after a light shower, when the conditions would be favorable to exertion.

"Annie," said I, "suppose, to relieve the deadly dullness of the afternoon, that we go out and pull the big watermelon, and send for Colonel Pemberton's folks to come over and help us eat it."

"Is it ripe, yet?" she inquired sleepily, brushing away a troublesome fly that had impudently settled on her hair.

"Yes, I think so. I was out yesterday with Julius, and we thumped it, and concluded it would be fully ripe by tomorrow or next day. But I think it is perfectly safe to pull it today."

"Well, if you are sure, dear, we'll go. But how can we get it up to the house? It's too big to tote."

"I'll step round to Julius's cabin and ask him to go down with the wheelbarrow and bring it up," I replied.

Julius was an elderly colored man who worked on the plantation and lived in a small house on the place, a few rods from my own residence. His daughter was our cook, and other members of his family served us in different capacities.

As I turned the corner of the house I saw Julius coming up the lane. He had on his Sunday clothes, and was probably returning from the afternoon meeting at the Sandy Run Baptist Church, of which he was a leading member and deacon.

"Julius," I said, "we are going out to pull the big watermelon, and we want you to take the wheelbarrow and go with us, and bring it up to the house."

115

"Does yer reckon dat watermillun's ripe yit, sah?" said Julius. "Didn'
'pear ter me it went quite plunk enuff yistiddy fer ter be pull' befo' termorrer."

"I think it is ripe enough, Julius."

"Mawnin' 'ud be a better time fer ter pull it, sah, w'en de night air an'
de jew's done cool' it off nice."

"Probably that's true enough, but we'll put it on ice, and that will cool
it; and I'm afraid if we leave it too long, some one will steal it."

"I 'spec's dat so," said the old man, with a confirmatory shake of the
head. "Yer takes chances w'en yer pulls it, en' yer takes chances w'en yer
don't. Dey's a lot er po' w'ite trash roun' heah w'at ain' none too good fer
ter steal it. I seed some un' 'em loafin' long de big road on mer way home
fum chu'ch jes' now. I has ter watch mer own chicken-coop ter keep chick'ns
'nuff fer Sunday eatin.' I'll go en' git de w'eelborrow."

Julius had a profound contempt for poor whites, and never let slip an
opportunity for expressing it. He assumed that we shared this sentiment, while
in fact our feeling toward this listless race was something entirely different.
They were, like Julius himself, the product of a system which they had not
created and which they did not know enough to resist.

As the old man turned to go away he began to limp, and put his hand
to his knee with an exclamation of pain.

"What's the matter, Julius?" asked my wife.

"Yes, Uncle Julius, what ails you?" echoed her sweet young sister. "Did
you stump your toe?"

"No, miss, it's dat mis'able rheumatiz. It ketches me now an' den in de
lef' knee, so I can't hardly draw my bref. O Lawdy!" he added between his
clenched teeth, "but dat do hurt. Ouch! It's a little better now," he said after
a moment, "but I doan' b'lieve I kin roll dat w'eelborrow out ter de watermil-
lun-patch en' back. Ef it's all de same ter yo', sah, I'll go roun' ter my house
en' sen' Tom ter take my place, w'iles I rubs some linimum on my laig."

"That'll be all right, Julius," I said, and the old man, hobbling, disappeared round the corner of the house. Tom was a lubberly, sleepy-looking
Negro boy of about fifteen, related to Julius's wife in some degree, and living
with them.

The old man came back in about five minutes. He walked slowly, and
seemed very careful about bearing his weight on the afflicted member.

"I sont 'Liza Jane fer ter wake Tom up," he said. "He's down in de
orchard asleep under a tree somewhar. 'Liza Jane knows whar he is. It takes
a minute er so fer ter wake 'im up. 'Liza Jane knows how ter do it. She tickles
'im in de nose er de yeah wid a broomstraw; hollerin' doan' do no good. Dat
boy is one er de Seben Sleepers. He's wuss'n his gran'daddy used ter be."

"Was his grandfather a deep sleeper, Uncle Julius?" asked my wife's
sister.

"Oh, yas, Miss Mabel," said Julius, gravely. "He wuz a monst'us pow'ful sleeper. He slep' fer a mont' once."

"Dear me, Uncle Julius, you must be joking," said my sister-in-law incredulously. I thought she put it mildly.

"Oh, no, ma'm, I ain't jokin'. I never jokes on ser'ous subjec's. I wuz dere w'en it all happen'. Hit wuz a monst'us quare thing."

"Sit down, Uncle Julius, and tell us about it," said Mabel; for she dearly loved a story, and spent much of her time "drawing out" the colored people in the neighborhood.

The old man took off his hat and seated himself on the top step of the piazza. His movements were somewhat stiff and he was very careful to get his left leg in a comfortable position.

"Tom's gran'daddy wuz name' Skundus," he began. "He had a brudder name' Tushus en' ernudder name' Cottus en' ernudder name' Squinchus." The old man paused a moment and gave his leg another hitch.

My sister-in-law was shaking with laughter. "What remarkable names!" she exclaimed. "Where in the world did they get them?"

"Dem names wuz gun ter 'em by ole Marse Dugal' McAdoo, w'at I use' ter b'long ter, en' dey use' ter b'long ter. Marse Dugal' named all de babies w'at wuz bawn on de plantation. Dese young un's mammy wanted ter call 'em sump'n plain en' simple, like 'Rastus' er 'Caesar' er 'George Wash'n'ton'; but ole Marse say no, he want all de niggers on his place ter hab diffe'nt names, so he kin tell 'em apart. He'd done use' up all de common names, so he had ter take sump'n else. Dem names he gun Skundus en' his brudders is Hebrew names en' wuz tuk out'n de Bible."

"Can you give me chapter and verse?" asked Mabel.

"No, Miss Mabel, I doan know 'em. Hit ain' my fault dat I ain't able ter read de Bible. But ez I wuz a-sayin', dis yer Skundus growed up ter be a peart, lively kind er boy, en' wuz very well liked on de plantation. He never quo'lled wid de res' er de han's en' alluz behaved 'isse'f en' tended ter his wuk. De only fault he had wuz his sleep'ness. He'd haf ter be woke up ev'y mawnin' ter go ter his wuk, en' w'enever he got a chance he'd fall ersleep. He wuz might'ly nigh gittin' inter trouble mo' d'n once fer gwine ter sleep in de fiel'. I never seed his beat fer sleepin'. He could sleep in de sun er sleep in de shade. He could lean upon his hoe en' sleep. He went ter sleep walk'n 'long de road oncet, en' mighty nigh bust' his head open 'gin a tree he run inter. I did heah he oncet went ter sleep while he wuz in swimmin'. He wuz floatin' at de time, en' come mighty nigh gittin' drownded befo' he woke up. Ole Marse heared 'bout it, en' ferbid his gwine in swimmin' enny mo', fer he said he couldn't 'ford ter lose 'im.

"When Skundus was growed up he got ter lookin' roun' at de gals, en' one er de likeliest un 'em tuk his eye. It was a gal name' Cindy w'at libbed

wid 'er mammy in a cabin by deyse'ves. Cindy tuk ter Skundus ez much ez
Skundus tuk ter Cindy, en' bimeby Skundus axed his marster ef he could marry
Cindy. Marse Dugal' b'long' ter de P'isbytay'n Chu'ch en' never 'lowed his
niggers ter jump de broomstick, but alluz had a preacher fer ter marry 'em.
So he tole Skundus ef him en' Cindy would 'ten' ter dey wuk good dat summer
till de crap was laid by, he'd let 'em git married en' hab a weddin' down
ter de quarters.

"So Skundus en' Cindy wukked hahd as dey could till 'bout a mont' er
so befo' layin' by, w'en Marse Dugal's brudder, Kunnel Wash'n'ton McAdoo,
w'at libbed down in Sampson County, 'bout a hunderd mile erway, come fer
ter visit Marse Dugal'. Dey wuz five er six folks in de visitin' party, en' our
w'ite folks need a new gal fer ter he'p wait on 'em. Dey picked out de likeliest
gal dey could fine 'mongs' de fiel'-han's, en co'se dat wuz Cindy. Cindy wuz
might'ly tickled fer ter be tuk in de house sarvice, fer it meant better vittles
en' better clo's en' easy wuk. She didn' seed Skundus quite as much, but she
seed 'im w'eneber she could. Prospe'ity didn' spile Cindy; she didn' git stuck
up en' 'bove 'sociatin' wid fiel'-han's, lack some gals in her place 'ud a done.

"Cindy wuz sech a handy gal 'roun' de house, en' her marster's relations
lacked her so much, dat w'en dey visit wuz ober, dey wanted ter take Cindy
'way wid 'em. Cindy didn' want ter go en' said so. Her marster wuz a good-
natured kind er man, en' would'a' kep' her on de plantation. But his wife
say no, it 'ud nebber do ter be lett'n' de sarvants hab dey own way, er dey
soon wouldn' be no doin' nuthin' wid 'em. Ole marster tole 'er he done promus
ter let Cindy marry Skundus.

" 'O, well,' sez ole Miss, 'dat doan' cut no figger. Dey's too much er
dis foolishness 'bout husban's en' wibes 'mongs' de niggers nowadays. One
nigger man is de same as ernudder, en' dey'll be plenty un 'em down ter Wash'-
n'ton's plantation.' Ole Miss wuz a mighty smart woman, but she didn' know
ev'ything.

" 'Well,' says ole Marse, 'de craps'll be laid by in a mont' now, 'en den
dey won't be much ter do fer ernudder mont' er six weeks. So we'll let her
go down dere an' stay till cotton-pickin' time; I'll jes' len' 'er ter 'em till den.
Ef dey wants ter keep 'er en' we finds we doan need 'er, den we'll talk furder
'bout sellin' 'er. We'll tell her dat we jes' gwine let her go down dere wid
de chil'en a week er so en' den come back, en' den we won't hab no fuss
about it.'

"So dey fixed it dat erway, en' Cindy went off wid 'em, she 'spectin' ter
be back in a week er so, en' de w'ite folks not hahdly 'lowin' she'd come back
at all. Skundus didn' lack ter hab Cindy go, but he couldn' do nuthin'. He
wuz wukkin' off in ernudder part er de plantation w'en she went erway, en'
had ter tell her good-by de night befo'.

"Bimeby, w'en Cindy didn' come back in two or th'ee weeks, Skundus
'mence ter git res'less. En' Skundus wuz diff'ent f'um udder folks. Mos' folks

w'en dey gits res'less can't sleep good, but de mo' res'lesser Skundus got, de mo' sleepier he 'peared ter git. W'eneber he wuz'n wukkin er eatin', he'd be sleepin'. W'en de yuther niggers 'ud be skylarkin' 'roun' nights en' Sundays, Skundus 'ud be soun' asleep in his cabin. Things kep' on dis way fer 'bout a mont' atter Cindy went away, w'en one mawnin' Skundus didn' come ter wuk. Dey look' fer 'im 'roun' de plantation, but dey couldn' fin' 'im, en' befo' de day wuz gone, ev'ybody wuz sho' dat Skundus had runned erway.

"Cose dey wuz a great howdydo 'bout it. Nobody hadn' nebber runned erway fum Marse Dugal' befo', en' dey hadn' be'n a runaway nigger in de neighbo'hood fer th'ee er fo' years. De w'ite folks wuz all wukked up, en' dey wuz mo' ridin' er hosses, en' mo' hitchin' up er buggies d'n a' little. Ole Marse Dugal' had a lot er papers printed en' stuck up on trees 'long de roads, en' dey wuz sump'n put in de noospapers—a free nigger f'um down on de Wim'l'ton Road read de paper ter some er our han's—tellin' all 'bout how high Skundus wuz, en' w'at kine er teef he had, en' 'bout a skyah he had on his lef' cheek, en' how sleepy he wuz, en' off'rin' a reward er one hunder' dollars fer whoeber 'ud ketch 'im. But none of 'em eber cotch 'im.

"W'en Cindy fus' went away she wuz kinder down in de mouf fer a day er so. But she went to a fine new house, de folks treated her well en' dere wuz sich good comp'ny 'mongs' her own people, dat she made up 'er min' she might 's well hab a good time fer de week er two she wuz gwine ter stay down dere. But w'en de time roll' on en' she didn' heared nothin' 'bout gwine back she 'mence' ter git kinder skeered she wuz'n nebber gwine ter see her mammy ner Skundus no mo'. She wuz monst'us cut up 'bout it, an' los' 'er appetite en' got so po' en' skinny, her mist'ess sont 'er down ter de swamp fer ter git some roots fer ter make some tea fer 'er health. Her mist'ess sont her 'way 'bout th'ee o'clock en' Cindy didn' come back till atter sundown; en' she say she b'en lookin' fer de roots, dat dey didn' 'pear ter be none er dem kin' er roots fer a mile er so 'long de aidge er de swamp.

"Cindy 'mence' ter git better jes' ez soon as she begun ter drink de root-tea. It wuz a monst'us good med'cine, leas'ways in her case. It done Cindy so much good dat her mist'ess 'cluded she'd take it herse'f en' gib it ter de chil'en. De fus' day Cindy went atter de roots dey wuz some lef' ober, en' her mist'ess tol' 'er fer ter use dat fer de nex' day. Cindy done so, but she tol' 'er mist'ess hit didn' hab no strenk en' didn' do 'er no good. So ev'y day atter dat Marse Wash'n'ton's wife 'ud sen' Cindy down by de aidge er de swamp fer ter git fresh roots.

" 'Cindy,' said one er de fiel'-han's one day, 'yer better keep 'way fum dat swamp. Dey's a ha'nt walkin' down dere.'

"Go way fum yere wid yo' foolishness,' said Cindy. 'Dey ain' no ha'nts. White folks doan' b'lieve in sich things, fer I heared 'em say so; but yer can't 'spec' nothin' better fum fiel'-han's.'

"Dey wuz one man on de plantation, one er dese yer dandy niggers w'at 'uz alluz runnin' atter de wimmen folks, dat got ter pest'rin' Cindy. Cindy didn' paid no 'tention ter 'im, but he kep' on tryin' ter co't her w'en he could git a chance. Fin'ly Cindy tole 'im fer ter let her 'lone, er e'se sump'n' might happen ter 'im. But he didn' min' Cindy, en' one ebenin' he followed her down ter de swamp. He los' track un 'er, en' ez he wuz a-startin' back out'n de swamp, a great big black ha'nt 'bout ten feet high, en' wid a fence-rail in its han's jump out'n de bushes en' chase 'im cl'ar up in de co'n fiel'. Leas'ways he said it did; en' atter dat none er de niggers wouldn' go nigh de swamp, 'cep'n Cindy, who said it wuz all foolishness—it wuz dis nigger's guilty conscience dat skeered 'im—she hadn' seed no ha'nt en' wuz'n skeered er nuffin' she didn' see.

"Bimeby, w'en Cindy had be'n gone fum home 'bout two mont's, harves'-time come on, en' Marse Dugal' foun' hisse'f short er han's. One er de men wuz down wid de rheumatiz, Skundus wuz gone, en' Cindy wuz gone, en' Marse Dugal' tole ole Miss dey wuz no use talkin', he couldn' 'ford ter buy no new han's, en he'd ha' ter sen' fer Cindy, 'en put her in de fiel'; fer de cotton-crap wuz a monst'us big 'un dat year, en' Cindy wuz one er de bes' cotton-pickers on de plantation. So dey wrote a letter to Marse Wash'n'ton dat day fer Cindy, en' wanted Cindy by de 'een er de mon', en' Marse Wash'-n'ton sont her home. Cindy didn' 'pear ter wanter come much. She said she'd got kinder use' ter her noo home; but she didn' hab no mo' ter say 'bout comin dan she did 'bout goin'. Howsomedever, she went down ter de swamp fer ter git roots fer her mist'ess up ter de las' day she wuz dere.

"W'en Cindy got back home, she wuz might'ly put out 'ca'se Skundus wuz gone, en' hit didn' 'pear ez if anythin' anybody said ter 'er 'ud comfort 'er. But one mawnin' she said she'd dreamp' dat night dat Skundus wuz gwine ter come back; en' sho' 'nuff, de ve'y nex' mawnin' who sh'd come walkin' out in de fiel' wid his hoe on his shoulder but Skundus, rubbin' his eyes ez ef he hadn' got waked up good yit.

"Dey wuz a great 'miration 'mongs' de niggers, en' somebody run off ter de big house fer ter tell Marse Dugal' hisse'f, mad as a hawnit, a-cussin' en' gwine on like he gwine ter hurt somebody; but anybody w'at look close could 'a' seed he wuz 'mos' tickled ter def fer ter git Skundus back ergin.

" 'Whar yer be'n run erway ter, yer good-fer-nuthin', lazy, black nigger?' sez 'e. 'I'm gwine ter gib yer fo' hunderd lashes. I'm gwine ter hang yer up by yer thumbs en' take ev'y bit er yer black hide off'n yer, en' den I'm gwine ter sell yer ter de fus' specilater w'at comes 'long buyin' niggers fer ter take down ter Alabam'. W'at yer mean by runnin' erway fum yer good, kin' marster, yer good-fer-nuthin', wool-headed, black scound'el?'

"Skundus looked at 'im ez ef he didn' understan'. 'Lawd, Marse Dugal',' sez 'e, 'I doan' know w'at youer talkin' 'bout. I ain' runned erway; I ain' be'n nowhar.'

" 'Whar yer be'n fer de las' mont'?' said Marse Dugal'. 'Tell me de truf, er I'll hab yer tongue pulled out by de roots. I'll tar yer all ober yer en' set yer on fiah. I'll—I'll—' Marse Dugal' went on at a tarrable rate, but eve'ybody knowed Marse Dugal' bark uz wuss'n his bite.

"Skundus look lack 'e wuz skeered mos' ter def fer ter heah Marse Dugal' gwine on dat erway, en' he couldn' 'pear to un'erstan' w'at Marse Dugal' wuz talkin' erbout.

" 'I didn' mean no harm by sleep'n in de barn las' night, Marse Dugal',' sez 'e,'en' ef yer'll let me off dis time, I won't nebber do so no mo'.'

"Well, ter make a long story sho't, Skundus said he had gone ter de barn dat Sunday atternoon befo' de Monday w'en he couln' be foun' fer ter hunt aigs, en' wiles he wuz up dere de hay had 'peared so sof' en' nice dat he had laid down fer take a little nap; dat it wuz mawnin' w'en he woke en' foun' hisse'f all covered up whar de hay had fell over on 'im. A hen had built a nes' right on top un 'im, en' it had half-a-dozen aigs in it. He said he hadn' stop fer ter git no brekfus', but had jes' suck' one or two er de aigs en' hurried right straight out in de fiel', fer he seed it wuz late en' all de res' er de han's wuz gone ter wuk.

" 'Youer a liar,' said Marse Dugal', 'en' de truf ain't in yer. Yer b'en run erway en' hid in de swamp somewhar ernudder.' But Skundus swo' up en' down dat he hadn' b'en out'n dat barn, en' fin'lly Marse Dugal' went up ter de house en' Skundus went on wid his wuk.

"Well, yer mought know day wuz a great 'miration in de neighbo'hood. Marse Dugal' sont fer Skundus ter cum up ter de big house nex' day, en' Skundus went up 'spect'n fer ter ketch forty. ·But w'en he got dere, Marse Dugal' had fetched up ole Doctor Leach fum down on Rockfish, 'en another young doctor fum town, en' dey looked at Skundus's eyes en' felt of his wris' en' pulled out his tongue, en' hit 'im in de chis', en' put dey yeahs ter his sides fer ter heah 'is heart beat; en' den dey up'n made Skundus tell how he felt w'en 'e went ter sleep en' how he felt w'en 'e woke up. Dey stayed ter dinner, e' w'en dey got thoo' talkin' en' eatin' en' drinkin', dey tole Marse Dugal' Skundus had had a catacornered fit, en' had be'n in a trance fer fo' weeks. En' w'en dey l'arned about Cindy, en' how dis yer fit had come on gradg'ly atter Cindy went away, dey 'lowed Marse Dugal' 'd better let Skundus en' Cindy git married, er he'd be liable ter hab some mo' er dem fits. Fer Marse Dugal' didn' want no fittified niggers ef 'e could he'p it.

"Atter dat, Marse Dugal' had Skundus up ter de house lots er times fer ter show 'im off ter folks w'at come ter visit. En' bein' as Cindy wuz back home, en' she en' Skundus wukked hahd, en' couldn' 'ford fer ter take no chances on dem long trances, he 'lowed em ter got married soon ez cotton-pickin' wuz ober, en' gib 'em a cabin er dey own ter lib in down in de quarters. En' sho' 'nuff, dey didn' had no trouble keep'n' Skundus wake f'm dat time fo'th, fer Cindy turned out ter hab a temper of her own, en' made Skundus walk a chalk line.

"Dis yer boy, Tom," said the old man, straightening out his leg carefully, preparatory to getting up, "is jes' like his gran'daddy. I b'lieve ef somebody didn' wake 'im up he'd sleep till jedgmen' day. Heah 'e comes now. Come on heah wid dat w'eelborrow, yer lazy, good-fer-nuthin' rascal."

Tom came slowly round the house with the wheelbarrow, and stood blinking and rolling his eyes as if he had just emerged from a sound sleep and was not yet half awake.

We took our way around the house, the ladies and I in front, Julius next and Tom bringing up the rear with the wheelbarrow. We went by the well-kept grapevines, heavy with the promise of an abundant harvest, through a narrow field of yellowing corn, and then picked our way through the watermelon vines to the spot where the monarch of the patch had lain the day before, in all the glory of its coat of variegated green. There was a shallow concavity in the sand where it had rested, but the melon itself was gone.

A Victim of Heredity

I had caught a chicken thief.

I had gone to North Carolina, a few years after the war, with some prejudices in favor of the colored people. It was my idea that with kind treatment
and fair opportunities they would improve their condition rapidly, and that
enjoying the privileges of freemen, they would learn in due time to appreciate
the responsibilities of citizenship. I am glad to say that my opinion was shared
by many of my Southern neighbors, and that observation and experience justified it in large measure.

There were a few of my colored neighbors, however, who did not readily
shake off the habits formed under the old system, and I suffered more or less
from petty thievery. As long as it was confined to grapes on the vine, or fruit
on the tree, or roasting-ears, or an occasional watermelon, I did not complain
very much; but when, one summer, I had suffered from several raids on my
hen-house, I determined to protect my property. I therefore kept watch one
night, and caught a thief in the very act of robbing my hen-roost. I locked
him up in a strongly built smokehouse until morning, at which time I expected
to deal with him.

I made up my mind, before I went to sleep, that an example must be
made of this Negro. I had learned that the laws of North Carolina were somewhat elastic, and that the degree of punishment meted out for crime was largely
dependent upon the vigor of the prosecution. I decided that five years in the
penitentiary would be about right for this midnight marauder. It would give
him time to break off the habit, and would strike terror to the hearts of other
thieves in the neighborhood.

When I got up in the morning I went down to the smokehouse to inspect
my captive. He was a somewhat insignificant-looking fellow, and seemed very
much frightened. I sent him down something to eat, and told him I was going
to have him taken to jail.

During breakfast I thought the matter over somewhat, and concluded that
five years in the penitentiary would be rather disproportionate to the actual
crime committed, and that perhaps two years would be equally effective as a
warning.

I was going to send one of my servants to town toward noon with a load of grapes, which were packed for shipment to the nearest market, and I decided to write a note to the sheriff, Mr. Weems, and ask him to send a constable out to my vineyard for the thief. By the time I had written the note it occurred to me that over-severity in the punishment of crime was often productive of harm, and had seldom resulted in any good, and that perhaps, taking everything into consideration, a year in jail in the neighborhood would be ample punishment, and a more impressive object lesson than a longer term in the distant penitentiary.

I sent the note to Mr. Weems. During the afternoon I learned incidentally that my captive had a large family and a sick wife, and, being of somewhat trifling disposition, had no steady employment but was dependent upon odd jobs for a livelihood. But while these might be subjects of consideration for the humanitarian, I realized that any false sentiment in the matter would be subversive of social order; that property must be protected, or soon there would be no incentive to industry and thrift. I determined that the thief should have at least six months in jail, if I had to support his family during that time.

Somehow or other, however, I could not dismiss the subject from my mind during the afternoon, and further reflection suggested that after all, while it might be politic, it was hardly just to punish a man as an example; that if an offender paid the penalty of his own misconduct, it would scarcely be fair to add to it a vicarious punishment for half a dozen hypothetical crimes which, if the theory of prevention were correct, would in all probability never be committed.

I therefore reached the final decision that Sam Jones, the prisoner, should spend, so far as my influence would secure this result, three months in the county jail.

I was sitting on the front piazza, indulging in a quiet smoke during the hot part of the afternoon, and had just arrived at this conclusion, when old Julius came around the house, and, touching his hat, asked at what time my wife wanted the rockaway brought around for our afternoon drive.

"I hardly think we shall go today," I replied, "until the constable has come and taken that thief to jail. By the way, Julius, why is it that your people can't let my chickens alone? Don't I employ a number of them, pay them good wages, befriend them in every possible way? It seems to me that common decency would require them to let my place alone."

The old man shook his head sadly.

"It's a myst'ry, suh," he answered with a sigh, "dat ev'ybody doan understan'. Ef dey did, some un 'em mought make mo' 'lowance."

My wife came out and took a seat in an armchair near me, behind the honeysuckle vine.

"I am asking Julius to explain why it is his people can't let chickens alone," I said to her.

"I think it unkind, John," returned my wife, "to charge the sins of one man on a whole race. There are thieves wherever there is portable property, and I don't imagine colored people like chickens any better than any one else."

Old Julius shook his head as a sign of dissent.

"I has ter differ from you dere ma'am," he said, with as much positiveness as he was capable of in conversation with white folks, "cullud folks is mo' fonder er chicken dan w'ite folks. Dey can't he'p but be."

"Why so?" I asked. "Is it in the blood?"

"You is hit it, suh, de fus' sta't-off. Yas, suh, en dat is de fac', tooby sho'."

"Why, Uncle Julius!" said my wife with some show of indignation, "I am ashamed of you, to be slandering your race in that way."

"I begs yo' pardon, ma'am, ef it hu'ts yo' feelin's, but I ain' findin' no fault wid dem. Dey ain't 'sponsible fer dey tas'e for chick'n-meat."

"Well," I said, "sit down and tell us all about it."

Julius took a seat on the top step, and with his ragged straw hat in his hand began:

"Long yeahs befo' de war dey wuz a monst'us rich w'ite genterman, name' Mars Donal' McDonal', w'at use' ter lib down on de yuther side er de Wim'-l'ton Road. Dis yer Mars McDonal' wuz a Scotchman. He hadn't alluz be'n rich, fer w'en he fus' come ter dis country he wuz po', en he wukked fer a year er so as oberseah fer ernudder w'ite man, 'tel he had save' money ernuff ter buy one er two niggers en den he rented a farm on sheers, en bimeby he had bought a plantation en bought some mo' niggers en raise' some, 'tel he 'mence ter be so well-off dat folks mos' fergot he had eber be'n a nigger-driver. He kep' on gittin' richer en richer, 'tel fin'lly he wuz one er de riches' men in de county.

"But he wa'n't sat'sfied. He had a neffy name' Tom, en Mars Donal' had be'n lef' gardeen fer dis yer neffy er his'n, en he had manage' so dat w'en young Mars Tom growed up dey wa'n't nuffin' lef' er de fine proputty w'at young Mars Tom's daddy had had w'en he died.

"Folks said Mars Donal' had rob' his neffy, but dey wa'n't no way ter prove it. En mo' d'n dat, Mars Donal' didn' 'pear ter lak Mars Tom a-tall atter he growed up, en turnt 'im out in de worl' ter shif' fer hisse'f widout no money ner nuffin.

"Mars Tom had be'n co'tin' fer lo dese many yeahs his secon' cousin, young Miss 'Liza McGuire, who useter lib on de yuther side er de ribber, en young Mars Tom wanted ter marry Miss 'Liza monstus bad. But w'en Mars Tom come of age, en Mars Donal' say all his proputty done use' up on his eddication, Miss 'Liza's daddy say he wouldn' 'low her ter marry Mars Tom 'tel he'd make some money, er show her daddy how he wuz gwineter suppo't Miss 'Liza ef he married her.

"De young folks wa'nt 'lowed ter see one ernudder ve'y often, but Mars

Tom had a bateau down on de ribber an' he use'ter paddle ober sometimes ter meet Miss 'Liza whuther er no.

"One eb'nin' Mars Tom went down ter de ribber an' untied his bateau an' wuz startin' ter cross, w'en he heared somebody holler. He looked roun' en he see hit wuz a' ole nigger 'oman had fell in de ribber. She had sunk once, an' wuz gwine down agin, w'en Mars Tom cotch 'er and pull't 'er out, en gin er a drink er sump'n he had in a flas', an' den tied his boat an' he'ped 'er up de bank ter de top, whar she could git long by herself.

"Now, dis yer 'oman w'at Mars Tom pull't outen de ribber des happen' ter be ole Aun' Peggy, de free-nigger cunjuh 'oman w'at libbed down by de Wim'l'ton Road. She had be'n diggin' roots fer her cunj'in', en had got too close ter de ribber, en had fell in wha' de water wuz deep en strong, en had come monst'us close ter bein' drownded. Aun' Peggy knowed all 'bout Mars Tom en his uncle ole Mars Donal', an' his junesey Miss 'Liza; en she made up her min' dat she wuz gwineter do sump'n fer young Mars Tom de fus' chanst she got. She wuz won'rin' wot kinder goopher she could wuk fer Mars Tom, w'en who should come ter see her one day but ole Mars Donal' hisse'f.

"Now, w'y Mars Donal' come ter go ter see ole Aun' Peggy wuz dis erway. Mars Donal' had be'n gittin' richer en richer, en closter en closter, 'tel he'd got so he'd mos' skin a flea fer his hide en taller. But he wa'n't sat's-fied, en he kep' on projickin' wid one thing en figg'rin' on ernudder, fer ter see how he could git mo' en mo'. He wuz a'ready wukkin' his niggers ez ha'd ez day could stan', but he got his 'count-book out one day an' 'mence' ter cack'late w'at it cos' 'imter feed his niggers, en it 'peared ter be a monstus sum. En he 'lowed ter hisse'f dat, ef he could feed his niggers fer 'bout half er w'at it had been costin' 'im, he'd save a heap er money ev'y yeah.

"Co'se ev'ybody knowed, an' Mars Donal' knowed, dat a fiel'-han' had ter hab so much bacon en so much meal en so much merlasses a week ter make 'im fittin' ter do his wuk. But Mars Donal' 'lowed dey mought be some way ter fool de niggers, er sump'n; so he tuk a silber dollar en went down ter see ole Aun' Peggy.

"Aun' Peggy laid de silber dollar on de mantelpiece en heared w'at he had ter say, en den she 'lowed she'd wuk her roots, en he'd hafter come back nex' day en fetch her ernudder silber dollar, en she'd tell 'im w'at he sh'd do.

"Mars Donal' sta'ted out, en bein' ez Aun' Peggy's back wuz tu'nt, he 'lowed he'd take dat silber dollar 'long wid 'im, bein' ez she hadn' tole 'im nuffin, an' he'd gin it ter her nex' day. But w'en he pick' up de silber dollar, it wuz so hot it burnt 'is han', he drapped it rale quick an' went off rubbin' his han' an' cussin' kinder sof' ter hisse'f. De nex' day he went back, en Aun' Peggy gin 'im a goopher mixtry in a bottle.

" 'You take dis yer mixtry,' sez she, 'en put it on yo' niggers rashuns de nex' time you gibs 'em out, en den stidder 'lowin' yo' han's a poun' er bacon en a peck a meal en a qua't er merlasses, you gin 'em half a poun' er bacon en half a peck er meal en a pint er merlasses, en dey won' know de diffe'nce. Fac', dis yer goopher mixtry'll make de half look des la'k de whole, an' atter de niggers has once eat some er dat conju'd meat en meal en merlasses hit's gwineter take dey appetites erway so dey'll be des' ez well sat'sfied ez ef dey had a side a bacon en a bairl er flour.'

"W'en Mars Donal' sta'ted erway Aun' Peggy sez, sez she:

" 'You done forgot dat yuther dollar, ain't yer, Mars Donal'?'

" 'Oh, yes, Peggy,' sezee, 'but here it is.' En Mars Donal' retch down in his pocket en pull't out a han'ful er gol' en silber, en picked out a lead dollar an' handed it to Aun' Peggy. Aun' Peggy seed de dollah wuz bad, but she didn' say nuffin'. But ez Mars Donal' wuz turnin' ter go 'way, Aun' Peggy sprinkle' sump'n on dat lead dollah, en sez she:

"O Mars Donal' kin I get yer ter change a twenty-dollah gol' piece for me?'

" 'Yas, I reckon,' sezee.

"Aun' Peggy handed him de lead dollar, en he looked at it en bit it en sounded it on de table, en it 'peared ter be a bran'-new gol' piece, so he tuk'n pulled out his pu'se an gin Aun' Peggy th'ee five-dollar gol' pieces en five good silber dollars, en den he tuk his goopher mixtry en went 'long home wid it.

"W'en Mars Donal' had gone, Aun' Peggy sont a mawkin-bird fer ter tell young Mars Tom ter come en see her.

"Mars Tom was gwine 'long de road one ebenin' w'en he heard a mawkin'-bird singin' right close ter 'im, an' de mawkin'-bird seem' ter be a-sayin':

" 'Go see ole Aun' Peggy,
She wants ter see you bad,
She'll show you how ter git back
De lan' yo' daddy had.'

"Mars Tom wuz studyin' 'bout sump'n e'se, en he didn' pay no 'tention ter w'at de mawkin'-bird say. So pretty soon he heahs de mawkin'-bird ag'in:

" 'Go en see Aun' Peggy,
She wants ter see you bad,
She's gwine ter he'p you git back
De gol' yo' daddy had.'

"But Mars Tom had sump'n e'se on his min' an' he wuz gwine on down de road right pas' whar Aun' Peggy libbed, w'en de mawkin'-bird come up en mos' pe'ched on his shoulders, an' sez, des' ez plain ez ef he wuz tawkin':

" 'Go see ole Aun' Peggy,
Er e'se you'll wush you had;
She'll show you how ter marry
De gal you wants so bad.'

"Dat happen' ter be des w'at Mars Tom wuz studyin' erbout, an' he 'mence' ter low dey mought be sump'n in w'at dis yer mawkin'-bird say, so he up'n goes ter see Aun' Peggy.

"Aun' Peggy tol' 'im how glad she wuz ter see 'im, en tol' 'im how she'd be'n wantin' ter do sump'n fer 'im. En den she 'splained 'bout Mars Donal', en tole Mars Tom sump'n w'at he mus' go en do.

" 'But I ain' got no money, Aun' Peggy,' sezee.

" 'Nemmine', sez Aun' Peggy, 'you borry all de money you kin rake en scrape, en git all de credit you kin, en I ain' be'n conj'in' all dese yeahs for nuffin', en I'll len' you some money. But you do des' ez I tell you, en doan git skeert, en ev'y thing'll tu'n out des exac'ly ez I say.'

"Ole Mars Donal' sprinkle' de goopher mixtry on his niggers rashuns, nex' Sunday mawnin', en den sarved out half rashuns, des' ez Aun' Peggy say, en sho' 'nuff, de niggers didn' 'pear ter notice no diffe'nce, des' ez Aun' Peggy say. En all de week none er de niggers didn' say nuffin' 'bout not habin' ernuff ter eat, en dey 'peared ter be des' ez well sat'sfied ez ef dey had got dey reg'lar rashuns.

"Mars Donal' figgered up his books at de een' er a week er so en foun' he had sabe' so much money dat he 'mence' ter wonder ef he couldn' save some mo'. En' bein' ez de niggers wuz all gittin' 'long so nice, en de cotton had be'n laid by, en de niggers wouldn' hab ter wuk so tarrible ha'd fer a mont' er so, Mars Donal' 'lowed he'd use Aun' Peggy's goopher some mo', en so he tuk'n sprinkle some mo' er de mixtry on de nex' week's rashuns en den cut de rashuns in two once mo'; stidder givin' de han's a half a peck er meal en a pint er merlasses, en half a poun' er bacon, he gin 'em a qua'ter er a peck er meal en half a pint er merlasses en fo' ounces er meat fer a week's rashuns. De goopher wukked des' de same ez it had befo', en de niggers didn' 'pear ter notice no diffe'nce. Mars Donal' wuz tickle' mos' ter def, en kep' dis up right along fer th'ee er fo' weeks.

"But Mars Donal' had be'n so busy fig'rin' up his profits an' countin' his money, dat he hadn' be'n payin' ez clos't 'tention ter his niggers ez yushal, en fus' thing he knowed, w'en de ha'd wuk begun ag'in, he 'skivered dat mos' er his niggers wuz so weak en feeble dat dey couldn' ha'dly git 'round' de plantation; 'peared es ef dey had jus' use' up all de strenk dey had, en den des' all gin out at once.

"Co'se Mars Donal' got skeert en 'mence' ter gin 'em dey reg'lar rashuns. But somehow er nuther dey didn' 'pear ter hab no appetite, en dey wouldn' come back fer dey rashuns w'en de week wuz up, but 'lowed dey had ernuff ter las' 'em fer a mont'. En meanw'iles dey kep' on gittin' po'er en po'er, en weaker en weaker, 'tel Mars Donal' got so skeert he hasten back ter see ole Aun' Peggy en ax' her ter take dat goopher off'n his niggers.

"Aun' Peggy knowed w'at Mars Donal' had done 'bout cuttin' down de rashuns, but she wa'n't ready ter finish up wid Mars Donal' yit, so she didn' let on, but des' gin 'im ernudder mixtry, en tol' 'im fer ter sprinkle dat on de niggers' nex' rashuns.

"Mars Donal' sprinkle it on, but it didn't do no good, en nex' week he come back ag'in.

" 'Dis yer mixtry ain' got no power, Peggy,' sezee. 'It ain' 'sturb' de yuther goopher a-tall.'

" 'I doan understan' dis,' sez Aun' Peggy; 'how did you use dat fus' mixtry I gin you?'

"Well, den Mars Donal' 'lowed how he sprinkle it on de fus' time, en how it wukked so good dat he had sprinkle it on de nex' time en cut de rashuns in two a'gin.

" 'Uh huh, uh huh!' 'sponded Aun' Peggy, 'look w'at you gone an' done! You wuz'n satisfied wid w'at I tole you, en now you gone en got ev'thing all mess' up. I knows how ter take dat fus' goopher off, but now you gone en double de strenk, en I doan know whuther I kin fin' out how ter take it off er not. Anyhow, I got ter wuk my roots fer a week er so befo' I kin tell. En w'ile's I is wukkin, you mought gib yo' niggers sump'n a little better ter eat, en dey mought pick up a little. S'posen you tries roas' po'k?'

"So Mars Donal' killed all 'is hawgs en fed his niggers on roas' po'k fer a week; but it didn do 'em no good, en at de een' er de week he went back ter Aun' Peggy ag'in.

" 'I's monst'us sorry,' she sez, 'but it ain' my fault. I's wukkin' my roots ez ha'd ez I kin, but I ain' foun' out how ter take de goopher off yit. S'pos'n you feed yo niggers on roas' beef fer a week er so?'

"So Mars Donal' killt all 'is cows an' feed de niggers on roas' beef fer a week. En all dis time dey wuzn' wukkin', an' Mars Donal's craps wuz gittin' 'way behin', en he wuz gwine mos' 'tracted fer fear he wuz bleedst ter lose dem five hund'ed niggers w'at he sot so much sto' by. So he goes back ter ole Aun' Peggy ag'in.

" 'Peggy,' sezee, 'you is got ter do sump'n fer me, er e'se I'll be in de po'-house fus' t'ing I know.'

" 'Well, suh,' sez Aun' Peggy, "I's be'n doin' all I knows how, but dey's a root I's bleedzed ter hab, en it doan grow nowhar but down in Robeson County. En I got ter go down dere en gether it on a Friday night in de full er de moon. En I won't be back yer fer a week er ten days.'

"Mars Donal' wuz mos' out'n his min' wid waitin' an' losin' money. 'But s'posen dem niggers dies on my han's w'iles you is gone,' sezee. W'at is I gwine ter do?'

"Aun' Peggy studied an' studied, den she up en sez, sez she:

" 'Well, ef dey dies I reckon you'll hatter bury 'em.'

" 'Dey is one thing you mought try, I spec's it's 'bout de only thing w'at'll keep yo' niggers alibe 'tel I gits back. You might see ef dey won' eat chick'n.

"Well, Mars Donal' wanted ter sabe his niggers. Dey wuz all so po' en so skinny en so feeble dat he couldn' sell 'em ter nobody, en dey wouldn' eat nuffin e'se, so he des' had ter feed 'em on chick'n. W'en he had use' up all de chick'ns on his place, he went roun' ter his nabers ter buy chick'ns en dey said dey wuz sorry, but dey'd sol' all deir chick'ns ter a man in town. Mars Donal' went ter dis yer man, en he say dem chick'ns doan b'long ter him but ter ernudder man w'at wuz geth'in' chick'ns, fer ter ship ter Wim'l'ton, er de Norf, er some'ers. Mars Donal' say he des' bleedzt ter hab chick'ns, en fer dat man ter see de yuther genterman en ax' 'im w'at he'd take fer dem chick'ns. De nex' day de man say Mars Donal' could hab de chick'ns fer so much, w'ich wuz 'bout twicet ez much ez chick'ns had be'n fetchin' in de mah-ket befo'. It mos' broke Mars Donal's hea't, but he 'lowed dem chick'ns would las' tel Aun' Peggy come back en tuk de goopher off'n de niggers.

"But w'en de en' er de week wuz retch' ole Aun' Peggy hadn' come back, en Mars Donal' had ter hab mo' chickens, fer chick'n-meat des barely 'peared ter keep de niggers alibe. En so he went out in de country fer ter hunt fer chick'ns. En en'ywhar he'd go, dis yuther man had be'n befo' 'im en had bought up all de chick'ns, er contracted fer 'em all, en Mars Donal' had ter go back ter dis man in town en pay two prices ter git chick'ns ter feed his niggers.

"De nex' week it wuz de same way, en Mars Donal' 'mence' ter git des-p'rit. He sont way off in two er th'ee counties, fer ter hunt chick'n, but high er low, no matter whar, dis yuther man had be'n dar befo', 'tel it 'peared lak he had bought up all de chick'ns in No'f Ca'lina.

"But w'at wuz dribin' Mars Donal' mos' crazy wuz de money he had ter spen' fer dese chick'ns. It had mos' broke his hea't fer ter kill all his hawgs, en he had felt wuss w'en he hatter kill all his cows. But w'en dis yer chick'n business begun, it come mighty nigh ruinin' 'im. Fu's he spent all de money he had saved feedin' de niggers. Den he spent all de money he had in de bank, er sto'ed away. Den he borried all de money he could on his notes, en he jes' 'bout retch' de p'int whar he'd hatter mawgidge his plantation fer ter raise' mo' money ter buy chicken fer his niggers, w'en one day Aun' Peggy come back f'um Robeson County en tol' Mars Donal' she had foun' de root she wuz lookin' fer, an' gun 'im a mixtry fer ter take de goopher off'n de niggers.

" 'Dis yer mixtry,' sez she, ' 'll fetch you' niggers appetites back en make 'em eat dey rashuns en git dey strenk back. But you is use' dat yuther mixtry so strong, en put dat goopher on so ha'd, dat I 'magines it's got in dey blood, en I's feared dey ain' nobody ner nuffin kin eber take it all off'n 'em. So I 'spec's you'll hatter gib yo' niggers chick'ns at leas' oncet a week ez long ez dey libs, ef you wanter git de wuk out'n 'em dat you oughter.'

"Dey wuz so many niggers on ole Mars Donal's plantation," continued Julius, "en dey got scattered roun' so befo' de wah en sence, dat dey ain' ha'dly no cull'ud folks in No'f Ca'lina but w'at has got some er de blood er dem goophered niggers in dey vames. En so, eber sence den, all de niggers in No'f Ca'lina has ter hab chicken at leas' once er week fer ter keep dey healt' en strenk. En dat is w'y cull'ud folks laks chick'n mo' d'n w'ite folks."

"What became of Tom and his sweetheart?" asked my wife.

"Yas'm" said Julius, "I wuz a-comin' ter dat. De nex' week atter de goopher wuz tuk off'n de niggers, Mars Tom come down ter Aun' Peggy, en paid her back de money he borried. En he tol' Aun' Peggy he had made mo' money buyin' chick'ns en sellin' em ter his Uncle Donal' dan his daddy had lef' 'im w'en he died, en he say he wuz gwine ter marry Miss 'Liza en buy a big plantation en a lot er niggers en hol' up his head 'mongs' de big w'ite folks des' lak he oughter. En he tol' Aun' Peggy he wuz much obleedzt ter her, en ef she got ti'ed cunj'in' en wanter res' an' lib easy, she could hab a cabin on his plantation en a stool by his kitchen fiah, en all de chick'n an' wheat-bread she wanter eat, en all de terbacker she wanter smoke ez long ez she lib."

I had occasion to visit the other end of the vineyard shortly after Julius had gone shambling down the yard toward the barn. I left word that the constable should be asked to wait until my return. I was detained longer than I expected, and when I came back I asked if the constable had arrived.

"Yes," my wife replied, "he came."

"Where is he?" I asked.

"Why, he's gone."

"Did he take the chicken-thief?"

"I'll tell you, John," said my wife, with a fine thoughtful look that furnished the best possible illustration of what she was saying, "I've been thinking more or less about the influence of heredity, and about the degree of our responsibility for what we do, and I concluded that if the slaves did contract the habit of stealing chickens and other little things to eat, they were not without some excuse for their conduct; and that we ought not to be too severe with them because they haven't outgrown the habit in a few years. So I told the constable that you had changed your mind, and that he might send in his bill for time lost and you would pay it."

"And what am I going to do with Sam Jones?" I asked.

"Oh," she replied, "I told Julius he might unlock the smokehouse and let him go."

Dave's Neckliss

"**H**ave some dinner, Uncle Julius?" said my wife.

It was a Sunday afternoon in early autumn. Our two women-servants had gone to a camp-meeting some miles away, and would not return until evening. My wife had served the dinner, and we were just rising from the table, when Julius came up the lane, and, taking off his hat, seated himself on the piazza.

The old man glanced through the open door at the dinner table, and his eyes rested lovingly upon a large sugar-cured ham, from which several slices had been cut, exposing a rich pink expanse that would have appealed strongly to the appetite of any hungry Christian.

"Thanky, Miss Annie," he said, after a momentary hesitation, "I dunno ez I keers ef I does 'tas'e a piece er dat ham—ef yer'll cut me off a slice un it."

"No," said Annie, "I won't. Just sit down to the table and help yourself; eat all you want, and don't be bashful."

Julius drew a chair up to the table, while my wife and I went out on the piazza. Julius was in my employment; he took his meals with his own family, but when he happened to be about our house at meal times, my wife never let him go away hungry.

I threw myself into a hammock, from which I could see Julius through an open window. He ate with evident relish, devoting his attention chiefly to the ham, slice after slice of which disappeared in the spacious cavity of his mouth. At first the old man ate rapidly, but after the edge of his appetite had been taken off he proceeded in a more leisurely manner. When he had cut the sixth slice of ham (I kept count of them from a lazy curiousity to see how much he *could* eat) I saw him lay it on his plate; as he adjusted the knife and fork to cut it into smaller pieces, he paused, as if struck by a sudden thought, and a tear rolled down his rugged cheek and fell upon the slice of ham before him. But the emotion, whatever the thought that caused it, was transitory, and in a moment he continued his dinner. When he was through eating, he came out on the porch, and resumed his seat with the satisfied expression of countenance that usually follows a good dinner.

"Julius," I said, "you seemed to be affected by something, a moment ago. Was the mustard so strong that it moved you to tears?"

"No, suh, it wa'n't de mustard; I wuz studyin' 'bout Dave."

"Who was Dave, and what about him?" I asked.

The conditions were all favorable to story-telling. There was an autumnal languor in the air, and a dreamy haze softened the dark green of the distant pines and the deep blue of the Southern sky. The generous meal he had made had put the old man in a very good humor. He was not always so, for his curiously undeveloped nature was subject to moods which were almost childish in their variableness. It was only now and then that we were able to study, through the medium of his recollection, the simple but intensely human inner life of slavery. His way of looking at the past seemed very strange to us; his view of certain sides of life was essentially different from ours. He never indulged in any regrets for the Arcadian joyousness and irresponsibility which was a somewhat popular conception of slavery; his had not been the lot of the petted house-servant, but that of the toiling field-hand. While he mentioned with a warm appreciation the acts of kindness which those in authority had shown to him and his people, he would speak of a cruel deed, not with the indignation of one accustomed to quick feeling and spontaneous expression, but with a furtive disapproval which suggested to us a doubt in his own mind as to whether he had a right to think or to feel, and presented to us the curious psychological spectacle of a mind enslaved long after the shackles had been struck off from the limbs of its possessor. Whether the sacred name of liberty ever set his soul aglow with a generous fire; whether he had more than the most elementary ideas of love, friendship, patriotism, religion—things which are half, and the better half, of life to us; whether he even realized except in a vague, uncertain way, his own degradation, I do not know: I fear not; and if not, then centuries of repression had borne their legitimate fruit. But in the simple human feeling, and still more in the undertone of sadness, which pervaded his stories, I thought I could see a spark which, fanned by favoring breezes and fed by the memories of the past, might become in his children's children a glowing flame of sensibility, alive to every thrill of human happiness or human woe.

"Dave use' ter b'long ter my ole marster," said Julius; "he wuz raise' on dis yer plantation, en I kin 'member all erbout 'im, fer I wuz ole 'nuff ter chop cotton w'en it all happen'. Dave wuz a tall man, en monst'us strong: he could do mo' wuk in a day dan any yuther two niggers on de plantation. He wuz one er dese yer solemn kine er men, en nebber run on wid much foolishness, like de yuther darkies. He use' ter go out in de woods en pray; en w'en he hear de han's on de plantation cussin' en gwine on wid dere dancin' en foolishness, he use' ter tell 'em 'bout religion en jedgemen'-day, w'en dey would haf ter gin account fer eve'y idle word en all dey yuther sinful kyarin'son.

"Dave had l'arn how ter read de Bible. Dey wuz a free nigger boy in de settlement w'at wuz munst'us smart, en could write en cipher, en wuz alluz readin' books er papers. En Dave had hi'ed dis free boy fer to l'arn 'im how ter read. Hit wuz 'g'in de law, but co'se none er de niggers didn' say nuffin ter de w'ite folks 'bout it. Howsomedever, one day Mars Walker—he wuz de oberseah—foun' out Dave could read. Mars Walker wa'n't nuffin but a po' bockrah, en folks said he couldn' read ner write hisse'f, en co'se he didn' lack ter see a nigger w'at knowed mo' d'n he did; so he went en tole Mars Dugal'. Mars Dugal' sont fer Dave, en ax' 'im 'bout it.

"Dave didn't hardly knowed w'at ter do; but he couldn' tell no lie, so he 'fessed he could read de Bible a little by spellin' out de words. Mars Dugal' look' mighty solemn.

" 'Dis yer is a se'ious matter,' sezee; 'it's 'g'in de law ter l'arn niggers how ter read, er 'low 'em ter hab books. But w'at yer l'arn out'n dat Bible, Dave?'

"Dave wa'n't no fool, ef he wuz a nigger, en sezee:

" 'Marster, I l'arns dat it's a sin fer ter steal, er ter lie, er fer ter want w'at doan b'long ter yer; en I l'arns fer ter love de Lawd en ter 'bey my marster.'

"Mars Dugal' sorter smile' en laf' ter hisse'f, like he 'uz might'ly tickle' 'bout sump'n, en sezee:

" 'Doan 'pear ter me lack readin' de Bible done yer much harm, Dave. Dat's w'at I wants all my niggers fer ter know. Yer keep right on readin', en tell de yuther han's w'at yer be'n tellin' me. How would yer lack fer ter preach ter de niggers on Sunday?'

"Dave say he'd be glad fer ter do w'at he could. So Mars Dugal' tole de oberseah fer ter let Dave preach ter de niggers, en tell 'em w'at wuz in de Bible, en it would he'p ter keep 'em fum stealin' er runnin' erway.

"So Dave 'mence' ter preach, en done de han's on de plantation a heap er good, en most un 'em lef' off dey wicked ways, en 'mence' ter love ter hear 'bout God, en religion, en de Bible; en dey done dey wuk better, en didn' gib de oberseah but mighty little trouble fer to manage 'em.

"Dave wuz one er dese yer men w'at didn' keer much fer de gals—least-ways he didn' 'tel Dilsey come ter de plantation. Dilsey wuz a monst'us peart, good-lookin', gingybread-colored gal—one er dese yer high-steppin' gals w'at hol's dey head up, en won' stan' no foolishness fum no man. She had b'long ter a gemman over on Rockfish w'at died, en whose 'state ha' ter be sol' fer ter pay his debts. En Mars Dugal' had be'n ter de oction, en w'en he seed dis gal a-cryin' en gwine on 'bout bein' sol' erway fum her ole mammy, Aun' Mahaly, Mars Dugal' bid 'em bofe in, en fotch 'em ober ter our plantation.

"De young nigger men on de plantation wuz des wil' atter Dilsey, but it didn' do no good, en none un 'em couldn' git Dilsey fer dey junesey,[1] 'tel

---

[1]Sweetheart.

Dave 'mence' fer ter go roun' Aun' Mahaly's cabin. Dey wuz a fine-lookin' couple, Dave en Dilsey wuz, bofe tall, en well-shape', en soopl'. En dey sot a heap by one ernudder. Mars Dugal' seed 'em tergedder one Sunday, en de nex' time he seed Dave atter dat, sezee:

"'Dave, w'en yer en Dilsey gits ready fer ter git married, I ain' got no rejections. Dey's a poun' er so er chawin'-terbacker up at de house, en I reckon yo' mist'iss kin fine a frock en a ribbin er two fer Dilsey. You er bofe good niggers, en yer neenter be feared er bein' sol' 'way fum one ernudder long ez I owns dis plantation; en I 'spec' ter own it fer a long time yit.'

"But dere wuz one man on de plantation w'at didn' lack ter see Dave en Dilsey tergedder ez much ez marster did. W'en Mars Dugal' went ter de sale whar he got Dilsey en Mahaly, he bought ernudder han', by de name er Wiley. Wiley wuz one er dese yer shiny-eyed, double-headed little niggers, sha'p ez a steel trap, en sly ez de fox w'at keep out'n it. Dis yer Wiley had be'n pesterin' Dilsey 'fo' she come ter our plantation, en had nigh 'bout worried de life out'n her. She didn' keer nuffin fer 'im, but he pestered her so she ha' ter th'eaten ter tell her marster fer ter make Wiley let her 'lone. W'en he come ober to our place it wuz des ez bad, 'tel bimeby Wiley seed dat Dilsey had got ter thinkin' a heap 'bout Dave, en den he sorter hilt off aw'ile, en purten' lack he gin Dilsey up. But he wuz one er dese yer 'ceitful niggers, en w'ile he wuz laffin' en jokin' wid de yuther han's 'bout Dave en Dilsey, he wuz settin' a trap fer ter ketch Dave en git Dilsey back fer hisse'f.

"Dave en Dilsey made up dere min's fer ter git married long 'bout Christmas time, w'en dey'd hab mo' time fer a weddin'. But 'long 'bout two weeks befo' dat time ole Mars 'mence' ter lose a heap er bacon. Eve'y night er so somebody 'ud steal a side er bacon, er a ham, er a shoulder, er sump'n fum one er de smoke-'ouses. De smoke-'ouses wuz lock', but somebody had a key, en manage' ter git in some way er 'nudder. Dey's mo' ways 'n one ter skin a cat, en dey's mo' d'n one way ter git in a smoke-'ouse—leastways dat's w'at I hearn say. Folks w'at had bacon fer ter sell didn' hab no trouble 'bout gittin' rid un it. Hit wuz 'g'in de law fer ter buy things fum slabes; but Lawd! dat law didn' 'mount ter a hill er peas. Eve'y week er so one er dese yer big covered waggins would come 'long de road, peddlin' terbacker en w'iskey. Dey wuz a sight er room in one er dem big waggins, en it wuz monst'us easy fer ter swop off bacon fer sump'n ter chaw er ter wa'm yer up in de winter-time. I s'pose de peddlers didn' knowed dey wuz breakin' de law, caze de niggers alluz went at night, en stayed on de dark side er de waggin; en it wuz mighty yard fer ter tell *wa't* kine er folks dey wuz.

"Atter two er th'ee hund'ed pounds er meat had be'n stol', Mars Walker call all de niggers up one eben', en tol' 'em dat de fus' nigger he cot stealin' bacon on dat plantation would git sump'n fer ter 'member it by long ez he lib'. En he say he'd gin fi' dollars ter de nigger w'at 'skiver' de rogue. Mars Walker say he s'picion one er two er de niggers, but he couldn' tell fer sho, en co'se dey all 'nied it w'en he 'cuse em un it.

"Dey wa'n't no bacon stole' fer a week er so, 'tel one dark night w'en somebody tuk a ham fum one er de smoke-'ouses. Mars Walker des cusst awful w'en he foun' out de ham wuz gone, en say he gwine ter sarch all de niggers' cabins; w'en dis yer Wiley I wuz tellin' yer 'bout up'n say he s'picion' who tuk de ham, fer he seed Dave comin' 'cross de plantation fum to'ds de smoke-'ouse de night befo'. W'en Mars Walker hearn dis fum Wiley, he went en sarch' Dave's cabin, en foun' de ham hid under de flo'.

"Eve'ybody wuz 'stonish'; but dere wuz de ham. Co'se Dave 'nied it ter de las', but dere wuz de ham. Mars Walker say it wuz des ez he 'spected: he didn' b'lieve in dese yer readin' en prayin' niggers; it wuz all 'pocrisy, en sarve' Mars Dugal' right fer 'lowin' Dave ter be readin' books w'en it wuz 'g'in' de law.

"W'en Mars Dugal' hearn 'bout de ham, he say he wuz might'ly 'ceived en disapp'inted in Dave. He say he wouldn' nebber hab no mo' conferdence in no nigger, en Mars Walker could do des ez he wuz a mineter wid Dave er any er de res' er de niggers. So Mars Walker tuk'n tied Dave up en gin 'im forty; en den he got some er dis yer wire clof w'at dey uses fer to make sifters out'n en tuk'n wrap' it roun' de ham en fasten it tergedder at de little een'. Den he tuk Dave down ter de blacksmif shop, en had Unker Silas, de plantation blacksmif, fasten a chain ter de ham, en den fasten de yuther een' er de chain roun' Dave's neck. En den he says ter Dave, sezee:

"'Now, suh, yer'll wear dat neckliss fer de nex' six mont's; en I 'spec's yer ner none er de yuther niggers on dis plantation won' steal no mo' bacon dyoin' er dat time.'

"Well, it des 'peared ez if fum dat time Dave didn' hab nuffin but trouble. De niggers all turnt ag'in 'im, caze he be'n de 'casion er Mars Dugal' turnin' 'em all ober ter Mars Walker. Mars Dugal' wa'n't a bad marster hisse'f, but Mars Walker wuz hard ez a rock. Dave kep' on sayin' he didn' take de ham, but none un 'em didn' b'lieve him.

"Dilsey wa'n't on de plantation w'en Dave wuz 'cused er stealin' de bacon. Ole Mist'iss had sont her ter town fer a week er so fer ter wait on one er her darters w'at had a young baby, en she didn' fine out nuffin' 'bout Dave's trouble 'tel she got back ter de plantation. Dave had patien'ly endyoed de finger er scawn, en all de hard words w'at de niggers pile' on 'im, caze he wuz sho' Dilsey would stan' by 'im, en wouldn' b'lieve he wuz a rogue, ner none er de yuther tales de darkies wuz tellin' 'bout 'im.

"W'en Dilsey come back fum town, en got down fum behine de buggy whar she b'en ridin' wid ole Mars, de fus' nigger 'ooman she met says ter her,

"'Is yer seed Dave, Dilsey?'

"'No, I ain' seed Dave,' says Dilsey.

"'Yer des oughter look at dat nigger; reckon yer wouldn' want 'im fer yo' junesey no mo'. Mars Walker cotch 'im stealin' bacon, en gone en fasten' a ham roun' his neck, so he can't git it off'n hisse'f. He sut'nly do look quare.' En den de 'ooman bus' out laffin' fit ter kill herse'f. W'en she got thoo laffin' she up'n tole Dilsey all 'bout de ham, en all de yuther lies w'at de niggers be'n tellin' on Dave.

"W'en Dilsey started down ter de quarters, who should she meet but Dave, comin' in fum de cotton-fiel'. She turnt her head ter one side, en purten' lack she didn' seed Dave.

" 'Dilsey!' sezee.

"Dilsey walk' right on, en didn' notice 'im.

" '*Oh,* Dilsey!'

"Dilsey didn' paid no 'tention ter 'im, en den Dave knowed some er de niggers be'n tellin' her 'bout de ham. He felt monst'us bad, but he 'lowed ef he could des git Dilsey fer ter listen ter 'im fer a minute er so, he could make her b'lieve he didn' stole de bacon. It wuz a week er two befo' he could git a chance ter speak ter her ag'in; but fine'ly he cotch her down by de spring one day, en sezee:

" 'Dilsey, w'at fer yer won' speak ter me, en purten' lack yer doan see me? Dilsey, yer knows me too well fer ter b'lieve I'd steal, er do dis yuther wick'ness de niggers is all layin' ter me—yer *knows* I wouldn' do dat, Dilsey. Yer ain' gwine back on yo' Dave, is yer?'

"But w'at Dave say didn' hab no 'fec' on Dilsey. Dem lies folks b'en tellin' her had p'isen her min' 'g'n Dave.

" 'I doan wanter talk ter no nigger,' says she, 'w'at be'n whip' fer stealin', en w'at gwine roun' wid such a lookin' thing ez dat hung roun' his neck. I's a 'spectable gal, *I* is. W'at yer call dat, Dave? Is dat a cha'm fer ter keep off witches, er is it a noo kine er neckliss yer got?'

"Po' Dave didn' knowed w'at ter do. De las' one he had 'pended on fer ter stan' by 'im had gone back on 'im, en dey didn' 'pear ter be nuffin mo' wuf libbin' fer. He couldn' hol' no mo' pra'r-meetin's, fer Mars Walker wouldn' low' 'im ter preach, en de darkies wouldn' a' listen' ter 'im ef he had preach'. He didn' eben hab his Bible fer ter comfort hisse'f wid, fer Mars Walker had tuk it erway fum 'im en burnt it up, en say ef he ketch any mo' niggers wid Bibles on de plantation, he'd do 'em wuss'n he done Dave.

"En ter make it still harder fer Dave, Dilsey tuk up wid Wiley. Dave could see him gwine up ter Aun' Mahaly's cabin, en settin' out on de bench in de moonlight wid Dilsey, en singin' sinful songs en playin' de banjer. Dave use' ter scrouch down behine de bushes, en wonder w'at de Lawd sen' 'im all dem tribberlations fer.

"But all er Dave's yuther troubles w'a'n't nuffin side er dat ham. He had wrap' de chain roun' wid a rag, so it didn' hurt his neck; but w'eneber he went ter wuk, dat ham would be in his way; he had ter do his task, how-somedever, des de same ez ef he didn' hab de ham. W'eneber he went ter lay down, dat ham would be in de way. Ef he turn ober in his sleep, dat ham would be tuggin' at his neck. It wuz de las' thing he seed at night, en de fus' thing he seed in de mawnin'. Wheneber he met a stranger, de ham would be de fus' thing de stranger would see. Most un 'em would 'mence' ter laf, en whareber Dave went he could see folks p'intin' at him, en year 'em sayin':

" 'W'at kine er collar dat nigger got roun' his neck?' er, ef dey knowed 'im, 'Is yer stole any mo' hams lately?' er 'W'at yer take fer yo' neckliss, Dave?'

"Fus' Dave didn' mine it so much, caze he knowed he hadn' done nuffin. But bimeby he got so he couldn' stan it no longer, en he'd hide hisse'f in de bushes w'eneber he seed anybody comin', en alluz kep' hisse'f shet up in his cabin atter he come in fum wuk.

"It wuz monst'us hard on Dave, en bimeby, w'at wid dat ham eberlastin' en eternally draggin' roun' his neck, he 'mence' fer ter do en say quare things, en make de niggers wonder ef he wa'n't gittin' out'n his mine. He got ter gwine roun' talkin' ter hisse'f, en singin' corn-shuckin' songs, en laffin' fit ter kill 'bout nuffin. En one day he tole one er de niggers he had 'skivered a noo way fer ter raise hams—gwine ter pick 'em off'm trees, en save de expense er smoke-'ouses by kyoin' 'em in de sun. En one day he up'n tole Mars Walker he got sump'n pertickler fer ter say ter 'im; en tole 'im he wuz gwine ter show 'im a place in de swamp whar dey wuz a whole trac' er lan' covered wid ham-trees.

"W'en Mars Walker hearn Dave talkin' dis kine er fool-talk, en w'en he seed how Dave wuz 'mencin' ter git behine in his wuk, en w'en he ax' de niggers en dey tole 'im how Dave be'n gwine on, he 'lowed he reckon' he 'd punish' Dave ernuff, en it mou't do mo' harm dan good fer ter keep de ham on his neck any longer. So he sont Dave down ter de blacksmifshop en had de ham tuk off. Dey wa'n't much er de ham lef' by dat time, fer de sun had melt all de fat, en de lean had all swivel' up, so dey wa'n't but th'ee er fo' poun's lef'.

"W'en de ham had be'n tuk off'n Dave, folks kinder stopped talkin' 'bout 'im so much. But de ham had be'n on his neck so long dat Dave had sorter got use' ter it. He look des lack he'd los' sump'n fer a day er so atter de ham wuz tuk off, en didn' 'pear ter know w'at ter do wid hisse'f; en fine'ly he up'n tuk'n tied a lighterd-knot ter a string, en hid it under de flo' er his cabin, en w'en nobody wuzn' lookin' he'd take it out en hang it roun' his neck, en go off in de woods en holler en sing; en he allus tied it roun' his neck w'en he went ter sleep. Fac', it 'peared Dave done gone clean out'n his mine. En atter a w'ile he got one er de quarest notions you eber hearn tell un. It wuz 'bout dat time dat I come back ter de plantation fer ter wuk—I had be'n out ter Mars Dugal's yuther place on Beaver Crick fer a mont' er so. I had hearn 'bout Dave en de bacon, en 'bout w'at wuz gwine on on de plantation; but I didn' b'lieve w'at dey all say 'bout Dave, fer I knowed Dave wa'n't dat kine er man. One day atter I come back, me'n Dave wuz choppin' cotton tergedder, w'en Dave lean' on his hoe, en motion' fer me ter come ober close ter 'im; en den he retch' ober en w'ispered ter me.

" 'Julius,' sezee, 'did yer knowed yer wuz wukkin' 'long yer wid a ham?'

"I couldn' 'magine w'at he meant. 'G'way frum yer, Dave,' says I. 'Yer ain' wearin' no ham no mo'; try en fergit 'bout dat; 't ain'gwine ter do yer no good fer ter 'member it.'

" 'Look a-year, Julius,' sezee, 'kin yer keep a secret?'

" 'Co'se I kin, Dave,' says I. 'I doan go roun' tellin' people w'at yuther folks says ter me.'

" 'Kin I trus' yer, Julius? Will yer cross yo' heart?'

"I cross my heart. 'Wush I may die ef I tells a soul,' says I.

"Dave look at me des lack he wuz lookin' thoo me en 'way on de yuther side er me, en sezee:

" 'Did yer knowed I wuz turnin' ter a ham, Julius?'

"I tried ter 'suade Dave dat dat wuz all foolishness, en dat he oughtn' ter be talkin' dat-a-way—hit wa'n't right. En I tole 'im ef he'd des be patien', de time would sho'ly come w'en eve'thing would be straighten' out, en folks would fine out who de rale rogue wuz w'at stole de bacon. Dave 'peared ter listen ter w'at I say, en promise' ter do better, en stop gwine on dat-a-way; en it seem lack he pick' up a bit w'en he seed dey wuz one pusson didn' b'lieve dem tales 'bout 'im.

"Hit wa'n't long atter dat befo' Mars Archie McIntyre, ober on de Wim'-b'le'ton road, 'mence' ter complain 'bout somebody stealin' chickens fum his hen-'ouse. De chickens kep' on gwine, en at las' Mars Archie tole de han's on his plantation dat he gwine ter shoot de fus' man he ketch in his hen-'ouse. In less'n a week atter he gin dis warnin', he cotch a nigger in de hen-'ouse, en fill' 'im full er squir'l-shot. W'en he got a light, he 'skivered it wuz a strange nigger; en w'en he call' one er his own sarven's, de nigger tole 'im it wuz our Wiley. W'en Mars Archie foun' dat out, he sont ober ter our plantation fer ter tell Mars Dugal' he had shot one er his niggers, en dat he could sen' ober dere en git w'at wuz lef' un 'im.

"Mars Dugal' wuz mad at fus'; but w'en he got ober dere an hearn how it all happen', he didn' hab much ter say. Wiley wuz shot so bad he wuz sho' he wuz gwine ter die, so he up'n says ter ole marster:

" 'Mars Dugal',' sezee, 'I knows I's be'n a monst'ous bad nigger, but befo' I go I wanter git sump'n off'n my mine. Dave didn' steal dat bacon w'at wuz tuk out'n de smoke-'ouse. *I* stole it all, en I hid de ham under Dave's cabin fer ter th'ow de blame on him—en may de good Lawd fergib me fer it.'

"Mars Dugal' had Wiley tuk back ter de plantation, en sont fer a doctor fer ter pick de shot out'n 'im. En de ve'y nex' mawnin' Mars Dugal' sont fer Dave ter come up ter de big house; he felt kinder sorry fer de way Dave had be'n treated. Co'se it wa'n't' no fault er Mars Dugal's but he wuz gwine

ter do w'at he could fer ter make up fer it. So he sont word down ter de
quarters fer Dave en all de yuther han's ter 'semble up in de yard befo' de
big house at sun-up nex' mawnin'.

"Yearly in de mawnin' de niggers all swarm' up in de yard. Mars Dugal'
wuz feelin' so kine dat he had brung up a bairl er cider, en tole de niggers
all fer ter he'p deyselves.

"All de han's on de plantation come but Dave; en bimeby, w'en it seem
lack he wa'n't comin', Mars Dugal' sont a nigger down ter de quarters ter
look fer 'im. De sun wuz gittin' up, en dey wuz a heap er wuk ter be done,
en Mars Dugal' sorter got ti'ed waitin'; so he up'n says:

" 'Well, boys en gals, I sont fer yer all up yer fer ter tell yer dat all
dat 'bout Dave's stealin' er de bacon wuz a mistake, ez I s'pose yer all done
hearn befo' now, en I's mighty sorry it happen'. I wants ter treat all my niggers
right, en I wants yer all ter know dat I sets a heap by all er my han's w'at
is hones' en smart. En I want yer all ter treat Dave des lack yer did befo'
dis thing happen', en mine w'at he preach ter yer; for Dave is a good nigger,
en has had a hard row ter hoe. En de fus' one I ketch sayin' anythin' 'g'in
Dave, I'll tell Mister Walker ter gin 'im forty. Now take ernudder drink er
cider all roun', en den git at dat cotton, fer I wanter git dat Persimmon Hill
trac' all pick' ober ter-day.'

"W'en de niggers wuz gwine 'way, Mars Dugal' tole me fer ter go en
hunt up Dave, en bring 'im up ter de house. I went down ter Dave's cabin,
but couldn' fine 'im dere. Den I look' roun' de plantation en in de aidge er
de woods, en 'long de road; but I couldn' fine no sign er Dave. I wuz 'bout
ter gin up de sarch, w'en I happen' fer ter run 'cross a foot-track w'at look'
lack Dave's. I has wukked 'long wid Dave so much dat I knowed his tracks:
he had a monst'us long foot, wid a holler instep, w'ich wuz sump'n skase
'mongs' black folks. So I followed dat track 'cross de fiel' fum de quarters
'tel I got ter de smoke-'ouse. De fus' thing I notice' wuz smoke comin' out'n
de cracks: it wuz cu'ous, caze dey hadn' be'n no hogs kill' on de plantation
fer six mont' er so, en all de bacon in de smoke-'ouse wuz done kyoed. I couldn'
'magine fer ter sabe my life w'at Dave wuz doin' in dat smoke-'ouse. I went
up ter de do' en hollered:

" 'Dave!'

"Dey didn' nobody answer. I didn' wanter open de do', fer w'ite folks
is monst'us pertickler 'bout dey smoke-'ouses; en ef de oberseah had a-come
up en cotch me in dere, he mou't not wanter b'lieve I wuz des lookin' fer
Dave. So I sorter knock at de do' en call' out ag'in:

" 'O Dave, hit's me—Julius! Doan be skeered. Mars Dugal' wants yer
ter come up ter de big house—he done 'skivered who stole de ham.'

"But Dave didn' answer. En w'en I look' roun' ag'in en didn' seed none
er his tracks gwine way fum de smoke-'ouse, I knowed he wuz in dere yit,
en I wuz 'termine' fer ter fetch 'im out; so I push de do' open en look in.

"Dey wuz a pile er bark burnin' in de middle er de flo', en right ober de fier, hangin' fum one er de rafters, wuz Dave; dey wuz a rope roun' his neck, en I didn' haf ter look at his face mo' d'n once fer ter see he wuz dead.

"Den I knowed how it all happen'. Dave had kep' on gittin' wusser en wusser in his mine, 'tel he des got ter b'lievin' he wuz all done turnt ter a ham' en den he had gone en built a fier, en tied a rope roun' his neck, des lack de hams wuz tied, en had hung hisse'f up in de smoke'ouse fer ter kyo.

"Dave wuz buried down by de swamp, in de plantation buryin'-groun'. Wiley didn' died fum de woun' he got in Mars McIntyre's hen-'ouse; he got well atter a w'ile, but Dilsey wouldn' hab nuffin mo' ter do wid 'im, en 't wa'n't long 'fo' Mars Dugal' sol' 'im ter a spekilater on his way souf—he say he didn' want no sich a nigger on de plantation, ner in de county, ef he could he'p it. En w'en de een' er de year come, Mars Dugal' turnt Mars Walker off, en run de plantation hisse'f atter dat.

"Eber sence den," said Julius in conclusion, "w'eneber I eats ham, it min's me er Dave. I lacks ham, but I nebber kin eat mo' d'n two er th'ee poun's befo' I gits ter studyin' 'bout Dave, en den I has ter stop en leab de res' fer ernudder time."

There was a short silence after the old man had finished his story, and then my wife began to talk to him about the weather, on which subject he was an authority. I went into the house. When I came out, half an hour later, I saw Julius disappearing down the lane, with a basket on his arm.

At breakfast, next morning, it occurred to me that I should like a slice of ham. I said as much to my wife.

"Oh, no, John," she responded, "you shouldn't eat anything so heavy for breakfast."

I insisted.

"The fact is," she said, pensively, "I couldn't have eaten any more of that ham, and I gave it to Julius."

The Marked Tree

I had been requested by my cousin, whose home was in Ohio, to find for him, somewhere in my own neighborhood in the pine belt of North Carolina, a suitable place for a winter residence. His wife was none too strong; his father, who lived with him, was in failing health; and he wished to save them from the raw lake winds which during the winter season take toll of those least fitted to resist their rigor. My relative belonged to the fortunate class of those who need take no thought today for tomorrow's needs. The dignity of labor is a beautiful modern theory, in which no doubt many of the sterner virtues find their root, but the dignity of ease was celebrated at least as long ago as the days of Horace, a gentlemen and philosopher, with some reputation as a poet.

Since my cousin was no lover of towns, and the term neighborhood is very elastic when applied to rural life, I immediately thought of an old, uncultivated—I was about to say plantation, but its boundaries had long since shrunk from those which in ante-bellum times would have justified so pretentious a designation. It still embraced, however, some fifteen or twenty acres of diversified surface—part sandhill, part meadow; part overgrown with scrubby shortleaf pines and part with a scraggy underbrush. Though the soil had been more or less exhausted by the wasteful methods of slavery, neglected grapevines here and there, and gnarled and knotted fruit trees, smothered by ruder growths about them, proved it to have been at one time in a high state of cultivation.

I had often driven by the old Spencer place, as it was called, from the name of the family whose seat it had been. It lay about five miles from my vineyard and was reached by a drive down the Wilmington Road and across the Mineral Spring swamp. Having brought with me to North Carolina a certain quickness of decision and promptness of action which the climate and *laissez faire* customs of my adopted state had not yet overcome, upon receipt of my cousin's letter I ordered old Julius to get out the gray mare and the rockaway and drive me over to the old Spencer place.

When we reached it, Julius left his seat long enough to take down the bars which guarded the entrance and we then drove up a short lane to the cleared space, surrounded by ragged oaks and elms, where the old plantation house had once stood. It had been destroyed by fire many years before and there were few traces of it remaining—a crumbling brick pillar here and there, on which the sills of the house had rested, and the dilapidated, ivy-draped lower half of a chimney, of which the yawning, blackened fireplace bore mute witness of the vanished generations which had lived and loved—and perchance suffered and died, within the radius of its genial glow.

Not far from where the house had stood, there was a broad oak stump, in a good state of preservation, except for a hole in the center, due, doubtless, to a rotten heart, in what had been in other respects a sound and perfect tree. I had seated myself upon the top of the stump—the cut had been made with the axe, almost as smoothly as though with a saw—when old Julius, who was standing near me, exclaimed, with some signs of concern,

"Excuse me, suh, I know you come from de No'th, but did any of yo' folks, way back yonder, come from 'roun' hyuh?"

"No," I returned, "they were New England Yankees, with no Southern strain whatever. But why do you ask?" I added, observing that he had something on his mind, and having often found his fancies quaint and amusing, from the viewpoint of one not Southern born.

"Oh, nothin', suh, leas'ways nothin' much—only I seed you settin' on dat ol' stump, an' I wuz kind er scared fer a minute."

"I don't see anything dangerous about the stump," I replied. "It seems to be a very well preserved oak stump."

"Oh, no, suh," said Julius, "dat ain' no oak stump."

It bore every appearance of an oak stump. The grain of the wood was that of oak. The bark was oak bark, and the spreading base held the earth in the noble grip of the king of trees.

"It is an oak, Julius—it is the stump of what was once a fine oak tree."

"Yas, suh, I know it 'pears like oak wood, an it 'pears like oak bahk, an' it looked like a oak tree w'en it wuz standin' dere, fifty feet high, fohty years ago. But it wa'n't—no, suh, it wa'n't."

"What kind of a tree was it, if not an oak?"

"It was a U-pass tree, suh; yes, sah, dat wuz de name of it—a U-pass tree."

"I have never heard of that variety," I replied.

"No, suh, it wuz a new kind er tree foun' hyuh. I nevah heard er any but dat one."

"Where did you get the name?" I asked.

"I got it from ol' Marse Aleck Spencer hisse'f, fohty years ago—fohty years ago, suh. I was lookin' at dat tree one day aftuh I'd heared folks talkin' 'bout it, an befo' it wuz cut down, an' ole Marse Aleck come erlong, an' sez I, 'Marse Aleck, dat is a monst'us fine oak tree.' An' ole Marse Aleck up an sez, sezee, 'No, Julius, dat ain' no oak tree—dat is a U-pass tree.' An'

I've 'membered the name evuh since, suh—de U-pass tree. Folks useter call it a' oak tree, but Marse Aleck oughter a knowd; it 'us his tree, an' he had libbed close to it all his life.''

It was evident that the gentleman referred to had used in a figurative sense the name which Julius had remembered so literally—the Upas tree, the fabled tree of death. I was curious to know to what it owed this sinister appellation. It would be easy, I knew, as it afterwards proved, to start the old man on a train of reminiscence concerning the family and the tree. How much of it was true I cannot say; I suspected Julius at times of a large degree of poetic license—he took the crude legends and vague superstitions of the neighborhood and embodied them in stories as complete, in their way, as the Sagas of Iceland or the primitive tales of ancient Greece. I have saved a few of them. Had Julius lived in a happier age for men of his complexion the world might have had a black Aesop or Grimm or Hoffman—as it still may have, for who knows whether our civilization has yet more than cut its milk teeth, or humanity has even really begun to walk erect?

Later in the day, in the cool of the evening, on the front piazza, left dark because of the mosquitoes, except for the light of the stars, which shone with a clear, soft radiance, Julius told my wife and me his story of the old Spencer oak. His low, mellow voice rambled on, to an accompaniment of night-time sounds—the deep diapason from a distant frog-pond, the shrill chirp of the cicada, the occasional bark of a dog or cry of an owl, all softened by distance and merging into a melancholy minor which suited perfectly the teller and the tale.

"Marse Aleck Spencer uster be de riches' man in all dis neighborhood. He own' two thousan' acres er lan'—de ole place ovuh yonduh is all dat is lef'. Dere wus ovuh a hund'ed an' fifty slaves on de plantation. Marse Aleck was a magist'ate an' a politician, an' eve'ybody liked him. He kep' open house all de time, an' had company eve'y day in de yeah. His hosses wuz de fastes' an' his foxhounds de swiftes', his gamecocks de fierces', an' his servants de impidentes' in de county. His wife wuz de pretties' an' de proudes' lady, an' wo' de bes' clo's an' de mos' finguh-rings, an' rid in de fines' carriage. Fac', dey alluz had de best er eve'ything, an' nobody didn' 'spute it wid 'em.

"Marse Aleck's child'en wuz de apples er his eye—dere wuz a big fambly—Miss Alice an' Miss Flora, an' young Marse Johnny, an' den some yeahs latuh, little Marse Henry an' little Marse Tom, an' den dere wuz ol' Mis' Kathu'n, Marse Aleck's wife, an' de child'en's mammy.

"When young Marse Johnny was bawn, and Aunt Dasdy, who had nussed all de child'en put de little young marster in his pappy's arms, Marse Aleck wuz de happies' man in de worl'; for it wuz his fus' boy, an' he had alluz wanted a boy to keep up de fambly name an' de fambly rep'tation. An' eve'-ybody on de plantation sheered his joy, fer when de marster smile, it's sunshine, an' when de marster frown, it's cloudy weather.

"When de missis was well enough, an' de baby was ol' enough, de christenin' come off; an' nothing would do fer Marse Aleck but to have it under de fambly tree—dat wuz de stump of it ovuh yundah, suh, dat you was settin' on dis mawnin'.

" 'Dat tree,' said Marse Aleck, 'wuz planted when my great-gran'daddy wuz bawn. Under dat tree eve'y fus'-bawn er dis fambly since den has be'n christen'. Dis fambly has growed an' flourish' wid dat tree, an' now dat my son is bawn, I wants ter hab him christen' under it, so dat he kin grow an' flourish 'long wid it. An' dis ole oak'—Marse Aleck useter 'low it wuz a oak, befo' he give it de new name—'dis ole oak is tall an' stout an' strong. It has weathe'd many a sto'm. De win' can't blow it down, an' de lightnin' ain't nevuh struck it, an' nothin' but a prunin' saw has ever teched it, ner ever shill, so long as dere is a Spencer lef' ter pertec' it.

" 'An' so my son John, my fus'-bawn, is gwineter grow up tall an' strong, an' be a big man an' a good man; an' his child'en and his child'ens child'en an' dem dat follers shall be as many as de leaves er dis tree, an' dey shill keep de name er Spencer at de head er de roll as long as time shall las'.'

"De same day Marse John wuz bawn, which wuz de fu'st er May— anudder little boy, a little black boy, wuz bawn down in de quahtahs. De mammy had worked 'roun' de big house de yeah befo', but she had give 'er mist'iss some impidence one day, an' 'er mist'iss had made Marse Aleck sen' her back ter de cotton-fiel'. An' when little Marse Johnny wuz christen', Phillis, dis yuther baby's mammy, wuz standin' out on de edge, 'long wid de yuther fiel'-han's, fuh dey wuz all 'vited up ter take part, an' ter eat some er de christenin' feas'. Whils' de white folks wuz eatin' in de house, de cullud folks all had plenty er good things pass 'roun' out in de yahd—all dey could eat an' all dey could drink, fuh dem wuz de fat yeahs er de Spencers—an' all famblies, like all folks, has deir fat yeahs an' deir lean yeahs. De lean yeahs er de Spencers wuz boun' ter come sooner er later.

"Little Marse Johnny growed an' flourish' just like the fambly tree had done, an' in due time growed up to be a tall an' straight an' smart young man. But as you sca'cely evuh sees a tree widout a knot, so you nevuh sees a man widout his faults. Marse Johnny wuz so pop'lar and went aroun' so much wid his frien's that he tuck ter drinkin' mo' dan wuz good for him. Southe'n gent'emen all drunk them days, suh—nobody had never dremp' er dis yer foolishness 'bout pro'bition dat be'n gwine roun' er late yeahs. But as a gin'ral rule, dey drunk like gent'emen—er else dey could stan' mo' liquor dan folks kin dese days. An' young Marse Johnny had a mighty quick temper, which mo' d'n once got 'im inter quarrels which it give 'im mo' or less trouble to make up.

"Marse Johnny wuz mighty fond er de ladies, too, an' wuz de pet of 'em all. But he wuz jus' passin' de time wid 'em, 'tel he met Miss Mamie Imboden—de daughter er de Widder Imboden, what own' a plantation down

on Rockfish. Ole Mis' Imboden didn' spen' much time on huh place, but lef'
it tuh a overseah, whils' she an' Miss Mamie wuz livin' in de big towns, er
de wat'rin'-places, er way up yonduh in de No'th, whar you and' yo' lady
come f'um.

"When de Widder Imboden come home one winter wid huh daughter,
Marse Johnny fell dead in lub wid Miss Mamie. He couldn' ha'dly eat ner
sleep fuh a week or so, an' he jus' natch'ly couldn' keep 'way f'um Rockfish,
an' jus' wo' out Marse Aleck's ridin' hosses comin' an' goin', day, night an'
Sunday. An' wharevuh she wuz visitin' he'd go visitin'; an' when she went
tuh town he'd go tuh town. An' Marse Johnny got mo' religious dan he had
evuh be'n befo' an' went tuh de Prisbyte'ian Chu'ch down tuh Rockfish reg'lar.
His own chu'ch wuz 'Piscopal, but Miss Imboden wuz a Prisbyte'ian.

"But Marse Johnny wa'n't de only one. Anudder young gent'eman, Marse
Ben Dudley, who come f'um a fine ole fambly, but wuz monst'us wild an'
reckless, was payin' co't tuh Miss Mamie at de same time, an' it was nip
an' tuck who should win out. Some said she favored one, and some said de
yuther, an' some 'lowed she didn' knowed w'ich tuh choose.

"Young Marse Johnny kinder feared fuh a while dat she like de yuther
young gent'eman bes'. But one day Marse Ben's daddy, ole Marse Amos Dudley, went bankrup', an' his plantation an' all his slaves wuz sol', an' he shot
hisse'f in de head, and young Marse Ben wuz lef' po'. An' bein' too proud
tuh wuk, an' havin' no relations ter live on, he tuck ter bettin' an' dicin' an'
kyard-playin', an' went on jes scan'lous. An' it wuz soon whispered 'roun'
dat young Mistah Dudley wuz livin' on his winnin's at kyards, an' dat he
wa'n't partic'lar who he played wid, er whar er how he played. But I is ahead
er my tale, fuh all dis hyuh 'bout Marse Ben happen' after Marse Johnny
had cut Marse Ben out an' ma'ied Miss Mamie.

"Ole Marse Aleck wuz monst'us glad when he heared Marse Johnny wuz
gwineter git ma'ied, for he wanted de fambly kep' up, an' he 'lowed Marse
Johnny needed a wife fuh tuh he'p stiddy him. An' Miss Mamie wuz one
of dese hyuh sweet-nachu'd, kin'-hearted ladies dat noboddy could he'p lovin'.
An' mo'over, Miss Mamie's Mammy wuz rich, an' would leave huh well off
some day.

"Fuh de lean yeahs er de Spencers wuz comin', an' Marse Aleck 'spicioned
it. De cotton crop had be'n po' de yeah befo', de cawn had be'n wuss, glanders
had got in de hosses an' most of 'em had had ter be killed; an' old Marse
Aleck wuz mo' sho't of money dan he'd be'n fur a long, long time. An' when
he tried tuh make it up by spekilatin', he jus' kep' on losin' mo' an' mo' an'
mo'.

"But young Marse Johnny had ter hab money for his weddin', an' the
house had to be fix' up fuh 'im an' his wife, an' dere had ter be a rich weddin'
present an' a fine infair, an' all dem things cos' money. An' sence he didn'

wanter borry de money, Marse Aleck 'lowed he s'posed he'd hafter sell one er his han's. An' ole Mis' Spencer say he should sell Phillis's Isham. Marse Aleck didn' wanter sell Isham, fur he 'membered Isham wuz de boy dat wuz bawn on de same day Marse Johnny wuz. But ole Mis' Spencer say she didn' like dat boy's looks nohow, an' dat his mammy had be'n impident tuh huh one time, an' ef Marse Aleck gwine sell anybody he sh'd sell Isham.

"Prob'bly ef ole Marse Aleck had knowed jus' what wuz gwineter happen he mought not 'a' sol' Isham—he'd 'a' ruther gone inter debt, er borried de money. But den nobody nevuh knows what's gwineter happen; an' what good would it do 'em ef dey did? It'd only make 'em mizzable befo' han', an' ef it wuz gwineter happen, how could dey stop it? So Marse Aleck wuz bettuh off dan ef he had knowed.

"Now, dis hyuh Isham had fell in love, too, wid a nice gal on de plantation, an' wuz jus' 'bout makin' up his min' tuh ax Marse Aleck tuh let 'im marry her an' tuh give 'em a cabin tuh live in by deyse'ves, when one day Marse Aleck tuck Isham ter town, an' sol' 'im to another gent'eman, fuh tuh git de money fuh de expenses er his own son's weddin'.

"Isham's mammy wuz workin' in de cotton-fiel' way ovuh at de fah end er de plantation dat day, an' when she went home at night an' foun' dat Marse Aleck had sol' huh Isham, she run up to de big house an' wep' an hollered an' went on terrible. But Marse Aleck tol' huh it wuz all right, dat Isham had a good marster, an' wa'n't many miles erway, an' could come an' see his mammy whenevuh he wanter.

"When de young ma'aid folks came back f'm dey weddin' tower, day had de infair, an' all de rich white folks wuz invited. An' dat same night, whils' de big house wuz all lit up, an' de fiddles wuz goin' an' dere wuz eatin' an' drinkin' an' dancin' an' sky-larkin' an' eve'ybody wuz jokin' de young couple an' wushin' 'em good luck, Phillis wuz settin' all alone in huh cabin, way at de fah end er de quarters, studyin' 'bout huh boy, who had be'n sol' to pay for it all. All de other cullud folks wuz up 'roun' de big house, some waitin' on de white folks, some he'pin' in de kitchen, some takin' keer er de guests' hosses, an' de res' swa'min' 'roun' de yahd, gittin' in one anudder's way, an' waitin' 'tel de white folks got th'oo so dey could hab somethin' tuh eat too; fuh Marse Aleck had open' de big blade, an' wanted eve'ybody to have a good time.

" 'Bout time de fun wuz at de highes' in de big house, Phillis heared somebody knockin' at huh cabin do'. She didn' know who it could be, an' bein' as dere wa'n't nobody e'se 'roun', she sot still an' didn' say nary word. Den she heared somebody groan, an' den dere wuz anudder knock, a feeble one dis time, an' den all wuz still.

"Phillis wait' a minute, an' den crack' de do', so she could look out, an' dere wuz somebody layin' all crumple' up on de do'-step. An' den somethin' wahned huh what it wuz, an' she fetched a lighterd to'ch f'um de ha'th. It wuz huh son Isham. He wuz wownded an' bleedin'; his feet wuz so' wid wal-kin'; he wuz weak from loss er blood.

"Phillis pick' Isham up an' laid 'im on huh bed an' run an' got some whiskey an' give 'im a drap, an' den she helt camphire tuh his nost'ils, mean-while callin' his name an' gwine on like a wild 'oman. An' bimeby he open' his eyes an' look' up an' says—'I'se come home, mammy,'—an' den died. Dem wuz de only words he spoke, an' he nevuh drawed anudder bref.

"It come tuh light nex' day, when de slave-ketchers come aftuh Isham wid deir dawgs an' deir guns, dat he had got in a 'spute wid his marster, an' had achully *hit his marster!* An' realizin' what he had done, he had run erway; natch'ly to'ds his mammy an' de ole plantation. Dey had wounded 'im an' had mos' ketched him, but he had 'scaped ag'in an' had reach' home just in time tuh die in his mammy's ahms.

"Phillis laid Isham out wid her own han's—dere wa'n't nobody dere tuh he'p her, an' she didn' want no he'p nohow. An' when it wuz all done, an' she had straighten' his lim's an' fol' his han's an' close his eyes, an' spread a sheet ovuh him, she shut de do' sof'ly and stahted up ter de big house.

"When she drawed nigh, de visituhs wuz gittin' ready tuh go. De servants wuz bringin' de hosses an' buggies an' ca'iges 'roun', de white folks wuz laffin' an' gwine on an' sayin' good-by. An' whils' Phillis wuz standin' back behin' a bunch er rosebushes in de yahd, listenin' an' waitin', ole Marse Aleck come out'n de house wid de young couple an' stood unduh de ole fambly tree. He had a glass er wine in his han', an' a lot er de yuthers follered:

" 'Frien's,' says he, 'drink a toas' wid me tuh my son an' his lady, hyuh under dis ole tree. May it last anudder hund'ed yeahs, an' den anudder, an' may it fetch good luck tuh my son an' his wife, an' tuh deir child'en an' deir child'en's child'en.'

"De toas' wuz drunk, de gues's depahted; de slaves went back tuh de quahtuhs, an' Phillis went home tuh huh dead boy.

"But befo' she went, she *marked de Spencer tree!*

"Young Marse Johnny an' his wife got 'long mighty well fuh de fust six mont's er so, an' den trouble commence' betwix' 'em. Dey wuz at a pahty one night, an' young Marse Johnny seen young Marse Ben Dudley talking in a cawnuh wid Miss Mamie. Marse Johnny wuz mighty jealous-natu'ed, an' didn' like dis at all. Endoyin' de same evenin' he overheard somebody say that Miss Mamie had th'owed Marse Ben ovuh beca'se he was po' an' married Marse Johnny beca'se he wuz rich. Marse Johnny didn' say nothin', but he kep' studyin' an' studyin' 'bout dese things. An' it didn' do him no good to let his min' run on 'em.

"Marse Ben Dudley kep' on gwine from bad ter wuss, an' one day Marse Johnny foun' a letter from Marse Ben in his wife's bureau drawer.

" 'You used ter love me,' says Marse Ben in dis hyuh letter—'you know you did, and you love me yit—I know you does. I am in trouble. A few hun'ed dollahs'll he'p me out. Youer totin' mo' d'n dat 'roun' on yo' pretty little fingers. Git the money fuh me—it'll save my honor an' my life. I swear I'll pay it back right soon.'

"Den all Marse Johnny's jealousy b'iled up at once, an' he seed eve'ything red. He went straight to Miss Mamie an' shuck de lettuh in her face an' 'cused her er gwine on wid Marse Ben. Co'se she denied it. Den he ax' huh what had become er huh di'mon' 'gagement ring dat he had give huh befo' dey wuz ma'ied.

"Miss Mamie look' at huh han' an' turn' white as chalk, fer de ring wa'n't dere.

" 'I tuk it off las' night, when I went tuh bed, an' lef' it on de bureau, an' I fuhgot tuh put it on dis mawnin.'

"But when she look' fer it on de bureau it wuz gone. Marse Johnny swo' she had give' it tuh Marse Ben, an' she denied it tuh de las'. He showed her de letter. She said she hadn' answered it, an' hadn' meant to answer it, but had meant to bu'n it up. One word led to another. Dere wuz a bitter quarrel, an' Marse Johnny swo' he'd never speak to his wife ag'in 'tel de di'mond ring wuz foun'. An' he didn'.

"Ole Marse Aleck wuz 'way from home dat winter, to congress or de legislator, or somewhar, an' Marse Johnny wuz de boss er de plantation whils' he wuz gone. He wuz busy all day, on de plantation, or in his office, er in town. He tuck moster his meals by hisself, an' when he et wid Miss Mamie he manage' so as nevuh to say nothin'. Ef she spoke, he purten' not to hear her, an' so she didn' try mo' d'n once er twice. Othe'wise, he alluz treated her like a lady—'bout a mile erway.

"Miss Mamie tuck it mighty ha'd. Fuh she was tenduh as well as proud. She jus' moped an' pined erway. One day in de springtime, when Marse Johnny wuz in town all day, she wuz tuk ill sudden, an' her baby wuz bawn, long befo' its time. De same day one er de little black child'en clum up in de ole Spencer tree an' fetch' down a jaybird's nes', an' in de nes' dey foun' Miss Mamie's ring, whar de jaybird had stole it an' hid it. When Marse Johnny come home dat night he found his wife an' his chile bofe dead, an' de ring on Miss Mamie's finger.

"Well, suh, you nevuh seed a man go on like Marse Johnny did; an' folks said dat ef he could 'a' foun' Marse Ben Dudley he sho' would 'a' shot him; but lucky fer Marse Ben he had gone away. Aftuh de fune'al Marse Johnny shet hisse'f up in his room fer two er three days; an' as soon as Marse Aleck come home, Marse Johnny j'ind de ahmy an' went an' fit in de Mexican Wah an' wuz shot an' kill'.

"Ole Marse Aleck wuz so' distress' by dese yer troubles, an' grieve' might'ly over de loss er his fus' bawn son. But he got ovuh it after a while. Dere wuz still Marse Henry an' Marse Tom, bofe un' 'em good big boys, ter keep up de name, an' Miss Alice an' Miss Flora who wuz bofe ma'ied an' had child'en, ter see dat de blood didn' die out. An' in spite er dis hyuh thievin' jaybird, nobody 'lowed dat de ole tree had anything ter do wid Marse Johnny's troubles, fer co'se nobody but Phillis knowed dat it had evuh been mark'.

"But dis wuz only de beginnin'.

"Next year, in the spring, Miss Alice, Marse Aleck's oldes' daughter, wuz visitin' the fambly wid her nuss an' chile—she had ma'ied sev'al yeahs befo' Marse Johnny—an' one day de nuss wuz settin' out in de yahd, wid de chile, under de ole tree, when a big pizen spider let hisse'f down from a lim' when de nuss wa'n't lookin', an' stung the chile. The chile swoll up, an' dey sent fer de doctuh, but de doctuh couldn' do nothin', an' the baby died in spasms dat same night, an' de mammy went inter a decline f'um grief an' died er consumption inside er six mont's.

"Of co'se de tree wuz watched close fer spiders aftah dis, but none er de white folks thought er blamin' de tree—a spider mought 'a' come from de ceilin' er from any other tree; it wuz jes' one er dem things dat couldn' be he'ped. But de servants commence' ter whisper 'mongs' deyse'ves dat de tree wuz conju'ed an' dere'd be still mo' trouble from it.

"It wa'n't long coming. One day young Marse Henry, de nex' boy ter Marse Johnny, went fishin' in de ribber, wid one er de naber boys, an' he clumb out too fah on a log, an' tip' de log up, an' fell in de ribber an' got drownded. Nobody could see how de ole tree wuz mix' up wid little Marse Henry's drowndin,' 'tel one er de house servants 'membered he had seed de boys diggin' bait in de shade er de ole tree. An' whils' they didn' say nothin' ter de white folks, leas'-ways not jes' den, dey kep' it in min' an' waited tuh see what e'se would happen. Dey didn' know den dat Phillis had mark' de tree, but dey mo' den half s'picioned it.

"Sho' 'nuff, one day de nex' fall, Miss Flora, Marse Aleck's secon' daughter, who wuz ma'ied an' had a husban', come home to visit her folks. An' one day whils' she wuz out walkin' wid her little boy, a sto'm come up, an it stahted ter rain, an' dey didn' hab no umbreller an' wuz runnin' ter de house, when jes' as dey got under de ole tree, de lightnin' struck it, broke a limb off'n de top, skun a little strip off'n de side all de way down, an' jump off an' hit Miss Flora an' de boy, an' killt 'em bofe on de spot—dey didn' have time ter draw anudder bref.

"Still de white folks didn' see nuthin' wrong wid de tree. But by dis time de cullud folks all knowed de tree had b'en conju'd. One un 'em said somethin' 'bout it one day ter old Marse Aleck, but he tol' 'em ter go 'long wid deir foolishness; dat it wuz de will er God; dat de lightnin' mought's well 'a' struck any yuther tree dey'd b'en under as dat one; an' dat dere wouldn' be no danger in de future, fer lightnin' nebber struck twice in de same place nohow.

"It wuz 'bout a yeah after dat befo' anything mo' happen', an' de cullud folks 'lowed dat mo' likely dey had be'n mistaken an' dat maybe de tree hadn' be'n mark', er e'se de goopher wuz all wo' off, when one day little Marse Tom, de only boy dat wuz lef', wuz ridin' a new hoss Marse Aleck had give 'im, when a rabbit jump 'cross de road in front er him, an' skeered dis hyuh young hoss, an' de hoss run away an' thowed little Marse Tom up 'gins' de ole Spencer tree, an' bu'st his head in an' killt 'im.

"Marse Aleck wuz 'mos' heartbroken, fer Marse Tom wuz de only son he had lef'; dere wa'n't none er his child'en lef' now but Miss Alice, whose husban' had died, an' who had come wid her little gal ter lib wid her daddy and mammy.

"But dere wuz so much talk 'bout de ole tree 'tel it fin'lly got ter ole Mis' Kathu'n's yeahs, an' she tol' Marse Aleck. He didn' pay no 'tention at fu'st, jes' 'lowed it 'uz all foolishness. But he kep' on hearin' so much of it, dat bimeby he wuz 'bleege' ter listen. An' he fin'lly 'lowed dat whether de tree was conju'd or not, it had never brought nuthin' but bad luck evuh sence Marse Johnny's weddin', an' he made up his min' ter git rid of it, in hopes er changin' de fambly luck.

"So one day he ordered a couple er han's ter come up ter de house wid axes an' cut down de ole tree. He tol' 'em jes' how ter chop it, one on one side an' one on de yuther, so's ter make it fall a partic'lar way. He stood off ter one side, wid his head bowed down, 'tel de two cuts had 'mos' met, an' den de tu'ned his eyes away, fer he didn' wanter see de ole tree fall— it had meant so much ter him fer so long. He heared de tree commence crackin', an' he heared de axemen holler, but he didn' know dey wuz hollerin' at him, an' he didn' look 'roun'—he didn' wanter see de ole Spencer tree fall. But stidder fallin' as he had meant it ter, an' as by rights it couldn' he'p fallin', it jes' twisted squar' 'roun' sideways to'ds ole Marse Aleck an' ketched 'im befo' he could look up, an' crushed 'im ter de groun'.

"Well, dey buried Marse Aleck down in de fambly buryin'-groun'—you kin see it over at de ole place, not fur from de house; it's all growed up now wid weeds an' briars, an' most er de tombstones is fell down and covered wid green moul'. It wuz already pretty full, an' dere wa'n't much room lef'. After de fune'al, de ole tree wuz cut up inter firewood an' piled up out in de yard.

"Ole Mis' Kathu'n an' her daughter, Miss Alice, an' Miss Alice's little gal, went inter mo'nin' an' stayed home all winter.

"One col' night de houseboy toted in a big log f'um de old Spencer tree, an' put it on de fire, an' when ole Mis' Kathu'n an' her daughter an' her gran'daughter went to bed, dey lef' de log smoulderin' on de ha'th. An' 'long 'bout midnight, when eve'ybody wuz soun' asleep, dis hyuh log fell out'n de fireplace an' rolled over on de flo' an' sot de house afire an' bu'nt it down ter de groun', wid eve'ybody in it.

"Dat, suh, wuz de end er de Spencer fambly. De house wuz nebber rebuil'. De war come erlong soon after, an' nobody had no money no mo' ter buil' houses. De lan', or what little wuz lef' after de mo'gages an' de debts wuz paid off, went ter dis hyuh young gent'eman, Mistuh Brownlow, down to Lumberton, who wuz some kinder fo'ty-secon' cousin er nuther, an' I reckon he'd be only too glad ter sell it."

I wrote to young Mr. Brownlow, suggesting an appointment for an interview. He replied that he would call on me the following week, at an hour stated, if he did not hear from me beforehand that some other time would be more convenient.

I awaited him at the appointed hour. He came in the morning and stayed to luncheon. He was willing to sell the old place and we agreed upon a price at which it was to be offered to my cousin.

He was a shallow, amiable young fellow, unmarried, and employed as a clerk in a general store. I told him the story of the Spencer oak, as related by old Julius. He laughed lightly.

"I believe the niggers did have some sort of yarn about the family and the old tree," he said, "but of course it was all their silly superstition. They always would believe any kind of foolishness their crazy imaginations could cook up. Well, sir, let me know when you hear from your friend. I reckon I'll drive past the old place on my way home, and take a last look at it, for the sake of the family, for it was a fine old family, and it was a pity the name died out."

An hour later there was an agitated knock at my library door. When I opened it old Julius was standing there in a state of great excitement.

"What is the matter, Julius?"

"It's done gone an' happen', suh, it's done gone an' happen'!"

"What has done gone and happened?"

"De tree, suh, de U-pass tree—de ole Spencer tree."

"Well, what about it?"

"Young Mistuh Brownlow lef' here an' went ovuh tuh de old place, an' sot down on de ole stump, an' a rattlesnake come out'n de holler an' stung 'im, an' killt 'im, suh. He's layin' ovuh dere now, all black in de face and swellin' up fas'."

I closed my deal for the property through Mr. Brownlow's administrator. My cousin authorized me to have the land cleared off, preparatory to improving it later on. Among other things, I had the stump of the Spencer oak extracted. It was a difficult task even with the aid of explosives, but was finally accomplished without casualty, due perhaps to the care with which I inquired into the pedigree of the workmen, lest perchance among them there might be some stray offshoot of this illustrious but unfortunate family.

The Dumb Witness

The old Murchison place was situated on the Lumberton plank road only about two miles from my vineyard on the North Carolina sandhills. Old Julius, our colored coachman, had driven me over one spring morning to see young Murchison, the responsible manager of the property, about some walnut timber I wished to purchase from him for shipment. I had noticed many resources of the country that the easy-going Southerners had not thought of developing; and I took advantage of them when I found it convenient and profitable to do so.

We entered the lane leading to the house by passing between two decaying gateposts. This entrance had evidently once possessed some pretensions to elegance, for the massive posts had been faced with dressed lumber and finished with ornamental tops, some fragments of which still remained, and the one massive hinge, hanging by a slender rust-eaten nail, had been wrought into a fantastic shape. As we drove through the gateway, a green lizard scampered down from the top of one of the posts, where he had been sunning himself, and a rattlesnake lying in the path lazily uncoiled himself and, sounding his rattle the meanwhile, wriggled slowly off into the rank grass and weeds.

The house stood well back from the road, on the crest of one of the regular undulations of the sandhill country. It was partly concealed, when approached from the road, by intervening trees and shrubbery, which had once formed a well-ordered pleasaunce, but now grew in wild and tangled profusion, so that it was difficult to distinguish one bush or tree from another. The lane itself was partially overgrown, and the mare's fetlocks swept the dew from the grass, where it had not yet been dried by the morning sun.

As we drew nearer, the house stood clearly revealed. It was apparently of more ancient date than any I had seen in the neighborhood. It was a large two-story frame house, built in the colonial style, with a low-pitched roof, and a broad piazza along the front, running the full length of both stories and supported by huge round columns, and suggesting distantly, in its general effect, the portico of a Greek temple. The roof had sunk on one side, and the shingles were old and cracked and moss-grown, while several of the windows in the upper part of the house were boarded up, and others filled with sash from which the glass had apparently long since been broken.

For a space of several rods on each side of the house the ground was bare of grass and shrubbery, and scarcely less forbidding than the road we had traveled. It was rough and uneven, lying in little hillocks and hollows, as though it had been dug over at hazard, or explored by some vagrant drove of hogs.

A casual glance might have led one to believe the place untenanted, so lonely and desolate did it seem. But as we approached we became aware of two figures on the long piazza. At one end, in a massive armchair of carved oak, was seated a man, apparently an old man, for he was bent and wrinkled. His long white hair hung down upon his shoulders, and his face was of a high-bred and strongly marked type. His eyes were turned toward the opposite end of the piazza, where a woman was seated in a splint-bottomed chair. She seemed but little younger than the man, and the face was enough like his to suggest that they were related in some degree, unless this fact were negatived by the woman's complexion, the hue of which disclosed a strong infusion of the blood of a darker race. She wore a homespun frock and a muslin cap and sat bolt upright, with her hands folded on her lap, looking toward her vis-a-vis at the other end of the piazza.

As we drew up a short distance from the door, the old man rose, as we supposed, to come forward and greet us. But, instead of stopping at the steps and turning his face outward, he continued his course to the other end of the piazza and halted before the woman.

"Viney," he said, in a sharply imperative voice, "my uncle says you will tell me where he put the papers. I am tired of this nonsense, I insist upon knowing immediately."

The woman made no reply, but her faded eyes seemed to glow for a moment, like the ashes of a dying fire fanned by some breath of air.

"Why do you not answer me?" he continued, with increasing vehemence. "I tell you I insist upon knowing. It is imperative that I should know, and know at once. My interests are suffering for every day's delay. The papers—where are the papers?"

Still the woman sat silent, though her figure seemed to stiffen as she leaned slightly toward him. He grew visibly more impatient at her silence, and began to threaten her.

"Tell me immediately, you hussy, or you will have reason to regret it. You take liberties that cannot be permitted. I will not put up with it," he said, shaking his fist as he spoke. "I shall have to have you whipped."

The slumbrous fire in the woman's eyes flamed up for a moment. She rose from her seat, and drawing herself up to her full height—she was a tall woman, though bowed somewhat with years—began to speak, I thought at first in some foreign tongue. But after a moment I knew that no language or dialect, at least none of European origin, could consist of such a discordant jargon, such a meaningless cacophony as that which fell from the woman's lips. And as she went on, pouring out a flood of sounds that were not words, and which yet seemed now and then vaguely to suggest words, as clouds suggest the shapes of mountains and trees and strange beats, the old man seemed to bend like a reed before a storm, and began to expostulate, accompanying his words with deprecatory gestures.

"Yes, Viney, good Viney," he said in soothing tones, "I know it was wrong, and I've always regretted it—always from the day I did it. But you shouldn't bear malice, Viney, it isn't Christian. The Bible says you should bless them that curse you, and do good to them that despitefully use you. But I was good to you before, Viney, and I was good to you afterwards, and I know you have forgiven me—good Viney, noble-hearted Viney!—and you are going to tell me. Now, *do* tell me where the papers are," he added, pleadingly, offering to take her hand, which lay on the arm of the chair.

She drew her hand away, as she muttered something in the same weird tones she had employed before. The old man bent toward her, in trembling eagerness, but seemed disappointed.

"Try again, Viney," he said, "that's a good girl. Your old master thinks a great deal of you, Viney. He is your best friend."

Again she made an inarticulate response. He seemed to comprehend, and turning from her, came down the steps, muttering to himself, took up a spade that stood at one end of the steps, passed by us without seeming conscious of our presence, and hastening with tottering footsteps to one side of the yard began digging furiously.

I had been so much interested in this curious drama that I had forgotten for the time being the business that brought me there. The old woman, however, when the man had gone, rose from her seat and went into the house without giving us more than a look.

"What's the matter with them, Julius?" I said, returning with a start to the world of reality.

The old man pointed to his head.

"Dey's bofe 'stracted, suh," he said, "out'n dey min'. Dey's be'n dat-a-way fer yeahs an' yeahs."

At that moment the young man of the house came out to the door, and greeted us pleasantly. He asked me to alight from the carriage and led me to the chair the old man had occupied. It was a massive oak affair, with carved arms and back and a wooden seat, and looked as though it might be of ancient make, perhaps an heirloom. I found young Murchison was a frank and manly young fellow, and quite capable of looking out for his own interests. I struck a bargain with him, on terms that were fair to both. When I had concluded my business and invited him to call and see me sometime, I got into the carriage, and Julius drove down the lane and out into the road again. In going out, we passed near the old man, who was still muttering to himself and digging rapidly, but with signs of weariness. He did not look up as we went by, but seemed entirely-absorbed in his strange pursuit.

In the evening, after supper, Julius came up to the house. We sat out on the porch, my wife and her sister and Julius and I. We cut a large watermelon, and when Julius had eaten the half we gave to him, he told us the story of old man Murchison's undoing. The air was cool, the sky was clear, the stars shone with a brightness unknown in higher latitudes. The voices of the night came faintly from the distant woods, and there could have been no more romantic setting for the story of jealousy, revenge and disappointment which the old white-haired Negro told us, in his own quaint dialect—a story of things possible only in an era which, happily, has passed from our history, as, in God's own time—and may it be soon!—it will from all the earth. Some of the facts in this strange story—circumstances of which Julius was ignorant, though he had the main facts correct—I learned afterwards from other sources, but I have woven them all together here in orderly sequence.

The Murchison family had occupied their ancestral seat on the sandhills for a hundred years or more. There were not many rich families in that part of North Carolina, and this one, by reason of its wealth and other things was easily the most conspicuous in several counties. The first great man of the family, General Arthur Murchison, had won distinction in the war of independence, and during all the Revolutionary period had been one of the most ardent of the Carolina patriots. After peace was established he had taken high place in the councils of the State, and had been elected a delegate to the Constitutional Convention which established the fundamental law of the land. His son became a distinguished jurist, whose name is still a synonym for legal learning and juridical wisdom in North Carolina. Roger Murchison, the son of Judge Murchison—the generations had followed one another rapidly in a country of warm skies and early marriages—was the immediate predecessor of Malcolm Murchison, the demented old man who was nominal owner of the estate at the time of my visit to the house.

In Roger Murchison the family may be said to have begun to decline from the eminence it had attained in the career of Judge Murchison. In the first place, Roger Murchison did not marry, thus showing, as far as mere actions could show, that he had not family pride enough to wish to continue the name in his branch of the house. Again, though his career in college had been brilliant; though the wealth and standing of the family gave him social and political prestige; and though he had held high office under the state and national governments, he had never while in public life especially distinguished himself for eloquence or statesmanship but had, on the contrary, enjoyed a life of ease and pleasure and had wasted what his friends thought rare gifts. He was fond of cards, of fast horses, of rare wines, and of gay society. It is not surprising, therefore, that he spent very little time on his property, preferring the life of cities to the comparative dullness of plantation life with such colorless distractions as a neighboring small town could offer.

He had inherited a large estate, including several plantations, and numerous slaves. During his frequent absences from home, in the last fifteen years of his life, he left his property under the management of a nephew, Malcolm Murchison, the orphan son of a younger brother, and his own prospective heir. Young Malcolm was a youth of unusual strength of character and administrative capacity, and even before he had attained his majority showed himself a better manager than his uncle had ever been. So well, indeed, did he manage the estate that his uncle left it for ten years practically in his hands, looking to him only for the means he required to lead his own life in other places. It is true he appeared periodically and assumed the role of proprietor, but Malcolm was the man whom the community and the slaves looked upon as both the present and the future master.

Young Murchison kept bachelor's hall in the great house. The only women about the establishment were an old black cook, and the housekeeper, a tall, comely young quadroon—she had too a dash of Indian blood, which perhaps gave her straighter and blacker hair than she would otherwise have had, and also perhaps endowed her with some other qualities which found their natural expression in the course of subsequent events—if indeed her actions needed anything more than common human nature to account for them. We like to speak of Negro cunning, of Indian revengefulness, of the low morality of inferior races, when, alas! our own race excels in them all, when it wishes, because it lends to evil purposes a higher intelligence and a wider experience than inferior races can command.

The duties of young Murchison's housekeeper were not onerous. The one conspicuous vice of this scion and heir of the Murchison house was avarice. If he had other failings they were the heritage of the period and he shared them with his contemporaries of the same caste. Perhaps it was this characteristic that kept him from marrying; it was cheaper to have his clothing and his table looked after by a slave than by a woman who would not have been content with her board and clothes. At any rate, for ten or fifteen years he remained single, and ladies never set foot in the Murchison house. Men sometimes called and smoked and drank, played cards, bought and sold produce or slaves, but the foot of a white woman had not touched the floor for fifteen years, when Mrs. Martha Todd came from Pennsylvania to the neighboring town of Patesville to visit a cousin living there who had married a Southern gentleman.

Malcolm Murchison met Mrs. Todd out driving on the road one day. He knew her companion, and lifted his hat in response to her somewhat distant bow. He was attracted by the stranger's appearance and made inquiries about her in the town, as a result of which he learned that she was a widow and rich in her own right. He sought opportunities to meet her, courted her, and after a decent interval of hesitation on her part—mourning for her first husband—received her promise to be his wife.

He broke the news to his housekeeper by telling her to make the house ready for a mistress. The housekeeper had been in power too long to abdicate it gracefully, or perhaps she foresaw and dreaded the future. Some passionate strain of the mixed blood in her veins—a very human blood—broke out in a scene of hysterical violence. She pleaded, remonstrated, raged. He listened calmly through it all, and said to her at the end:

"You had better be quiet and obedient. I have heard what you have to say—this once—and it will be useless for you to repeat it. If you are reasonable, I will send you to the other plantation. If not, I will leave you here, with your new mistress."

She was silent for the time being, but raged inwardly. The next day she stole away from home, went to the town, sought out the new object of Murchison's devotion and told her something—just what she told no one but herself and the lady ever knew.

When Murchison called in the evening, Mrs. Todd sent down word that she was not at home. With the message came a note:

"I have had my wedded happiness spoiled once. A burnt child dreads the fire—I do not care to go twice through the same experience. I have learned some things about you that will render it impossible for me ever to marry you. It is needless to seek an explanation."

He went away puzzled and angry. His housekeeper wore an anxious look, which became less anxious as she observed his frame of mind. He had been wondering where Mrs. Todd had got the information—he could not doubt what it was—that had turned her from him. Suddenly a suspicion flashed into his mind. He went away early the next morning and made investigations. In the afternoon he came home with all the worst passions of weak humanity, clad with irresponsible power, flaming in his eyes.

"I will teach you," he said to his housekeeper, who quailed before him, "to tell tales about your master. I will put it out of your power to dip your tongue in where you are not concerned."

There was no one to say him nay. The law made her his. It was a lonely house, and no angel of mercy stayed his hand.

About a week later he received a letter—a bulky envelope. On breaking the seal, he found the contents to consist of two papers, one of which was a letter from a friend and political associate of his uncle. It was dated at Washington, and announced the death of his Uncle Roger as the result of an accident. A team of spirited horses had run away with him and thrown him out of the carriage, inflicting a fatal injury. The letter stated that his uncle had lingered for a day, during which he had dictated a letter to his nephew; that his body had been embalmed and placed in a vault, to await the disposition of his relatives or representatives. His uncle's letter was enclosed with the one above and ran as follows:

"My dear Malcolm: This is the last communication I shall ever make to you, I am sorry to say—though I don't know that I ought to complain, for I have always been a philosopher, and have had a good time to boot. There must be an end to all things, and I cannot escape the common fate.

"You have been a good nephew and a careful manager, and I have not forgotten the fact. I have left a will in which you are named as my sole heir, barring some small provision for my sister Mary. With the will you will find several notes, and mortgages securing them, on plantations in the neighborhood—I do not need to specify, as they explain themselves; also some bonds and other securities of value and your grandmother's diamond necklace. I do not say here where they are, lest this letter might fall into the wrong hands, but your housekeeper Viney knows their hiding place. She is devoted to you and to the family—she ought to be for she is of our blood—and she only knows the secret. I would not have told her, of course, had I not thought of just some such chance as this which has befallen me. She does not know the value of the papers, but simply that they are important.

"And now, Malcolm, my boy, good-by. I am crossing the river and I reach back to clasp your hand once more—just once.

"Your dying Uncle,

"Roger Murchison"

Malcolm Murchison took this letter to Viney. She had been banished from the house to a cabin in the yard, where she was waited on by the old black cook. He felt a little remorseful as he looked at her; for, after all, she was a woman, and there had been excuses for what she had done; and he had begun to feel, in some measure, that there was no sufficient excuse for what he had done.

She looked at him with an inscrutable face as he came in, and he felt very uncomfortable under the look.

"Viney," he said, not unkindly, "I'm sorry I went so far, and I'm glad you're getting better."

Her expression softened, a tear rolled down her cheek, and he felt correspondingly relieved. It is so easy to forgive our own sins against others.

"Your old Master Roger is dead. I have just received a letter telling me how it happened. He was thrown from a buggy in a runaway and injured so badly that he died the same day. He had time to write me a letter, in which he says you can tell me where he put certain papers that you know about. Can you tell"—he remembered her condition—"can you show me where they are?"

A closer observer than Malcolm Murchison might have detected at this moment another change in the woman's expression. Perhaps it was in her eyes more than elsewhere; for into their black depths there sprang a sudden fire.

Beyond this, however, and a slight quickening of her pulse, of which there was no visible manifestation, she gave no sign of special feeling, and even if these had been noticed they might have been attributed to the natural interest felt at hearing of her old master's death.

The only answer Viney made was to lift her hand and point it to her mouth.

"Yes, I know," he said hastily, "you can't tell me—not now at least, but you can surely point out the place to me."

She shook her head and pointed again to her mouth.

"Is it hidden in some place that you can't lead me to when you are able to get up?"

She nodded her head.

"Will it require words to describe it so that I can find it?"

Again she nodded affirmatively.

He reflected a moment. "Is it in the house?" he asked.

She shook her head.

"In the yard?"

Again she made a negative sign.

"In the barn?"

No.

"In the fields?"

No.

He tried for an hour, naming every spot he could think of as a possible hiding place for the papers, but with no avail. Every question was answered in the negative.

When he had exhausted his ingenuity in framing questions he went away very much disappointed. He had been patiently waiting for his reward for many years, and now when it should be his, it seemed to elude his grasp.

"Never mind," he said, "we will wait until you are better, and then perhaps you may be able to speak intelligently. In the meantime you shall not want for anything."

He had her removed to the house and saw that she received every attention. She was fed with dainty food, and such care as was possible was given to her wound. In due time it healed. But she did not even then seem able to articulate, even in whispers, and all his attempts to learn of her the whereabouts of the missing papers, were met by the same failure. She seemed willing enough, but unable to tell what he wished to know. There was apparently some mystery which only words could unravel.

It occurred to him more than once how simple it would be for her to write down the few words necessary to his happiness. But, alas! She might as well have been without hands, for any use she could make of them in that respect. Slaves were not taught to write, for too much learning would have made them mad. But Malcolm Murchison was a man of resources—he would have her taught to write. So he employed a teacher—a free colored man who had picked up some fragments of learning, and who could be trusted to hold his tongue, to teach Viney to read and write. But somehow she made poor progress. She was handicapped of course by her loss of speech. Ignorant people learn with their voices as well as with their minds. It was unfamiliar work, too, for the teacher, who would not have been expert with a pupil equipped with all the normal faculties. Perhaps she had begun too old; her mind was too busily occupied with other thoughts to fix it on the tedious and painful steps by which the art of expression in writing is acquired. Whatever the reason, she manifested a remarkable stupidity while seemingly anxious to learn, and in the end Malcolm was compelled to abandon the attempt to teach her.

Several years passed in vain efforts to extract from Viney in some way the wished-for information. Meantime Murchison's affairs did not prosper. Several other relatives claimed a share in his uncle's estate, on the ground that he had died intestate. In the absence of the will, their claims could not be successfully disputed. Every legal means of delay was resorted to, and the authorities were disposed, in view of the remarkable circumstances of the case, to grant every possible favor. But the law fixed certain limits to delay in the settlement of an estate, and in the end he was obliged either to compromise the adverse claims or allow them to be fixed by legal process. And while certain of his own rights were, he was compelled to see a large part of what was rightfully his go into hands where it would be difficult to trace or recover it if the will were found. Some of the estates against which he suspected the hidden notes and mortgages were held were sold and otherwise disposed of. His worry interfered with proper attention to his farming operations, and one crop was almost a failure. The factor to whom he shipped his cotton went bankrupt owing him a large balance, and he fell into debt and worried himself into a fever. The woman Viney nursed him through it, and was always present at his side, a mute reproach for his cruelty, a constant reminder of his troubles. Her presence was the worst of things for him, and yet he could not bear to have her out of his sight, for in her lay the secret he longed for and which he hoped at some time in some miraculous way to extract from her.

When he rose from his sick-bed after an illness of three months, he was but the wreck of the strong man he had once been. His affairs had fallen into hopeless disorder. His slaves, except Viney, were sold to pay his debts, and there remained to him of the almost princely inheritance he had expected only the old place on the sandhills and his slave, Viney, who still kept house for him. His mind was vacant and wandering, except on the one subject of the hidden will, and he spent most of the time in trying to extract from Viney the secret of its hiding place. A young nephew came and lived with him and did what was necessary to hold the remnant of the estate together.

When the war came Viney was freed, with the rest of her brethren in bondage. But she did not leave the old place. There was some gruesome attraction in the scene of her suffering, or perhaps it was the home instinct. The society of humankind did not possess the same attraction for her as if she had not been deprived of the power of speech. She stayed on and on, doing the simple housework for the demented old man and his nephew, until the superstitious Negroes and poor whites of the neighborhood said that she, too, shared the old man's affliction. Day after day they sat on the porch when her indoor work was done, the old man resting in the carved oaken armchair and she in her splint-bottom chair; or the old man commanding, threatening, expostulating, entreating her to try, just once more, to tell him his uncle's message— she replying in the meaningless inarticulate mutterings that we had heard; or the old man digging, digging furiously, and she watching him from the porch, with the same inscrutable eyes, though dulled somewhat by age, that had flashed upon him for a moment in the dimly lighted cabin where she lay on her bed of pain.

The summer following the visit I made to the old Murchison place I accompanied my wife North on a trip to our former home. On my return several weeks later I had occasion again to visit young Murchison, and drove over one morning to the house. As we drove up the lane I noticed a surprising change in the surroundings. A new gate had been hung, upon a pair of ugly cast-iron hinges. The grass in the path had been mowed, and the weeds and shrubs bordering it had been cut down. The neglected pleasure-garden had been reduced to some degree of order, and the ground around the house had been plowed and harrowed, and the young blades of grass were just shooting up and covering the surface with a greenish down. The house itself had shared in the general improvement. The roof had been repaired and the broken windows mended, and from certain indications in the way of ladders and pails at one side of the house I inferred that it was intended to paint it. This, however, was merely a supposition, for house-painting is an art that languishes in the rural districts of the South.

Julius had been noticing my surprise at these signs of thrift, with a pleased expression that boded further surprises.

"What's been going on here, Julius?" I asked.

"Ole Mars Murchison done dead, suh—died las' mont', an' eve'thing goes ter young Mistah Roger. He's done 'mence' ter fix de ole place up. He be'n ober ter yo' place lookin' 'roun' an' he say he's gwineter hab his'n lookin' lak yo'n befo' de yeah's ober."

We stopped the rockaway in front of the house. As we drew up an old woman came out in whom I recognized one of the strange couple I had seen on the porch on my former visit. She seemed intelligent enough, to judge by her appearance, and I ventured to address her.

"Is Mr. Murchison at home?"

"Yes, sir," she answered, "I'll call him."

Her articulation was not distinct, but her words were intelligible. I was never more surprised in my life.

"What does this mean, Julius?" I asked, turning to the old man, who was grinning and chuckling to himself in great glee at my manifest astonishment. "Has she recovered her speech?"

"She had nebber lost it, suh. Ole Viney could 'a' talked all de time, ef she had had a min' ter. W'en Ole Mars Malcolm wuz dead she tuck 'n' showed young Mistah Roger whar de will an' de papahs wuz hid. An' whar you reckon dey wuz, suh?"

"I give it up, Julius. Enlighten me."

"Dey wa'n't in de house, ner de yahd, ner de bahn, ner de fields. Dey wuz hid in de seat er dat ole oak ahm-cheer on de piazza yonder w'at Ole Mars Ma'colm be'n settin' in all dese years."

A Virginia Chicken

The Rev. Samuel Thompson was born a slave in Virginia, and remained in bondage until the war broke out, when he ran away and joined the Union army, where he was received as contraband of war. He was perfectly able and willing to handle a musket, and by reason of his generous physical proportions, would have made an excellent target for Confederate bullets. But as Congress in its almost infinite wisdom, had not yet seen fit to trust the Negroes with guns, the Rev. Samuel—at that time plain Sam—was assigned to duty in the camp kitchen; and many a hungry officer's burden of care was lightened, and his stomach and heart expanded by the savory soups which Sam served up to the mess. It was often a mystery where he got the materials to make them, for the rules against foraging were very strict, the country impoverished, and the disaffected natives not at all inclined to sell to the hated Yankees at any price.

Sam got through the war with a whole skin, and was then seized with the universal thirst for learning which prevailed among his race just after the war. He began attendance at one of the schools established by the Freedmen's Bureau, and by dint of hard study qualified himself to enter a school of higher grade. Here he attracted the attention of a wealthy patron of the school, who helped him through college. He was ordained some years ago as Presbyterian minister, and went to work as missionary and teacher among his people in the South. He was subsequently appointed by President Grant to a government position of some importance. He drew his salary with commendable regularity, and filled the office with credit to himself and to the government he served. The energy and perseverance which helped him up the rugged path of preferment were the same qualities which at an earlier period of his history and in a different sphere, had enabled him to keep the officers' mess supplied with palatable food when the source of supplies seemed as bare as the widow's cruse. I heard him relate one of his adventures during that period, and I will let him tell it in his own language, though at the time I heard it education had destroyed the fine flavor of the Virginia dialect which his language would probably have possessed some years before:

164

"We were on the march southward just after the battle of------. The rebels had passed through the country a few days before, and had cleaned up the supplies along their route like a swarm of locusts. There was not a pig to be met with, a cow was a whole show in herself, and the occasional sight of a chicken scurrying through the woods was calculated to make a lover of chicken meat weep with longing. The chickens had been hunted so much that they were shy as partridges. For two or three days my mess had been living on salt pork and army beans, and I could perceive that the diet was beginning to pall on their stomachs. I saw that my reputation was at stake, and I determined to save it. One morning after breakfast I sallied forth on a foraging expedition, determined to find something good to eat if there was anything in the neighborhood.

"We were pushing the Johnnies pretty close, and as they had been hurrying so much in the last day or two, I hoped they might have left behind them as much as a roasting pig, or a chicken or a goose. Our pickets were stationed a mile from camp. I struck out southward and had reached the line before I found anything. A little beyond the line, however, I came across a cabin, and creeping through the bushes toward it, what was my delight to see two or three hens feeding before the door. I picked up a stone and threw it at the group. This startled the hens and they began to cackle, which brought to the door a tall, poor white woman, with a green checked bonnet on her head and a pipe in her mouth. She began to call the chickens, and finally tried to drive them into the open door of the hen-house; but the chickens were not well drilled, and scattered about the clearing. One of them came in my direction, and I made a dash and secured the prey.

"The woman was very angry.

" 'Put that chicken down, nigger,' she said.

" 'Sorry I can't do it, ma'am, but men must eat, and chickens is made for it.'

"Then she opened the flood gates of her wrath, and poured out a volume of abuse which one would hardly have expected from such a source. She wished me all kinds of lingering deaths, consigned me to eternal tortures in perdition, and had about used up her breath and her imagination before I could get out of sight in the direction of the camp. I told her it was no use to get mad— that the Southe'n people had brought on this war, and that those who danced must pay the fiddler. But, Lord bless you, argument didn't seem to have the least effect upon her.

"When I got a little nearer camp, I sat down on a log and began to pick the chicken. I was just revolving in my mind how I could best cook it, when I heard the click of a musket, and looking up, found myself confronted by a hungry, gray-bearded Johnny, whose musket was pointed directly at me.

" 'Drap that chicken, nigger.'

"I dropped it.

" 'Stan' up ag'in that tree.'

"I stood.

"Two or three other graybacks came out of the woods. They were evidently bushwhackers, and had seen hard luck. One of them secured the chicken; a fire was quickly started, and in about three minutes the chicken was spitted on a bayonet and cooking nicely.

" 'What shill we do with the nigger?'

" 'Shoot 'im,' answered a fierce-looking one-eyed fellow.

"I began to feel weak in the knees.

" 'Run 'im down ter Richmon' an' sell 'im,' suggested a second. 'Niggers is bringing fifteen hundred dollars in gold at Richmon'.'

"I breathed easier.

" 'Too much trouble,' said number three, a stoop-shouldered, long-haired chap. 'Keep 'im to wait on us,' at which there was a laugh, and I didn't know exactly how to feel.

" 'We cain't do it,' said the first speaker. 'We ain't got nuthin' ter feed 'im on, an' we hain't got no time ter sell 'im. There's nuthin' ter do but to shoot 'im,' whereat my heart sank down into my boots, went out at the toes, and ran off in the woods.

"The others wouldn't agree to this at once, and the question was argued a while longer. Meanwhile the chicken was cooking nicely.

" 'Let's decide the question by a game o' seven-up,' said number two. 'Jim kin ten' ter the chicken, an' me'n you play. I win, we keeps the nigger, an' sells 'im when we kin; you win, we shoots 'im,' to which they all agreed.

"I never watched a game with greater interest, and when I saw the hand the shooting fellow got, I knew my game was up. A minute later they rose.

" 'Say yo' prayers, nigger, and say 'em quick,' said the man with the long beard. I began to pray in a loud voice.

" 'That'll do' he said after a minute, raising his gun; 'you take too durn long.'

"I closed my eyes to receive the expected shot. I heard the click of muskets, and— " 'Halt!' sounded clear and sharp from the woods behind me.

"I opened my eyes. The Johnnies had dropped their guns and looked by no means pleased. A dozen Yankees swarmed out of the woods. It was a reconnoitering part from our camp. Some secured the bushwhackers, others secured the chicken. In a moment I was at liberty, and I never appreciated liberty so much before or since. But the funniest thing about it was the way the prisoners looked at our soldiers eat that chicken.

"We kept them in camp several weeks. A guard was placed over them, and I spent most of my spare time walking around outside of the guard, asking the Johnnies what they were going to do with the nigger, and how they liked the chicken, and what was the price of niggers down at Richmond. They were the maddest men you ever saw, and I had to dodge many a brick and clod of dirt which they threw at me. And cursing me—but I couldn't blame them much. Finally we moved our camp, and they were exchanged a few weeks later. I got off a parting fire at them as they went away, and one of them threw a pebble which struck me and left its mark. I never look in a glass and see that scar on my forehead but what I have to laugh at the way those bushwhackers looked at that chicken."

Uncle Peter's House

Ever since the broad column of Sherman's army swept through central North Carolina, leaving the whites subjugated and impoverished and the blacks free and destitute, it had been Peter's dearest wish to own a house—a two-story white house, with green blinds. From his earliest childhood such a house had been to him the symbol of power, prosperity, and happiness. From the little group of cabins which made up the slave quarters of the large plantation on which he was born could be seen, at a short distance, the large white house, surrounded by broad piazzas, upon which opened the long windows guarded by green Venetian blinds. Standing on the highest part of the plantation, in a grove of patriarchal elms, it was the most conspicuous object in the landscape. From it the eye of the little autocrat who ruled this broad domain could overlook the acres of cotton stretching out to the edge of the distant forest, and the dark-green masses of waving corn which covered the meadows, and toward it the ear of the tired slave was turned at evening, to listen for the sound of the horn which announced a few hours' respite from the hard toil which made up his daily life. When Peter was a little pickaninny he occasionally went up to the great house with the old mammy who had nursed the children of the quarters, to get a dose of castor oil or Epsom salts, the sovereign remedies of the plantation for sick children. The glimpses of life in the great house which he got on those occasions were like revelations of the supernatural and filled his little soul with wonder and awe. And it is not strange when old Aunt Lyddy told him stories of heaven and the angels, that he should ask if heaven was like the great house and the angels like the white folks. And he could not understand, at that tender age, why the old woman's dim eyes flashed and her voice trembled as she pushed him out of the cabin with "G'long out in de ya'd 'n' play, chile!"

As Peter grew older he envied the lot of his young master's little yellow valet, and his young mistress' maid in her calico gown. They wore clothes, and, in cold weather, shoes, while Peter's wardrobe consisted of a change of the only garment plantation etiquette required for the children of the quarters. But Peter met with no such good fortune as theirs, for he was black, and not

168

comely, and the house servants were selected for ornament as well as use. When he was old enough, the stern exigencies of plantation life sent him out into the fields with the other hands to pick up cotton and drop corn, and, as his arms grew stronger, to wield the hoe and guide the plow; and, while the fierce heat beat down upon his back as he bent over the hoe, the great white house, glittering in the sunlight, looked like New Jerusalem in the pictures. He ceased, however, after a little experience, to think of its inmates as angels. He loved; his master's son took a fancy to the same girl. The girl, very absurdly, preferred Peter. But the facility with which it settled such little domestic difficulties was one of the glories of the peculiar institution, and the matter was speedily arranged by selling Peter to a distant part of the state. He soon forgot the girl; but the picture of the great white house, around which clustered the most vivid impressions of childhood, remained fresh in his memory.

At the close of the war Peter found himself free, along with several millions of his brethren. There was no Moses to lead them into a land flowing with milk and honey, and there was very little left in the flesh-pots of Egypt. But as affairs adjusted themselves, and the freed people learned to assume the burdens as well as enjoy the sweets of liberty, Peter found work and tasted the first substantial fruits of freedom when his horny hand closed upon a greenback. It was a dirty, foul-smelling bit of paper, but it represented power and made Peter feel a capitalist. He found, after a while, that he could earn more than he was obliged to spend, and the reflection that his masters had got these surplus earnings when he was a slave, and with them had bought their houses and lands, led by an easy transition to the thought, Why should I not buy land and build a house? He became accustomed to think of the subject, the thought grew into a purpose and the purpose brought forth a plan. The plan was simplicity itself; he would save money enough to buy the land; then he would get the lumber; then with his own work—for he was handy with tools— and the occasional assistance of a good carpenter he would build his house.

There was nothing wrong about the plan. As a plan it was perfect, but in working it out several difficulties presented themselves. First, it was not easy to save the money. Peter had not long been accustomed to the use of money, and the temptation was very strong to spend it for some of the good things which were now, for the first time, within his reach. But his purpose gave him strength, and slowly the roll of bills in the stocking in the "chist" increased in size, until Peter had money enough to buy a piece of land.

The next step was to buy the land. And here Peter was confronted by what seemed at first an insuperable obstacle—no one would sell him the land. There was plenty of land that did not produce enough to pay the taxes, but the landowners did not care to sell to Negroes. They would rent to them on shares or for a fixed rent, but they would not sell—it was against their principles. Several of them, however, expressed a desire to borrow Peter's money and were surprised, not to say indignant, at his declining to dispose of it in that way; it seemed like a reflection on the honor of Southern gentlemen. At length Peter succeeded in buying a piece of land just beyond the limits of the little town in which he lived. A Northern man who had bought a large tract of land to work the turpentine woods, and had used it up for that purpose, was glad to dispose of it at a low figure, and was not particular about the purchasers, if they paid the price. So, for the sum of seventy-five dollars in current paper of the country, Peter found himself a lord of the soil—the proud possessor of fifteen acres of land fronting on the Lumberton plank-road. It was a poor soil—"Jis' 'bout strong 'nuff to sprout cow peas," the natives would have said. The tall pines had been stripped of their bark as far up as the turpentine "hacks" would reach, and were now good for hardly anything but firewood. There was a little ridge toward the front which would make an excellent building site, and behind it bubbled up a spring of clear, cool water; and the sighing of the wind through the tops of the tall pines and the rustling of the rabbit in the scanty underbrush were sweet music to Peter's ears. In the intervals of his toil for daily bread the sound of his ax could be heard in the woods, and the hill where he expected to build was gradually denuded of its garrisons of battle-scarred veteran pines. But people in the South have their peculiar notions about hurrying, and it was a year or two before Peter had two acres cleared. He built a log cabin for temporary occupation, a little to one side of the place where he meant to build the big house, and into it moved his household goods. An old-fashioned, four-posted bedstead, a few splint-bottomed chairs and wooden stools, and an ironbound, wooden "chist" made up most of his furniture, while perhaps the most valued articles of his personal property were the two sharp-snouted, slab-sided, spindle-shanked hogs and three yellow dogs of assorted sizes. Some parts of North Carolina are admirably adapted to sheep raising, but no Legislature has yet been elected in that state which would consider favorably a bill to abate the dog nuisance. The denizen of the sandhills is joined to his dogs—like the dog to his fleas. He is conservative, too; his fathers kept dogs, and he prefers to go slowly about removing the ancient landmarks. Uncle Peter did not move the pigs into the house, but they were quite near enough to make their presence felt, while the dogs had beds of pine straw under the house. The clearing was surrounded by a rail fence and planted in corn, pending the accumulation of a building fund.

Work at fifty cents a day and find yourself is not a rapid way to wealth. When Peter had nothing these wages seemed ample. But now he had aspirations and his earnings had not kept pace with them. So he fell an easy prey to the plausible eloquence of a big land owner, who persuaded him to buy a mule on time and rent a farm on shares. Peter gave his note for the value, or rather the price, of the mule at 15 per cent interest, secured by a mortgage on the mule and the prospective crop. By an arrangement with his landlord, he had a credit at a store while the crop was making. The land was cleared swamp land, and better than the ordinary sandhill land, and in the early part of the season the crop flourished. Uncle Peter used his credit at the store pretty freely, and the goods he bought were charged at certainly no less than their full value. But toward the end of the season the rust got into the cotton and damaged the staple, eventually diminishing the yield at least one-third, and the mule—an old army mule, who bore the legend "C.S.A." (Confederate States of America) conspicuously branded on his side, and had been through half a dozen campaigns—succumbed to a prevailing epidemic, and kicked his last kick just after the last plowing, in spite of all the rubbings and drenchings which his master's skill could administer. When Peter divided the crop with his land-lord and settled up accounts for the year, he found that of his two-thirds of the crop, the note and interest due for the purchase money of the mule took one half, and the bill at the store absorbed the balance, and left him twenty dollars in debt. The store bill would probably have eaten up the mule, too, if that patient animal had not already been eaten by the buzzards.

When Peter came out of bondage he brought with him a wife. She had been the servant of a planter whose land adjoined that of Peter's master. The two children which she had found time in the intervals of plantation work to bring into the world would probably have been sold to the far South, if the war had not interfered somewhat with the slave-breeding industry. As it was, they remained on the plantation until the close of the war. When freedom came, Peter, his wife, and his children, in addition to the natural ties which bound them, formed those social ties which are incompatible with slavery, and became a family. But the plantation was not a good school in which to learn how to raise a family. Peter brought up his boys as well, perhaps, as he knew how, but, unfortunately, the elder of the two did not develop in his character those qualities which are essential to good citizenship. Peter had hardly paid the debt entailed by the failure of his agricultural experiment, and got together a few dollars to start his building fund, when Peter, Jr., in a drunken brawl, fatally stabbed one of his associates, was arrested and thrown into jail. His father retained the best lawyer in the county for the defense, and, like a great many other unfortunate people, found the law an expensive luxury. Uncle Peter cut down the pines on his land and sold the wood; Aunt Dinah took in washing; but the earnings of the ax and washboard were not large enough, and Peter was at length compelled to mortgage his land to pay the lawyer's fees. His sacrifices were partly rewarded; the boy's neck was saved, but he was convicted of manslaughter and sentenced to imprisonment in the penitentiary for ten years. Perhaps the skill and eloquence of his lawyer helped to bring about this result; possibly, too, the jury were influenced by the consideration that to hang him would be an expense to the county, while the ten years' penal term could be utilized for the public good in building the railroads which were at that time beginning to stretch across the State and bring it into closer communication with the rest of the world.

It took another year to pay off the mortgage. Then Uncle Peter took a fresh start. He bought an ox, and every day the figure of this ungainly steed, followed by a load of split pine or black-jack saplings, and guided by Peter's second son, who was very inconsistently named Primus, found its way into the little town, and the sale of the wood added forty or fifty cents to the building fund. A few big trees were cut down and hewn into sills for the foundation of the proposed house, and a few others were hauled to the nearest saw mill and sawed into beams, but most of the lumber was bought outright. The pile of lumber grew slowly; the sun and rain to which it was exposed would have spoiled the soft white pine of the North before the pile grew large enough, but they only seasoned the resinous Carolina pine.

When he had lumber enough to finish the frame Uncle Peter began his house. The sills were mortised and placed in position. There was no preliminary excavation for a cellar, and no extensive brick or stone foundation. Cellars are rarely met on the Carolina sandhills, and the houses frequently stand on wooden blocks a long time before the brick or stone pillars are built. Week after week went by, and piece by piece the framework was prepared. In the fall of the year, when the crops had been gathered, Uncle Peter made a feast and invited his neighbors to the house-raising. A good carpenter was engaged to superintend the work; the strong arms of Uncle Peter's friends reared the beams and fastened them in their places and the skeleton of the house was set up. Then the assembled guests adjourned to the cabin and ate the 'possum and sweet potatoes, the cornpone, and the biscuits, and the fried chicken and the big hominy, and drank the persimmon beer which Aunt Dinah's skillful hands had brewed, with the characteristic appreciation of their race for good victuals.

The house grew slowly during the winter, the work being done as Peter had the money to buy lumber or time to use it. He did the rough parts himself and employed a carpenter from time to time for the particular jobs.

The house was perhaps two-thirds done when, one dark night, a party of jolly young fellows comprising a detachment of the recently organized local camp of the Ku Klux Klan, at that time a new thing, started out to have a little fun. Mounted on fleet horses and clad in long black robes, ornamented with grotesque devices in white, they struck terror to the hearts of the ignorant and superstitious. The masks, which hid their identity, and the oath of secrecy which bound them, made these midnight riders practically irresponsible, and irresponsible power is dangerous in any hands. This particular company, however, had no desperate or bloody purpose, but merely meant to amuse themselves. They fired a couple of volleys from their shotguns over the cabin of a superannuated Negro couple on the outskirts of the town "just to stimulate their old blood a bit," as a young physician in the crowd remarked. Then they attached to the gate of a prominent citizen of opposite political opinions a placard ornamented with what was intended as the picture of a coffin, and containing a notice to leave the country in thirty days, on pain of the consequences, which, it was intimated, might be tar and feathers, a whipping, or worse. Then they surprised on his way home from church a young colored man, who had recently made some indiscreet political remarks at a camp-meeting, and gave him a sound whipping with hickory switches, wound up with a little wholesome advice from a young limb of the law, who was ambitious to represent the county in the Legislature, to the effect that "the Southe'n people don't approve of mixin' politics with religion."

But these little diversions only whetted their appetite for fun. They had no special program for the evening, and when they saw the tall, unpainted frame of Uncle Peter's house standing by the road it suggested possibilities for more fun. They rode up the lane to the cabin and silently surrounded it. One of them knocked at the door.

"Who dar?" asked Peter, and as he opened the door, thinking no harm, a half dozen seized him and drew him out into the yard.

"What are you building here, old man?" asked one.

"Jes' a little house to lib in, marse," answered the trembling Peter, now thoroughly frightened.

"Now yer lyin', ain't yer?" said another; "It's a nigger school house, ain't it?"

"No, Marse, I 'clare to de Lo'd it's jes' my own house."

"The idee of a nigger livin' in a two-story house is jes' ridiculous," remarked a tall "Klucker" with some warmth.

"Ownin' land, too," said another; "what with niggers runnin' the guv-'ment, and niggers buyin' the lan', I'm durned if I see what's to become o' the white people."

"It's chilly tonight," suggested a little fellow, with a skull and cross-bones elaborately embroidered on the front of his gown, "let's have a fire."

He raked up a little pile of shavings under the side of the new house and asked for a match. One or two voices demurred to such summary proceedings, but the flask which had gone the round of the crowd several times during the evening had left them a little reckless. With a halter from one of the horses Peter was tied to a tree a little distance from the house, with his face turned toward it. The little "Klucker" lit the match and stuck it to the shavings, and soon the house was in a fine blaze. And poor Peter, in mortal terror from the shotgun at his ear, suffered in silence, save the low moan which from time to time forced itself from his lips, while he saw the dream of his youth, the toil of his maturer years, and what he had hoped to be the solace of his old age, go up in smoke. There was no attempt to put the fire out. The few people who saw it from a distance saw at the same time the ghostly figures flitting about, and took care to increase the distance. At length the little group rode off, and when the last beat of their horses' hoofs had died away, and their gay laughter was lost in the distance, the trembling Dinah emerged from the cabin, and released the victim of this little practical joke.

"It was a little rough on the old nigger to burn his house," said one of the party in relating the circumstance to a friend who had not participated, "but, by granny, it was as good as a circus to see the ole nigger's eyes roll while the house was a-burnin'."

Such an experience would have discouraged most men. Few, however, came out of the school of slavery without having learned the lesson of patience. The Ku Klux Klan, like Peter's house, became a thing of the past, it was the unquiet spirit of slavery hovering about the body from which it had been driven out. When the ghost was laid, Peter took fresh courage. He was a faithful Christian, and while his standard of religion as applied to everyday life was perhaps not the highest, the element of faith was not lacking. Too ignorant of letters to do more than spell out the simpler chapters of the Bible, he had a faith in God which would have put many a better-natured soul to the blush, a simple, unquestioning belief that God knows what is best for his children— a faith as superior to the blind fatalism of the Mohammedans as the ethics of Christianity are to the sanguinary creed of the Arabian prophet. He thought, with a literal application of the metaphor, that perhaps it was better for him to have gone through the fiery furnace of affliction, and he found comfort in the history of ancient Job, the man of Uz, who had such a hard time, and yet came out all right in the end. Peter "accepted the situation." The ashes of the burnt house manured the crop of corn which he had planted in the clearing, and the work of accumulating lumber was begun anew, though carried along with somewhat less energy, for time and toil had not been without their effect even upon Peter's robust frame. Again the sills were laid, again the neighbors were called in to the feast, and again the skeleton of Uncle Peter's house was outlined against the dark background of pines. A year elapsed; the house was weather-boarded and the sheathing nailed to the rafters; the roof was shingled; and the only thing now necessary to make the house habitable, after the Southern fashion, was to build the chimney and put in the windows. Uncle Peter husbanded his resources for a grand coup. It was his intention to have the chimney built and the windows put in during the same week.

In getting everything in readiness for this supreme effort, he climbed to the roof of the house one morning to saw the opening in the top for the chimney. The scaffolding, not having been securely put up, broke under his weight, and he fell to the ground, unfortunately striking on the pile of bricks which had been placed near the house for the use of the masons. His groans brought Aunt Dinah to the door, and with the help of her son Primus, she carried the wounded man into the cabin and laid him on the bed.

A physician was summoned, who came immediately. Peter lay half conscious, groaning in pain. Upon examination the doctor found an arm and a rib broken. He set the broken arm, wrote a prescription and went away, promising to return later in the day. He came and found no apparent improvement in the patient's condition. He felt Peter's pulse, and gravely said that he feared there was some internal injury which might prove more serious than the broken arm and rib. A subsequent visit only confirmed this opinion; the case did not develop favorably. In a few days, despite what medical skill and good nursing could do, the old man felt the end approaching, and sent for the colored preacher of his church to come and pray with him for what he believed would be the last time.

It was late in the afternoon. The bed of the sick man was so placed that he could look out of the open window at the unfinished house beyond. Up the white strip of sandy road that led to the town toiled a slow ox cart, with its load of turpentine barrels, and beyond this the dusky pines waved in the gentle wind, and seemed to sigh in sympathy with the sufferer, while from the deep recesses of the forest came the faint sound of chopping, and the melancholy croak of frogs, which the approach of evening had already aroused from their silence. About the bedside of the dying man were grouped his wife and son, the preacher and a few other friends who had been hastily summoned.

The preacher knelt and prayed a fervent prayer, and Peter murmured "Amen" as he concluded.

The eyes of the dying man were directed through the open window to the unfinished house a few yards away. The unpainted pine rafters were gilded by the glory of the setting sun.

"Elder," said Peter faintly to the preacher, "I didn' finish dat house."

"My brudder," said the preacher, "you shall have a better house on de udder sho'."

"Yas, bless de Lo'd," murmured the old man, "a house not made with hands, but eternal in de hebbens." Then, after a pause, to his younger son, "Primus, it's de las' thing I kin ax yer to do; take care o' yer po' ole mammy, and finish dat house, dat de good Lo'd didn' 'low me to finish."

"Yes, my brudder," said the preacher, after Primus had given the required promise, "de Lo'd didn' 'low David to buil' de temple, but his son Solermun built it after his father died."

The dying man faintly smiled assent, then whispered: "Good-by, ole 'ooman; I can't finish dis house fer you, but dere'll be one ready fer you when you jine me on de othe' sho'." Then he tried to sing,

"A mansion in hebben I see."

The watchers joined softly in the simple refrain, the old man's voice failing after the first line. He lay quietly with closed eyes for a few minutes, his breathing so faint that it seemed to have ceased altogether; then his eyes opened and a sudden glory came into them.

"See!" he exclaimed in a strong, clear voice, with a rapt look which seemed to penetrate beyond the veil, "I see de angels comin' to carry me home; and on de othe' side of de ribber I see dat hebbenly mansion—a big white mansion, wid green blin's on de winders, and broad piazzas all 'roun' it— and de tree of life grows over it, and the ribber of life flows by it." Then turning his eyes earthward—"Good-by, ole 'ooman; good-by, Primus; good-by, Elder," and then he fell asleep, and not the passionate weeping of the bereaved wife, nor the prayers of the preacher, nor anything earthly could wake him.

They made his grave under the pines on his own land, a stone's throw from the unfinished house. Several years have elapsed. Primus, true to his promise, has had the windows put in and the chimney built and is now lathing the interior. Aunt Dinah is growing old, but is still hale and hearty, and may yet live to see the house finished. The grove of young elms which Peter planted is thriving and will probably shade the yard nicely by the time the house is painted and the green blinds hung.

The Fall of Adam

Brother Gabriel Gainey was the founder, patron, chief elder and preacher of the colored Baptist Church in 'Possum Hollow. Before the war "Bre'r Gabe" was the slave preacher on a large plantation, and his pulpit powers were developed under circumstances somewhat unfavorable to a thorough knowledge of the Scriptures or to any acquaintance with the rules of grammar. He had strong lungs, however, and a powerful imagination, and could depict the horrors of sheol with a rude realism which was very effective in bringing plantation sinners to repentance, and it was a tradition of the neighborhood that even a white man had once been converted under his preaching.

In a great crisis genius always comes to the front. Napoleon would never, perhaps, have been Emperor, had General Menou been able to restore order in the streets of Paris. In the breaking up of society which followed the abolition of slavery, Brother Gabriel saw his chance, and determined to have a church of his own. With a little help from the Freedmen's Bureau he bought a small strip of land, and chiefly with his own hands put up the rude structure where his followers worshipped. In the fullness of his joy he christened it Hallelujah Chapel, which name it bears to this day. He gathered about him a fair-sized congregation and performed his pastoral duties with a lively zeal. He earned his living as a carpenter, the church contributions being just about sufficient to keep him in Sunday clothes. The dignity and importance of leadership were enough to satisfy the elder's moderate ambition.

One evening Elder Gainey sat by the fireplace in his little frame dwelling-house, slowly and patiently studying out a hymn which he wished to learn by heart in order to line it out the more readily the following Sabbath. A blazing pine-knot supplied him with light, and cast flickering and fantastic shadows on the walls. The elder had just decided upon a satisfactory pronunciation for a word of four syllables with which he had been wrestling, when there was a knock at the door, and he arose to admit a visitor.

"Good-evenin', Elder," said the new arrival, a tall, angular Negro, with a peculiar cranial development known as a "double head," by no means uncommon among the Southern Negroes, and generally accompanied with more than ordinary intellectual activity. Elder Gainey greeted the visitor with becoming gravity, and the usual inquiries concerning the health of their two families and the state of the weather were exchanged, when the visitor continued:

"I 'lowed you'd be home tonight, elder, so I thought I'd come over an' ax you a few questions on one or two p'ints in de Bible, what's be'n botherin' my mind."

Brother 'Lijah Gadson, the anxious inquirer, was an active and valuable member of the elder's church. He had but one serious fault—he was fond of asking hard questions. As not a few of these fell to Elder Gainey's share as spiritual guide of the congregation, the worthy elder was frequently reminded of a certain old and popular proverb in reference to the difficulty which a wise man may sometimes find in answering the questions of a fool.

Brother 'Lijah was provided with a rush-bottomed rocking-chair, and the elder, after placing a couple of sweet potatoes before the fire, seated himself on the other side of the hearth and announced his readiness to impart information.

"Bre'r Gab'l," said 'Lijah, interrogatively, "you's pretty well acquainted wid de Bible?"

"Yas, Bre'r 'Lijah," replied the elder modestly, "dat is, I knows a little sump'n 'bout de Bible."

"Well, elder, da's one thing 'bout de Bible I never couldn' understan' and dass de fall of Adam. Now I'se hearn a good 'eal 'bout dis subjic': I'se sarched de Scriptures, an' axed udder folks, but after all my sarchin's an' my axin's, I ain't never yit be'n able to find out whar Adam fell from, nuh how he come to fall?"

"I think," said the elder reflectively, "dat Adam fell 'case he didn' min' de Lawd."

"I knows dat, Bre'r Gab'l, but dass not de p'int. De words used is dat Adam fell, an' I believe de Bible mean jes' what it say. So what I'se tryin' to fin' out is whar he fell from, how far he fell."

Elder Gainey's face assumed an expression of deep thought, and after a few moments' pause, he replied:

"Well, Bre'r 'Lijah, I's be'n studyin' de Scriptures for many years, but dass de fus' time I had de question put in jes' dat way 'zackly. I'll think de question ovah, an' by nex' Sunday mawnin' I hopes to be able to answer it satisfac'ry. Some o' dese deep p'ints requi'es studyin' an' prayin' ovuh. Is yuh had dat wood hauled to de chu'ch yit, Bre'r Gadson?"

"Anothuh p'int what's be'n worryin' me," continued Brother Gadson, not noticing the diversion, "is what caused de diffe'nce 'twix' white folks an' black folks. I be'n 'flectin' dat subjic' over a long time, and axin' 'bout it; but nobody doan' seem to know nuffin' surtin 'bout it. Some says it's de cuss o' Caanyun but I never could'n' understan' bout dis here cuss o' Caanyun. I can see how de Lawd could turn anybody black jes' by cussin' 'im; 'case 'fo I j'ined de church—dat was 'fo de wah—I use' ter cuss de overseah on ole marse's planta-tion awful bad—when he was'n' da—an' all de darkies on de plantation use'ter cus 'im, an' it didn' make de leas' changes in 'is complexion. 'Peahs to me somebody must 'a done sum'in' to make black folks, 'case de Lawd is good, an' I dorn' b'lieve He made anybody black at fus'."

Brother Gabriel gazed earnestly into the fire.

"De ways of de Lawd, Bre'r Gadson, is pas' findin' out. Dat is a deep question, but I have no doubt I kin fin' a chapter in de Bible what'll throw some light on it, if it doan 'splain it all. I will also tech on dat p'int in my sermon nex' Sunday mawnin'. Bre'r Gadson, is yuh hauled dat wood to de chu'ch yit?"

Brother 'Lijah, having relieved his mind of these weighty matters, was now in a condition to talk business. He was the "section" or sexton of Hallelu-jah Chapel, and attended to the fires, sweeping, and other similar duties. The matter of the wood disposed of, Brother 'Lijah discussed one of the sweet pota-toes which by this time was done to a turn, and bidding the elder good-night, took his way homeward.

Whenever he had very knotty questions to discuss, Brother Gabriel went into a trance. On these occasions the elder would retire to his chamber, or to the woods,, and remain for a long time engaged in prayer. These prayers were delivered aloud, and would gradually increase in energy and vociferous-ness until the neighbors all knew that "Bre'r Gab'l was "ras'lin' in pra'r." When he had wrought himself up into a state of excitement bordering on frenzy he would relapse into unconsciousness. In an hour or so he would come to and have a vision, more or less marvelous to relate to his wondering auditors. Between the date of the conversation reported and the Sunday after, the elder indulged in a "rastle" which supplied the material of his great sermon.

II

The next Sabbath dawned fair and beautiful. The great blue vault stretched far above, as clear and soft as a Venetian sky. Along the country roads, bor-dered with fields of yellowing corn and snowy cotton, the congregation streamed from all directions. It was a big day. There were several candidates for baptism. After the baptism it was the intention of the church to start a revival. There was also a collection to be taken up for the benefit of the preacher. With all these incentives to effort, Bre'r Gabriel was anxious to do his best.

The services did not begin until half-past eleven. The appointed hour was an hour earlier, but the colored people in their new-found freedom were like the sturdy Saxons of long ago, who, Blackstone tells us, "held it beneath the condition of a freeman to arrive or do anything at the appointed time." Bre'r 'Lijah had circulated the information that Elder Gainey would preach on the two subjects of "Adam's Fall" and the "Origin of Races," and there was considerable curiosity to hear the sermon—especially that part of it which related to the latter subject.

As the weather was fine and the church small, the services were held in the open air, under a temporary shelter of pine boughs. The pulpit and benches were brought out, and supplementary seats were extemporized by laying pine slabs across logs of wood. While the congregation was gathering, Brother 'Lijah led those present in a new song of his own composition, sung to a simple and not unpleasing melody. The song was a running commentary on the lives and virtues of "Ole Moses," "Ole David," and other Old Testament characters, and was sung by 'Lijah as a solo, the music-loving audience soon catching the swing of the rather rollicking chorus and joining in heartily.

The regular service began when Elder Gainey ascended the pulpit and gave out the opening hymn. This hymn was sung by the choir, which was composed of young people, equipped with large, yellow-covered notebooks, having the music printed in character notes. The choir sang with the spirit, though their understanding of the tune (an old-fashioned fugue) was occasionally open to doubt.

Then followed the opening prayer, an appeal to the Deity by a gifted brother, whose effusion equalled in comprehensiveness the Morning Prayer in the Episcopal service. It almost equalled the Morning Prayer in length, must have been tiresome to the congregation, who were all devoutly kneeling. Several indiscreet sisters encouraged the orator by groans and exclamations, and under this stimulus it seemed hard to say when he would stop. He might have gone on and on forever, like the Wandering Jew or the Phantom Ship, had not Brother Gabriel, mindful of the other services, and watching his chance, at last brought the prayer to a close by interjecting a sonorous "Amen" when the eloquent and perspiring orator paused to breathe.

Then followed the second hymn, lined out by the preacher, and led by Brother 'Lijah, who always acted as precentor. The hymn concluded, Elder Gainey stood up behind the pulpit, carefully adjusted his spectacles, poured out a glass of water from the pitcher which graced the stand, opened the Bible at random, took out his handkerchief—a large square of snowy linen— sonorously blew his nose in a dignified manner, placed the handkerchief under one side of the Bible and announced his text—a familiar passage from the book of Revelations—and began his sermon as follows:

"I's gwine tuh preach to yuh dis mawnin', breth'n an' sistern, 'bout two mighty deep an' powerful subjec's. Las' Wednesday evenin' one o' de members o' de chu'ch axed me two questions dat sot me to sea'ch de Scripters." (Here he stated the questions substantially as propounded by Brother Gadson.) "I sea'ch de Bible day by day, but couln' fin' nothin' sartin in it. I 'cluded dey wan' no use readin' no mo'—de subjec' was too deep fur readin'. Pra'r was what was wanted. An', breth'n an' sistern, I ras'led in pra'r 'tell I fell into a trance, an' in dat trance I had a vision what made the whole thing plain as de sunlight. Dem two questions might 'peah to be mighty diffe'nt, but dat vision showed me that de two b'longed right close togeddah, dat one growed right out'n de yuthuh.

"It seemed to me, when I fell into dat trance, I see a tall white angel comin' right down f'om hebben to wha'r I wus. He had a golden harp in his han', golden slippuhs on his feet, and a crown of gold upon his head. He flewed right down 'side o' me an' says: 'Rise up, Gab'l, an' go along wid me, an' all will be made cla'r to you.' I followed de angel th'ough de aiah, ovuh de mountains an' valleys an' oceans 'tel we come to a big gyahden where all kin's o' trees an' flowuhs was growin! Den de angel says to me: 'Dis is de gyahden of Eden. Look! Den de angel lef' me an' I looked, an' see Adam an' Eve in de gyahden jes' es dey wus when de wuhld was made.

"I seen de sarpen' crawl up to Eve an' talk to her, an' den she et de apple. Bimeby Adam come 'long. Eve give Adam de apple, an' Adam did eat. Bimeby Eve seen de Lawd a comin'. 'Adam,' says Eve, 'yander come de Lawd!' Den Adam turn' pale an' begun to trimble. 'De Lawd'll be mad with us 'case we et dat apple,' says he, 'what for you make me eat dat apple, Eve?' 'You mighty big cowya'd, Adam, you done et dat apple, an' tain' no use talkin'. Yander come de Lawd, an' he look mad.' 'Less hide, Eve,' said Adam. So dey hid in de bushes. Bimeby 'long come de Lawd wid a big hick'ry in 'is han'. 'Adam, wha'r is you?' says he. Adam never said a word. But de Lawd knowed wha'r Adam wus, an' he come right straight towa'ds 'im.

"Adam started to run—de Lawd right aftuh 'im; Adam jumped ovuh de tree of life—de Lawd right aftuh 'im; run roun' de worl'—de Lawd right aftuh 'im; swum ovuh de sea—de Lawd right aftuh 'im; jumped ovuh Jupiter—de Lawd gainin' on 'im; jumped ovuh de moon—de Lawd close behin'. When he got to de sun, he was so tired he couldn' jump high 'nuff, an' de bright light blind' 'im so he couldn' see whar' he was goin', an' he fell—fell right down into the rivuh Jordan; an' befo' he could pull hisse'f out'n de mud at de bottom, de Lawd cotch 'im—an' sich anuthuh whippin' de Lawd give Adam de worl' have nevuh hearn tell uv sence. An' dat 'splains, bro'rs an' sisters, de fall of Adam.

"De yuthuh p'int what was 'splained to me at de same time by de vision, was what made de diffe'nce 'twix' white folks an' black folks; an' what I larn' convince' me dat de Lawd nevuh made nobody black. 'Fac' de Lawd nevuh made nobody but Adam an' Eve—de yuthuhs wus all bawn. O' co'se if Adam uh anybody else gwine' do anything to make deyse'ves black, de Lawd wan' gwine have nothin' tuh do wid it; he made 'em once, an' he nevuh do his wuk twice. So dis 'splains de diffe'nce. When Adam jump' ovuh de sun, de fiah wus so hot, it scawched 'im black as a crips, an' curled up his ha'r so he nevuh couldn'n't git it straight agin. An', 'cawdin' to de laws ob nachah

Jes' so de tree fall, jes' so it lie.
Jes' so de sinner jib, jes' so he die.

An' so Adam nevuh turn' white no mo', but stayed black all de rest of 'is life. All Adam an' Eve's chillun bawn fo' de Fall wus white, an' dey wus de fo'fathers ob de white race o' people—all Adam an' Eve's chillun bawn aftuh de Fall wus black, an' dey wus de fo'fathers ob de black race of people."

The close of the sermon was followed by a ripple of excitement and a subdued murmur, which showed the interest with which the statements of the elder had been listened to and it was not at all certain that the murmur was one of unqualified approval. One brother over in the amen corner was so deeply moved that he forgot the etiquette of the service, and startled the congregation by standing up and addressing the elder.

"Elder, did I understan' you to say dat all Adam's chillun bawn befo' de Fall was white?"

"Yas, dass what de vision say."

"An' Adam libbed wid Eve aftuh de Fall?"

"Ob co'se—dey wan't nobody else to lib wid."

"Well, it kindah 'peahs to me, elder, dat unduh all de sarcumstances ob de case dem chillun bawn aftuh de Fall oughtah be'n mullatahs."

"Bre'r Isham," said the elder sternly, "I wants dis tawkin' in de chu'ch stopped. De collection will now be lifted. Bre'r Needham, set de table out. Bre'r 'Lijah, sta't a hyme."

McDugald's Mule

Mr. Dugald McDugald was ready to start home. He had sold his turpentine, bought his tea and coffee, and laid in his weekly supply of whiskey and tobacco. His round-shouldered, sallowy-complexioned son, a sandhill lad of sixteen summers, had mounted the mule.

"G'long, Beauregard," said Mr. McDugald, touching the mule's flanks with a hickory switch which he took from a hole in one of the cross-pieces of the cart.

Beauregard started off down the street, but stopped on the corner a few paces away.

"Git up," drawled Archie, sticking his bare heels in the mule's flank.

"G'long, Beauregard," said Mr. McDugald, emphasizing the command by a vigorous application of the 'hick'ry'.

But words and blows were both unavailing. Several of the loafers so common in Southern towns had by this time gathered about the cart. The mule's face wore a dogged expression, which, with the peculiar manner in which his feet were planted, clearly indicated his intention not to move a peg. Several of the bystanders offered suggestions:

"Twist 'is tail," said one.

"You kin do that," replied Mr. McDugald. But the dispenser of gratuitous advice evidently knew something about the peculiar ways of the mule and refrained from operating. Another loafer, with a sudden inspiration, suggested that a fire be built under the mule.

"No, gen'lemen, I hain't a-goin to do nothin' o' the sort. Archie, unhitch the mule and we'll camp over in the bank lot."

Archie unharnessed the mule, that stubborn animal moving readily enough when the shafts were let down. Mr. McDugald and Archie drew the cart over into the bank lot. This had been the site of the Clarendon Bank, of which nothing but the bare walls, with here and there the charred end of a beam or the twisted iron framework of a door remained.

In the evening while Archie remained by the campfire and watched the cart, Mr. McDugald came over to the store. Business was dull, and I occupied a splint-bottomed chair on the sidewalk in front of the store. Mr. McDugald sat down on an empty tobacco box, and after a few observations on the state of the weather and the prospects of the cotton crop, continued in his usual high-pitched drawl:

"You mought wonder, Cholly, why I 'lowed that mule to git the better o' me. But I had a reason for it. I'm under obligations to that mule. I have had him nigh on to ten year now, an' I feel sorter attached to him. But more'n that, he saved my life once, and I ain't likely to forgit it soon.

"It was 'long in sixty-eight. I had had Beauregard pushing' three year then. You mought say, pushin' four year. An' I must say, that I never had a better mule; even his faults are virtues, as my story will prove. I guess his difference from other mules comes from his great experience. He's been in the wah, an' he's branded in two places, 'U.S.A.' and 'C.S.A.,' showin' that he served on both sides. I found him down in the swamp on my place just after Sherman went through, an' I have had him ever sence. I named him Gin'l Beauregard.

"Well, as I was a tellin' you, he saved my life once. You don't mind the big fresh in '68? No; I recall your pappy hadn't moved here then. Wal, it was the biggest fresh we had sence eighteen forty-five. The Cape Fear riz forty feet, an' all the river bottoms from here to Wilmington was flooded an' the crops entirely spiled. It rained every day in June, and the ground was too wet for us to plow even our watermillioms.

"I had some business down to Lumberton on a Wednesday. I think it was the twenty-fifth of June. Yes; I remember now; I was goin' to fetch Archie from his granny's where he had been spending his birthday. He was only six years old, if my memory serves me right. I had to cross Lumber river over the old bridge. You never seen the old bridge, Cholly."

"I seed it," said one of the bystanders, or rather bysitters, for no Southerner will stand when he can find a place to sit, "it was carried away in that very fresh."

"Yes," continued the old man, "as I was a-sayin', I crossed Lumber river on the old bridge, stayed the night at Archie's granny's, and started back in the mornin', me an' Archie. I had this very mule, Beauregard. He hadn't be'n workin' much on account of the rain, an' I had to drive him pretty hard the day before. We started back next mornin', and 'long about nine o'clock we had got mighty nigh to the river. The river had be'n risin' durin' the night and was almost up to the bridge. Howsomedever, I went ahead a piece an' looked at the bridge keerful, an' as I couldn't see no signs of weak'nin' I decided to drive over. I hollered back to Archie, who was with the kyart, to come on. Archie jerked the lines an' tried to start the mule, but he wouldn't go.

" 'Why don't you come on?' says I.

" 'The durn mule's a-balkin',' says Archie.

"Wal, now, I never knowed Beauregard to balk like that. I went back, tuk hold o' the bridle, patted him on the head, an' tried to coax 'im along. But it didn't do no good. Bimeby I got mad. I stepped off into the woods an' cut a big hick'ry. Jest as I got back a kyart come up to us on the road. The driver stopped and said he'd help us start the mule. So down he got, an' ketchin' the mule by the tail, begins to twist. An' when he gin a twist, the mule gin 'is hind leg a twist an' the next minute my frien' was layin' in the ditch side'n the road. When I had helped him on his kyart, he 'lowed he had business over the river and couldn' stay no longer, so he reckoned he'd git along.

"In about two minutes, 'long come another farmer and sidgested that I build a fire under the mule. I got some sticks and prime-straw, an' lit a fire, and as it got to burning Beauregard lifted his huff and planted it right in the fire, scatterin' it all around. A burnin' stick struck my frien' in the eye, after which he diskivered that he was in a powerful hurry.

"Wall, I was jist a-settin' there a-wond'rin' what to do next. By that time the fust kyart ahead of us which wa'n't loaded an' had be'n goin' pretty fast got over the bridge. The las' kyart was jest about to the middle o' the bridge. The bridge was more'n a quarter of a mile long—when I hearn a crashin' and a creakin' an' when I looked I seen the bridge abowin' an' abendin', and in less than two minutes it had broken in two in the middle, an' was floatin' off down the river, the water a-foamin' an' a-bilin' around it. The pore feller with the cinder in his eye was right where the bridge broke, and him an' his hoss was drownded. It was a fine hoss, too; it was a shame to see a critter like that drownded.

"Me an' Archie went back an' stayed at his granny's a day or two till the river went down, an' then we crossed at McMillan's ford, about two miles further up the river.

"The mule seemed to know what had happened and as soon as the bridge fell, went right along without no further trouble.

"Ever since then," continued Mr. McDugald with a sigh, "me nor Archie have never hendered that mule from havin' his own way. He don't often balk but when he does we jest onhitches 'im and waits till he gets ready to go.

"Wal, I reckon I'll lay down," said the old man in conclusion as he sauntered off towards the camp.

Tom's Warm Welcome

Mr. Dugald McDugald had completed his purchases. He had carefully arranged the boxes and bags on his cart, and was filling his pipe with a handful of "home-made," which he had extracted from his capacious trousers pocket. His old gray mule had pricked up his long ears, and the yellow hound under the cart had got up, yawned, stretched and shaken himself. Mr. McDugald stopped in the doorway to light his pipe with an old-fashioned sun-glass. Just as the faint blue smoke began to curl up from the bowl of the pipe, old Tom MacDonald passed by on the other side if the street. Everybody called him "Old Tom MacDonald," not from any lack of respect, for he was a rich and highly respected citizen, but merely by way of description.

"Well, if there hain't ole Tom MacDonal' " said Mr. McDugald. "I hain't seen 'im for a coon's age. Don't look no more dried upper than he did ten year ago. Did I ever tell you 'bout how Tom went to ole Dunkin Campbell's ball?"

Mr. McDugald was fond of telling stories, of which he knew a great many, and he indulged his fondness whenever he could find an auditor.

As there were no customers in the store for the moment, I was willing to listen. Mr. McDugald seated himself leisurely in a splint-bottomed chair, while I reclined gracefully on a sack of salt. The mule observed these movements through the open door, and, with an air of relief, composed himself for a standing nap.

"About forty years ago Louis, his ole daddy, lived out on Rockfish Crick— jes' beyant where I lived. He didn't own no lan', but rented from old Gin'l McGee, who owned all o' Rockfish Township in them days. Ole MacDonal' was mighty no 'count; he never could git money enough to buy a nigger, and nobody would take his note, so he had to work hisself nearly to death. Tom was a pore shote, mightily lack his daddy, and nobody thought much of him. Me an' him was about one age, an' 'bout that time was both courtin' the same gal.

"Jinnie Campbell, that was her name—I can see her now," said the old man with a far-away look in his faded gray eyes, "big blue eyes, the plumpest figger and the sooplis' dancer in the settlement. Her daddy run a gris' mill on Rockfish, and the boys fotch their corn all the way from Beaver Crick an' Peg's Pocoson to Dunkin's mill, jist to git a sight of Jinnie. An' she was wuth it, too.

"Tom wa'n't no igception, 'ceptin' that he was wuss smitten than any of us. She didn't keer nuthin' for him, an' showed it plain. But the more Jinnie slighted 'im the wusser he got. He would hide in the bushes, and peep at her when she passed, and he tended the Sandy Run Presbyterian Church reglar, 'ca'se she sung in the choir, for everybody knowed his folks was Baptis'.

"Well, gittin' aroun' to my story, ole Dunkin Campbell give a dancin'. It was to be on a Wednesday night, an' most o' the young folks in the settlement was 'vited. But Tom MacDonal' wa'n't. At that time he hadn't seen Jinnie for two weeks, and he made up his mine to go, anyhow.

"He had to fix up some igscuse, so Monday mornin' at sun-up he saddled his mare an' rode off to Lumberton. He got back Wednesday evenin', fix hisself up and trotted over to Dunkin's as big as anybody. He rode up the lane, hitched his mare, an' knocked at the door. Ole Dunkin come out.

" 'Well, Lord bless me,' says he, shakin' Tom's han', 'if taint Tom McDonal'. Come right in, Tommy, come right in.'

"The strains of the fiddle came through the open door.

" 'No, thankee,' says Tom, 'I didn' know ye had comp 'ny or I'd waited tell to-morrer. I jes get back from Lumberton this evenin', and while I was there young Archie McMillan axed me to tell you to come down sometime an' look at a new kind of millstone he wants you to try.'

" 'Yes, I will, Tommy, an' much obliged to you.' Jes' then somebody called him from the inside, an' he added, 'But come in, Tom, come in, the boys an' gals is havin' a little dance, an' they'll be glad to have ye jine 'em.'

"Tom felt somethin' like backin' out at the las' minute, but the fiddles goin', an' the ole man shuk hans so hearty, an' he happened to see Jinnie dance across the floor; so he hung up his hat on one of the wooden pegs in the passage, and followed ole Dunkin into the hall, where the dancin' was goin' on. Jest as he reached the door the fiddles stopped at the end of the set an' ole Dunkin sung out:

" 'Boys an' gals, here's Tom MacDonal'; he wa'n't invited here tonight, but he's just as welcome as ef he had a' been.'

"Some o' the gals snickered, and one or two of the boys lafft out. But Tom wa'n't a bad lookin' feller, and was a good dancer; there was nothin' agin 'im, 'ceptin' his bein' pore and no 'count, so the gals wa'n't sorry to see 'im. An' as he would fight when he got his dander up, the boys was afeared to laff much. When the music started up ag'in, Tom mixed in with the crowd an' got to talkin' an' dancin', and had almost forgot he wa'n't ax' to the dancin', when the old man Dunkin, who had'n' forgot it, come in to call em to supper.

"The boys an' gals paired off. Jinnie was dancin' with me, an' I tuk her in. The ole man stood by the door, between the hall an' the dinin' room incouragin' the young folks to go in. Tom hung back a little, remembering he wa'n't invited, an' all the gals had pardners before he begun to look around for one. But Ole Dunkin had his eye on 'im, and when he noticed Tom holdin' back, he sung out, kind o' hearty and cheerful, 'come 'long, Tommy, come right 'long. There's plenty to eat. Don't be back'ard. You wa'n't invited to the dancin', but Lord bless me, you're jest as welcome as ef you had a' been.'

"Tom winced at this, wuss'n my mule Beauregard does when I hit 'im on a raw spot. He looked aroun' but there wa'n't no way o' gittin' out jes then. He hadn't bin able to speak to Jinnie yit, nuther; an' the long table, loaded down with chicken an' possum an' cake an' sellabub, looked mighty temptin'. So he reckoned he'd stay a little while an' then manage to slip off. The boys couldn't help laffin', though they purtended to be tickled at somethin' else, an' the gals snickered.

"Tom waited till the supper was started good an' then slipped out in the passage, meanin' to git away without bein' noticed. He hadn't spoke to Jinnie the hull evenin', but he had seen her, which was somethin'. But even the chance o' talkin' to her wa'n't temptation enough to make 'im resk any more o' ole Dunkin's welcomin'—it was too warm, he said to himself—it made him feel a hankerin' for fresh air. He hadn't more'n got out into the passage and tuk his hat down, when ole Dunkin come out of a side door openin' on the passage between Tom an' the door.

" 'Why, Lord bless me, Tommy,' says 'e—he allus talked loud, bein' 'customed to the noise o' the mill—'you hain't goin'?' The house was open, an' the talkin' round the table stopped while the compiny all listened to the ole man out in the passage. Tom begun to stammer out somethin', havin' to go to town in the mornin' an' gittin' up early. 'Why, there'll be lots o' dancin' yet, Tommy, an' ef you wa'n't invited here, you're jest as welcome as ef you had a' been.'

"Human natur', even the pore quality Tom had, couldn't stan' no more, an' Tom made a break for the door. He could hear the boys an' gals laffin' fit to kill—*they* couldn't stan' no more. Tom mounted his mare, an' as he started down the lane ole Dunkin stood in the door, an' called after 'im:

" 'Well, good-night, Tommy; hope you enjoyed yerself. You wa'n't invited here, but you was jest as welcome as ef you had a' been.'

"Tom run the mare all the way home, an' laid awake all night cussin' hisself. He kept close for more'n a month afterwards, and for a long time he would turn outen the road whenever he see one o' them gals comin'."

"Who married Jinnie?" I asked with a boyish interest in the blue-eyed beauty, as Mr. McDugald picked up his molasses jug.

"Well, now, who do you reckon?"

"You married her yourself, didn't you, Mr. McDugald?"

"Well, no, I didn't, I'm sorry to say, though I wouldn't have my ole 'ooman hear me say so. Tom MacDonal' married her. They didn't notice Tom much more'n dirt 'till his Uncle Archie died down in Sampson county and left 'im a plantation an' a likely lot o' niggers. Not only the Campbells, but everybody tuk 'im up then, and he married her inside o' six months. She's dead now, pore critter, an' ole Tom's be'n married twice since. But that oldes' boy o' his'n, young Tom, is hern."

Mr. McDugald swung the molasses jug under the cart, in close proximity to another jug, of somewhat smaller proportions; and mounting his mule, which, after the fashion of the Carolina sandhills, wore a saddle and drew the cart at the same time, started off down the Lumberton plank-road.

"Well, Cholly," he said, "I reckon it'll be sun-down afore I git over them sandhills. G'long, Beauregard."

How a Good Man Went Wrong

The Treasurer of Wayup left town somewhat unexpectedly the other day, and in order to explain his absence to his family, sent a note home by a District Messenger boy.

The Treasurer had been gone about two weeks, when it began to be rumored about the City Hall that nobody knew where he was. An enterprising newspaper got wind of the affair, and a morning edition of the *Daily Screecher* came out with a four-column article, inquiring in guarded but significant language: "Where is Treasurer Barnstable?"

By noon the report was pretty general that the City Treasurer had absconded. By two o'clock a meeting of the city finance committee had been held, and an examination of the books had disclosed the fact that there was three hundred thousand dollars of the city's money in the Treasurer's possession.

At three o'clock an expert was called in to open the Treasurer's vault, of which the absconded official alone knew the combination. By four o'clock the rumored defalcation had been telegraphed to the four quarters of the globe.

In the gray dawn of the following morning, after a night of ceaseless toil, the expert succeeded in opening the vault. It was empty!

This discovery intensified the prevailing excitement. The defaulting Treasurer's bondsmen attached all his property. A warrant was issued charging him with embezzlement, and a description of his person was telegraphed all over the world. A crop of lawsuits sprang up; the newspapers flourished like a green bay tree.

When, on the morning of the eighteenth day of his absence, Treasurer Barnstable walked into his office, set his grip-sack on the floor, and hung his hat on its accustomed nail, you would have thought from their looks that the clerks in the office had seen a ghost. The news of his return spread like wildfire. In thirty seconds the Mayor was in the office.

"Barnstable, old man!" he exclaimed; "where *have* you been?"

"Why, I've been down in New Jersey, fishing. What's been going on? I hope I haven't been missed?"

The Mayor groaned.

190

"Where is the three hundred thousand dollars?" he inquired, as soon as he could command his voice.

"The three hundred thousand dollars? Why, it's in the vault; where else should it be?"

"Don't ask me now, Barnstable, but show me the money; I'll tell you why afterward."

The Treasurer was mystified; but he knew his friend the Mayor too well to think he would ask anything of the kind except for some good reason. He unlocked the vault, entered it; and, taking down an old cigar box from an upper shelf, unwrapped a bundle covered with brown paper, and revealed to the glad eyes of the Mayor three hundred thousand dollars worth of cash and good securities.

An explanation followed; and, as soon as the astounded Treasurer could pull himself together, he took a carriage and was driven rapidly to his home.

As he mounted the steps of his house, he met the messenger boy coming down; he had just delivered the message.

THE SHORT STORIES

A Limb of Satan

Old Uncle Ebenezer was sitting in a rickety splint-bottomed chair, under the shade of the china tree in his back yard, smoking his clay pipe with the long reed stem, and dreaming over, in a state between sleeping and waking, the days of his long-vanished youth. The sun was setting over a hill that sloped gently upward from the rear of his house, and the cabin beyond the garden across the back fence stood silhouetted against a glorious background of purple and gold.

Uncle Ebenezer recalled, with a singular vividness of detail, the plantation upon which he had been brought up, as a slave, down in North Carolina. He had been named Napoleon, contracted, plantation fashion, to 'Poleon. His master had not been a hard one, as masters went, and 'Poleon might have lived quite comfortably, with his wife and family, whom he loved very much, but for the haunting fear, never absent from the slave's heart, of what eventually happened in 'Poleon's case. His master died, the estate was divided, and 'Poleon and his family were separated, with no reasonable hope of reunion. Shortly after this, 'Poleon ran away from his new owner, and in the course of time, with the aid of friends, found himself in the Northern town where he had since lived, for many years, in the little frame house behind which he now sat smoking his pipe and, incidentally, nursing his rheumatism.

Upon his arrival in the Free States, 'Poleon, who was of a religious turn of mind, placed himself under the spiritual ministrations of a colored preacher who presided over a small congregation of his own people. At their first interview the minister naturally asked 'Poleon his name.

" 'Poleon Pearsall, suh," was the reply.

"My deah brother," rejoined the elder solemnly—he only knew two books, The Bible and The Pilgrim's Progress—"you won' nevuh be able ter squeeze thoo de peahly gates wid no sech name as dat. In yo' ign'ance you has be'n kyarin' roun' a name hitch' ter you w'at has be'n a millstone roun' de neck er yo' soul. Dat name er yo'n means Apollyon"—the elder pronounced the *o* long—"which is anotheh name fer de Ole Debbil hisse'f. You better look in de Good Book an' fin' yose'f a new name, fer ter take off de cuss er dat one. An' you betteh change yo' other name, too, er you'll hab de slave-ketchers aftuh you fus' thing you know."

As a result of this conference, the new arrival was received in the church the following Sunday under the name of "Ebenezer P. Johnson." The "P." meant nothing in particular, but was merely thrown in for general effect, unless it might be regarded as a lingering flavor of the old appellation.

One of the first steps taken by Ebenezer, *nee* 'Poleon, upon finding employment, had been to buy himself a home. He had bought it upon a land contract, on long time; and upon the occasion referred to, when he was sitting in the garden, he had finally succeeded, after nearly twenty years, in meeting the last installment of principle and interest upon his little home. The agreed period of payment had been lengthened by several causes. Ebenezer had never heard of his plantation wife, nor of their children. Your Negro does not, as a rule, like to live alone, and when Ebenezer became established as a freeman, he had married a woman who promised well, but proved to be afflicted with fits, and, after some years, departed for another and a better world, after putting Ebenezer to a great deal of trouble and expense. A union was formed in the trade at which he worked, and he found himself, by reason of his color, excluded from membership. This deprived him of employment, and of the hope of advancement by reason of skill and experience. With the patient philosophy of his race, he had taken to carrying the hod, and falling one day from a defective scaffold, had broken a leg. A lawyer brought suit against the contractor, but an abler lawyer defended him, and Ebenezer recovered no damages. The fracture healed imperfectly, and when Ebenezer got out and around again, he walked with a pronounced limp. Since that time, too, the injured limb had been extremely susceptible to changes in the weather; it was as sensitive as a barometer—the least dampness in the air brought on rheumatic twinges.

These and others of the small misfortunes which form so large a part of the life of the poor had necessarily retarded the payment for the house; but "All's well that ends well," and Uncle Ebenezer, who had that day received a clear deed for his property, would have been happy, he thought, but for two things. First, he sadly reflected, he had no furniture worthy of the name. His wife, years before, had wished him to buy furniture, and let the house wait. She had argued that they would both be old before the house was paid for, and that they might as well be comfortable while they were young enough to enjoy life. Ebenezer had resisted this logic, which turned out to be sound enough in his wife's case, for an unusually severe fit carried her off while the house was yet furnished with only the barest necessaries. Anticipating his freedom from debt, Ebenezer had for several months had his eye upon a set of furniture, upholstered in red, blue and green plush, displayed in a neighboring show window, and which he had thought would set off his house finely; but the furniture had been purchased by one of his neighbors a few weeks before Ebenezer had finished paying for the property.

The question of furniture, then, would of itself have been sufficient to cloud slightly the serenity of the afternoon, even had there not been another and more acute source of discomfort. For instance, as Uncle Ebenezer took his pipe from his mouth and was running a long broom-straw through the stem to clear out the ambeer, a pebble, swiftly propelled from some hidden source, by an unseen power, struck the stem and knocked the pipe from the old man's hand.

"Drat dat boy!" he muttered angrily, as he stooped to pick up the fallen pipe-stem. "Ef I had sich a chile er gran'chile, I'd break eve'y bone in 'is body, but w'at I'd make 'im behave hisse'f. Oh-h-hh!" he muttered, in a voice trembling with rage, as he shook his gnarled and knotted fist toward a small black head projected cautiously above the rear fence, "ef I could jes' lay my han's on dat boy, I'd—I'd—"

Emotion rendered the rest of his speech inarticulate. The small black lad in the yard behind his own was the bane of his life. For several weeks there had been an active feud between Ebenezer and this boy—a situation the more exasperating to the old man because so one-sided. A sling-shot—at best an invention of the Evil One—becomes in the hands of a small boy a weapon proscribed by law in all well-governed cities. Uncle Ebenezer's flowers had had their heads shot off; his chickens had been killed one by one. His cat, after incredible hardships, had been driven into exile. A window in the rear of his house had been broken, and now even his personal dignity and security were assailed by this little *limb of Satan*.

"A lim' er Satan—dat's w'at he is, sho's you bawn! Ef he wuz my boy, I'd l'arn 'im ter rispec' ole age, ef I had ter string 'im up by his thumbs, er t'ar 'im, limb f'm limb, er roas' 'im befo' a slow fier.

"I s'pose he's got a mammy. W'at kin' er 'oman is it w'at'll stan' 'sponsible fer a young un lack dat? Some low-down, no-'count triflin' critter she is, no doubt, w'at ain' wuth de power an' shot it'd take ter kill 'er. Dat boy is ernuff by hisse'f ter prove dat his daddy and his grandaddy en all his antcisters oughter be'n in jail. De Debbil is put his mark all ober dat boy's count-'nance. Dar's dat 'oman stan'in' in her back do' now! I'm gwine down ter de een' er de gyahden an' gin her a piece er my min'."

Uncle Ebenezer rose to his feet with many a groan, and took several hobbling steps toward the rear of the yard before he hesitated, and then stopped short.

"Ef I does," he muttered, "jes' ez lack ez not she'd th'ow somethin' at me, er e'se jump over de fence wid a broom er a rollin' pin; an' dis yer rheumatiz is twistin' my laig so I'm 'feard I couldn' 'fen' myse'f, er git in de house befo' she'd mos' killt me—er e'se she'd fall down in a fit an' sw'ar I knocked her down. Now she's gone—an' dere goes ernudder one er my winder-panes! De p'liceman on dis yer beat oughter be 'long in fo' er five minutes. I'm gwine ter hab dat boy 'rested, ef it's de las' ac' I ever does!"

Sis' Jane was bending over the ironing-board, where she had toiled since early morn. It was not every day that Sis' Jane, as her friends called her—her other name was Walker—could work at home, for poverty compelled her to accept employment wherever it might be found, at whatever a healthy, able-bodied, willing woman could turn her hand to. Sis' Jane's lot in life had been a hard one, judged even by the standard prevailing among her own people. Born a slave upon a Southern plantation and freed by the Civil War, she had married, when but little more than a child, a husband who as a breadwinner had proved a complete failure, the support of the family devolving mainly upon Jane. After a period of wandering they had settled in this town, so far as people who lived from hand to mouth could be said to settle anywhere. Numerous children had come with the years, and finding the battle of life too severe, had retired early from the struggle, except little Sam, who, by virtue of a strong constitution, had survived cold, hunger, bad air, poor food and insufficient clothing, and having thus proved his right to live, was now the sole joy and comfort of his mother, who loved him much and spoiled him not a little.

Sis' Jane's troubles had been various. Her husband, after having lived for years upon her earnings, had fallen a victim to evil courses and died after a lingering illness, leaving a doctor bill for his wife to liquidate. Jane liked a nice house, and having paid, by small installments, the doctor's and undertaker's bills, had invested in a beautiful set of furniture, upholstered in red, blue and green plush, which had been temptingly displayed for several months in the show window of the Great American Installment Furniture Emporium at a near-by corner. The price, forty dollars, was prohibitive if demanded all at once; but on the installment plan, at two dollars per week, with interest at ten per cent monthly on the deferred payments, seemed ridiculously low. She had undertaken the purchase with a light heart and for several months had paid the installments promptly. Then one of her best and most liberal patrons, who paid her three dollars a week for washing and ironing, moved away from the town. Her boy, too, had the measles, and required nursing and medicine. Mr. Baumgartner had been accommodating about the furniture, but after receiving no money for several weeks, began to show signs of impatience. The rent, moreover, became due with heartless regularity, and the landlord knew too well the difficulty of meeting it currently to permit his tenants to fall behind. Sis' Jane, for these various reasons, was considerably troubled in mind as she stood, this summer day, perspiring over the ironing-board.

Just then, as the weight of her misfortunes seemed to press most heavily, little Sam came running into the house. He had carefully hidden his sling-shot—a modified form of catapult—behind the ash-barrel, and presented to his mother's eye a perfect picture of injured innocence.

"Mammy!" he cried, in shrill childish treble, his eyes bulging with fright, "O mammy! dat ole man back er ou' lot is shakin' his fis' an' makin' faces at me, an' say he's gwine ter skin me alive—jes' 'cause I wuz lookin' over de fence at 'im."

Sis' Jane set her iron down and proceeded to relieve her mind:

"Ez ef a po' widder 'oman didn' hab trials ernuff, here comes dis ole nigger man fer ter make mo' trouble. My little Sammy, de sweetes'-tempered, lovin'es'-natered, bes'-behaved boy in dis neighborhood, can't go out in his own gyahden an' look ober his own back fence, widout bein' 'bused an' th'eaten' by a triflin' ole nigger w'at 'low he's too good ter be looked at. What he wanter put on airs erbout? He ain' got no fu'nicher in his house—Liza Jones say dey ain' but two cheers an' a stool in de place. He ain' got no wife ner no housekeeper, ner no child'en, ner nobody at all erbout 'im. I reckon he's one er dese yer mean ole debbils dat nobody won' lib wid nohow.

"But he sha'n't impose on my Sammy! I'm gwine out dere in de ya'd an' gib 'im a piece er my min', an' ef dat don' stop 'im, I'll jes' 'po't 'im ter de p'liceman on dis beat, an' he'll fix 'im, I don' doubt w'atsomeber."

While his mother was indulging in this monologue, Sammy had disappeared. Going out by the front door, he ran around the house, secured the hidden weapon, and took another shot, through a crack in the fence, at the old man's pipe, the clay bowl of which he shattered to fragments, one of which Uncle Ebenezer had some trouble in getting out of his eye.

When Sis' Jane, hearing some further commotion, went to the back door, she saw her old neighbor standing at the line fence, brandishing a large stick, and hurling violent denunciations at her offspring. Sis' Jane took her way majestically down the garden walk.

"Look-a-here, 'oman," Uncle Ebenezer sputtered as she drew near the fence, "I want you ter keep dat little lim' er Satan er yo'n chained up, er I'm gwine ter beat de life outer 'im de fus' time I kin lay my han's on 'im. He shoots de heads off'n all my flowers, he's killt all er my chickens, he's broke two panes er glass outer my winder, an' he's jes' dis minute knock' my pipe outer my mouf an' nigh erbout put my eye out—an' den he stan's here by de fence an' grins at me! Ef he teches anything er mine any mo', I'm gwine ter lamm 'im, er e'se hab 'im tuck up—dat's w'at, an' you better 'member it!"

Jane had listened to his harangue with an air of weariness, mingled with contempt.

"Is you thoo?" she asked, when the old man paused for lack of breath, and shook his stick at Sam, who had prudently retreated to a safe distance.

"Yas, I'm thoo talkin'. Fum now on I speaks wid deeds, not wo'ds. Jes' le' me lay my han's on you, you little black rascal, an' I'll l'arn you manners, er my name ain' Ebenezer Johnson!"

"I wants ter say, w'en you get thoo blowin' off steam," said Sis' Jane, squaring herself off—she was a large, fullbreasted woman, and loomed up considerably over the old man, whom age had bowed—"I wants ter say dat ef I wuz a po' ole, cripple', wo'n-out shadder of a man, lack you is, wid one foot in de grave an' de other totterin' on de edge, dat I'd try ter fin' somethin' better ter do dan ter be tormentin' de life out'n a po' little o'phan boy, wid nobody but a po' ha'd-wo'kin' widder 'oman ter pervide fer his keep an' clo's an' schoolin'. De idee of a man er yo' age pickin' at a feeble little chile! I'm 'shame' ter hab you in dis neighbo'hood; I'm gwine ter move an' git 'way from dat."

"Good excuse!" retorted the old man, with something between a snort and a chuckle. "I doubt ef you kin pay de rent."

Sis' Jane turned pale beneath her ebony integument. The old man perceived the effect of his speech and followed up his advantage.

"Dese yer cheap people, w'at rents," he went on, "is de ruination of a neighbo'hood; dey ain' got no intrus' in keepin' it up. Ef dey loses dey repitation, er goes in debt at de groc'ry, dey kin move whar folks don' know 'em. Dey lets dey no-'count child'en run de streets an' git inter all so'ts er debilment, an' don' keer fer nobody ner nuffin'."

"Ef I didn' hab no mo' ter brag erbout dan you has," broke in Sis' Jane, placing her arms akimbo, "ef I didn' hab no mo' d'n dis two-by-fo' lot, on dis yer low-down alley, an' dat ten-foot dog house wid nuffin' in it but a kitchen table an' two wooden cheers, I wouldn' be talkin' so biggety ez you is! A pusson mought hab misfortunes an' come ter lib in dis neighbo'hood fer a mont' er so, an' den move erway; but I considers it a sign er mighty low tas'e w'en anybody delib'ately buys a house in dis yer—dis yer—cow-pen," she ejaculated with a fine scorn, casting a contemptuous glance around the neighboring back yards.

"You kin thank yo' lucky stars," rejoined Uncle Ebenezer, "ef you don' hab ter go lower yit; some folks gits ter do po'-house. An' ez fer dat little black lim' er Satan, I kin see his finish now, on de scaffol'! He's got all de marks on 'im—dey've crapped out soon, but I kin read 'em—I kin read 'em. I prophesies a bad een' for dat boy! Ef he ain' killt befo' he grows up, he'll be hung higher'n Haman w'en he is. Ef I had a gran'son lack dat, I'd—I'd pizen 'im ter sabe de fam'ly fum disgrace."

"You is a evil-hea'ted ole sinner," retorted Sis' Jane, losing some of her coolness. "Nebber, sence I lef' my ole marster's plantation down in Jeffe'son County, No'th Ca'lina, has I eber met wid ez mean a' ole nigger ez you is. You er mos' lackly too ole ter hang in dis worl'—you've l'arnt how ter cover up yo' crimes, no doubt—but you'll bu'n in de nex' worl', all right ernuff, I kin hear yo' ole dry bones a-cracklin' now!"

"I don' know who could 'a' raise sech a specimen as you down in Jeffe'son County, No'th Ca'lina," retorted Uncle Ebenezer. "W'at po' w'ite man did you b'long to down dere?"

"I didn' b'long ter no po' w'ite man," replied Jane, "I b'long ter de fines' genterman in Jeffe'son County, an' he bought me fum ole Mars Peter Pearsall jes' atter de wah broke out."

"Huh!" rejoined the old man, looking at her with greater interest, "w'at wuz yo' mammy's name?"

"Her name wuz Dilsey."

"An' w'at yo' daddy's name?" asked the old man.

"I don' see w'at it is ter you, but ef it'll do you any good ter know, his name was 'Poleon Pearsall. Ef he wuz heah now, he wouldn' 'low no cross grain', half-crazy ole nigger lack you ter be 'busin' his gran'chil' an' th'eatenin' his life!"

"No," replied the old man with something like a smile, "I 'spec' he wouldn'. An' ef I had my gal, Jane, w'at I ain' seed fer twenty yeah's en mo', ter come an' keep house fer me, I wouldn' haf ter lib all by myse'f in dis yer lonesome house er mine—on dis yer *low-down* alley—in dis yer ole cattle-pen er a neighbo'hood. Did yo' mammy ever tell you w'at become er yo' daddy?"

"W'at you know 'bout my daddy?" asked Sis' Jane curiously.

"I knows all erbout 'im, chile," replied the old man. *"I'm yo' daddy an youer my gal."*

It was easy to make a hole in the fence by pulling off three or four palings. In a few minutes Uncle Ebenezer was seated in a green plush patent rocker, relating the incidents of his life to the wide-eyed and excited Jane.

"An' now," said the old man, looking around, "whar's dat boy?"

"Sammy" called his mother, "you Sammy, come hyuh!"

A small black face, with white and shiny eyes apparently twice their usual dimensions, peered cautiously round the edge of the door-jamb.

"Come in here, boy," commanded his mother, sadly but resignedly. "Ef yo' gran'daddy wants ter beat you fer yo' misdoin's, he's got de right, fer we're gwine ter move in his house termorrer. Come in an' git yo' lickin', fer I don' doubt you desarve it."

"Bless yo' life, honey," chuckled the old man, holding out his arms, "come here ter yo' ole gran'pappy! He wouldn' lay a finger on you fer all de worl'! You er jes' de spit an' image er me w'en I wuz yo' age, an' jes' ez chock-full er playfulness an' debilment. Now dat I'm thoo huggin' you, take dis yer ten-cent piece an' go an' buy yo'se'f some candy, an' den come ober to my house thoo dat hole in de fence an' see yo' gran' pappy!"

Aunt Mimy's Son

Not the least important member of our household on the sandhills was our colored cook, Mrs. Jemima Belfontaine. I happen to know that this was her name, for I wrote it down in our household account-book when we first set up our establishment, and I saw it once again in the address of a letter I read for her. When she first came to work for us, my wife, who was not familiar with Southern customs, was doubtful how to address her, and to be on the safe side, called her Mrs. Belfontaine.

"Law, ma'am," she said, after the first day or two, "I ain' use' to bein' call' Mis' Belfount'n, an' it kind o' 'fuses me! Ef I gets to thinkin' o' myse'f as Mis' Belfount'n, I'll be so proud I won't be able to cook. Dey doan' nobody call me Mis' Belfount'n. Dat's w'at dey use' to call my ole missis. Ev'ybody calls me 'Mimy,' or 'Aun' Mimy,' or 'Sis' Mimy,' an' I feels mo' comf'table w'en I'm call' by a name I'm use' to."

So we called her "Aunt Mimy."

Nature was in a generous mood when she planned Aunt Mimy, for she could not have weighed less than three hundred pounds. She was of chocolate-brown complexion, and possessed the cheerful disposition of her race and the genial good nature that usually characterizes fat people. Aunt Mimy generally wore a gay bandana head-handkerchief when about her work in the kitchen, but on Sundays she blossomed out in a bonnet of antique style and decoration, a gift from the former mistress, of whom she always spoke with respectful affection.

Aunt Mimy had been recommended to us by an acquaintance in the neighboring town. We were boarding for a few weeks at the principal hotel while the process of installation into our new domain was going on. There were repairs to be made on the fine old house we had bought, furniture to be purchased, and servants to be hired. For us, as strangers to the country and the people, the task of obtaining competent domestic help was a difficult one, and we accepted with gratitude the kindly advice of the warm-hearted people among whom we had come to settle. We mentioned to one of them, a gentleman of position and standing, and who, by the way, had been brought up in the neighborhood where my farm was, that we wondered where we could get a good cook.

"I think I know just the woman you want," he said, after a moment's reflection. I know of no better cook than old Aunt Mimy, who used to belong to old Colonel Belfontaine, my wife's father. Her mother once belonged to Major McAdoo, whose place you have bought, and Colonel Belfontaine got her with his wife. She has been cooking in town here, but the people have moved away, and I think you can get her. She was at our house the other day, and told my wife she was tired of town, and wanted to move back into the country, in the neighborhood of the old place. Negroes are like cats, you know. I don't mean the young Negroes, who like to wander, but the old generation, who cling to the old customs and the old places. I'm sure Aunt Mimy would be delighted to go, for it would take her right back into the neighborhood where she was born and raised. I'll send her around, if you'd like to talk to her."

I thanked my kind informant, and the next day Aunt Mimy appeared at the hotel. She was introduced into our sitting room by way of the back stairs, which must have been of unusual width to accommodate her. I was indeed somewhat frightened at her bulk, and she seemed to surmise the direction of my thoughts.

"Yas, suh," she said, "I know I'm big, but I'm a mighty light eater. You see I've done got my growth, an' it doan' take much ter keep me up."

Our interview was satisfactory. We were pleased with Aunt Mimy. She seemed neat, respectful, and intelligent. Her skill had been vouched for, and we engaged her to cook for us at the wages she named, which seemed to us ridiculously small, although apparently quite up to the local standard.

Aunt Mimy entirely justified our good opinion of her, and more than met our expectations in the matter of her art. She could not only cook most of the dishes we were accustomed to, but made us acquainted with numerous Southern delicacies, some of which would tempt the palate of an epicure. We had suggested that she live in the house with us, but she said that was not the Southern custom, and she was not used to it; she would prefer a house of her own, where she could receive her friends and provide a home for a young niece who lived with her. There were several small houses on the estate, most of them log cabins, and we assigned her one of these, situated near the main road, about a quarter of a mile from our own house. She was in our kitchen by daylight in the morning, and except when she was off duty, remained until after the supper table had been cleared away and the kitchen work completed. She had a young colored girl to assist her; but she had small confidence in the powers of most young people, and insisted on seeing for herself that everything was properly done.

"Dese young folks," she was wont to say at times, "is not good fer much.

Dey ain' had de trainin'. Dem ole times wuzn't ev'thing dey wuz cracked up fer, but dey did do one thing—dey l'arnt cullud folks how to wuk, an' some of 'em has mos' forgot how, sence dey ben free."

She made one exception to this general rule as to the worthlessness of young people, and that was in the case of her son Tom. We first learned of this son shortly after she came into our service.

" 'Scuse me, suh," she said to me one day in the dining room, "but is you evuh run 'cross my son Tom at de No'th?"

"Why, no, Aunt Mimy; at least I don't know that I have."

"Well, suh, dat 'peahs to me kinder quare. He's be'n at de No'th three or fo' yeahs, an' I wuz mos' sho' you'd 'a' met 'im somewhar."

"What part of the North is he in?" I asked, "You know the North is a pretty big place, Aunt Mimy."

"He's be'n in Noo Yo'k an' Boston an' Providence an' Rhode Islan'. He wuz in Cleveland w'en I got my las' lettuh from 'im."

"How does he like the North?" I asked, with mild curiosity.

"He likes it fus'-rate, suh. He says cullud folks gits 'long jes' like w'ite folks, long as dey got de money an' behaves deyse'ves."

"What is your son doing?" I said, somewhat interested in this philosopher who had succeeded in discovering the true secret of prosperity and progress—thrift and good conduct.

"He said in his las' lettuh dat he wuz in de hotel business—runnin' a hotel, I s'pose, like de Jeff'son House, whar you put up in town yonduh."

"He must be a pretty bright man," I said, "to have succeeded so well."

"Oh, yas, suh," she said, mistaking my meaning, "he's sev'al shades brighter'n I is. My husban' wuz a yaller man. An' he's smaht, too, or he nevuh would 'a' clumb up so fas'. I'm proud o' my Tom. Ef dese yuther good-for-nothin' young boys would do like my Tom, dey'd he'p deir race to git out'n de land o' Egyp' an' de house er bondage, an' be somebody, like w'ite folks."

It was some time after this conversation before Aunt Mimy's son's name was mentioned again in my hearing. One day I asked her, casually, if she had heard from her son lately.

"Yas, suh," she answered, "I got a lettuh f'om 'im las' week."

"How's the hotel getting on?" I asked.

"He's done quit de hotel business, suh. He says dey wa'n't money enough in it. He's gone into de railroad business now. I 'spec' he's runnin' one o' dem big railroads up dere in de No'th. He couldn' 'spec' to get nothin' like dat to do down heah, 'cause dey ain' enough for all de w'ite folks to do; an' co'se it's nach'ul for de w'ite folks not to want our folks crowdin' 'em, for dey wuzn' raise' dat-a-way. W'at dese young cullud folks wants to do, is to git out'n heah an' go to de No'th, whar Tom says dey's plenty o' room an' plenty o' money, an' dey kin have a chance like other folks."

Some months later the subject came up again, I have forgotten in just what connection.

"How's your son Tom getting along?" I asked. "Has he run his railroad into the hands of a receiver yet?"

She did not understand my last allusion, so she answered only the first question.

"He's gittin' along fine, suh, climbin' up de ladder ev'y yeah he stays at de No'th. He's made so much money in de railroad business dat he's quit dat an' stahted a bank. Banks is whar dey makes money, ain' it, suh?"

"Yes," I said, "sometimes." I had painful memories of a bank where I had lost a considerable sum.

"Uh, huh!" she said in triumph. "Dat's w'at I 'lowed." She put her hand in her pocket and fished out an old fashioned knitted purse, from which she extracted a new bank-note.

"I reckon he made dat five-dollah bill, doan' you, suh?"

I glanced at the money. It was a note of an Ohio national bank.

"Yes," I said. "I suppose he did make it, in a way."

She put it carefully away.

"Your son doesn't forget his mother in his prosperity," I remarked.

"Oh, no, suh, he always sot a heap o' store by his mammy. An' I'm proud o' him, for dey ain' no yuther young cullud man w'at evuh went from dis place dat evuh sent back as much money to de ole folks as my Tom has, an' he's de only one sent back any money he made hisse'f."

Several months later, Aunt Mimy brought me a letter to read.

"It's f'om my Tom, suh, she said. "I know de han'write. My niece reads my lettuhs, but she's gone to town to stay wid her mammy a day or so, so I 'lowed you or Mis' Annie wouldn' mind readin' it to me."

I took the letter. It was written in a large hand, with some faults of grammar and spelling, but on the whole a creditable production. I did not think it quite a commercial hand, however, nor was the style that of a man accustomed to weighty affairs.

Among other things it said, in substance, that the writer had found banking a somewhat uncertain business, that it had its ups and downs, that it had opened the way for him, however, to a place in a state institution, where he would be sure of steady employment for a year or two, and would know what his earnings would be, and that he expected to be so busy that he might not be able to write to her with his usual regularity.

Aunt Mimy listened with a pleased expression to the reading of the letter, and when I handed it back, took it as tenderly and held it as carefully as if it had been a live thing.

"I reckon he's done be'n 'lected to de legislature or sump'n," she said with conviction. "I always knowed f'om his cradle dat my Tom would git along in de worl'."

"You ought to feel proud of him," I said. "It's true he changes his business pretty often, but then he seems to get into something better every time."

"Oh, yas, suh," she replied, "dat wuz alluz de way wid Tom—nevuh

satisfied, alluz tryin' to fin' sump'n bettah. But nevuh did I 'spec' to see a
boy o' mine a' officuh o' de state. Do you reckon he might git to be gov'nor?"
she asked, a little doubtfully.

"I don't know, Aunt Mimy. Time works wondrous changes. But whether
he ever does or not, as long as he is an honest man, and earns a living, and
doesn't forget his mother, you have reason to be proud of him."

Aunt Mimy did not hear from her son for some time after the receipt
of this letter; at least, she made no mention of him in our hearing. Eight or
nine months later she asked my wife one day if she could be spared from the
house a half-day in the morning and another in the afternoon, if she would
make it up by coming earlier and staying later. When asked the reason for
the request, she said:

"I got a sick man at my house. I use' to know his mammy w'en he wuz
a baby. Fac', we b'longed to de same w'ite folks an' wuz raised on de same
plantation. He's be'n away a long time an' he's come back to de ole neighbo-
'hood, an' all his folks wuz gone, so I done tol' 'im I'd take keer o' 'im till
he got well. He gits out'n his head oncet in a w'ile, an' my niece Sally is
too young ter be lef' 'lone wid 'im all de time. It ain' nothin' ketchin', for
the doctuh says so."

"What doctor has he had?" I asked.

"Doctor Hay, suh. He's be'n to see 'im twice, an' he's comin' ag'in dis
evenin'."

My wife gave her the required permission. We asked her, from time to
time, how the sick man was getting along. For a while she seemed to think
he was mending, but later her answers were not reassuring. She took a warm
interest in the patient, and we thought she must have loved his mother very
much, for she seemed quite sad at times, and we knew of nothing else to mar
her usual serenity.

Doctor Hay was called to our house one day to see my wife. Before leaving
the house after his visit, he spoke of Aunt Mimy's guest.

"By the way," he said, "I have a very interesting case down here on the
road, at your cook's house. It is a young mulatto, of unusually fine physique
and more than average intelligence—just the kind of man who, with fair opportunities and some strength of character might have been of some use in the
world. But he took a wrong turn somewhere, and dissipation and disease have
simply used him up. He is practically dying of debility; he hasn't vitality
enough left to recruit his losses.

"It's a queer case, too, in other respects. Occasionally the man is delirious,
and from his ravings, one can imagine what a variety of experiences he has
undergone. He would seem to have been a hotel bell-boy, a sleeping-car porter,
and an attendant in a gambling den. But the most curious phase of his delirium
is a constant fear of pursuit, as if he had escaped from prison and were afraid

of recapture. Poor creature! In just about ten days he will be confined in a narrow cell from which there will be no escape."

One day, a week or two later, Aunt Mimy did not appear in the morning at the usual hour, but sent word by her niece that her guest had died the night before, and asked that we excuse her for a day or two, to attend to the preparations for the funeral.

Of course we acquiesced, and Aunt Mimy's young assistant did the kitchen work until her return.

Early next morning Aunt Mimy came up to the house. Her eyes were swollen with weeping, and we sympathized with her distress, which we imagined grew out of the natural tenderness of her heart, either at the mere presence of death, or at the loss of the son of her old friend.

"I come up to ast you an' Mis' Annie if you had any objections to my buryin' de young man w'at died at my house in de ole plantation buryin'-groun' over yondeh on de hill?"

There was an old burying-ground on the place, where the slaves of former days had laid their tired limbs to rest when their long day of toil was over. It was surrounded by a dilapidated picket fence, and overgrown with weeds and long grass, amid which, here and there, a sunken place or a rotting headboard showed the purpose for which the enclosure had been used. I did not much like the idea of making further interments there, and I suppose Aunt Mimy read the objection in my eyes.

"His gran'mammy use' to b'long on dis plantation, suh, an' all his folks is buried dere, an' I know he wouldn' res' easy in his grave 'less'n he wuz laid 'longside of 'em."

I reluctantly gave the required consent, and she thanked me effusively and went away somewhat comforted. The funeral took place the next day and was largely attended by the colored people, with the usual melancholy delight of their race in mortuary exercises. We could see the cortege wind across the field in the distance until it reached the low hill where the ashes were laid to ashes and dust to dust.

Aunt Mimy came back to work the morning after the funeral. She was very quiet during the rest of the week, and sad of face. Once or twice my wife found her weeping softly in a corner of the kitchen, but respecting her grief, appeared not to notice it.

On Sunday afternoon of the next week, my wife and I took a walk over to the old burying-ground. We did not speak as we approached it, and our progress over the soft earth made no perceptible noise. Before we reached the ruined fence, and while yet outside of the fringe of trees and bushes that surrounded it, we heard the sound of low sobs which seemed to come from someone inside of the enclosure.

We drew softly near and peered through the bushes. Our old cook, dressed in the deepest black, had thrown herself across the low mound of a newly made grave, in an attitude of utter abandonment.

"Oh, my po' boy!" she said between her sobs, unconsciously borrowing almost the words of an ancient Hebrew king, who had a wayward son. "Oh, my po' boy, my po' Tom, why couldn' you stay wid yo' po' ole mammy? She'd 'a' wukked for you, she'd 'a' hid you, she'd 'a' died for you—Oh, Tom, my po' boy, my po' boy!"

We stepped softly away so as not to intrude upon her grief, and after that, we asked her no more about her son.

Aunt Lucy's Search

"**Y**as, honey, I keeps a-goin', goin', goin'."

"And when do you expect to stop, Aunt Lucy?"

"Doan nebber 'spect ter stop 'tel I fines de las' one. Dere's only one lef' now. Dey tell me he's 'way up Norf somewhar, an' I's gwine ter keep a-goin' 'tel I fines 'im. Good-by, honey."

The lady's hand sought her pocket before she extended it to the old colored woman; when she drew it back there was something hard and white left in Aunt Lucy's palm.

"T'ank'ee, honey, de Lawd bless yer," said the old woman, with a curtsy. Then she took up her stick and bundle, drew her scanty shawl closer about her bent shoulders, and hobbled out into the chill November air, muttering to herself, "Goin', a-goin', goin'."

Aunt Lucy was known far and wide as a "character." She had been a slave, and in early womanhood had become the property of a North Carolina farmer—it would be absurd to call him a "planter," for he was but one degree removed from the condition of a poor white man. She married, after the broomstick ritual, a slave upon a near plantation. When he was sold away from the neighborhood, she found another husband without the formality of divorce proceedings. In the course of time and of these alliances, she presented her master with six children, each of whom raised him one degree higher in the social scale. These six young slaves, with their mother, constituted the bulk of his property.

In an evil hour Lucy's master mortgaged his slaves to raise money for a speculation. He invested the proceeds of the mortgage in the stock of a projected canal, from which great things were looked for. Work on the canal began with a flourish of trumpets, and progressed finely for a little while; then the treasurer ran away with the company's money, the work was abandoned, and Lucy's master was ruined. His creditors foreclosed their mortgage, and Lucy and her children were sent to the auction block. Her master and her mistress, and her young masters and mistresses, shed bitter tears, as well they might, for the loss of their slaves cut the tie which bound them to "society." Henceforth, alas! they could hope to be nothing more than "poor whites."

In the ordinary course of events the whole slave family might have been bought by one person, or, if separated, by people in the neighborhood, and they would thus have been able to see one another, at least now and then. But, unfortunately, a "speculator"—a Negro trader—happened to be in the town on the day of the sale. He attended the auction and bought four of Lucy's children—boys ranging in age from twelve to twenty. The other two children, a boy and a girl, both under twelve, were sold to people in the county, and Lucy herself to the gentleman who had hired her from her master for several years, and who was willing to pay a round sum to obtain a cook without an equal.

The monotonous going, going, going, of the auctioneer fell upon the mother's heart like the lash upon quivering flesh, and the stroke of the hammer as each child was knocked down to the trader fell upon her heart like the knell of doom. She did not cry out; she let them take her children unresistingly; the slave could suffer and be silent. The expression of her grief was restrained by a pride which revealed itself in a stoical semblance of indifference; only an occasional gleam of love or hate flashed from her eyes as they rested, now upon her children, now upon the idle crowd who stood listening to the jocular remarks of the auctioneer as he expatiated on the good points of his merchandise. There is no pride like that of hopelessness; but in her cabin at night, Lucy gave vent to her tears, and besought of her Heavenly Master help to bear the burdens which earthly masters imposed upon her. Shallow sciolists may consider the essence of Christianity with its excrescences; this poor woman grasped its inner meaning; she could endure all this at her Christian master's hands, and then seek consolation at the altar of her master's God.

The speculator carried the four young slaves to the far South, and sold them, some in one state, some in another. Of the children left near their mother, the daughter died, and the son was shot and killed far away from home, while attempting to escape from slavery. When the war left Aunt Lucy free, she did not know the whereabouts of any of her children—except the one buried down by the swamp—a sunken grave filled with stagnant water, where frogs croaked a melancholy requiem, and noisome serpents trailed their slimy length along.

Aunt Lucy's last "husband" celebrated his new-found freedom by going as far away from home as the first impulse of his altered situation would carry him; he got as far as Baltimore and never came back to North Carolina. Aunt Lucy stayed at home and worked for her late master. He had always treated her kindly, and now paid her liberal wages. Advancing age had silvered her hair, and the objectless toil of slavery had made her seem older than she really was. A severe attack of rheumatism had left her permanently lame, and rendered walking difficult even with the aid of a stick.

Aunt Lucy's first thought after her "freedom" was of her children; her mother heart had always yearned for them—slavery could not crush this instinct. What seemed a visionary idea took possession of her mind, and could not be dislodged by argument or opposition; she determined to find her children. But how? She had no money to employ detectives, to advertise; she could command none of that machinery of civilization by which at the present day a man can be traced to the very ends of the earth, even when life or liberty depends upon concealment. Aunt Lucy knew of but one way to find her children, and that was to go and look for them.

"She knowed de worl' was big," she said, "but she knowed de Lawd was good."

Aunt Lucy had no ideas whatever about geography; she had never been out of her native county; but she knew that where her children had gone she could go, and that if she lived long enough and kept going she could find them. She had no more stopped to balance probabilities than she would have done to argue the existence of a God. And at fifty this crippled woman took her staff in hand and with little money in her purse, went forth into the wide world upon a quest more hopeless than that of the Holy Grail by Arthur's knights.

But somehow fortune seemed to favor the old woman. She traveled by rail or steamboat when she had money, and walked when she had none. She was a good cook, and at times paused in her search and worked for the means to pay her fare to the next city. Kindly white mothers, who had lost their beardless sons, past finding, on Southern battlefields, sympathized with the old woman, and helped her out of their scanty store. Her own people fed and lodged her when she came among them, and took up collections for her in their churches. She advertised in such papers as colored people were most likely to read.

At the end of two years she had found one son—in Alabama. He had a family, and was very poor. Aunt Lucy did not stay with him long, but resumed her search, strengthened in her faith by this partial success. She found another son in Georgia. But, alas! she found him in a prison camp, a ball and chain on his leg, sentenced for some petty offense to a long term of punishment. She saw him several times, tried to comfort him, and to plant in his heart some seeds of faith and repentance, and then sadly continued her endless journey. This seemed the end of her good luck. She would meet here and there some one who had known a colored man by the name of Sam or Dan or Caesar Johnson; but when she followed up the clue it proved delusive, and five years elapsed before she found another of her children. At one time she went to her old home to rest awhile.

"Better stay home, Aunt Lucy," said her friends, "and not be ramblin' 'roun' de worl' dis way. You'll meet yo' chillen in hebben."

"I doan know 'bout dat," Aunt Lucy would reply with a shake of her head; "dey mought not all git dere. I's got ter fine 'em on dis side'n de ribber, and I mus' keep a goin,' goin,' goin' 'tel I comes across 'em somewhar."

And the queer old figure in faded calico dress, thin woolen shawl, and gingham sunbonnet would take up her stick and go again upon her errand.

She found one other son in Richmond, Virginia. He was better off than any she had hitherto found; he was a preacher, and owned a home to which he made his mother welcome. She remained with him a year—two years— and then the old longing came upon her and she left her comfortable home to look for the last son. She went back to North Carolina, then farther South, toward where her children had first been carried. Diligent searching and in- quiry finally resulted in her tracing the other son to Chicago. Thither she turned her tottering footsteps. An emigrant train hurried her through the moun- tains, across the prairies, and into the great city of the West.

It was late in the afternoon of a cold damp day in the early part of Decem- ber when Aunt Lucy arrived in Chicago. The chill air struck through her thin clothing, and she drew her shawl closer about her as she stepped down on the platform. She looked around among the throng in the crowded depot for a black face. Presently she found one, and in its owner a sympathetic listener. The porter heard her story attentively. Yes, he knew just such a man as she described, whose name was Caesar something, he didn't know his last name, who had been born in North Carolina, had been sold and carried to New Or- leans when a boy, had served in the Union army and had come North at the close of the war. He had heard him speak about it often; he kept a barber shop not far from the depot.

"Just step over there to the waiting room, Auntie, and stay there a few minutes until I get off duty, and I will go up there with you."

Someone called the porter and he hurried away. Aunt Lucy started toward the waiting room, to reach which she had to cross several tracks. The tracks were not fenced nor guarded. Nobody noticed the poor old colored woman. A train shot into the depot. Nobody saw just how it happened; but the old woman, bewildered by the confusion, deafened by the noisy bells, and blinded by the unaccustomed glare of the electric lights, stepped in front of the ap- proaching train. The engine struck her and threw her to the ground.

A crowd quickly surrounded her. The friendly porter came to seek her and found them carrying her into the baggage room. A surgeon was hastily summoned; he pronounced her injuries fatal; she might live an hour or two if kept quiet; any attempt to remove her would only hasten the end.

"Fetch my son," faintly murmured Aunt Lucy. "Let me fine de las' one befo' I go. I's be'n a-goin', goin', goin', dese many years, an' now I's almost gone, an' when I sees him I'll be willin' ter go."

The porter hastened away, and soon returned with the barber, a stalwart black who towered half a head above the men about him. Eager questions were asked and answered, and Aunt Lucy's withered face lit up with solemn joy when she realized beyond a doubt that she had found her last child.

"Lif' me up, honey," she said, "an' put yo' arms aroun' me, and lemme look into yo' face. Is you my little Caesar? Yo' po' ole mammy done trabble all ober de worl' ter fine yer, honey. Been goin', goin', goin', for lo! dese many years, but bless de Lawd, I done foun' de las' one."

The son kissed his mother's cheek as he lifted her to a sitting posture on the rude couch which had been improvised for her reception. Even the surgeon, who had stood by a hundred deathbeds, was touched by this meeting; and the eyes of the rough trainmen who stood about were dim with unaccustomed moisture.

"T'ank de Lawd, I's done foun' de las' one," murmured the dying woman. The tide of life flowed swiftly out. She breathed heavily. They laid her down, and in a moment the spirit which had kept this frail body going, going, going, had gone. Aunt Lucy's mission was accomplished—the hammer of death had fallen.

The March of Progress

The colored people of Patesville had at length gained
the object they had for a long time been seeking—the appointment of a committee of themselves to manage the colored schools of the town. They had argued,
with some show of reason, that they were most interested in the education of
their own children, and in a position to know, better than any committee of
white men could, what was best for their children's needs. The appointments
had been made by the county commissioners during the latter part of the
summer, and a week later a meeting was called for the purpose of electing
a teacher to take charge of the grammar school at the beginning of the fall
term.

The committee consisted of Frank Gillespie, or "Glaspy," a barber, who
took an active part in local politics; Bob Cotten, a blacksmith, who owned
several houses and was looked upon as a substantial citizen; and Abe Johnson,
commonly called "Ole Abe" or "Uncle Abe," who had a large family, and
drove a dray, and did odd jobs of hauling; he was also a class-leader in the
Methodist church. The committee had been chosen from among a number of
candidates—Gillespie on account of his political standing, Cotten as representing the solid element of the colored population, and Old Abe, with democratic
impartiality, as likely to satisfy the humbler class of a humble people. While
the choice had not pleased everybody—for instance, some of the other appli-
cants—it was acquiesced in with general satisfaction. The first meeting of
the new committee was of great public interest, partly by reason of its novelty,
but chiefly because there were two candidates for the position of teacher of
the grammar school.

The former teacher, Miss Henrietta Noble, had applied for the school.
She had taught the colored children of Patesville for fifteen years. When the
Freedmen's Bureau, after the military occupation of North Carolina, had called
for volunteers to teach the children of the freedmen, Henrietta Noble had offered her services. Brought up in a New England household by parents who
taught her to fear God and love her fellow men, she had seen her father's
body brought home from a Southern battlefield and laid to rest in the village

cemetery; and a short six months later she had buried her mother by his side. Henrietta had no brothers or sisters, and her nearest relatives were cousins living in the far West. The only human being in whom she felt any special personal interest was a certain captain in her father's regiment, who had paid her some attention. She had loved this man deeply, in a maidenly, modest way; but he had gone away without speaking, and had not since written. He had escaped the fate of many others, and at the close of the war was alive and well, stationed in some Southern garrison.

When her mother died, Henrietta had found herself possessed only of the house where she lived and the furniture it contained, neither being of much value, and she was thrown upon her own resources for a livelihood. She had a fair education and had read many good books. It was not easy to find employment such as she desired. She wrote to her Western cousins, and they advised her to come to them, as they thought they could do something for her if she were there. She had almost decided to accept their offer, when the demand arose for teachers in the South. Whether impelled by some strain of adventurous blood from a Pilgrim ancestry, or by a sensitive pride that shrank from dependence, or by some dim and unacknowledged hope that she might sometime, somewhere, somehow meet Captain Carey—whether from one of these motives or a combination of them all, joined to something of the missionary spirit, she decided to go South, and wrote to her cousins declining their friendly offer.

She had come to Patesville when the children were mostly a mob of dirty little beggars. She had distributed among them the cast-off clothing that came from their friends in the North; she had taught them to wash their faces and to comb their hair; and patiently, year after year, she had labored to instruct them in the rudiments of learning and the first principles of religion and morality. And she had not wrought in vain. Other agencies, it is true, had in time cooperated with her efforts, but anyone who had watched the current of events must have been compelled to admit that the very fair progress of the colored people of Patesville in the fifteen years following emancipation had been due chiefly to the unselfish labors of Henrietta Noble, and that her nature did not belie her name.

Fifteen years is a long time. Miss Noble had never met Captain Carey; and when she learned later that he had married a Southern girl in the neighborhood of his post, she had shed her tears in secret and banished his image from her heart. She had lived a lonely life. The white people of the town, though they learned in time to respect her and to value her work, had never recognized her existence by more than the mere external courtesy shown by any community to one who lives in the midst of it. The situation was at first, of course, so strained that she did not expect sympathy from the white people; and later, when time had smoothed over some of the asperities of war, her work had so engaged her that she had not had time to pine over her social exclusion. Once or twice nature had asserted itself, and she had longed for her own kind, and had visited her New England home. But her circle of friends was broken up, and she did not find much pleasure in boarding-house life; and on her last visit to the North but one, she had felt so lonely that she had longed for the dark faces of her pupils, and had welcomed with pleasure the hour when her task should be resumed.

But for several reasons the school at Patesville was of more importance to Miss Noble at this particular time than it ever had been before. During the last few years her health had not been good. An affection of the heart similar to that from which her mother had died, while not interfering perceptibly with her work, had grown from bad to worse, aggravated by close application to her duties, until it had caused her grave alarm. She did not have perfect confidence in the skill of the Patesville physicians, and to obtain the best medical advice had gone to New York during the summer, remaining there a month under the treatment of an eminent specialist. This, of course, had been expensive and had absorbed the savings of years from a small salary; and when the time came for her to return to Patesville, she was reduced, after paying her traveling expenses, to her last ten-dollar note.

"It is very fortunate," the great man had said at her last visit, "that circumstances permit you to live in the South, for I am afraid you could not endure a Northern winter. You are getting along very well now, and if you will take care of yourself and avoid excitement, you will be better." He said to himself as she went away: "It's only a matter of time, but that is true about us all; and a wise physician does as much good by what he withholds as by what he tells."

Miss Noble had not anticipated any trouble about the school. When she went away, the same committee of white men was in charge that had controlled the school since it had become part of the public-school system of the State on the withdrawal of support from the Freedmen's Bureau. While there had been no formal engagement made for the next year, when she had last seen the chairman before she went away, he had remarked that she was looking rather fagged out, had bidden her good-by, and had hoped to see her much improved when she returned. She had left her house in the care of the colored woman who lived with her and did her housework, assuming, of course, that she would take up her work again in the autumn.

She was much surprised at first, and later alarmed, to find a rival for her position as teacher of the grammar school. Many of her friends and pupils had called on her since her return, and she had met a number of the people at the colored Methodist church, where she taught in the Sunday school. She had many friends and supporters, but she soon found out that her opponent had considerable strength. There had been a time when she would have withdrawn and left him a clear field, but at the present moment it was almost a matter of life and death to her—certainly the matter of earning a living—to secure the appointment.

The other candidate was a young man who in former years had been one of Miss Noble's brightest pupils. When he had finished his course in the grammar school, his parents, with considerable sacrifice, had sent him to a college for colored youth. He had studied diligently, had worked industriously during his vacations, sometimes at manual labor, sometimes teaching a country school, and in due time had been graduated from his college with honors. He had come home at the end of his school life, and was very naturally seeking the employment for which he had fitted himself. He was a "bright" mulatto, with straight hair, an intelligent face, and a well-set figure. He had acquired some of the marks of culture, wore a frock-coat and a high collar, parted his hair in the middle, and showed by his manner that he thought a good deal of himself. He was the popular candidate among the progressive element of his people, and rather confidently expected the appointment.

The meeting of the committee was held in the Methodist church, where, in fact, the grammar school was taught, for want of a separate schoolhouse. After the preliminary steps to effect an organization, Mr. Gillespie, who had been elected chairman, took the floor.

"The principal business to be brought befo' the meet'n' this evenin'," he said, "is the selection of a teacher for our grammar school for the ensuin' year. Two candidates have filed applications, which, if there is no objections, I will read to the committee. The first is from Miss Noble, who has been the teacher ever since the grammar school was started."

He then read Miss Noble's letter, in which she called attention to her long years of service, to her need of the position, and to her affection for the pupils, and made formal application for the school for the next year. She did not, from motives of self-respect, make known the extremity of her need; nor did she mention the condition of her health, as it might have been used as an argument against her retention.

Mr. Gillespie then read the application of the other candidate, Andrew J. Williams. Mr. Williams set out in detail his qualifications for the position: his degree from Riddle University; his familiarity with the dead and living languages and the higher mathematics; his views of discipline; and a peroration in which he expressed the desire to devote himself to the elevation of his race and assist the march of progress through the medium of the Patesville grammar school. The letter was well written in a bold, round hand, with many flourishes, and looked very aggressive and overbearing as it lay on the table by the side of the sheet of small notepaper in Miss Noble's faint and somewhat cramped handwriting.

"You have heard the readin' of the application," said the chairman. "Gentlemen, what is yo' pleasure?"

There being no immediate response, the chairman continued:

"As this is a matter of consid'able importance, involvin' not only the welfare of our schools, but the progress of our race, an' as our action is liable

to be criticized, whatever we decide, perhaps we had better discuss the subjec'
befo' we act. If nobody else has anythin' to obse've, I will make a few remarks."

Mr. Gillespie cleared his throat, and, assuming an oratorical attitude, proceeded:

"The time has come in the history of our people when we should stand
together. In this age of organization the march of progress requires that we
help ourselves, or be left forever behind. Ever since the war we have been send-
in' our child'n to school an' educatin' 'em; an' now the time has come when
they are leavin' the schools an' colleges, an' are ready to go to work. An' what
are they goin' to do? The white people won't hire 'em as clerks in their sto's
an' factories an' mills, an' we have no sto's or factories or mills of our own.
They can't be lawyers or doctors yet, because we haven't got the money to
send 'em to medical colleges an' law schools. We can't elect many of 'em to
office for various reasons. There's just two things they can find to do—to preach
in our own pulpits, an' teach in our own schools. If it wasn't for that, they'd
have to go on forever waitin' on white folks, like their fo'fathers have done,
because they couldn't help it. If we expect our race to progress, we must educate
our young men an' women. If we want to encourage 'em to get education,
we must find 'em employment when they are educated. We have now an opportunity to do this in the case of our young friend an' fellow-citizen, Mr. Williams, whose eloquent an' fine-lookin' letter ought to make us feel proud of
him an' of our race.

"Of co'se there are two sides to the question. We have got to consider
the claims of Miss Noble. She has been with us a long time an' has done
much good for our people, an' we'll never forget her work an' frien'ship. But,
after all, she has been paid for it; she has got her salary regularly an' for
a long time, an' she has probably saved somethin', for we all know she hasn't
lived high; an', for all we know, she may have had somethin' left her by her
parents. An' then again, she's white, an' has got her own people to look after
her; they've got all the money an' all the offices an' all the everythin'—all
that they've made an' all that we've made for fo' hundred years—an' they sho'ly
would look out for her. If she don't get this school, there's probably a dozen
others she can get at the North. An' another thing: she is gettin' rather feeble,
an' it 'pears to me she's hardly able to stand teachin' so many child'n, an'
a long rest might be the best thing in the world for her.

"Now, gentlemen, that's the situation. Shall we keep Miss Noble, or shall
we stand by our own people? It seems to me there can hardly be but one
answer. Self-preservation is the first law of nature. Are there any other remarks?"

Old Abe was moving restlessly in his seat. He did not say anything, however, and the chairman turned to the other member.

"Brother Cotten, what is yo' opinion of the question befo' the board?"

Mr. Cotten rose with the slowness and dignity becoming a substantial citizen, and observed:

"I think the remarks of the chairman have great weight. We all have nothin' but kind feelin's fer Miss Noble, an' I came here tonight somewhat undecided how to vote on this question. But after listenin' to the just an' forcible arguments of Brother Glaspy, it 'pears to me that, after all, the question befo' us is not a matter of feelin', but of business. As a businessman, I am inclined to think Brother Glaspy is right. If we don't help ourselves when we get a chance, who is goin' to help us?"

"That bein' the case," said the chairman, "shall we proceed to a vote? All who favor the election of Brother Williams—"

At this point Old Abe, with much preliminary shuffling, stood up in his place and interrupted the speaker.

"Mr. Chuhman," he said, "I s'pose I has a right ter speak in dis meet'n'? I *s'pose* I is a member er dis committee?"

"Certainly, Brother Johnson, certainly; we shall be glad to hear from you."

"I s'pose I's got a right ter speak my min', ef I is po' an' black, an' don' weah as good clo's as some other members er de committee?"

"Most assuredly, Brother Johnson," answered the chairman, with a barber's suavity, "you have as much right to be heard as anyone else. There was no intention of cuttin' you off."

"I s'pose," continued Abe, "dat a man wid fo'teen child'n kin be 'lowed ter hab somethin' ter say 'bout de schools er dis town?"

"I am sorry, Brother Johnson, that you should feel slighted, but there was no intention to igno' yo' rights. The committee will be please' to have you ventilate yo' views."

"Ef it's all be'n an' done reco'nized an' 'cided dat I's got de right ter be heared in dis meet'n', I'll say w'at I has ter say, an' it won't take me long ter say it. Ef I should try ter tell all de things dat Miss Noble has done fer de niggers er dis town, it'd take me till termorrow mawnin'. Fer fifteen long yeahs I has watched her incomin's an' her outgoin's. Her daddy was a Yankee kunnel, who died fightin' fer ou' freedom. She come heah when we—yas, Mr. Chuhman, when you an' Br'er Cotten—was jes' sot free an' when none er us didn' have a rag ter ou' backs. She come heah, an' she tuk yo' child'n an' my child'n, an' she teached 'em sense an' manners an' religion and book-l'arnin'. When she come heah we didn' hab no chu'ch. Who writ up No'th an' got a preacher sent to us, an' de fun's ter buil' dis same chu'ch-house we're settin' in ternight? Who got de money f'm de Bureau to s'port de school? An' when dat was stop', who got de money f'm de Peabody Fun'? Talk about Miss Noble gittin' a sal'ry! Who paid dat sal'ry up ter five years ago? Not one dollah of it come outer ou' pockets!

"An' den, w'at did she git fer de yuther things she done? Who paid her fer teachin' de Sunday school? Who paid her fer de gals she kep' f'm throwin' deyse'ves away? Who paid fer de boys she kep' outer jail? I had a son dat seemed to hab made up his min' ter go straight ter hell. I made him go ter Sunday school, an' somethin' dat woman said teched his heart, an' he behaved hisse'f, an' I ain' got no reason fer ter be 'shame' er 'im. An' I can 'member, Br'er Cotten, when you didn' own fo' houses an' a fahm. An' when yo' fus' wife was sick, who sot by her bedside an' read de Good Book ter 'er, w'en dey wuzn' nobody else knowed how ter read it, an' comforted her on her way across de col', dahk ribber? An' dat ain' all I kin 'member, Mr. Chuhman! When yo' gal Fanny was a baby, an' sick, an' nobody knowed what was de matter wid 'er, who sent fer a doctor, an' paid 'im fer comin', an' who he'ped nuss dat chile, an' tol' yo' wife w'at ter do, an' save' dat chile's life, jes' as sho' as de Lawd has save' my soul?

"An' now, aftuh fifteen yeahs o' slavin' fer us, who ain' got no claim on her, aftuh fifteen yeahs dat she has libbed 'mongs' us an' made herse'f one of us, an' endyoed havin' her own people look down on her, aftuh she has growed ole an' gray wukkin' fer us an' our child'n, we talk erbout turnin' 'er out like a' ole hoss ter die! It 'pears ter me some folks has po' mem'ries! Whar would we 'a' be'n ef her folks at de No'th hadn' 'membered us no bettuh? An' we hadn' done nothin', neither, fer dem to 'member us fer. De man dat kin fergit w'at Miss Noble has done fer dis town is unworthy de name er nigger! He oughter die an' make room fer some 'spectable dog!

"Br'er Glaspy says we got a' educated young man, an' we mus' gib him sump'n' ter do. Let him wait; ef I reads de signs right he won't hab ter wait long fer dis job. Let him teach in de primary schools, er in de country; an' ef he can't do dat, let 'im work awhile. It don't hahm a' educated man ter work a little; his fo'fathers has worked fer hund'eds of years, an' we's worked, an' we're heah yet, an' we're free, an' we's gettin' ou' own houses an' lots an' hosses an' cows—an' ou' educated young men. But don't let de fus' thing we do as a committee be somethin' we ought ter be 'shamed of as long as we lib. I votes fer Miss Noble, fus', las', an' all de time!"

When Old Abe sat down the chairman's face bore a troubled look. He remembered how his baby girl, the first of his children that he could really call his own, that no master could hold a prior claim upon, lay dying in the arms of his distracted young wife, and how the thin, homely, and short-sighted white teacher had come like an angel into his cabin, and had brought back the little one from the verge of the grave. The child was a young woman now, and Gillespie had well-founded hopes of securing the superior young Williams for a son-in-law; and he realized with something of shame that this later ambition had so dazzled his eyes for a moment as to obscure the memory of earlier days.

Mr. Cotten, too, had not been unmoved, and there were tears in his eyes as he recalled how his first wife, Nancy, who had borne with him the privations of slavery, had passed away, with the teacher's hand in hers, before she had been able to enjoy the fruits of liberty. For they had loved one another much, and her death had been to them both a hard and bitter thing. And, as Old Abe spoke, he could remember, as distinctly as though they had been spoken but an hour before, the words of comfort that the teacher had whispered to Nancy in her dying hour and to him in his bereavement.

"On consideration, Mr. Chairman," he said, with an effort to hide a suspicious tremor in his voice and to speak with the dignity consistent with his character as a substantial citizen, "I wish to record my vote fer Miss Noble."

"The chair," said Gillespie, yielding gracefully to the majority, and greatly relieved that the responsibility of his candidate's defeat lay elsewhere, "will make the vote unanimous, and will appoint Brother Cotten and Brother Johnson a committee to step round the corner to Miss Noble's and notify her of her election."

The two committeemen put on their hats, and, accompanied by several people who had been waiting at the door to hear the result of the meeting, went around the corner to Miss Noble's house, a distance of a block or two away. The house was lighted, so they knew she had not gone to bed. They went in at the gate, and Cotten knocked at the door.

The colored maid opened it.

"Is Miss Noble home?" said Cotten.

"Yes; come in. She's waitin' ter hear from the committee."

The woman showed them into the parlor. Miss Noble rose from her seat by the table, where she had been reading, and came forward to meet them. They did not for a moment observe, as she took a step toward them, that her footsteps wavered. In her agitation she was scarcely aware of it herself.

"Miss Noble," announced Cotten, "we have come to let you know that you have be'n 'lected teacher of the grammar school for the next year."

"Thank you; oh, thank you so much!" she said. "I am very glad. Mary"—she put her hand to her side suddenly and tottered—"Mary, will you—"

A spasm of pain contracted her face and cut short her speech. She would have fallen had Old Abe not caught her and, with Mary's help, laid her on a couch.

The remedies applied by Mary, and by the physician who was hastily summoned, proved unavailing. The teacher did not regain consciousness.

If it be given to those whose eyes have closed in death to linger regretfully for a while about their earthly tenement, or from some higher vantage-ground to look down upon it, then Henrietta Noble's tolerant spirit must have felt, mingling with its regret, a compensating thrill of pleasure; for not only those for whom she had labored sorrowed for her, but the people of her own race, many of whom, in the blindness of their pride would not admit during her life that she served them also, saw so much clearer now that they took charge of her poor clay, and did it gentle reverence, and laid it tenderly away amid the dust of their own loved and honored dead.

Two weeks after Miss Noble's funeral the other candidate took charge of the grammar school, which went on without any further obstacles to the march of progress.

The Sway-Backed House

Whether or not Uncle Solomon Grundy, like his famous namesake of the nursery rhyme, was born on Monday, I have no means of knowing; nor am I informed as to the days of the week on which the other principal events of his life took place. I do know, however, that he was a tall, shapely, and very dark man, with a straight nose, thin lips, and blue eyes. From his color and the quality of his hair one would have been inclined to regard him as a full-blooded Negro; but his features, his blue eyes—a remarkable anomaly—and the fact that he was free-born, made it seem probable that he might have a distant strain of white blood, which, by reversion, had come to the surface through the overlying dark strata. He had been known to say that he was the descendant of an African king—these sable royalties may yet become as numerous, for purposes of pedigree, among dark Americans of the future as the ancient kings of Ireland. Whether for this or some other reason, he manifested a very distinct scorn for ordinary blacks. Perhaps this sentiment had something to do with his marriage, when about thirty years old, to a light-brown woman with a daughter much fairer of complexion than herself.

This little yellow girl became the apple of the old man's eyes. His wife bore him no children, and Solomon, who was of a very affectionate disposition, lavished upon Julia all the love which he might have distributed among a large family. He lived, with his wife and the child, in a small North Carolina town, where, being a free man and a skilled bricklayer and plasterer, he enjoyed a good income, for a man of simple tastes and humble station, and was able to provide comfortably for his wife and adopted daughter. The girl grew to womanhood and married a free colored man of the town, whereupon she left her mother's house and went to live with her husband.

Julia's marriage was as prolific as most unions of the poor, whose families are likely to increase in inverse ratio to their ability to support them. Some years later she died, leaving, among half a dozen children, a little daughter who resembled Julia very much. Solomon's wife, the grandmother, took the child to bring up. The father soon married again, and the girl was not missed from the crowded household, where her absence was a relief rather than a loss.

223

The little Isabella took the place, in the mind of Solomon and his wife, of the lost daughter Julia. She was dressed better than most colored children of the town, was sent to school regularly—she grew up just after the war—and showed herself appreciative and grateful for her opportunities. When she neared womanhood, her grandmother died, and Isabella, who continued to live with the old man, became known as the sole heiress of the sway-backed house, which, with the land about it, constituted the bulk of Uncle Solomon's estate. This was no mere surmise, but had for its foundation the old man's personal statement.

"Yas, suh," he would say, "Isabella is de only one I keer fer, an' she's gwine ter be my heir. Ef she'll stay here an' keep house for me while she's single, er live here wid her husban' when she marries, she shall have all I got."

"You haven't any relatives of your own, Uncle Solomon, have you?" asked a neighbor, one day.

"No," he answered, somewhat shortly. "I had a sister once, but she married a low-down, good-fer-nothin' black nigger, an' I ain't seen her ner heared from her fer twenty years. She may be dead fer all I know er keer."

The old man's house stood on a corner, on the bank of a creek. It was a frame house, large for the neighborhood, and some two stories in height. Owing to some miscalculation of strains or misplaced economy of material, the middle of the roof had sagged considerably below the ends, thus giving the house a decidedly sway-backed appearance. When Uncle Solomon bought the house and lot, he plastered all the rooms and had the roof reshingled, but the principal defect could not, in his opinion, be remedied without an entire reconstruction of the house, which he did not feel able to afford. Viewed from the end, the bend in the roof was not noticeable; and one gets accustomed to anything, so that the irregularity of outline did not detract a great deal, in the public eye, from the value or desirability of Isabella's inheritance. The house was much larger than the shabby one-story tenements in the neighborhood, and there was nothing at all the matter with the acre of land to which it appertained.

A pretty yellow girl could not grow up in Patesville without several suitors, and Isabella was no exception to the rule. The aspirants to her favor, however, had to pass the inspection, not only of Isabella's somewhat critical taste, but of the old man's more robust prejudices. Some were too old for Isabella, and some too young. Some were too dark to make a good match, and some too trifling to suit the old man. For a while the balance hung trembling between Professor Revels, of the grammar school, and Tom Turner, the blacksmith, who lived just a short distance from Uncle Solomon's. Isabella had, at first, a sneaking fondness for the blacksmith, a sturdy, brown young man, whose bare arms, shining in the light of his forge, revealed the knotted muscles of a Hercules. He was a good-natured fellow, too, and very fond of Isabella, though somewhat slow of speech and diffident in manner. Professor Revels, however, proved a powerful rival to Turner. He was not only by nature a shade lighter than the blacksmith, but, by the free use of soap and water, and certain cosmetics recommended for the purpose, looked at least a shade lighter than he really was; while the blacksmith, by reason of his trade, seemed darker than he ought. These integumentary details seemed really of more importance to the old man than to Isabella, who was more strongly impressed by the difference in the clothes of her two admirers. The Professor—he did not use the title himself, but his friends thrust it upon him—wore, every day in the week, clean, well-fitting garments, high collars and bright neckties, which contrasted strikingly with the sooty garb and open shirt-front of the young blacksmith, who, donning his good clothes more seldom, did not, for want of practice, wear them with the ease and grace of the Professor. To the advantages already stated, Revels added what seemed to the old man the most powerful argument in his favor—a very remarkable thrift. He owned already two small houses, and, having commended himself to the town authorities by abstention from politics and deference to the white people, seemed likely to hold his position indefinitely. Uncle Solomon admired the teacher's exceptional prosperity. The Professor shared the general knowledge of Isabella's expectations, and was willing to add the sway-backed house to his growing possessions. It was worth, with the land attached, at least eight hundred dollars, and possibly nine. Revels, it must be said in all fairness, was by no means indifferent to Isabella's personal attractions, though it is likely that he would have looked further before committing himself had it not been for the expected inheritance. The result of this balancing of personal and social advantages was the engagement of Isabella and Professor Revels, early in the spring of 187–. The marriage was set for a date late in June, at the end of the school year, and the couple were to take a trip to Washington on a half-rate summer excursion ticket for their wedding journey. The Professor's brother, who held a clerkship in one of the Government departments, would entertain them gratis, thus reducing materially the expenses of the visit.

Toward the latter part of May, Uncle Solomon was taken ill with a severe attack of acute rheumatism, a disease to which he had long been subject in a milder form. Isabella attended him faithfully, and was very much shocked and pained when the doctor told her one day that he feared the rheumatism might reach the old man's heart, in which event the illness would in all probability have a fatal termination; for Isabella was really fond of her grandpap, as she affectionately called him, and would have been quite content to wait indefinitely for her inheritance.

She was somewhat surprised one day when a very dark young man, of good manners and neatly though poorly dressed, called at the house and announced himself as the old man's nephew. The visitor stayed to dinner, and conversed more or less with his uncle while Isabella prepared the meal. Uncle

Solomon did not seem at all elated by the appearance of this hitherto unknown and unsuspected relative, though he listened patiently enough to the young man's account of his widowed mother's family, which was large, and her circumstances, which were poor, and asked the visitor to call again in case he should be passing through the town. The young man, according to his own story, was on his way to an institution of higher learning in another town, where he hoped to work his way through. He very gratefully accepted a present of five dollars which his uncle extracted, with painful effort, from a wooden chest under the head of his bed. The old man subsequently made but slight reference to his relations, merely remarking to Isabella that if the boy was a fair specimen of the family, they must be very black; that, for his part, he believed in lightening up the breed, and that his sister had made a serious mistake.

Isabella was not especially interested in the visitor, and under the pressure of household cares soon forgot his very existence; for her grandpap grew steadily worse from day to day. In the early part of June the enemy attacked the citadel of his life; his heart succumbed to the disease, and he went the way of all the earth, including even landed proprietors. The doctor must have warned him, however, or he had felt some presentiment of his impending fate; for, a week or two before his demise, he sent for Mr. Henry Williams, the colored lawyer of the town, and made a will in due form, it being necessary to devise his property if he wished Isabella to have it—for, it will be remembered, she was not a blood relation, and her adoption had never taken a legal form. The will was left in the lawyer's hands for safe-keeping, under a strict injunction of secrecy as to its contents.

Upon Isabella, as the person standing nearest to the deceased, devolved the responsibility for the funeral arrangements. Owing, however, to her youth and inexperience, to say nothing of her very sincere grief, she relied more or less for assistance upon her affianced husband. The Professor counseled a modest funeral; he was opposed, he said, to ostentation in funerals, which was a race weakness that ought to be combatted. He felt quite sure that Mr. Grundy himself, a man of simple tastes, would have preferred a neat pine coffin to the more elaborate and expensive velvet-lined casket with silver-plated handles and a glass top, of which Isabella had first thought. She would have liked to have the sermon preached at the colored Methodist church, of which Uncle Solomon had been an occasional attendant, though not a regular member; but the Professor suggested that, as the colored cemetery was only a short distance from the house, it would be much more convenient to have the sermon preached at the residence, from which the pallbearers, if carefully selected for their strength, could carry the body directly to the grave, thus saving the expense of a hearse and carriages, and setting an example of simplicity and good taste in a quarter where it was very much needed. Isabella could not dispute the wisdom of a teacher whom she had obeyed as a pupil a year before, and whom she was soon to obey as a wife; she yielded her own wishes, and carried out the Professor's ideas, even at the cost of some adverse criticism from others.

The funeral was, nevertheless, largely attended. The lawyer, who was among those present, had caused it to be known among the near neighbors and intimate friends of the deceased that he would produce and read the will at the house immediately after the interment. At the conclusion of the obsequies, Isabella and her relatives, the Professor, and several near neighbors, including the young blacksmith, gathered in the sitting room and waited, with becoming gravity, until Mr. Williams produced and read, with professional unction, the last will and testament of Solomon Grundy. The estate, as itemized in the will, consisted of the sway-backed house and the land surrounding it, one hundred and ten dollars in money, and a claim of three hundred and seventy-five dollars against the defunct Freedman's Savings Bank. This last item, as the lawyer explained, was practically valueless. The receivers of the bank had paid one dividend, and there was small prospect of another. By the terms of the will the property, after the payment of debts, funeral expenses, and cost of administration, was to be sold at private sale, upon the best terms obtainable, and the proceeds to go, share and share alike, to Isabella Reynolds and the ten children of the decedent's sister, Elizabeth Goins, of Tarboro, North Carolina.

"This afternoon," said the lawyer, as he folded the paper, "I shall have the will admitted to probate, and the estate will be settled as soon as the court shall direct."

Professor Revels, who had listened closely to the reading of the will, could hardly conceal his chagrin at the disposition of the property. Nevertheless, with an effort at self-control strengthened by his schoolroom experience, he mastered his feelings sufficiently to take a formal farewell of Isabella, being among the first to leave. The others did not remain long; the will gave them something to talk about, and it seemed hardly becoming to discuss the dead man in the room where his coffined remains had stood an hour before.

Tom Turner was the last to leave.

"I'm sorry, Isabella," he said, holding her hand meanwhile, "that you should lose your grandpap. He was a good man, and we shall all miss him. I know a fellow who would have been glad to do all he did for you, and more, if you had given him the chance. But he doesn't bear malice. It isn't always best for us to have what we want. If I can be of any use to you, call on me— you haven't far to come."

Isabella involuntarily contrasted this magnanimous sympathy with the abrupt departure of her affianced lover, to the disadvantage of the absent one. She was, nevertheless, a sensible girl, and was able to appreciate the disappointment which so thrifty a young man as the Professor must have felt upon hearing the will. He would doubtless be around the next day, however, for, while the expected inheritance was not to be despised, he had loved her, she felt, for herself as well, and would return to console her in her loneliness and take counsel with her about the future.

Several of the neighbors called next day to see how Isabella took the will, and to condole with her over the loss of the inheritance.

"It's a shame," said one ardent sympathizer, "a burnin' shame. Dat ole man's promisin' all dese years ter leabe you dat house an' lot. I sh'd think he'd be feared ter go befo' de jedgement th'one wid sech a lie on his lips."

"Please don't talk that way about grandpap," replied Isabella. "He was good to me for many years. He fed and clothed and reared my mother, and did the same for me, and neither of us had any claim upon him. If on his deathbed his conscience smote him because of his poor sister and her children, whom he had neglected so many years, and he felt that he ought to leave something to his own flesh and blood, I surely have no good right to complain. They need it quite as much as I, and more, for I am going to marry a school-teacher and a man of property, who is able to give me all I need. I owe the old man nothing but respect and affection, and while I appreciate your good intentions, I'd rather not hear anything said against him. If I am satisfied, no one else need be troubled."

Isabella was somewhat disappointed when the day passed without a visit from her lover. She received a note from him next day, in which he explained that the work of preparation for the school examination would occupy him for a few days, so that he would not intrude upon her grief immediately, but would leave her alone with her sorrow for a little while.

The little while lasted for a week, and stretched out into two. Meantime the court appointed Mr. Williams, the lawyer, as administrator of the Grundy estate. There being no reason for delay, the property was promptly sold. When the funeral expenses and costs of administration had been paid, there remained for distribution among the eleven legatees the sum of six hundred and sixty dollars and some odd cents, or about sixty dollars each.

Isabella received this money on Monday morning. She had been notified by the lawyer, several days before, that the purchaser of the property wished to take possession on Wednesday. The two weeks that had passed since the funeral had given Isabella ample time for reflection about her lover. When the third day after the funeral had passed without his reappearance, she had casually walked by the schoolhouse, but had seen nothing of Professor Revels. Once again, a few days later, while coming out from the lawyer's office, where she had called upon business of the estate, she had seen Revels passing upon the opposite side of the street. She felt piqued that he should go by without seeing her—he had hitherto been able to make out her figure at the distance of half a mile. She did not shed any tears, however, but went thoughtfully on her way.

On the Sunday before the Monday on which she received her shrunken legacy, Isabella went to church. She had not put on regular mourning for the old man, but was soberly clad, and wore a black necktie, and a black ribbon upon her sailor hat. She saw Professor Revels sitting upon the men's side of the church, and perceived that he gave a glance, now and then, in her direction—not exactly an ardent glance, but one in which conflicting emotions presented their respective claims in an orderly manner. At the close of the service Isabella left the church slowly. She confidently expected that Professor Revels would walk home with her. She was, indeed, sorely in need of counsel and comfort. In two days she must leave her home. There was nowhere for her to go, except the small house occupied by her father and his family, in which there was positively no room for her. Her marriage with the Professor was set for the following week. She might, under more auspicious conditions, have postponed it out of respect to the old man's memory; but under the circumstances, there being no tie of blood between them, the question of her own future became of paramount importance. Until her relations with the Professor should be definitely settled—and it must be admitted that Isabella had felt some misgivings since the funeral—her future movements must, of course, remain undecided. She had been offered, for instance, a country school to teach, and was at a loss what response to make. She had thought a great deal of Professor Revels; respect for his position had been as much an element of her regard as any warmer feeling. She felt that he had treated her rather coldly of late; but if he should come forward after church and walk home with her, she was willing to overlook his neglect and resume their former relations.

The congregation left the church, at the close of the service, by two different doors, most of the men passing out through one and the women through the other, though there was some mingling of the sexes in the vestibule. Isabella went out by the women's door. Her path homeward required her to turn to the right and pass the other door at an angle. She saw the Professor standing by the men's door, and gave him a full and frank look of invitation, which she might very properly do, he being her affianced husband. He started, came a few steps toward her, hesitated, lifted his hat, and turned back, as though he had left something in the church for which he must return. Isabella had observed his movements and felt distinctly disappointed; she nevertheless preserved her outward calm and proceeded on her way with even a little more than her usual dignity, the accession being due to the fact that she had observed several curious persons watching Revels and herself.

When she had descended the hill near the church and reached the bridge across the creek, she saw Tom Turner leaning against the railing, and was conscious of a decided feeling of pleasure at sight of her sturdy young neighbor, who looked quite well in a new suit of clothes. She appreciated, too, the delicacy which had made him wait at the bridge rather than, by joining her at the church, interfere with other plans which she might have had. He walked home with her, and invited her to dinner at his mother's. She accepted the invitation, after some little demur; she had always liked Tom's mother, who was an even-tempered woman, and a peaceable neighbor.

On the following Monday afternoon about five o'clock, shortly after school hours, Isabella, who was getting ready to leave the sway-backed house, heard a familiar step on the piazza. She opened the door, and admitted Professor Revels. He put out his hand and took her own, which she gave him mechanically. If he contemplated any warmer greeting, she did not encourage it by her manner.

"Good evening, Isabella," he said, laying his hat upon the table and taking a seat without further invitation. "I hope you are feeling well."

"Yes, sir," answered Isabella—he had been her teacher a year before, and Isabella always addressed him in terms of respect—"as well as could be expected."

"As well, no doubt," he rejoined with a sigh, "as could be expected after so painful an experience. I had always regarded Mr. Grundy as a gentleman— a man of no education, it is true, through no fault of his own—but a man of correct habits and sound principles. I could never have imagined him guilty of such gross injustice and such unfeeling cruelty as to bring you up as his heir and then leave his property to distant relatives who had no claim upon him whatever."

"Please do not speak harshly of him," said Isabella. "His property was his own—he worked hard for it—he could do with it as he liked. He had already done much for me."

"It is very kind of you to talk that way, Isabella; it speaks well for your heart, but not well for your sense of justice. There were others besides you to be considered."

"Yes, it is true, there were others," rejoined Isabella, thinking of the ten fatherless nephews and nieces.

"It was because I could not control my feelings toward Mr. Grundy," continued Revels, conscious that some explanation would be gracefully appropriate, even if not really called for, "that I have not been around since the funeral. We have both been disappointed, Isabella."

"I will admit that *I* have," murmured Isabella.

"Yes, and so have I. Many a man in my place would feel entirely justified in breaking off our engagement. When I offered you my hand, you were the prospective heiress of this handsome house, and of this spacious lot, upon which four or five other houses might easily be built. Thoughtless people have smiled at the sway-backed roof, but my brother, the carpenter, assured me that it could easily be straightened. But you have been well raised, Isabella, and I think, after all, in spite of your loss, that you please me better and would make a more suitable schoolteacher's wife than any other young woman in town."

"You are paying me a high compliment," said Isabella.

"It may seem so," he went on, "but I am sincere. I have figured that, by careful economy, you will be able to save for me, during the next ten years, as much as the inheritance of which you have been robbed would have amounted to."

"Thank you, sir," rejoined Isabella, humbly. "I have never been considered extravagant. Grandpap was saving, and taught me the value of money."

Revels looked moodily satisfied. "Do you know yet what your share of the estate will amount to?" he asked.

"Sixty dollars and eight and one-eleventh cents. I had to throw off the fraction to make change."

"Sixty dollars and eight cents," he repeated, meditatively. "I had supposed it would be a little more—but no matter. With so recent a death in the family you would not want a wedding—we can be married quietly, and save the expense. Laid out prudently, the sixty dollars will furnish our house. I presume that under the circumstances you would be willing to forego the trip to Washington—we can go down to Wilmington for a day or two on the boat."

"Yes," she replied, "I have given up the Washington trip for the present."

"Very well, then, Isabella; I am convinced that, on the whole, it will be for the best. We will be married next Monday night at eight, according to our original plan. Will you be here, or at your father's?"

"I shall be at my husband's, Professor Revels," replied Isabella, rising, with a cold glitter in her eyes and a triumphant ring in her voice which made Revels shiver with vague alarm.

"Your-your husband's?" he stammered, rising involuntarily the while.

"At my husband's," repeated Isabella distinctly, lingering upon the words—"at my husband's, Mr. Thomas Turner's, around the corner. You are too slow about making up your mind, Professor Revels. I was married to Mr. Turner after church last night. There he is coming up the walk now. He will need all my attention, and I wish you a very good evening."

Wine and Water

The people of Wellington had voted on the prohibition question, and a majority of them had declared that decorous and prosperous little town thenceforth "dry." A Baptist college and a Methodist female seminary were flourishing local institutions, and their influence had been largely instrumental in bringing about the temperance reform.

Of course such a measure could not be entirely popular, and a number of hard drinkers felt deeply injured by the closing of the few saloons which the town had formerly supported; they had no place to loiter, no "free lunch" to nibble at, and but limited opportunities for getting into that beatific condition of "gloriously drunk."

The saloon-keepers were indignant, but powerless. They closed out their business and one of them set up a grocery with a drug-store attachment. The new grocery was largely patronized, and soon became extremely popular with the former frequenters of the defunct saloons. These found Walker's a convenient lounging place. A barrel of peanuts and a box of red herrings did duty as "free lunch" and the drug clerk was often suspiciously busy.

One evening about nine o'clock Israel Higgins, sexton of the Baptist church, called at the grocery and bought a gallon of wine for communion purposes.

"Give the best, Mr. Pillroller," said Israel to the clerk, "our folks are able to pay for it."

The clerk poured a gallon of port wine into the sexton's big brown jug, and charged the item on his daybook against the Baptist church. Israel took his departure, jug in hand.

The transaction between Israel and the drug clerk had been witnessed by several people in the store, and among them old Peter Hardcase. From long indulgence in the habit of drinking, Peter had become unconsciously interested in any transaction which involved the transfer of alcoholic beverages. The sparkle of liquor in a glass charmed him like the eye of a serpent. Its trickle from cask or bottle was music in his ears; and when he had no money he at least liked to be where its aroma would not be denied him.

The magnitude of Israel's purchase had, therefore, appealed to the strongest side of Peter's nature. A gallon of wine! What possibilities of pleasure were bound up in it! How gloriously drunk he could get if he had a gallon of liquor.

Guided by a sort of instinct, and without any definite end in view, Peter followed Israel as he left the grocery. Israel walked down Main Street a short distance, and then turned into College street, on which the church was situated, Peter following, unperceived, a short distance behind.

The sexton unlocked the church, entered, and striking a match, lit a gas-jet, throwing the still smoking match upon the floor. He then went to the rear of the room, and entering a small apartment to the left of the pulpit, which we will call the vestry room, deposited the jug in a cupboard.

Peter Hardcase had divined Israel's purpose in entering the church and as the sexton's footsteps resounded with a hollow echo in the dim depths of the large auditorium, Peter slipped within the open door and concealed himself behind a pew. Peter Hardcase had long passed the period when the fear of committing sacrilege would have moved him, or where there was any lingering trace of early training, although his parents had been church members, and had brought him up religiously.

The sexton, having disposed of his jug, retraced his steps down the aisle, turned out the gas, and left the church, locking the door behind him. At this Peter, seeing the coast clear, emerged from his hiding place and found his way to the vestry room, which he entered, and, closing the door behind him, lighted the gas. It required but a moment to force the lock of the cupboard, and with trembling hands and eager eyes Peter lifted the jug from the shelf and raised it to his lips.

While he is resting, let us look for a moment at the manner in which the church was built. Of somewhat recent construction, and erected by a wealthy congregation, it was built of brick and stone, in approved modern style. It fronted on College street, the right side of the building along a street which crossed College street at right angles. The building was lighted from this side. On the left the church was separated by a solid brick party wall from one of the buildings of the Baptist college; there was no opening on this side, the light being supplied by a skylight in the roof. The only exit in the rear was a door which led from the vestry room to a small court surrounded by brick walls and opening through a stout oaken door upon the college grounds. Its key was kept by the president of the college, who acted as pastor and usually came in that way from his residence.

When Israel had lighted the gas on entering the church, he had carelessly tossed the match aside. It was a sulphur-match—one of the sort which burn until extinguished or burnt out. Had it fallen on the hard floor it would probably have gone out immediately. But the Christmas holidays had just gone by, and the work of cleaning the church of its evergreen decorations was in progress. There was a little pile of withered leaves and dry festoons of cedar which had been swept up by Israel in the afternoon lying to the right of the door. The match fell upon this pile of rubbish. It caught, and the fire smouldered for several minutes, during which Israel had time to place his jug in the cupboard and leave the church.

The fire then burst into a little flame, slowly consuming the pile of half-dried rubbish. This only whetted its apppetite. It seized a bit of carpet on the floor, and, crawling under the nearest pew, reached up to the cushions on the seats, and greedily devoured them. Then, running along the carpet in the aisle on the right, it caught the ends of the pews, and, wrapping itself around the pillars, reached long tongues of flame up toward the gallery, which extended along the sides of the church.

Meanwhile Peter Hardcase had taken another drink, and was beginning to feel the effect of the rich liquid. A dreamy languor stole over him—a sense of comfort which the poor quality of the whisky he usually drank had for a long time been powerless to evoke. He had raised the jug for one drink more, when a dull roar proceeding from the body of the church fell upon his ear and made him pause with the uplifted jug in his hands. The roaring increased and the now distinct crackling of the burning woodwork made it impossible to mistake the meaning of the sounds. Quickly setting the jug down, Peter opened the door and saw the interior of the church in flames.

Peter was not too far gone to realize that his safety required an immediate adjournment to the outer air, and he looked around for a way of escape. He first tried the door in the rear, but found it locked hard and fast. He tried to force it, but the lock was set in the door, and the bolt ran into the frame in such a way that it was impossible to reach it without breaking the door down. Then he turned back to the auditorium to find that the flames had cut off all access to the front and the side where the windows were. The little door in the vestry was his only hope. He tried to batter it down with a heavy chair. But the little door was stout. A valuable communion set was kept in the cupboard, and with a view to its safety the door had been strongly constructed.

Meanwhile the flames crept steadily towards the platform, and Peter soon realized that if help did not arrive he would have taken his very last drink. He was growing desperate, when a thought struck him. There must be a baptismal tank under the pulpit, as in most Baptist churches. Perhaps there was water in it. It took but a moment to find the opening and to raise the lid. The tank was dry!

Peter sprang down, and, feeling along the side, found the faucet which supplied the tank with water. The water flowed! He rushed back into the vestry room, secured the jug, and returning, crouched in the tank and closed the door above him. The tank was of brick, with a cement lining, and rested on the ground, so that Peter's only danger was from overhead if the floor began to burn.

He could hear the flames crackling above him, and now the alarm had been given, and the welcome noise of fire engines and the shouts of the gathering crowd, fell faintly, as from a distance, upon his ear. About this time the fire fastened its fangs into the pulpit floor, and began to eat through the stout planking. With his battered hat Peter dipped up water, and throwing it upward, kept the flames at bay. If the firemen could get the fire under control before the roof fell in and crushed his frail covering, he thought he could hold out until then.

With the assurance of safety from fire, Peter began to think of danger from other sources. If he made his presence in the tank known he would have to explain how he got there, and he would find it hard to convince other people that he had not fired the church. Besides, he would lose the wine, for which he had undergone so much. Moved by these considerations, he kept quiet. He tried to find the valve which emptied the tank, but in vain, and he was compelled to remain crouching in the water.

The fire was finally put out, the crowd went home to bed. The whole of the interior of the church had been burned out. It was long past midnight when Peter Hardcase emerged from the ruins, and all drenched and smoke-begrimed, crept shivering homeward under the friendly veil of darkness.

It would be a fitting ending for this tale, to record that Peter's experience led him to think seriously of the manner of life he was leading, and to give up his evil courses. But alas! the cold, hard facts will not admit of any such perversion. Peter took the jug home with him, and finished up the wine within the next two days.

The Prophet Peter

"**I**t will rain at a quarter pas' three."

It was then eleven o'clock in the morning. The speaker was one of a gang of paupers at work on the "poor-farm" as it was called, run in connection with the county infirmary; weak-featured, dull-eyed men, failures all, victims of misfortune, with too little brain, or energy, or self-control, to make their way in the world. They were in charge of a "boss" or overseer by the name of David Walker, a man of very different type, who held his place by virtue of a political appointment.

For weeks the land had been smitten by drought. Day after day the summer sun had run its course through a cloudless sky. The corn was dying. The smaller water-courses had dried up entirely, or dwindled to mere sluggish threads of moisture. Even the river, a mile or two away, was shrunk to so small a volume that half its sandy bed was exposed. The men had been fighting a fire, which had broken out in the woods adjoining the farm, and threatened to reach the standing crops, which were dry enough to invite destruction. To the lips of every man there, had the question been asked of each what he would most like to see, the answer would have risen instinctively, "Rain."

And yet Pete Gump's remark was greeted with derision. The butt of the poorhouse, despised for his dullness and sloth, the clod-faced Peter was left mainly to himself or to the society of his lank, stoop-shouldered wife—herself an inmate of the institution. Both were mountain whites who had drifted down from the Blue Ridge, plainly visible, on clear days, in the distance. Pete had little to say, and seemed generally about half asleep. If the overseer cursed him, as happened at times, he showed no sign of resentment. More intelligent paupers, whose poverty was due to their mistakes, or their vices, looked down upon Pete as beneath them.

"Pete says it's goin' ter rain," said one, jerking his thumb over his shoulder toward the object of their ridicule.

"At a quarter pas' three," laughed another. "We'll watch the clock."

"We'll 'p'int you a committee ter hol' a bucket an' ketch the rain, Pete."

But their jeers were interrupted and Pete's prophecy forgotten when a loud hail from behind told them that the fire had broken out anew. At a sharp word of command from the overseer they were off again, grumbling their protests. What was the advantage of being in the poorhouse, if one had to work as hard as those outside?

At three o'clock in the afternoon the fire was still smouldering. A lunch had been brought out to the men, which they ate standing. There was not a cloud in the sky. Within five minutes a breeze sprang up, the temperature fell sharply, and a streak of nimbus appeared in the southwest. The sky was quickly overcast. At a quarter past three there was a heavy rain, which the thirsty earth drank greedily. The fire was extinguished, the crops were saved, and the weary laborers suspended work for the day.

The overseer, after the rain, washed, shaved, and changed his clothes, and leaving the poor-farm took his way down the road to where a white house gleamed through surrounding shrubbery. This, with the broad expanse of pleasant fields beyond it, covered with rich harvests, and stocked with much blooded cattle and many fine horses, belonged to old Squire Doremus, bedridden now for several years, whose only daughter, Hazel, would inherit them. Walker knew their value, and had long cast an envious eye upon them.

Just before the overseer turned into the yard, a tall young man standing beside Miss Doremus upon the piazza, kissed her tenderly, sprang lightly to the ground, and disappeared by a footpath leading through the shrubbery. Not having witnessed this incident, Walker scarcely perceived the slight and swift change of expression with which the young woman turned and faced him as he addressed her, after a noiseless approach over the soft, water-soaked earth.

"Good evening, Miss Hazel."

"Good evening," she returned, civilly, but coolly.

"How is the Squire today?"

"Father is about the same," she replied. "He gets neither better nor worse, except for short spells. But the doctor thinks he will improve."

She had not asked her visitor to be seated. He placed a chair for her. "Sha'n't we sit down?"

"No, thank you," she said, "I don't care to sit down."

The overseer was tired; but he could only remain standing.

"You're a very dutiful daughter," he said, "but you need someone to help you."

"Thank you," she replied, innocently, "I have four servants in the house already, and a good overseer."

Walker's face flushed. "I'm not speaking of servants," he said sulkily. "You know what I mean."

"How should I know your meaning, Mr. Walker, except from what you say?"

"I suppose," he continued, while he tapped the floor nervously with the toe of his boot, "I suppose I am not good enough for you?"

She made no reply, but being a girl of spirit, showed signs of rising anger.

"Some younger, and richer, and handsomer man is in favor?" he sneered.

"If that is a question," she said, restraining herself, "to which you insist upon an answer, I would say that it cannot possibly be any concern of yours. I have tried to let you see that before. But since you cannot take a hint, and since I will not permit you to speak to me in the tone you have used today, I will simply say that you have worn out your welcome here, Mr. Walker, and if you come again, I shall not see you."

She turned, as she spoke, to leave him.

"Very well, Miss Doremus," he retorted with a vindictiveness which he made no effort to conceal. "You have shown me the gate. I'll go, but the time may come when you'll be glad to see me."

He swept the Squire's domain with a covetous glance as he turned away; nor, being a persistent fellow, did he entirely relinquish the hope of sometime calling it his own.

The sun was hot again next day, but the heavy rain had left the soil in excellent condition to work. The overseer got his gang out early, and still smarting under his rebuff of the day before, drove the men to their utmost capacity. Toward noon one of them fell into a fit. The rest stopped work and gathered around their fallen comrad, who, with contorted features and foaming lips, lay writhing upon the ground.

It was the overseer's first experience of the sort—the sufferer was a new inmate. The infirmary doctor had gone to town that day and would not be back until evening. Various remedies were suggested by members of the party, but all agreed that no matter what was done, the attack would have to run its natural course, which would extend over several hours and leave the patient weak and unable to work. While the discussion was in progress, Pete Gump came forward, knelt by the patient, and stroked his hands and his face. This had continued only a few minutes, when the stiffened limbs relaxed, the eyes resumed their normal position, and the man sat up and looked around, with a somewhat dazed expression, and called for water.

He was given a drink, dashed with the contents of a flask from the overseer's pocket, and immediately resumed his place in the ranks and proceeded with his work as though nothing had happened.

Next morning one of the men complained of a splitting headache. A few passes of Pete's hands drove the pain away. In the afternoon another sprained his ankle—they were all a set of incompetents, the prey of every wandering disease germ, the constant victims of their own carelessness or inefficiency. Peter rubbed the sprained joint, the pain disappeared as if by magic, and there was no resulting inflammation.

On the following Sunday, in accordance with custom, such inmates of the infirmary as cared to attended the Methodist church. An itinerant evangelist preached a stirring sermon. In the experience meeting that followed, brother

Peter Gump, who had never been known to utter five consecutive sentences, gave eloquent and burning testimony. Walker and a friend of his by the name of John Skedd were in the congregation. Neither of them was spiritually inclined; they went to church, when they went at all, for social reasons.

"Pete Gump surprised folks today," said Skedd. "Who'd 'a' ever dreamt it was in him?"

"There's something the matter with Pete," returned the overseer. "He's got some kind of power that's come on him all of a sudden." And he related to Skedd the events of the past week in which Gump had figured.

Skedd slapped his thigh suddenly. "I know what's the matter with him!" he exclaimed. "I've seen it before! Pete is a healer, a divine healer, and a prophet as well. He's got the power, and if he knew how to use it, there'd be a fortune in it. Look at that man Slatter, or Slaughter, or whatever his name was—he made a pile of money. But Pete!—oh, hell!—Pete ain't got sense enough to come in out of the rain."

Walker was reflective. "John," he said "Pete has got the power. We have got the sense. Why can't we put the two together? There was a travelin' doctor in town last week that carried away five thousand dollars in cash and promissory notes. We couldn't call Pete a doctor, for he don't know enough to talk about their complaints. But a divine healer don't need to know nothing—the less he knows, the more mirac'lous his power'll be."

In a few weeks the fame of the Prophet Peter had spread throughout the countryside. The chief instrument of its dissemination were the Apostles David and John, as they soon began to be called. Pete no longer resided on the poor-farm. Walker, having resigned as overseer, devoted himself to the exploitation of the prophet, assisted by his friend Skedd, who found in his new career a stimulating occupation for a mind that shrank from anything like real work. Meetings were held at various points. The sick and the afflicted, the halt and the lame, were invited to come and be healed. The Apostle David, who was fluent of speech, was the chief spokesman. The prophet did the laying on of hands. Silent for the most part, in the excitement of a meeting, amid the hymns and the shouting, the power would come, his face would be transfigured, and he would utter the words of inspiration. The Apostle John, jealously watched by his partner, held the purse and received the offerings of the faithful, who were urged to give freely for the maintenance of the work. No public report was ever made of the amount collected. The money was presumably expended for the support of the apostles and the prophet, and his wife Ma'y Liz', a simple-minded, suspicious soul who disapproved of her husband's career of healing, and brooded over him with a jealous tenderness. She had no illusions concerning him; but he had been good to her, and he was hers and she loved him.

"Pete air a fool—I've lived with 'im ten year and oughter know," she declared to the apostles, "an' I ain't got no confidence in you all. I don't know where he got this power er his'n; it's jest as liable to 'a' come from the Devil as from the Lo'd. But as long as we git our rashuns, an' I kin go 'long an' see that no harm don't come to Pete, I reckin I ain't keerin' much."

The apostles mollified her with a new calico gown, and furnished her each week with a few dollars of spending money, which seemed like wealth to her. She followed the band, a silent and watchful attendant at the meetings.

For the first few weeks of the prophet's mission, he healed many hundreds by the laying on of hands. Some strange power he possessed, either to drive away disease, or to stir, in the hearts of those willing to believe, such a glow of faith and hope that pain melted away before it. But whatever the influence was, the apostles, much to their concern, began to notice, after a few weeks, that it was declining. Whether the whole thing was merely fleeting and temporary, or whether the prophet must stop now and then to let the cisterns refill, they could not know. Nor, being hardheaded men, were they inclined to take many chances. Were the prophet's power to disappear entirely, they would, by waiting, lose the benefit of what remained; if it could be strengthened by a brief rest, the gain would be theirs. By way of experiment they announced that the prophet would retire into the wilderness for five days of prayer and meditation. The time was spent in a secluded cabin in the woods, where the prophet was waited upon by his wife and guarded by the apostles from intrusion. When the period of retreat was ended, he came forth, accompanied by the apostles, and for a few days preached and healed with his usual accustomed efficiency. But one day the power failed to manifest itself; the prophet sat through the meeting in a dull trance; there was no laying on of hands, and many went away disappointed.

The apostles met for consultation.

"The meetin's don't stimulate him like they used to," said Walker. "What can we do?"

"Why not try some other stimulant?" suggested Skedd.

"Whiskey?"

"No, folks would notice it, and a prophet has got to be above ord'nary human weaknesses. We must give him somethin' different, and we mustn't let 'im know what it's for. To do good work, a prophet must believe in himself."

So they suggested to the prophet that he was not well, and needed medical treatment; and thereafter, from time to time they gave him, before the meetings, small doses of narcotics, with excellent results. But as time passed, the drugs, at first resorted to only occasionally, became a matter of constant necessity, and the sluggish powers of the prophet would not awake without them. As it became necessary to increase the dose, the apostles, foreseeing a point beyond which this method would be ineffective, put their heads together to devise some plan by which to gather, at one stroke, the whole harvest which they might have hoped to reap through several years.

In the early part of their connection with the prophet, they had sought by close questioning to fathom the secret of his power. The only thing they could learn was that sometimes, at night, he had visions, in which pale and luminous shapes appeared and conversed with him, though he could never remember clearly what they said.

"He must have another vision," declared the Apostle David, "and a definite revelation. People like something new, and we'll make it good and strong."

So one night the prophet had a vision. Awakened from a deep sleep, he was confronted by a white-clad figure, which told him in sepulchral tones, in scriptural phrase, and with a profusion of trite imagery, that the Lord, grown weary of man's wickedness, had commissioned him to proclaim the end of the world, that he should warn all men to flee from the wrath to come and make their peace with an offended God; and that he should advise them to sell all they had and turn the proceeds into the prophet's treasure, to be used for the spread of this the Lord's message and commandment. In the morning the prophet told his apostles of the vision and the revelation, neither of which was any news to them. The vision, he said, was more clear and distinct than any which had appeared before; the message had been more definite and certain, and he burned with zeal to accomplish his mission.

The apostles spread the news and arranged the meetings, and the prophet set the countryside on fire with his eloquence. Not John the Baptist, clad in camel's hair, and feeding on locusts and wild honey, had preached with more consuming fervor the coming of his Lord, than did this modern prophet, clad in blue jeans and living on bacon and corn bread. He baptized people in the creeks and the river; he healed the sick; or, if he did not, he promised them, if they were faithful, and believed, that on the thirty-first day of October they should leave behind them all the ills of the flesh, and, with beautified and glorified bodies, rise to heaven in the train of their triumphant Lord.

The new doctrine spread like wildfire among the simple country people. The revelation had been skillfully planned for a time when the crops had in the main been gathered but not yet sold and the farmers had leisure to talk and attend the meetings. The winter would have been cold, and spiritual fire might have found a rude antagonist in snow or ice or mountain winds. Spring was a lean season, and summer a busy one. The apostles had planned their harvest to follow closely that of the thrifty farmers thereabouts.

Nor had they planned in vain. An eclipse of the moon was accepted as a portent, confirmed by the appearance of a comet which waxed for a few days and then waned again. The apostles did not fail to emphasize the importance of spreading the faith, and of giving to that end. Gathered crops were sold, mostly at a sacrifice; for who would need them after the fateful day? Money poured in upon the apostles. Day after day they announced that preachers had been sent out to proclaim the end of the world. When the farmers sold their crops, they parted with their livestock. Why keep cows that would never calve again, pigs that would never see another killing season, horses and oxen that would never plow another crop? They kept enough to live upon until the judgment day, after which nothing more would be needed. There were skeptics enough, seemingly, to absorb all the offerings; and there was little bargaining. Had it not been for the command to spread the news, many would not have sold at all; for they knew they were giving what would soon be nothing. They consoled themselves with the reflection, on the other hand, that money was but dross, and would last no longer than its consideration, while it might in the meantime be made useful in spreading the gospel of the second coming of the Lord. Millions of sinners had not yet been warned.

"We have sent out messengers far an' wide," declared the Apostle David, "an' these in turn have sent out others; and the word is being carried to the ends of the earth. But the time is short, my brethren. Only a few brief days remain between the unrepentant and eternal destruction. You cannot enjoy unclouded happiness in paradise unless you have done all you can to save others. Sell your houses, sell your farms—the Lord will raise up buyers—and cast your all into the treasury!"

They sold their lands. Buyers were forthcoming, and many deeds changed hands. Fine farms went for a song. There were some timid believers, but the prophet and the apostles kept the enthusiasm at fever heat, and those who hesitated preserved at least a shamed silence and did nothing to discourage the faithful.

Not only the poor, but the well-to-do, were affected. Miss Doremus, the Squire's daughter, was among the last to succumb. Her lover had been a constant scoffer, and with him she had followed the meetings from time to time from mere curiosity—there were few social distractions at best in the country life, and these had all been abandoned because of the new religious movement. But Miss Doremus's skepticism at length gave way; she was swept into the emotional vortex which surrounded her, and became an ardent believer, much to her lover's disgust. They quarrelled, and she went to the meetings with neighbors or servants, while he hung gloomily around the outskirts and watched her with a jealous eye. Because of this estrangement, he did not learn that she had induced her invalid father to sell, for a fraction of its value, the land which was to constitute her inheritance. For in all the land sales the buyers had magnanimously waived the possession until after the thirty-first of October, thereby relieving the sellers from the trouble and distraction of moving, and leaving them free to prepare their hearts and minds for the great day.

The thirty-first of October dawned clear and beautiful. At break of day the Prophet Peter and a host of his disciples, all clad in white robes, and singing hymns as they walked, took their way to a high hill which had been selected for the purpose, there to wait the coming of the Lord. Their minds were prepared for great signs and wonders; but they were firm in their belief in their own salvation, and looked forward with hope rather than with dread—the only cloud being upon the minds of those who, like Lot's wife, looked behind, concerned about some unregenerate loved one. The Apostles David and John had said their farewell words at a meeting the night before, and had gone, they said, to lead other bodies of the faithful to other heights, in other places, to await the coming of the Lord.

It was a motley gathering. All ages and colors and grades of social standing were represented; and in anticipation of the dread presence which should pass that way, there was no longer any distinction of persons. Master and man, black and white, rich and poor, stood side by side, hand in hand, and lifted their voices together in hymns of praise. Not all the faithful were there. Strength and inspiration were doubtless to be found near the prophet and his more intimate disciples but the Lord would come everywhere, and he would save the believers wherever they might be. Hazel Doremus, for instance, sat by her father's bedside. Whatever came to pass, she would be found at her post of duty; what higher warrant could she have for higher salvation?

The prophet had not announced, because there had not been revealed to him, the exact hour at which the final catastrophe should take place; nor had he ventured any opinion. But it was the general impression that it would come early in the day. Many had watched all night, by the light of lanterns which they kept trimmed and burning. The hilltop was already covered with people when the sun rose, bright and beautiful, above a low bank of feathery clouds which lay along the eastern horizon. When the first purple beams shot upward, a thrill passed through the gathering. It might be the familiar sun that would appear, or it might be the flaming sword of the Sun of Righteousness come to judge the earth.

It proved to be the former, and as the orb of day rose above the horizon, the thin clouds were dispersed by the growing heat, and the sun mounted through a cloudless, fleckless sky. Not in the first watch was the Lord to come.

Several hours passed, spent mostly in prayer and song and exhortation. The prophet said little these first hours, but sat somewhat apart, absorbed in his own emotions. His whole being was in a state of exaltation that lifted him above the height on which he sat, above the far-away blue mountain peaks, sending his soul forth to meet its Lord. One of the brethren gained his attention with an inquiry about the fateful hour.

"It is not yet, my brother," he answered, "not until the sun is higher in the heavens. We are in God's hands. He has not vouchsafed to name to me the hour."

At nine o'clock the sky was still clear. A light breeze had sprung up, a breath of the Indian Summer which had painted the leaves of the trees with brown and crimson and yellow, making them a marvelous and beautiful tapestry.

"Doubtless," said one of the brethren, in the course of an exhortation, "doubtless the Lord has sent this bright and beautiful day that the wicked, when they are condemned to everlasting fire, may look back upon what they forfeited because of their sins, and that the faithful may know how much greater is the least of heaven than the best of earth."

At ten o'clock many eyes were turned towards the heavens. Still there was no sign. At eleven o'clock the sky was not less serene; the sun shone even more brightly. Few of those on the hilltop had eaten that morning, and most had fasted through the night and the long hours of waiting had begun to tell upon them. Water from a nearby spring was passed around, but no one would go away for food. A woman, thinking that the prophet might work a miracle, brought him a loaf.

"No, sister," he said, misconstruing her intent, "take thou and eat, if thy flesh is weak. But I am on my Master's business, and have no need of meat for the body."

"When will the Lord come?" they asked him again.

"Surely not until the sun is at its height," he replied. "We are in the hands of the Lord. With Him time is nothing, and a thousand years are but a day."

Noon came. The sun had climbed to the zenith. Every eye was cast upward. Even those of the prophet himself were turned expectantly toward the heavens. Surely this would be the ideal hour! How could the Lord of earth and Heaven better display his power than by eclipsing with his glory the midday effulgence of his greatest work? But there was still no sign. The sun shone as brightly as before, the sky remained serene.

Some of the more timid souls, until then uplifted by the zeal of their comrades, began to waver. It was recalled that other prophets had predicted the end of the world, and it had not come. But the faithful reproved these weak ones, and their feeble voices were drowned in a hymn of praise and faith. When three o'clock was passed the stronger spirits were unable to keep down the murmurs. A sickly woman fainted from hunger and fatigue. Children were crying. Widows who had sold their homes, old men who could no longer work and had parted with their all, were confronted by the possibility that the sacrifice had been for naught, and that they were reduced to beggary.

But the prophet was firm. The Lord had appeared to him in a vision and had announced the end of the world for this day, and the day was not finished.

"Courage, my brethren! Patience, my sisters! Let us watch and wait even until the going down of the sun. Perhaps the Lord is waiting to come over the mountains in the glory of the sunset!."

More hymns were sung, with less enthusiasm. A few, overcome by hunger, began to slip away. On the edge of the greater gathering a small knot of bearded men were collected.

"My cattle are gone," said one, gloomily.

"My horses are sold," said another.

"My wheat and corn," added a third.

"My house and farm," said yet another.

"And the Lord has not come," said a fifth.

"Suppose," said the first, "that this prophet is a false prophet?"

"Where," asked another, ominously, "are the apostles? They ought to be here. They have held the scrip and the purse; they have taken the money for our farms and our cattle and our crops. Who knows what they have done with it, they and their prophet?"

The group of malcontents grew larger as the sun declined. The murmuring became general. Even the prophet was troubled. Could he have been deceived? Could the Devil have appeared in the guise of an angel of light? If he were mistaken, if he had been the dupe of the Father of Lies, then what would it mean to these deluded people, who had given up everything at his command?

Slowly the sun declined in the cloudless West. There had been no earthquake, no lightnings, no thunder, no last trump, no fire from heaven, no celestial host. Slowly the crowd melted away from the hilltop. Slowly the prophet's spirits sank and his faith faltered. Slowly at first, and then faster as the sun fell to the horizon, a group of bearded men, with fierce faces, and curses on their lips, and various improvised weapons in their hands, moved toward where the prophet still sat surrounded by a faithful few. And as the sun set peacefully and gloriously, a discredited prophet, with fear in his heart that lent wings to his feet, was in full flight, with a mob of angry and desperate men at his heels.

In the gray dawn of the following day Pete Gump stood by the river bank. He had eluded his pursuers, and had taken refuge in the heart of a swamp, where he had fallen from exhaustion and slept until morning. On awaking he had made his way to the river, in which he had bathed his haggard face and his bloody hands, torn by the thorns through which, in his hasty flight, he had forced his way.

What was he to do? But yesterday a prophet, today he was a fugitive. Not entirely for nothing had his sluggish soul been exercised; and there in the chill morning air, beside the cold river, his thoughts were more collected and more logical than ever in his life before, and there flashed upon him something more than an intuition of the part the apostles had played in his undoing. What would be his future? Should his enemies find him, they would put him to a shameful and violent death. For he knew of what fierce rages they were capable. They had trusted him, and while he had meant to help them and save them, he had ruined them. If he should remain hidden until the storm blew over, it would be only to return to the poor-farm, if they would even receive him there, to become again the butt of rude raillery, the scorn of the quicker-witted, to which would be added the ignominy of failure. No, he could not. Though it may have deserted him, he had felt the divine flame. That which it had sanctified must not become the sport of mean men. There were footsteps approaching, and he heard the sound of voices. Already his enemies were at hand. In a moment they would be upon him. With a murmured prayer for forgiveness, he walked out upon an overhanging log and just as his pursuers emerged from the wood, sprang into the swift current where the river was deepest.

Two weeks after the flight of the prophet, David Walker made his way cautiously along the road to Squire Doremus's, looking on all sides to see that he was not observed. He entered the yard and directed his footsteps toward the front piazza where Miss Doremus sat, in a rocking chair, in a drooping and disconsolate attitude. She did not look up until he addressed her.

"Good evening, Hazel."

She flashed him an indignant look.

"Three months ago," he said, "I begged you to marry me, and you repulsed me with scorn and contempt. Then you were the heiress of a wealthy father, and I was the overseer of the poor-farm, a man of little property. Today you are poor and I am rich. This farm and everything on it; this house and everything in it, belong to me."

"Impossible!" she exclaimed with genuine surprise. "They were sold to a stranger."

"He was my agent. And not only this farm, but half the farms in the county belong to me. Did you suppose that I was in the apostle business for nothing? People sold their crops and their stock, and gave the money to me to advance the cause. I advanced the cause—*my* cause. With the offerings of cash I bought the land."

"But nobody ever heard of you as a buyer," she insisted.

"For obvious reasons," he replied. "And the deeds are not even yet recorded. They are here in this bundle," he said, taking a bulky parcel out of his pocket. "This paper on top is a deed from William Doremus to my agent; the next is from my agent to me. Here are the deeds for twenty thousand acres of land, with a hundred good houses upon them—rich farms, fat pastures— and the stock upon them is mine. When I have settled my business with you, I shall go down to the county seat and put these deeds on record."

"You have not dared to do so before," she rejoined with a spirit which disaster had not quenched.

"But I shall do so now. Moreover, this fat wallet which I show you, contains thousands of dollars—thousands of dollars!—my share of the remaining offerings of the faithful—the foolish faithful! You treated me with scorn, but I bear no malice. I am of a forgiving disposition. I had no desire to see you or the Squire suffer. I am willing to marry you still if you will say the word, and to take care of your father for the rest of his life."

He awaited his answer in confident expectancy.

Absorbed in their talk, neither of them had observed a tall young man who had approached and stood concealed behind a thick syringa bush which stood a couple of yards away. And of course neither of them saw the air of suspense with which he awaited Miss Doremus's reply, nor the joyful expression which overspread his countenance when Miss Doremuss rose to her feet, and drawing herself up to her full height, exclaimed with withering contempt.

"Dave Walker, I never liked you, nor thought you honest! I would not marry you if every one of your stolen acres was plated with gold! I can work for my living and my father's. Leave this yard, and if you do not go at once, I'll send the servants out to raise the neighborhood and have you treated as you deserve. This may be your house, but as long as I stay here I'll be mistress of it!"

"Very well," said Walker, "if you ever come to want, you'll have yourself to thank. I've given you a chance."

"And I'll give *you* a chance," said a voice from behind, as Will Thornton stepped out from the shelter of the syringa bush. Walker, turning on his heel, faced the threatening muzzle of a revolver.

"I'll give you a chance," repeated the young man. "There are a dozen men within ten minutes walk of where we are, who would be just delighted to take you out and put a rope around your neck and string you up to a tree. I'm going to send for them, and stand here until they come, unless you do exactly as I say. First, hand over that bundle of deeds."

Walker was thinking rapidly. The young man had spoken the truth, and of his sincerity there could be no reasonable doubt—a glance at his stern, set face made this very clear. Reluctantly he passed over the bundle of deeds. Thornton tossed them to Miss Doremus.

"Burn them up," he said. "Not one of them has been recorded. I looked at the records an hour ago."

Hazel stepped through the open door, into the hall, where a wood fire was burning in the open fireplace. They saw her throw the bundle into the fire.

"Now hand over that wallet. By your own confession you have filled it by robbing the widow and the fatherless. Every dollar shall be returned to those from whom it was stolen. Now, go, and if you go fast enough, you may be able to get away."

Walker went, and stood not upon the order of his going. He must have saved some remnant of his ill-gotten gains, for he moved to an adjoining state and changed his name, and was subsequently elected to Congress. Miss Doremus married her lover.

Nor was the prophet drowned after all. The footsteps and voices he had heard were those of Ma'y Liz' and a few faithful followers, who had been seeking him all night. They reached the river in time to see him plunge into the water, and to rescue him, with some difficulty, before he had gone down the third time. But the shocks and strains of his public career had proved too much for the prophet's poor mind, which thereafter remained little more than a blank. He was kept out of sight for a time, and when the duplicity of the apostles was exposed, and Thornton had made restitution to some, and others found that they were not to lose their lands, the prophet came to be regarded more as a fellow victim than as an accomplice of the swindlers. He returned to the poorhouse, where he became a favored inmate, asked for by visitors, pointed out with pride, the recipient of many small gifts of money or tobacco. Ma'y Liz' shone by his reflected light. "Pete alluz were a fool," she would say, placidly—"I lived with him long enough to know—an' now he ain't got no sense at all." And then she would add, with a certain naive pride, "But he were a big prophet an' a healer one time, he shore were."

How Dasdy Came Through

"**W**hat's de matter wid yer, Dasdy?" asked Aunt Zilpha, looking up from the washtub at her good-looking daughter.

"Dey ain't nuthin' de matter wid me," replied Dasdy, slamming her iron viciously on the ironing board, where a limp mass of snowy linen was gradually assuming form and substance under her skillful hand.

Aunt Zilpha rubbed away for several minutes, and then asked another question:

"Is yer gwine ter chu'ch ter-night, Dasdy?"

"I dunno as I is," replied Dasdy (short for Desdemona) gloomily.

"Better g'long, honey," continued Aunt Zilpha. "Elder Smith gwine to preach ter-night."

Dasdy worked away vigorously at the ironing board. Presently she said: "'Lizah Davis had on dat new silk dress and velvet bonnet las' night."

"Wonder whar dat gal got de money ter buy a silk dress?" asked Aunt Zilpha, contemptuously; "it mus' be dis here cheap silk."

"I 'spect it's secondhand," remarked Dasdy, as she changed her iron. "She never had no silk dress 'fo' she went to C'lumbia. She say her sister give 'er dat dress—but I dunno."

"Did 'Dolphus ax yer to go to ch'uch wid 'im ary night dis week?" asked Aunt Zilpha, after a pause.

"No, he's be'n gwine wid dat 'Lizah Davis all de week. She was shoutin' las' night."

"Umph!" grunted Aunt Zilpha, "dat's all 'pocrisy—dat gal ain't got no religion." She wrung out a few more pieces, and then continued:

"Better g'long to chu'ch, honey. Good religion better dan sweethearts."

There was a great revival in progress at the Mt. Gilead Baptist Church, the chief tabernacle of worship for the colored people of Patesville. The interest had been kept up for six weeks, and was still unabated, and the number of conversions and additions to the church was something unprecedented. The elder in charge had not been able to do half the work, and preachers had come from distant towns to assist him. Meetings were held nightly, and on Sundays

249

five times a day—beginning at sunrise and ending only at midnight. In fact the religious enthusiasm of the colored people at Patesville, who constituted half the population, was at fever heat.

Adolphus Sampson was among the earliest converts. Adolphus was head waiter at the Clarendon House, the leading hotel of the town, and being yellow and rather goodlooking, was very popular among the young women who were willing to fulfill their duty to society by getting married.

Before the revival began 'Dolphus had for a long time kept company with Dasdy Williams, one of the best-looking of the girls that attended the Baptist church. He had hesitated a little at one time between Dasdy and 'Lizah Davis, another dusky belle. But Dasdy was more attractive in person and could earn more money as a laundress than 'Lizah as a nurse, and 'Dolphus' susceptible heart had prudently succumbed to this combination of attractions.

But now everything was changed. Soon after the revival 'Dolphus had been converted, and his zeal for religion had temporarily overshadowed his fondness for Dasdy's company. She was still a sinner, and the callow saint was fond of trying his new wings. He found in Dasdy a poor listener to that kind of conversation—she preferred the old style. A slight coolness had thus sprung up between the lovers, when 'Lizah Davis appeared upon the scene with all the prestige of a visit to Columbia, and with the additional charms conferred by a new silk dress and a velvet bonnet. Moreover, she was converted during the second week of the revival and 'Dolphus hence found in her a sympathetic listener, and enjoyed at the same time the somewhat worldly satisfaction of going to church with the best-dressed girl in the congregation.

Of course this was gall and wormwood to Dasdy. She was in love with 'Dolphus and did not at all approve of the turn affairs had taken. The condition of her mind at this time predisposed her to sentimental impressions. A powerful sermon by Elder Smith affected her considerably, and one evening she left her seat in church and went forward to the mourners' bench. The next day the impressions of the evening before seemed to have passed away entirely. Dasdy tried to think of her sins, but the figure of 'Dolphus intruded itself persistently, and instead of reflecting on her own shortcomings, she could not keep her mind from the meanness of 'Lizah Davis, who had stolen her lover. At night Dasdy did not feel the least inclination to go forward when the mourners were invited up to the front seats. But curious eyes were watching her, and consistency required that she should not give up soon.

While she hesitated 'Dolphus came into the church at the right door and 'Lizah Davis at the left, resplendent in her new dress and bonnet; they had evidently come to church together.

Dasdy struggled for a moment between two powerful emotions—love for 'Dolphus, which made her feel like crying, and hatred for the other girl, which made her feel like tearing her eyes out.

Then another motive for going to the mourners' bench suggested itself:

If she could only get religion 'Dolphus might come back to her; and she liked to think of Brother 'Dolphus bending over her at the mourners' bench, encouraging her in tones of love and religion combined. Yielding to the impulse of this idea, she went forward and knelt at the front seat. Now it happened that during the whole evening 'Dolphus had not come near her. There was a large congregation and many mourners; and 'Dolphus did not know she was at the mourners' bench for some time, and then could not reach her for the crowd of women standing around.

Dasdy prayed mechanically, but her heart was not in it; and she went home in a worse frame of mind than that in which she had gone to church. The next day she had the conversation with her mother, and this good old woman persuaded her to go to church and continue her prayers.

At eight o'clock Dasdy got ready for church. She put on her plainest dress, and a starched gingham sunbonnet instead of her Sunday hat. Her face wore an expression which indicated some determined purpose. As she left the house her mother said:

"Try to get through dis week, Dasdy. De big baptizin' gwine ter come off next Sunday, an' ef I was you I rudder be baptized at a big baptizin'."

"I feel dat I'm gwine ter git through dis night," said Dasdy firmly.

The church was crowded that night, and the enthusiasm ran high. Dasdy did not go forward at the first call; but when 'Lizah Davis came in and took her seat in front of the pulpit, just behind the last of the benches reserved for mourners, Dasdy's eyes glistened with something which was not a tear nor yet religious feeling. She went forward and knelt a short distance from 'Lizah's seat. Prayers and hymns followed each other in rapid succession. By and by somebody started one of the popular and stirring revival songs. During this hymn Dasdy was observed to slip from the seat where she was kneeling and fall to the floor, where she lay at full length, with half closed eyes, moaning and groaning, with occasional writhings and spasmodic movements of the limbs.

"Sister Dasdy Williams under conviction," ran round the room. A circle was formed about her, a special prayer was offered, and a special hymn sung for her benefit. One or two sisters knelt beside her and poured exhortations into her ears. Others in the background exchanged opinions as to whether she would get through that evening or not. Dasdy through her half-shut eyes saw 'Lizah Davis join the circle about her. Then her movements became more violent.

"I b'leeve she's comin' through," said one sister, breathlessly, looking over the shoulder of the woman in front of her.

"I knowed she'd git through in time fur de big baptizin'," whispered another young woman, sarcastically, pressing forward into the circle. The spectators in the gallery were leaning over toward the crowd below. Suddenly Dasdy sprang to her feet, her face beaming. Uttering a loud shout she jumped straight up and down for a dozen times.

"Glory!" she cried; "oh, so happy! praise de Lamb!" She threw her arms out sidewise. One hand struck a sister on the nose, and the crimson tide proceeding from that organ compelled her to retire. Then as a backward movement in the circle indicated a disposition on the part of the more timid to seek safety, Dasdy sprang in the direction of 'Lizah Davis, and seizing her new velvet bonnet, swung it once or twice on high; then, still shouting and as though unconscious of what she did, dropped it to the floor and trampled it under foot. Another hat shared the same fate. Half a dozen officious women grasped her arms and tried to hold her. Meanwhile 'Lizah, with an angry look, was trying to get her bonnet. Dasdy slipped down between the encircling arms of those who held her, and reaching out caught the overskirt of 'Lizah's silk dress.

Rip! r-r-rip! went the fragile fabric—it was cheap silk—and as 'Lizah attempted to escape, the fastenings of the overskirt gave way at the waist, and the devoted garment fell under the feet of the women who tried to hold the still writhing Dasdy. 'Lizah finally escaped with the fragments of her finery, and with feelings far different from what a religious meeting should have inspired, forced a passage through the crowded aisles and hastened homeward, to weep scalding tears of rage and grief. Her bonnet was entirely ruined, and the silk dress never entirely recovered its pristine splendor.

Dasdy was baptized the following Sunday, and established her reputation for piety by the fine exhibitions of shouting she gave on that occasion. Her designs on Adolphus were successful; she had added one more to the long list of those who have stolen the livery of heaven to serve their own selfish ends; those who believe that all is fair in love may perhaps find excuse for her. The Sunday after the baptizing she appeared at church in a new blue silk dress, with satin trimmings, and a hat gorgeous in the wealth of feathers and ribbons that adorned it. The susceptible but inconstant 'Dolphus could not resist this new combination of gorgeousness and sanctity, and returned to his former allegiance. And from the following announcement which recently appeared in the local newspaper, it may be inferred that the course of true love ran thenceforth smoothly to its proper goal: "Last Wednesday evening the efficient and scholarly head waiter of the Clarendon House led to the hymeneal altar the lovely and accomplished Miss Desdemona Brown, one of our most popular young society ladies. The ceremony was performed at Mt. Gilead Baptist Church by Elder Smith, and the happy pair left the following morning for a two weeks' bridal tour, after which they will reside temporarily with the bride's mother. Mr. Sampson will still continue to preside over the Clarendon dining room."

The Partners

Among the human flotsam and jetsam that followed in the wake of the Civil War, there drifted into a certain Southern town, shortly after the surrender, two young colored men, named respectively William Cain and Rufus Green. They had made each other's acquaintance in a refugee camp attached to an army cantonment, and when the soldiers went away, William and Rufus were thrown upon their own resources. They were fast friends, and discussed with each other the subject of their future.

"Well, ez fer me," said William, "my marster had put me ter de bricklayer's an' plasterer's trade, an' I'd wukked at it six weeks befo' I come away. I hadn' larnt eve'ything, but I reckon I knows ernuff ter make a livin' at it."

"Ez fer me," returned Rufus gloomily—he was not of the most cheerful temperament—"I don't know how ter use nuffin' but a hoe."

"I has ter use de hoe in my bizness, too," rejoined William. "De mo'tar has ter be mix' wid a hoe. W'y can't we go in podners? You kin mix de mo'tar, an' I'll put it on, tel I've larnt you all I knows. We'll keep ou' money tergether, an' w'at I makes shill be ez much yo'n ez mine, an' w'at you makes shill be ez much mine ez yo'n, an' w'at we bofe makes shill belong ter bofe of us. How would dat 'rangement suit you?"

Rufus, having felt some alarm at the prospect of facing the world alone—slavery had not been a good school for training in self-reliance—found this proposition a very agreeable one, and promptly expressed his willingness to accept it.

"And now," said William, who thus early in the affair assumed the initiative, "we ought to hab somethin' ter show ou' agreement—dat's de way w'ite folks does bizness, an' we'll hafter do de same. I knows a man roun' here w'at kin write, an' we'll git some paper an' hab him draw up de articles."

The scribe and the paper were found, and William dictated the following agreement, the phraseology of which is reminiscent of certain solemn forms which he had heard used from time to time, being town-bred and accustomed to the ways of the world:

253

"William Cain and Rufus Green is gone in partners this day to work at whatever their hands find to do. What they makes shall belong to one as much as the other, and they shall stand by each other in sickness and in health, in good luck and in bad, till death shall us part, and the Lord have mercy on our souls. Amen."

This was written in a doubtful hand, on each of two sheets of foolscap paper, and signed by the partners with their respective marks. Each received a copy of the agreement, and they promised the man a half-dollar for his services, to be paid out of their first earnings.

Having found a place to live, William and Rufus settled down as well as their uncertain fortunes would permit. It soon became apparent that William was the more capable of the two, and equally clear—to his patrons at least—that he had not worked at his trade long enough to learn to do fine work. In consequence of this discovery, the partners soon themselves engaged almost solely in the whitewashing and patching business, at which they were fairly successful. Even here, however, William's relative superiority manifested itself, and he generally wielded the brush while Rufus mixed the whitewash. When business was slack, they engaged in such manual labor as they could find. They ate together, slept together, and had a common purse, from which they supplied their necessities and had a little left for amusements and tobacco.

They were living thus, in a hand-to-mouth way, but with the cheerful contentment characteristic of their race, when a Northern philanthropist, filled with the fine, post-bellum zeal for the freedmen, purchased at a low price an extensive plantation in the vicinity of the town, which he cut up into small farms, and, for the encouragement of industry and thrift among the Negroes, sold to them at prices little more than nominal. All but two of the farms had been disposed of before he discovered William and Rufus. Learning that they lived in what they called partnership, he informed them that such a relation was incompatible with the development of self-reliance and strength of character, and that their best interests would be promoted by their learning each to fight his own battle. A thoughtful student of history might have suggested to the philanthropist that the power of highly developed races lies mainly in their ability to combine for the better accomplishment of a common purpose. The good man meant well, however, and his method was admirably adapted to separate the wheat from the chaff. His arguments, or his liberal offer, proved effective; William and Rufus put away the whitewash pails and brushes and became freeholders and farmers upon adjoining tracts of land.

The soil was fertile, and the new owners were filled with the buoyant hopefulness and zeal which characterized the colored people immediately after their emancipation, when there seemed to be a rosy future for their race, not in some distant generation, when the memory of their bondage should have become dim and legendary, but for themselves and their children. The good philanthropist, waiving for the moment his theory of self-reliance—of which indeed his whole generous scheme was a contradiction—gave his beneficiaries advice and oversight for several years, during which William and Rufus, in company with their neighbors, throve apace. In much less time than even the philanthropist had anticipated, both farms were paid for, and William and Rufus tasted the pleasures which any healthy-minded man feels when he first knows himself owner, in fee simple, by metes and bounds, of a piece of the soil which, in a broader sense, is the common heritage of mankind.

During the first years of their separation William and Rufus remained fast friends. The friendship, like their former partnership, was of more practical benefit to Rufus than to William. It was largely due to William's advice about plowing and planting and harvesting, to William's superior knowledge of horses and cattle and hogs, and his more trustworthy intuitions about wind and weather, that Rufus had been able to pay for his farm and procure his deed at the same time with William. This aid, too, was rendered spontaneously, and so much as a matter of course, that Rufus, who was a man of slow perceptions, flattered himself upon being a very successful farmer, and on the highroad to substantial wealth.

Nevertheless, as the years rolled on, William's greater prosperity became apparent even to Rufus, who began gradually to appreciate the fact that William's fields bore larger crops, that his cows calved oftener and gave more milk, that his hogs were fatter and better bred, that his hens laid more eggs and suffered less from fox or hawk, or other thieves.

Shortly after becoming a landowner Rufus had married a wife, who in time bore him several children. William, too, had selected a helpmeet, with a like effect upon his household. The first rift in the long friendship came one day when one of William's children and one of Rufus's had a juvenile dispute, which, if left to themselves, they would have forgotten in an hour. Their mothers, however, took up the quarrel, and having longer memories, became somewhat estranged over it. Since the families were near neighbors and had long been dependent upon one another for the exchange of neighborly courtesies, a quarrel was irksome to say the least. At first William and Rufus paid no attention to the misunderstanding, its only effect upon them being that they met and talked along the turnrows and across fences rather than by each other's firesides. As it was, the trouble would probably soon have been smoothed over, had not the demon Envy, with its train of malice and all uncharitableness, taken possession of Rufus's wife and passed from her to her husband.

Mrs. William Cain came out to church one Sunday in a new frock. Rufus was unable, at the momennt, to buy his wife a garment equally handsome. To make matters worse, William drove Mrs. Cain to church the same day in a new buggy, a luxury in which Rufus, who, like William himself, had hitherto walked to church or driven thither in his cart, could not as yet afford to indulge.

"Dat Cain 'oman is puttin' on mo' airs 'n ef she own' somebody," sniffed

Mrs. Rufus. "She jes' displayin' dem clo's, an' he's jes' bought dat buggy—
he must 'a' got it on credit—jes' ter show off an' make us feel po' an' mean.
Rufus, ef you are de man I take you fer, you won' have nothin' mo' ter do
wid dem people!"

When William next saw Rufus working near the fence and walked down
to pass the time of day, Rufus saw him coming and moved farther away. For
the first few times that this occurred, William supposed it to be a mere coincidence; but when Rufus one day passed him on the road without speaking, even
the pretense of deep absorption in thought did not deceive William. His old
friend had turned against him, and he felt sore at heart. Surely a friendship
of such long standing ought not to be broken because of a few hard words
by two quick-tempered women on account of a children's quarrel.

It occurred to William that perhaps he might pour oil upon the troubled
waters. One Saturday evening he sent his hired man over to Rufus's house
with a message.

"My boss wants ter know," said the messenger, "ef you wouldn' lack
ter borry his buggy termorrer afternoon an' take a ride somewhar."

This seemed to Rufus very kind of William, and he was on the point
of accepting the offer, when Mrs. Green broke in:

"You kin go an' tell William Cain dat we don' go ridin' in borried buggies; dat w'en we git able ter pay fer a buggy, we'll ride, an' not be trapesin'
roun' de country showin' off in buggies w'at ain't paid fer!"

This message, delivered with fidelity both to language and spirit, aroused
some righteous resentment in William's bosom. If Rufus preferred enmity to
friendship, William concluded that he would at least not force his good offices
upon his neighbor, but would hereafter wait until they were requested. He
knew from past experience that Rufus would need them sooner or later. As
a consequence of this mutual coolness, the breach between the neighbors became, if not wider, at least more pronounced.

The purchase of the buggy and the incidents growing out of it had taken
place in the autumn, after the crops had been gathered and sold. During the
following winter Rufus's sweet potatoes, which had not been properly put up,
began to rot, and almost his entire supply was spoiled before he became aware
of their condition. During any other winter, William, whose potatoes always
kept well, would have lent him, at a nominal price, enough potatoes to tide
him over the season. This time, however, Rufus was compelled to pay winter
prices for his potatoes, and cart them home from the town, five miles away.

Henceforth misfortune seemed to follow Rufus. His cows went dry, and
the family had to get along without milk, while they could see, as they drove
along the road, William's pigs feeding upon the surplus of his dairy. One of
Rufus's two horses was taken sick. Upon a similar occasion, the winter before,
William had suggested treatment which had cured the complaint. Rufus admin-
istered the same remedy for a different disease, and the horse died. So far had

the ill-feeling toward his neighbor gone that Rufus ascribed the death of the horse to William, instead of to his own folly in giving the medicine without a proper understanding of the ailment.

William would have been willing at any moment to resume their former relations, upon proper advances from Rufus, of whose misfortunes he was indeed not fully informed, for intercourse between the two families had entirely ceased and even the children were forbidden to play together. The line that separated their farms marked as well the boundary between two school districts, and the children went in opposite directions to different schools. But there came a time when even William's patience was exhausted, and he began to feel something like anger toward his whilom friend.

The rear part of William's farm consisted of a low meadow, through which ran a small stream. With the instinct of a wise farmer seeking to diversify his crops to the best advantage, William had planted this meadow in rice, with very good results. In the cultivation of this cereal it was necessary, now and then, to flood the meadow. This had heretofore been accomplished easily by damming up the stream at the point where it left William's land, whereby it overspread its banks and overflowed the low ground. This had resulted also in flooding Rufus's meadow, which was of similar location and extent, and through which the stream flowed before reaching William's land; but as Rufus had hitherto followed William's advice and example in the matter of planting rice, this overflow was mutually satisfactory and profitable to both.

In the season that followed the beginning of this alienation of an old friendship, Rufus planted his meadow in rice, but lacking William's wisdom, and not having the benefit of his advice, Rufus's crop proved a failure, and the following year he determined to plant the meadow in corn. Having received no notice of his neighbor's intention to change the crop, William planted rice as usual, and in due time dammed up the stream in order to flood the meadow. When Rufus saw the water coming upon his corn, he said nothing to William, but went to consult a lawyer, who advised an injunction. A lawsuit was accordingly begun, and William restrained from backing up the water on the adjoining land.

It was this unneighborly conduct on the part of Rufus that turned the milk of William's friendship into the gall of enmity. He employed the best lawyer in the county, and instructed him to fight the lawsuit to the bitter end.

A quarrel between adjoining land-owners is usually a tedious affair, with many collateral complications, and the law's delays are proverbial. In the course of the next year or two it became necessary, at a certain stage of the proceedings, to make a detailed plat of Rufus's farm, for which purpose a surveyor was employed. In order to perform his work properly, the surveyor went to the county records and procured an exact copy of the description in Rufus's deed. When with his instruments he went to survey Rufus's lines he made a remarkable discovery—the deed did not convey that piece of land at all, but contained a repetition of the description of another parcel in the philanthropist's allotment, previously sold to a different purchaser.

The surveyor was—he believed unjustly—a poor man. His ancestors had once been rich in land and slaves. His grandfather had once owned the very plantation out of which Rufus's farm had been carved. The family had been ruined by the war. Driving past these flourishing farms, the surveyor had often thought they ought to be his own. Now he had discovered that one of the best of them was occupied by a Negro who held it under a clouded title. After a very brief struggle with his conscience, the surveyor made a long journey. In a distant Northern city he found a descendant of the philanthropist, who had met with reverses and had died in comparative poverty. Upon certain plausible representations the surveyor procured, for a small sum, a quit-claim deed of all the right, title and interest of the philanthropist's heir in the land occupied and improved for many years by Rufus. Armed with this document he returned home and began an action in ejectment.

The writ served upon Rufus fell like a bombshell in the heart of his household. Never had he so needed the advice and moral support of his former friend as when he first comprehended the import of the proceedings now begun against him. If he had followed his first impulse, he would have gone and begged his friend's pardon for his own past conduct, to which, he obscurely realized, the alienation of recent years was almost entirely due. Some such suggestion to his wife evoked, however, a torrent of indignant protest.

"Beg his pa'don indeed!" she cried. "He's 'sponsable fer all ou' troubles. Ef he hadn' dammed up dat creek you never would 'a' gone ter law, an' den you wouldn' 'a' hi'ed no su'veyor, an' all dis trouble wouldn' 'a' come on us. He's 'sponsable fer it all, an' you shan't go nigh 'im."

So Rufus went for advice to his lawyer, who tried the case and lost it on a technicality. A better advocate might have won it. A rich man, properly advised, might have taken the case to a higher court with a fair prospect of ultimate success. But Rufus's misfortunes, including the expenses of litigation, had exhausted his cash and his credit, both of which had been derived from the property now decreed to be no longer his. He lost the spring of hope, and yielded to what seemed the inevitable. His wife took the blow as hard, but in a different manner.

"You're no 'count at all," she said to Rufus bitterly. "I ma'ied a man wid land an' hosses an' cows an' hawgs. Now after ten years er slavin', w'at is I got? A man wid nuthin', an' not much er dat! I've wukked myse'f ter skin an' bone, fer who? Fer a w'ite man! I mought as well never 'a' be'n freed. But I'll do so no longer! Hencefo'th you c'n go yo' way an' I'll go mine."

She went away in anger, taking her two children and moving to the neighboring town, where she rented a small room and took in washing for a living. Rufus still lingered at the farm, which he had received a two-weeks' notice to vacate. Several times during the first week he had seen William near the line fence, looking toward the house that must soon be occupied by strangers. Perhaps William was sorry for his old friend—more likely he was gloating over his fallen enemy. Rufus hardened his heart and stiffened his neck, and when he saw William, looked the other way.

On the last day of the second week Rufus harnessed up the old sore-backed horse, his sole remaining beast of burden, to the rickety spring wagon which in the apathy of hopelessness he had not cleaned or repaired for several months. Only the day before he had seen the new owner riding along the road with his wife, inspecting their future domain. Rufus had rented an abandoned log cabin in the woods not far away, where he could hide his diminished head in shame; and he hoped to procure day's work on the neighboring farms, whereby to keep body and soul together. He would resign his deaconship in the church, and henceforth lead the life of obscurity for which alone his meager talents qualified him. It was hard, nevertheless, to leave the land that he had labored upon for so many years, the house he had built with his own hands, and in which he had expected to spend his declining years in peaceful comfort— it was very, very hard.

He loaded the wagon with his few remaining chattels—his wife had taken some, and others had been sold. When he had brought the last piece out of the house, he sat down upon the doorstep and buried his face in his hands. In that moment of self-examination the true source of his misfortunes became entirely clear to him. Long he sat there, until even the sore-backed horse turned his head with an air of mild surprise in his lack-lustre eye.

"Rufus!"

So deeply had Rufus been absorbed in his own somber thoughts that he had not seen William climb over the fence and approach the house. At the sound of his voice so near at hand, Rufus looked up and saw William standing before him with outstretched hand.

"No, William," said Rufus, shaking his head slowly, "I couldn' shake han's wid you."

"Stop yo' foolishness, Rufus, an' listen ter me? Gimme yo' han'!"

"No, William," returned Rufus sadly, "I ain' fitten ter tech yo' han'. You wuz my bes' frien'; you made me w'at I wuz; an' I tu'ned my back on you, an' ha'dened my heart lak Farro of ole Egyp' ter de child'en er Is'ael. You had never done me nuthin' but good; but I went ter de law 'g'inst you, an' den de law come ter me—an' I've be'n sarved right! I ain' fitten' ter tech yo' han', William. Go 'long an' leave mer ter my punishment!"

"You has spoke de truf, Rufus, de Lord's truf! but ef I kin fergive w'at you done ter me, dey ain' no 'casion fer you ter bear malice 'g'inst yo'se'f. Git up f'm dere, man, an' gimme yo' han', an' den listen ter my wo'ds!"

Rufus rose slowly, and taking each other's hands they buried their enmity in a prolonged and fervent clasp.

"An' now, Rufus," said William drawing from his pocket an old yellow paper, through which the light shone along the seams where it had been folded, "does you reco'nize dat paper?"

"No, William, you 'member I never l'arned ter read."

"Well, I has, an' I'll read dis paper ter you:

"William Cain an' Rufus Green is gone in partners this day to work at whatever their hands find to do. What they makes shall belong to one as much as the other, and they shall stand by each other in sickness and in health, in good luck and in bad, till death shall us part, and the Lord have mercy on our souls. Amen."

"Ou' old podnership paper, William," said Rufus sadly, "ou' ole podnership, w'at wuz broke up ten years ago!"

"Broke up? Who said it wuz broke up?" exclaimed William. "It says 'in good luck an' in bad, till death shall us part,' an' it means w'at it says! Do you suppose de Lord could have mussy on my soul ef I wuz ter fersake my ole podner at de time er his greates' trouble? He wouldn' be a jes' God ef he did! Come 'long now, Rufus, an' we'll put dem things back in yo' house, an onhitch dat hoss. You ain' gwine ter stir one foot f'm dis place, onless it's ter go home ter dinner wid me. I've seen my lawyer, an' he says you got plenty er time yit ter 'peal you' case an' take it ter de upper co't, wid eve'y chance ter win it—an' he's a hones' man, w'at knows de law. I've got money in de bank, an' w'at's mine is yo'n till yo' troubles is ended, an' f'm dis time fo'th we is podners 'till death shall us part.' "

Mr. Taylor's Funeral

Mr. David Taylor had been for many years chief steward, during the season of navigation, upon a steamboat running between Groveland and Buffalo, on one of the Great Lakes. The salary and perquisites made the place a remunerative one, and Mr. Taylor had saved considerable money. During the winter time he ran a coal yard, where he supplied poor people with coal in small quantities at a large profit. He invested his savings in real estate, and in the course of time became the owner of a row of small houses on a side street in Groveland, as well as of a larger house on the corner of the adjacent main street.

Mr. Taylor was a stout mulatto, with curly hair and a short gray mustache. He had been a little wild in his youth, but had settled down into a steady old bachelor, in which state he remained until he was past forty-five, when he surprised his friends by marrying a young wife and taking her to live with him in the corner house.

Miss Lula Sampson was a very personable young woman, of not more than twenty-two or twenty-three. She had not been without other admirers, but Mr. Taylor's solid attractions had more than counterbalanced the advantages of these others in the way of youth and sprightliness. For Miss Sampson, while not without her sentimental side, had a practical vein as well, and concluded that on the whole it would be better to be a rich old man's darling than a poor young man's slave.

They lived together very comfortably in the corner house, and Mrs. Taylor enjoyed to the full such advantages as regular rents and savings-bank dividends carried in their train. Mr. Taylor had been for many years a leading member of the Jerusalem Methodist Church, in which he had at various times acted as class-leader, trustee and deacon, and of which he had been at all times the financial backer and manager. Mrs. Taylor had been brought up, so to speak, in the Mt. Horeb Baptist Church, and had at one time sung in the choir; but after her marriage she very dutifully attended service with her husband, only visiting the Baptist church on special occasions, such as weddings or funerals or other events of general public interest.

One day in May, 1900, a month or more after the opening of navigation in the Spring, Mr. Taylor left Groveland on the steamer *Mather* for Buffalo, on one of her regular semiweekly trips to that port. When the steamer returned several days later without him, his wife and friends felt some concern at his non-appearance, as no message had been received from him in the meantime. Inquiry on the steamer merely brought out the fact that Taylor had not been on hand when the boat was ready to leave port, and that she had sailed without him; in fact, he had not been missed until the *Mather* was some miles out.

When several days more elapsed without news from the absent man, his wife's uneasiness became a well-defined alarm. She could account for his absence on no hypothesis except that some harm had befallen him. And upon reading an item in a newspaper, about a week after Mr. Taylor's disappearance, to the effect that the body of a middle-aged mulatto had been found floating in Buffalo harbor, she divined at once that her husband had been the victim of accident, or foul play, and that it was his body that had been recovered. With a promptitude born of sincere regret and wifely sorrow, she requested the company of Deacon Larkins, the intimate personal friend and class-leader of her husband, and with him took the train for Buffalo. Arriving there they found the body at an undertaking establishment. It had evidently been in the water several days, and the features were somewhat disfigured, but nevertheless Mrs. Taylor had no difficulty in identifying the body as that of her late husband. She had the remains prepared for shipment, and the day after her arrival at Buffalo accompanied them back to Groveland. She had telegraphed for a hearse to be at the depot, and when she saw the coffin placed in it she took a carriage with Deacon Larkins and drove to her home.

"Brother Larkins," she said, in grief-stricken accents, as she thought of her good friend and husband and of the narrow cell in which he must soon be laid, "I wish you would t-t-take charge of the arrangements for the f-f-funeral. I know my dear dead David loved you, and would have wished you to attend to it."

"I shall be glad to, Sister Taylor. It is the last service I can perform for my dear friend and brother. His loss will be a sad blow to the church, and to us all."

In pursuance of his instructions Deacon Larkins engaged an undertaker, inserted in the newspapers a notice announcing the date of the funeral, requested six of the intimate friends of the deceased to act as pallbearers, and telegraphed the pastor of the Methodist church, who was out of town, to be on hand on Wednesday, at two o'clock in the afternoon, to conduct the services and preach the funeral sermon.

Several friends of the family called on Mrs. Taylor during the day preceding the funeral, among them the Reverend Alonzo Brown, pastor of the Mt. Horeb Baptist Church. Mr. Brown was a youngish man, apparently not more than thirty, and had himself suffered a bereavement several years before, in the loss of a wife to whom he had made a model husband, so excellent a husband indeed that more than one lady had envied his wife when living, and when she died, had thought that her successor would be indeed a fortunate woman. In addition to possessing these admirable domestic qualities the Reverend Alonzo was a very handsome man, of light-brown complexion, and with large and expressive black eyes and very glossy curly hair. Indeed, Mrs. Taylor herself had several times thought that if an overruling Providence in its inscrutable wisdom should see fit to remove her dear David from his earthly career while she was yet a young woman—which was not at all unlikely, since he was twenty-five years her senior—there was no man of her acquaintance with whom she could more willingly spend the remainder of her days and the money her good David would leave her than the Reverend Alonzo Brown. Of course this had been only one of the vague day-dreams of a lively imagination; but it is not surprising, when the central figure in this vision called on her upon the heels of the very event upon which the day-dreams had been predicated, that the idea should penetrate even the veil of grief that surrounded her, and assume something of the nature of a definite probability.

Mr. Brown was a man of tact, and consoled the widow very beautifully in her bereavement.

"Yes, Sister Taylor," he said, pressing her hand with soothing friendliness, "your loss is indeed great, for your husband was a man of whom any woman might have been proud. You displayed excellent taste and judgment, too, Sister Taylor, in selecting as your companion a man of steady habits and settled character, who could leave you suitably provided for during the rest of your life."

The widow sobbed at the magnitude of her loss, but was not unmindful of the compliment to her own taste and judgment.

"But the saddest feature about our dear brother's taking off is not your loss," he said, again pressing her hand consolingly, "it is what he himself has lost—the companionship of one who made his household a model for his friends to imitate, and the despair of those who could not hope to be so fortunate. It is true," he added, with proper professional consistency, "that he has gone to his reward, but I am sure he would willingly have waited for it a few years longer in this terrestrial paradise."

The minister, as he said this, looked around appreciatively at the very comfortable room in which they sat. There was handsome paper on the walls, a bright red carpet on the floor, lace curtains at the windows, a piano, a well-filled bookcase—and in fact all the evidences of solid prosperity, based on landed proprietorship. And by his side, too, sat the weeping young widow, to whom tears and weeds were by no means unbecoming.

While he had been speaking an idea had occurred to Mrs. Taylor. She was before her marriage a member of his church. The pastor of the Methodist church, she had learned since her return from Buffalo, was out of town, in attendance on the general conference of his denomination in session at New

York. It would be a very nice thing indeed to have Mr. Brown preach the funeral sermon.

"Brother Brown," she said, on the impulse of the moment, "I want you to do me a favor. Will you preach my dear David's funeral sermon?"

He reflected a moment. It was an opportunity to secure that influence which would enable him to lead back into his fold this very desirable sheep.

"If you don't think it will be taken amiss by his own church," he answered, "it would give me great pleasure to perform the last sad rites over our departed friend."

"There will be no trouble about that," she replied. "Elder Johnson has gone to general conference, and there is no one else whom I would prefer to yourself. I ask it as a personal favor."

"It shall be done at any cost," he said determinedly, again pressing her hand in farewell.

"And if you will ask the choir to sing, I shall be under still greater obligation," she said. "They are all my friends, and I have often joined with them on similar occasions, before I was married, and I'm sure you would prefer them."

About an hour after Mr. Brown went away, Deacon Larkins called to make a final report of the arrangements he had made.

"I've requested several of the brethren to act as pallbearers," he said, naming them, "and have asked the choir to furnish the music. Elder Johnson telegraphed this afternoon that he would be here in time to preach the sermon. He has already started, and will get here by half-past one and come right up from the depot."

Mrs. Taylor scented trouble. "But I thought he couldn't come, and I've invited Elder Brown to preach the sermon," she said.

Deacon Larkins looked annoyed. "There'll be trouble," he said. "You asked me to make arrangements and I acted accordingly."

"What can we do about it?" she asked anxiously.

"Don't ask me," he said. "I'm not responsible for the difficulty."

"But you can help me," she said. "I see no way out of it but to explain the situation to Elder Brown and ask him to retire. Please do that for me."

Deacon Larkins grumbled a little and went away, intending to do as requested. But the more he thought about the matter the more displeased he felt at the widow's action. She had not only been guilty of disrespect to him, in asking a minister to conduct the services without consulting the man in whose charge she had placed the arrangements, but she had committed the far more serious offense of slighting the Methodist church. He could hardly think of a graver breach of propriety than to ask the minister of a rival denomination to officiate at this funeral. If it had been some obscure member of the congregation the matter would have been of less consequence; but to request the Baptist minister to preach Brother David's funeral sermon was something like asking

Martin Luther to assist at the Pope's interment. The more Deacon Larkins thought of it the less he liked it; and finally he concluded that he would simply wash his hands of the entire business—if the widow wanted to call off Elder Brown she would have to do it herself.

He wrote a note to this effect and sent it by his youngest son, a lad of ten, with instructions to deliver it to Mrs. Taylor. The boy met a companion and went off to play, and lost the note. His father was away when he got back home. In the meantime the boy had forgotten about the note, and left his father to infer that it had been delivered.

About a quarter of two on the day of the funeral the friends began to arrive. The undertaker in charge seated them. When the Baptist choir came it was shown to the place provided beforehand for the singers. When a few minutes later the Methodist choir arrived and stated what their part in the service was to be, the undertaker, supposing they were an addition to the number already on hand, gave them the seats nearest those occupied by the Baptist choir. There was some surprise apparent, but for a while nothing was said, the members of the two bodies confining themselves to looks not altogether friendly. Some of them thought it peculiar that, if the two choirs had been asked to cooperate, there had been no notice given and no opportunity to practice together; but all awaited for the coming of the officiating minister to solve the difficulty. Meantime the friends of the family continued to arrive, until the room where the remains were placed was filled to overflowing, and there were people standing in the hall and seated in other rooms from which they would be able to see or hear very little of the exercises.

At just five minutes to two a livery carriage drove up to the gate and deposited on the pavement a tall, dark man, wearing a silk hat, a high vest, and a coat of clerical cut—it was Elder Johnson of the Jerusalem Methodist Church. The elder paid the driver his fee and went in at the front gate. At the same moment the pastor of the Baptist church came in at the side gate and drew near the front door. The two preachers met on the porch and bowed to one another stiffly. The undertaker's assistant came forward and took their hats.

"Which of you gentlemen is to conduct the service?" asked the undertaker, with a professionally modulated voice.

"I shall conduct the service," answered Elder Johnson in a matter-of-fact tone.

"I am to conduct the service," said Mr. Brown firmly, in the same breath.

Elder Johnson looked surprised, Mr. Brown looked determined, and they glared at each other belligerently.

"May I ask what you mean, sir?" said Elder Johnson, recovering somewhat from his surprise.

"I mean, sir, that I'm going to conduct the funeral exercises," replied the other.

The undertaker began to feel uneasy. It was his first funeral in that neighborhood, and he had expected to make a reputation by his success in directing it.

"There's evidently some misunderstanding here," he said, in a propitiatory tone.

"There's no misunderstanding on my part," said Elder Johnson. "I was telegraphed to by Deacon Larkins, at the widow's request, and have left important business and come five hundred miles at considerable expense to preach this funeral, and I intend to preach it, or know the reason why."

"There can be no possible misunderstanding on my part," replied Mr. Brown. "People may send telegrams without authority, or under a mistaken impression; but I was asked by the widow, personally, to conduct the funeral services, and I propose to do so."

"The deceased was a member of my church before the widow was born," retorted Elder Johnson, making in his warmth a mistake of several years. "I was requested by the widow's agent to conduct this service, and have come here prepared to do it. Every consideration of duty and decency requires me to insist. Even the wishes of the widow should hardly be permitted to stand in the way of what, in this case, is the most obvious propriety."

"The widow," said Mr. Brown, "is the principal one concerned. Her wishes should be sacred on such an occasion, to say nothing of her rights. I'll not retire until I am personally requested by her to do so. I received my commission from her, and I'll resign it to her only."

"Wait a moment, gentlemen," said the undertaker, hopefully, "until I go and speak to the widow."

The colloquy on the porch had not gone unnoticed. Through the half-closed Venetian blinds a number of the guests had seen the group apparently engaged in animated discussion, though their voices had been pitched in low tones; and there was considerable curiosity as to what was going on.

In a few moments the undertaker returned. "Gentlemen," he said in desperation, "something must be done. I can't get anything out of the widow. She is almost hysterical with grief, and utterly unfit to decide on anything. You must come to some agreement. Why can't you divide the services between you?"

The rival clergymen set their faces even more rigidly.

"I can submit to no division," said Elder Johnson, "that does not permit me to preach the sermon. No man could know Brother Taylor as well as I did, and no man could possibly be so well prepared to pronounce a fitting eulogy on his life. It would be an insult to my church for anyone but Brother Taylor's pastor to preach his funeral; in fact, it seems to me not only in bad taste, but bordering on indecency for the pastor of another church, of another denomination, to take advantage of a widow's grief and irresponsibility, and try to force himself where the most elementary principles of professional courtesy would require him to stay away. However, I'm willing to overlook that, under the circumstances, if Brother Brown will be content to read the Scriptures and lead in one of the prayers."

"I repel Brother Johnson's insinuations with scorn; their animus is very plain," said the Baptist minister, with some heat. "I will accept of no compromise that does not allow me to deliver the discourse. I was personally requested to do so; I have prepared a sermon with special reference to the needs of this particular case. If I don't use it my labor is wasted. My brother seems to think there's nobody to be considered in this matter but the deceased, whereas I am of quite the contrary opinion."

It was very apparent that no such compromise as the one proposed was possible. Meanwhile the curiosity on the inside was rising to fever heat; a number of eyes were glancing through the blinds, and several latecomers had collected about the steps leading up to the porch and were listening intently.

Pending this last statement by the reverend gentlemen of their respective positions, the undertaker had had time to think. He was a man of resources and the emergency brought out his latent powers. A flash of professional inspiration came to his aid.

"Gentlemen," he said soothingly, "I think I can see a way out of this difficulty which will give each of you an opportunity to officiate and prevent the funeral from being spoiled. Here are two large rooms, opening by wide doors from opposite sides of a central hall. There are people enough to fill the two rooms easily. The remains can be placed in the hall between the two rooms, where they can be seen from both. Each of you conduct a service in a separate room, and all the guests can be comfortably seated in a position to hear or participate in one service or the other."

The proposition was a novel one, but it possessed the merit of practicability, and after some brief demur, both ministers reluctantly consented to the arrangement. The body was quickly removed to the hall, and disposed in a position where it would be visible from both rooms. The undertaker made a brief statement of the situation and announced that two services would be held. The company divided according to their individual preferences, some taking seats in the other room, others remaining where they were. The Baptist choir, of course, went with their own minister; the Methodist choir remained with theirs. When the widow came out, clad in deepest weeds and sobbing softly, she took her seat, whether by inadvertence or choice did not appear, in the room where Mr. Brown had elected to conduct his part of the ceremony.

Each service opened with singing. The Methodist choir sang "Rock of Ages." The Baptist choir softly chanted "Asleep in Jesus," until they were compelled to sing louder in order to be heard at all. Each of the ministers then read a passage of Scripture; there was no conflict in this, as they were far enough apart to avoid confusion.

Each then offered prayer. The Methodist minister rendered thanks for the blessing of a beautiful life that had been spared so long among them as an example of right living. Mr. Brown, on the other side of the hall, with equal fervor asked for comfort to the sorrowing widow in her bereavement. And each in his own words prayed that the event they had come together to mourn over might be a warning to those present of the transitoriness of all earthly good, and that by calling attention to the common mortality it might humble their souls and drive out jealousy and envy and malice and all uncharitableness.

At the close of the prayers there was another musical number—or rather two of them. The Baptist choir rendered an anthem breathing resignation and comfort. The Methodist choir sang a hymn of triumph over death and the grave. Someone discreetly closed one of the doors during the singing, so that no discord marred the harmony of this part of the service.

When the two addresses were well under way, a man came up the street and entered the premises by the front gate. There had been several late arrivals, but until this one appeared they had all found seats in the house. As the new-comer approached he saw the crepe upon the door, noted the half-drawn blinds, and glanced across the lot at the row of carriages drawn up on the side street. With an expression of mingled wonder and alarm, he drew nearer the door and heard the sound of preaching. He stepped softly upon the porch but paused before he reached the door and, after hesitating a moment, came down again, and going around to the side of the house stood on tiptoe and peered curiously through the half-closed blinds at the scene within. First he noticed the coffin, piled high with flowers. Then the sermon fixed his attention, and clutching the window sill with his elbows he stood listening for several minutes.

"Indeed, my dear brethren and sisters," Elder Johnson was saying, "we may well mourn the death of our dear brother, and look upon it as an irrepara-ble loss. Where will we find a man who was so generous in his contributions to the church, so devoted to his family, or who set a better example of the Christian life? In him we have lost a leader in every good work, a faithful friend, a dear brother, a strong pillar in the church, a champion of his race, a man whom we all loved and admired. Cut off in the prime of life, in the full tide of his usefulness, we mourn his departure, and we rejoice that he has lived—we celebrate his virtues and we revere his memory."

The man outside dropped from his somewhat constrained position, and the puzzled expression on his face became even more pronounced. But he had heard the voice, though indistinctly, of the minister across the hall, and he went softly around the rear of the house and, picking up a small box which lay in the yard, placed it under a window of the other room. Looking through the slats, he saw a woman dressed in deepest mourning. Her face was concealed by the heavy crepe veil that fell before it, but her form was shaken by convulsive sobs. Grouped around the room was an audience equally as large as the one across the hall, and the young Baptist minister was saying, with great unction:

"There are no words, my hearers, by which we can adequately express the sympathy we feel for this bereaved widow in this, her hour of deepest earthly sorrow. Our hearts go out to this beloved sister, whose mainstay has been cut off, and who has been left to tread the thorny path of life in loneliness and desolation. I know that if the departed can look down from that upper sphere which he now adorns, upon this scene of his late earthly career, no more painful thought could mar the celestial serenity of his happiness than the reflection that he had left behind him in inconsolable grief the companion of his earthly joys and sorrows. We feel for our sister; we commend her to the source of all comfort; we assure her of such friendly offices as are within our weak power. And we hope in time the edge of her grief will lose its sharpness, and that she may feel resigned to the decree of Heaven and find such consolation as a life of usefulness may yet have to offer her."

The two sermons came to an end almost simultaneously, and again the two audiences were led in prayer. While the eyes of the two ministers were raised on high in supplication, and those of their hearers were piously turned to earth, the man on the outside, unable to restrain his curiosity longer, stepped down from his box, came around to the front door, opened it, walked softly forward, and stopped by the casket, where he stood looking down at the face it contained.

At that moment the two prayers came to an end, the eyes of the ministers sought a lower level, while those of the guests were raised, and they saw the stranger standing by the coffin.

Some nervous women screamed, several strong men turned pale, and there was a general movement that would probably have resulted in flight if there had been any way out except by passing through the hall.

The man by the casket looked up with even greater wonderment than he had before displayed.

"Whose funeral is this, anyhow?" he asked, addressing himself to nobody in particular.

"Why," responded several voices in chorus, "it's your funeral!"

A light dawned on the newcomer, and he looked much relieved.

"There's some mistake here," he said, "or else if I'm dead I don't know it. I was certainly alive when I came in on the train from Buffalo about thirty minutes ago."

The drowning in Buffalo harbor of a man resembling Taylor had been, of course, a mere coincidence. It might be said, in passing, that Mr. Taylor never explained his prolonged absence very satisfactorily. He did tell a story, or rather a vague outline of a story, lacking in many of the corroborative details which establish truthfulness, about an accident and a hospital. As he is still a pillar in the Jerusalem Methodist Church, and trying hard to live up to the standard set by his funeral sermons, it would be unbecoming to do more than suggest, in the same indefinite way, that when elderly men who have been a little wild in their youth are led by sudden temptation, when away from the restraining influences of home, to relapse for a time into the convivial habits of earlier days, there are, in all well-governed cities, institutions provided at the public expense where they may go into retreat for a fixed period of time, of such length—say five or ten or twenty or thirty days—as the circumstances of each particular case may seem to require.

A Bad Night

My wife has perhaps more good qualities than any woman I am acquainted with. I shall not attempt to enumerate them, but will merely say for the purposes of this story that she has only one fault. In accordance, however, with the universal law of compensation, she possesses that one fault in such measure as to counterbalance a great many of her virtues—she is the most suspicious of women.

Nature has given her a fairly symmetrical figure and a very pleasant face. Her features are not cast exactly in the ancient Greek mold, but are above the average in these degenerate days, and on the whole she is a very good-looking woman. She does not wear the finest fabrics, but always dresses in good taste. Yet whenever she sees anyone looking at her intently, she at once becomes indignant because she imagines that her appearance is being criticized—that her dress does not fit smoothly, or her hat is awry. She has a mortal terror of dogs and canine beauty and fidelity have no existence for her, for in every dog she sees either an actual or a probable case of hydrophobia. The pleasure of rapid motion, which Dr. Johnson so long ago stamped with his approval, she never enjoys, for if the horse gets out of a walk, she thinks he is running away.

Beggars and peddlers never come to our house but once, for in every one of them she sees a tramp or a sneak thief. She has had a wicket put in the kitchen door, through which she can look at anyone knocking and transact any business she may have with strangers. She has even had iron bars put on the lower windows, and nearly bankrupted me once by putting burglar alarms and a telephone into the house—a rented house at that. In vain I have assured her that there is nothing in our humble establishment for the sake of which even an amateur burglar would risk his life or his liberty. She cannot be convinced that my silver watch, the plated teaspoons, and the silver ice pitcher, which was the most valuable of our wedding presents, are not a standing temptation to thieves. We once, during the temporary illness attendant upon the birth of our first child, hired a girl to help with the housework; but my wife kept such a close surveillance over Biddy that the high-spirited scion of

Hibernian royalty left in a huff, forgetting to pay back the two-weeks' wages I had advanced her to buy a new bonnet.

On one occasion my venerable uncle, who lives in the country and whom my wife had never met, came in to pay us a visit. He modestly went round to the back door and knocked. My wife opened the wicket, gave him a hasty glance, jumped at the conclusion that he was a tramp or a peddler, ordered him out of the yard, and slammed the wicket in his face before the astonished old gentleman had time to introduce himself. We have since had to buy all our Christmas and Thanksgiving turkeys, and did not spend the next summer on my uncle's farm, a visit which we had looked forward to with pleasant anticipation.

But these were small matters, and I could afford to laugh at most of them, until the incident occurred which would have rendered my wife's fault unbearable and compelled me to resort to extreme measures (the nature of which it is unnecessary for me to state) if it had not at the same time opened her eyes to her own folly, the first step, I hope, to a permanent cure.

This incident took place one evening in summer. I had said to my wife at noon that I might not be home for supper, as I should probably be detained at the office an hour or two in the evening, and if so, would get a lunch downtown. As it happened I did not have to stay down in the evening, but started home about the usual hour. While I was waiting for a street car I heard a gruff voice pronounce my name, and before I could turn felt a stunning blow on my shoulder—evidently intended for a friendly clap—and as I wheeled around in some trepidation, found myself face to face with Spratt. Spratt was an old college classmate and former chum of mine whom I had not seen for a year as he had been running a cattle ranch down in Texas.

"Hello, Spratt, old man," I exclaimed, as soon as I had recovered my breath, "I haven't seen you since the flood!"

Spratt immediately consigned me to the infernal regions in the emphatic language of the Texas cowboy, while the painful grasp of his hand and the unaffected cordiality of his manner showed the pleasure he felt at meeting me. My first impulse was to ask Spratt to supper. But then I remembered that my wife hardly expected me to supper; and while I was mentally balancing the pros and cons, Spratt thrust his hand in my arm, and exclaimed:

"I'm stopping at the National, and I'm going up to dinner. Come up and have a bite. I want to talk to you, and I've got to leave the city in the morning."

Under ordinary circumstances I would not, by remaining away from supper, have subjected myself to the unjust and degrading suspicions to which my unexplained absence would have surely given rise; yet, reflecting that my wife did not expect me, I thought I might risk it in this instance. I went with Spratt to the hotel, and we had supper served in a private room where we could talk over old times without restraint. The soup was good, the fish was excellent, the roast was superb. We had a couple of bottles of wine, and Spratt, who had acquired the tastes of the frontiersman with marvelous facility, must have some Kentucky whiskey. I merely took the least bit of this at Spratt's request to try the flavor.

When I parted from Spratt about nine o'clock, I felt extremely comfortable and never was in better spirits in my life. I took a streetcar and soon reached home. In a fit of absent-mindedness I tried to open the door with my pocket knife for a while, but discovering my mistake, applied the latch-key and gained admittance. I hung, or meant to hang, my hat on a hook, but it fell on the floor and rolled over into a corner. I did not think it worthwhile to pick it up, as a slight feeling of languor stealing over me made me disinclined to any unnecessary exertion. I took off my overcoat and hung it over the back of a chair which stood in a corner. It slipped off the chair and fell behind it on the floor, but as it was just as safe there, I did not think it necessary to pick it up. I was feeling very sleepy by this time, and lay down on the lounge in the sitting room.

That is to say, I meant to lie down on the lounge, but through some miscalculation or mistake, or misfortune, I missed the lounge and lay on the floor. My memory is a little indistinct about the matter now, but I remember I thought it would require a good deal of exertion to get up and lie down on the lounge, to say nothing of the possibility of another failure. I concluded that under the circumstances the floor was good enough for me. As the position I lay in was not very comfortable, I turned over toward the lounge and rolled under it; the chintz cover, which fell in a curtain to the floor, shaded my eyes from the light, and I went to sleep almost immediately. My memory is almost an utter blank as to the subsequent events of the evening, and what happened during the next hour I relate as it was told to me afterwards.

My wife, not expecting me home until somewhat late in the evening, had stepped across the street to a progressive euchre party at the house of an intimate friend, where she stayed until about eleven o'clock. On coming home, she did not, for reasons above stated, see my hat or overcoat, and naturally supposed I had not yet come in. My sister-in-law, who was staying with us, had gone to a party with her young man, and thus leaving my wife alone in the house. As time passed and I did not put in an appearance, she became a little restless and nervous, as was but natural for a woman of her disposition. In looking around the room for some object that was misplaced she caught site of my feet protruding from under the lounge. She had no idea that I was in the house, and she needed but a glance at the boots, which had become very dirty in my homeward meandering, to convince her that a burglar had secreted himself under the lounge with the intention of robbing the house when all the inmates were asleep.

Most women, under like circumstances, would have screamed or fainted, or in some way exhibited their emotions. But my wife, as I have said, was no ordinary woman, but possessed a firmness and strength of character which is by no means common, even among the sterner sex, and rarely met with in women. She did not scream or faint, but went quietly out of the room, ran upstairs to the library, closing the doors behind her softly, so as to prevent the noise from being heard below, and telephoned the nearest police station, stating that a burglar was concealed in the house and asking that a policeman be sent to arrest him. Then she got my revolver out of a bureau drawer, went downstairs, and sat down by the worktable, within ten feet of the supposed burglar. I question whether one woman in a thousand would have been capable of as much.

In about five minutes a knocking was heard at the door, and my wife admitted the two guardians of the peace—an Irishman and a Negro.

"Whar is de bugglar, ma'am?" whispered the colored policeman.

"Under the sofa in the next room," she said, pointing to the open door of the sitting room.

"Go in front," suggested the Irishman to the colored man, "and Oi'll have the nippers ready whin ye've grabbed the spalpeen."

They entered the room, and my wife's nerves not being equal to any further tension, she fainted. When she came to, the Irishman was holding a glass of water to her lips, and as she opened her eyes he said:

"Faith, mum, an' we arristed 'im. The spalpeen attimpted to resist the officers of the law, and we clubbed him over the head a bit. It'll make him sleep the sounder tonight."

My wife's sister came in a few minutes later, and the two women sat and waited for me far into the night. My sister-in-law first went to bed, and my wife followed shortly after, but not to sleep, as she was worried at my non-appearance and tormented with fears for my safety.

In the cold gray dawn I awoke from a troubled sleep. I was not at first sure that I was awake. My head felt very queer, and, as I discovered by passing my hand over it, was covered with contusions of various degrees of magnitude and tenderness. My clothes were torn and muddy, and taking me altogether, I looked as though I had been tossed by an angry bull or run over by a fire engine. I found myself in a small apartment, with a narrow, grated window and an iron door in the stone wall. It required no second glance to show me that I was in prison. I was, in fact, immured in a cell of the Central Police Station.

I endeavored to recall the events of the previous evening. I remembered, somewhat vaguely, all that took place up to the time when I went to sleep under the lounge. What happened afterwards I could recall only as a dream, in which, like a lost spirit, I had been tormented by devils who clubbed me with telegraph poles and prodded me with red-hot pitchforks.

But why was I here? Had I imbibed too freely of Spratt's Kentucky whiskey, and in a fit of alcoholic mania murdered my wife or one of the children, or the whole family? I pictured to myself the bloody corpses of my children, slain by a father's ruthless hand. Had I gone out in my sleep and unwittingly committed arson or burglary or some other heinous offense? Or had I merely been run in for disorderly conduct? I gave it up, but my reflections were not pleasant while I waited for enlightenment.

About eight o'clock a turnkey put in an appearance with a plate of coarse food and a brown mug of what purported to be coffee, and shoved them through a wicket in the door of my cell.

"I say," I anxiously inquired, "where am I anyway?"

"You're in a very fine place compared with where you will be before long," was the gruff response. "You're in the Central Station now, but the chances are that you will be in jail in about two hours."

This information was not very reassuring. "But what am I in for?" I asked.

"Burglary and resisting the officers. You know what you're in for; the old thing, no doubt. Hurry up and eat your breakfast, if you want any, for the court will open in half an hour, and your case is the first or second on the docket."

I was horror-struck—crushed—almost annihilated! What a position! A life which so far had been at least honest, a reputation without a flaw, to be blasted in a single night by the well-meant, but ill-timed hospitality of Spratt! I am afraid that in the excitement of the moment I referred to Spratt in language which would not bear repetition.

But the all-important question was, how to get out of the scrape, if possible. Of course a lawyer was the first thing needed, and after some solicitation I induced the turnkey, who was naturally inclined to consider me a rather desperate and irresponsible character, to send for an attorney of my acquaintance, on whose skill and secrecy I could rely.

I had hardly time to give my attorney a hasty and somewhat incoherent account of such events of the preceding evening as I could recollect, when the presiding genius of the institution reappeared, and called out in a sing-song tone:

"Number three, burglary and resisting officers," and I was hurried up a flight of stone steps, through a long corridor, and into a dingy court room, where sat a somewhat austere-looking judge, with hair and whiskers slightly streaked with gray, and a mustache clipped straight across the upper lip. As the day was wet and disagreeable, the number of spectators was small, for which I was devoutly thankful.

"What is your name?" asked the court.

"John Smith," whispered my legal adviser, and I unblushingly gave the time-honored response.

"You are charged with two offenses. The first charge against you is burglary. Are you guilty or not guilty?"

"Not guilty," I answered, at the instance of my attorney.

"Mr. Bailiff, call Patrolman Sullivan."

Patrolman Michael Sullivan, being first duly sworn, testified that on the evening before he had been on duty at the Forest Street Police Station; that at eleven o'clock he had been detailed by Sergeant Donnelly, in response to a telephone call, to go with Patrolman Caesar Johnson to No. 375 Birch Street and arrest a burglar who was concealed on the premises; that they had been admitted to the house by the front door, and had found the prisoner concealed or partly concealed under a lounge in the sitting room; that he was evidently under the influence of liquor at that time; that—

When I heard the number of the house I began to understand the situation, and the subsequent disclosures made it all clear to me. I remembered rolling under the lounge, and knowing my wife's peculiar temperament, I saw that I had been the innocent victim of circumstances. I hurriedly whispered to my lawyer, and as I told him how things were, a broad grin slowly diffused itself over his face. Interrupting the witness he exclaimed:

"May it please the court, this whole affair is a most ridiculous mistake, as I can convince your honor in two minutes' private conversation, if your honor will grant me that."

Our police court is not very ceremonious and the coveted two minutes was granted; and in the adjacent witness room the court was soon informed that I had been arrested in my own house, on the complaint of my own wife. The judge was a little incredulous at first, but on the assurance of my attorney the cases against me were dismissed. The court gave me a few words of advice which I received in a spirit of proper humility, and I was once more a free man.

I begged my attorney to call a hack for me, as an appearance on the street in my condition at that time would have occasioned some remarks to say the least, even if some zealous policeman had not re-arrested me on general principles. Even the hackman was suspicious, and demanded his fare in advance. I paid it and was soon driven home.

I alighted from the vehicle and ran up the steps as quickly as possible, to avoid the eyes of inquisitive neighbors. A jerk at the doorbell brought my wife, who uttered a shriek of joy and literally threw herself upon me. In my weakened physical condition I was obliged to brace myself up against the wall in order to sustain the shock.

"Oh, Paul, Paul, my dear husband! Where have you been? Oh, my poor husband! How did you escape?"—and so on, kissing me hysterically the while.

I calmly endured these demonstrations of joy for a few moments, and then putting her from me, I said sternly:

"Madam, behold the consequences of your folly! You have accomplished your work! In me you see a nervous wreck, a blasted reputation, blighted prospects, and a ruined life. Unhand me, madam," and I stalked as majestically as was possible under the circumstances into the house.

I glanced hastily into the first mirror I came to, to see if my hair had not turned gray in a single night; and I cannot tell yet whether it was a relief or a disappointment to find that it had not. I shall always hereafter be a little skeptical about the time-honored literary expedient; for according to all the canons of fiction, my sufferings certainly ought to have had that result.

While I was dressing my wounds and changing my clothes, my wife and I were mutually enlightened as to the events of the night. Of course I heaped reproaches upon her head, and with such a pointed illustration at hand, I was not slow in pointing out to her the absurdity of that suspiciousness which was her one fault. In her mortification at my arrest and the possible social and financial consequences, she did not, as I feared she would, make any allusion to my inebriated condition at the time that I came home; which was, I am reluctantly forced to admit, the primary cause of this unfortunate affair. I need not here stop to say that she has mentioned it several times since then.

But this was not the end. Some sharp-nosed reporter had learned of the arrest of a supposed burglar at No. 375 Birch Street the night before, and had the whole disgusting details dished up in the *Morning Swill Barrel*, together with several circumstances which seemed to connect me with a notorious band of criminals. This brought the scavengers of the evening papers around to learn more about the matter, and in the course of their inquiries they learned that I had not been seen since leaving the hotel the night before. This fact was duly chronicled in the evening papers under the conspicuous title of "A Mysterious Disappearance," and the theory was put forward that I had been put out of the way by the burglar before reaching home, in order to facilitate the commission of the burglary. When I hurried down to the office about three o'clock I found the proprietor and the assistant bookkeeper deeply immersed in the accounts, and I knew from the look of relief that came into the proprietor's face that my reappearance had lifted a load from his mind.

I remained closeted with him for half an hour. I made a clean breast of the matter, for I did not want to have him hear a garbled edition of it from some other source. He was a fair man—not too good to sympathize with the weakness of others—and the matter was overlooked. I took a week's vacation while my wounds were healing and while a tailor was making me a new suit. I am happy to state that the story never got out. My lawyer was discreet, and the wretched creature who had appeared in the Police Court would never have been recognized as the elegant Paul _____. My disappearance was accounted for to inquisitive acquaintances by a sudden summons to a neighboring town to attend the dying bed of my aged great-grandfather.

As I remarked at the beginning of this story, which I publish as a warning to young married people, the most important result of the affair—and one which consoles me for all the annoyance and expense in the way of doctor's, lawyer's, and tailor's bills—has been a gradual change for the better in my wife's disposition. At the present rate of improvement, I hope to see her one vice thoroughly eradicated, when I shall be able to present to the world that rarest of creatures:

> "A perfect woman, nobly planned,
> To warn, to comfort, and command."

The Doctor's Wife

T he wind was whistling shrilly around the corners of the house, sobbing and sighing through the evergreens in the yard, and howling dismally up among the chimney-tops, as Dr. Baird, one winter evening, turned up the collar of his overcoat, drew on his gloves, and pulled his sealskin cap down over his ears.

"I shall not be in again until morning, Mary," he said to Mrs. Baird, who sat by a low table in front of the grate, reading a newspaper by the light of a shaded lamp. "Mrs. Murray is no better, and requires constant attendance. Dr. Graves has been with her all day, and I must relieve him tonight. Her condition is quite serious, but I think she will pull through. However, the crisis will hardly be reached before tomorrow noon."

Mrs. Baird laid down the newspaper, and sighed. Twenty years of wedded happiness had not fully reconciled her to the conditions of a busy physician's life; and she often longed for the time when her husband could retire from the active practice of his profession. But as Dr. Baird was still what is called a young man, and by no means as rich as he hoped to become, Mrs. Baird had resigned herself to the inevitable, and endured the discomfort of irregular meals and broken sleep without murmuring. So she merely looked up and sighed as her husband made this announcement.

"Have you set the burglar alarm?" she asked.

"Yes, for all the lower floor except the side door to the library. I shall take the key to that door, so that I can come in without disturbing you. I shall try to get back by six in the morning. Good night." And the Doctor took his way across the grounds, toward the sanitarium.

The burglar alarm had been placed in the house some time before, at Mrs. Baird's suggestion. A man-servant had formerly slept in the house, but he had moved to a room in the sanitarium; and in view of the Doctor's frequent absence from home, Mrs. Baird had persuaded him to have a burglar alarm put into the house. The Doctor had laughed at her fears, and had to be reminded of the burglar alarm, for he frequently forgot to adjust it. She would not touch it herself; it made her nervous, she said.

The sanitarium was a local institution, in which the people of the village of Wellington took a great deal of pride. It was owned by a syndicate of wealthy men, who had selected the town on account of its healthy location, pastoral surroundings, and fine scenery, as the site of a large hotel, which, by virtue of these attractions, supplemented by a competent medical staff and judicious advertising, had become quite a popular health resort. Dr. Baird was resident physician-in-chief of the establishment, and with his family occupied a cottage on the opposite side of the extensive grounds, and several minutes' walk from the main building.

Mrs. Murray was one of the nurses at the sanitarium, who had herself been taken ill. Dr. Baird entered the sickroom and inquired of Dr. Graves:

"How is she now?"

"Sinking rapidly," was the reply. "I do not think she will live until morning."

A short consultation followed, and it was decided that both doctors should remain by the patient's side until there was some further change in her condition.

After the Doctor left, Mrs. Baird finished her newspaper, and then looked over the latest fashion-plates with her daughter Mollie, a trim-looking lass of sixteen summers, who was trying to solve the important problem of how to make a new dress. At nine o'clock, with a caution to Mollie about the fire and the lights, Mrs. Baird went upstairs to bed.

Mollie dawdled over her fashions a little while longer, and then sought her room, which was a small apartment on the lower floor, and opening off the sitting room.

About midnight the burglar alarm went off with a great racket and woke Mrs. Baird from a sound sleep.

She realized, of course, that someone was in the house, or attempting to gain entrance. Her second thought was for Mollie's safety. Mollie was downstairs, and her room one which a burglar would be most likely to enter in any search for valuables. Hastily opening a drawer in the chiffonier which stood in her bedroom, Mrs. Baird took out a revolver and glanced at it by the light of the night-lamp to see if it were loaded. Weapon in hand, she went softly and swiftly down the stairs, her heart a prey to a thousand apprehensions. Every instant she expected to hear a scream. Suppose Mollie should cry out, or resist the burglars? Suppose her youth and beauty should tempt them to a worse crime than burglary? As she neared the foot of the stairs she heard voices in the parlor! Horror of horrors! The burglars were really in the house! They must have known beforehand that her husband was away.

A few steps farther brought her to the parlor door opening upon the hall into which the staircase descended. It stood partly open, and looking in she saw that the folding doors which separated the parlor from the sitting room stood open, and beyond off the sitting room she could see the open door of Mollie's chamber.

But what riveted her attention and froze her blood was the scene she saw in the parlor. Two men were standing in the middle of the room, and bending over a white-clad figure which they were laying on the floor.

Was her daughter dead? Had she fainted? Had she been chloroformed? Had the fiends—she raised her revolver and fired it at the nearest man, and then her over-wrought nerves gave way, and with a wild shriek she fell fainting to the floor.

When she recovered consciousness, it was to see her husband bending over her, with a vinaigrette in his hand, from which he had been administering a restorative.

"Mollie, Mollie," she gasped.

"Here, mamma," and Mollie was at her side, alive and well, and showing no sign of distress except concern for her mother.

When Mrs. Baird had recovered sufficiently to listen, her husband explained to her what had taken place. There had been no burglary, and Mrs. Baird had made, naturally enough, a mistake that had nearly proved fatal.

The two doctors had remained by the bedside of the sick nurse until after midnight, when she took a sudden turn for the worse and died a few minutes before one o'clock. The two of them had wrapped her body in a sheet from the bed, and placing it on a shutter had brought it to Dr. Baird's house to be laid out. Funerals were never held from the sanitarium, and though sometimes a patient died, the body was generally taken away as soon as possible, because of the depressing effect which the presence of a corpse in the house would have upon its inmates.

The two doctors had brought the body to the front of the cottage, which was the entrance nearest the sanitarium. The key to the side door would also unlock the front door. He hardly thought of the burglar alarm, knowing of course that his presence in the house would be known immediately, and not anticipating any such heroic measures on the part of his wife. They had borne the body through the hall into the parlor, and were just in the act of depositing it on the floor, when Mrs. Baird, seeing them in the dim light from a shaded gas-jet turned down low in the adjoining sitting room, had mistaken them for strangers and the white-robed body for the unconscious figure of her daughter Mollie, and had fired her pistol.

But the excitement of the moment had confused her aim, or the dim light had rendered it uncertain, and the bullet, which at such close quarters would have been dangerous coming from any hand, had sped on its way without further damage than nipping Dr. Graves' ear and shattering a fine *Sèvres* vase which stood on the mantle opposite the door. It was a close call, however.

Dr. Baird now has great confidence in the efficacy of burglar alarms, and has since applied to them the old maxim about playing with edge tools. He has also secretly substituted blank for ball cartridges in Mrs. Baird's revolver, as his business still calls him out at night very often, and he does not care to run any unnecessary risks. On the whole, his view of the matter is a very sensible one.

How He Met Her

Frank Hatfield was feeling very comfortable as the Chicago express sped swiftly and smoothly westward along its iron track. He was off on a week's vacation and was going to Chicago to meet his sweetheart, who was coming with her mother from a far Western state.

Frank had first met Minnie West some years before at the home of her married sister in his native town, and the acquaintance then formed had been kept up by occasional visits which Frank made on his trips to the West in the interest of the large manufacturing establishment which he represented as traveling salesman. Frank was not the gay, careless drummer we read so much about in the funny papers, but a long-headed, ambitious young fellow, who went on the road because it paid well, and because he expected at some future time to be at the head of a business where his traveling experience and extensive acquaintance would be of great commercial value.

His acquaintance with pretty Minnie West had ripened into love. Minnie was not merely pretty; she was talented and industrious, and as teacher of a Western school had for several years been the sole support of a widowed mother—a gentle, inefficient woman of middle age who could easily enough manage their small domestic establishment, but who would have been utterly incapable of engaging single-handed in the struggle for existence. Minnie's industry, accomplishments, and devotion to duty, joined to a pretty face and a graceful figure, formed a combination of attractions which even the prospective burden of a mother-in-law could not offset, and to which Frank had willingly succumbed. A brief courtship, supplemented by frequent correspondence, had culminated in an engagement. Minnie had resigned her school and was on the way East to her old home, where the wedding was to take place the following month. Frank had arranged to meet them in Chicago and accompany them on the remainder of their journey.

Frank arrived in Chicago about eight o'clock in the evening. He went to a hotel, registered his name, ate supper, wrote a few letters, smoked a cigar, and about ten o'clock went to bed. The house was rather full, and the best room to be had was on the fourth floor. But Frank was a veteran traveler, and a varied experience of hotels had rendered him callous to considerations of altitude, amplitude or temperature; so when the bell-boy led the way to a room in which the traditional cat could with difficulty have been swung, and of a temperature more frigid than was exactly comfortable, Frank went calmly to bed without indulging in any unnecessary profanity, and was soon sleeping the sleep of youth and good digestion.

His dreams were pleasant. He dreamed that his marriage was taking place in a vast cathedral whose venerable aisles were filled with dim religious light which came through ancient stained glass windows. A priest, clad in his sacred vestments, performed the marriage ceremony, and a white robed acolyte swung a perfumed censer to and fro. Once he swung it too far, and the pungent smoke got into Frank's nostrils and made him sneeze.

The sneeze awoke him, and he found his room full of smoke—not from a perfumed censer, but from burning carpets and woodwork. Then the electric bell in his room began to ring, and as he hurriedly threw open the window, the roar of rushing engines and clanging fire-bells greeted his ear. The hotel was on fire. A glance along the side of the building showed that there was no fire escape within reach. Going back to the door, he opened it for an instant, and the cloud of smoke rushing in nearly blinded him. Closing the door quickly, he hurriedly drew on a portion of his clothing. Then, opening his valise, he took from it a coil of cotton rope, small, closely twisted, and knotted at intervals of a foot or more; he always carried this rope in his valise, though he had never heretofore had occasion to use it. Then drawing the bedstead close to the window, he was in the act of fastening the rope, when he heard a scream which sounded very near him. Hastily looking out of the window, he saw at another window a short distance from his own two women leaning out—one an elderly woman, who was frantically screaming, and the other a young woman with her hair done up in curl papers. Both women were in their night-dresses, and the younger woman was with one hand trying to throw a shawl around the elder woman's shoulders, while with the other hand she firmly grasped the arm of the elder woman, who looked as though she would jump from the window to certain death on the stone pavement beneath. Far below the crowd surged, the engines throbbed, and the streams of water rose into the air. The fire was yet mainly in the interior of the building, and the firemen were trying to reach it from the lower floors.

When Frank saw the women he paused in the work of fastening his rope, and rushing back to the door, perceived that in a moment the fire would reach his own room. He made a rapid estimate of the distance of the room where the women were from his own, and seizing the rope, rushed out into the thick smoke, and holding his breath, felt his way along the side of the passage until he reached what he thought to be the right door. He turned the knob, but the door did not yield. Looking back, he saw the fire almost upon him, and threw himself with desperate energy against the door. By this time the inmates of the room had heard him and unlocked the door, which he entered and closed quickly behind him.

"Just keep cool," he said quietly to the excited women, "and you will get down all right. Here is a rope."

Then with the aid of the younger woman he drew the bedstead to the window, fastened the rope, and threw the end out of the window.

"Now, then, be quick," he said to the elder woman, "you go first. The rope is strong, and the knots will keep it from hurting your hands."

But the old lady protested that she could never do it. There was no time for argument, so Frank drew up the rope, and fastening it under her arms, with the help of the younger woman lowered her to the ground. Then while the people below were untying the rope, he assisted the young woman out of the window and saw her nearly to the ground. Meanwhile the fire had burnt through the thin door of the room and long tongues of flame were reaching toward the window. There was no time to be lost; Frank thought the rope would bear the weight of two. If he did not go at once the fire would reach the upper end of the rope and cut off all hope of escape. So he climbed out of the window and started downwards.

The young woman had reached the bottom safely, and Frank was about half-way down, when what he had feared took place. The rope was burned at the top, and giving way, precipitated him to the pavement below.

When he recovered consciousness he saw a fair and familiar face bending over him, in which tears gave place to a joyful smile as he opened his eyes and looked up wonderingly.

"O, Frank!" cried Minnie, "I am so glad! I thought you were dead, and that I had killed you." And a pair of soft white arms encircled his neck and a shower of warm kisses fell upon his face.

The Wests had arrived a few hours earlier than they had expected to, and had just retired when the alarm of fire was given. They had put up at the same hotel, and had seen Frank's name on the register, but in the confusion and terror of their flight from the burning building, had not recognized his face, begrimed as it was with smoke. For similar reasons Frank had not recognized them, especially as he had not expected them until the next day.

"I cannot understand," said Minnie, sometime after their marriage, with mock reproachfulness, "why you did not recognize me on the night of the fire."

"I had never seen you in evening costume before," replied Frank mischievously. "And why was it that you did not know me?"

"O!" she said, severely, "you had just come through the smoke, and you know I had never seen you in your true colors before."

A Metropolitan Experience

I had come to New York to seek my fortune. The path over which I was to pursue the fickle goddess was but vaguely defined, at least in regard to details. But I know what I wanted to do, and that was to practice my profession.

I had just finished a three years' course in a New Jersey medical college, during which time I had spent the greater part of my modest patrimony, which had consisted of three thousand dollars realized from an insurance on my father's life. My father had been a physician of fine skill, high ideals, and small practice, a not uncommon combination. I had no mother or sisters to keep me at home; our town was abundantly supplied with physicians; and, as I did not care to wait half a lifetime for a practice which would have barely supported me during the remaining half, I had determined to seek my fortune elsewhere.

On leaving a small town, it was natural that I should come to a large one. I knew that the greatest success, other things being equal, was only possible where the largest opportunities existed; and if I did not succeed in a large city, I could not reproach myself with the lack of opportunity. Hence I came to New York.

I secured board at a second-rate boarding house in the neighborhood of Washington Square. It was part of my plan of operations to study the city a while before hanging out my shingle.

With this object in view I spent a good deal of time on the streets and in public parks; and on pleasant evenings I frequently sat for an hour or two in Washington Square. Seated there, on one of the public benches, often in close proximity to some bottle-nosed and ill-odored tramp, I would study the strange jumble of types in the stream of humanity that rolled through the park, which is more of a thoroughfare than a pleasure-ground.

Most of those who passed belonged to the shabbier classes of the metropolis; you could see there every variety of New Yorker, from the above-mentioned tramp to the shabby genteel clerk; only the wealthy and prosperous-looking were seldom met with.

One evening as I sat in my accustomed seat, absorbed for the moment in a calculation as to how long the human stomach could endure the food at Mrs. Van Hashelar's boarding house, I was dimly conscious of a female figure passing by. I looked up, but the lady had gone too far for me to see her face. What I did see was a slender figure, set off by a blue silk dress of a stylish cut, and though walking somewhat briskly, borne along with a graceful motion quite different from the usual wobble of a woman in a hurry; a charming back, above which rose a well-turned neck, surmounted by a head of hair of the color poets are popularly supposed to rave about, a ruddy gold, on top of which in turn reposed a most bewitching bonnet. This somewhat elaborate description but faintly pictures the impression she made upon me at the time.

I felt a sudden desire to see the lady's face; I was sure it would be beautiful and I have always been a great admirer of beautiful women, or rather of the beautiful in women—the distinction is obvious. I rose from my seat, and started down another path, running in the same general direction as she was going, intending to execute a sort of flank movement and meet her face to face on the other side of the park, where the two paths converged after a long curve. Just as I approached the point where the paths came together the lady slipped and fell, uttering a little scream. I rushed forward and assisted her to rise.

"Are you badly hurt?" I inquired in a sympathetic voice.

"Oh, no," she replied, thanking me, "it is nothing at all." But as she started off she came near falling a second time. I caught her and placed her arm in mine.

"Shall I call a carriage?" I asked.

"Oh, no," she said, "it is hardly worthwhile. I live only a short distance, and—if you will—"

"Certainly," I said, not waiting for her to finish the sentence, "I shall be very glad to assist you."

A few minutes' walk, and one or two turns brought us to a brick house of conventional style, and I helped her up the high stoop and rang the doorbell. As she did not release my arm when the door was opened, I could do nothing less than help her into the house. I deposited my fair burden on a cushioned armchair in the parlor, and, hat in hand, was beginning an elaborate parting bow, when she exclaimed:

"Oh, do sit down and rest a moment. How tired you must be carrying poor me such a distance."

I sat down. I may say here that she was quite as pretty as I had imagined her to be.

"I suppose we ought to be introduced," she said. "I am Miss Preston."

"And I am Dr. Scott, at your service," I replied. Our conversation had not advanced beyond this preliminary stage when the doorbell rang, and the servant girl entered a moment later with a telegraph message. Excusing herself, Miss Preston hurriedly tore open the envelope and glanced at the message. Her face took on a look of concern, and she said to the servant:

"Katy, is papa at home?"

"No, ma'am, he went to Boston this afternoon."

"Then telephone Uncle George's house and see if he is at home," and when the girl had gone out she continued, turning to me: "It's all about my Cousin Harry. He is at Yale, and I am afraid is just a little wild. He tells me that through an unfortunate mistake he has got into a scrape, without any fault of his own, and that if I don't send him a telegraph money order for fifty dollars by nine o'clock, he is likely to be disgraced, and perhaps expelled from college."

I murmured my sympathy. The girl returned and announced that Uncle George had gone to Philadelphia, and would not be back until the next night. At this intelligence the expression of concern in Miss Preston's face deepened into dismay.

"Papa away—Uncle George out of town—and only twenty-five dollars in the house," she exclaimed. "Oh, what shall—"

I interrupted her: "If I can venture to offer you my assistance I shall be glad to lend you the money."

"Oh, no," she said, "I couldn't think of accepting a loan from a stranger— or, such a recent acquaintance," she corrected herself, blushing.

I assured her with some eloquence of speech that in a crisis like this the ordinary conventionalities of polite society should yield to the exigency of the moment; and in the end I persuaded her to accept a loan of twenty-five dollars.

"Papa will send a check when he returns tomorrow," she said, "or I will send the money by Katy, if you will leave me your card."

I felt for my card-case, but I had left it at home. I said it didn't matter; I often walked down that way, and would stop in in a day or two, and see if she had recovered from her injury.

"Very well," she replied with a fine blush and an entrancing smile, "I shall expect you."

I went home with my head in a whirl. What a divine creature! What beauty! What grace! What refinement of sentiment! And to think that I had been able to serve this beautiful creature and to place her under an obligation to me, and that I was expected to call again. I felt much like a knight-errant of the olden time when he had rescued some captive princess, and had been rewarded for his valor with permission to wear her colors. My ecstatic condition was the more excusable by reason of the fact that I had no lady acquaintances in New York—barring Mrs. Van Hashelar—and had been for three years immersed in the dry details of my medical studies, and entirely without ladies' society.

I concluded that two days would be a reasonable time to elapse before I called to see Miss Preston. I spent the next two days in dreamland. If I sought my accustomed seat in Washington Square it was only to compare the women who passed with Miss Preston. It was very annoying to have to think of such an adorable creature in such a formal way. "Dear Miss Preston" would have looked very well on an envelope, or even as a spoken address; but to think of her as "Miss Preston" was maddening. I tried to supply the hiatus, and ran over all the pretty names I could think of without being able to decide upon any one which expressed all I thought her name ought to suggest. I suppose If I had known her name was Sarah, or Jane, or even Sarah Jane, I would have thought it very nice, but I gave up in despair the attempt to name such loveliness. To find relief from my restlessness I went up to the Astor Library and tried to read a bulky treatise on macrobiosis, which was my favorite study; but somehow the subject was less interesting than usual, and I finally found temporary distraction from my thoughts in Ouida's latest novel.

The two days finally ran out, and with winged feet I sought the home of my fair acquaintance. I was at first a little doubtful about the place, as on my former visit my absorption in the young lady had been such that I had failed to notice either street or number. However, by following the same course as before, I soon found the house and rang the doorbell. A servant girl admitted me, and asking my name, ushered me into the parlor. I had been seated but a moment when a somewhat elderly woman of angular build and severe countenance entered the room. In answer to her inquiring look I said that I had called to ask how Miss Preston was.

"Miss Preston? Why, there's no Miss Preston here," she said.

I looked around the room. It was surely the same room in which I had seen her last. There was the same ugly steel engraving of Abraham Lincoln signing the Emancipation Proclamation; the same chromo of Charles Sumner between the front windows, the piano occupied the same corner, and on it stood the same open sheet of music, the latest popular catch, "When the Chickens Come to Roost," or some similar title.

"But, madam," I said, "is not this the residence of Mr. Preston?"

"No, indeed," she replied, "this is Mrs. Ledbetter's boarding house."

"This is surely where I saw Miss Preston. But perhaps I am mistaken in the house, though it seems hardly possible."

"There are no Prestons in the block," she said, positively. Then a thought seemed to strike her. "Perhaps you mean Miss Weston; she and her father went away yesterday."

"Was she a blond, with dark blue eyes and very fine teeth, and did she wear a blue silk dress?" I inquired.

"Her exact description, only those fine teeth were false. They left yesterday, without paying their board bill. Twenty-six dollars, young man, is a large sum for a poor widow to be swindled out of."

I began to have an idea. "Do you know where they lived?" I asked.

"They said they were going to Boston, where they were expecting remittances, and all that. But it's my belief that they live wherever they can get board. That sort of people don't have any homes."

My idea had by this time developed into a theory. I remembered the stories I had read of the female sharpers of New York. I had been swindled. The sprained ankle was only a trap, into which I had fallen, like any common greenhorn. I made my theory known to Mrs. Ledbetter, and her opinion readily coincided with mine, which was further strengthened by several circumstances which she related. My theory became a conviction. I had been taken in, and I had myself to thank for it.

"Well, young man," said Mrs. Ledbetter, "you have my sympathy, but I don't see that that helps either of us. Where are you boarding?"

Having found out that I did not wish to change my boarding house, Mrs. Ledbetter at length permitted me to wish her good afternoon.

I was cruelly undeceived. My faith in humanity had received a shock from which I feared, in my youthful pessimism, that it would never recover. Henceforth woman lost her charm for me, and in every fair face I saw a possible Miss Preston. I steeled my heart against feminine attractions; I even changed my boarding house because I discovered in myself signs of weakening toward a pretty shorthand writer who came to board at Mrs. Van Hashelar's. My mind was made up; I would live and die a bachelor.

However, this sternness wore off, or, at least became softened with time, which takes the edge off the sharpest pain. I resumed my walks and character studies; but as my experience of Washington Square had been so painful I got into the habit of going up to Central Park to pursue my observations. One afternoon I sat on an iron bench just at the intersection of a carriage drive and a footway reading a copy of the *Herald*, which contained a graphic account of a great ball on Fifth Avenue the night before. I was wondering how long it would be before I could gain admittance to that enchanted sphere—I confess that I am given to day-dreams—when a carriage drew near, and an exclamation in a feminine voice caused me to look up. A hansom cab had stopped a few yards away, in which sat an elderly gentleman and a very good-looking young lady.

"Yes, papa," said the lady, "it is surely he; I cannot be mistaken." When she spoke I recognized Miss Preston. In the light of those eyes and the charm of that voice I forgot that I had been swindled, and blushed to the roots of my hair—I am not sure that my hair did not blush, but as it is naturally red I cannot be certain. I lifted my hat and advanced to the carriage, as her attitude showed that she expected me to do.

"Papa," she said, turning to the portly, well-dressed gentleman who sat beside her, "this is Dr. Scott, who so kindly helped me to rescue Harry from that very disagreeable predicament the other day; my papa, Mr. Preston. We have been looking for you ever since, and I have been, oh, so mortified that I could not learn your address. We got the directory and looked up all the Dr. Scotts, but could not find you. How could you be so cruel as to leave us under such a burden of obligation for so long?"

As I was trying to collect my thoughts, and to tell the truth without referring to my manifestly absurd suspicions, the portly and respectable father invited me to enter the carriage. I complied, and as we drove through the shaded drives on the beautiful metropolitan pleasure-ground, I explained that I had been unable to find the house.

"A very natural mistake," observed Mr. Preston, oracularly, "for one who is not familiar with great cities. To find a needle in a hay-mow is an easy task compared with searching for a person in New York without an address"— in which opinion I agreed with him; indeed, he could not at that moment have expressed an opinion in which I would not have concurred.

But why prolong the story? I accompanied them home; I got my money, though that was a small matter. My first visit was but one of many, and I now have an office in the basement of my father-in-law's residence. Mr. Preston is an alderman, and is interested in city contracts. He is already rich, and when his term of office expires we expect to move up on Fifth Avenue. As my wife is her father's only child, and will undoubtedly inherit his wealth, I am not obliged to enter the feverish race for money. I am at present engaged in the preparation of a work on macrobiosis which I expect will make me famous. There is but one drawback to our wedded happiness—Mr. Preston is a widower and I have no mother-in-law.

The Shadow of My Past

When I had known Ethel about a year, I declared my love, and found, to my intense joy, that it was returned.

"I will speak to your father at once," I said.

Her face took on a thoughtful expression.

"I shouldn't be precipitate," she said. "It will be real nice to be engaged, but papa has very decided notions about marriage, and you'd better let me handle him."

I deferred to her wishes. Indeed I was glad to be relieved of a formidable task. I had been employed for a year or two as teller in the bank of which her father was a stockholder and director. He was a rather reserved and stern-looking old gentleman, and our occasional communications at the bank had been of the briefest. I had met Ethel at an evening party, and had been calling at the house for some time, but had seldom met Mr. Parker. He, it seemed, had a library upstairs where he spent most of his time. When I had run across him in the hall now and then he had nodded curtly, and had thrown me a glance which seemed to ask what the devil I was doing there. I was a self-made man, however, and used to overcoming difficulties. As long as he did not translate his looks into words and forbid me the house, I continued to go. I was therefore secretly relieved that Ethel should undertake the labor of bringing him around.

When I saw her next evening, I inquired how matters were progressing.

"Be patient, Hal," she said. "Papa is a man of moods, and must be approached carefully. As soon as I think it safe, I will bring the subject up."

It was a week before she reported.

"I have spoken to papa," she said, "and while he doesn't say no—he doesn't say yes."

"What does he say?" I asked in pained suspense.

"He says I'm too young."

"Preposterous! You are twenty-two."

"He doesn't believe that girls should marry before they are twenty-five. Now, Hal, don't look as though you were sentenced to death. I'm not going to wait until I am twenty-five."

"My darling!" I ejaculated, intensely relieved.

"But I'll tell you," she continued, "what I *am* going to do. Papa, mamma and I are going to Europe in May. We shall be back in October. After we return, papa is going down to the town you came from, and if he finds that your career from the beginning has been a consistently worthy one, he will take up the question of our marriage say a year hence. He has a theory that a man's character is a unit, and must be a harmonious unit; that if it is defective or weak at one point, or at any time in his life, it is marred all the way through."

There was nothing to do but submit. I made some tentative suggestion about her being old enough to know her own mind and about the loneliness of a summer without her; but she did not choose to see the drift of my remarks.

"I expect to have a lovely time, Hal, and you'll be too busy with your work to do more than answer my letters. I told papa where you were born and spent your boyhood. I'm not afraid of anything he may find out about you."

"You will have no cause to be," I replied with conviction.

I was a self-made man; not entirely finished, but not ashamed of the job, so far as it had gone. As I looked back over my career, after my last conversation with Ethel, I could recall no place at which an accusing finger could be pointed. I had begun my business career as a district messenger, and had become an office boy. I had attended night school and had qualified myself for a clerkship. I had worked hard, and had risen in proportion, doubtless, to my merits. Certainly nothing but merit had helped me on, for I had no influential relatives or friends.

But if my life in the city had been an open book, my life before was a closed chapter; at least I had not opened it for thirteen years. My recollections of it were none too distinct, and some of them none too pleasant. Suppose Ethel's father should be absurd enough to go down to Greenville to look up my early life, what would people say of me—the people who had known me only as a child and had lost sight of me so long?

My childhood had not been fortunate. My father, a man of more than average intelligence, and of considerable energy, had lacked the judgment to combine these effectively, and had therefore remained always a poor man. My mother, I have been told, was a woman of fine parts, and fitted by nature for something better than the life of drudgery to which her condition as a poor man's wife condemned her. I had three brothers and two sisters, of whom all but one brother died while children.

When I was about twelve our family met with a series of misfortunes which seemed to mock at the doctrine of chances and the laws of life. My father, while out hunting, accidentally shot and killed himself. The sod on his grave had not taken root before my brother was poisoned by eating ice cream at a Sunday-school picnic. While we were at his funeral our house took fire and burned to the ground. My mother, bereft of her husband and her home, was obliged to take in sewing for a living. My own support was provided for by binding me out to Josiah Gormully, a prosperous butcher who kept a shop in our neighborhood. Gormully had a son, Tom, about two years my senior, and a daughter of about my own age who, to impress upon me their own superiority, conspired to make my life as miserable as possible. I endured this while my mother lived, but when she at last succumbed to her troubles and a hemorrhage, I found my lot too hard to bear. One day when Tom Gormully was more than usually exasperating, I gave him a sound thrashing, notwithstanding that his sister Mary undertook to help him out. Gormully had gone away for several days to buy cattle. After my passion had cooled, I looked forward with some apprehension to his return. The nearer it approached, the more apprehensive I became, and, the night before his expected arrival, I packed my slender wardrobe in an old oilcloth valise, and between two days shook the dust of Greenville from my feet.

Fifteen years had passed, and time had long since softened any animosity I had felt against the Gormullys. When vacation time arrived, it occurred to me that it might be well to anticipate Ethel's father's investigation and visit the old town and learn for myself whether I was remembered, and in what manner. It would be an easy way to dispose of a week of the two to which I was entitled. I bought a ticket to Greenville.

Reclining luxuriously in the parlor car, I felt a pleasant glow of anticipation. I thought of my old master the butcher, and imagined the cordial handclasp with which he would greet me. How heartily he would laugh at the memory of my little "scrap" with the children! I pictured Mary a plump and rosy matron, recalling with pleased surprise, in the handsome and well-dressed gentleman who stood before her, the lean and shabby apprentice upon whom she had looked down so many years before. Old Jim Prout, the village shoemaker, in whose shop, next door to Gormully's, I had spent so many spare hours, would be delighted to see the boy who had listened so patiently to his stories, and whose hard lot he had pitied. There rose before my mind the image of Mrs. Betsy Barker, who kept the little millinery shop of the village and gave me cake and apples and other good things, and sympathized so deeply with my mother in her misfortunes. I should be glad to shake hands with my Sunday-school teacher, Deacon Hardacre, of the Free Will Baptist Church, to which my parents had belonged, and to let him know that his work had not been entirely barren of results. But the person I looked forward with most pleasure to meeting was Miss Celina Hawkins, a distant relative of my mother's and the only individual in Greenville with whom I could claim the tie of blood. Often had I run errands, chopped wood, drawn water, and worked in the garden for Cousin Celina. Once when the roof of her house caught fire I had climbed up and put it out, at the imminent risk of my own physical integrity. I was sure that Miss Hawkins, if living, would be overjoyed to see me; nor had I come to the end of these pleasing reflections when the train drew up at Greenville station.

There were many changes in the town. I left the train at the same little wooden depot that had been there when I went away, but walking up the street I noticed many new buildings, and missed some that I remembered. The modest inn that had sheltered travelers in my boyhood had given place to a pretentious brick building designated by a large sign in gilt letters as the Commercial Hotel.

The service, however, was scarcely in keeping with the exterior. There was no one at the desk when I went in, and the boy who took my valise explained that the clerk had been subpoenaed into court with the register, to give evidence in a lawsuit; that he would return shortly, when I could register. Meantime I could have supper, which was ready.

I had been at the table but a few minutes when I was engaged in conversation by the man opposite me. From his familiarity with the waiters I inferred that he was no stranger to the hotel. We exchanged some remarks about the weather, and then I asked him if he lived in the town.

"Yes, sir," he answered, "my name is Gormully—Thomas J. Gormully, editor of the *Weekly Torchlight*. You're in tobacco, I presume—or are you in liquor?"

I don't know why he should have thought me in tobacco or liquor, unless it might be that they were the principal commodities dealt in by the local tradespeople. But the mention of his name diverted my mind from any annoyance I might otherwise have felt at the suggestion that I looked like a whiskey drummer.

I had an inspiration. Tom Gormully had not suspected my identity, nor had he asked my name. Before revealing it, I might, by a question, learn the real estimation in which I was held by the Gormully family.

"No," I replied, "I am not in any commercial line. To be candid," I said, "I am here to look up the record of a man who was brought up in this town, I believe. He was known in those days as Henry, sometimes called Hank, Skinner."

My companion leaned forward eagerly, resting both hands on the table, with his knife and fork pointing upward.

"Hank Skinner!" he exclaimed. "Why I know all about Hank Skinner! What is it this time—murder?"

I was so taken aback at this outburst that I could only murmur confusedly that my mission was a confidential one; I simply desired to ascertain the facts.

"I'm the man to give them to you," he said with enthusiasm. "Nothing that he has done or is suspected of will surprise the people of Greenville. To speak the literal truth, Hank Skinner, even as a boy, was a desperate character. Several years my elder, one day he assaulted me and in spite of my feeble resistance, nearly killed me. My sister, who was present, implored him to desist. In an access of brutal rage he turned upon her with such ferocity that she was laid up for a month from the shock. Father was away from home at the time and Skinner escaped before his return. Father offered a reward for his capture, but he was never apprehended. I supposed he had died a violent death or was in the penitentiary long ago. Well, well, I'll take you down to the house after supper. The old man will tell you more about him."

This was a trifle discouraging. To disclose my identity now would likely prove even more embarrassing. I felt curious to know what, if anything more, the old man *could* say to my detriment. If it should prove to be any worse, I might hesitate to make myself known at all. When I had finished supper, I registered as "John H. Smith, Chicago," and then walked with my new acquaintance a couple of blocks to a fine, large new house, which he pointed out as his father's residence.

"Father," he said, introducing me to the portly and well-clad individual who came forward to meet us, "this is Mr. Smith, a gentleman from Chicago, who is looking up the record—the black record—of Hank Skinner, our Hank, you know. Mr. Smith, my father, the Honorable Josiah Gormully, Mayor of Greenville."

"I welcome you to our city, Mr. Smith, said the mayor. "I am indeed glad to know you, and to render you any assistance within my power. Hank Skinner was a most depraved, indeed a most dangerous character."

The mayor then repeated in substance what his son had said, with somewhat fuller detail, and expressed regret that he could not have one more meeting with Hank Skinner—just one.

"I am quite willing," he added, "to appear as a witness in the trial or to give my deposition."

I thanked him, and said I would communicate with him later. As we were getting up to go out, a large, showily dressed woman of twenty-eight or thirty came into the room.

"Good evening, Mary," said Tom Gormully. "Mr. Smith, my sister, Miss Gormully. Mr. Smith is looking up the early record of Hank Skinner, *our* Hank."

Miss Gormully, who had given me a winning smile at first, now frowned and shuddered.

"That is a painful subject with me," she answered. "I can even now see his murderous look bent upon me, and feel the blows he aimed at me with his brutal fists. My poor nerves never recovered fully from the effects of his fury. His very name makes me shudder. Has he murdered somebody, now that he is strong enough?"

I was sufficiently hardened, by this time, to retain my self-possession. I replied that my mission being a confidential one, I was not at liberty to disclose it.

"Oh, I see," said the mayor, nodding sagaciously, "he might take alarm and escape. Well, I hope you may convict him and send him over the road."

The mayor mentioned the names of several of my former acquaintances and suggested that I call on them. I bade him and his interesting offspring good-night, found my way back to the hotel, smoked a cigar, and then went to bed. My past record, as developed so far, was scarcely one to be proud of. But the Gormullys could hardly be expected to hold me in a grateful remembrance, and therefore their statements did not greatly interfere with my night's rest.

After breakfast next morning, I started out to find Mrs. Betsy Barker. The house that had formerly been her millinery shop was now used as a coal office, and in the window where the creations of Mrs. Barker's genius had once been displayed, there now stood a row of pine boxes containing samples of coal. I inquired of the clerk behind the desk the whereabouts of the former tenant.

"I don't know," he said, "I've only been in town a few weeks. But there's an old shoemaker around the corner who seems to know everybody; you'd better ask him."

I found the shoemaker, whom I recognized immediately, in spite of some changes wrought by time, as my old friend, Jim Prout. He made room for me by brushing the waxed ends from a three-legged stool, and asked me to sit down, glancing meanwhile at my feet. But the glossy sheen of my patent leathers must have raised a doubt as to the object of my visit, and he looked at me inquiringly as I sank cautiously down upon the stool. I will own to a slight feeling of disappointment at perceiving that he did not recognize me. A friendship so sincere as his had been should have a keener memory. But of course age might have dulled his faculties. The mention of my name would doubtless open his eyes.

"I am from Chicago," I said with a smile, "and am trying to find out something about the past life of one Henry Skinner—Hank Skinner, they used to call him—who was brought up in Greenville. I am led to believe that you knew him, some fifteen years ago."

The old man turned a blank and lack-luster eye upon me, took off his glasses, wiped them, put them on again, and planted his elbows on his knees.

"Skinner—Hank Skinner? I disremember any sich name. Who did he work for?"

"I understand he was bound to the mayor, Mr. Gormully."

"Le'me see," he said reflectively. "There wuz a boy by the name of Jeems—Jeems Jinkins, that worked for Gormully when he run the tannery. Mebbe that wuz the boy ye mean?"

"No, this boy's name was Hank—Hank Skinner. He worked for Gormully when he kept a butcher shop down on Jackson Street."

"Oh, I reckon I ricollec' the boy now—a tall, stoop-shouldered boy with red hair, and cross-eyes."

"No," I said, "that isn't the boy. This boy was short and thin, and had black eyes and hair."

"Le'me see. Seems ter me there wuz sich a boy druv' Gormully's butcher cart 'long 'bout twenty years after the war. Do yer know anything 'bout his folks?"

"His father accidentally shot himself."

"Oh, yes, I remember the boy distinc'ly now. He was a son of ole Joe Skinner, a worthless kind o' cuss, that spent most of his time huntin' an' fishin' an' hangin' roun' barrooms. I did hear it said that Hank shot his daddy and then put out a report about his havin' shot hisself. There was some difficulty 'bout provin' it, an' so there wuz nothin' done. But it wuz more'n likely so, for it wa'n't long before he sot fire to his mammy's house, and run away to 'scape the consequences. He wuz a desp'rit character, and it wuz a good riddance o' bad rubbish when he made hisself skeerce. And so you're lookin' up his record, air ye? What's he be'n doin' now?"

"I am not at liberty to state at present," I replied, "but I thank you for the information. Do you know where I can find a Mrs. Betsy Barker, an old lady who is said to have once kept a millinery store around the corner here?"

"Ole Mis' Betsy Barker? Wal, I sh'd say I could! Mis' Barker lives out by the fair grounds, the fust house on the left-han' side after ye pass Eccles' mill-pond. Just keep on down Gillespie Street, and ye can't miss it. I don't know whether ye can get anything sensible from ole Mis' Barker. She's gettin' on to'ds her second chil'hood, but now an' then she has a glimmerin' o' reason an' ricollection. Have ye got any terbacker with ye?"

I gave the old man a cigar, and left his shop decidedly chagrined, comforting myself, however, with the reflection that the old man was in his dotage. Mrs. Barker was ten years younger; her memory could scarcely be worse. I crossed the bridge over the mill-pond, and reached the little cottage to which I had been directed. A knock at the door brought out Mrs. Barker herself, a little thinner, a little more bent, the veins in her hands a little more prominent, but with the same keen eyes peeping out of her wrinkled face. It was clear by this time that I had changed much more in appearance than my former friends, for Mrs. Barker showed no sign of recognition.

I lifted my hat, and stated that I had been directed to her as one who might remember a boy by the name of Henry Skinner, commonly called Hank, who had run away from Gormully the butcher some fifteen years before.

"Laws yes! I remember Hank Skinner perficly well. Won't you sit down? Hank's mother was a friend of mine when I was a gal. But pore Mandy was unfortunate. Her husband wa'n't worth shucks. He got shot in a quarrel down at Bill Syke's barroom, an' left Mandy a widder with two boys, one named Bill, and this Hank. Bill was a good boy, but Hank was the black sheep o' the flock. He p'isoned his brother, and ran away before they could take him up. I believe he did work for Gormully the butcher a little while, but was discharged for stealin'. Is he be'n forgin' a note or robbin' a bank?"

"I am not at liberty to state the exact nature of his offense at present," I replied mechanically, "but I am much obliged to you for your information."

This was appalling. My record was growing blacker and blacker. And yet in spite of my chagrin, there was a certain grim humor about the situation. I felt a reckless curiosity to fathom the greatest depth of depravity I had reached in the memory of my former acquaintances. I had concealed my identity at first upon the impulse of the moment, expecting at each subsequent meeting to declare myself. It now seemed uncertain whether a favorable opportunity would present itself. I still cherished, however, a lingering hope that my old Sunday-school teacher, Deacon Hardacre, would remember some good thing of me, and that my distant relative, Miss Celina Hawkins, had preserved some kindly thought of the orphan boy who had fled from a harsh and cruel service. It was well I did not build upon this hope.

Deacon Hardacre had prospered with the growth of the town. I found him at his office, where he transacted a real estate and insurance business. He glanced at me keenly, and inquired in what way he could serve me. I stated the object of my visit.

"Hennery Skinner?" he said, dropping into what I recognized, even after the lapse of years, as his Sunday-school tone. "Oh, yes, I remember Hennery. Your inquiry confirms my fear that he had succumbed to temptation. No wonder, when his temperament and inherited tendencies were so much against him! How often have I trembled for his future! For I realized that only a large outpouring of divine grace could save him from destruction. But, alas! I could never see any comforting signs in Hennery. He was neglectful of his lessons, and gave me more trouble than any boy in Sabbath school; and I have heard that he was a sore trial to his poor mother. My fears were confirmed when he committed a brutal assault on the children of his employer, our present mayor, and fled from the restraining influences of home and friends. May I inquire the nature—"

I murmured some vague reply and escaped, sick at heart. Could I have been so grossly self-deceived? My last hope of rehabilitation lay in my old friend Cousin Celina. I found her seated on the front porch of the same old house where she had lived when I was a child. The same old elm cast its shade over her. There was a difference, though; twenty years had left their mark on Miss Celina, while the elm did not seem a day older.

I had hardly expected her to know me, and when I had convinced her that I was not a tramp, or an agent of any kind, I made the usual inquiry, whether she remembered anything about Hank Skinner's boyhood.

"Hank Skinner? Yes, I recollec' Hank. I heard there was a detective in town lookin' him up. I reckon you must be the detective? Well, I can tell you this much—none o' the Skinners was ever worth the powder and shot it would take to kill 'em. My third cousin, Amanda Simpson, married this Hank Skinner's father, and it was a sad day for her. He never amounted to anything, and his boys were jus' like him. This Hank used to hang roun' my house for somethin' to eat, and I had to keep things locked up while he was about.

As it was, I missed one o' my spoons that's never been accounted for, and I'm positive he took it. This Hank had a fearful temper. He had to run away for somethin'—let me see, what was it? His brother—no, his brother p'isoned a man. Oh, I remember now—my memory ain't as good as it used to be, but I remember quite distinc'ly now! Hank knocked his mother down, and then set fire to the house before she came to. There wa'n't no evidence, but everybody knowed Hank must 'a' done it. And so he's suspected o' killin' somebody else, is he? Well, I always said he'd come to a bad end!''

My last hope had failed. Miss Celina maundered on in a disconnected way, while I sat for a few minutes like one oppressed with a hideous nightmare. How I got out of the house I hardly know, but a little later I found myself sitting on the bridge over the mill-pond, where I had so often gone swimming and fishing in my boyhood. Fixing my eyes upon the quiet water, I reviewed my past in detail.

Had I really been such a scoundrel as my old friends pictured me? Of course I had not poisoned my brother, or shot my father, or burned my mother; but brushing aside these absurdities, had I been so much worse than other boys as to forfeit the toleration extended toward the faults of youth? Had I possessed no single redeeming trait? It was strange that they should all have misjudged me so greatly; and yet it would have been more remarkable that a sane person could have so greatly misjudged himself. A fool may not perceive his own folly, but a liar must know when he lies, and a thief when he steals.

I spent the remainder of the day in finding out all I could about myself. I heard nothing worse than I had heard already, but I collected elaborate details of my misdoings. I learned the motives which had prompted them. Not only was I made out the author of the misfortunes which had overwhelmed my family, but other mysterious crimes occurring about that time were imputed to me. People whom I had never known gravely bore witness to my precocious depravity. Such was my reputation as it would be gathered by my prospective father-in-law, who believed in the unity of character; who maintained that one serious moral lapse argued a permanently defective character.

I left Greenville by the night train, without having disclosed to anyone my identity. I found a quiet place, with good fishing, where I finished my vacation, and thought out a plan for the redemption of my reputation. It was before the war, and the path to fame was not so easy as in peacetime. But it was still four months or more before Ethel and her father would return from Europe, and in four months an energetic man, with his future happiness at stake, can accomplish wonders. Not only was my love in jeopardy from the shadow that rested on my past. I was ambitious for large success; I had dreamed of a public career. Could I hope for either with such a cloud hanging over me?

My plan involved a campaign for publicity. Hitherto I had been the most retiring of men. I didn't start a newspaper, but I cultivated the acquaintance of newspaper men. When I attended a ball or reception, I saw that my name was in the list of guests. I joined the Chamber of Commerce, and deliberately worked for a place on an important committee. Seizing every opportunity to speak, I began to develop forensic ability. During the fall I read a paper to the Chamber on "The Relation of National Banks to National Prosperity," upon which I received many compliments. As my various successes were from time to time mentioned in the newspapers, I sent marked copies to Thomas Gormully, Esq., Editor of the *Greenville Torchlight*. A struggling weekly published my address in full—I confess I paid for the composition—accompanied by a short biography, prepared with an especial view to its reaching the eyes of the Greenville public, and so worded as to make clear my identity with the Hank Skinner who had formerly worked for the mayor. Shortly after I had forwarded copies of this paper to Editor Gormully, I received through the mail a marked copy of the *Greenville Torchlight* containing the following editorial:

A Distinguished Fellow Townsman

The older citizens of Greenville especially, and some of the younger ones as well, will be pleased to note the success which has attended the career of one of our former citizens, the Honorable Henry Skinner. We are proud to number ourselves among the friends of Mr. Skinner's boyhood, and to remember that at one period of his life the same roof sheltered both our heads. The career of Mr. Skinner, the principal events of whose life are set forth elsewhere in this number, in an excerpt from a metropolitan journal, is one that reflects credit upon our city, and should be an incentive to every ambitious young man among us, as well as a matter of local pride. The editor is one of a committee of prominent citizens who have united in requesting Mr. Skinner to deliver an address to the people of Greenville at an early date.

The next week I received the invitation. I accepted, went to Greenville, and delivered an address. I was met at the depot by a committee and escorted in a carriage to the hotel. The hall in which I spoke was filled to overflowing. The rostrum was decorated with a magnificent bouquet of roses to which was attached the card of Miss Mary Gormully. The Mayor, attired in a suit of black broadcloth, with a glittering diamond in his shirt-front, introduced me in the following language, as reported in the next week's edition of the *Torchlight:*

Ladies and gentlemen: I have the honor of presenting to you this evening a young man whom some of you have known in other days, a gentleman who typifies in his career the genius of American civilization; who epitomizes in his life the growth and progress of our country. I remember him when but a child, the comfort of his widowed mother, upon whom misfortune had laid its hard hand. It was my privilege at one period of his young life to receive him under my own roof, and I feel proud today of the small share I contributed to his prosperity. But our town was not large enough to hold him. His mind even then soared beyond our confines, and sought in the outer world wider opportunities for development. He found them, and made the best use of them. His career has been one of uninterrupted success, and while yet a young man, he is the recipient of honors which most of us consider ourselves fortunate to attain toward the close of life. I have the honor of introducing to you our friend and fellow townsman, the Honorable Henry Skinner, who will now address you.

I spoke and spoke well. My remarks were received with favor, and with each recurring sign of appreciation I waxed more eloquent, until I finally sat down amid a perfect storm of applause. For half an hour after the meeting closed I was surrounded by prominent citizens who came forward to shake my hand and claim old acquaintance. They congratulated me on my address and on my success in life. Old Jim Prout, in his Sunday clothes, was among the first to come forward and shake my hand, his face beaming with pleasure. I may say right here that no one seemed to connect me in the slightest degree with the John H. Smith who had visited Greenville a few months before. I could account for this partly by psychological reasons, partly by some difference in dress, and by my having shaved off my mustache.

"Well, well," said old Jim, "but I am glad to see ye, Hank. I always knowed you'd git along in the world. It was only the other night I was saying to my old woman, 'Liza,' says I, 'I'm goin' ter hear Hank Skinner speak if I have to crawl there on my han's an' knees.' "

I was going out of the hall with Tom Gormully, when we passed an old woman seated near the door.

"You ain't going by without speaking to yo'r old friends, be ye?" said a piping voice which I recognized as that of Mrs. Betsy Barker.

"I'm too old to scrouge up there on the platform," she added, putting out her hand "but I was determined to speak to ye if I had to be the last one goin' out. Yo'r mother was my best friend, and I remember what a good boy you was and what a help and comfort to her! Old Deacon Hardacre was out to my house the other day tryin' to buy my lot, and we got to talkin' about how smart you used to be, and how you always knowed yo'r Sunday-school lessons, and how he had often wondered what had become of you. I allowed that I always knowed you'd git along; and he said yes, that a boy of yo'r talents and yo'r character couldn't be kep' down, and that you was one of the Lord's chosen vessels. I hear the deacon's sick, else he'd surely be here tonight."

At the hotel I received a note from Miss Celina Hawkins, expressing regret that her rheumatism prevented her from coming to hear me speak, but hoping I would not leave town without visiting my old friend and cousin.

Thus the shadow of my past was lifted and I was able to face my *fiancée* and my future without fear. I never judged my old friends harshly. Human nature is much the same at all times and in all places, and my experience illustrates the consequences of giving a dog a bad name. But the reverse of the proverb is also true, although it takes a little longer time to make, and a little harder work to keep, a good name.

A Secret Ally

Colonel Brierson was very angry. He had received a letter from his son Tom, who was away at college. To make a long story short, the letter will explain itself. It ran as follows, written in a bold, round hand, not yet completely formed, but revealing in every line a frank and manly nature:

"My dear Father—I write to you upon a subject which I have not mentioned before, not from any want of filial respect, but because I feared, though I trust my fears were without foundation, that your views on the subject would not agree with mine, and I hated to incur your displeasure. But things have reached that point where an explanation must be made. In brief, I am in love, and moreover, I am engaged to be married.

"The young lady is not of just our standing in society, but she is prettier and more intelligent than any other young lady I know. She has been well educated, having attended the seminary here, and would make anyone a good wife.

"I would not have spoken to her so soon or without consulting you; but her mother—a widow—died a few weeks ago and left her alone in the world, and I tried to comfort her in her distress—with the result that I asked her to marry me and she consented.

"I write to ask your consent to our speedy union. I am sorry to interrupt my college course, but I am willing to do what duty requires, and I go to work without further preparation.

"I hope, dear sir, that you will approve of my choice and consent to our marriage. I am, as ever, your affectionate son,
Thomas"

"Nonsense!" the colonel had exclaimed as he read this letter. "Calf love! Some boarding house keeper's brat! Married, indeed! Why he couldn't earn money enough to support himself! I wouldn't think of allowing him to commit such a folly!"

The colonel fretted and frowned and finally poured a glass of wine from the bottle before him and drank it. Then he leaned back in his easy chair and began to think.

He had fallen into a reverie, when he heard a slight cough, and looking up saw a young man standing on the other side of the hearth, hat in hand. It was a fresh-looking young fellow, with a respectful air, and a slight flush on his face as he addressed the colonel.

"Good morning—sir," he said hesitatingly.

There was something strangely familiar about this young man, and the colonel looked at him curiously without rising from his chair.

"Good evening," he replied, "sit down."

The young man drew a chair up to the other side of the grate and sat down.

"It's a pretty cold night," he said, rubbing his hands and speaking modestly, as was becoming in the presence of an older person. The colonel still looked at his visitor curiously. He had seen that face somewhere, but couldn't exactly place it. The young man was dressed in a style in vogue twenty-five years before—very tight trousers, a very short coat and an embroidered silk waistcoat. The colonel remembered having had a similar waistcoat when he was young.

"By your leave, colonel, I will try a glass of your wine. It will take off the chill of the night air. I came a long distance tonight to see you." And he poured out a glass of the rich wine and tossed it off.

"Aha!" he resumed, mellowing under the influence of the rare liquor. "That reminds me of the vintage of '27 we had at the wine supper on Scribbins' birthday. Wasn't that a jolly time, though! I remember you got very drunk— pardon me—I mean you became very jolly, and finally got so sleepy that you fell under the table and had to be carried off to your room. Ah! you were a sad fellow in those days."

"You seem to know a great deal about those old days," said the colonel, somewhat stiffly, and not relishing the familiar allusions to his college life, at least from the lips of a stranger.

"Well, I should say so," said the young fellow, "and then what fine times we used to have in your room when Jones and Brown and the other boys would come up to play poker. Ah, the glorious game! Do you ever try a hand nowadays?"

The colonel could not help feeling some of the enthusiasm of this voluble young man, who kept on a little more seriously:

"And the girls! The pretty girls, the darling creatures! Oh, but how you loved the girls! The stolen dances up in old Ritter's barn, and the cozy evenings when we played checkers with pretty Rose. Poor Rose! Do you know, I hope you'll excuse me for mentioning it. I never did think you treated Rose just right."

"Who are you," asked the colonel, "and what do you know about Rose?"

"Ah, well, I know all about it. Your parents didn't approve of your marrying the janitor's daughter, and you broke your promise to her. They said she died of consumption, but I know better—she died of a broken heart."

It must not be supposed that Col. Brierson could sit unmoved and hear this impudent young intruder call up these scenes of his vanished youth. He remembered Rose—sweet Rose! He remembered the pretty frilled apron she used to wear; the charming dressing cap her French mother had made for her; her timid face, bold only in the consciousness of her lover's fidelity. He remembered the note he had written, bidding her farewell, and he remembered, too, with a bitter pang, the last glimpse he had caught of her, as the train which bore him out of the college town flashed by her mother's house. She had been standing at the door and her white face and sunken cheeks had haunted him all through the foreign tour on which he had accompanied his father.

"Who are you?" he inquired angrily as the visitor rose to go, "and where did you get your information about my private affairs? I must say that your manners—"

"Why, didn't I introduce myself?" said the young man, laughing softly. "You ought to have remembered me. Don't you recollect this coat? Baker made it. Why, I am the ghost of your youth. I came a distance of thirty years tonight to see you, and I'm glad to find you looking so well. Good night!" And with a familiar gesture of farewell, the young man opened the door and went out.

As he opened the door, the strong draft from the outside blew down the tongs, which fell on the hearth with a noisy clatter. The colonel started and rubbed his eyes.

"Bless my soul," he said, "it's ten o'clock, and I haven't written that letter to Tom."

So saying he poured out another glass of wine, of which he took a sip, and then indited the following epistle, which brought joy to two young hearts:

"My dear Tom—I won't say that I am pleased at the contents of your letter, though I was at first very much surprised. I will be down at the college next week, and will look into the matter you write about. If I find the young woman what you represent her to be, I do not know that I shall be inclined to oppose your wishes. In the meantime, do not neglect your studies.

"Your affectionate father,
J. H. Brierson"

The Kiss

Mrs. Cartwright left the streetcar at the nearest corner, and walked the half of a city block that led to her own gateway, and up the flower-bordered flagged walk across the green lawn to the verandah where her two children, Talbot and Cecile, were playing, under the supervision of a white-capped nurse. They were beautiful children, fashionably dressed. It was a beautiful home, upon a beautiful street, and Mrs. Cartwright was a beautiful woman.

Beautiful, and young. She had been less than twenty when Eustace Cartwright had first met her. Her family had been poor, and in financial difficulties. Cartwright had rescued them from ruin, and, fascinated by Hilda's beauty and her wit, had taken her from an eight-room house in a shabby suburb, had bestowed his old and honored name upon her, and, after a summer in Switzerland, had brought her home to the handsome residence on Euclid Avenue which his grandfather had built forty years before. It was not in the latest style, but was possessed of a spaciousness, a dignity and a comfort which suited Cartwright's quiet, scholarly tastes.

They had been very happy for several years. Hilda's two children had occupied her mind and her time. She appreciated to the full her good fortune; never more than when, while driving in her carriage or her automobile, she passed her former friends on foot, or, when, while shopping, she saw them standing behind the counter. She wore the airs and graces of a fine lady in a manner to satisfy even her husband's friends, who had been not entirely certain that Cartwright had not stooped to marry her.

The serpent had entered Eden when Cartwright's nephew, Carroll Deane, the son of his only sister, became a member of the household, after the death of his mother, already a widow. Cartwright was fond of the handsome, blue-eyed youth, whose liveliness was in marked contrast to his own taciturn sedateness. He showered the boy with benefits, and found a keen pleasure in seeing him enjoy the things for which the elder man had never greatly cared. Carroll was a convenient escort for Hilda when Cartwright did not care to go to a ball or party, a function which Carroll seemed more willing to perform than most young men to wait upon their female relatives. The beauty of the two young people—their vivacity, their youthful zest for pleasure, their freedom of intercourse, brought about the old result. There was a fierce insurrection of primal passions, a few months of guilty pleasure, and then Carroll had gone away to college.

Carroll and Hilda corresponded during his absence. He came home for the Christmas holidays. He went away again, and the correspondence continued. He returned for the Easter vacation, and had left that morning, a day late, for the East. She had accompanied him to the station, on a streetcar, and they had parted with a handclasp and a few whispered words—their real parting had taken place, an hour before, at the house. She was conscious, when the train pulled out, of a loss, and yet of a relief. The mantle of deceit did not rest lightly upon her shoulders—she had not sinned without suffering.

She was glad, as she went up the walk that day, that Carroll was gone. She had quite decided to break off their affair. It was too wicked, too treacherous, too dangerous. Eustace had been easy to deceive, but once enlightened, was not the man to endure lightly such an offense at the hands of the objects of his own bounty. Carroll had agreed with her. He was going to Europe in June, to be gone all summer. They would write, now and then, friendly letters—that was all.

As an earnest of her reformation, which was to begin as soon as he had gone, she had given him his letters and demanded hers.

"I destroyed them," he said, "last night."

She was obliged to take his word, though she had not always found him truthful—light love is apt to take liberties with truth. A lingering doubt had assailed her at the railroad station.

"You are sure, dear," she said, "that you burnt my letters?"

"Quite sure," he returned. "I hated to, but we had agreed that it was best."

It was sweet to have him hate to; but it was best, and she felt relieved, and tried to be glad—that he had burnt her letters, and that he was gone, and that she would not see him again for many months, by which time it would be easy for them to meet as friends and relatives, and with no other thought.

This feeling had grown in strength during her return homeward on the streetcar. The sight of her beautiful home, the outward and visible sign of physical comfort and assured position; the merry greeting of her rosy-cheeked children—the pledges of her wifehood—strengthened her renewed sense of virtue and conjugal fidelity.

She had laid off the last of her wraps, together with the last lingering consciousness of her sins, and had entered upon her role of ideal wife, when the telephone bell rang. She was near the instrument and took down the receiver.

"Hello, is this East 897-B?"

"Yes, is that you, Eustace?"

"Yes, Hilda. I have bad news, Carroll's train met with an accident, about twenty miles out. Many were killed or injured."

Her heart stopped beating.

"And Carroll?" she breathed.

"Is among the killed."

She dropped the receiver and sat for a moment like one dazed. Then the instinct of self-preservation returned, and she picked up the receiver and placed it to her ear.

"Hello, hello, hello!" came her husband's voice. "Are you there, Hilda?"

"Yes—yes!"

"I thought they'd cut us off. I wanted to say that a relief train is leaving the Union Station in ten minutes, and I am going out on it. If he is dead, I will bring his body home. It is terrible—poor boy, just on the threshold of life—facing its struggles and its joys—my sister's only child, whom I loved as my own son."

Hilda had been thinking with lightning-like rapidity (an electric wave, it is said, would flash around the earth an incredible number of times a second, could it last so long). Carroll was dead, and he had not destroyed her letters— she knew instinctively that he had not destroyed them—and they were either on his person or in his luggage. Eustace would go to the scene of the wreck, and he would find them, and she would be disgraced and ruined. A wild thought seized her.

"Can I go with you?" she demanded anxiously.

She would go with him, and perhaps she could get the letters, so that Eustace would never see them.

"I don't think it necessary, dear. The scene would only harrow your feelings."

"I might be of some use," she insisted.

"You can be of more use in preparing for our reception. And you haven't time. I've barely five minutes to make the station, and it would take you twenty, if you had an automobile at the door."

She hung up the receiver, despair in her heart. Never before had her sin appeared so hideous. She felt a foreboding, not dim and distant, but vivid and imminent, that her punishment was at hand—that she would lose everything that made her life worth living. She would lose husband, children, home— her position, her good name—all the things for which women strive, and which few of whom attain in such full measure as they had come to her. She could not even retain the solace of guilty love—for her lover was dead—dead in his youth and his beauty and his sins, with the proofs of his treachery upon his person. She would have nothing left, except her beauty, and the flower of that was gone; nor was it a commodity that could go twice to such a market. She wished that she were dead.

But she took no steps to carry out the wish. Perhaps, after all, Carroll had destroyed the letters. They might have been lost in the wreck. Perhaps Eustace would not search Carroll's luggage. She would hope against hope—even against the cold fear which clutched her heart and told her there was no escape.

Cartwright returned home in the afternoon, bringing the body of his nephew. Hilda awaited her fate in agonized suspense. But there was nothing unusual in Cartwright's manner, unless it were an added gravity, for which the occasion was sufficient to account. Hilda had very little opportunity for conversation with him during the day—he was fully occupied with preparations for the funeral and with communications from and to friends of Carroll.

Carroll's trunk and valise had been brought to the house, and Hilda, during her husband's absence, examined their contents thoroughly. She found many souvenirs of their love—a lock of hair, a ring, half a dozen photographs, a ribbon, a glove, a stolen slipper—each with its tender associations. Had she been less anxious, she would have wept her eyes out, but even the tragedy of death faded in importance beside the tragedy of the life which would face her should Eustace find her letters.

She felt a measure of relief when she did not find them. Would she have felt more relieved at finding them? She did not know—there was always the possibility that Eustace might have found them first and read them. On the whole, she thought she would rather have found them; she would have destroyed them, and the chances were that her husband had not examined Carroll's luggage.

She even overcame her emotions enough to make sure that the letters were not upon Carroll's body. He must have destroyed them, as he had said. She had misjudged the poor boy. He had told the truth, and had made a sacrifice, for her sake. She would cherish a tender memory of him, for their love's sake.

The funeral took place next day. Eustace's manner reassured Hilda. Nothing was omitted which the dignity and position of the family required. Eustace wore a band of crepe upon his hat, and, with Hilda and the children in deep mourning, followed the body to the family vault in Lake View Cemetery.

Hilda felt greatly relieved when all was over. Her husband had shown no sign of suspicion. It was inconceivable that he could have done what he had that day, with knowledge of the dead youth's treachery. Hilda swore a silent and solemn oath that never again would she run such a risk—never again would she be tempted to deceive this loyal and courteous gentleman who had done so much for her. She would prove, by her devotion, how much she loved and respected him, and she would atone, so far as in her lay, for the wrong she had already done him. The atonement, of course, must be secret, as the sin had been. Confession would be worse than useless; it could do no one any good—it would not only destroy her husband's happiness but deprive her of opportunity for reparation.

She felt, as she sat opposite Eustace at dinner that night, a chastened gladness that Carroll was gone. He had, in a sense, deserved his fate, and she was free, from her sin and from its consequences—free to tread the straight and pleasant path of honest happiness by the side of a gentleman who loved her—free through no merit of her own, it was true, but by the decree of a kind fate which had spared her while taking her fellow sinner.

When the dessert was served, she rang for the nurse, who took the children away.

"Will you come into my study?" said Eustace, quietly, when they were gone. "I have something to say to you."

The color left her face, the light forsook her eyes. Her panoply of self-absolution and future immaculateness slipped, like a dropped garment, from her sinful soul and left it bare, as she rose mechanically and followed the accusing figure of her husband from the room.

His study lay across the hall. As she entered, he placed a chair for her, with formal courtesy. He then unlocked a drawer of his desk and took from it a bundle of letters, tied with narrow blue ribbon. She recognized the ribbon and remembered vividly when and from where it had been taken.

"These, I think" said Cartwright, in calm and even tones, "are yours—it is the law, I believe, that letters belong, first to the recipient, then to the writer. My interest, I think, was sufficient to justify my having read them—or some of them—enough of them. I now return them—to their lawful owner."

He put out his hand. She took the letters mechanically and laid them on her lap. An hour earlier, had she laid hands on them, she would have concealed them in her bosom. Now they had been read. Then they had been pregnant with immense possibilities—now they were dead—a spent rocket—dead as the body of her lover in the vault—dead as her hope for future happiness. They might lie on her lap, or on the floor, or in Eustace's desk, so far as he and she were concerned.

She heard him speaking, as though from a distance, and it was with an effort, at first, that she grasped the purport of his speech.

"Of course you realize, Hilda, what the result of this discovery must be. You can no longer be wife of mine, or I husband of yours. I have lost, at one blow, wife and nephew—both of whom I loved—what more I have lost I leave for you to imagine; you have a keen mind and a judgment riper than your years.

"I shall not attempt to fix or to distribute the blame for this deplorable affair which has worked my misfortune. Carroll is dead—as the result of his own folly, in all likelihood, for had he left yesterday, as he ought to have done, he would not have been a passenger upon the wrecked train. But you were the older of the two. You were a mother—you had your children to consider. And you were a wife, and held my honor in your hands."

He had not lifted his voice in the least, but upon her quivering conscience every word fell like the lash of a whip. She shrank together, and almost cowered before him, while her eyes sought the floor, but could get no further than the damning bundle of letters upon her lap.

"I shall not reproach you," he went on, "now or ever. When this interview is ended, I shall never mention the matter again—it will not be a pleasant subject. As I have said, you can no longer be my wife. But neither would I have you leave me. There are the children—I must consider them, if you did not; they must never, by any act of mine, have occasion to hold their mother in disrespect. Carroll was my sister's child; to blacken his memory would be to reflect upon her and upon all of us; nor do I care to become a subject of pity or ridicule."

She wondered vaguely, and dully, what he was going to—what he *could* do that would carry out his purpose and yet leave undone the things he did not wish to do.

"You will continue," he said, "that is, if my wishes prevail—to occupy your place in the household. To the world—to the servants even, there will be no change. If there should be at first some slight and inevitable constraint, and you think the servants might take notice, you can discharge them all and take on new ones who will know no past with which to compare our future. You will doubtless be glad to share with me the effort to keep the children in the dark—for their sakes?"

He seemed to wait for an answer, and she murmured something inarticulate which he apparently took for acquiescence.

"This, of course, will limit our intercourse. The house is large, and we need not interfere at all with one another. A very slight difference of arrangement will effect all the change that is necessary."

Her fingers were mechanically picking at the folds of her gown. The bundle of letters had slipped to the floor. Something within her shrank from what the life to which he condemned her might become. Nor had her husband ever seemed so noble, so worthy of love and respect as now when he sat in judgment upon her, and she had lost him.

Perhaps he noticed her change of expression.

"You shall be free," he said, "to come and go. I shall not interfere with your movements—except that I shall exercise a certain supervision over your company, for both our sakes. Upon formal occasions, when it is conventionally required, I will attend you—perhaps I have neglected my duty in that regard, and am myself to blame, in part, for what has happened.

"If you find life unendurable under these terms," he added, rising as though to dismiss her, "doubtless we can find a remedy. You could travel, or reside abroad, for your health. Or if you should wish, sometime, to seek a divorce—such things can be quietly arranged, with no scandal.

"And now, if there is nothing you wish to say, or ask, shall we terminate this painful interview?"

She rose, and with desperate effort, stepped firmly forward—had she faltered, he would, she knew, have offered her his arm—and she was unworthy to take it. He stooped, however, picked up the packet of letters, and, as he opened the door of the library with one hand, extended the bundle with the other.

"Permit me," he said, "you were leaving your letters."

How many lifetimes Hilda Cartwright lived in the next five years, she never stopped to figure out, but the time was long. From the very beginning she accepted, as a finality, the situation and her husband's terms. To the outside world, they were husband and wife, living in conventional harmony—if conjugal harmony be any longer conventional. If friends of their own social circle suspected anything between them, they were courteous enough not to mention it—to their faces; and when curiosity had nothing new to feed upon, it soon died away.

Their divided life was rendered easier by a gradual change in their habits. Cartwright had never cared a great deal for society, and Hilda began to go out less and less, until she became, in time, almost as much a recluse as her husband.

As the best atonement she could make for her offense, she sought to become what she imagined Eustace would have liked her to be, had she never disappointed him. She was a perfect housekeeper, an ideal mother. Such social duties as she still undertook were performed with effectiveness, grace and dignity, and Mrs. Cartwright became known as one of the most respected and admired of the younger matrons of her set. She was active in the work of her church, and a liberal contributor, both of time and money, to a number of good charities. Her benefactions fell like dew upon many a thirsty soul, because they felt in what she did the subtle sympathy with weakness or misfortune which comes only from those who have trod the same path.

Time dealt gently with her. She grew in the noble virtues which take their root in self-sacrifice. They left their impress upon her face, which became more beautiful with the passing years. At thirty she was in a young matronly prime which put her youthful and more immature beauty to the blush.

During all the years of her atonement, Cartwright had never, by a single word, recalled the subject of their estrangement. Nor were they much together, except in the presence of others. He was always courteous—too courteous, one shrewd lady said, for a man who loved his wife—and sometimes almost kind. But while Hilda loved him well enough to have thrown herself at his feet and placed his heel upon her neck, she was ever conscious of the impalpable barrier which separated them—a barrier as impenetrable as the shirt of chain mail which gentlemen of the romantic past wore under their silken doublets when dining with their friends. She did not attempt to pass this barrier—it would turn a smile, or a fond word, she felt instinctively, as surely as the steel jacket would stop a dagger-thrust. If he would ever change she did not know. If so, she would be there, beside him; if not, she must bear her punishment as best she could.

She knew he was not happy—and the knowledge was part, the greater part—of her punishment. Nor had he quite her resources to ward off unhappiness. Companionship was in large measure denied him. She had her children, nor did she realize, in her absorption, the extent to which she monopolized their society. He threw himself eagerly into affairs, and devoted himself, in his hours of relaxation, to the studies of which he was so fond.

But Hilda saw he was not happy, and, at last, that he was not well. His cheeks grew thinner, his hair was more than touched with gray, he lost some of the spring of life. Hilda watched him silently, with a yearning love, and with a growing fear. If he should die, it would be of unhappiness, and she would have murdered him as surely as though she had dropped poison in his cup.

In the spring of the fifth year of their estrangement, Cartwright fell ill. The doctor diagnosed the case as one of fever, possibly malignant, and ordered isolation and a trained nurse.

"I shall nurse him myself," said Hilda firmly.

"Impossible, madam. You will be liable to infection. And there are the children to consider."

"They can be sent away, if necessary," she declared. "For myself I do not care—and I am strong. I shall nurse him."

She could not be dissuaded, but took her place by Cartwright's bedside. At the height of the fever he became delirious, and said some things which tore her heart—not altogether with pain. She had a trained nurse to assist her, but at these times she sent the nurse out of the room.

He seemed to be mending, when, one morning, he took a turn for the worse. The doctor made a careful examination.

"Astonishing," he said, as he finished. "I never knew of such a combination. He has developed diphtheria, of a malignant type."

She knew what this implied. "Is there no hope?" she whispered hoarsely.

"None," he replied, "without a miracle—and the age of miracles is past. At his age, he could scarcely hope to recover even in good health; in his present weakened condition there is no power of resistance whatever—it is only a matter of a day or two. Meanwhile it is dangerous for you to be near him—you have denied yourself sleep and rest—you are in none too good condition yourself to resist disease."

"I shall stay beside him," she declared, "to the last moment. I wish to be near him when he—if he—recovers consciousness. If it were only for a moment, and I were away, I should never forgive myself."

He protested, but in vain. Finding she would stay, he gave her minute directions how to avoid infection.

"Above all things, guard your mouth. Don't let your lips touch anything—

not even your hands—that could possibly convey the contagion. I think you are running an unnecessary risk, but willful woman—"

"Must have her way," said Hilda, closing the conversation.

The doctor went away, but returned in an hour, remained two, and went away again.

"I'll be back in another hour. He'll last till morning, perhaps."

While the doctor was gone, Cartwright opened his eyes and looked up at his wife. The nurse was asleep in the next room.

"Hilda," he said, "is it you, dear?"

"Yes, Eustace," she returned, dropping on her knees beside the bed and taking his thin hand in hers.

"I am ill, am I not, Hilda?"

"Yes, dear, you are very ill."

"I am going to die, Hilda. I haven't cared a great deal about living, for several years."

"Spare me, Eustace, and spare yourself. If you die, I shall not care to live."

His face lit up with a rare smile.

"Do you love me?" he whispered, with his failing breath.

"I would give my life for you—and give it twice for one word of love."

"One word, my darling—one word? I have loved you always—I have never ceased to love you, and I am dying of my love. I wish now that I could live, but I suppose it is too late. But kiss me, Hilda, before I die!"

Then bravely, and without a moment's hesitation, she took her life into her hands and bent her face to his. He threw his arms, hot with fever, about her neck, and their lips met in a long, lingering caress.

They ought to have died, of course, and given their story a dramatic ending. But the doctor came back, an hour later, with a new culture which dissipated the gathering membrane.

They spent their new honeymoon in the Engadine—it was long before the war—and were as happy as chastened remorse, upon one side, and complete forgiveness, upon the other, and fervent love, upon both, would permit.

Cartwright's Mistake

I was sitting on the hotel piazza, following with my glass the movements of a steamer in the offing. As she disappeared around a distant bend of the shore, I turned my head toward the left, from which I heard footsteps approaching. My gaze rested upon the portly figure of a gentleman who stood a short distance from me, his hand resting on top of the balustrade. My eye instinctively settled upon the broad abdominal expanse which the skill of a fashionable tailor had not been able to prevent from being the most striking feature of the gentleman's appearance, for he was very fat.

The gentleman evidently perceived the objective point of my glance, for he gave a faint apologetic sort of a smile, as though he were somewhat ashamed of himself, and advanced toward me.

"Well, Walton," he said, extending his hand, "don't you know me?"

I had not recognized his figure, but the voice was the familiar one of an old college friend.

"Why, it's Cartwright! How are you, old boy? I'm ever so glad to see you," I exclaimed, grasping his outstretched hand and shaking it with genuine pleasure. I had been at this particular hotel of this particular seaside resort (which we will call Cliffdale) for two whole days without meeting a single acquaintance. Cartwright's advent was a decided relief to what threatened to be a solitary exile instead of a pleasant vacation. There were many people at the hotel, but I am not much of a hand at making new acquaintances.

"No wonder you didn't recognize me," said Cartwright, glancing downward at himself as far as his waistband, which formed his horizon in that direction. "I am getting so abominably fleshy that life is almost a burden to me. I thought a course of sea-bathing might reduce my weight somewhat and so I concluded to run down here for a few weeks. I'm ever so glad to meet you, Walton. What have you been doing with yourself since we left old Yale?"

We conversed awhile on topics of mutual interest and then went to walk along the beach. Though Cartwright's weight, as he informed me, was two hundred and fifty pounds, yet he was no mere vulgar bundle of adipose tissue. He possessed a strong and vigorous mind, and carried his flesh in such a way that after the novelty of his appearance wore off it did not provoke mirth or even remark. He was very well proportioned, and while his chin was not disproportionate to the rest of his body, it had not put on the extra folds which disfigure so many fat people. His walk was dignified, at least, if not graceful. His frank good-nature was irresistible.

We parted at bedtime, to meet at breakfast next morning. After a cigar on the piazza, we took a stroll along the beach together. A short distance from the hotel an open carriage dashed by, in which were seated two ladies, one middle-aged and of rather distinguished appearance, the other young and beautiful. I had scarcely time to lift my hat before the carriage had passed us.

"What a beautiful girl!" exclaimed Cartwright, looking after the phaeton; the hood was down, and over it he could see the nodding plume of the young lady's hat. "Who is she?"

"That," I replied, calmly, "is Miss Florence Gaylord, of Clearport. She is rich and accomplished; her charms of person speak for themselves; she is an excellent catch, and so far as I can learn, is still unappropriated."

"She is certainly very beautiful," he rejoined, with a thoughtful air.

The Gaylords, mother and daughter, had arrived at Cliffdale the night before, and this was my first sight of them. They were old acquaintances of mine. We saw them every day during the next few weeks. Cartwright became very attentive to Miss Gaylord, and it soon grew obvious that he was very much in love. I do not know what tricks my own heart might have played me, for Florence was very charming; but there was another young woman, then spending the summer in Europe, who had a first mortgage on my affections, and the arrangements had been made for a foreclosure shortly after her return in October. I was therefore out of the race, and Cartwright had nothing to fear from my rivalry. Of course he would have had no chance whatever had I been in a position to enter the contest.

I could see with half an eye that Miss Gaylord was partial to Cartwright. She walked with him, talked with him, rode with him, danced with him— he could dance well, in spite of his obesity; she sang to him, and discussed books and authors with him, for they were both cultivated people, and fond of literature. I could not see how any self-respecting, modest young woman could offer a man more encouragement than she gave Cartwright.

But he was singularly obtuse. He labored under the impression that no woman could love him with a genuine affection.

"No, Walton," he would say, "no young and pretty woman could love such a mountain of flesh as I am. A widow with a large family, or an old maid who had exhausted all her hopes, might put up with me. A young woman might pity me, and in her generosity seem to encourage me, but she wouldn't mean anything by it. They smile on me for the same reason that they pat the back of a prize ox at a county fair."

"Nonsense," I said, "the woman who catches you will win a prize in the matrimonial lottery and Florence Gaylord knows it. You are worth half a dozen of these feather-weight dudes who are fluttering around her."

"Yes," he rejoined with a rueful smile, "I suppose I would be, by the pound."

One afternoon I strolled down the beach with a paper novel in my hand, and finding a comfortable seat in a rustic pagoda a little way from my hotel, I settled myself for a quiet half hour. I had not read more than one chapter when two ladies approached the pavilion and seated themselves on the other side of the lattice-work, vine-covered screen that divided the pavilion into two parts. I was lying stretched on the seat, the back of which concealed the most of my body, while a mass of vines hid my head from observation. I glanced up from my novel, but did not stir, nor did I recognize the ladies until one of them spoke, with the voice of Florence Gaylord.

"I love Mr. Cartwright very much, and I think he loves me in return, although he is awfully shy. I mean to catch him if I can though it sounds dreadfully vulgar for me to say so." She glanced around her quickly as she made the remark, but fortunately did not perceive me.

Of course the proper thing for me to do would have been to make my presence known. But she had already spoken, and I had already heard, and I spared her blushes by remaining quiet, hoping they would go away before burdening my conscience with any further weight of ill-gotten information. I could not now escape without being seen by them; the most I could do was to feign sleep, to provide against possible discovery.

"He is so ridiculously fat," said Mrs. Gaylord, who was evidently on very familiar terms with her daughter, "that everybody will laugh at you for marrying him. Charlie Puddinghead is just as rich, and much better looking, and is dying for you."

"Why, mamma! How shameful for you to speak of Mr. Cartwright in that way! What you find fault with only makes him more attractive to me. I have always intended to marry a fat man. Charlie Puddinghead is no larger than a well-grown sparrow. Fat men are always good-natured; and one can feel, during the storms of life, that one is anchored to something substantial, that the first rough wind of sorrow or misfortune will not blow away. I despise lean men."

I could scarcely restrain my laughter at this unique confession. I ought perhaps to have been angry, for I myself am lean almost to emaciation, but Miss Gaylord's views were too deliciously droll to wound my sensibilities.

The ladies finally went away, and after waiting until they were some distance away, I went back to the hotel.

I meant to tell Cartwright a part at least of what I had heard. But he had latterly grown somewhat sensitive on the subject of his obesity, and I went up to my room after supper to meditate upon the best way in which to give him the benefit of what I had heard, without disclosing too much, or the exact manner in which I had acquired my information. An hour or two later I went to his room, but he was not there, and I did not see him until morning.

"Walton," he exclaimed, grasping my hand with painful warmth, "congratulate me. Florence has promised to be mine."

"I congratulate you from the bottom of my heart," I said, "I am sure you will be happy."

In my surprise at the suddenness of the announcement, I forgot all about the conversation I had overheard on the bench, which, of course, was now of no consequence. The lovers were quite as much absorbed in each other as lovers usually are, and I was left to a certain extent to my own devices. I had utilized my opportunity by making some sketches which I had planned, but had up to this time been too lazy to execute.

A few days after the announcement of the engagement, Cartwright was called away from Cliffdale on urgent business. He went immediately, promising to return in two weeks.

My vacation lasted somewhat longer than I had originally intended. I was still at the hotel when the two weeks of Cartwright's expected absence had elapsed. The Gaylords had been away a week, visiting some friends, but had returned to the hotel, where they expected to remain until September. When Cartwright had been away two weeks I received from him the following letter:

"My Dear Walton! I shall be detained here a week or two longer than I expected. I could perhaps finish up my business and get back sooner, but I am preparing a surprise for Florence and my other friends. You will hardly guess the nature of it, but you will open your eyes when you see what it is. Don't say anything about it, for I mean it to be a complete surprise to the others.

"Yours, etc.,

D. CARTWRIGHT"

There was nothing in this mysterious communication that would afford a clue to the nature of the projected surprise. I said nothing to Miss Gaylord about the letter. Cartwright himself kept her informed of his movements.

The last two weeks of my vacation passed pleasantly enough. A day or two before I left Cliffdale, I received the following note from Cartwright:

"Dear Walton: Will be down on the eight o'clock express. Arrange it so that I can meet you alone with Florence and her mother. Leave word with the clerk what room you are in. Don't let them know you expect me.

"Yours, Cartwright"

More mystery, and no clue to unravel it! As fortune would have it, I had received by express that morning a portfolio of etchings and engravings which I had purchased for a certain house I had built for a certain young woman (already mentioned) who was expected to return from Europe in a few weeks. By some mistake they had been sent to me at the seaside. I invited the ladies down to my sitting room at eight o'clock to look at the engravings, and left word at the clerk's desk that Mr. Cartwright would find us there.

The ladies came promptly. They examined the pictures and criticized them with rare good taste, for they had both traveled widely and were familiar with art and the relative merit of artists.

At a quarter past eight I heard a quick step, which sounded somewhat familiar, pass along the hall and stop at my door, at which there was a knock.

"Come in," I exclaimed.

The door was opened, and a gentleman stood in the doorway—a tall, symmetrical young man, without an ounce of superfluous flesh upon him, attired in a faultlessly fitting suit of gray tweed. The ladies and I looked at him for a moment in puzzled curiosity; there was something familiar about him though he was evidently a stranger. There was no sign of recognition on the part of anyone, nor could I imagine who he was until he spoke.

"Well?" he exclaimed, "I thought I would surprise you!"

The wish was father to the thought, for up to that time we had not shown any signs of surprise.

It was Cartwright. He beamed upon us in an ecstasy of pleasure, and laughed gleefully at our evident amazement as we realized who he was.

Meanwhile I watched the effect of his changed appearance upon Florence. She had started at the sound of his voice. When the fact dawned fully upon her that the slender boy before her was but a few weeks before the man whom she loved, she turned as pale as though she had seen a ghost.

"Mamma," she said, in a voice scarcely audible, "take me to my room. The gentlemen will excuse us."

"Why, Florence," answered her mother, "you will be better in a moment. Mr. Cartwright's return was so sudden. You should have prepared us," she said, with a note of reproach, addressing Cartwright.

"Take me to my room, please," urged Florence.

Mrs. Gaylord led her away with murmured excuses. Cartwright offered his arm to assist her.

"No thanks," she said, with a perceptible shudder, "mamma will help me."

When they had gone, Cartwright turned to me, his face white and miserable, his elation all departed.

"What does it all mean?" he groaned. "I thought she would like it." He cast a comprehensive look over his altered person.

"What have you been doing with yourself?" I inquired.

"I've been under treatment for obesity," he replied. "I found a famous physician who has reduced my weight about half in four weeks. But what's the matter with Florence?"

"The surprise was too great for her," I said. "She will be all right in the morning." But I remembered the conversation I had overheard on the beach, and I feared for the result of Cartwright's experiment.

At nine next morning Cartwright came into my room.

"They have gone," he said; "read this."

He tossed me this note, which I opened and read:

"Dear Mr. Cartwright:—Pardon my seeming rudeness of last evening. But permit me to explain it by saying that my feelings were beyond control. We leave this morning on the early train, and I beg of you to release me from my engagement. It is difficult for me to express my meaning, but you are so different from what you were when we met and when we became engaged, that it is hard to realize that you are the same person. I fear I could never be happy with you now. Feeling as I do, I think it best for us not to meet. I only wish you greater happiness than I could ever have brought you.

FLORENCE GAYLORD"

A Fool's Paradise

Went to the ball at Mrs. Granville De Puyster's last night (December 15, 1878). It was a brilliant affair. The air was heavy with the perfume of rare flowers; the music throbbed voluptuously; the soft light of the multitudinous wax candles fell upon beautiful women and splendid men. The scene was elysian in its beauty. How can I thank Jenkyns for this invitation. It has opened up to me a new world. Hereafter I shall move upon a higher social plane, from which I can look down with generous pity upon my former associates. I shall treat them politely when we chance to meet *noblesse oblige*—but so far as society is concerned, we must henceforth be strangers.

Jenkyns has procured me an invitation to Mrs. Merriwether's for next Thursday evening. (By the way, I hope he will not ask me for another loan before that time; he is not as prompt in his payments as I could wish.) I wonder if Miss Ferrand will be there. I must find out who she is. Such a charming freshness and simplicity! The moment she entered the drawing-room door I was struck by her appearance. She is a blonde, tall and stately, with eyes of deepest blue, from which truth seems to look out inquiringly upon an unfamiliar world. She wore a high-cut gown of dove-colored silk, with violets in her hair and at her throat. Jenkyns tells me it was her first ball. It is no wonder, then, that a blush should overspread her face as she looked around the room at the elaborate display of shoulders. What conventional purity! Women like her are the salt of society! Would that there were more of them to exercise a restraining influence upon the growing laxity of fashionable morals.

I had the inexpressible pleasure of taking her out to supper. How will I ever be able to pay my debt of gratitude to Jenkyns! It was interesting to hear Miss Ferrand's *naive* opinions on the ways of fashionable society. "Do ladies really drink wine?" she asked me in a horror-struck whisper.

"See for yourself," I answered.

"It is disgraceful," she continued, her cheeks aflame with indignation. I noticed that she did not take wine herself, and that she went away early. A glorious creature! I hope she will be at Mrs. Merriwether's.

January 10, 1879.—I met Miss Ferrand last night for the fourth time. She is more charming each time I see her. Last night her beauty was heightened by an elaborate full-dress toilet. She wore a gown of white satin, with a bunch of yellow roses at her waist. What superb shoulders she has! Her arms would put a Venus to the blush.

A short acquaintance with fashionable society brings a pretty woman out wonderfully. Miss Ferrand waltzes divinely. I understand she has been taking dancing lessons since she came to the city. She and young Van Dusen make a handsome couple. I saw no reason, however, for his clasping her so closely during the waltz. I have never heard any good of that fellow. He is a rich snob; his money is his only redeeming quality. His touch is pollution to a pure and unsullied soul like that of Miss Ferrand. She surely has not heard of his habits, or she would not dance with him.

I waltzed with her later in the evening, and—but I cannot describe my feelings. Let me confess it here in these pages, which no profane eye will ever desecrate: I am in love—deeply, desperately in love. Dearest Ida—Ida!—my pen lingers lovingly upon the name—could you not read my secret in my eyes— in every tone of my voice? I am thirty-five and this is the first time I have ever been really in love.

Van Dusen took her out to supper. Lucky scoundrel! I gave my arm to a faded wallflower, to whom I could not reasonably be expected to talk a great deal. I succeeded in getting seats opposite Miss Ferrand at the supper table, and feasted my eyes upon her from behind the pyramid of hothouse flowers that rose in front of my plate. I am afraid my companion was somewhat neglected.

Van Dusen was very attentive to Ida; he must be in love with her himself. The thought is maddening! In her innocent good-nature she seemed to encourage him. She laughed at his clumsy wit and appeared to listen—what a bore it must have been!—to the bits of stale gossip he had picked up at the clubs, about people she did not know, and events in which she could not have been interested. The fellow has not a single original idea. He piled her plate with dainties, and I watched her tapered fingers carry to her lips the champagne he forced upon her. Do I hate or envy him most?

I have found out all about her. She comes of a poor but highly cultivated family; her father is a professor in a theological seminary, and her mother writes articles for the magazines. I can seek her hand without incurring the imputation of mercenary motives. I shall call this evening with Jenkyns, who is acquainted with the family she is stopping with.

11 P.M.—Called with Jenkyns. Delightful time. Will go again by myself next Thursday evening. Miss Ferrand is as accomplished as she is beautiful. She plays brilliantly upon the piano and sings with a cultivated and very sympathetic voice. I could scarcely refrain from weeping at her rendition of "Way Down Upon de Swanee Ribber." She sang the ballad with a pathos and deli-

cacy that redeemed it from its minstrel associations and appealed to the finer feelings of the heart. I looked over a number of her drawings; they show signs of unusual talent. She is familiar with the best literature of the day, and spoke of several authors with whose names I am unacquainted. I fear I am not worthy of her, and yet I will make the effort to win her love. I think she must have perceived something of my feeling toward her; I do not see how she could have failed to do so.

March 10.—Black despair has fallen upon me. I have been refused—kindly, but firmly. Nothing could have been more delicate than her way of putting it; but, alas! the blow is not less crushing because the hand that gave it was wrapped in velvet.

"Mr. Dunlap," she said, "I regret this exceedingly—more, indeed, than language can express. But, while I esteem you highly, I do not feel for you the affection which I must have for the man whom I marry."

"Is there no hope that your feelings toward me may change?" I asked.

"I am afraid not," she replied. "No, Mr. Dunlap, it is better for you not to cherish false hopes. But we can still be friends. Some other and better girl will make you happier than I could."

A decent self-respect would require me to forget her. But, groveling in the depths of self-abasement, I confess that I love her still, and shall ever love her.

April 15.—My worst fears are realized. Is it reserved for gilded vice and emptiness always to triumph over honorable poverty? Miss Ferrand has become Mrs. Van Dusen. I went to see her married. The brilliantly lighted church was crowded to the doors. From an obscure corner I watched the bride float down the aisle upon Van Dusen's arm, while the organ pealed forth a joyful wedding march. It was like seeing a lamb led to the sacrifice. The music ran together in a jumble of discords. I could bear no more, and hurried out of the church by the side door. I had received an invitation to the reception, but could not trust myself to attend; my heart was too full. May Ida never repent the step she took tonight.

May 20.—I have tried in vain to tear this unholy love from my heart. Ida is now the wife of another. But did she not say we might be friends? It cannot be wrong for me to watch over her; she may yet need a friend. I do not believe Van Dusen will make her a good husband, and I may yet have an opportunity to prove my friendship.

I met Mrs. Van Dusen last night.

"Why did you not come to my reception?" she said, reproachfully.

"Do not ask me," I replied; "I could not."

"Poor Mr. Dunlap!" she sighed.

What divine pity! It almost consoled me for my misery; and when she asked me to bring her fan from the sofa in the other room I felt an elation that lasted me all the evening.

August 1, 1881.—It has been a long time since I have written in my journal. I attended the *soirée* at Mrs. Van Dusen's last night. I suspect that my fears were well founded. Ida does not look happy, and there is an expression of sullen savagery about Van Dusen's heavy face that bodes ill for his wife's peace of mind.

I conversed with my hostess a few minutes at supper. She surely has some secret sorrow. She swallowed several glasses of wine with almost feverish haste. Would that I could comfort her—my poor darling! She must suffer, and I can do nothing.

March 2, 1882.—I can scarcely restrain my joy, and yet the sentiment is almost inhuman. Van Dusen is dead—killed in a railway accident. Ida is free! Having waited so long, I can wait a little longer, but when the period of her mourning is over I will again tempt my fate. If humble and patient devotion can win her love, she shall yet be mine.

March 10.—Fortune favors me. Van Dusen's affairs were found to be fearfully involved, and in all probability there will be nothing left for the widow and child. I have volunteered my services in straightening out the books of the estate, and getting her business in order. This brings me into frequent contact with Ida. Her resignation is almost divine; and the pensive smile that lights up her face now and then is like a ray of light escaping through a rift in the walls of paradise.

May 10.—My task is completed. There is scarcely anything left of the fine estate Van Dusen inherited. He has run through it all in a few brief years. Ida will have to find something to do to support herself and her child. What a shame that conventionality will not permit me to assume the burden; I would work my fingers to the bone for her.

May 20.—I have bestirred myself to find music pupils for Ida. She is a skillful musician, and will make, I think, an excellent teacher. Some of her former fashionable associates have interested themselves in her behalf, and she will be able to earn enough to live in comfort until the time arrives when I can offer her a humble home.

June 1, 1883.—When I called at Mrs. Van Dusen's last evening I found a tall, handsome fellow there. He is a Mr. Courcy, a banker, and the father of one of Ida's music pupils. I have learned today that he is a widower. How rapidly I hope the next few months may fly, so that I may put the momentous question upon which my future happiness depends!

October 12.—I am dazed, dumbfounded, stupefied. All last night I tossed upon my bed in sleepless misery. I have not been to the office today, but went for a long walk in the park this morning, hoping that the fresh air and the sight of the green trees might give my throbbing brain relief. Perhaps I can get rid of some of my pain by pouring it out upon the pages of my journal. When I called upon Ida last evening, she said to me:

"Mr. Dunlap, I believe you are a true friend of mine, indeed my best friend, and I wish to confide in you with respect to a matter of vital importance to me. I am alone in the world, except for Nellie. My earnings are small at the best, and while at present adequate for my simple needs, they will not, even supposing them to remain constant, be sufficient to educate Nellie as the Ferrands have always been brought up."

"Dear Mrs. Van Dusen," I cried at this point, "let me—"

She interrupted me and continued: "Mr. Courcy has offered to marry me. He can give me wealth and luxury, a home for Nellie, and the means to educate her properly. I believe he loves me dearly, and I have accepted him. I hope you think I have acted wisely. Will you not congratulate me?"

For an answer I poured out my own love in a torrent of words. She looked pained and surprised.

"I did not dream that you felt such sentiments for me, Mr. Dunlap," she said, and with downcast eyes she continued, "You said nothing; what might have been if you had spoken sooner it would not be right for me now to say. But my word is given and I cannot break it. Can we not still be friends? I know I can never repay you for all your kindness to me."

I could not resist so much dignity, such integrity of character. With a sublime self-denial she had sacrificed her love for me to what she believed to be her duty. What might have been she would not say—she had plighted her word and I must go on in the dreary routine of my lonely life—cheered somewhat by a ray of friendship, when, if I had only spoken sooner, I might have basked in the sunshine of love.

January 3, 1884.—I see Mrs. Courcy occasionally. The happy intimacy of her widowhood is mine no more. I sometimes imagine that she tries to avoid me when we meet. I fear that she sacrificed too much to an abstract conception of duty, and that her loveless marriage is not a happy one.

March 10, 1886.—I see from the *Morning Bugle* that Mrs. Courcy met with an accident last night. In going to her carriage from Mrs. Merriwether's reception, she slipped upon the icy pavement and sprained her ankle.

March 12.—I have had quite a painful experience today. I was coming out of the club when I met Jenkyns.

"Hello, Dunlap!" he exclaimed, "did you hear about the accident to Mrs. Courcy?"

"Yes," I said, "I hope it is not serious."

"Do you know how it happened?" He leaned over me and whispered to me: "She was drunk—drunk as a fish."

I do not know whether horror or indignation was the stronger sentiment in my mind at that moment. As soon as I could command my voice, I replied hotly:

"Jenkyns, you are no gentleman. You slander as pure and noble a woman as ever walked upon the earth."

"Ah, well, old boy, if you're going to get huffy about it I can't help it, you know. That's what everybody says, and I have seen her take a drop too much myself."

I gave the fellow a look, into which I tried to throw all the contempt I felt for him, and then turned upon my heel. I did not wish to create a public scandal by treating him as he deserved to be treated. I regret that the code has fallen into disuse among us; if it were in force I should call him out.

March 18.—I learn that the injury sustained by Mrs. Courcy the other night is more serious than was at first supposed, and that her walk will always be characterized by a limp.

I saw her last night, for the first time since the accident, and I thought the slight limp added individuality to her movements, and did not in the least detract from her beauty. The defect is scarcely perceptible in her dancing. She looks a little pale and *distrait*. I fear her domestic life is not happy. How my heart bleeds for her!

September 13, 1887.—Mrs. Courcy is in distress; it can no longer be concealed. I met her at Mrs. Merriwether's several evenings since, and she told me the whole story in strictest confidence. Her husband no longer loves her; his affections have been alienated by another woman. As a consequence, he has treated his wife shamefully; he has even accused her—I blush to write it even in the privacy of my own journal—of unfaithfulness. This is a mere subterfuge, a transparent pretext by which he means to procure a divorce. He has employed private detectives, who watch his wife's movements and make her life miserable.

I could only advise her to suffer patiently; I assured her of my sympathy, and that I would stand by her if Courcy should attempt to carry out his plan.

October 18.—The blow has fallen. Today Mr. Courcy filed his petition in court, asking a divorce and the custody of his children. The affair has got into the newspapers, and is the all-absorbing topic of conversation. How Ida must suffer! I sought her out in her distress. She seemed glad to see me again, and to know that she had at least one true friend. She has left her husband's house, and says she will never return to it; nothing could induce her to enter the presence of the monster who has thus vilified her.

I implored her to accept my aid, and she has permitted me to retain as counsel for the defense Messrs. Snap & Doubleday, the eminent attorneys. Of course my connection with the matter is kept secret, as my poor stricken one must not give her enemies any material which they can distort into evidence against her.

I have read a copy of the divorce petition. It comprises a series of shameful attacks upon the character of a woman whom the plaintiff believes to be defenseless. But he shall find himself deceived. I will spend the savings of a lifetime before I will allow that saint to be imposed upon. He charges her with things that I cannot write—it is enough to say that he tries to saddle upon her his own crimes. I have notified Snap & Doubleday to spare no expense in defending her. They have filed a cross-petition, asking for a divorce and alimony. It will serve Courcy right if he loses her forever, and has to pay a sum which will secure her independence, and be a well-merited punishment for his infamous conduct. Such men are most easily affected through their pockets.

Ida is grateful to me. When I called last evening I found her with disheveled hair and eyes red with weeping. She told me, somewhat incoherently, of her great distress of mind. She had sought temporary relief in stimulants, but without avail. I comforted her as best I might, and left her somewhat calmer.

December 10.—The iniquity is accomplished. Perjury and villainy have prevailed against truth and virtue. Is there any such thing as justice upon the earth? In spite of the unrighteousness of his cause, in spite of all the skill of Messrs. Snap & Doubleday, the court has granted Mr. Courcy a divorce from his wife, and has given him the custody of their two children. It is an iniquitous decision, from which, alas! the law gives no appeal.

I am alarmed about the effect this decision may have upon Mrs. Courcy. I called this afternoon, but could not see her. As I went up to the door I met the servant-girl coming from the opposite direction. She had been out to get a bottle of wine for Ida to take her medicine in. I gave the girl some money, and begged for tidings of Ida. She said the poor creature was unwell, and that she had just fallen into a much-needed sleep. Of course I would not disturb her. I will ask her to let me send Dr. Barnes, the eminent specialist in nervous troubles, to visit her.

Courcy has left the city. Rumor says he is brokenhearted; that he has sold out his business, and gone where his children will never hear of their mother's shame; but I have it on good authority that he has gone to join the woman who is the cause of all Ida's misfortunes.

Ida has recovered somewhat from the depression into which she was thrown by the decision in the divorce case. She is trying to bear her troubles with resignation. It must be a hard thing for a woman to hold up her head under such a blow. But the consciousness of innocence gives Ida strength, and she will not bend before an unrighteous verdict.

I have determined to give her the right to look to me for protection. This very day I will offer her a refuge for her poor bruised heart. I will not let my chance slip a second time.

March 3, 1888.—At last—at last I have reaped the reward of my patient fidelity! Ida has promised to be mine; next week my happiness will be complete. I called yesterday afternoon. I sat down upon the sofa beside her, and, taking her little hand in mine, told her the story of my love.

"I have loved you since I first saw you," I said. "Time has only strengthened my passion. Your misfortunes have only served to make you dearer to me. You are still young and beautiful—I am fast growing old. Come to my waiting heart. Let me say to the world, 'This is my wife; I believe in her.' Let me give you a home, humble it is true, but a place where you can be at peace, and where, perhaps, when time has healed the wounds your poor heart has received, you may find a measure of happiness."

Her hand trembled with emotion as it lay in mine.

"Dearest Paul," she murmured, "I have loved you ever since your kindness to me during my widowhood. Your friendship and assistance during my recent period of trial have endeared you to me still more. Can the fragment of my life that is left compensate you in any degree for your years of devotion? But no, I scarcely dare burden you with a woman whose name has been dragged, as mine has, before the eyes of a heartless world."

"Forget it, darling," I interrupted her, "as I have forgotten it. I have saved a little money. I cannot give you the wealth and luxury you have been accustomed to, but I will share with you what I have; I can keep you from want, and shield you from calumny."

She laid her head upon my shoulder. "Oh, Paul," she gently murmured, "such as I am, take me."

For the first time in our acquaintance of ten years I strained her to my bosom. That moment of happiness was compensation for all my weary years of waiting.

We spent an hour in sweet communion of soul. She told me how she had loved me during all those years, and how soon she had realized the fatal mistake of her second marriage. Before I left her she went to make me a cup of tea.

While she was gone from the room I noticed the corner of a newspaper sticking out from under a sofa cushion that had been carelessly thrown upon it. I pulled it out. It was a copy of the *Evening Bugle*. As I glanced carelessly down its columns, what was my delight to read the following paragraph:

> DIED—At Westfield, Kan., Jabez Dunlap. Mr. Dunlap was one of the pioneers of Westfield, and leaves an estate valued at several hundred thousand dollars. We learn from good authority that he died intestate, and that his nearest relative is a Mr. Paul Dunlap, of - - - - - -, at present a bookkeeper in the employ of the Barton Iron Company of that city.

Do you wonder at my delight? I am Paul Dunlap. I had never met this uncle of mine, and could not be expected to weep over the death of a stranger who had left me very rich. I shall testify my respect to his memory by the erection of a handsome monument.

I could not conceal my elation when Ida returned with the tea. "Do you think you will be content to share my poverty?" I asked.

"Yes, dear," she answered, looking at me with love-lit eyes, "poverty with you will be affluence after the loveless marriages that mine have been."

"Have you read the *Evening Bugle?*"

"No," she said, "except merely to look over the advertising columns in the hope of finding something by which I could increase my earnings. But I have a permanent situation now," she added playfully.

"Read this item." I handed her the paper.

"Oh, Paul," she cried, her eyes big with wonder, "is it you?"

"It is I," I replied, catching her in my arms. "Darling, the world is ours. We will sail for Europe as soon as I can get the estate settled up."

Am I not the most fortunate of men? Ida, wealth, leisure—all are mine! What have I done to deserve such happiness?

* * * * *

Extract from *Chicago Daily News,* September 3, 188–

* * * Yesterday Judge Dailey, after the briefest trial on record (it lasted just five and a quarter minutes by our reporter's reliable Waterbury chronometer) granted a divorce in the case of *Dunlap* vs. *Dunlap,* on the petition of the husband. The grounds on which the application was made were drunkenness and gross neglect of duty. And thus the wheel goes merrily round.

A Grass Widow

"**C**HICAGO, April 14—The body of an unknown woman, well-dressed, but having a dissipated look on her face, was found in an alley, near West Wood street, Thursday. No marks of violence were found on the body, and a post-mortem will be necessary to determine the cause of death. The woman was apparently about twenty-five years of age, slightly above the middle height, with wavy brown hair, and strikingly beautiful in face and figure. There are no marks on the clothing and no papers were found on the person of the deceased by which she might be identified. A peculiar cross-shaped birthmark, high on the left temple and partly covered by her hair, may give a clue to the friends, if she has any. The body will remain at Holmes & Hartman's morgue during tomorrow."

An ordinary newspaper item, which some poor hack of a reporter had picked up on his daily round among the purlieus of a great city. Ordinarily I should have glanced casually over the paragraph, and then have turned my attention to the next column of the paper.

But there was something in it which caught my attention. And, as I reread the description grew more familiar, and I remembered a woman who had not been twenty-five nor dissipated when I knew her, but who was a little above the middle height (I had described her once as "divinely tall"), with wavy brown hair, and "strikingly beautiful in face and figure." I remembered, too, that once when I had been in her company, a passing breeze had lifted the fringe of hair worn low upon her broad, white forehead, and had revealed a tiny, blood-red cross high upon the temple. I determined to go and look at the body of this unknown woman. It might be the woman I knew; stranger things had happened.

The next morning, after breakfast, I started to the office a little earlier than usual, going a few streets out of the way in order that I might pass the morgue, which was an attachment of a large undertaking establishment. I took my place in the line of waiting visitors. There were morbid curiosity seekers, the same class who frequent murder trials and police courts—intellectual ghouls, feeding their depraved imaginations on the dead and decaying things of society; sharp-eyed young reporters, plying their nimble pencils in little red-covered notebooks; one or two old people, shabbily clad, who went in with anxious looks, and came out with lighter steps and more cheerful countenances—they had not found something they had feared to find.

I passed into the room. There were several bodies there, each lying on a marble slab, with a stream of water trickling over its face. One of these was the body of a woman. The newspaper description was correct; she had been young and fair. My presentiment had also been correct; it was the woman I had known. And now I will tell when and where.

*   *   *   *   *

I had finished my course at college. I had read for honors and achieved them, but at the imminent risk of my health. I graduated at the head of my class, but I left college pale and nerveless. My physician said that I had been on the verge of brain fever, and advised me to take a long rest, and to spend the summer if possible either in the country or at the seaside. I chose the former and went to visit my brother, who lived in a village twenty miles from the city where I had attended college.

George and I were the only surviving members of a once numerous family. Two of our brothers had been killed in the civil war. Our mother and two sisters had gone the way of all the earth, and only recently had our beloved father joined the silent circle of the dead, snatched away by a remorseless disease, just when the active labors of his life were over, and he was preparing to enjoy the leisure and freedom from care which the training of a large family and the exacting demands of a professional career had hitherto kept beyond his reach. My brother and I were drawn closer together by each of the successive losses, and concentrated on each other the affections which we had shared with the larger family circle. George had married several years before I left college, and his home thenceforth became mine whenever I chose to make it so. He had invested the greater part of his modest patrimony in a stone quarry, on the line of a great railroad, and was doing a flourishing business. He had a wife, handsome, accomplished and lovable: gentle in demeanor, generous in sentiment, and worshipping in her husband an ideal quite different from what he really was. For while affectionate and good-tempered, George had one or two vulnerable points in his character and was easily tempted in certain directions. Though I was several years his junior my influence had more than once kept him out of serious entanglements. Since he had married, however, he had led an exemplary life, and the most exacting wife could not have demanded greater devotion than he had displayed to Madge.

Their house was situated some distance from the business part of the town, on a suburban continuation of the main street of the town, and behind it, at the rear of the large kitchen garden, ran a shallow brook. A lane ran from the street to the brook, which it crossed by a rustic bridge. I mention these details of the location of the house because they have an important bearing on my story.

The place was old-fashioned in construction and appearance. It was a charming old fashion, however, and George had wisely determined not to disfigure it with modern additions, and except for such interior changes as comfort had demanded the house remained unaltered. A profusion of shrubbery adorned the spacious yard, and a broad piazza, in front of which grew two stately elms, furnished a pleasant lounging place for summer days.

For several weeks I did nothing but read newspapers. The rest of the time I spent rambling about the woods and fields, reveling in the pure country air and the beauty of sky and verdure.

After a few weeks of idleness, however, my health grew better, the color returned to my cheek, and I felt equal to the task of beginning my novel, a work which I had long contemplated, and which I imagined I could dash off in a few weeks. I set to work upon it, and had completed the first two or three chapters, when the introduction of a new member into our household interfered somewhat with my plans.

"George," said Madge one morning as we sat at a late breakfast, "I am going to invite Laura Wharton to visit us. Poor dear! I know she must find it dreadfully lonely out there among strangers."

"Where is she?" asked George, indifferently.

"In San Francisco. Her husband is in Japan, you know."

"Oh, yes, I remember now. He went over as agent for a firm. When is he coming back?"

"Laura says he will be gone for a year, as the condition of the firm's Japanese business will require his presence at least that much longer."

"Wonder why he didn't take her with him?" asked George.

"Oh, her letter explains that. She was dreadfully anxious to go, but she is rather delicate and her physician feared that the long voyage and the unaccustomed surroundings might have an unfavorable effect upon her health."

"Well," remarked George, as he rose from the table, "invite her by all means. An interesting young grass widow, in delicate health, will make an excellent companion for our pale student here. Besides, she'll furnish him with literary material; he can put her in his novel." Thus the matter was settled. The invitation was sent and promptly accepted. The letter of acceptance brought a request for George's aid in securing passes over the railroads. The large shipping business of the quarry gave George a claim on the railway companies to courtesies of this description. In due time he handed two handsomely engraved bits of pasteboard to Madge, who forwarded them to her distant friend.

One afternoon, a few weeks later, Madge drove down to the depot to meet the visitor. I was seated in the library, my table drawn close to the long window, and working hard on a personal description of the heroine of my novel.

I was still debating the point whether to make her a statuesque blonde or a magnificent brunette, when I heard the crunching of wheels on the graveled drive, and looked up from my manuscript. The window in front of which I sat was open, and on the other side of the piazza a climbing vine had been trained, forming a leafy screen, through which I could gratify my curiosity unperceived. As I looked out a clear, musical voice exclaimed, in tones of unmistakable sincerity:

"Oh, do stop, Madge! What a lovely old place! It looks just like a picture."

I looked at the speaker through my leafy veil, and mentally exclaimed: "What a beautiful woman! I will use her for my heroine!"

Seated by Madge, and leaning slightly forward in the eagerness of her admiration, she did not appear to be nineteen; a half brunette, with wavy brown hair peeping coquettishly from beneath a charming bonnet; her dark eye sparkling with artistic appreciation of the quaint old brick house in its setting of flowers and shrubbery.

"Oh, Madge!" she exclaimed. "How delightful it must be to live in such a charming old place."

Then Madge drove up to the steps, and the guest alighted, and I saw her no more until evening. When she appeared at supper my first impression was strengthened. The traces of travel had been removed, and a becoming evening dress set off to advantage her charms of person. Her conversation was cultivated and witty. I began to think that this delicate grass widow would prove a delightful adjunct to a summer vacation, and that Mrs. Wharton's grace and beauty would add immeasurably to the somewhat colorless abstraction which had hitherto done duty as the heroine of my novel.

II

Mrs. Wharton's presence caused several changes in our domestic habits, but principally in my own. As the only unencumbered person about the house, it naturally came about that the entertainment of the visitor devolved largely upon me. I went out riding with her, and found her by no means averse to a sharp canter along a smooth stretch of road. She rode so well that I immediately inserted an equestrian scene in my novel. I went driving with her, and she handled the reins so well that I wrote up a runaway episode, in which my heroine's skill and presence of mind prevented what might have been a dire catastrophe.

On rainy days we read together in the old library. George was generally absent at the quarry, which lay on the other side of the town. Madge was usually occupied with her household affairs. On warm afternoons Mrs. Wharton reclined in a Mexican hammock swung in the piazza, and dawdled over a novel or a book of poems.

Of course it would have been unnatural for a young man, thus thrown in daily and familiar intercourse with a young and pretty woman, not to become more or less interested in her. I will confess that I thought her charming. There was a clinging tenderness in the manner in which she held my arm, for instance, when we visited the quarry and walked too near the edge of a stonepit, that was quite exhilarating. I should doubtless have fallen violently in love with her if she had been a widow or unmarried. There were several reasons why I did not. In the first place, I had been well bred. In the second place, my novel acted as an escape valve for my imagination. Besides, there was a blue-eyed little fairy with whom I had taken many long walks during my last year at college, and her image was too recently and too firmly impressed upon my youthful heart to be driven out even by the charming Mrs. Wharton. I no more dreamed of scaling the barrier which matrimony had built between us than I would have dreamed of scaling Mt. Shasta.

One day I asked her if she had heard from her husband lately.

"Have I a husband?" she asked dreamily, shooting a glance at me from beneath her long eyelashes.

"Twelve thousand miles is a long distance."

Several other remarks, uttered at various times when we were alone together, led me to think that her relations with her husband might not be as pleasant as perfect connubial bliss would require.

"George," I said one evening, when we were smoking on the piazza and Mrs. Wharton and Madge were indoors, "what sort of a fellow is Mrs. Wharton's husband?"

"Don't know," he replied laconically. He was a man of few words and many cigars.

"Do you get many letters for her?" The mail for the family always went to the office.

"Haven't got any from Japan, so far."

"I imagine she don't care much for her husband," I remarked, stating my reasons for this opinion.

"Likely enough," said George. "It's a beastly shame. A woman like that ought not to be running about the world alone. A woman like that was made to be loved. Wonder you aren't in love with her yourself before now."

I denied the soft impeachment with a blush.

A week or two after this conversation George met with an accident. A heavy fall of rain had softened the earth around the top of one of his quarry-pits, and, stepping carelessly too near the edge, the earth caved, and he was precipitated ten or fifteen feet to the bottom of the pit. His injuries were not serious, but several bruises and a sprained ankle made it necessary for him to keep quiet for a week or two. He therefore remained at home, and I attended to as much of his business at the quarry as could be done in his absence. This kept me away from the house, except for a short time before and after meals.

I noticed that during the week Mrs. Wharton occupied her usual place on the verandah, and I suppose she did her best to entertain George during his convalescence. As for George, he did not seem to take his enforced inactivity as hard as he usually would have done. Ordinarily he would have fretted and fumed, would have smoked innumerable cigars, would have read a few novels and a great many newspapers. He would probably have begun to hobble about before his ankle had gained sufficient strength, with the result of making him somewhat surly and short of speech.

On the contrary, however, his confinement to the house produced none of these results. He was cheerful and even animated. The occasional hitches in his business, resulting from my inexperience, did not disturb his equanimity. I even found him reading Byron one afternoon.

"Cultivating the muses, George?" I inquired.

"Reading about this fellow Beppo," he replied carelessly. "Deuced interesting thing. Didn't know Byron had so much life in him." From which it may be inferred that George's tastes were not strictly literary.

I sat down on the chair which Mrs. Wharton had risen from before I came out on the piazza.

"Don't you think Mrs. Wharton has a beautiful voice?" he said, knocking the ashes from his cigar.

"Decidedly so," I said. "She sang with spirit and understanding to Madge's accompaniment."

"Her figure is perfect," he added, reflectively.

I assented to this.

"And then she has such a charming manner, and dresses in such exquisite taste."

"Have you expressed your opinion of her to Madge?" I inquired with a tinge of sarcasm.

"I can't say I have," he answered shortly. "Women are peculiar about these things. A man can admire a handsome woman without making a fool of himself about her. Madge is all well enough in her way, but she hasn't got Laura's chic."

"Look out, old boy," I said, laughing, "you know your weakness."

A few days later I came home from the quarry a little earlier than usual. Instead of entering at the front gate, I came down the lane which ran alongside of the yard, leading to the brook below, and came in at the side gate. As I stopped to pluck a flower, I heard Mrs. Wharton's voice speaking in a low tone. The voice came from the piazza, and on the other side of the screen of vines I could see the glimmer of her white dress.

"He was too slow," she was saying. "If he had been more like you, George, I might have loved him. He has been with me every day for three weeks, and has not said a word of love, or even kissed so much as my hand. He's a good little fellow, too good for this world. I'm afraid your brother Frank will die early, George."

This conversation promised to become interesting. I kept quiet.

"Frank is young yet, Laura. He'll grow wiser as he grows older. Your love would be wasted on a boy, even so good a boy as Frank."

I crept a little further away from the piazza, and then went around to the front steps. When I went upon the piazza George was deeply absorbed in his volume of Byron, and Mrs. Wharton was knitting with more than usual energy on the fancy sacque she was making for Madge's child, while a slight blush heightened the glow of her cheek.

Of course I said nothing of my discovery. It was clear as day to me now that Mrs. Wharton had been making love to me ever since she had been in our house. It was equally clear that she had used her charms on George with greater effect. I felt oppressed by the weight of my secret, so much so, indeed, that I did not even think of the dramatic effect with which I could work it up in my novel. I had no right to speak to Mrs. Wharton; I would not for the world have spoken to Madge, for I instinctively felt that a nature like hers would not overlook such a fault in a husband. I imagined how terrible it must be for a woman to have her dearest ideal shattered. I spoke to George. I did not tell him what I had overheard, but I intimated that I saw the drift of things very clearly. He turned the subject of conversation as soon as he could, and ridiculed the idea that there was anything serious between himself and Mrs. Wharton.

III

A week passed. I saw no further indications of any secret understanding between George and Laura, and I began to think that my advice had borne fruit in recalling George to his senses. It is true that they were much together for several days. Then George's ankle got better, though it seemed to me longer in recovering its strength than the nature of the injury required. At length, however, he got out to his business again, and his tete-à-tetes with the fair Laura were after that less frequent. Of course they met at table and in the family circle, and occasionally, when Mrs. Wharton had some shopping to do, she would accept a seat in George's buggy when he drove through the business part of the town on his way to the quarry.

My novel was progressing finely, and I had got the heroine involved in a position from which it would require something decidedly improbable to extricate her, when, one morning at breakfast, Mrs. Wharton announced that she had received a letter from her husband.

"I am afraid," she said, regretfully, "that I must bring my visit to an end. Ralph writes that he will arrive on *The Mikado,* which is due in San Francisco next week."

"How happy you must be at the prospect of meeting your husband," said Madge. "But I shall be awfully sorry to lose you," she continued.

"It's too bad you can't finish your visit," remarked George, politely, but with almost too apparent unconcern. I observed, however, that he did not look at her as he spoke.

"I'm sure I never spent a more delightful summer," she murmured, leaning over to feed a lump of sugar to Madge's little boy, Johnnie, of which precocious infant Laura seemed very fond. This stuffing with sweets was a breach of domestic discipline only allowed in view of Mrs. Wharton's approaching departure.

"You'll want passes, of course," remarked George as he unfolded his napkin.

"Pray don't trouble yourself," she cried, deprecatingly. "I could not allow you to bother so much on my account."

"Oh, it's no trouble at all," protested George as we rose from the table. "When do you go?"

"I think I had better leave Friday," she replied. *"The Mikado* is due at San Francisco the latter part of next week, and that will give me plenty of time to get there before the steamer arrives."

During the two or three days intervening before Mrs. Wharton's departure I worked away diligently on my novel, and made some progress in extricating the heroine from the disagreeable predicament into which her enemies had forced her. To accomplish this intellectual feat required a great deal of thought on my part, and I therefore did not trouble myself about Mrs. Wharton's affairs.

Thursday evening we all met at supper. Mrs. Wharton was somewhat pale and distrait. Madge was regretfully sympathetic—the regret at losing her visitor—the sympathy in Laura's anticipated pleasure at meeting her husband after such a long absence. George seemed somewhat preoccupied, and gave random answers to several questions which I asked during the meal. The conversation turned on Mrs. Wharton's journey.

"By the way," George remarked, "I have your passes," and he drew out of his pocket an envelope from which he took several papers. One was yellow, and as he opened the envelope I noticed another slip like it in color and size, which he returned to his pocket.

The next morning Mrs. Wharton, assisted by Madge, was busy with preparations for her departure. I did not feel like working on my novel that morning, so I went over to the quarry to spend an hour in watching the workers blasting out the solid rock. To my surprise I found very few at work. I spoke to a workman standing near.

"What's the matter?" I asked. "Why are not the men at work?"

"We haven't been doing anything for several days," he replied. "There don't seem to be any contracts on hand, and business has been slack ever since the boss was laid up with his sprained ankle. The men don't like it either."

This was news to me. George had said nothing at home about the condition of his business, or I would surely have heard of it. I walked up to the office. George was seated at his desk, an open letter before him. As I came in he carelessly threw the letter on the desk face downward.

"What's the matter with the business, George?" I asked. "The men say they haven't been doing anything for several weeks."

"Awfully dull for the past three weeks or so," he answered. There was a note in his voice, however, which somehow savored of insincerity.

"I have just got an order, though," he continued, "which will keep us busy for three months. I made a bid to furnish the stone for a new public building at Caldwell, and I think I'll get it. I have just received a letter from the contractor, asking for a conference at his office tomorrow morning. I guess I shall have to run down there tonight."

"You can see Mrs. Wharton a part of the way on her journey," I remarked.

"Yes, that's a fact; so I can. She'll be pleasant company. I wish you would ask Madge to have my valise packed for me."

When I went home to lunch I delivered the message to Madge. She did not evince any surprise, as George's business frequently called him away from home. "It will be pleasant for Laura to have company as far as Caldwell," she said.

When George came home to dinner he explained more fully the object of his journey. He seemed very much elated, but there was a suppressed excitement in his manner which was very unusual, and which a successful stroke of business seemed hardly sufficient to account for; and I still noticed that tone of insincerity in his voice. I do not think that Madge perceived it. It was like a slight discord in a piece of music is to an unmusical ear. I was conscious of it, but could not define it nor account for it.

The hour for the departure of the travelers approached. The train left at seven, and the depot was at least a mile from the house, on the other side of the town. Just before the time to start it began to rain. This necessitated a change in our plan, which had been to walk to the depot in a family party. It was therefore decided that Madge and I should remain at home, and George would drive Mrs. Wharton to the depot in his covered buggy. The buggy would be brought back by a servant who had gone with the trunks on an express wagon. Mrs. Wharton came down, clad in a gray traveling dress of some clinging material, which fitted her elegant figure perfectly.

"Good-by, dear Madge," she murmured, as the two women embraced. "I cannot find words to tell you how I have enjoyed my visit."

I bade Mrs. Wharton farewell, and assisted her into the buggy, which rolled off down the graveled drive and out into the street. As we turned to go into the house Madge called her little boy.

"Johnnie! where are you? Come to mamma!"

The child did not come nor answer. He had been in the hall a few minutes before, and Mrs. Wharton had kissed him before she went out on the piazza. Madge went into the house to look for the child. A few minutes later she reappeared.

"Frank," she said, anxiously, "I wish you would help me look for Johnnie. I don't know where he can have gone. Please look out in the lane and down toward the brook; he may have strayed in that direction."

I went out of the side gate and down the lane toward the brook. As I neared the rustic bridge I heard a splash and a faint scream. Fear lent wings to my feet, and I reached the bridge in a moment. Looking down the stream I saw a small figure floating a few rods away. The water was shallow, but the child was only three years old. Besides, there was an eddy a short distance below, and beyond it a pool of deep water where the boys of the neighborhood were wont to disport themselves. If I could only reach the child before he got to this spot I might save him.

Springing over the low railing I made my way down the stream as rapidly as possible. Every swimmer knows how hard it is to run even in shallow water. But I could not have reached the boy any quicker by running on the bank, for the brook was fenced on each side, and I would have lost more time climbing fences than I would have gained by running on land. My efforts were only partially successful. The child reached the eddy, was whirled around once or twice, and sank, coming up a moment later in the deep water beyond. By this time I had reached the spot and caught his little skirt as he came up. A moment later and I had drawn the dripping and apparently lifeless body to the bank. I knew that prompt measures must be taken, and clasping the limp little frame in my arms I ran as fast as I could homeward.

Madge met me at the gate. She looked at me approaching, and she divined from the manner in which I held the child that something was wrong. With a wild scream she sprang toward me, and seizing the lifeless form of her child, ran toward the house.

"Don't be excited," I exclaimed as calmly as my own excitement would permit. "A few simple steps will restore him to consciousness. He was under the water only a minute."

My familiarity with the books in the library was such that I could put my hand on book or page where instructions were given for resuscitating drowned persons. By the time I found them Madge had recovered somewhat of composure, and her strong good sense asserted itself in the manner in which she carried out the instructions I gave.

"The girl will help you," I said, "and I will go at once for Dr. Greene, and then go to the depot and see if I can catch George before the train leaves."

These events had not occupied a quarter of an hour from the time George and Mrs. Wharton had left for the depot. They had fully half an hour to reach it, and I hoped I could get there on foot in the fifteen minutes remaining.

I dashed out of the house and down the street. The doctor's residence was but a half dozen doors from our own. As I drew near I saw his buggy standing at the gate and his rotund figure disappearing in the shrubbery.

"Doctor!" I screamed; "for God's sake, come quick!"

He turned and came back to the gate.

"George's child is drowned," I said, "and they are trying to resuscitate him. His father is going away on the seven o'clock train, and I have but fifteen minutes to reach him."

"Have you a horse?"

"No."

"Take my buggy and I will go to the house on foot. Bring him back if you can. It is not always easy to restore drowned people."

I sprang into the buggy, and seizing the whip, astonished the good doctor's easy-going old gray mare. She seemed to recognize the seriousness of the emergency, however, and responded nobly.

We reached the depot in ten minutes. I sprang out, and ran into the station house. There was no train there. I glanced at the depot clock, and it marked five minutes after train time.

"Plenty of time, sir," said a blue-clad porter, coming up behind me. "Train twenty minutes late."

I ran to the waiting room. There were several people sitting there, but all were strangers.

"Have you seen a lady and a gentleman together?" I inquired of the porter.

"Lady in gray-blue bonnet?" he asked.

"Yes."

"They've gone up the park," he answered. "Those are their things." He pointed to a pile of valises and bundles. I recognized them.

"In what direction did they go?" I asked.

"Didn't notice. Best way to catch 'em now is to wait right here. Train'll be along pretty soon now, and if you go one way they may come another, and you'll miss 'em."

This was true. I could only wait. The depot stood at one side of an ornamental park, used for picnic parties and excursions. The light rain had ceased by this time, and George and Mrs. Wharton, tempted by the delicious coolness of the evening air, and having plenty of time, had strolled off down one of the winding paths. I sat down by the pile of luggage, and instinctively put my hand in my pocket for someting to read—I remembered having stuck a newspaper in the inner pocket of the light overcoat which I had snatched up as I left the house. Instead of the newspaper I drew out a folded paper, which I opened with some curiosity, not remembering to have seen it before. It was a letter addressed to my brother George. I involuntarily glanced at the first few lines, when I became interested, and read the letter through. It ran as follows:

DEAR SIR: Your figures for the quarry are pretty steep. However, it is a valuable property and we think we can get our money out of it by prudent management. As requested by you, we will have deed prepared according to your instructions, and will be at depot with notary public to meet ten o'clock train. We have procured draft on Denver, which will be delivered on execution of deed.

Yours truly,

The letter was signed by a prominent stone merchant in Caldwell, with whom George had frequently had business transactions.

My first sensation was one of astonishment, and it was several moments before the full meaning of the situation dawned upon me. George's alleged business in Caldwell was fictitious. He had been closing up his own business, and had sold out the quarry. He had procured passes for himself as well as for Mrs. Wharton. There could be but one reason for so much deception and secrecy. The wicked woman who was with him had wound her toils about his weak nature, and a wife's love, a successful business career, even honor itself, had been thrown to the winds for a pretty face.

I heard the whistle of the approaching train. The porter ran into the waiting room and gathered up the luggage.

"This way, sir. Lady and gentleman just steppin' on train."

In a moment I was in the car. "George," I cried. "Johnnie has fallen into the brook and drowned. For God's sake, come home."

He turned a ghastly white with emotion, while a look, which I cannot define, came into Mrs. Wharton's eyes. Reading it in the light of my recent discovery, it expressed baffled love and disappointed hopes.

"I will go at once," said George, in a voice which sounded strange and unnatural. "Good-by," he added, turning to Laura. "I—I will—"

"I will go back with you," she said. "I ought not to leave Madge in her affliction."

George had already left the car.

"I do not think it necessary," I said coldly, as she rose from her seat. "Perhaps you had better go on and meet your husband. And as you pass through Caldwell, you might explain to the gentleman at the depot why George is not there to sign the deed for the quarry."

She saw that I knew all. She sank back into her seat, and her eyes blazed with hatred and pent-up rage. The train started and I left the car. I sprang into the buggy and soon overtook George, who had started up the street on foot. The doctor's mare made a record that evening which she has not beaten since.

The doctor and Madge were still working at the child, and it was some

minutes after we arrived before the first faint signs of returning animation rewarded their efforts. Finally, however, the child breathed, then opened his eyes,
and the danger was over.

George stood looking on with haggard face. When Madge had carried
the child off to bed, and the good doctor had gone to his well-earned supper,
I drew the letter from my pocket and handed it to George.

"You have on the wrong overcoat," I said. "You left this in your pocket."

He took the letter mechanically, but as he recognized it, his face fell.

"You read it?" he asked. I nodded assent.

He did not attempt to blame me or to excuse himself. "For God's sake,
do not tell Madge," he whispered hoarsely. "It's all over now and it would
kill her to know."

I never told Madge. The sale of the quarry fell through, and George had
to pay a round sum to prevent a lawsuit.

I did not see Mrs. Wharton again. We learned more of her afterwards—
that her marital relations were not pleasant, and that her husband had exiled
himself to Japan in order to get as far away from her as possible. Madge received a note from her a week or two later to the effect that her husband had
been met by dispatches at Honolulu, and had turned back to Japan. Madge
did not invite her to resume her visit.

I lost sight of her from that time. What kind of life she led, through what
vicissitudes of fortune or misfortune she passed, how she sank step by step from
respectability to shame, I never knew. The look on the marble face in the
morgue; the mysterious death in the worst quarter of a great city; the shabby
finery of her attire—these things furnished the outline of a story which the
imagination may fill in.

I wrote an unsigned letter to the undertaker, enclosing an amount sufficient
to pay for her decent burial. I did not wish to appear personally in the matter,
nor did I make my recognition of the body known to the public. She had long
been lost to the world in which her early life had been passed. Better let her disappear, like a fallen star, in the darkness of oblivion.

Jim's Romance

A tall office building on a busy street in a crowded city: a human hive, where lawyers, brokers, architects, real-estate dealers, civil engineers, worked and schemed with varying degrees of success or failure—everyone in Groveland knows the Blackstone Building. There are other structures that overtop it, and are more elaborately fitted up, but for favorable location and convenient access there is no more desirable building in the city.

Perkins' new office boy was going down in the elevator one day.

"Soft snap yer got here, Jim," he said to the elevator man, "settin' down and ridin' all day long."

"Humph! A mighty soft snap!" growled Jim. "It's hard work and small pay, and I'd earn my money if I didn't have nothin' to do but listen to the chestnuts worked off in this elevator every day. You ain't in no hurry, Billy; your boss won't be back for half an hour. You don't know this block yet. Just ride up and down a trip or two and listen."

An attorney's clerk got into the elevator at the next floor.

"Down, derry, down," he observed as the elevator started.

Quite a crowd were waiting at the bottom for the upward trip. One passenger came into the hall on a run and crowded in just as Jim was shutting the door.

"There's always room for one more in a streetcar and an elevator," he panted cheerfully, as he pushed a fat woman up against the office boy and squeezed against the wall. By the time the car reached the second floor, the last man in remembered that he had forgotten something, and getting off, started down the stairs.

"The King of France with forty thousand men
Went up the hill and down again,"
quoted the young lawyer.

"And w'en 'e was up, 'e was up, up, up,"
gasped the office boy in smothered tones, from behind the fat woman.

Just then the man who had got off—he could be seen from the elevator as he ran downstairs—slipped when near the bottom step and finished his descent with more speed than dignity.

"And when he was down, he was down, down, down,"
cried the passengers in chorus.

"That's what I have to listen to," said Jim, when the elevator was cleared at the top floor, "day in and day out, year in and year out. My coat was ripped on the shoulder yistiddy. Forty-seven men durin' the day—I kept tally—asked me if I knowed my coat was ripped. Seventeen gals asked me what I'd give 'em to mend it; and 'leven men inquired if I was sheddin' that coat. It's worth a hundred a month to stand it. It's worse'n a streetcar conductor's job. And there ain't nothin' in it—thirty dollars a month, and no chance for a raise! I've been here goin' on six years, and I've got to have thirty-three dollars a month next year, or I'll quit—that's all there is about it."

Jim's dissatisfaction with the amount of his salary was chronic and of long standing, and all the tenants were aware of it. They all liked Jim, partly from sympathy—he was a cripple, and only able to walk with the aid of a stick and with an awkward dragging of one leg—and partly because he was of an accommodating disposition and generally of a cheerful temper. He lived with his mother, whom he helped support. He was quite communicative at times, especially to young people; his physical imperfection seemed to give him a sort of affinity for other kinds of weakness and immaturity. He was a thrifty fellow, and every junior clerk and office boy about the Blackstone knew that Jim had seven hundred dollars in the bank, the savings of many years, dating back to a period before he took the elevator, and when he had sold papers on the street.

When the elevator had made several trips, half a dozen working girls got on at the top floor. The Blackstone was connected at the rear with a power block, which had its main entrance on a side street. There was a passage between the office building and the power block, and the employees in the latter were in the habit of coming through the passage to the elevator to enjoy the luxury of a ride.

Some of the girls sat, others remained standing. They were all ordinary-looking girls, except one, a tall, fair girl, more neatly dressed and finer-featured than the rest. They were laughing and joking with one another.

"Now, Mamie, just keep your eyes off Jim," said one of them with assumed anger. "He's my feller, and I won't stand it!"

"Nev' mind, Nell, I'm going to cut you out; ain't I, Jim?" said the tall girl caressingly. She stood behind him, looking in the mirror on the side of the car; as she raised her hand to adjust her hat, her arm brushed his head lightly. Jim flushed, laughed fatuously, and pulled his cap on more tightly as he thought of the little bald spot on his crown.

"Who's that tall gal, Jim?" asked the office boy when the girls had trooped out. Their gay laughter was still ringing along the hallway.

"Her name's Mamie. She works in Jepson's, the book publishers."

"I've never seen her before," said the office boy.

"She's only been working here this week."

"She's a fine-lookin' gal," continued the office boy judicially.

Jim was usually very ready with his opinions on women and things in general, but he made no reply to this observation.

In two or three weeks Jim was hopelessly in love with the tall, fair-haired Mamie. He became confidential with the office boy, and discussed with him the expedience of marrying on thirty dollars a month.

"Provided, you know, Billy, that a feller's got a little somethin' laid by."

"Yes," said the office boy, with a fine assumption of experienced wisdom, "if a feller's got 'bout six or seven hundred dollars, he might risk it. But matter-mony's a lottery, Jim, and there's more blanks 'an prizes."

"That's so," assented Jim. "It takes a man that knows somethin' about women to pick out a wife. There ain't no place like an elevator to learn all that's worth knowin' about the female sex."

The girl, with a woman's intuition, soon saw how the land lay. At first she was inclined to look at the matter as a good joke, and when the girls teased her about her "mash," she replied in the same spirit:

"Never mind; me and Jim's all right."

One day Jim took the tall girl up alone. "Mamie," he said tenderly, "won't you marry me?"

He had not meant to speak to her there, but she looked so tempting, in a light flower-figured dress, with a bunch of violets in her fluffy yellow hair, that he couldn't help it.

Mamie laughed constrainedly. She knew he was in earnest, but she chose to take it lightly. "You don't want to marry me, Jim; you don't know enough about me"—this a little wistfully—"and I don't know enough about you"—this saucily.

"We can get better acquainted," suggested Jim. "We mightn't improve on acquaintance. And I should have to think about it."

She threw him back a laugh as she stepped out of the elevator. Another passenger was waiting, so he could not detain her. His eyes followed her as he started the elevator slowly downwards. She had gone but a few steps when she met Jepson's bookkeeper, Fitzgerald, who said something to her in a low tone. Jim could not hear what he said nor did he see the scornful look she flashed on the speaker. The bookkeeper stepped into the elevator.

"The girls say you are mashed on Mamie," he said, as he flipped the ash off his cigarette with his little finger. The nail was edged with black, and the finger disfigured with a large cameo ring with a female face. There were signs of dissipation in the dead yellow of his skin and the dark circles round his eyes.

Jim had never liked this bookkeeper. He could not have given any particular reason for it, perhaps, except an instinctive aversion, for he liked others who were much worse, so far as he knew, than the bookkeeper. He was a dark, slender man, of about thirty, and wore a black mustache which he cared for sedulously. When he spoke about other people—he seldom said any good of them—his flippant criticisms were generally accompanied by a cynical smile.

"The gals are talkin' through their hats!" said Jim gruffly. "When I get mashed I'll publish it in the newspapers."

"She's a fine girl!" said the bookkeeper. "They say she thinks lots of you. Wish you luck, my boy."

"He's too fresh." growled Jim fiercely to himself when the bookkeeper had gone. "If old Jepson just knowed about them poker games and champagne suppers up in the Crouse Block, Mr. Smarty Fitzgerald would be out of a job quick enough."

For several days after Jim's proposal Mamie did not use the elevator. Jim cast many an anxious look towards the rear door leading from the power block, which was visible from the elevator. Other girls came and went, and laughed and chaffed, but Jim was preoccupied, and paid no more attention to any of them than his business required.

"What's become of Mamie?" he asked one of the girls one afternoon, with a painful attempt at disinterestedness.

"She's walking up and down the stairs for exercise," said one of the girls.

"She's mad with Jim," another said.

Several days more elapsed and still Mamie did not come that way. Jim became low-spirited. He had an hour for lunch at noon each day, when he was relieved by one of the janitors. Walking was not easy or graceful to him, but for several days he limped around to the side entrance of the power block and watched for Mamie. One day his heart leaped as he saw her coming. But as she came up from one direction Jepson's bookkeeper approached from the other.

"Hello, Mamie!" said Jim.

"Hello, Jim!" she said and nodded pleasantly. She seemed to be thinking of something and did not offer to stop. Jim would have spoken and detained her, but the bookkeeper was in the way. She went on up the stairs, Fitzgerald following a few steps behind her. But Jim could not see that he caught up with her around the first turn in the stairway and kept beside her while they walked slowly up the four flights of stairs.

One evening of the following week Jim quit work at the usual hour and started towards home. He had left the main streets, and was passing along a quiet thoroughfare, when a woman brushed past him in the twilight. He felt a momentary thrill; there was something familiar in the outline and movement of the hurrying figure. When she had reached the next corner a man stepped out and stood directly in her path. She moved from side to side several times, but he always blocked her way. Jim had drawn nearer in the meantime, and had recognized the woman as Mamie. There was something familiar about the man, too, but his overcoat collar was turned up and Jim could not make out his face. The two had been so absorbed by what was going on between them that they had not observed the cripple's approach. Jim was almost upon them when the man seized Mamie rudely by the arm and tried to draw her down the cross street from which he had come. She resisted with some vigor but in a moment received unexpected aid. Jim with one blow of his stick sent her assailant senseless into the gutter.

"Thank you, oh, thank you!" panted the girl. At that moment a belated electric light flashed out on the night above them and showed the girl all flushed and trembling with indignation and excitement.

"Why, it's Jim!" she cried, and clutched his arm. "Oh, how glad I am that you came up. I can never thank you enough."

"You'd better let me see you home," said Jim. "These tramps and beggars are getting so bold a person can't walk along the streets in broad daylight, to say nothing of night. But I'll go and call a policeman and have this fellow locked up."

"Oh, no," she said hurriedly, "please don't. We'd have to be witnesses and it would be a lot of trouble, and he's been pretty severely punished already. He was only a beggar, who insisted on my giving him money, when I really didn't have it to give."

She took Jim's arm—more for company than support. They walked on for a while, and turning into a narrow street, stopped at the door of a mean house. The sound of loud voices came from within.

"I'd ask you to come in, Jim," she said, "but father's blowing up the boys, and it might not be pleasant. I'm ever so much obliged to you. Good night."

Jim limped away. "It's a shame," he thought, "that such a girl should have to live with a crowd like that. But never mind. I know a little house on a little side street in a respectable neighborhood that will just suit Mamie. I could be happy in a cellar with her, but there's nothing too good for a girl like that."

During the next month Mamie often rode in the elevator. Gratitude, perhaps, or caprice, or possibly some softer feeling, made her kinder to Jim. Sometimes, when they happened to be alone, he pleaded his cause, with such earnestness and success that one day he told Perkins' office boy, in the strictest confidence, that he was going to be married.

"I know the gal," said the office boy. "It's Mamie. Well, Jim—you know I told you mattermony is a lottery—you may draw a prize and you may draw a blank."

"She's a big prize, Billy," said Jim with conviction.

"She's a fine-lookin' gal," said the office boy.

"Fine as silk," said Jim softly.

"When'll it be?"

"Next month," answered Jim. "We're goin' to housekeepin' right away."

The news of Jim's engagement spread with the rapidity of a confidential communication. Jim bought furniture, a suit of fine clothes for himself, a ring and a gold watch for Mamie, with the result of a perceptible shrinkage in his seven hundred dollars.

"A gal like that, Billy," he said to the office boy, "is worth all you can spend on her. I feel like a millionaire when I go to buy anything for her."

Several weeks before the month was up a subscription list was quietly passed around the block, and more than fifty dollars was contributed to buy a wedding present for Jim and his bride. And the manager of the building, at the suggestion of several of the best tenants, decided to raise Jim's salary after his marriage, in recognition of his faithful service and increased responsibilities. Mamie gave up her job a week before the day set for the wedding and went home to prepare for it.

On the afternoon of the third day before Jim's wedding, Perkins' office boy came out to the elevator about five o'clock.

"D'you hear the news, Jim?" he asked.

"No. What's the news?"

"Jepson's dude bookkeeper Fitzgerald has skipped with five thousand dollars."

"You don't say! When did he go?"

"Well, they just discovered it this afternoon. He didn't show up this morning and about noon his wife came down to the office to see him and he wasn't there. Old Jepson got suspicious and opened up the safe and looked over the books in a hurry and found out that the office was about five thousand in the hole. The way he humped himself to the police headquarters was a caution."

Jim went off duty at six o'clock and immediately after supper called at Mamie's home.

"My land, Jim!" said her mother, "Mamie's not at home. She left at two o'clock to go to her sister's, over on the West Side, to get her to help her make a waist. I guess they haven't finished it yet."

"I'll go after her," he said.

Jim was very much depressed as he took the streetcar on the next corner to go to the West Side. Mamie must have expected him, and it wasn't like her to disappoint him. He felt vaguely uneasy lest some evil had befallen her, and when he got off the car he hurried to the house where her sister lived.

"Is Mamie 'most ready to go home?" he asked of the woman who opened the door.

"Why, Mamie ain't here," she answered. "I haven't seen her since yesterday."

Jim felt sick at heart, and his feeling of uneasiness took well-defined shape. He recalled certain things he had noticed at times when Mamie and the defaulting bookkeeper had been together in the elevator, and remarks he had overheard from others and had not noticed in his blindness now became full of meaning. By a flash of intuition he identified the muffled figure he had knocked into the gutter six weeks before as Fitzgerald, and he recalled Mamie's reluctance to have him arrested and her anxiety to get away. And yet it had seemed plain enough that night that she did not care for the bookkeeper, for her anger was undoubtedly genuine and her relief apparent when Jim had come to the rescue. If she had gone away with Fitzgerald, it had not been of her own free will—she had been coerced, or over-persuaded, or in some way taken advantage of.

Jim got off at police headquarters and inquired if anything had been learned of the defaulter's movements. He could ascertain nothing definite. Then he rode down to the Union Depot to make inquiries on his own behalf.

Fortune favored him. As he entered the station he met Perkins' office boy coming out.

"You're too late, Jim," said Billy. "The train's just gone. I came down to see my mother off—she's goin' to Chicago—and Mamie got on the same car. I asked where she was goin', and she said to spend the night with her sister out at Berea."

Jim knew that Mamie had no sister at Berea, a suburban town about fifteen miles from the depot. A few moments of rapid thinking convinced him that the bookkeeper was either on the train, or that Mamie had gone to join him.

He inquired about the next train for Chicago and was told that it was due to leave at nine o'clock. He had time to go home, get what money he had in the house, and tell his mother he might not be back until late. On his way downtown he stopped at a pawnbroker's and bought a revolver and a box of cartridges of a size to fit it. He reached the station just in time to buy a ticket for Chicago and catch the nine o'clock express.

The train rumbled out of the station and slowly dragged its length through the city and past the suburbs, and then shot away across the open country with all the speed that coal and water and intelligent human skill and attention could give it, leaving behind a trail of fire and smoke. Jim sat in the most secluded seat that he could find, and when the conductor had come and gone, cautiously loaded the revolver. He had no well-defined plan of action. He was going to find Mamie and bring her back; and if the bookkeeper interfered to prevent him, he would kill him. Perhaps he might kill him anyway.

For two or three hours the train rushed on tirelessly through the night with very few stops. Jim sank back into the corner of the seat and fell into a doze. How long he had slept he did not know, when he was awakened by the sudden stopping of the train. He looked up and saw the passengers peering out of the windows and some of them hastily leaving the car. There were voices outside and when he looked out he saw lights moving to and fro.

He spoke to a man who passed by his seat: "What's the matter?"

"There's a wreck," replied the other. "The train ahead of this has been smashed to kindling wood."

Jim's heart leaped to his throat. "Anybody hurt?" he gasped.

"Lots," said the other. "Six or eight killed, and they are getting out more. Don't know how many are wounded. We'll be tied up here an hour or two."

Jim hastened out of the car. A crowd composed of passengers and people from the neighborhood had gathered around the wrecked cars. A spreading rail, or some obstruction placed on the track—it was not yet certain which—had caused the engine to leave the rails. The cars had piled into one another and lay in one great miscellaneous heap of shattered wood and twisted iron. The road at this point ran through a very shallow cut, and on one side, on the top of the grassy slope, the bodies of the dead had been laid awaiting the arrival of the relief train which was momentarily expected. The wounded had been carried to the other bank, where a physician who had been on the wrecked train and had escaped injury was giving them such attention as he could in the absence of instruments and medicines. Men with lanterns and torches were still working to extricate the wounded from the debris, and one poor wretch, caught beneath a heavy beam which it was difficult to move because of the weight upon it, was filling the air with his shrieks and groans. Fortunately the wreck had not taken fire and the unfortunates involved in the catastrophe were spared this added horror.

Jim walked over first to where the wounded lay, and with sickening expectation looked down into the faces twisted with pain or disfigured by their wounds. He breathed easier when he saw Mamie was not among them. But his feeling of relief was only momentary, for, as he walked around the wreck to the other side, his fear that he would find her among the dead grew stronger. Someone had built a bonfire on that side with fragments from the wreck, and the flame now shot up and cast a lurid glare over the scene. With trembling limbs and eager eyes Jim passed along the row of bodies, decently disposed side by side. The first two were women. One of them had been crushed out of all semblance to humanity; the other, a young and handsome woman, had died of some internal injury, for her face was not marred, and there was no visible sign of violence, and the light from the fire tinged her full round cheek with a ruddy glow. A glance down the rest of the row showed Jim that the remaining six were men. With a weight lifted from his heart he walked slowly past them, gazing curiously into the face of each. By one of them a woman knelt weeping; and by another a little child, startled and excited, but all unaware of the weight of its misfortune, sat sobbing in infantile distress. When Jim reached the last, he started and trembled with a mingled feeling which he did not stop to analyze. There at his feet lay the body of Jepson's bookkeeper. With the exception of a wound behind the temple, over which the hair had helped to stanch the flow of blood, his face was not disfigured, but seemed set in the satirical smile Jim had so often noticed upon it. He wore the coarse clothes and shoes of a workingman, evidently assumed as a disguise. His hands had been crossed upon his bosom, and on the little finger of his left hand was the cameo ring with a woman's face which he had been so fond of displaying.

"I'm too late here," said Jim to himself. Acting upon a sudden impulse, he drew the revolver and the box of cartridges from his pocket and threw them both as far into the night as his strength would carry them. Then he turned away to look for Mamie.

He sought through the crowd, but could not find her for several minutes. Finally, huddled in a heap beside a fence off to one side, he thought he saw something which might be a woman. Drawing nearer, he heard muffled sobs, and when he touched the figure on the shoulder and a woman looked up, he saw that it was Mamie.

"Get up, Mamie," he said. "I've come after you."

When she recognized his voice she burst into a wilder fit of weeping, buried her face in her hands, and turned away from him.

"Oh, I can't," she sobbed, "I can't. I'm not fit for you to look at, Jim. Go away and leave me to my punishment. Why wasn't I killed, like he was? You can kill me now if you want to, for deceiving you so."

"Don't excite yourself, Mamie." he said soothingly, "but come along with me, and we'll take the next train back, and I'll get you home before morning and nobody'll know anything about it."

She grew calmer by degrees, and after a while rose to her feet. "Why did you come for me?" she asked. "Why didn't you let me go, Jim, and take the consequences of my foolishness?"

"I wanted to save you from that scoundrel," said Jim, "but Somebody Else has attended to that. Of course, after this. . . ."

"Of course, after this, you couldn't marry me," she said quickly, taking the word from his lips. "But I'm not as bad as I seem, though," she added eagerly, her pale face flushing red. "He was going to take me to Chicago and find me a job, and when he got a divorce he was going to marry me. I'm not as bad as you think me, Jim"—this pitiably—"and I would have kept him at his distance until he married me. I didn't want to go with him, but he made me; I couldn't resist him. I'm telling you the truth, Jim; I don't expect you to marry me, but I don't want you to hate me and despise me."

By this time they were drawing near the wreck. In the distance they heard the long, wierd shriek of a locomotive whistle, and, rounding a curve in the distance, the head-light of the approaching relief train flashed into view. As they came in range of the lights about the wreck, Mamie glanced timidly into Jim's face, and what she saw there made her lose sight of herself for a moment.

"Oh, Jim," she said, "I'm so sorry I treated you so. You've been too good to me, and when I get home I'll thank you and—and pray for you all my life."

Following the wrecking train came another that took on the passengers and mails. In a little while she pulled away, and at the next station Jim and Mamie got out. An hour later they took the eastbound express, which would land them at home again at six o'clock in the morning.

There were not many people in the car and the lights were turned down low. They said nothing to one another, but when Mamie after a while crept timidly closer to him, Jim did not shrink away. By and by the reaction from her past hours of excitement set in and she dozed and nodded, and finally her head fell over on Jim's shoulder.

He looked down at her face a moment sadly, and then a great wave of love—of forgiving and self-forgetful love—invaded him and swept over him. He put his arm gently around her, and glancing back to see that no one was looking, bent over and softly kissed her.

The Exception

The Marguerite Duval Stock Company was stranded at Waiteville, seventy-five miles from Kalamazoo. They had been playing one-night stands in repertoire—also in hard luck—on the ten-twent'-thirt' circuit. Owing to unfavorable weather and rival attractions, their Waiteville performance the night before had been a rank failure—from every point of view. Their trunks had been attached for their hotel bill, and they had literally slept in their clothes, so as to be sure of having something to wear.

The company had an engagement at Kalamazoo for that night. To reach Kalamazoo in time for the performance, it would be necessary to catch the ten o'clock train—there was no other until five, which would be too late. Counting the ties, the last resort of stranded Thespians, was out of the question—there was not time enough, and the snow was three feet deep—in the drifts. They had been ejected, breakfastless, from the hotel, and were gathered about the red-hot stove at the railroad station.

There were Patsy McGuire, or Percy Duval, the manager; his daughter Maggie—Miss Marguerite Duval—the star; Wilkins, the leading man—stage name immaterial; Mrs. McGuire, the first old lady; Polly Jones, the soubrette, and a couple of others. The only other person in the station was a tall, dark young man, whose hair hung down to his shoulders. He wore a slouch hat and a long black beaver overcoat with astrakhan collar and cuffs, and was smoking a very offensive Wheeling stogie. While seemingly looking out the window, he was watching, out of the corner of his eye, the group around the stove.

"We can't walk," declared McGuire, "that's a sure thing."

"No," assented Maggie, "I am on my uppers—and my rubbers are locked up in my trunk, at the hotel."

"No," repeated the manager, "we can't walk. We can't even send the ladies ahead, and walk ourselves—it's the whole company, or we can't do business in Kalamazoo tonight, and the company will have to disband. We can't walk, and the odds are against our riding. There's just six dollars in the treasury, barring the quarter Jim has gone to buy sausage with. The fare to Kalamazoo for seven people is eleven dollars and ninety cents. We are five dollars and ninety cents to the bad."

"Can't we get a rate?" asked Wilkins, the leading man.

"I don't know," returned the manager, gloomily. "This reform legislation has spoiled a lot of good things. But I'll talk to the ticket agent."

He strolled over toward the window, behind which the agent was checking his accounts and filing his orders.

"Hello, Bill," said the manager, with forced joviality—he was accustomed, in the practice of his art, to assuming emotions which he did not feel.

The agent glanced at him shrewdly. Perhaps he suspected something— Waiteville was not a large town.

"Why, hello, Patsy! Going in this morning?"

The tall, dark young man had left his seat by the window and was standing just behind McGuire, looking over his shoulder.

"Bill," said the manager, "we're hard up—snowed under last night, trunks attached for the hotel bill, and unless we can take this train for Kalamazoo, where we're billed to appear tonight, and the house has been sold out— the company will be busted. We've got six dollars—there's seven of us. Can you make us a rate?"

The agent seemed to be hesitating.

"We've spent hundred of dollars on this line, Bill, in the last ten years," argued McGuire. "We're regular customers. You can fix it, if you want to."

The tall young man broke into the conversation.

"I forbid it," he said. "The new two-cent fare law makes no exceptions. The Marguerite Duval Stock Company are entitled to no more favors than I am. If they get a lower rate than two cents, I'll file a complaint with the authorities."

"Now, what right have you to interfere here, Kelly?" said McGuire, turning to the speaker. "This is none of your funeral."

"I have the right of every citizen to see that the laws are enforced. I expect to pay my fare to Kalamazoo—I have the money here in my pocket, and more besides. *My* hotel bill is paid. My trunk is standing outside on the platform. I shall buy my ticket when I get good and ready, and have my trunk checked, and at ten o'clock I shall board the train. And I do not intend that any— bunch of—deadbeats shall get for nothing what I have to pay for."

"I don't see how I can do anything, Patsy," said the agent. "That's the law, as he says. My hands are tied—I've no leeway at all."

The manager returned disconsolately to the circle around the stove.

"Nothing doing," he sighed. "I might have made a dicker with Bill, for the sake of 'Auld lang syne,' if Kelly hadn't butted in. By Jove," he exclaimed, slapping his knee. *"He* gave us away to the hotel keeper—it must have been he—or we couldn't have been subjected to the dastardly outrage of an attachment before breakfast."

Kelly had resumed his seat and his sneer. Wilkins walked over to him.

"Say, Kelly," he demanded, "I want that ten dollars you borrowed from me."

"Sir," returned Kelly, haughtily, "the trifling amount that you mention is a professional debt, which is understood between gentlemen to be paid only when convenient. Your loan is amply secured. As you know, I have stock in a Colorado mining company, and in a Texas oil company; I am the owner of real estate, and my reputation is worth a great deal. What has the company done since McGuire discharged me—me, Reginald DeCourcey, the eminent tragedian, to give my roles to a—a scene-shifter?"

"Your mining stock never paid a dividend; your Texas oil company was a fake—the papers were full of it last week—and your real estate is a cemetery lot, which is pretty nearly full. I want the money. You've got it—I just heard you say so."

"And you heard me say I was going to pay my fare with it, to Kalamazoo. If you have any fears about your money, I'll give you my note."

"Your note," retorted Wilkins, "wouldn't be worth the paper it was written on. Your note would be as bad—as your Hamlet. You won't pay me that ten?"

"Certainly not—not now. I'd be a pretty fool to stay here, and let you go to Kalamazoo."

"You're little better than a thief, Mike Kelly, and you ought to be behind the bars."

"Imprisonment for debt has been abolished for a long time," returned Kelly, "or you and the rest of your company would be doing time."

For some reason the quarrel did not reach the stage of blows. Perhaps actors are so accustomed to mimic rages that they are seldom capable of real ones. Wilkins walked back to the stove and sat there in moody abstraction.

"If we could just get rid of Kelly before the train comes," said McGuire, "I could make a dicker with Bill—I'm sure I could."

Wilkins was cogitating deeply. Kelly had said that imprisonment for debt was abolished. It might seem, superficially considered, that this must be true, for the Marguerite Duval Stock Company were in debt, but at liberty. But every rule has its exceptions. Wilkins had been office boy in a lawyer's office, before he yielded to the fascination of the footlights. He was cudgelling his brain for some obscure memory lodged somewhere in his brain cells. When he found it, he rose hurriedly and left the station, taking his way toward the center of the town, a couple of blocks away.

The shrill whistle of the train at the water tank two miles down the track had pierced the winter air, and Kelly was standing at the window to buy his ticket when Wilkins returned, accompanied by an individual wearing a cap, a badge, and bi-colored chin whiskers, who laid his hand on the tragedian's arm.

"Is your name Michael Kelly?"

Kelly looked at him superciliously.

"*Alias* Reginald DeCourcey?"

"I am Reginald DeCourcey," returned Kelly, unbending.

"Is that your trunk out there on the platform?"

"It is."

"Then you're under arrest. Come along with me."

"Upon what charge, pray?" demanded the tragedian.

"On the suit of J. P. Wilkins, for ten dollars, money had and received."

"But you can't imprison me for debt," declared the tragedian.

"Not as a rule," said the constable, "but there's an exception. We can attach your person for absconding and taking away from the county money or property with which you might pay your debts."

"It's an outrage," protested Kelly, shaking his fist at Wilkins. "I'll get even with you for this."

"You can pay the money, and the three dollars costs now, if you like," said the constable, "and that'll make you even."

"I'll not pay," declared Kelly. "I—I haven't got money enough."

"Then come along," said the constable. "You're blockin' the way, an' the train's comin'."

As soon as Kelly was out of the room, McGuire secured the agent's ear again. When the train drew up at the platform, the conductor came into the station for orders. The agent held a brief colloquy with him, as the result of which the Marguerite Duval Stock Company piled into the smoking-car and whirled away to Kalamazoo.

A Miscarriage of Justice

The case of *Carey vs. Westbrook* was set down for trial at the September term of court. Jim Carey was talking the case over with Perkins, his lawyer. A number of papers were spread out upon the table in Perkins's private office.

"It's a dead open-and-shut case, Jim," said the lawyer. "We're sure to win. These papers make your case, and, of course, kill Westbrook's counterclaim."

"There he goes now," said Carey looking out of the window.

The lawyer involuntarily turned his eyes in the same direction, and as involuntarily compared the two antagonists. On the one hand, old Colonel Westbrook, tall, straight and slim, as neat as though he had just stepped out of a bandbox, driving down Main Street in a dog-cart drawn by a high-stepping bay—a gentleman of the old school, with aristocrat written on every line of his sharp-featured, high-nosed face, with its white mustache and imperial—for a generation Colonel Westbrook had been the great man of the county, and his agricultural implement factory—his father's before him—the chief industry of Illyria. Jim Carey short, stout, almost burly, with a smooth-shaven, brick-red face, a broad hand with spatulate fingers—keen, hard blue eyes, in which flashed now and then a gleam of humor—who knew the business from the ground up, sometime a workman, then a foreman in this same factory; now the proprietor of a rival establishment which was slowly but surely, by force of superior energy and ability, driving the older concern to the wall. Perkins, like the rest of Illyria, had watched the struggle. With the calmness of assured strength, Westbrook had ignored Carey's day of small things. Latterly it had dawned upon his consciousness that his ancestral business was threatened by a dangerous rival. They were the past and the future—Westbrook the old order, Carey the new to which the old must give place, in accordance with the law of life and the spirit of this age. Physically and mentally each was the embodiment of his type—of however much he might become possessed, Carey would always remain Jim to his friends and a democrat, and however much the colonel might lose, he would never be anything but an aristocrat the most unbending.

The same thought was in Carey's mind as he watched his enemy from the window. Carey had never been envious, and was not vindictive. He was proud of his small beginnings. He had enjoyed climbing; his vigorous but not overtrained mind, which matched his sturdy body, had exulted in the struggle and gloried in the victory. He had nothing against the colonel. The colonel had always treated him well enough, in a condescending, patronizing way— not offensively patronizing, for the colonel was a model of courtesy—but with the condescension of a superior to an inferior. It had rankled, just a little, at times, that Carey's success had not perceptibly changed the colonel's attitude. If they had chanced to meet, in the encounters which were inevitable in a small town where two men were rivals in the same business, Carey had remained "Carey" and the colonel had never seemed to think it necessary to shake hands with his former foreman. Carey had felt it a little, those first years, but as his fortunes rose and Westbrook's declined by comparison, his annoyance had given place, for the most part, to an amused tolerance. Any lingering resentment he might feel now and then was mainly impersonal, and less at the lack of respect for Jim Carey than at the implied slight of the great god Success— the refusal to see the obvious, which is always an offense to direct minds. This lawsuit was in fact the outcome of this feeling. He simply wanted to wake Westbrook up and make him realize that there were two agricultural implement factories in Illyria.

"He looks as sure of winning as he is of losing," observed Perkins.

"Oh, he'll look just the same after he's lost," said Carey, "only he'll sit a little straighter and walk a little stiffer. I wouldn't have started the case if he had'nt been so darned stiff. He can't read the signs of the times—he still thinks of me as Jim the molder, or Carey the foreman. The world stopped moving for him just before I got started He had already cooled in his mold while I was being poured into mine."

"He don't realize what he's up against."

"He *would* get in the way," returned Carey, "and he'll have to abide by the consequences. It's a case where the best man wins."

"And you win," said Perkins. "There goes the judge, Carey. I guess we'd better be going over."

They went downstairs to the street. Carey's buggy was hitched in front of the door. They both got in. The horse a young, high-spirited two-year-old, started off rapidly, shied at a newspaper lying on the street, but was brought down to a level gait by Carey's firm hand on the reins.

"A fine colt, Carey, but full of ginger."

"Yes," returned Carey. "I have to keep a tight rein on him. He's only been driven a few months."

The judge was just taking his seat on the bench when Perkins and his client reached the court room, and they remained standing while the crier opened Court. Colonel Westbrook and his attorney, Sawyer, were in their places at the trial table. *Carey vs. Westbrook* was the first case called. The jury box was filled from the waiting panel.

Both sides exercised great care in the selection of the jury. Each talesman was examined as to his knowledge of the parties and of the dispute, and his relations of business or friendship with the attorneys in the case. Since the parties were the two best-known men in the county and their attorneys the most prominent of their profession, it took nearly an hour to fill the panel with men whose knowledge of men and affairs was presumably slight enough to qualify them to sit in judgment upon a weighty matter. During this process Sawyer watched Perkins and Perkins watched Sawyer, consulting now and then with Carey.

When the jury had been sworn, Perkins stated the case for the plaintiff. His client, Mr. Carey, had at one time been an employee of the Westbrook Manufacturing Company. While thus employed, as a bench hand, he had invented a certain plow. A patent for same had been taken out in the name of the company. Mr. Carey had been promoted to the position of foreman, with an agreement that if his employment with the company should ever terminate, he should receive a royalty on all plows subsequently manufactured containing his invention. He prayed judgment in the sum of fifty thousand dollars or whatever amount the proof should show.

Sawyer read the answer. It admitted the invention, but denied the contract, or the plaintiff's right to recover. Carey had invented the plow in the course of his regular employment, and had made the models in the company's time and of the company's materials. The company's right to the invention had been evidenced by its taking out the patent and manufacturing the plow for years, with the acquiescence of the plaintiff and without any demand for royalties. Defendant maintained that the appointment of Carey as foreman had been in full satisfaction of any equitable interest he may have had in the invention. This employment had terminated at Carey's own volition, with no resulting liability on the part of the defendant.

By way of counterclaim, the Westbrook Manufacturing Company sued Carey for ten thousand dollars, or whatever sum the proof should show, for royalties on plows manufactured under the same patent by Carey, in his own factory, since leaving the Westbrook employment.

Carey was the first witness. He testified to the main facts as outlined in Perkins' statement of the case, and detailed certain conversations between himself and Colonel Westbrook's brother, the general manager of the company at the time the plow was invented.

"Did you," asked Perkins, "receive any written communication, or exchange any correspondence, bearing upon the subject matter of this action?"

"I did, yes."

"Will you produce it?"

Carey drew from the inside breast pocket of his coat a brown leather pocketbook—from from which he took certain papers. They were the same papers which had rested on the table in Perkins' law office that morning, before the opening of Court.

Carey passed one of the papers to Sawyer, who looked it over and handed it back.

"Do you know the handwriting of that document?"

"Yes, sir."

"Whose is it?"

"Mr. Charles Westbrook's."

"Under what circumstances did you receive it?"

"At the time of my appointment as foreman, after a conversation with Mr. Westbrook about my future status with the company."

"You may read the paper."

Sawyer objected to the introduction of the paper, for various ingenious but specious reasons, which did not find favor with the Court—which overruled the objection, to which the defendant took an elaborate exception.

The paper, when read, seemed, unless it could be successfully refuted, to be an acknowledgment of Carey's claim to royalties when he should cease to be foreman. The other documents were of similar tenor.

Several witnesses testified that ten cents on each plow would be a reasonable royalty. Colonel Westbrook admitted that the Westbrook Manufacturing Company had made, under the patent, and sold, since Carey left the company, at least five hundred thousand plows. Carey's figures were sixty thousand, the bulk of his product having been in other articles.

By the noon adjournment the plaintiff had rested his case. The prima facie presentment had seemed irrefutable, and Carey and Perkins went to lunch serenely confident of victory. Perkins was jubilant.

"I hadn't expected any such figures," he exulted. "I supposed he'd concede about two hundred thousand, or force an accounting. He's given us the full amount of our claim—the old idiot!"

"He doesn't expect us to win," returned Carey. "He doesn't realize the situation at all. He made the figures big on purpose—it reflects more glory on the company, and he'll imagine he's won a bigger victory."

The two parties lunched at the same hotel, at opposite ends of the dining room. The colonel, Perkins observed, preserved his air of tranquil assurance, but Sawyer seemed worried. Sawyer clearly had not expected the documentary proofs.

The defense occupied the afternoon, and proved that Carey had never, until the bringing of the suit, demanded any royalties. Mr. Charles Westbrook was called. His testimony was directed to a different construction of the letters than what seemed their obvious intent as interpreted by Carey. Sawyer was alert, clever, even able, but, as Perkins observed, not less anxious. Only the colonel seemed as calmly confident as ever—he knew his cause was just, and that Carey's claim was preposterous. Why Carey had once been a workman in his factory!

The testimony was all in by four o'clock, and the argument was set for the following morning. Upon the adjournment Perkins gathered up the papers from the stenographer's desk and handed them to Carey.

"Take care of these until morning," he said. "They are worth $50,000.00 to you, and we don't want them to get lost."

When Colonel Westbrook, driving into Illyria next morning from his country place, approached the bridge over the river, which he must cross to get within the city limits, he saw Jim Carey's buggy on the bridge ahead of him. Just at that moment a tug, passing under the bridge sent out a cloud of dense black smoke which overflowed the bridge, and at the same time emitted, in quick succession, several sharp, short blasts of a weird whistle. The combination proved too much for Carey's two-year-old, and the two-year-old proved too much for Carey. The colt bolted, with the bit in his teeth, and dashed the buggy into the railing of the bridge. Carey was pitched over the railing and fell fifteen or twenty feet into the shallow water near the river's edge.

The colonel, who had instinctively increased his speed when he had seen Carey lose control of the colt, was at the end of the bridge almost by the time Carey struck the water. The depth was not over two or three feet at that point, and the colonel sat in his buggy waiting for Carey to emerge, none the worse for his ducking. But when he saw no movement on Carey's part, he sprang from the buggy down the hill with a speed and lack of dignity very foreign to his usual manner, waded unhesitatingly into the river, and dragged Carey out, unconscious. He had probably struck the bridge railing in going over, or the water had not been deep enough to break the impact of his fall. As Colonel Westbrook deposited Carey's form upon the bank, he saw Carey's brown pocketbook floating slowly down the stream, and sinking slowly as it floated. The colonel was human. He had seen Carey, the evening before, place the only material evidence in the case in that brown pocketbook. The colonel had spent a night in reflection. He was no less sure of the justice of his case than ever, and no less confident of the outcome. But if the papers yonder should never get to the jury, assurance would be rendered doubly sure; and if Carey should, after his defeat, secure a re-hearing, he would have no evidence whatever for a second trial.

But the colonel's hesitation was only momentary. He waded a little deeper into the river and rescued the pocketbook.

By this time a crowd had gathered, among them a policeman, and Carey was showing signs of recovery. The colonel handed the pocketbook to the officer.

"Take care of this," he said, "It belongs to Mr. Carey, and contains papers which he regards as valuable. I would suggest that you call a doctor at once and send for Attorney Perkins."

Whereupon the colonel climbed the hill to the street by a roundabout path which required no sacrifice of his dignity. His horse and trap were standing where he had left them, and a few minutes' drive brought him to Sawyer's office.

The accident delayed the opening of Court, and when Carey, having meanwhile exchanged his clothes for dry ones and recovered somewhat from the shock of his fall, appeared with Perkins in the courtroom, it was nearly eleven o'clock. The judge and jury, and Westbrook and Sawyer, were in their places.

"We have been waiting an hour and a half, Mr. Carey," said the judge, pleasantly, "but we are very glad we didn't have to dismiss the case for lack of a party plaintiff."

"Thank you, your Honor," returned Carey, with a twinkle in his blue Irish eyes. "It was the fault of my two-year-old. He ought to be fined for contempt of court."

Sawyer advanced to the bench and spoke to the Court in a low voice.

"Gentlemen of the jury," said the judge, "you may be at your ease for fifteen minutes."

"May I speak to you, Sawyer," said Perkins.

They stepped aside together.

"Sawyer," said Perkins, "after what happened this morning Carey doesn't want to go any further with the case. He says he couldn't collect a judgment from a man who had saved his life. He wouldn't enjoy the money. And you know, as well as I do, how the verdict will go. We never expected to get so much; and you know, even better than I do, what shape the Westbrook Company is in—they couldn't pay $50,000 and escape bankruptcy. Carey simply can't do it. It wasn't only saving his life—he'd have drowned in two feet of water if he'd been pulled out a minute later—but when Westbrook rescued that pocketbook, with the exhibits in it, Carey simply couldn't go on. Westbrook's money would be dirty money, and he don't want it. We are going to dismiss the case. Tell Westbrook."

Sawyer felt and looked distinctly relieved. He had no hope of winning the suit, and defeat would mean well-nigh ruin for his client, the Westbrook Manufacturing Company. He walked over to the colonel at the trial table.

"Carey's going to dismiss the suit."

"Why?" demanded the colonel, astonished.

"Gratitude. He doesn't want your money, after what happened this morning."

The colonel's eyes glowed with the zeal of fanaticism.

"Tell Mr. Carey, with my compliments, that I shall not permit him to dismiss the case, after I have won it. I wish my rights to rest upon a judicial determination, and not upon Mr. Carey's gratitude. He doesn't owe me anything at all for what took place this morning—I would have done what I did for any human being—and I shall not let a mere accident be made an excuse for cheating me of a verdict. I don't impugn his motive—but that would be the result. There shall be no miscarriage of justice here by my connivance."

"But we can't prevent them from dismissing the action, any time before verdict," returned Sawyer.

"We will fight it on the counterclaim—they can't dismiss that."

"They are suing for a large sum, colonel, and juries are uncertain."

The colonel looked at Sawyer coldly.

"It is a matter of principle," he said. "I hope, Sawyer that you are not weakening at the end?"

Sawyer flushed. He had made a good fight, against heavy odds. It was not his fault that he had a fool for a client. He merely wished to see the responsibility fixed where it belonged.

"Not at all," he replied. "If it is your wish, we'll fight it to a finish."

He conveyed the colonel's ultimatum to Perkins, who looked his astonishment at hearing it.

"Well, all I can say, Sawyer, is that your client is crazy. I know you wouldn't advise such a course."

"I've done my best," said Sawyer. "I guess we'll have to fight it out. If you dismiss the main case, he'll try out the counterclaim."

Sawyer turned to Carey, and stated the situation.

"Whew!" whistled Carey, softly. "What are we going to do? Can't we sort of lie down, and let ourselves be licked by default?"

"Well, you see, Carey, I've a reputation to keep up: I can't afford to lose lawsuits."

"That's right," returned Carey, musingly, "you've got a personal interest—that's why I hired you, and I can't complain."

"Besides," added Perkins, "we couldn't lose the case now if we tried. The Court will do everything but charge the jury directly to bring in a verdict in our favor. Even that jury couldn't do otherwise. They're under oath to try the case by the law and the evidence."

Carey was absorbed in thought.

"Go ahead," he said, finally. "Do your darndest."

The arguments proceeded. Perkins presented his case convincingly. Sawyer made the best he could of the weaker side.

The noon adjournment intervened between the arguments and the charge. Most of the jurymen lived in town and went home to lunch.

When court reconvened, the jury were charged strongly in favor of the plaintiff on all the issues. They retired, and in thirty minutes returned a verdict in favor of the defendant on the main case, giving him a verdict of ten thousand dollars on the counterclaim.

Perkins was furious.

"Your Honor," he sputtered, "I demand that the jury be polled."

The Clerk called the name of each juror and put to each one of them separately the question--

"Is this your verdict?"

Each one gave an affirmative answer. They were then dismissed by the Court.

Colonel Westbrook stood up and looked across the trial table. "Mr. Carey," he said, putting out his hand, "you have acted like a gentleman and a man of feeling in this matter today. I shall say nothing about the kind of advice you had in bringing the suit—the least said, I think the better. But I can't permit you, sir, to excel me in magnanimity. I shall mark the judgment on the counterclaim satisfied, and, so far as our company is concerned, you may continue to manufacture the plow, which was your invention, after all."

Carey was so overcome with surprise that he took the colonel's proffered hand mechanically and murmured something incoherent. The colonel construed it as an expression of gratitude, and moved away with his head in the air.

One of the jurymen had remained in the room, a little to one side, where he stood listening aghast at Perkins, who was raving bitterly at the stupidity of juries in general and this one in particular. The juryman beckoned to Carey, who walked over to him.

"What's the matter with Sawyer, Jim?" he asked anxiously. "Wasn't it like you wanted it?"

"You needn't have given him the ten thousand on the counterclaim," said Carey, in an aggrieved tone.

"But you said you wanted to lose the case."

"Yes, but I didn't want to pay anything. However, Billy, it's all right—mum's the word."

He told Perkins about it later—not all about it, but enough to enlighten that astute limb of the law, who would not have cared for any completer information.

"You see, Perkins," was the way he put it, with a twinkle in his eye, "the boys got the idea, somehow, that I wanted to lose the case. The foreman, Burns, used to be a bench-mate of mine, years ago. They got balled up a little on the counterclaim, but it turned out all right. The trial did one thing—the colonel gave me his hand and 'mistered' me. But the darned old aristocrat had got the better of me all along the line. I gave him fifty thousand dollars for my life, and he gave me ten thousand for nothing."

"We'll upset the verdict on a new trial," said Perkins, eagerly.

"No, we won't," returned Carey; "there'll be no new trial."

Stryker's Waterloo

Napoleon Stryker had sought fortune from his youth up. He had been carefully reared by parents of moderate means, who had put him to work in a wholesale coal dealer's office when he left high school. But the work did not suit Napoleon: it was not exciting, consisting mainly as it did in entering and footing up weights in long columns in a small book and transferring them to other long columns in a large book. Napoleon did not think his opportunities for advancement were large enough in the coal business. He therefore quit his place and took the agency for a subscription book. This not proving the mine of wealth he had anticipated, he went into the manufacture of a patent medicine, guaranteed to cure all diseases, from chilblains to spinal curvature. But this, too, proved a failure, for want of sufficient capital to advertise it. Then he devoted several years to the invention of a shifting-keyboard for the piano, by means of which all music could be played in one key, thus effecting a vast saving of the time of learners; but when he had got it perfected and patented no one seemed to want it. In fact, Napoleon Stryker had tried almost every plan for capturing fortune except the only certain way—by means of a regular business and a settled life. In the meantime he had accumulated nothing except a wife and six children, and a little household furniture. He had just begun to work up a scheme for supplying public places with automatic peanut roasters on the drop-a-nickel-in-the-slot-plan, when fortune, in disguise it is true, came knocking at his door. On the fifteenth of June, 1887, he was injured in a wreck at Silver Creek on the Riverside Railroad.

Others suffered in this accident; some were killed, and several more or less severely hurt. But it was found that Stryker had received the worst injuries. He was taken from the wreck to a hospital, where an examination showed that his skull was fractured. In addition to this he had sustained a compound comminuted fracture of the left humerus, a simple fracture of the right femur, numerous painful contusions, and a severe concussion of the spine. It was thought he could not live; but he pulled through, almost by a miracle, and in the course of three months' time was able to be wheeled about in an invalid's chair, and a little later to crawl about out-of-doors occasionally on sunny days, with the aid of a couple of crutches.

In the meantime he did not suffer for want of attention. Every advantage of the best medical attendance and the most careful nursing was provided by the railroad company. When consciousness returned to him after the wreck, almost the first thing he saw was the anxious face of the company's claim agent, bending sympathetically over him, and the first sound that fell upon his ear was the claim agent's voice giving orders to spare no skill and no expense. And two or three times a week thereafter, while Stryker was in the hospital, the genial claim agent would call and bring with him a bouquet of flowers, or some delicacy to tempt the sick man's palate.

"My dear Mr. Stryker," he would say in substance, not all at once, but from time to time, "the company wants your every need provided for. Of course we expect to make this thing right with you. But we don't want you to think of it as a mere cold, commercial transaction. Ill-natured people are fond of saying that corporations have no souls, but that you know is not true of the Riverside. The road is virtually bankrupt and hasn't paid a dividend for several years. Everybody who knows anything about it knows that the rails are worn out, the cross-ties are rotten, the engines are only fit for scrap-iron and the cars for kindling wood. But nobody can say we were ever mean in settling for injuries. I don't want to worry you about these matters now, but whenever your nerves get strong enough to talk business, you'll find us disposed to be liberal." And then the claim agent, whose name was Hall, would tell a funny story or two, and go away leaving Stryker feeling decidedly more cheerful.

But somehow or other the invalid never seemed strong enough to talk about settlement, and when Hall would delicately lead the conversation toward the subject, Stryker would say his poor head was too muddled to think about business, or his poor back too weak to stand the nervous strain of attending to it.

In the meantime he was visited by various friends, among them several enterprising young lawyers of his acquaintance, who during conversation casually mentioned the subject of damages. But Stryker did not seem to care to talk about the matter, and to any such suggestions only replied that the railroad company wanted to settle with him, and that he should probably make some kind of a deal with them.

But Napoleon Stryker had found his opportunity and intended to make the most of it. As soon as he was able to leave the hospital he called on Judge Daniel W. Badger, a lawyer of reputation for skill and experience and after a consultation or two began a suit against the Riverside Railroad Company for one hundred thousand dollars damages for personal injuries sustained in the Silver Creek collision.

The claim agent was more than disappointed at the turn affairs had taken. He viewed Stryker's conduct in the light of a personal grievance. He had counted on this settlement, had built hopes upon it. He had expected to pay a large figure, somewhere from five to ten thousand dollars, to settle this claim; but that Stryker would bring a suit in this underhand manner he had not anticipated. The settlement of the Stryker case was not merely a matter of professional pride with Hall—his personal interests were also involved. He stood well with the management of the company, but he did not think that his value had received adequate practical recognition, and he had determined, as soon as he should have settled all the Silver Creek accident cases, to ask for a substantial increase in his salary. But this movement of Stryker in suing the company had marred the continuity of his plan, and he feared that the pendency of the suit would interfere with his chances. Of course, on the usual theory of damage suits, the plaintiff had asked for much more than he could hope to get; but dividing one hundred thousand by two, or three, or four, the quotient would still be a large sum. And even a fifty-thousand-dollar verdict in such a case was not improbable, for a dangerous precedent had just recently been established in another case against another railroad in the same state, in which a verdict of forty-eight thousand dollars and costs had stood the test of all the courts and had been finally paid by the defendant company.

"It's a durned, mean, low-lived, sneaking piece of business for Stryker to sue us," said Hall to the assistant solicitor of the company in discussing the suit; and that astute official agreed with him, but suggested a further attempt at settlement.

Hall called at Stryker's house and asked to see him. Mrs. Stryker said that her husband was feeling very poorly and his back was bad and he was lying down and couldn't see anyone, and if it was anything in reference to the lawsuit he should consult Mr. Stryker's attorney, as Mr. Stryker had left the matter entirely in his hands.

"I thought I was mad before," said Hall in reporting this interview to the assistant solicitor, "but I hadn't known anything about the feeling till then. I'll get even with him yet for the time and money I've thrown away on him. I have a presentiment that in the long run we'll beat him."

The filing of a petition claiming damages is only the first step in a legal duel, merely the challenge to combat. The ordinary and unavoidable delays of the law are proverbial, but when these are enhanced to the utmost by every expedient within the knowledge of learned and experienced counsel, a lawsuit is not a matter of days or months, but of years. The case of Stryker against the Riverside Railroad Company was contested bitterly. No pleading was filed until the very last moment of the time limited by law for filing it. Demurrers, motions and amendments were interposed at every possible point. When in the course of time the railroad company had exhausted every means of delay, the case came up for trial in the Common Pleas Court. There was a preliminary skirmish of several days over the empaneling of a jury, and when the testimony was finally reached, the case was fought inch by inch, day after day, for a whole month, with a skill and pertinacity that kept the courtroom filled with spectators and made the case memorable in judicial annals.

The witnesses for the plaintiff made out a strong case in his favor. Stryker himself was in court, and his battered condition was palpable. He was accompanied by his wife and the six children dependent upon him. Numerous expert witnesses testified as to the extent of Stryker's injuries and their probable effect upon his future health and ability to earn money. The main struggle in the case was over the injury to Stryker's spine. The plaintiff's experts were unanimous in the opinion that the injury to his spine was permanent and that he would never be able to walk without artificial support or to engage in any business which would require prolonged exertion of any kind. In their opinion Stryker's nervous system was hopelessly shattered, and his vitality so undermined that he could not hope to live out more than half his days. The defense introduced testimony to the effect that injuries to the spine or to the nervous system were very deceptive; that they might seem very severe and yet be liable to take a sudden turn and improve rapidly. But though the defense was ably and ingeniously conducted, the jury, composed of twelve presumably intelligent men, brought in a verdict for the plaintiff, assessing his damages at $45,000.00.

The effect of the verdict was favorable in more ways than one, as under its inspiring influence Stryker felt much better than he had since the injury was received, and he began to hope that with the $45,000.00 once paid and within his possession his recovery would be only a matter of time.

But it is one thing to get a verdict and another thing to collect the money. The company made a motion for a new trial, which was argued to the court and overruled. The case was then taken up on error to the Circuit Court, the next tribunal in the ascending series. With the enormous mass of testimony to be transcribed by the stenographer, and other unavoidable delays, it was six months from the rendition of the verdict before the Circuit Court passed upon the case, affirming the verdict in the Common Pleas Court. This was victory number two for Mr. Stryker, and the cheerful emotions succeeding this decision made him feel very much stronger. Fortune was no longer a distant, tantalizing vision, but a substantial reality almost within his grasp.

To a man of Stryker's sanguine temperament the pleasures of anticipation were but little less than those of possession. And he had the happy faculty of inspiring others with his own views. Under the influence of the favorable aspect of his affairs he found his credit materially enhanced, and was able to surround his family with luxuries to which they had theretofore been strangers. The $45,000.00 he regarded as working capital for a great financial scheme, which he was elaborating with a renewed mental vigor corresponding to the improvement in his physical strength.

"Stryker," said his attorney, Judge Badger, to him one day, "it seems to me that you are walking a little easier than you did when the case was tried."

"Yes, I am," said Stryker, "I am feeling a great deal better and I suppose I show it."

Judge Badger looked alarmed. "This will never do, Stryker," he said. "Of course, I hope you'll recover in the course of time, but I wouldn't advise you to get well until this case is finally out of the way. The railroad people have given notice that they are going to take the case up to the Supreme Court. Of course, we'll beat 'em, but there's always a chance that we won't, and if we don't, the case will have to be tried over again."

The effect of this caution was to retard Stryker's recovery. That is to say, he really did not feel so well after this view of the case was put to him as he had felt before. What subtle connection there was between the state of his lawsuit and the condition of his spinal column is a matter for scientific explanation, but nevertheless the fact remains that he did not feel so well. He suffered no relapse, but merely remained in status quo.

Of course, the Riverside Railroad Company carried the case up to the Supreme Court, and as that body was, as it is in nearly every state, a long way behind with its docket of cases, a number of months elapsed before the case of *Stryker vs. The Riverside Railroad Company* was taken up by the Court and argued before it. In an elaborate opinion, covering forty pages of the State Reports, the Supreme Court reversed the decision of the lower courts and remanded the case for a new trial.

This defeat, coming upon the heels of a series of victories, was not only bitter, but discouraging to Stryker. The decision of the Supreme Court did not in any way affect the merits of the case, it having been based upon technical error in the trial. But it was like a storm that had blown down a carefully constructed building; the material was all there, but the patient labor of months had gone for naught. It simply meant that the fight must be made over again, with whatever advantages had been gained by experience, and whatever disadvantages might arise by reason of the lapse of time.

Of these latter there was one that was inevitable and that filled Napoleon Stryker with dismay. For in spite of the depressing effect of this setback, he could no longer deceive himself with regard to the fact that he was rapidly recovering from his injuries. As his strength returned, he felt a physical longing for the exercise essential to the comfort as well as to the health of those who are in good condition. Before the accident he had been a man of active habits, accustomed to long walks, the swinging of Indian clubs, and other forms of athletic enjoyment. The discomfort therefore, in prospect, to say nothing of the long course of deception which seemed necessary, in order to keep himself in apparently the same condition as at the former trial, was appalling to a degree. But Stryker argued that he had virtually won this case, that he was entitled to the forty-five thousand dollars, that the contumacy of the railroad company in prolonging the fight was an injustice which he was fairly entitled to meet by deception. He was quite willing, in fact would have preferred, under the circumstances, to remain an invalid, but if health *would* return, though unwelcome, he should not permit it to spoil his fortunes. After thinking the matter carefully over, he concluded that the only safe plan was to keep his own counsel, and to inform no one, not even his lawyer or the wife of his bosom, of the altered condition of his health.

The officials of the Riverside Railroad Company were of course delighted at the decision of the Supreme Court.

"We'll beat him yet," said the claim agent. "It's a long lane that has no turning, every dog has his day, and the mills of the gods grind slowly, but they grind exceeding small. I've kept my eye on Stryker, and I'm convinced that if we can stave off this second trial long enough, he'll get well. In fact, I'm dead certain he's shamming now, and, if I'm authorized, I'll make it a point to prove it."

As the result of an interview with the Chief Counsel of the company, the Claim Agent received carte blanche in the matter of ways and means, and the case of Stryker against the Riverside Railroad Company thenceforth resolved itself into a duel between Napoleon Stryker and Edgar Hall.

From this time forth Stryker found his footsteps hounded by detectives. If he happened to be picking his way laboriously along a back street or alleyway, and unconsciously straightened himself up or lifted one of his feet a little higher than usual, the sight of a man standing on a corner or in a doorway would alarm him, and his progress would become slower and the curve in his back more decided. He rented a house in the suburbs of the city, with a high board fence around the back yard; but the first time that he sallied cautiously out after supper to take a little turn in the cool of the evening, he saw a hat rising above the fence, and retreated into the house. If he took a little excursion to his father-in-law's in the country to escape for a while from the strain under which he was laboring, there was sure to be some fellow-traveler on the train who would stop at the same station and put up at the village hotel or a neighboring farmhouse. And of course his fears magnified these dangers. In every book agent who called to sell an illustrated edition of the *Household Guide* or the *Family Realm* or Cooper's novels, in every tramp, in every passing countryman, he saw a detective in disguise. And the more he felt himself beset with spies, the stronger became his longing to throw down his crutches, straighten himself up and run a mile or two.

The only place where he could find relief was in the privacy of his own chamber. There, after the rest of the household had retired to slumber, with the shades closely drawn, the light turned down low, the door locked, and the keyhole plugged up, he would pound a rubber bag, swing Indian clubs, and exercise vigorously with dumbbells. And then in the morning the stalwart athlete of the night before would creep along in the sunshine, a decrepit invalid, the mere wreck of what had once been a man. The dumbbells and Indian clubs, the rubber bag and the manual of instruction—the silent accomplices of these midnight revels—he kept carefully locked up in a closet to which no one else had access. When Mrs. Stryker tearfully protested that she was excluded from his confidence, he told her some unsatisfactory story, with the result that domestic unhappiness was added to his other troubles.

But there soon developed a new source for alarm. The exercise thus surreptitiously indulged in by Stryker began to manifest itself in the glow of returning health and the filling out of his relaxed muscles. He tried cosmetics to disguise this, but every curious glance he encountered alarmed him. He sought for a while to counteract these symptoms by eating chalk and drinking vinegar, but without avail. He tried dieting himself, but the results were not satisfactory. Finally he had to give up his nocturnal exercise, and with inaction and starvation combined he was able to get down to the time of the second trial without, as he imagined, a living soul being aware of any material change in his physical condition.

But Stryker was reckoning without his Hall. In the meantime it must be admitted that Hall had not been able to get any tangible proof that Stryker had improved in health. Nevertheless, he was as firmly convinced as ever that Stryker was shamming. As the time for the trial approached, Hall began to fear that the company would have to fight the case with no better weapons than before, when an idea struck him. Rome was once saved by a goose, Scotland by a thistle, and an object of but little more importance in the economy of nature and the conduct of human affairs, was made the instrument of Napoleon Stryker's downfall.

When an idea struck Edgar Hall it was very soon transmuted into a fact. Hall lived in Vestibula, a small town on the Riverside Railroad, some miles away from the city. He made the city his headquarters, but spent Sundays and holidays at home. When he next went to Vestibula he carried with him a dog. This dog had been carefully selected—for his breed, his intelligence, his knowledge of various tricks, and his great docility. He also purchased and had sent to him at Vestibula, by express, a pair of crutches. With the aid of his son, a bright lad of about sixteen, for four weeks prior to the date set for the second trial of the Stryker case, he put the dog through a careful course of training. A day or two before the trial Hall and his son went up to town and had several consultations with half a dozen trustworthy men who were detailed by the railroad company to assist him. The evening before the trial Hall and his men took a walk in the neighborhood of the Court House, and carefully noted the surroundings.

When the Stryker case was called there were only a few people in the courtroom, but the news that the famous struggle was about to be renewed soon drew a large crowd. Stryker was on hand, with pale face and drawn features, moving painfully along on his crutches, and accompanied as before by his wife and children. His attorney placed a chair for him. Mrs. Stryker produced a cushion and carefully adjusted it to rest his back. A bottle of smelling salts was placed at his elbow. The windows were carefully looked after, to prevent drafts, and a physician took a seat near Stryker, in case the excitement should prove too much for the invalid. The railroad attorneys were on hand in full force. The trial table was heaped with books and papers, and it was apparent that a desperate struggle was at hand.

The morning was devoted to securing a jury, and in the afternoon Judge Badger made the opening statement. He drew a picture of Stryker before the accident, a stalwart, handsome man, firm of step, keen of intellect, filled with high hopes, and engaged in important transactions, on the road to fortune and to fame. He referred in terms of glowing panegyric to Stryker as a husband, affectionate, tender and faithful; as a father, guiding his children with firm hand among the perilous pitfalls of life. Then in moving language he referred to the accident, the criminal carelessness of the railroad company, the pain and suffering, the long tedium of convalescence.

"We expect to prove," he said, "by the testimony of the most expert physicians in this community, that my client's injuries are of such a nature that he can never walk erect again. By the gross and criminal carelessness of this grasping and merciless corporation, he is henceforth compelled to creep along the earth like a worm in the dust. We expect to prove that mentally he is not what he once was; that the intellectual vitality that once impelled him forward to grand enterprises has departed, and he is left what you see here, a physical and nervous wreck, floating down the stream of life to the sea of oblivion. Gentlemen, we shall ask a verdict at your hands which will in some degree compensate my client for his ruined life, which will make up to his wife and children—to this widow and these orphans, I might say—for some part of what they have lost, and which will force this soulless monopoly to understand that it cannot trifle with the lives of the public by whose sufferance alone it exists."

At the close of Judge Badger's statement Court adjourned until ten o'clock the next morning, at which time the defendant was to make a statement in reply.

On the eighteenth of June, 1890, the seventy-fifth anniversary of the battle of Waterloo, at half past nine o'clock in the morning, Napoleon Stryker, accompanied by his attorney, Judge Badger, approached the Court House. To reach it from the lawyer's office they had to pass through a narrow street, a few rods in length, flanked on one side by a brick building with no openings near the ground, and on the other side by a high iron fence surrounding the county jail. This street, known as Equity Lane, ran past the Court House and into the Public Square, at the corner of which the Court House stood. When Stryker and Judge Badger turned into Equity Lane there were perhaps as many as a dozen men walking along at different points in the street, and a small group standing by the iron fence and looking through it into the window of the county jail. Stryker was absorbed in earnest conversation with his attorney, and making painfully slow progress as he crept along. For very possibly there were jurors in the groups of men around the Court House door and others whom they might meet.

They had gone about half the length of the street when they heard a startled cry behind them, which was taken up immediately by a number of frightened voices:

"Mad dog! Mad dog! Run for your lives!"

Stryker and his companion turned and saw coming directly toward them, a few yards distant, a big black dog, with blood-shot eyes, foaming at the mouth and barking viciously. People in front of them were running, people behind them were running. One man who had apparently been bitten was lying on the ground, surrounded by sympathizing friends. Judge Badger dropped his law books and ran.

As it happened, the fear of being bitten by a mad dog was something which had weighed like a nightmare on Stryker's mind since his childhood. When a small boy he had once been attacked by a ferocious bulldog, and something of the terror he then felt had always remained with him. He dropped his crutches and ran and ran and ran, in an agony of fear, past the Court House, past half a dozen witnesses stationed along his path by the Claim Agent, past half a dozen doctors subpoenaed as experts in the case, past the trial judge, who at that moment was approaching the Court House, and whom he almost ran over, and finally took refuge in the branches of a tree, to which he climbed with surprising agility, and where he remained in mortal fright until the dog had been secured.

The second trial of *Stryker vs. the Railroad Company* was never finished. When it was called at ten o'clock, counsel for the plaintiff asked for an adjournment of a few hours, which was granted by the court. Before the time had expired the case was settled for five thousand dollars, and Stryker signed a release in full of all claims against the company. His attorney took half of this for fees and a part of the remainder for money loaned his client. With the pittance that was left Stryker resumed the quest of fortune. He is now engaged in promoting the organization of a secret mutual benefit assessment society, for a per capita commission on the members he secures.

Hall's great feat became famous in railroad circles, and the company made an unsolicited advance in his salary of more than he had meant to ask for.

Walter Knox's Record

The high school commencement exercises had taken place before the usual admiring audience of parents, friends and schoolmates. The valedictorian, Walter Knox, had made the hit of the evening with his address on "Our Duty as Citizens." The class prophet, in forecasting Walter's future, had made the pleasing prediction that he would sometime occupy a high place in the ranks of our lawmakers. Walter had been, during his senior year, president of the high school debating society, and was noted among his classmates for his knowledge of public affairs, of which, indeed, he had an unusual grasp for a boy of eighteen.

"Now, Walter," said his uncle the following morning, at the breakfast table, "what do you wish to do with yourself? I should like above all things to send you to college, for you are my only sister's child, and I love you as though you were my own; but you know that I cannot afford it."

"I know quite well, uncle, that you have already done for me more than you could really afford, and I shall never be able to thank you enough. I am willing and anxious to go to work."

"It is perhaps more important just now," continued Mr. Terry, "that you do *something* and do it well, than that you do any particular thing. Nevertheless, it would be just as well to find some employment that you like, so that the knowledge you acquire may lay the foundation for a future career. Have you any pronounced inclination? Is there any work which you would prefer to work of any other kind?"

"I should like, sir," replied Walter hesitatingly, "to go into public life. Of course, I don't mean," he continued, blushing slightly as he detected a somewhat quizzical smile on his uncle's face, "of course I don't mean that I want to run for office, for I'm not of age. But I should like to get into some one of the city or county departments, where I can learn the routine work of public administration, so that I may be prepared to perform properly the duties of a citizen, and to serve the public intelligently when I am old enough to ask for their suffrages."

"And would you look forward to public life as a profession?" asked his uncle—a broad-minded man, who respected the ideals of youth, while measuring them by the standards of experience.

"Yes, sir," replied Walter. "I think there is no greater career than to be a leader of men, and no higher cause than the promotion of good government."

"I quite agree with you, Walter. You might add, also, that there is no more difficult task, no work in which more men fail, or fall short of success, and none in which the hope and the realization lie so far apart. But it is nevertheless a work which should be courageously attempted, and never given up; and the ambition to participate in it is a worthy as well as a daring one. In your case, too, it suggests the field in which I can perhaps most easily secure employment for you. I will see what I can do."

"My dear Walter," said Mr. Terry the following day, "I have found a place for you. It may not lead to the White House, but it will give you some clerical experience and knowledge of municipal affairs, and will pay you a very handsome salary for a person of your age."

"Thank you, uncle. I am much obliged to you, as I am for all that you have done for me. What is the place?"

"A clerkship in the Public Works Department of the city. The Director is under some little obligation to me, and is willing to repay it in that way. You will start in at fifty dollars a month, with a chance of promotion. I think you will be able to fill the place."

"I'll do my best, sir," responded Walter, gratefully.

The first of the following week found Walter at a desk in the accounting office of the Public Works Department of the large western city where he lived. For several days his work was not well defined, but by the end of the week certain specific duties had been assigned to him. They were not onerous, nor did they seem to involve any considerable responsibility, and Walter really felt slightly disappointed that he was not to have a larger share in the government of the municipality. The work at his desk formed one simple link in the chain of accounting. By the system in use, when an order for supplies for the department was given out to a contractor, a duplicate of the order was filed in the office, and pasted in a large book, which was placed in Walter's custody during the daytime, and locked in the vault at night. When bills for supplies furnished came in, it was Walter's duty to compare and check the bills with the duplicate orders, and certify to the correspondence of the quantities and amounts.

Walter found that his position brought with it the opportunity to make some very agreeable acquaintances. There was only one other clerk in the room where he sat, a very quiet fellow of about thirty, by the name of Smith, who was amiable enough, but inclined to be taciturn. Mr. Street, of the firm of

Howe & Street, which filled large orders for iron for the department, was very cordial to Walter. Mr. Street came into the office often to collect bills, and proved to be a very pleasant fellow. One day he gave Walter a couple of theater tickets, which he himself was unable to use because of an unforeseen business engagement. Walter's desk was partly furnished with handsome paperweights, erasers, and similar articles, presented with the compliments of Howe & Street. Walter could have smoked all the time at Street's expense, if he had used tobacco; and when Street one day invited Walter to dine with him at a popular hotel restaurant, Walter felt very much elated at having won the friendship of a business man so much older than himself.

The dinner was an elaborate one, and of a kind to which Walter was not accustomed. Seated before a snowy cloth glittering with silver and cut glass, eating to the sound of soft music, fawned upon by obsequious waiters, his tastes consulted and deferred to, Walter felt as never before the power of money to acquire the comforts and luxuries of life.

"My dear boy," said his host when the meal was well under way, "what will you have to drink?"

"Thank you," replied Walter, "I never take anything."

"Oh, pshaw!" exclaimed Street, "a glass of sherry will warm your heart and give you new and broader views of life. Nothing is more despicable than a drunkard; but we men of the world know when to drink and when to abstain. A glass of good wine at mealtime makes one feel like a new man. Here's to your success in life!"

Walter drank the toast, and soon felt an unaccustomed glow stealing over him. Street filled his glass again, in spite of a faint protest, and before they left the table Walter had emptied it.

"And now," said Street, "let's go out and have a little fun. Have you ever been up to Jerry Black's?"

"No," answered Walter. "I've been at work so short a time that I haven't really had the time to get well acquainted down town."

"Now is your chance, then" rejoined his mentor, "to see a phase of life to know which is part of a liberal education. Of course no gentleman will form the habit of visiting such places, but a man of the world, especially a man in public life, should know something of everything. No one can make a successful politician unless he is familiar with the weaknesses of mankind, for it is by these that they are most easily managed."

To a mind in the exhilarated and slightly confused state of Walter's, this advice seemed the flower of wisdom. A few minutes walk, ending with a climb up two flights of stairs, saw them in a gilded gambling den, within a stone's throw of the city hall. A number of men were gathered round a table, watching the progress of the game with intense excitement.

"Notice that little fellow put his money on the red," whispered Street to Walter, "and see what happens. There, he has quadrupled his stake! I'm going to try my luck, just for fun."

He laid a dollar on the board, and took away five. Another bet resulted favorably.

"Try a chance," he said to Walter, "it's once in a lifetime. You'll find it a novel sensation."

Walter bet a dollar and lost.

"Try again," urged Street. "Better luck next time. If you never risk, you'll never win."

"I haven't the money," stammered Walter, with a blush.

"I'll lend you ten," replied Street. "Whatever is mine belongs to my friends."

When Walter, somewhat sobered by his losses, left Jerry Black's he owed Street one hundred dollars. With the reaction from the excitement of the gambling room, he realized something of what this meant.

"Mr. Street," he said, "I don't know when I'll ever be able to pay that back."

"Don't worry about that," replied Street. "Pay it out of your next winnings."

"I shall play no more," rejoined Walter stoutly.

"Then just don't think about it at all," said Street. "What is money between friends? Pay it at your leisure—a year hence, or two. I could live comfortably if you never paid it."

Street did not appear at the office again for a week. In the meantime Walter's first month's salary had been paid. His uncle and aunt, who had reared him, were people of moderate means, and Walter had offered to pay for his board while he should be working. He needed some clothes, too, so that it was difficult to see how he could spare more than five dollars to apply on his debt to Street, which weighed upon Walter's mind. When he next saw Street, Walter tendered him the five-dollar note.

"My dear boy," said Street genially, pushing the note back, "don't let that little bill trouble you. You'll be getting a 'raise' in salary before long, and then we talk business. How do you like my new suit?"

"It's very handsome," replied Walter, looking ruefully at his own somewhat shabby clothes; "I wish I had one like it."

"There's nothing easier," replied Street promptly. "They were made by Turner, just round the corner—he's made my clothes for years. Very reasonable, too; this suit cost only twenty-five dollars—dirt cheap, when one considers how long Turner waits for his money."

"How long does he wait?" asked Walter with interest. He really needed a new suit of clothes.

"No gentleman pays his tailor under three to six months. They don't expect it. It would demoralize the business to pay them too promptly. I shall probably not pay for this suit before Christmas. I'll take you round and introduce you to old Turner. You may want to do business with him sometime."

Walter accepted the offer. Turner was cordial, and invited Walter to come in and look over his summer suitings, of which he had a fine line. Mr. Knox might have whatever he wanted, and take his own time about paying.

"It's very tempting," said Walter as they left the tailor's, "if one doesn't mind being in debt."

"My dear boy," replied Street, " 'debt' is the same thing as 'credit,' viewed from the opposite standpoint. Commerce is based on credit. The city is ten million dollars in debt. Every commercial house does much of its business on borrowed capital. Half the sales of our firm are on the books from thirty to ninety days. No man can ever get a start in life, or make any money worth speaking of, without going into debt."

This was comfortable doctrine. Next day Walter stepped into Turner's and left his measure for a new suit and a light overcoat. This brought his debts up to the amount of a hundred and fifty dollars; but Street's account was not pressing, and he could easily pay the tailor in three or four months. When his new suit was sent home he found several other things needed in order to make the rest of his dress in keeping with it, so that by the end of the month he was in debt twenty-five dollars more.

About a week after the next payday Street presented a bill to Walter for approval. Strictly speaking, the bill should have come from the receiving clerk, whose desk was in another room, and who stamped the bills with the date of receipt and sent them to Walter by a messenger. Street, however, was on familiar terms with the office force, and often took the bills himself from one clerk to the other.

"That's all right, Walt," he said carelessly, throwing the bill on Walter's desk. "Just stick your O. K. on it. I want to get it up to the auditor before the office closes."

Walter was about to follow this very unbusinesslike suggestion, when he noticed the amount of the bill. He had an excellent memory for figures, and it struck him that he had filed no duplicate of an order on Howe & Street for just that amount. This called to mind another fact which he had discovered in the course of his work.

"Just a moment, Mr. Street," he replied, taking down the book in which the orders were pasted, "and I'll make certain that it checks."

Walter was immersed in the order book, and therefore did not observe that for a moment Street's face wore a very black look. It took but a moment to find the order. "It seems to be but one hundred and twenty-five dollars in the order, Mr. Street," he said.

"There is a mistake then," replied Street, positively. "Your duplicate is wrong. The original order was for two hundred and twenty-five, and you see that the amount is checked by the engineer of the waterworks, who received the goods. You had better change the figure on the order."

"I'm afraid I couldn't do that," replied Walter, with some natural reluctance to disoblige a friend, "without looking the matter up."

"I think you had better change the figure to correspond with this, and then O. K. the bill," said Street, showing signs of irritation.

Walter was silent. He was under obligations to Street, who might be entirely right about the matter; he knew, too, that even if he were not, the discrepancy would in all probability never be discovered. But he felt instinctively that he ought not to approve the bill.

"However," said Street, observing his reluctance, "I'll let the bill go over for today. On second thoughts, I can get along without the money for a while. I'll look the matter up, so you needn't trouble yourself about it until I present the bill again."

"Very well," said Walter, much relieved. "I've no doubt it's all right."

If Walter had been less fundamentally honest, he would probably have approved with but little hesitation the bill presented by Street, and would have corrected the duplicate order to correspond. Not only was it likely that Street was correct, but Walter had long ago discovered that the system of bookkeeping in use in the department was so loosely constructed that by the collusion of one or two employees in the department it would be possible to manipulate bills against the city in any manner desired, within reasonable limits, with hardly a chance of discovery. A mistake was just as likely to pass unnoticed. He had once said something of the sort to Smith, who had remarked that it was no business of clerks to run the department, and that critics were apt to prove unpopular. This had thrown cold water on Walter's half-formed purpose of mentioning his views upon the matter to one of his superior officers.

Street did not make his appearance at the office for several days. He came in one morning, and after some conversation with Smith, whose desk was at the other end of the room, stopped a moment at Walter's desk.

"By the way, Knox," he said carelessly, "I've got a little personal bill to meet in a day or two, and I'm rather short of funds. I suppose you could help me out a little on that hundred you owe me?"

Walter felt decidedly embarrassed. "I—I'm sorry, Mr. Street, but I can't do anything before the end of the month. I—I understood that there was no hurry about it."

"Oh, n—o," responded the other, somewhat discontentedly, and looking Walter straight in the eye, "of course one doesn't like to hurry one's *friends;* but when a fellow has to pay his own debts, he naturally thinks of what's coming to him. We'll let it stand a day or two."

This interview disturbed Walter considerably. His equanimity was further shaken by the receipt, the following day, of a duplicate bill from his tailor, suggesting that as quarterly accounts would soon fall due, a check for the amount would be very acceptable. To add still further to his troubles, he received, the same day, by a messenger, a note from the Director of the Department of Public Works, requiring him to go to the Director's private office. He could think of no good reason why the Director should wish to see him, and it was with the most dismal forebodings that he followed the messenger upstairs, to the Director's private office. He was shown a seat, and waited about fifteen minutes, until the Director looked up from his desk and deigned to notice Walter's presence.

"Your name is Knox?"

"Yes, sir."

"Mr. Knox, complaint has been made that you have been discourteous to persons transacting business with the department. Don't let it occur again."

"There must be some mistake, or some misapprehension, sir," replied Walter, with a strong feeling of indignation at so unjust a charge. "May I ask what I am charged with, and by whom?"

"It is against the policy of the department to give such information. You may not have intended any discourtesy; but clerks in public office should conduct themselves so that there can be no misapprehension as to their manners. Those who wish to succeed in public life should make friends, and not enemies. You have not been in the service very long. Here is a copy," he added, handing Walter a small pamphlet, "of some rules for employees, which it will pay you to study. That is all."

Walter left the Director's office in some tumult of feeling, which was not allayed when he glanced over the book of printed rules. One of them warned employees against running into debt beyond their means of payment, under penalty of dismissal. Another forbade employees from frequenting gambling houses, under a similar penalty.

The injustice of the charge made against him rankled in Walter's breast to such an extent that he must speak about it to someone; so he made a confidant of Smith, to whom he related his interview with the Director, intimating at the same time that he suspected Street of having made the complaint, and stating his reasons for the suspicion.

"You'd better be careful," said Smith. "Street was one of the Director's chief backers for his own appointment, and has the strongest 'pull' of any contractor in the city. I'd give him the benefit of the doubt every time. I would advise you to keep on the good side of Street."

Smith's suggestion that the Director of Public Works was under obligations to Street was well founded. Indeed these obligations had proved so burdensome that the Director would willingly have rid himself of them. When he learned, through Smith, who was a personal friend of his, that Walter suspected Street of having complained against him because he had refused to approve an incorrect bill, the Director sent for Walter a second time.

"Mr. Knox," he said, "information has come to my ears which makes me think that perhaps I was misled with regard to the subject of our conversation the other day. I have decided, upon second thoughts, that you ought to know who made the charge. It was Mr. Street, of Howe & Street, who claimed that you had treated him discourteously with regard to a certain bill. I should like to know all the circumstances of the case."

Walter stated the facts as they had occurred. "I have no doubt, sir, that it was a mistake, but I felt it my duty to be sure."

The Director had listened musingly. He was sincerely tired of Street, who had demanded more favors of the department than his support had really been worth. He was not at all sure that there had been a mistake in the bill, but suspected the contrary. If he could disable Street through Walter, he would by the same stroke disembarrass himself of a troublesome friend, and render Street harmless to injure him in the future.

"Mr. Knox," he said to Walter, "your conduct has been entirely proper, and deserves commendation instead of blame. I take pleasure in making the acknowledgment. This information puts me in a position to offer you a rare opportunity—that of rendering the city an important public service. From this and other things that have come to my knowledge, I am inclined to believe that there is a conspiracy on foot to defraud the city, by tampering with the honesty of certain employees. You having proved incorruptible, it is deemed necessary to bring about your discharge by complaints of your conduct. This plot against the city can be frustrated and the tables turned upon the conspirators in a very simple manner."

"How, sir?" asked Walter eagerly. He felt proud to have won the commendation of his superior; he was not without a natural feeling of resentment at the attempt to make use of him as a catspaw; and he had always wished that he might render some distinguished public service, for which the dull routine of his daily work had thus far seemed to offer no opportunity.

"We must fight fire with fire, Mr. Knox, and meet fraud with dissimulation. Men like Street are public enemies; but they are too astute to be fought in the open—it is necessary to trap them like rats or wild beasts. Once unmasked, their power for evil is at an end. They can be reached in only one way—by encouraging them to commit some overt act, and then letting them face the consequences.

"For instance," he continued, "when you next see Street, treat him cordially. Suggest that you are ready to approve his bill. Follow the same course for a month or two; carefully note the discrepancies on a private memorandum, keep a still tongue in your head, and Street will be thwarted in his criminal design, and other dishonest persons warned against similar attempts. You will not only have the reward of a good conscience, but will also have become entitled to promotion."

The scheme thus outlined seemed at the moment a very alluring one. By it, Walter could keep Street in a good humor for some time to come; when the disclosure came, Street's power for injury through the debt due him would be more than offset by his service to the city; and the advance in salary that he might expect would soon enable him to pay all that he owed.

Walter had been carefully grounded, however, in correct principles, and possessed a very clear intelligence for so young a man. His second thoughts upon the Director's proposition were by no means so comfortable. Street had as yet committed no crime. Walter had been asked to do something without which no crime was possible—to perform one act in a series of acts which would constitute a crime, in order that a comtemplated offense might become a real one. Should one do evil that good might come? He saw, too, that to approve the bills as suggested would place him in a false position, from which even the Director's word might not be able to release him. It seemed to Walter that it would be much better to watch the public treasury and keep thieves out, than to admit them in order that they might be caught. The longer he studied the situation the less he liked it, and he finally made a desperate resolve. He wrote the Director a note, stating that he could not perform the service required. The reply, as he expected, was a long yellow envelope, containing his discharge from the Public Works Department.

Walter made a clean breast to his uncle, who heard him patiently to the end.

"Your record is not perfect, Walter," said Mr. Terry gravely. "You have acted very weakly and wickedly in permitting yourself to be led into ways which you surely knew were dangerous, and in getting so deeply into debt. I am glad to see, however, that when you were put to the sterner test of principles, you were wise enough to see the right and strong enough to do it. I will advance the money to pay your debt to Street, and will at the same time give him a piece of my mind. You have gained some costly experience of public life, which may be of value to you when you grow older. For the present I think you had better find some employment where your youth and inexperience will not tempt others to corrupt your character."

Some of this was bitter medicine, but Walter knew that he had deserved it. He spent the next year of his life as clerk in a grocery store. By strict economy he paid his debts, including the hundred dollars paid by his uncle to Street. When he read in the newspapers, a few weeks after his dismissal, that a new and safer system of accounts had been introduced into the Public Works Department, he was comforted by the thought that in all probability he *had* accomplished some good during his brief experience in the office; and while undergoing the penance of the grocery store, he did not relinquish the hope that at some future time he might find a worthy career in public life.

The Averted Strike

Mr. Philetus Strong sat in his private office, at the Strongville Rubber Works, about ten o'clock in the morning, looking over the mail that had been delivered a few minutes before. Some of the letters were pleasant reading—those enclosing checks, for instance—and especially one containing a very larger order for an expensive grade of goods. One letter he tossed aside with a gesture of impatience. It was a notice from the municipal authorities requiring him to equip the main building of the factory with fire escapes of a prescribed design. Mr. Strong's first impulse was to ignore the notice, or to refer it to his lawyers.

"It's an imposition," he muttered, "an outrage. Fire escapes are not needed on the mill. It is of slow-burning construction, and our own apparatus will put out any fire in five minutes. It will be money thrown away. But it's the law," he decided, "and I suppose must be obeyed. It's cheaper to put them up than to fight the city."

Having reached this conclusion Mr. Strong opened the next letter. It was from the general foreman, or superintendent, of the factory, a naturalized Englishman named Armitage, announcing his resignation of the position. Armitage had been foreman of the factory for ten years, and had filled the place admirably; but a brother in England had died recently, and left him a small estate, and he wished to go to the old home to settle up the property, which would be sufficient, he said, to place him thereafter above the necessity for hard work.

Armitage had been away for a week on leave of absence, to consult a lawyer in an Eastern city. His place had been taken temporarily by one of the most experienced and capable workmen, a man by the name of Walker, the only colored man employed in the factory. As Mr. Strong had not expected to lose Armitage's services, the question of securing permanently another foreman had not until now presented itself.

So important a matter required careful consideration. Should he promote a man from the ranks of his own workmen, or would the ends of discipline be better subserved by employing an outsider? While Walker was a good work-

man, and an intelligent, steady fellow, did he possess the firmness, the judgment, the readiness of decision necessary in a man to be trusted with responsibilities so considerable, and would a colored man command the respect of several hundred white operatives to the extent necessary to maintain discipline
among them?

While Mr. Strong was weighing this matter he became aware of a rustle
of silken skirts, an odor of violets, and, as he looked up, of a couple of young
ladies who had entered the office without ceremony.

"Papa," said one of them, a tall, stylishly dressed girl with blue eyes and
fair hair, "I'm going to take Mabel through the factory and show her everything, and then we'll go up in the tower and look out at the view. Of course,
I had to show Mabel first the center of the web—the office."

"Ah, I see," said Mr. Strong, as he shook hands with his daughter's
friend, "where the old spider sits and sucks the life-blood of his victims. Thank
you. But I'm afraid you two will interfere with the business," he added. "The
operatives will stop to look at you for at least five minutes each. Two hundred
times five minutes equals one thousand minutes. At sixty minutes to an hour
that makes upwards of sixteen hours, which at eight hours a day amounts to
more than two days' time your visit will cost me."

Alice bent over and kissed him. "That makes the loss good," she said,
"and now we won't disturb you any longer."

"Shall I send a man with you?" asked her father.

"Oh, no, papa," said Alice, "it isn't at all necessary. I know the way
perfectly."

Mr. Strong had scarcely resumed his train of thought, when a party of
five or six men filed into the office. Mr. Strong looked up and saw they were
operatives from the mill.

"Well, men," he asked, "what's the trouble? It must be something serious
that would bring you from your work at this hour."

"One of the belts broke, sir, and while it was being repaired we thought
we would come and speak to you. We are a committee of the workmen, sir,
and we want to ask a question and perhaps make a suggestion."

Mr. Strong had been in business many years and had long ago learned
that it was good business policy to treat his workmen courteously and fairly,
and to consider suggestions they might make from to time. If he did not always
grant their wishes, he at least did not ignore them. As a consequence he seldom
had any trouble with his workmen, and agitators who tried to stir up discontent
among them met with but slight encouragement.

"All right, Ludlow," said Mr. Strong, addressing the spokesman of the
party, "go ahead."

"Well, sir," replied Ludlow, "the question is whether you are going to
appoint Walker foreman."

"Suppose I were going to do so—and I have been thinking of it—what then?"

"Then we should want to suggest," rejoined Ludlow, "that you don't do it."

"Humph!" said Mr. Strong, "and what objection have you to Walker?"

"Well, sir, we're not used to working under niggers—perhaps I should say colored men—and we don't like it, and don't want to keep it up. We didn't mind it so much for a week. But we've learned that Armitage is not coming back and we thought that we'd let you know our way of thinking, in case you might have any notion of giving Walker the job permanently."

"You've worked with Walker for several years," said Mr. Strong, "and no one has objected to him. He's the same color now that he has been all along."

"Yes, sir," rejoined the spokesman, "and we haven't objected to working *with* him; what we don't want is to work under him."

Mr. Strong did not reply for a moment. Meanwhile the men sat silently waiting.

"Have you seriously thought over what you are asking me to do?" Mr. Strong said, when he broke the silence. "Here you ask me to rob of well-earned promotion an experienced and competent workman in whom I may have found the very qualities that I need in a foreman. You are not only unjust to him, but you are doing me an injury. And you ask this for what reason? Simply because God has planted under Walker's skin the color you get on the outside of yours by the day's work. You talk of the rights of labor, and yet you come and ask me to deprive an industrious and faithful man of the highest right of labor—the right to an opportunity to do the best he is capable of, and to obtain the proper reward for it."

"Well, sir," replied Ludlow, somewhat shamefacedly, but not yielding the point, "we think you put it rather strongly. We don't object to his earning a living, or to his working with us. But we don't like the idea of having him over us. Put yourself in our place. You're a white man yourself. You've fought in the army. How would you have liked to have a black officer over you?"

"Whenever our government gives one of them an opportunity to demonstrate that he is a better soldier and more capable leader than I, then I will face the question. But this man has had his chance and proved his quality. I am willing to say that before you came in I doubted the expediency of appointing Walker foreman, although I had thought about it. But since you men, who ought to know what makes a good foreman, come in and frankly ask me to keep him back solely on account of his race, I feel even more strongly inclined to believe that I ought to appoint him. I'll take the matter under consideration. Perhaps he might not care to be foreman in a mill where the workmen were unfriendly to him. I'll only say now that I'll think about it."

"We hope you'll think our way, sir. There's a lot of us, and we've got our minds pretty well made up."

"Is that a threat?" asked Mr. Strong, sharply.

"Well, no, sir, not exactly. We haven't been authorized to make any threats, but merely to make a request and report your answer."

Mr. Strong was tempted for a moment to use harsh language. He resented the interference in the first place—the factory was not yet a union factory—and in the second place he revolted at the narrow prejudice displayed by the workmen.

Strongville was not in New England, but in the southern part of a state of the Middle West, and not far from the old line that in former years had separated free labor from labor enslaved; and while himself New England bred, Mr. Strong knew that old social customs and habits of thought are not easily changed, and that old prejudices need but a breath to revive them. He did not wish to precipitate a strike, in view of the large order he had received in the morning's mail. He did not wish to yield the point too easily, nor, if possible to avoid it without disaster, did he wish to yield it at all.

"I'll consider your proposition," he repeated, as the men rose to go, "and do what I think right, and best for all concerned."

"We hope, sir," said Ludlow, "that you'll decide this week. The Labor Day parade takes place next week, and our foreman is always appointed as one of the marshals. We don't want to change the rule, and we don't want to give you any trouble."

"You're giving me more than you think," replied Mr. Strong. "But as I say, I'll think the matter over."

Ludlow and his companions filed out, and left their employer seriously annoyed. He was entirely familiar with labor conditions and it had been his settled policy to consult the interests, and where possible, the wishes of his employees. But there was a higher principle involved in this question, which Mr. Strong could not ignore, the very principle, indeed, which had governed his dealings with his workmen. For he had been taught from his youth up to love justice and to try to do it. His father had been a pronounced abolitionist at a period when to help the oppressed was both a glory and a shame. He recalled how he had fed runaway Negroes in his father's attic, and how when a lad he had thrilled beneath the passionate eloquence of anti-slavery orators pleading the cause of the slave.

For a man of these antecedents, a fair-minded, just, and withal somewhat obstinate man, to treat an employee unjustly because of his color, was not a thing to be done off-hand. And yet the emergency was a serious one. In the event of a strike his business would be seriously embarrassed, for the workmen were skilled laborers, and the industry was one in which the supply of labor was not in excess of the demand. He could not fill the order just received if his working force should be disorganized by a strike, and unless he filled it he would probably lose what promised to become his best business connection. Mr. Strong realized with a sigh (and not for the first time) that wealth and position carried with them serious responsibilities; and that he had before him the somewhat difficult task of harmonizing his principles with the requirements of business.

Mr. Strong was occupied in the office until the whistle blew that marked the hour of noon. The operatives filed out of the mill and scattered, most of them, to their homes in the neighborhood for their midday meal, leaving in the mill only a few who had brought their lunches with them. Mr. Strong looked up at the clock, and was pulling down the top of his desk to go home for luncheon when a confused noise of voices in the yard caught his attention. As he rose from his chair a workman rushed into the office.

"Mr. Strong," he exclaimed excitedly, "the mill's on fire."

"Has the water been turned on from the tank?"

"No, the fire caught in the tower and we can't get to the levers."

The mill was equipped with a system of pipes extending along the ceilings of the various rooms, and connecting with a tank on the roof, from which by a system of levers the water could be turned on at any point desired, or over the whole of the factory at once. Unfortunately the location of the fire rendered the mechanism for working the apparatus unavailable. Besides this arrangement there were fire extinguishers and buckets about the mill with which an incipient fire could have been easily extinguished. But the fact that the mill was practically deserted at noon had given the flames an opportunity to gain some headway before any steps could be taken to fight them.

It was the work of a moment for Mr. Strong to turn in the city fire alarm from his office and place himself at the scene of the fire. The mill building which stood a few rods distant from the office was of brick, and the main portion of it of slow-burning construction. The tower, however, in which the fire had started, formed a sort of offset to the main building, and was less solidly built, and the rooms on the several floors were used largely for packing goods. There were quantities of pine boxes, filled and empty, and paper wrappers and packing material of various kinds, so that when the fire got under way it found plenty of inflammable material to feed upon. The fire engines, because, it was learned afterwards, of a fire elsewhere, were slow to respond to the call, and the fire had made considerable progress by the time the operatives, disturbed at their dinners, came flocking back to the mill.

Mr. Strong had scarcely begun to give directions about getting as much machinery, goods and material as possible out of the burning building, when he heard a shriek, and turning his eyes upward, simultaneously with two hundred other pairs of eyes, saw a sight that froze his blood. Standing on the edge of the tower, which had a flat roof above which the side walls projected upward for about eighteen inches, stood his daughter, and by her side her companion to whom he had spoken an hour and a half before. As he learned afterwards, they had been on the topmost floor of the tower, which was six stories high, when the ascending smoke warned them of the fire below. They had tried to descend the stairs, and had only just found their way through a trap door to the roof. Mr. Strong had supposed them gone an hour before.

"My God!" he exclaimed with agonized voice. "How can we get them down? Bring ladders, men, bring ladders!"

"There's no ladder long enough to reach up so far," said Ludlow, who happened to be standing near.

"Then someone must go up the stairs."

He made a rush for the door, but the interior of the first floor was a fiery furnace and the stair had already fallen. Even in his distraction he could see there was no possible way of rescue in that direction. He rushed back into the yard, glanced upward, and saw his daughter's friend weeping and wringing her hands, and Alice quietly looking downward to see what steps would be taken for their rescue. From the window in the roof the smoke was already pouring.

"Can nobody get them down?" cried Mr. Strong. "I will give a thousand dollars, ten thousand dollars—anything—everything—to anyone who will save them."

The men looked on eagerly. They would willingly have helped without reward if there had been any feasible way. And Mr. Strong was rich and generous, and the prospect of a liberal reward would have been an inducement to take desperate chances. But apparently every avenue of access to the tower was cut off; part by the flames, which were pouring out of the windows on one side, but the rest quite as effectively by dense volumes of smoke. While a dozen voices discussed so many wild plans of rescue, none of them practicable, a man came running through the crowd, with a coil of small rope in his hand. It was Walker, the foreman.

"Help me put this ladder at the corner of the tower," he said. "I'll go up there."

A dozen willing hands placed the ladder at the spot designated. The man fastened the coil of rope so that it hung at his back and would not interfere with his movements.

"You'll never get up, Walker," they cried, wondering what he meant to do. "The ladder doesn't reach within twenty feet of the roof."

"Never you mind," said the colored man, "I didn't sail the ocean seven years for nothing. I can almost climb a straight wall. Somebody get a stronger rope to tie onto this line when I let it down, and hurry!"

When Walker reached the top of the ladder, which he climbed with surprising agility, the plan which he meant to adopt was at once apparent. The end of the ladder rested against one side of an ornamental projection extending downward on the corner of the building from the roof for the depth of two stories. This projection was simply an extra course of brick four inches in thickness and lapping each side of the corner about a foot, resembling almost exactly the reinforcing pieces on the corners of a dry-goods box or packing case. Walker left the ladder, and clasping one arm and knee against the inner side of the projection and the others around the corner of the tower, began to work his way slowly upward.

The brick was common brick with a rough surface, so that he could get friction enough to hold on, though only by great effort, because of the very narrow space in which to move his right arm and knee. To those who watched him breathlessly from below, his position seemed one of extreme peril. Suppose he should lose his hold? Three lives would be sacrificed instead of two. Interest in the man and his daring attempt almost eclipsed anxiety for the position of the two girls, which was every moment becoming more perilous. When at length Walker reached the top and drew himself over the wall, the tension was relieved by a wild shout of joy and applause.

To fasten one end of the line to the flagstaff on the tower, and throw the coil down, was the work of a moment. Then while Miss Strong, who had never for a moment lost her nerve, pulled up the stout rope which was immediately tied on below, Walker ran to the water tank and released the mechanism that let the water into the fire-extinguishing pipes in the workrooms and storerooms of the building below. To tie the rope around the almost fainting form of Miss Strong's friend and with a turn of the rope around the flagstaff to lessen the strain, to lower her into the waiting arms below, took but a few minutes. Miss Strong's turn came next, and then the crowd saw Walker coming down the rope hand over hand, with the ease and rapidity of an old salt. As he touched the ground the fire-engine dashed into the yard.

"Walker," said Mr. Strong, as he grasped the panting but smiling rescuer by the hand, "I owe you more than my own life. I can never repay you."

"That's all right, sir, you don't owe me anything. Anybody that knew how to climb as well as I do could do what I did. I was in the Navy, sir; any able seaman could do as well."

By this time the fire engine had begun to play on the flames, and combined with the action of the extinguishing apparatus, and got the fire under control before any material damage had been done to the main part of the building.

"You have saved my daughter and saved the mill, Walker. I can only thank you now, but henceforth you are my friend, and friendship with me is not an empty name."

That evening, Walker dressed in his best clothes and, much to his discomfort, was overwhelmed with gratitude by two beautiful young ladies, who had partially recovered from the shock of their adventure, and lionized by his employer and his wife, and a host of their friends who had asked an opportunity to meet the brave rescuer. Some men are born heroes, some achieve heroism, and some have heroism thrust upon them. To Walker all these parts were assigned at once. Soft hands pressed his horny palm. Fair faces smiled into his, and sweet voices said flattering words, and he would have been less than human, as he went home that night, if he had not felt the world a pleasant place to live in, and himself a very acceptable member of its population.

About nine o'clock next morning the same committee of workmen, with Ludlow at their head, called on Mr. Strong at the office. The mill had been shut down for a few days, until the slight damage by fire and water could be repaired.

Mr. Strong had quite made up his mind as to the answer he would give them in reference to Walker.

"Well, my men," he said, "what can I do for you today?"

"You can forget what we said about Walker yesterday, sir," answered the spokesman, "and we hope you won't mention it to him at all. We've taken the sense of the mill-hands about it, and they all want you to make him foreman. We realize that he saved your daughter's life, and probably saved our jobs. And he's a good fellow, and we like him, and don't want any better man to work under. And next Saturday we're going to elect him one of the marshals of the Labor Day parade, and we'll be proud to march behind him."

"My friends," replied Mr. Strong, with emotion, "you do honor to yourselves, to humanity, and the cause of labor. I shall be glad to forget your visit of yesterday, and to remember only your appreciation of and desire to reward character and courage. I shall be happy to appoint Mr. Walker foreman, and shall tell him it was done at your request."

Walker was informed of his appointment the same day.

"I owe you more than I can repay, Walker," said Mr. Strong, "but I am going to give you some substantial evidence of my appreciation. The appointment as foreman you have earned, and are entitled to by the rule of promotion. But my personal acknowledgment shall take a different form. I had a talk with the other directors last night. We are going to reorganize the company, and have decided to credit you with five thousand dollars of the new company's stock, in acknowledgment of your courage and coolness, and the service you have rendered us all."

Walker was overwhelmed. "I haven't done anything to deserve all this, sir. I only did my duty, and it was easy for me to do. You don't need to give me anything, sir."

"It is sometimes hard to do one's duty, Walker. You have a family to provide for and bring up, and you cannot afford to throw away your chances; and I certainly cannot afford, on my part, to do less than I think right in the matter. Your interest in the business will make you a better foreman and be to our mutual advantage."

And being a man of good, hard sense, whose chances in life had been few, Walker had no further objections to make, but thanked his employer and Another for the good fortune that had befallen him.

White Weeds

Students of Danforth University during the late Nineties may remember the remarkable events following the death of Professor Carson of that institution.

At three o'clock one afternoon Professor Carson left his own apartments in Merle Hall and crossed the university campus toward the president's house. It was obvious to the few students whom he encountered during his short walk that Professor Carson was deeply absorbed in thought, because, ordinarily a model of politeness, upon this occasion he either passed them as though unaware of their presence, or responded to their respectful salutations with a very palpable perfunctoriness. There was reason enough, the students knew, for a certain degree of preoccupation on the part of Professor Carson, but hardly sufficient to account for an agitation so extreme as not only to disturb his usually grave and composed countenance but to make him forget his punctilious manners. A man might well be absent-minded upon his wedding day, but he need not look as though he were under sentence of death and straining every effort to secure a reprieve. For Professor Carson, as everyone knew, was to be married at 7 o'clock in the evening to Miss Marian Tracy, by common consent of the university faculty and the student body the most beautiful woman of her years in Attica.

It was a noble campus that Professor Carson crossed. Founded by a wealthy merchant of a past generation, before the days of colossal and burdensome fortunes, the university had never been regarded as a medium of self-advertisement, but as the contribution of an enlightened philanthropist to the training of youth and the advancement of science. There was a broad quadrangular sweep of velvety turf, crossed by two intersecting avenues of noble elms, while distributed symmetrically around the square were a dozen stately stone buildings, some ivy-clad, others beginning already to show, though the institution was only fifty years old, the markings of frost and snow and sun and rain which in a strenuous Northern climate so soon simulate the mellowness of age.

Professor Carson found the president at home and was ushered into his presence. President Trumbull of Danforth University was a suave and learned gentleman of fifty, in whom a fine executive mind had not overborne a zeal for scholarship, in which he had achieved deserved renown before assuming the cares of administration. A more striking contrast than that between the two men it would be difficult to imagine; physically they were almost the antitheses of each other. Professor Carson was tall and slender with fair hair, which he wore much longer than most men; the president was sturdy and his hair dark, with a very slight sprinkling of white, and ruddy of complexion. The professor's forehead was high and narrow, the president's lower but broader. The president's eye was gray, keen and steady; the professor's blue, weak and wavering. The one was the face of a man of affairs, who welcomed responsibilities as a fit exercise for high powers; the other that of a man lacking resolution and prone, in the crises of life, to seek the support and direction of stronger minds. It was, indeed, Dr. Trumbull's well-known decision of character which had brought Professor Carson, torn by conflicting emotions, across the campus to the president's house. Both were men of striking appearance, not to say handsome men, Professor Carson's manner being marked by a certain distinction, accounted for in some measure by his consciousness that he was of an old and distinguished ancestry. He was deeply wedded to his work, and punctiliously conscientious in its performance; he was professor of mathematics, a science governed by exact rules and requiring little exercise of judgment or imagination. He had been connected with the school longer than President Trumbull and was loyal to its ideals and traditions, with the tenacity of a vine which has thrust its slender roots into the interstices of a rock.

President Trumbull was in his study, in company with his daughter Marcia, a handsome and intelligent child of twelve who sat beside a window reading, while her father wrote at his desk. At a glance from his visitor, the president, with another glance, dismissed Marcia. Professor Carson, murmuring a request for permission, closed the door of the room and sat, or rather sank into a chair near the president.

"Well, Professor Carson, what can I do for you? I see that you have something on your mind."

"Dr. Trumbull," said the other, "I am in the greatest trouble of my life."

"Bless me, Professor! What can it be? Nothing serious, I hope?"

"Serious is hardly the name for it—it is more than serious. It is a matter that concerns my whole future—almost a matter of life and death. As you know, I am—I was to be married tonight."

"Yes, and to an exceedingly beautiful and charming lady."

This statement was made in all sincerity, and not without a certain degree of regret. Dr. Trumbull was a widower of less than a year's standing. Had Professor Carson waited a while longer, he would not have been without a formidable rival.

"Exactly," said Professor Carson, extending his hand with a gesture unconsciously tragic, "and an hour ago I received this letter."

Dr. Trumbull took the letter, and as he read it an air of astonishment overspread his features.

"An extraordinary statement," he exclaimed, "most extraordinary! But surely it is not true—surely you cannot believe it?"

"I—don't—know what to believe. It is possible—most things are possible."

"But, my dear sir, this is an anonymous letter—the weapon of malice—the medium of slander."

"I know it, sir. In the ordinary affairs of life I should have tossed it into the fire. But this is a matter vital to my happiness. And there is always the possibility that someone might wish to tell another the truth, without seeming to do an unkind thing. An anonymous letter *might* be written with the best of motives."

"The method throws suspicion on the motive. Is there no clue to the writer? Have you any enemy?"

"None that I know of," replied Professor Carson promptly. "I don't know of a man in the world who should wish me other than well."

"Or a woman?"

"Or a woman," came the reply with equal promptness.

"It is more calculated to injure the lady than you," said the president reflectively. "*She* may have enemies."

"She is the soul of candor, and popular with her own sex."

"She is beautiful, and popular with the other sex—sufficient reasons why she might be the object of envy or malice."

"The letter is from another city. It is postmarked 'Drexel.' "

"Drexel is forty miles away," returned the president. "One might take the ten o'clock train from here, post the letter at Drexel, and be back here by twelve o'clock. The letter would be here for afternoon delivery."

Professor Carson examined the envelope.

"It was post-marked at Drexel at eleven o'clock. The receiving stamp shows it delivered at the post office here at 12:15. It reached me in the afternoon delivery. It is typewritten, so there is no penmanship to afford a clue."

"I have passed the point of concern about its origin," returned Professor Carson. "It is the fact itself that worries me. The mere suggestion is torture. If the statement be true, it means the ruin of my happiness. If it be false—and pray God it is—I have no time, before the hour set for the wedding, to ascertain the fact. I must decide now, with such light as I have. As my friend and superior in office, what would you advise me to do?"

"Why not ask the lady?"

"I could not do it. If it were true, I could not marry her."

"Nor, as I understand, would you wish to. And if it were false, your mind would be at ease."

"But if I should ask her, she might not marry me; and if it is false, I would not lose her for the world."

"You would trust her word?"

"Implicitly. She is too proud to lie."

"Then, my dear Professor Carson, if you feel that way. . . ."

"Then you would advise me?"

"Is it so important?" asked the president, perplexed. "The world would never know it, even if it were true."

"Someone knows it—if it be true," returned the other. "And then, I should wish to have children, and it is of them I should have to think—it would be criminal not to think of them. The time is so short that I don't know what to do nor where to turn. I thought you might advise me—you are so prompt, so resourceful. I should wish to adopt a course that would protect myself, and yet in no way reflect upon the lady, or upon the university, or impair my usefulness here."

"Such delicacy was to be expected of you, Professor Carson. If it were my own affair, I could decide it promptly, but unless I could put myself exactly in your place, as perhaps I should be unable to do, I should hesitate to advise a man upon a matter so vital. Your problem is a difficult one from your own point of view—perhaps from any man's. You are engaged to be married, within a few hours, to a most charming woman, in whose worth and worthiness you have had entire confidence. The wedding preparations are made, the guests invited. Even now, in all probability, the bride is dressing for the wedding. At this moment you receive an anonymous letter, purporting to convey information which, if true, renders the lady ineligible for marriage with you. I see but three courses open to you as a gentleman—and those who know you would expect you to consider the subject first from that point of view. You can take the letter to the lady, ask her frankly if the charge be true, and marry her or not, as she may answer. A less frank but at least forgivable step would be to postpone the marriage on account of sudden indisposition—you are looking far from well just now. If she confirmed the statement of the letter, you would have to make some such excuse, in order to spare her feelings. A third course, which a man—some men at least—who loved the lady well enough would follow, would be to throw the letter into the fire and marry her."

"But which do you think—" began Professor Carson desperately, "which do you think—"

"I think," said the president, interrupting him, "that you had better choose between the three. A gentleman of your character and antecedents can hardly fail to select a course consistent with—"

"With honor," murmured the poor professor. "Thank you, sir," he added with dignity, "I shall trouble you no further. But whatever course I decide upon, I may ask you to hold in strict confidence all that I have said, and the contents of this letter?"

"You need hardly ask it. It is not a matter to be repeated. Whether the marriage take place or no, we should have no right to compromise the lady."

At 7 o'clock the same evening the marriage of Professor John Marshall Carson to Miss Marian Tracy took place at the latter's residence. Miss Tracy was alone in the world, having neither parents nor near relatives living. She had been a teacher in a ladies' seminary, and made her home with a distant connection who lived in the town. To the college world the event was a notable one. Professor Carson was, if not exactly popular, at least very highly esteemed by his colleagues. If he seemed at times to hold himself aloof from the other professors, his attitude was instinctively ascribed to a natural reserve rather than to undue self-esteem. If any new-fledged tutor or professor ever attempted to be familiar with the professor of mathematics, he was brought back to the conventional by a tact so delicate, a courtesy so refined, that no offense was taken, and respect took the place of what, at a ruder rebuff, might easily have been dislike. The wedding was attended by all of the professors and their wives, as well as by many of the townspeople.

The house was decorated for the wedding with red and white roses. Festoons of smilax ran from the chandeliers in the center to the corners of the rooms. The floors were covered with white canvas. Gorman and McAlee's orchestra, screened behind palms in the back hall, played a varied program of classical and popular music, ranging from Mendelssohn to ragtime. These details are mentioned because they are important to the remainder of the story. The bride,

> "Clothed in white samite,
> Mystic, wonderful,"

as Dr. Trumbull murmured when the vision dawned upon him—was radiant in the well-preserved beauty of thirty years, for Miss Tracy was no longer in her first youth. When she entered the front parlor upon the arm of her cousin, to the strains of the wedding march, there was not a man present who did not think Professor Carson an extremely lucky man. It was observed, however, by those who paid the bridegroom any attention, that he did not seem as happy as the occasion demanded; that the voice with which he spoke the irrevocable vows had not the vibrant ring that might be expected from the virile man united to his mate; that the hand which he gave to those who congratulated him was limp and cold; that while from time to time during the evening his eyes sought the bride's face with a look of longing, behind this lay a haunting distrust—that he seemed to be seeking something which he did not find; that at other times his manner was *distrait* and his smile forced; and that when the last guests were departing, his expression alternated between anticipation and dread. President Trumbull, the most distinguished guest, responded at the supper table to a toast in which he wished the couple every felicity. At no time during the evening did Professor Carson allude to the interview of the afternoon, nor did the president mention it to him then or thereafter. There had been no scandal, no sensation, and Dr. Trumbull had no disposition to pry into another's secrets.

If there were any lingering curiosity on Dr. Trumbull's part concerning which of the two possible courses open to him besides postponement of the marriage Professor Carson had adopted, it was not lessened by his observation of the married couple during the succeeding months. He went to Europe for the summer, but upon his return in the autumn to his duties, he met Professor Carson daily, in the routine of the university work, and the lady from time to time in the social life of which the university was the center. Only a few meetings were necessary to convince him that neither husband nor wife was happy. Professor Carson, at the end of what should have been a restful vacation, had visibly declined in health. Always slender, he had become emaciated. His natural gravity had developed into an almost sepulchral solemnity, his innate reserve into a well-nigh morbid self-absorption. The rare smile which had at times flickered upon his features seemed to have gone out forever.

His efforts to overcome this melancholy were at times very apparent. Mrs. Carson was fond of society, and they often went out together. On such occasions their bearing towards one another was perfect, of its kind. Professor Carson was the embodiment of chivalrous courtesy—a courtesy so marked that in the bearing of any other man toward his own wife it would have provoked a smile. The lady, in her demeanor toward her husband responded in a manner so similar as to seem at times ironical. In a free and familiar society of intimates they were, when together, conspicuous. The lady when alone could unbend; but Professor Carson after his marriage never appeared in society alone.

In spite, however, of this elaborate deference toward one another, more than one observer besides Dr. Trumbull suspected that their union was not one of perfect happiness. Dr. Trumbull wondered, more than once, whether Carson had asked her, before their marriage, the question suggested by the anonymous letter, and, receiving a negative answer, had had his faith shaken after marriage, or whether he had loyally burned the letter, but had been unable to divest himself of the hateful doubt it had engendered, which was slowly sapping his vitality. That some cause was producing this unfortunate result became more and more apparent, for before the next summer vacation came around, Professor Carson took to his bed, and, after a brief illness, was enrolled among the great majority.

The number of those who were interested in the Carsons household was largely increased during the two days succeeding the professor's death. Announcement was duly made that the funeral services would take place on Saturday afternoon—Professor Carson had died on Thursday—and were to be conducted by old Dr. Burridge, rector emeritus of St. Anne's. This in itself was a novelty, for Dr. Burridge was purblind and hard of hearing, and rarely performed any priestly function except some service where sight and hearing were not prime essentials. Some surprise being expressed that Dr. McRae, the rector in charge, had not been requested to officiate, it was learned that Dr. Burridge would act by special request of the widow.

This, however, was a trivial preliminary. The real surprise began when those who entered the house shortly before the hour fixed for the service, found none of the customary trappings of woe, but on the contrary, a house decked as for a wedding ceremony. It required only a moment for those who had been present at Professor Carson's marriage a few months before to perceive with a sort of dazed wonder, that an effort had seemingly been made to reproduce, as near as the plan of the rooms would permit, the decorations upon that occasion. Roses, white and red, were banked in the corners; long streamers of smilax ran from the chandeliers to the corners of the room, and were twined around the stair railing. Where, at the wedding ceremony a floral altar had been reared, the body of Professor Carson, in immaculate evening dress, lay upon a bier, composed of a casket the sides of which were let down so as to resemble more a couch than the last narrow house of a mortal man.

The troubled wonder of the funeral guests was still further augmented when in the rear hall, behind a screen of palms. Gormand and McAlee's orchestra began to play Wagner's "O du mein holder Abendstern." For a moment, while the gathering audience were realizing that a band associated only with pleasure parties was playing music, which, while not exactly profane, was certainly not religious—for a few moments the audience was silent, and then the room was as murmurous with whispered comment as a wheat-field shaken by the wind.

One of the professors spoke to the undertaker, who was hovering, like a bird of prey, around the hall.

"What is the meaning," he asked, "of this extraordinary performance?"

"Don't ask me, sir. It is the widow's orders. I don't approve of it, sir, but business is business with me. It is the widow's orders, and, as the person chiefly interested, the widow's wishes are sacred."

While Dr. Burridge, in full canonicals, having taken his place before the bier, to which he was led by one of the ushers, was reading the first part of the beautiful Episcopal service for the burial of the dead, there was opportunity for those present to reach in some degree the frame of mind befitting so solemn an occasion. At that point, following the first lesson, where a hymn is sung or an anthem, the discomfort returned with even greater force when a hired quartet, which some of those present recognized as belonging to the neighboring town of Drexel, began to sing, to a soft accompaniment by the orchestra, not the conventional and the expected "Abide with Me" or "Lead, Kindly Light," but Graben Hoffman's exquisite love song, "Der schoenste Engel." As the words were German only a few understood them, but in the bosoms of the rest there was a vague intuition that the song was of a piece with the other unusual features of the occasion.

Good old Dr. Burridge, however, to whose dull hearing all music was the same, had neither seen nor heard anything to mar the solemnity of the service. He repeated the Creed, in which he was joined by those who were sufficiently collected, and added the fitting prayers. When he had concluded the portion of the service which could be performed at the home, and the undertaker had announced that the remainder of the service would take place at the cemetery, the guests instead of rising returned to their seats as though by a common premonition that there was something more to happen. Nor were they disappointed, for almost immediately the orchestra struck up the "Wedding March" from *Lohengrin,* and Mrs. Carson, clad not in widow's weeds but in bridal array, her face set in a tragic smile, entered the back parlor and moved in time to the music down the narrow lane which had been left between the chairs, and pausing before the bier took off her wedding ring and placed it in her dead husband's hand; took off her wreath of orange blossoms and laid it among the flowers by his side. Then, turning, she left the room by the side door. A few moments later, when the casket had been closed and the body was ready for sepulture, she came downstairs dressed in an ordinary street costume of dark cloth, took her place in the mourner's carriage, and followed the remains to the grave, by the side of which she stood like any ordinary spectator until ashes had been consigned to ashes, and dust to dust, after which she immediately entered her carriage and was driven away, leaving the mystified throng morally certain that nothing but a pronounced mental aberration on the part of Mrs. Carson could account for so extraordinary, not to say shocking a funeral. To more than one the mad scene in Hamlet occurred as at least a distant parallel, though no one of them had ever dreamed that the stately Mrs. Carson had loved her middle-aged husband so deeply as, like Ophelia, to go mad for love of him.

So paralyzed with amazement had been everyone at the funeral, and brief had been Mrs. Carson's appearances, that not anyone had uttered a word of condolence or spoken to her during the afternoon. That very night she left Attica. Her house was closed and her affairs settled by her distant cousin, and it was learned that she had gone abroad for an indefinite sojourn. By the will of Professor Carson, which was presented for probate shortly after his decease, he left to his widow the whole of his estate, which amounted to some $20,000 in money and securities.

A little more than a year after Professor Carson's death, at the close of the school year, Dr. Trumbull, accompanied by his daughter Marcia—he had been a widower now for three years—left home to spend the summer in Europe. A few weeks later, upon stepping aboard the steamer at Mainz for the trip down the Rhine, he saw seated upon the deck, at a little distance, a lady whose outlines, though her face was turned away, seemed familiar. Having seen his daughter comfortably seated and their hand baggage placed, he went over to the lady, who, upon his addressing her by name, looked up with a start, and then extended both her hands.

"Why, Dr. Trumbull, what a surprise! You are the last person whom I should have expected to see!"

"And, I suppose, the one whom it gives you the least pleasure to see?"

"By no means! Indeed, I am glad to see you. One's home friends are never so welcome as when one meets them in a foreign land."

"Yes, I believe it is understood that a mere bowing acquaintance at home becomes an intimate friend abroad."

"Now, doctor, I shall not follow your very palpable lead; you must take my friendship at its face value."

"My dear Mrs. Carson, I am only too glad to do so, and am sincerely delighted, on my part, that our paths have met."

The president's daughter, finding herself deserted, and recognizing Mrs. Carson, came over at this juncture, and was duly hugged and kissed.

"How tall you are growing, dear!" said the lady. "It is only about a year since I saw you, and you look three years older."

"My dresses are longer," said Marcia ingenuously. "Oh, I'm so glad we've met you. You know, I always liked you, Mrs. Carson, even before you were married."

"You dear child! And as for you, who could help loving you? But, there, how selfish I am! In my pleasure at our meeting, I had forgotten all about Professor and Mrs. Gilman. I'm traveling with them, you know. Professor Gilman has had his 'sabbatical year,' and I've been with them ever since they came over last July. At school Mrs. Gilman was my dearest friend, and they have been very good to me."

"And you never give up your friends?"

"Never! So long as they are good to me. But excuse me a moment, and I will look them up."

She returned shortly with her friends. The two gentlemen were old acquaintances and former intimates. Professor Gilman, an authority on medieval history, had been a colleague of Dr. Trumbull's at Brown, many years before. After the exchange of cordial greetings, the ladies, accompanied by Marcia, went over to the side of the boat, leaving the gentlemen together.

They spoke of their work and their travels, and then the conversation turned on Mrs. Carson.

"She is looking well," said President Trumbull.

"A fine woman," returned Professor Gilman, "a woman of character, capable of forming a definite purpose, and of carrying it out; and yet not at all hard, and in some ways exceedingly feminine. My wife loves her dearly, and we have enjoyed having her with us."

"I never thought," said Dr. Trumbull, "that she was quite happy with Carson."

"Happy! Far from it! I suppose, after Carson's remarkable funeral, that all Attica imagined her out of her mind?"

"Her conduct was unusual, certainly, and in default of explanation, such a suspicion might really have seemed charitable."

"Did it ever occur to you that there might be a reasonable explanation, without that hypothesis?"

"Frankly, yes, though I could never have imagined what it was. I happened to know something of Carson's antecedents, and of certain events preceding his marriage, which I have thought might in some obscure way have accounted for Mrs. Carson's eccentric conduct upon that occasion. But the knowledge came to me in such a manner that I shall probably never know any more about it."

"Did it concern a letter?"

"Yes."

"An anonymous letter?"

"Yes."

"Then I know it already. Mrs. Carson is my wife's other self—even I play only second fiddle. They have no secrets from one another. I know that Mrs. Carson values your good opinion, and since you know so much, I imagine she would not be unwilling for you to know all the facts—if you could dream them, say. Indeed, you ought to know them."

It was a warm day. Their cigars were good. The ladies left them alone for half an hour. The steamer glided smoothly down the Rhine. Two gentlemen in middle life, upon their vacation, might have dozed and might have dreamed. At any rate, before the ladies rejoined them, each knew all that the other knew of Mrs. Carson's story, and what they did not know required no supernatural wisdom to divine it.

When, after the wedding, the guests had departed and the wedded pair were left alone, the bride observed that Professor Carson was ill at ease, and that his embarrassment was serious. For a while he wandered about the room. At length he sat down beside her and began to speak.

"Marian," he said, "I have a very painful duty to perform. This afternoon, only a few hours ago, I received through the mail an anonymous letter, containing a certain statement with reference to yourself."

To say that his wife was surprised is a mild statement. She was not a child, but a mature woman, and the inference seemed plain; a wedding, an anonymous letter upon the eve of it. That he had not believed the statement, whatever it had been, was apparent, for he had married her. But right upon the heels of this conviction came the first false note in her conception of Professor Carson's character—a doubt of his taste. She had considered him the flower of courtesy—had looked upon his chivalrous deference for women as a part of his Southern heritage. It was this attribute of his, which, more than anything else, had attracted her. That having loyally ignored such a letter, he should now tell her of it was hardly to have been expected of him.

"I could not believe the statement," he went on, "and therefore, as honor required of me, I threw the letter into the fire, and fulfilled my contract."

Again the lady winced. It hardly required a sensitive mind to infer, from his language, that he had married her because of their previous engagement. His choice of words was at least unfortunate.

"I am sorry," she said with spirit, "that you should have felt under any compulsion."

"There was none," he replied, "except that of my love. And I did not believe the story."

"Then why mention it?"

"Because I must know," he replied, "and yet I dared not run the risk of losing you. Had I asked you the question before our marriage, your pride, which in my eyes is one of your greatest charms, might have made you refuse to marry me."

"Quite likely," she replied, with rising anger. "But, since you ignored the letter, and disbelieve the story, why, oh, why, do you tell me now?"

"Because," he said wildly, "because I love you, and because my happiness is so bound up in you, and because this charge is of such a nature, that I can never shake off its memory until I learn from your own lips that it is false. I know it is false—I am sure it is false—it must be false; but I want your lips to give it the lie. Whatever you say, I shall believe."

She was a woman, and for a moment curiosity replaced indignation.

"And what," she asked, "is this terrible charge which I must meet, this crime I must deny?"

"It is a monstrous calumny. Could anyone, looking at your fair face, at your clear eye, your frank and noble countenance, believe that one drop of Negro blood coursed through your veins? Preposterous!"

His words were confident, but his voice scarcely rang true, and she could read the lingering dread in his eyes. This, then, that some unknown person had said of her, was the offense with which she was charged!

She was silent. He watched her anxiously.

"Suppose," she answered with a forced smile, "suppose, for the sake of the argument, it had been true—what then?"

"Ah, dearest," he replied, reassured by her smile, and drawing nearer to her, while she retreated behind a convenient chair. "I should have suffered a severe shock. For the sake of the university, and to avoid scandal, I should have lived with you, had you been willing, and to the outer world we should have been husband and wife; but to ourselves the relationship would have existed in name only."

"And you married me." she said coldly, "with such a doubt in your mind, and with such a purpose, should the doubt be wrongly resolved? It seems scarcely fair to me. I might have answered yes."

He explained his state of mind, or at least endeavored to make it clear, plainly surprised that he should find it necessary; for to his mind, the mere statement of the fact was its own explanation.

His father had been a planter, with wide estates and numerous slaves.

His mother had suffered deeply in her pride and her affections, because of some poor unfortunate of color. With his mother's milk he had drunk in a deadly antipathy to the thought of any personal relation between white people and black but that of master and servant. The period of his adolescence had coincided with the tense years during which the white South, beaten on the field, had sought in a fierce and unreasoning pride a refuge from the humiliation of defeat, and with equal unreason, but very humanly, had visited upon the black pawns in the game, who were near at hand, the hatred they felt for their conquerors. Most of this feeling Professor Carson had overcome, but this one thing was bred in the bone.

"It is part of me," he said. "Nothing could ever make me feel that the touch of a Negress was not pollution. Beside my mother's deathbed I swore a solemn vow that this sin should never be laid at my door."

His bride was not flattered by the suggestion. She, a Negress, to whom his vow might apply!

"How white," she asked, "must one be, to come within the protection of the code of Southern chivalry?"

"There are no degrees," he explained. "To me, and those who think like me, men and women are either white or black. Those who are not all white are all black. Were I married in fact to a woman even seemingly as white as you, yet not entirely white, I should feel guilty of mortal sin. I should lie awake at night, dreading lest my children should show traces of their descent from an inferior and degraded race. I should never know a moment's happiness."

"Pardon my curiosity," she said, "but this is interesting—at least. What, may I ask, was to have been—my attitude in this marriage? In this state there would have been no legal objection to our union. We are both Episcopalians, and our church looks upon divorce with disfavor. Was I to have submitted without protest to a plan which left me married, yet no wife?"

"It would have been for you to say," he replied. "I could not blame you for concealing your antecedents. For me to seek a divorce would have been to reveal your secret, which honor would scarcely have permitted, and the same reason, I imagined, might constrain you. But, let us thank heaven! I am spared the trial, and with your assurance that all is well we shall be happy all the rest of our lives."

He moved toward her to take her in his arms.

"You forget," she answered quickly, and still evading him, "that I have given you no such assurance."

Professor Carson turned white to the lips. She thought he would have fainted at her feet; he clutched the table beside him for support. She would have pitied him, had she despised him less.

"What," he faltered, "can it be possible?"

"I shall certainly not deny it," she replied.

And she never did. They lived together according to his program. He was never certain, and in his doubt he found his punishment. When he died, she yielded to a woman's weakness. She was not a widow, but a bride. She owed Professor Carson no affection and felt for him no regret. He had outraged her finest feelings, and she had stooped to a posthumous revenge, which had satisfied her mind, while it only mystified others; indeed, she had cared very little, at the time, for what others might think. That having known her, and loved her, and married her, a prejudice which reflected in no wise upon her character, her intelligence or her beauty could keep them apart, was the unpardonable sin. She must be loved for what she was.

"It is curious," said Dr. Trumbull, reflectively, "how the fixed idea dominates the mind. Perfectly reasonable and logical and fair-minded upon every other topic, upon one pet aversion a man may skirt the edge of mania. Nature has set no impassable barrier between races. A system which, assuming the Negro race to be inferior, condemns Mrs. Carson, because of some remote strain of its blood, to celibacy and social ostracism, or throws her back upon the inferior race, is scarcely complimentary to our own. The exaggerated race feeling of men like Carson is more than a healthy instinct for the preservation of a type; it is more than a prejudice. It is an obsession."

"A disease," returned Professor Gilman. "In all probability, had she given Professor Carson the answer he wanted, it would never have satisfied him. The seed had been planted in his mind; it was sure to bring forth a harvest of suspicion and distrust. He would in any event have worried himself into a premature grave. His marriage, while the doubt existed, was a refinement of Quixotry—and of unconscious selfishness; to spare the feelings of the possible white woman, and to save her for himself, he deliberately contemplated the destruction of the happiness of the possible—Negress."

Across the deck, Dr. Trumbull studied the graceful contour of Mrs. Carson's figure, the fine lines of her profile. A widow, and yet no wife! It was interesting. It would be a brave man who would marry her—but surely she had never loved Carson.

Dr. Trumbull had always admired her, since he had known her. Had she been willing, and had she waited a little longer, she might have been spared the somewhat tragic interlude with Carson.

"I had always wondered," he said, reflectively, "which of the three courses open to Carson he adopted—to postpone the marriage—to burn the letter— or to ask her frankly whether its contents were true. It seems that he did all three—he asked whether or not the statement was true; he burned the letter and married her without mentioning it; and—he deferred the marriage—the real marriage. It was the order in which he did them that destroyed his happiness and shortened his life."

"And all," said Professor Gilman, "for nothing, absolutely nothing. What malicious mind conceived and wrote the letter, Mrs. Carson never learned, but there was not a word of truth in it! Her blood is as entirely pure as Professor Carson's could have been. My wife knew her people, and her line of descent for two hundred years is quite as clear, quite as good, as that of most old American families. But here come the ladies."

"Oh, papa," cried Marcia, "you and Professor Gilman have been so busy talking that you have missed the most beautiful scenery—the Lorelei, and Bingen, and Ehrenbreitstein, and—oh, my! If it hadn't been for Mrs. Carson, who has been telling me all the legends, I shouldn't have known anything about them."

"I saw you with her and Mrs. Gilman, dear, and knew it was all right. Perhaps Mrs. Carson will show them to me—some other time."

The Doll

When Tom Taylor, proprietor of the Wyandot Hotel barber shop, was leaving home, after his noonday luncheon, to return to his work, his daughter, a sprightly, dimunitive brown maid, with very bright black eyes and very curly black hair, thrust into his coat pocket a little jointed doll somewhat the worse for wear.

"Now, don't forget, papa," she said, in her shrill childish treble, "what's to be done to her. Her arms won't work, and her legs won't work, and she can't hold her head up. Be sure and have her mended this afternoon, and bring her home when you come to supper; for she's afraid of the dark, and always sleeps with me. I'll meet you at the corner at half-past six—and don't forget, whatever you do."

"No, Daisy, I'll not forget," he replied as he lifted her to the level of his lips and kissed her.

Upon reaching the shop he removed the doll from his pocket and hung it on one of the gilded spikes projecting above the wire netting surrounding the cashier's desk, where it would catch his eye. Some time during the afternoon he would send it to a toy shop around the corner for repairs. But the day was a busy one, and when the afternoon was well advanced he had not yet attended to it.

Colonel Forsyth had come up from the South to attend a conference of Democratic leaders to consider presidential candidates and platforms. He had put up at the Wyandot Hotel, but had been mainly in the hands of Judge Beeman, chairman of the local Jackson club, who was charged with the duty of seeing that the colonel was made comfortable and given the freedom of the city. It was after a committee meeting, and about four in the afternoon, that the two together entered the lobby of the Wyandot. They were discussing the platforms to be put forward by the two great parties in the approaching campaign.

"I reckon, judge," the colonel was saying, "that the Republican party will make a mistake if it injects the Negro question into its platform. The question is primarily a local one, and if the North will only be considerate about the matter, and let us alone, we can settle it to our entire satisfaction. The Negro's place is defined by nature, and in the South he knows it and gives us no trouble."

"The Northern Negroes are different," returned the judge.

"They are just the same," rejoined the colonel. "It is you who are different. You pamper them and they take liberties with you. But they are all from the South, and when they meet a Southerner they act accordingly. They are born to serve and to submit. If they had been worthy of equality they would never have endured slavery. They have no proper self-respect; they will neither resent an insult, nor defend a right, nor avenge a wrong."

"Well, now, colonel, aren't you rather hard on them? Consider their past."

"Hard? Why, no, bless your heart! I've got nothing against the nigger. I like him—in his place. But what I say is the truth. Are you in a hurry?"

"Not at all."

"Then come downstairs to the barber shop and I'll prove what I say."

The shop was the handsomest barber shop in the city. It was in the basement, and the paneled ceiling glowed with electric lights. The floor was of white tile, the walls lined with large mirrors. Behind ten chairs, of the latest and most comfortable design, stood as many colored barbers, in immaculate white jackets, each at work upon a white patron. An air of discipline and good order pervaded the establishment. There was no loud talking by patrons, no unseemly garrulity on the part of the barbers. It was very obviously a well-conducted barber shop, frequented by gentlemen who could afford to pay liberally for superior service. As the judge and the colonel entered, a customer vacated the chair served by the proprietor.

"Next gentleman," said the barber.

The colonel removed his collar and took his seat in the vacant chair, remarking, as he ran his hand over his neck, "I want a close shave, barber."

"Yes, sir; a close shave."

The barber was apparently about forty, with a brown complexion, clean-cut features and curly hair. Committed by circumstances to a career of personal service, he had lifted it by intelligence, tact and industry to the dignity of a successful business. The judge, a regular patron of the shop, knew him well and had often, while in his chair, conversed with him concerning his race— a fruitful theme, much on the public tongue.

"As I was saying," said the colonel, while the barber adjusted a towel about his neck, "the Negro question is a perfectly simple one."

The judge thought it hardly good taste in the colonel to continue in his former strain. Northern men might speak slightingly of the Negro, but seldom in his presence. He tried a little diversion.

"The tariff," he observed, "is a difficuult problem."

"Much more complicated, suh, than the Negro problem, which is perfectly simple. Let the white man once impress the Negro with his superiority; let the Negro see that there is no escape from the inevitable, and that ends it. The best thing about the Negro is that, with all his limitations, he can recognize a finality. It is the secret of his persistence among us. He has acquired the faculty of evolution, suh—by the law of the survival of the fittest. Long ago, when a young man, I killed a nigger to teach him his place. One who learns a lesson of that sort certainly never offends again, nor fathers any others of his breed."

The barber, having lathered the colonel's face, was stropping his razor with long, steady strokes. Every word uttered by the colonel was perfectly audible to him, but his impassive countenance betrayed no interest. The colonel seemed as unconscious of the barber's presence as the barber of the colonel's utterance. Surely, thought the judge, if such freedom of speech were the rule in the South the colonel's contention must be correct, and the Negroes thoroughly cowed. To a Northern man the situation was hardly comfortable.

"The iron and sugar interests of the South," persisted the judge, "will resist any reduction of the tariff."

The colonel was not to be swerved from the subject, nor from his purpose, whatever it might be.

"Quite likely they will; and we must argue with them, for they are white men and amenable to reason. The nigger, on the other hand, is the creature of instinct; you cannot argue with him; you must order him, and if he resists shoot him, as I did."

"Don't forget, barber," said the colonel, "that I want a close shave."

"No, sir," responded the barber, who having sharpened his razor, now began to pass it, with firm and even hand, over the colonel's cheek.

"It must have been," said the judge, "an aggravated case, to justify so extreme a step."

"Extreme, suh? I beg yo' pardon, suh, but I can't say I had regarded my conduct in that light. But it was an extreme case so far as the nigger was concerned. I am not boasting about my course; it was simply a disagreeable necessity. I am naturally a kind-hearted man, and don't like to kill even a fly. It was after the war, suh, and just as the Reconstruction period was drawing to a close. My mother employed a Negro girl, the child of a former servant of hers, to wait upon her."

The barber was studying the colonel's face as the razor passed over his cheek. The colonel's eyes were closed, or he might have observed the sudden gleam of interest that broke through the barber's mask of self-effacement, like a flash of lightning from a clouded sky. Involuntarily the razor remained poised in midair, but, in less time than it takes to say it, was moving again, swiftly and smoothly, over the colonel's face. To shave a talking man required a high degree of skill, but they were both adept, each in his own trade—the barber at shaving, the colonel at talking.

"The girl was guilty of some misconduct, and my mother reprimanded her and sent her home. She complained to her father, and he came to see my mother about it. He was insolent, offensive and threatening. I came into the room and ordered him to leave it. Instead of obeying, he turned on me in a rage, suh, and threatened me. I drew my revolver and shot him. The result was unfortunate; but he and his people learned a lesson. We had no further trouble with bumptious niggers in our town."

"And did you have no trouble in the matter?" asked the judge.

"None, suh, to speak of. There were proceedings, but they were the merest formality. Upon my statement, confirmed by that of my mother, I was discharged by the examining magistrate, and the case was never even reported to the grand jury. It was a clear case of self-defense."

The barber had heard the same story, with some details ignored or forgotten by the colonel. It was the barber's father who had died at the colonel's hand, and for many long years the son had dreamed of this meeting.

He remembered the story in this wise: His father had been a slave. Freed by the Civil War, he had entered upon the new life with the zeal and enthusiasm of his people at the dawn of liberty, which seem, in the light of later discouragements, so pathetic in the retrospect. The chattel aspired to own property; the slave, forbidden learning, to educate his children. He had worked early and late, had saved his money with a thrift equal to that of a German immigrant and had sent his children regularly to school.

The girl—the barber remembered her very well—had been fair of feature, soft of speech and gentle of manner, a pearl among pebbles. One day her father's old mistress had met him on the street and, after a kindly inquiry about his family, had asked if she might hire his daughter during the summer, when there was no school. Her own married daughter would be visiting her, with a young child, and they wanted some neat and careful girl to nurse the infant.

"Why, yas ma'am," the barber's father had replied. "I reckon it might be a good thing fer Alice. I wants her ter be a teacher; but she kin l'arn things from you, ma'am, that no teacher kin teach her. She kin l'arn manners, ma'am, an' white folks' ways, and nowhere better than in yo' house."

So Alice had gone to the home of her father's former mistress to learn white folks' ways. The lady had been kind and gracious. But there are ways and ways among all people.

When she had been three weeks in her new employment her mistress's son—a younger brother of the colonel—came home from college. Some weeks later Alice went home to her father. Who was most at fault the barber never knew. A few hours afterward the father called upon the lady. There was a stormy interview. Things were said to which the ears of white ladies were unaccustomed from the lips of black men. The elder son had entered the room and interfered. The barber's father had turned to him and exclaimed angrily:

"Go 'way from here, boy, and don't talk ter me, or I'm liable ter harm you."

The young man stood his ground. The Negro advanced menacingly toward him. The young man drew his ready weapon and fatally wounded the Negro—he lived only long enough, after being taken home, to gasp out the facts to his wife and children.

The rest of the story had been much as the colonel had related it. As the barber recalled it, however, the lady had not been called to testify, but was ill at the time of the hearing, presumably from the nervous shock.

That she had secretly offered to help the family the barber knew, and that her help had been rejected with cold hostility. He knew that the murderer went unpunished, and that in later years he had gone into politics, and became the leader and mouthpiece of his party. All the world knew that he had ridden into power on his hostility to Negro rights.

The barber had been a mere boy at the time of his father's death, but not too young to appreciate the calamity that had befallen the household. The family was broken up. The sordid details of its misfortunes would not be interesting. Poverty, disease and death had followed them, until he alone was left. Many years had passed. The brown boy who had wept beside his father's bier, and who had never forgotten nor forgiven, was now the grave-faced, keen-eyed, deft-handed barber, who held a deadly weapon at the throat of his father's slayer.

How often he had longed for this hour! In his dreams he had killed this man a hundred times, in a dozen ways. Once, when a young man, he had gone to meet him, with the definite purpose of taking his life, but chance had kept them apart. He had imagined situations where they might come face to face; he would see the white man struggling in the water; he would have only to stretch forth his hand to save him; but he would tell him of his hatred and let him drown. He would see him in a burning house, from which he might rescue him; and he would call him murderer and let him burn! He would see him in the dock for murder of a white man, and only his testimony could save him, and he would let him suffer the fate that he doubly deserved! He saw a vision of his father's form, only an hour before thrilling with hope and energy, now stiff and cold in death; while under his keen razor lay the neck of his enemy, the enemy, too, of his race, sworn to degrade them, to teach them, if need be, with the torch and with the gun, that their place was at the white man's feet, his heel upon their neck; who held them in such contempt that he could speak as he had spoken in the presence of one of them. One stroke of the keen blade, a deflection of half an inch in its course, and a murder would be avenged, an enemy destroyed!

For the next sixty seconds the barber heard every beat of his own pulse, and the colonel, in serene unconsciousness, was nearer death than he had ever been in the course of a long and eventful life. He was only a militia colonel, and had never been under fire, but his turbulent political career had been passed in a community where life was lightly valued, where hot words were often followed by rash deeds, and murder was tolerated as a means of private vengeance and political advancement. He went on talking, but neither the judge nor the barber listened, each being absorbed in his own thoughts.

To the judge, who lived in a community where Negroes voted, the colonel's frankness was a curious revelation. His language was choice, though delivered with the Southern intonation, his tone easy and conversational, and, in addressing the barber directly, his manner had been courteous enough. The judge was interested, too, in watching the barber, who, it was evident, was repressing some powerful emotion. It seemed very probable to the judge that the barber might resent this cool recital of murder and outrage. He did not know what might be true of the Negroes in the South, but he had been judge of a police court in one period of his upward career, and had found colored people prone to sudden rages, when under the influence of strong emotion, handy with edged tools, and apt to cut thick and deep, nor always careful about the color of the cuticle. The barber's feelings were plainly stirred, and the judge, a student of human nature, was curious to see if he would be moved to utterance. It would have been no novelty—patrons of the shop often discussed race questions with the barber. It was evident that the colonel was trying an experiment to demonstrate his contention in the lobby above. But the judge could not know the barber's intimate relation to the story, nor did it occur to him that the barber might conceive any deadly purpose because of a purely impersonal grievance. The barber's hand did not even tremble.

In the barber's mind, however, the whirlwind of emotions had passed lightly over the general and settled upon the particular injury. So strong, for the moment, was the homicidal impulse that it would have prevailed already had not the noisy opening of the door to admit a patron diverted the barber's attention and set in motion a current of ideas which fought for the colonel's life. The barber's glance toward the door, from force of habit, took in the whole shop. It was a handsome shop, and had been to the barber a matter of more than merely personal pride. Prominent among a struggling people, as yet scarcely beyond the threshold of citizenship, he had long been looked upon, and had become accustomed to regard himself, as a representative man, by whose failure or success his race would be tested. Should he slay this man now beneath his hand, this beautiful shop would be lost to his people. Years before the whole trade had been theirs. One by one the colored master barbers, trained in the slovenly old ways, had been forced to the wall by white competition, until his shop was one of the few good ones remaining in the hands of men of his race. Many an envious eye had been cast upon it. The lease had only a year to run. Strong pressure, he knew, had been exerted by a white rival to secure the reversion. The barber had the hotel proprietor's promise of a renewal; but he knew full well that should he lose the shop no colored man would succeed him; a center of industry, a medium of friendly contact with white men, would be lost to his people—many a good turn had the barber been able to do for them while he had the ear—literally had the ear—of some influential citizen, or held some aspirant for public office by the throat. Of the ten barbers in the shop all but one were married, with families dependent upon them for support. One was sending a son to college; another was buying a home. The unmarried one was in his spare hours studying a profession, with the hope of returning to practice it among his people in a Southern state. Their fates were all, in a measure, dependent upon the proprietor of the shop. Should he yield to the impulse which was swaying him, their livelihood would be placed in jeopardy. For what white man, while the memory of this tragic event should last, would trust his throat again beneath a Negro's razor?

Such, however, was the strength of the impulse against which the barber was struggling that these considerations seemed likely not to prevail. Indeed, they had presented themselves to the barber's mind in a vague, remote, detached manner, while the dominant idea was present and compelling, clutching at his heart, drawing his arm, guiding his fingers. It was by their mass rather than by their clearness that these restraining forces held the barber's arm so long in check—it was society against self, civilization against the primitive instinct, typifying, more fully than the barber could realize, the great social problem involved in the future of his race.

He had now gone once over the colonel's face, subjecting that gentleman to less discomfort than he had for a long time endured while undergoing a similar operation. Already he had retouched one cheek and had turned the colonel's head to finish the other. A few strokes more and the colonel could be released with a close shave—how close he would never know!—or, one stroke, properly directed, and he would never stand erect again! Only the day before, the barber had read, in the newspapers, the account of a ghastly lynching in a Southern state, where, to avenge a single provoked murder, eight Negroes had bit the dust and a woman had been burned at the stake for no other crime than that she was her husband's wife. One stroke and there would be one less of those who thus wantonly played with human life!

The uplifted hand had begun the deadly downward movement—when one of the barbers dropped a shaving cup, which was smashed to pieces on the marble floor. Fate surely fought for the colonel—or was it for the barber? Involuntarily the latter stayed his hand—instinctively his glance went toward the scene of the accident. It was returning to the upraised steel, and its uncompleted task, when it was arrested by Daisy's doll, hanging upon the gilded spike where he had left it.

If the razor went to its goal he would not be able to fulfill his promise to Daisy! She would wait for him at the corner, and wait in vain! If he killed the colonel he himself could hardly escape, for he was black and not white, and this was North and not South, and personal vengeance was not accepted by the courts as a justification for murder. Whether he died or not, he would be lost to Daisy. His wife was dead, and there would be no one to take care of Daisy. His own father had died in defense of his daughter; he must live to protect his own. If there was a righteous God, who divided the evil from the good, the colonel would some time get his just deserts. Vengeance was God's; it must be left to Him to repay!

The jointed doll had saved the colonel's life. Whether society had conquered self or not may be an open question, but it had stayed the barber's hand until love could triumph over hate!

The barber laid aside the razor, sponged off the colonel's face, brought him, with a movement of the chair, to a sitting posture, brushed his hair, pulled away the cloths from around his neck, handed him a pasteboard check for the amount of his bill, and stood rigidly by his chair. The colonel adjusted his collar, threw down a coin equal to double the amount of his bill and, without waiting for the change, turned with the judge to leave the shop. They had scarcely reached the door leading into the hotel lobby when the barber, overwrought by the long strain, collapsed heavily into the nearest chair.

"Well, judge," said the colonel, as they entered the lobby, "that was a good shave. What a sin it would be to spoil such a barber by making him a postmaster! I didn't say anything to him, for it don't do to praise a nigger much—it's likely to give him the big head—but I never had," he went on, running his hand appreciatively over his cheek, "I never had a better shave in my life. And I proved my theory. The barber is the son of the nigger I shot."

The judge was not sure that the colonel had proved his theory, and was less so after he had talked, a week later, with the barber. And, although the colonel remained at the Wyandot for several days, he did not get shaved again in the hotel barber shop.

Baxter's Procrustes

Baxter's *Procrustes* is one of the publications of the Bodleian Club. The Bodleian Club is composed of gentlemen of culture, who are interested in books and book-collecting. It was named, very obviously, after the famous library of the same name, and not only became in our city a sort of shrine for local worshipers of fine bindings and rare editions, but was visited occasionally by pilgrims from afar. The Bodleian has entertained Mark Twain, Joseph Jefferson, and other literary and histrionic celebrities. It possesses quite a collection of personal mementos of distinguished authors, among them a paperweight which once belonged to Goethe, a lead pencil used by Emerson, an autograph letter of Matthew Arnold, and a chip from a tree felled by Mr. Gladstone. Its library contains a number of rare books, including a fine collection on chess, of which game several of the members are enthusiastic devotees.

The activities of the club are not, however, confined entirely to books. We have a very handsome clubhouse, and much taste and discrimination have been exercised in its adornment. There are many good paintings, including the portraits of the various presidents of the club, which adorn the entrance hall. After books, perhaps the most distinctive feature of the club is our collection of pipes. In a large rack in the smoking-room—really a superfluity, since smoking is permitted all over the house—is as complete an assortment of pipes as perhaps exists in the civilized world. Indeed, it is an unwritten rule of the club that no one is eligible for membership who cannot produce a new variety of pipe, which is filed with his application for membership, and, if he passes, deposited with the club collection, he, however, retaining the title in himself. Once a year, upon the anniversary of the death of Sir Walter Raleigh, who, it will be remembered, first introduced tobacco into England, the full membership of the club, as a rule, turns out. A large supply of the very best smoking mixture is laid in. At nine o'clock sharp each member takes his pipe from the rack, fills it with tobacco, and then the whole club, with the president at the head, all smoking furiously, march in solemn procession from room to room, upstairs and downstairs, making the tour of the clubhouse and returning to the smoking-room. The president then delivers an address, and each member is called upon to say something, either by way of a quotation or an original sentiment, in praise of the virtues of nicotine. This ceremony—facetiously known as "hitting the pipe"—being thus concluded, the membership pipes are carefully cleaned out and replaced in the club rack.

As I have said, however, the *raison d'être* of the club, and the feature upon which its fame chiefly rests, is its collection of rare books, and of these by far the most interesting are its own publications. Even its catalogues are works of art, published in numbered editions, and sought by libraries and book-collectors. Early in its history it began the occasional publication of books which should meet the club standard—books in which emphasis should be laid upon the qualities that make a book valuable in the eyes of collectors. Of these, age could not, of course, be imparted, but in the matter of fine and curious bindings, of hand–made linen papers, of uncut or deckle edges, of wide margins and limited editions, the club could control its own publications. The matter of contents was, it must be confessed, a less important consideration. At first it was felt by the publishing committee that nothing but the finest products of the human mind should be selected for enshrinement in the beautiful volumes which the club should issue. The length of the work was an important consideration— long things were not compatible with wide margins and graceful slenderness. For instance, we brought out Coleridge's *Ancient Mariner,* an essay by Emerson, and another by Thoreau. Our *Rubáiyát of Omar Khayyám* was Heron-Allen's translation of the original manuscript in the Bodleian Library at Oxford, which though less poetical than FitzGerald's was not so common. Several years ago we began to publish the works of our own members. Bascom's *Essay on Pipes* was a very creditable performance. It was published in a limited edition of one hundred copies, and since it had not previously appeared elsewhere and was copyrighted by the club, it was sufficiently rare to be valuable for that reason. The second publication of local origin was Baxter's *Procrustes.*

I have omitted to say that once or twice a year, at a meeting of which notice has been given, an auction is held at the Bodleian. The members of the club send in their duplicate copies, or books they for any reason wish to dispose of, which are auctioned off to the highest bidder. At these sales, which are well attended, the club's publications have of recent years formed the leading feature. Three years ago, number three of Bascom's *Essay on Pipes* sold for fifteen dollars—the original cost of publication was one dollar and seventy-five cents. Later in the evening an uncut copy of the same brought thirty dollars. At the next auction the price of the cut copy was run up to twenty-five dollars, while the uncut copy was knocked down at seventy-five dollars. The club had always appreciated the value of uncut copies, but this financial endorsement enhanced their desirability immensely. This rise in the *Essay on Pipes* was not without a sympathetic effect upon all the club publications. The Emerson essay rose from three dollars to seventeen, and the Thoreau, being by an author less widely read, and by his own confession commercially unsuccessful, brought a somewhat higher figure. The prices, thus inflated, were not permitted to come down appreciably. Since every member of the club possessed one or more of these valuable editions, they were all manifestly interested in keeping up the price. The publication, however, which brought the highest prices, and, but for the sober second thought, might have wrecked the whole system, was Baxter's *Procrustes*.

Baxter was, perhaps, the most scholarly member of the club. A graduate of Harvard, he had traveled extensively, had read widely, and while not so enthusiastic a collector as some of us, possessed as fine a private library as any man of his age in the city. He was about thirty-five when he joined the club, and apparently some bitter experience—some disappointment in love or ambition—had left its mark upon his character. With light, curly hair, fair complexion and gray eyes, one would have expected Baxter to be genial of temper, with a tendency toward wordiness of speech. But though he had occasional flashes of humor, his ordinary demeanor was characterized by a mild cynicism, which, with his gloomy pessimistic philosophy, so foreign to the temperament that should accompany his physical type, could only be accounted for upon the hypothesis of some secret sorrow such as I have suggested. What it might be no one knew. He had means and social position, and was an uncommonly handsome man. The fact that he remained unmarried at thirty-five furnished some support for the theory of a disappointment in love, though this the several intimates of Baxter who belonged to the club were not able to verify.

It had occurred to me, in a vague way, that perhaps Baxter might be an unsuccessful author. That he was a poet we knew very well, and typewritten copies of his verses had occasionally circulated among us. But Baxter had always expressed such a profound contempt for modern literature, had always spoken in terms of such unmeasured pity for the slaves of the pen, who were dependent upon the whim of an undiscriminating public for recognition and a livelihood, that no one of us had ever suspected him of aspirations toward publication, until, as I have said, it occurred to me one day that Baxter's attitude with regard to publication might be viewed in the light of effect as well as of cause—that his scorn of publicity might as easily arise from failure to achieve it, as his never having published might be due to his preconceived disdain of the vulgar popularity which one must share with the pugilist or balloonist of the hour.

The notion of publishing Baxter's *Procrustes* did not emanate from Baxter—I must do him the justice to say this. But he had spoken to several of the fellows about the theme of his poem, until the notion that Baxter was at work upon something fine had become pretty well disseminated throughout our membership. He would occasionally read brief passages to a small coterie of friends in the sitting room or library—never more than ten lines at once, or to more than five people at a time—and these excerpts gave at least a few of us a pretty fair idea of the motive and scope of the poem. As I, for one, gathered it, it was quite along the line of Baxter's philosophy. Society was the Procrustes which, like the Greek bandit of old, caught every man born into the world, and endeavored to fit him to some preconceived standard, generally to the one for which he was least adapted. The world was full of men and women who were merely square pegs in round holes, and vice versa. Most marriages were unhappy because the contracting parties were not properly mated. Religion was mostly superstition, science for the most part sciolism, popular education merely a means of forcing the stupid and repressing the bright, so that all the youth of the rising generation might conform to the same dull, dead level of democratic mediocrity. Life would soon become so monotonously uniform and so uniformly monotonous as to be scarce worth the living.

It was Smith, I think, who first proposed that the club publish Baxter's *Procrustes*. The poet himself did not seem enthusiastic when the subject was broached; he demurred for some little time, protesting that the poem was not worthy of publication. But when it was proposed that the edition be limited to fifty copies, he agreed to consider the proposition. When I suggested, having in mind my secret theory of Baxter's failure in authorship, that the edition would at least be in the hands of friends, that it would be difficult for a hostile critic to secure a copy, and that if it should not achieve success from a literary point of view, the extent of the failure would be limited to the size of the edition, Baxter was visibly impressed. When the literary committee at length decided to request formally of Baxter the privilege of publishing his *Procrustes,* he consented, with evident reluctance, upon condition that he should supervise the printing, binding, and delivery of the books, merely submitting to the committee, in advance, the manuscript, and taking their views in regard to the bookmaking.

The manuscript was duly presented to the literary committee. Baxter having expressed the desire that the poem not be read aloud at a meeting of the club, as was the custom, since he wished it to be given to the world clad in suitable garb, the committee went even farther. Having entire confidence in Baxter's taste and scholarship, they, with great delicacy, refrained from even reading the manuscript, contenting themselves with Baxter's statement of the general theme and the topics grouped under it. The details of the bookmaking, however, were gone into thoroughly. The paper was to be of handmade linen, from the Kelmscott Mills; the type black-letter, with rubricated initials. The cover, which was Baxter's own selection, was to be of dark green morocco, with a cap-and-bells border in red inlays, and doublures of maroon morocco with a blind-tooled design. Baxter was authorized to contract with the printer and superintend the publication. The whole edition of fifty numbered copies was to be disposed of at auction, in advance, to the highest bidder, only one copy to each, the proceeds to be devoted to paying for the printing and binding, the remainder, if any, to go into the club treasury, and Baxter himself to receive one copy by way of remuneration. Baxter was inclined to protest at this, on the ground that his copy would probably be worth more than the royalties on the edition, at the usual ten per cent, would amount to, but was finally prevailed upon to accept an author's copy.

While the *Procrustes* was under consideration, someone read, at one of our meetings, a note from some magazine which stated that a sealed copy of a new translation of Campanella's *Sonnets,* published by the Grolier Club, had been sold for three hundred dollars. This impressed the members greatly. It was a novel idea. A new work might thus be enshrined in a sort of holy of holies, which, if the collector so desired, could be forever sacred from the profanation of any vulgar or unappreciative eye. The possessor of such a treasure could enjoy it by the eye of imagination, having at the same time the exaltation of grasping what was for others the unattainable. The literary committee were so impressed with this idea that they presented it to Baxter in regard to the *Procrustes.* Baxter making no objection, the subscribers who might wish their copies delivered sealed were directed to notify the author. I sent in my name. A fine book, after all, was an investment, and if there was any way of enhancing its rarity, and therefore its value, I was quite willing to enjoy such an advantage.

When the *Procrustes* was ready for distribution, each subscriber received his copy by mail, in a neat pasteboard box. Each number was wrapped in a thin and transparent but very strong paper, through which the cover design and toolings were clearly visible. The number of the copy was endorsed upon the wrapper, the folds of which were securely fastened at each end with sealing-wax, upon which was impressed, as a guaranty of its inviolateness, the monogram of the club.

At the next meeting of the Bodleian a great deal was said about the *Procrustes,* and it was unanimously agreed that no finer specimen of bookmaking had ever been published by the club. By a curious coincidence, no one had brought his copy with him, and the two club copies had not yet been received from the binder, who, Baxter had reported, was retaining them for some extra fine work. Upon resolution, offered by a member who had not subscribed for the volume, a committee of three was appointed to review the *Procrustes* at the next literary meeting of the club. Of this committee it was my doubtful fortune to constitute one.

In pursuance of my duty in the premises, it of course became necessary for me to read the *Procrustes.* In all probability I should have cut my own copy for this purpose, had not one of the club auctions intervened between my appointment and the date set for the discussion of the *Procrustes.* At this meeting a copy of the book, still sealed, was offered for sale and bought by a non-subscriber for the unprecedented price of one hundred and fifty dollars. After this a proper regard for my own interests would not permit me to spoil my copy by opening it, and I was therefore compelled to procure my information concerning the poem from some other source. As I had no desire to appear mercenary, I said nothing about my own copy, and made no attempt to borrow. I did, however, casually remark to Baxter that I should like to look at his copy of the proof sheets, since I wished to make some extended quotations for my review, and would rather not trust my copy to a typist for that purpose. Baxter assured me, with every evidence of regret, that he had considered them of so little importance that he had thrown them into the fire. This indifference of Baxter to literary values struck me as just a little overdone. The proof sheets of "Hamlet," corrected in Shakespeare's own hand, would be well-nigh priceless.

At the next meeting of the club I observed that Thompson and Davis, who were with me on the reviewing committee, very soon brought up the question of the *Procrustes* in conversation in the smoking-room, and seemed anxious to get from the members their views concerning Baxter's production, I supposed upon the theory that the appreciation of any book review would depend more or less upon the degree to which it reflected the opinion of those to whom the review should be presented. I presumed, of course, that Thompson and Davis had each read the book—they were among the subscribers—and I was desirous of getting their point of view.

"What do you think," I inquired, "of the passage on Social Systems?" I have forgotten to say that the poem was in blank verse, and divided into parts, each with an appropriate title.

"Well," replied Davis, it seemed to me a little cautiously, "it is not exactly Spencerian, although it squints at the Spencerian view, with a slight deflection toward Hegelianism. I should consider it an harmonious fusion of the best views of all the modern philosophers, with a strong Baxterian flavor."

"Yes," said Thompson, "the charm of the chapter lies in this very quality. The style is an emanation from Baxter's own intellect—he has written himself into the poem. By knowing Baxter we are able to appreciate the book, and after having read the book we feel that we are so much the more intimately acquainted with Baxter—the real Baxter."

Baxter had come in during this colloquy and was standing by the fireplace smoking a pipe. I was not exactly sure whether the faint smile which marked his face was a token of pleasure or cynicism; it was Baxterian, however, and I had already learned that Baxter's opinions upon any subject were not to be gathered always from his facial expression. For instance, when the club porter's crippled child died, Baxter remarked, it seemed to me unfeelingly, that the poor little devil was doubtless better off, and that the porter himself had certainly been relieved of a burden; and only a week later the porter told me in confidence that Baxter had paid for an expensive operation, undertaken in the hope of prolonging the child's life. I therefore drew no conclusions from Baxter's somewhat enigmatical smile. He left the room at this point in the conversation, somewhat to my relief.

"By the way, Jones," said Davis, addressing me, "are you impressed by Baxter's views on Degeneration?"

Having often heard Baxter express himself upon the general downward tendency of modern civilization, I felt safe in discussing his views in a broad and general manner.

"I think," I replied, "that they are in harmony with those of Schopenhauer, without his bitterness; with those of Nordau, without his flippancy. His materialism is Haeckel's, presented with something of the charm of Omar Kayyam."

"Yes," chimed in Davis, "it answers the strenuous demand of our day— dissatisfaction with an unjustified optimism—and voices for us the courage of human philosophy facing the unknown."

I had a vague recollection of having read something like this somewhere, but so much has been written that one can scarcely discuss any subject of importance without unconsciously borrowing, now and then, the thoughts or the language of others. Quotation, like imitation, is a superior grade of flattery.

"The *Procrustes,*" said Thompson, to whom the metrical review had been apportioned, "is couched in sonorous lines, of haunting melody and charm; and yet so closely interrelated as to be scarcely quotable with justice to the author. To be appreciated the poem should be read as a whole—I shall say as much in my review. What shall you say of the letter-press?" he concluded, addressing me. I was supposed to discuss the technical excellence of the volume from the connoisseur's viewpoint.

"The setting," I replied judicially, "is worthy of the gem. The dark green cover, elaborately tooled, the old English lettering, the heavy linen paper, mark this as one of our very choicest publications. The letter-press is of course De Vinne's best—there is nothing better on this side of the Atlantic. The text is a beautiful, slender stream, meandering gracefully through a wide meadow of margin."

For some reason I left the room for a minute. As I stepped into the hall, I almost ran into Baxter, who was standing near the door, facing a hunting print, of a somewhat humorous character, hung upon the wall, and smiling with an immensely pleased expression.

"What a ridiculous scene!" he remarked. "Look at that fat old squire on that tall hunter! I'll wager dollars to doughnuts that he won't get over the first fence!"

It was a very good bluff, but did not deceive me. Under his mask of unconcern, Baxter was anxious to learn what we thought of his poem and had stationed himself in the hall that he might overhear our discussion without embarrassing us by his presence. He had covered up his delight at our appreciation by this simulated interest in the hunting print.

When the night came for the review of the *Procrustes* there was a large attendance of members, and several visitors, among them a young English cousin of one of the members, on his first visit to the United States; some of us had met him at other clubs, and in society, and had found him a very jolly boy, with a youthful exuberance of spirits and a naive ignorance of things American that made his views refreshing and, at times, amusing.

The critical essays were well considered, if a trifle vague. Baxter received credit for poetic skill of a high order.

"Our brother Baxter," said Thompson, "should no longer bury his talent in a napkin. This gem, of course, belongs to the club, but the same brain from which issued this exquisite emanation can produce others to inspire and charm an appreciative world."

"The author's view of life," said Davis, "as expressed in these beautiful lines, will help us to fit our shoulders for the heavy burden of life, by bringing to our realization those profound truths of philosophy which find hope in despair and pleasure in pain. When he shall see fit to give to the wider world, in fuller form, the thoughts of which we have been vouchsafed this foretaste, let us hope that some little ray of his fame may rest upon the Bodleian, from which can never be taken away the proud privilege of saying that he was one of its members."

I then pointed out the beauties of the volume as a piece of bookmaking. I knew, from conversation with the publication committee, the style of type and rubrication, and could see the cover through the wrapper of my sealed copy. The dark green morocco, I said, in summing up, typified the author's serious view of life, as a thing to be endured as patiently as might be. The cap-and-bells border was significant of the shams by which the optimist sought to delude himself into the view that life was a desirable thing. The intricate blind-tooling of the doublure shadowed forth the blind fate which left us in ignorance of our future and our past, or of even what the day itself might bring forth. The black-letter type, with rubricated initials, signified a philosophic pessimism enlightened by the conviction that in duty one might find, after all, an excuse for life and a hope for humanity. Applying this test to the club, this work, which might be said to represent all that the Bodleian stood for, was in itself sufficient to justify the club's existence. If the Bodleian had done nothing else, if it should do nothing more, it had produced a masterpiece.

There was a sealed copy of the *Procrustes,* belonging, I believe, to one of the committee, lying on the table by which I stood, and I had picked it up and held it in my hand for a moment, to emphasize one of my periods, but had laid it down immediately. I noted, as I sat down, that young Hankin, our English visitor, who sat on the other side of the table, had picked up the volume and was examining it with interest. When the last review was read, and the generous applause had subsided, there were cries for Baxter.

"Baxter! Baxter! Author! Author!"

Baxter had been sitting over in a corner during the reading of the reviews, and had succeeded remarkably well, it seemed to me, in concealing, under his mask of cynical indifference, the exultation which I was sure he must feel. But this outburst of enthusiasm was too much even for Baxter, and it was clear that he was struggling with strong emotion when he rose to speak.

"Gentlemen, and fellow members of the Bodleian, it gives me unaffected pleasure—sincere pleasure—some day you may know how much pleasure—I cannot trust myself to say it now—to see the evident care with which your committee have read my poor verses, and the responsive sympathy with which my friends have entered into my views of life and conduct. I thank you again, and again, and when I say that I am too full for utterance—I'm sure you will excuse me from saying any more."

Baxter took his seat, and the applause had begun again when it was broken by a sudden exclamation.

"By Jove!" exclaimed our English visitor, who still sat behind the table, "what an extraordinary book!"

Everyone gathered around him.

"You see," he exclaimed, holding up the volume, "you fellows said so much about the bally book that I wanted to see what it was like; so I untied the ribbon and cut the leaves with the paper knife lying here and found—and found that there wasn't a single line in it, don't you know!"

Blank consternation followed this announcement, which proved only too true. Everyone knew instinctively, without further investigation, that the club had been badly sold. In the resulting confusion Baxter escaped, but later was waited upon by a committee, to whom he made the rather lame excuse that he had always regarded uncut and sealed books as tommy-rot, and that he had merely been curious to see how far the thing could go; and that the result had justified his belief that a book with nothing in it was just as useful to a book-collector as one embodying a work of genius. He offered to pay all the bills for the sham *Procrustes,* or to replace the blank copies with the real thing, as we might choose. Of course, after such an insult, the club did not care for the poem. He was permitted to pay the expense, however, and it was more than hinted to him that his resignation from the club would be favorably acted upon. He never sent it in, and, as he went to Europe shortly afterwards, the affair had time to blow over.

In our first disgust at Baxter's duplicity, most of us cut our copies of the *Procrustes,* some of us mailed them to Baxter with cutting notes, and others threw them into the fire. A few wiser spirits held on to theirs, and this fact leaking out, it began to dawn upon the minds of the real collectors among us that the volume was something unique in the way of a publication.

"Baxter," said our president one evening to a select few of us who sat around the fireplace, "was wiser than we knew, or than he perhaps appreciated. His *Procrustes,* from the collector's point of view, is entirely logical, and might be considered as the acme of bookmaking. To the true collector, a book is a work of art, of which the contents are no more important than the words of an opera. Fine binding is a desideratum, and, for its cost, that of the *Procrustes* could not be improved upon. The paper is above criticism. The true collector loves wide margins, and the *Procrustes,* being all margin, merely touches the vanishing point of the perspective. The smaller the edition, the greater the collector's eagerness to acquire a copy. There are but six uncut copies left, I am told, of the *Procrustes,* and three sealed copies, of one of which I am the fortunate possessor."

After this deliverance, it is not surprising that, at our next auction, a sealed copy of Baxter's *Procrustes* was knocked down, after spirited bidding, for two hundred and fifty dollars, the highest price ever brought by a single volume published by the club.